PRAISE FOR ANNIE PROULX'S
BARKSKINS

"*Barkskins* is an awesome monument of a book, a spectacular survey of America's forests dramatized by a cast of well-hewn characters. Such is the magnetism of Proulx's narrative that there's no resisting her thundering cascade of stories. A vast woods you'll want to get lost in . . . *Barkskins* is a towering new work of environmental fiction."

—*THE WASHINGTON POST*

"*Barkskins* is masterful, full of an urgent, tense lyricism, its plotting beautifully unexpected, its biographical narratives flowing into one another like the seasons. . . . A marvel . . . A long novel worth your time."

—*USA TODAY*

"Towering . . . With gorgeous imagery, clean prose and remarkable sensitivity, *Barkskins* is as powerful and important as any literary work produced on this continent in the three centuries spanned by the story."

—*PITTSBURGH POST-GAZETTE*

"*Barkskins* encompasses a breadth of themes and history rarely approached by any writer, girded by peerless research and Proulx's X-ray vision into the human heart. But the triumph of the novel lies in sentences that burst from the page, ideas that move and breathe with mission."

—*O, THE OPRAH MAGAZINE*

More Praise for

Barkskins

"Monumental . . . a potently imagined chronicle of mankind's dealings with the North American forests."

—*The Wall Street Journal*

"Like the best realists, Proulx can make us see the world and its inhabitants with greater clarity. Juggling so many different plotlines and characters becomes easier when you have, as Proulx does, a Dickensian gift for quick portraiture."

—*The Boston Globe*

"Few authors are as uniquely qualified as Annie Proulx to sustain a novel as long as *Barkskins*. Pages melt away as readers zoom through the decades. . . . This is Proulx at the height of her powers as an irreplaceable American voice."

—*Entertainment Weekly* (Grade A)

"An intricately detailed narrative of geography, history and humanity that is both exhilarating and mesmerizing . . . [T]his is not a novel to peck at or flick through, but one to read slowly and to savor as a long and fulfilling feast."

—*The Economist*

"Fearless . . . Delicious . . . *Barkskins* has a large cast, but that's a showcase for Proulx's gift for creating lively, complex characters. Proulx's style is inimitably her own, but it echoes here with those of great influences: Dickens, Melville, Twain, Faulkner and more."

—*Tampa Bay Times*

"Proulx's characters are vivid, insistent, captivating. . . . [N]ary a page goes by without a few exquisitely observed historical details. . . . A narrative so grand in spatial and temporal scope, so broad in theme, that it cannot conceivably be strictly American. Her pitch-perfect sentences, instead, encompass the entire Western world, and its ever-growing concern with ecological and environmental change."
—*The New Republic*

"Proulx's greatest novel yet. [Her] talent for bringing individuals alive with a single perfectly turned line has never been sharper than in these pages."
—*The Christian Science Monitor*

"Stunning . . . Proulx is a writer's writer, and one whose deep interest in history provides the long view of how our environmental recklessness has brought us to a point of reckoning."
—*The Seattle Times*

"Proulx sketches each person with vigorous, unforgettable strokes. . . . [R]ead it, absorb its urgent message."
—*NPR*

"An epic capstone to eighty-year-old Proulx's impressive career, *Barkskins* surpasses even the extraordinary *The Shipping News* as her finest novel."
—*St. Louis Post-Dispatch*

"Epic . . . Violent, monumental and often breathtaking, *Barkskins* is a colossal achievement."
—*The Columbus Dispatch*

"Captivating . . . Proulx's prose is often glorious, her several protagonists unforgettable. She taps a vein here, helping to make *Barkskins* one of the most exciting books I have read in years. Proulx has pulled out all the stops."

—*The Buffalo News*

"Enthralling . . . Vividly conceived. *Barkskins* brims with a granular sense of human experience over a period of three hundred years. . . . Proulx's beautiful prose renders an exultant view of the life of forest worlds lost to us."

—*BookPage*

"Remarkable not just for its length, but for its scope and ambition. It's a monumental achievement, one that will perhaps be remembered as her finest work. . . . Despite the length, nothing seems extraneous, and not once does the reader sense the story slipping from Proulx's grasp, resulting in the kind of immersive reading experience that only comes along every few years."

—*Publishers Weekly* (starred review)

"Part ecological fable à la Ursula K. Le Guin, part foundational saga along the lines of Brian Moore's *Black Robe* and, yes, James Michener's *Centennial,* Proulx's story builds in depth and complication without becoming unduly tangled and is always told with the most beautiful language. Another tremendous book from Proulx, sure to find and enthrall many readers."

—*Kirkus Reviews* (starred review)

"Rigorously researched, intrepidly imagined, complexly plotted and vigorously written . . . nothing less than a sylvan *Moby-Dick* . . . Proulx's commanding, perspective-altering epic will be momentous."

—*Booklist* (starred review)

Also by Annie Proulx

Heart Songs and Other Stories
Postcards
The Shipping News
Accordion Crimes
Close Range
That Old Ace in the Hole
Bad Dirt
Fine Just the Way It Is
Bird Cloud

Barkskins

A NOVEL

Annie Proulx

SCRIBNER

New York   London   Toronto   Sydney   New Delhi

SCRIBNER
An Imprint of Simon & Schuster, Inc.
1230 Avenue of the Americas
New York, NY 10020

First Scribner trade paperback edition April 2017

SCRIBNER and design are registered trademarks of The Gale Group, Inc.,
used under license by Simon & Schuster, Inc., the publisher of this work.

For information about special discounts for bulk purchases,
please contact Simon & Schuster Special Sales at 1-866-506-1949
or business@simonandschuster.com.

The Simon & Schuster Speakers Bureau can bring authors to your live event.
For more information or to book an event, contact the Simon & Schuster Speakers Bureau
at 1-866-248-3049 or visit our website at www.simonspeakers.com.

Interior design by Erich Hobbing

Manufactured in the United States of America

1 3 5 7 9 10 8 6 4 2

The Library of Congress has cataloged the hardcover edition as follows:
Proulx, Annie.
Barkskins : a novel / Annie Proulx.—First Scribner hardcover edition.
pages cm
I. Title.
PS3566.R697B37 2016
813'.54—dc23
2015030152

ISBN 978-0-7432-8878-1
ISBN 978-0-7432-8879-8 (pbk)
ISBN 978-1-4767-7182-3 (ebook)

To the memory of my high school teacher
Elizabeth Ring,
Maine historian, scholar and educator,
who excited in me a lifelong interest in historical change
and shifting disparate views of past and present.

To the memories of my sister Joyce Proulx Kostyn,
brother-in-law John Roberts,
writers Ivan Doig, Dermot Healy, Aidan Higgins
and wildlife biologist Ronald Lockwood.

And for barkskins of all kinds—
loggers, ecologists, sawyers, sculptors, hotshots,
planters, students, scientists, leaf eaters, photographers,
practitioners of shinrin-yoku, land-sat interpreters,
climatologists, wood butchers, picnickers, foresters,
ring counters and the rest of us.

Why shouldn't things be largely absurd, futile, and transitory? They are so, and we are so, and they and we go very well together.

George Santayana

In Antiquity every tree, every spring, every stream, every hill had its own genius loci, its guardian spirit. These spirits were accessible to men, but were very unlike men; centaurs, fauns, and mermaids show their ambivalence. Before one cut a tree, mined a mountain, or dammed a brook, it was important to placate the spirit in charge of that particular situation, and to keep it placated. By destroying pagan animism, Christianity made it possible to exploit nature in a mood of indifference to the feelings of natural objects.

Lynn White, Jr.

Contents

CONTENTS

CONTENTS

CONTENTS

Barkskins

I

forêt, hache, famille

1693–1716

I

Trépagny

In twilight they passed bloody Tadoussac, Kébec and Trois-Rivières and near dawn moored at a remote riverbank settlement. René Sel, stiff black hair, slanted eyes, *yeux bridés*—in ancient times invading Huns had been at his people—heard someone say "Wobik." Mosquitoes covered their hands and necks like fur. A man with yellow eyebrows pointed them at a rain-dark house. Mud, rain, biting insects and the odor of willows made the first impression of New France. The second impression was of dark vast forest, inimical wilderness.

The newcomers, standing in the rain waiting to be called to make their marks in a great ledger, saw the farmers clumped under a sheltering spruce. The farmers stared at them and exchanged comments.

At his turn René made not only an X but the letter *R*—marred by a spatter of ink from the quill—a letter which he had learned in childhood from the old priest who said it was the beginning of René, his name. But the priest had died of winter starvation before he could teach him the succeeding letters.

Yellow Eyebrows regarded the *R*. "Quite the learned fellow, eh?" he said. He bawled out "Monsieur Claude Trépagny!" and René's new master, a shambling, muscular man, beckoned him forward. He carried a heavy stick like a cudgel. Drops of rain caught in the wool of his knitted cap. Thick brows couldn't shadow his glaring eyes, the whites so white and flashing they falsely indicated a vivacious nature. "We must wait a little," he said to René.

The damp sky sagged downward. They waited. Yellow Eyebrows, the deputy whom his new master called Monsieur Bouchard, again bawled "Monsieur Trépagny!" who this time fetched a familiar; Charles Duquet, a scrawny *engagé* from the ship, a weakling from the Paris slums who during the voyage often folded up in a corner like a broken stick. So, thought René, Monsieur Trépagny had taken two servants. Perhaps he was wealthy, although his sodden *droguet* cloak was tattered.

Monsieur Trépagny tramped up the muddy path toward a line of black mist. He did not so much walk as hurl himself along on his varied legs, one limber, one stiff. He said *"Allons-y."* They plunged into the gloomy country, a dense hardwood forest broken by stands of pine. René did not dare ask what services he would be performing. After years of manly labor chopping trees in the Morvan highlands he did not want to be a house servant.

In a few hours the sodden leaf mold gave way to pine duff. The air was intensely aromatic. Fallen needles muted their passage, the interlaced branches absorbed their panting breaths. Here grew hugeous trees of a size not seen in the old country for hundreds of years, evergreens taller than cathedrals, cloud-piercing spruce and hemlock. The monstrous deciduous trees stood distant from each other, but overhead their leaf-choked branches merged into a false sky, dark and savage. Achille, his older brother, would have gaped at New France's trees. Late in the day they passed by a slope filled with shining white trunks. These, said Monsieur Trépagny, were *bouleau blanc,* and the *sauvages* made houses and boats from the bark. René did not believe this.

The big trees made him think again of Achille, a *flotteur* who had spent his brief years plunging in and out of the cold Yonne, guiding logs down the river. He had been powerful, immune to the water's chill, had worked until a log with a broken limb, sharpened and polished to a spear by the friction of its travels, had pierced his bladder, carrying him along like a gobbet of meat on a spit. René now wore his brother's underwear and wool trousers and his short coat. He wore Achille's sabots, though a barefoot life had given him callused feet tough as cow hooves, hardened against French cold. In this new world he would learn the cold was of a different order.

The *engagés,* dizzy with the narcotic effect of deep forest, stumbled on sprawling spruce roots. *Bébites* assailed them, minuscule no-see-ums like heated needles, blackflies with a painless bite that dispersed slow toxins, swarms of mosquitoes in such millions that their shrill keening was the sound of the woods. At a bog Monsieur Trépagny told them to smear mud over their exposed skin, especially behind the ears and on the crown of the head. The insects crept through the hair and stabbed the scalp. That, said Monsieur Trépagny, was why he wore a tuque in this damnable country. René thought an iron helmet would be a better choice. Monsieur Trépagny said the *sauvages* made a protective salve from spruce needle oil and animal fat but he had none. Mud would do. They walked on through the dim woods, climbing over mossy humps, passing under branches drooping like dark funeral swags. The *engagés'* legs, weakened by the long ocean voyage, cramped with fatigue.

"How big is this forest?" asked Duquet in his whinging treble voice. He was scarcely larger than a child.

"It is the forest of the world. It is infinite. It twists around as a snake swallows its own tail and has no end and no beginning. No one has ever seen its farthest dimension."

Monsieur Trépagny stopped. With his stick he smashed out dry spruce twigs at the base of a tree. From beneath his cloak he took a fire bundle and made a small blaze. They crouched around it, stretching out their purple hands. He unfolded a cloth wrapping revealing a piece of moose meat, cut pieces for each of them. Famished, René, who had only hoped for bread, bit and tore at the meat. The grey mosquitoes hummed at his ears. Duquet looked out from puffed slits and, unable to chew, he sucked the meat. Beneath Monsieur Trépagny's generosity they sensed contempt.

They walked on through a chaos of deadfalls, victims of some great windstorm, Monsieur Trépagny following no discernible path but frequently looking upward. René saw he was following cut marks on certain trees, marks ten feet above the ground. Later he learned someone had blazed the trees in winter striding high above the earth in snowshoes like a kind of weightless wizard.

The forest had many edges, like a lace altarpiece. Its moody darkness eased in the clearings. Unknown plants and curious blossoms caught their eyes, funereal spruce and hemlock, the bright new-growth puffs at the tips of the pine branches, silvery tossing willow, the mint green of new birch—a place where even the sunlight was green. As they approached one opening they heard an irregular clacking sound like sticks—grey bones tied in a tree, stirred by the wind. Monsieur Trépagny said that the *sauvages* often hung up the bones of a killed animal after thanking its spirit. He led them around beaver ponds protected by almost impenetrable alder queaches, warning that the narrow pathways were moose runs. They passed through wet country. Hollows brimmed with tea-colored rainwater. The quaking sphagnum, punctuated with pitcher plants, sucked at every step. The young men had never imagined country so wild and wet, so thickly wooded. When an alder branch tore Duquet's jacket he swore in a low voice. Monsieur Trépagny heard him and said he must never curse a tree, especially the alder, which had medicinal powers. They drank at streams, crossed shallow riffles curved like damascened scimitar blades. Oh, how much longer, muttered Duquet, one hand to the side of his face.

They came again to open forest, where it was easy to stride under the trees. *Sauvages* burned away the underbrush, said their new master in a disparaging tone. In late afternoon Monsieur Trépagny cried *"porc-épic!"* and suddenly hurled his walking stick. It whirled once and struck the porcupine a blow on the nose. The animal pitched down like a falling star, trailed by blood drops. Monsieur Trépagny built a big fire and when the flames subsided into purple rods suspended the gutted animal over the coals. The burning quills stank, but when he took the carcass off the fire, beneath the blackened crust the meat was good. From his bottomless pockets Monsieur Trépagny drew a bag of salt and gave them each a pinch. The leftover meat he wrapped in a greasy cloth.

The master built up the fire again, rolled into his cloak, lay down under a tree, closed his fiery eyes and slept. René's legs cramped. The cold, the pines hissing in the wind, wheedling mosquitoes and owl cries kept him awake. He spoke softly to Charles Duquet, who did not answer, and then he was silent. In the night something half-wakened him.

Morning began with fire. Though it was late spring it was colder than cold France. Light crawled into the gloom. Monsieur Trépagny, gnawing on leftover meat, kicked Duquet and bawled *"Levez-vous!"* René was up before Monsieur Trépagny could kick him. He looked at the meat in Monsieur Trépagny's hand. The man tore off a piece and threw it to him, tore another and threw it to Duquet as one might throw scraps to a dog, then headed out with his tireless, lurching gait, following the cuts high on the trees. The new servants saw only darkness except to their rear, where the abandoned fire winked beguilingly.

The day was cold, but dry. Monsieur Trépagny racked along a dim trail, but by noon the rain returned. They were stuporous with fatigue when they reached snarling water, a black river, yet transparent as dark chert. On the far side they saw a clearing filled with stacks of cordwood and the omnipresent forest pressing in. Smoke rose from a hidden chimney. They could not see the house, only mountains of wood and outbuildings.

Monsieur Trépagny shouted. A woman in a mooseskin tunic painted with curling designs came around the end of the nearest woodpile and called out—*"Kwe!"*—then turned away. René Sel and Charles Duquet exchanged stares. An Indian woman. *Une sauvage!*

They followed Monsieur Trépagny into the frigid river. René slipped on a round river rock and half-fell, thinking of Achille, of the icy Yonne. Fish veered around them, shot past, so many fish the river seemed made of hard muscle. On the muddy shore they passed a fenced garden plot of weeds. Monsieur Trépagny began to sing:

"Mari, Mari, dame jolie . . ." The *engagés* kept silent. Duquet's mouth was pinched as if the air burned, his eyes swollen almost shut.

Beyond the woodpiles they saw Monsieur Trépagny's house, their first sight of the timber *pièce-sur-pièce* style, the steep-hipped roof, the shape of the bell-cast eaves familiar from France. But every part was wood except for three small windows set with expensive French glass. Against the trees they saw a *wikuom,* which they learned the next day was the *sauvage* woman's bark house, where she retreated with her children at night.

Monsieur Trépagny took them to his storehouse. The interior stank of rotting potatoes, marsh hay and cow shit. One end was partitioned off and behind it they heard the breathing of a beast. They saw a black fire pit, a forge. Monsieur Trépagny, enamored of his own voice, continued to sing, made a fire in the pit and left them. Outside his voice receded, *"Ah! Bonjour donc, franc cavalier . . ."* The rain began again. René and Duquet sat in darkness except for the light of the dying fire. There were no windows in the building and when Duquet opened the door to let in light, clouds of savage midges and mosquitoes rushed them. They sat in the near dark. Duquet spoke. He said that he was suffering from *mal aux dents*—toothache—and would run away at his first chance and return to France. René was silent.

After a time the door opened. The *sauvage* woman and two children came in, their arms full. The woman said *"bien, bien,"* and gave each of them a beaver robe. She pointed to herself and said "Mali," for like most Mi'kmaqs she found it difficult to pronounce the letter *r.* René said his name and she repeated it—Lené. The larger child set down a wooden bowl of hot cornmeal. They disappeared. René and Duquet scooped the mush out of the bowl with their fingers. They wrapped themselves in the robes and slept.

It was not light when Monsieur Trépagny wrenched open the door and shouted in a hard voice, *"Allons-y!"* Behind the partition came the sound of jets of milk hitting the bottom of a wooden bucket. He tossed them pieces of smoked sturgeon and took his steel-bladed ax from the wall, gave them each a short-hafted dulled ax. René's had a great chip missing from the cutting edge. In the dripping dawn Trépagny led them past a maize garden and into a small clearing. He swung his arm in an arc and in an ironic voice called the cramped space his big clearing—*"le grand défrichement"*—then began to chop at a tree with skillful strokes. He commanded them to do the same. He said today they would cut logs to build their quarters, an enlargement of his *domus,* so that they might vacate his storehouse as quickly as possible. René swung the short-handled trade tool, felt the jolt of the tree's resistance, swung again, embarking on his life's work of clearing the forest of New France. Duquet nibbled at a tree with his hatchet, a yellow discharge leaking from his bitten eyes. They limbed the fallen trees, rolled and dragged them to the edge of the clearing. The branches went aside to be chopped later into cordwood.

The ax was dull. In the time it took René to fell one smallish tree, the master brought down three larger and was at work on a fourth. There must be a way to sharpen an ax with a quarter of the cutting edge gone, he thought. He would refresh its sharpness; with doubts he chose a river cobble and began to grind with circular motions. There was no visible progress and he soon began chopping again. Monsieur Trépagny picked up the useless cobble and threw it into the forest, took the ax from René and flourished it. "To sharpen," he said, "we use sandstone—*grès.*" He pantomimed the sharpening. René wanted to ask where Monsieur Trépagny kept his sharpening stones but the man's glaring expression kept him quiet.

Monsieur Trépagny twisted his lips at Duquet's whittle marks. He regarded Duquet's lopsided face. "Open your mouth," he said, tapped the rotten tooth with the blade of his knife and muttered that he would pull it at the end of the day. Duquet made a negative sound.

At the height of the sun the *sauvage* woman brought a pot of steaming maize. René had rarely eaten food at midday. With a wood chip

Monsieur Trépagny scooped out a glob. In the center of the maize melted a creamy substance. René took some on his wood chip, was overcome by the richness. *"Ah!"* he said and took more. Monsieur Trépagny said tersely that it was *cacamos,* moose bone marrow. Duquet barely ate even this and leaned against a tree breathing noisily.

At twilight they left the clearing. Monsieur Trépagny clattered through his smithy tools until he found a pair of ironmonger's pliers. Duquet sat openmouthed on a stump and Monsieur Trépagny seized the tooth with the tool and wrenched. He dropped the yellow fang on the ground. Duquet spat blood and pus, his lower lip split from the weight of the pliers. *"Allons-y,"* said Monsieur Trépagny, moving toward his house. René saw him pick up Duquet's tooth and put it in his pocket.

The men entered the single room and their masculine stench blended into the human funk of the north woods. The pockmarked Mari noticed René's nostrils flare at the smell of the house and threw an aromatic juniper branch on the fire. In the hubhub of brats they heard some names—Elphège, Theotiste, Jean-Baptiste—but they all looked the same and so like their Mi'kmaw mother that René forgot them immediately. Mari spoke a patois of mixed Mi'kmaq and terse French with a few Portuguese phrases in a curious rhythm. The children had French names.

She brought them a pot of unsalted stewed goose cooked with wild onions and herbs. The meat fell off the bone though Duquet could manage only a little of the broth. A small dish of coarse salt stood in front of Trépagny and he pinched it up with thumb and two fingers.

"Mari does not cook with *sel,* the Mi'kmaq say it spoils the food. So always carry your own *sel,* René Sel, unless you can put your thumb in the victuals and season them with your name—ha-ha." Then came a plate of hot corn cakes. Monsieur Trépagny poured an amber syrup on his cakes and René did the same. The syrup was sweet and smoky, better than honey, and he could not believe it came from a tree, as the master said. Duquet, exhausted by his ordeal, bent his head. Mari went to her cupboard and stirred something. She brought it to Duquet. Monsieur Trépagny said perhaps it was a potion made from green alder catkins, the very alders Duquet had cursed, so then the medicine would not work for him. Mari said, "willow leaf, willow bark good medicine Mali make," and Duquet swallowed it and slept that night.

Day after day the chopping continued and their hands swelled, blistered, hardened, the rhythm of chopping seized them despite the dull axes. Monsieur Trépagny watched René work.

"You've held an ax before; you have a woodsman's skill." René told him about the Morvan forest where he and Achille had cut trees. But already that life was unmoored and slipping sidewise out of memory.

"Ah," said Monsieur Trépagny. The next morning he took their wretched axes from them and went off, leaving them alone.

"So," said René to Duquet, "what is Monsieur Trépagny, is he a rich man? Or not?"

Duquet produced a hard laugh. "I thought that between you and Monsieur Trépagny all the knowledge of the world was conquered. Do you not know that he is the *seigneur* and we the *censitaires*?—what some call *habitants*. He is a *seigneur* but he wants to be a nobleman in this new country. He apportions us land and for three years we pay him with our labor and certain products such as radishes or turnips from the land he allows us to use."

"What land?"

"A fine question. Until now we have been working but there has been no mention of land. Monsieur Trépagny is full of malignant cunning. The King could take the *seigneurie* from him if he knew. Did you really not understand the paper you signed? It was clearly explained in France."

"I thought it concerned only a period of servitude. I did not understand about the land. Does that mean we are to be farmers? Landowners?"

"*Ouais,* plowmen and settlers, not landowners but land users, opening the forest, growing turnips. If people in France believed they could own land here outright they would rush in by the thousands. I for one do not wish to be a peasant. I don't know why you came here but I came to do something. The money is in the fur trade."

"I'm no farmer. I'm a woodsman. But I would like to have my own land very much."

"And I would like to know why he took my tooth. I saw him."

"And I, too, saw this."

"There is something evil there. This man has a dark vein in his heart."

Monsieur Trépagny returned a few hours later with iron axes for them, the familiar straight-hafted *"La Tène"* René had known all his life. They were new and the steel cutting edges were sharp. He had brought good whetstones as well. René felt the power in this ax, its greedy hunger to bite through all that stood in its way, sap spurting, firing out white chips like china shards. With a pointed stone he marked the haft with his initial, *R.* As he cut, the wildness of the world receded, the vast invisible web of filaments that connected human life to animals, trees to flesh and bones to grass shivered as each tree fell and one by one the web strands snapped.

After weeks of chopping, limbing and bark peeling, of dragging logs to Monsieur Trépagny's clearing with his two oxen, cutting, notching and mortising the logs as the master directed, lifting them into place, chinking the gaps with river mud, the new building was nearly finished.

"We should be building our own houses on our assigned lands, not constructing a shared lodging next to his *ménage,*" Duquet said, his inflamed eyes winking.

Still they cut trees, piling them in heaps to dry and setting older piles alight. The air was in constant smoke, the smell of New France. The stumpy ground was gouged by oxen's cloven hooves as though a ballroom of devils had clogged in the mud: the trees fell, their shadows replaced by scalding light, the mosses and ferns below them withered.

"Why," asked René, "do you not sell these fine trees to France for ship masts?"

Monsieur Trépagny laughed unpleasantly. He loathed René's foolish questions. "Because the idiots prefer Baltic timber. They have no idea what is here. They are inflexible. They neglect the riches of New France, except for furs." He slapped his leg. "Even a hundred years ago de Champlain, who discovered New France, begged them to take advantage of the fine timber, the fish and rich furs, leather and a hundred other valuable things. Did they listen to him? No. Very much no. They let these precious resources waste—except for furs. And there were others with good ideas but the gentlemen in France were not interested. And some of those men with ideas went to the English and the seeds they planted there will bear bloody fruit. The English send thousands to their colonies but France cannot be bothered."

As spring advanced, moist and buggy, each tree sending up a fresh fountain of oxygen, Duquet's face swelled with another abscess. Monsieur Trépagny extracted this new dental offense and said commandingly that now he would pull them all and Duquet would waste no more time with toothaches. He lunged with the blacksmith's pliers but Duquet dodged away, shook his head violently, spattering blood, and said something in a low voice. Monsieur Trépagny, putting this second tooth in his pocket, spun around and said in a silky, gentleman's voice, "I'll have your skull." Duquet leaned a little forward but did not speak.

Some days later Duquet, still carrying his ax, made an excuse to relieve his bowels and walked into the forest. While he was out of earshot René asked Monsieur Trépagny if he was their *seigneur*.

13

"And what if I am?"

"Then, sir, are we—Duquet and I—to have some land to work? Duquet wishes to know."

"In time that will occur, but not until three years have passed, not until the *domus* is finished, not until my brothers are here, and certainly not until the ground is cleared for a new maize plot. Which is our immediate task, so continue. The land comes at the end of your service." And he drove his ax into a spruce.

Duquet was gone for a long time. Hours passed. Monsieur Trépagny laughed. He said Duquet must be looking for his land. With vindictive relish he described the terrors of being lost in the forest, of drowning in the icy river, being pulled down by wolves, trampled by moose, or snapped in half by creatures with steaming teeth. He named the furious Mi'kmaw spirits of the forest—*chepichcaam,* hairy *kookwes,* frost giant *chenoo* and unseen creatures who felled trees with their jaws. René's hair bristled and he thought Monsieur Trépagny had fallen too deeply into the world of the savages.

The next day they heard a quavering voice in the distant trees. Monsieur Trépagny, who had been limbing, snapped upright, listened and said it was not one of the Mi'kmaw spirits, but one that had followed the settlers from France, the *loup-garou,* known to haunt forests. René, who had heard stories of this devil in wolf shape all his life but never seen one, thought it was Duquet beseeching them. When he made to call back Monsieur Trépagny told him to shut his mouth unless he wanted to bring the *loup-garou* closer. They heard it wailing and calling something that sounded like *"maman."* Monsieur Trépagny said that to call for its mother like a lost child was a well-known trick of the *loup-garou* and that they would work no more that day lest the sound of chopping lead the beast to them.

"Vite!" Monsieur Trépagny shouted. They ran back to the house.

2

clearings

With Duquet gone—"eaten by the *loup-garou*," said Monsieur Trépagny with lip-smacking noises—the *seigneur* became talkative, but told differing versions of his history while he chopped, most of his words lost under the blows of the ax. He had a skilled eye that could see where small trees stood more or less in a row, and these he would notch, then fell the great tree at the end, which obligingly took down all the small trees. He said his people came from the Pyrenees, but another time he placed them in the north, in Lille, nor did he neglect Paris as his source. He described his hatred of villages and their lying, spying, churchy inhabitants. He despised the Jesuits. Monsieur Trépagny said he, his brothers and their uncle Jean came to New France to enter the fur trade, although he himself had better reasons.

"Our people in earlier times were badly treated in France. The popish demon church called us heretics and tortured us. They believed they had conquered us. They were wrong. We have held to our beliefs hand, head, heart and body in secret for centuries and here in New France we will grow strong again." He extolled the new land, said it would surpass Old France in richness and power.

"A new world that will become greater than coldhearted old France with its frozen ideas. Someday New France will extend all the way to Florida, all the way to the great river in the west. Frontenac saw this."

René thought of it and agreed, New France was a prize if England kept away. But he did not often think of such things. He saw himself as a dust mote in the wind of life, going where the drafts of that great force carried him.

"What," asked Monsieur Trépagny, "is the most important thing? After God, of course."

René wanted to say land, he wanted to say seeds, he wanted to say stolen teeth. He didn't say anything.

"Blood!" said Monsieur Trépagny. "Your family. Your blood people."

"They are all dead," said René, but Monsieur Trépagny ignored him and continued his history. He and his brothers, he said, went first up the mysterious Saguenay River "to barter with the Hurons for furs, and later with the Odaawa, building up trust, but we avoided the Iroquois, who love the English and who, from childhood, practice testing themselves against horrible tortures. They enjoy inflicting pain on others. The *voyageurs'* life is a good life for my brothers, who still ply the rivers. For me, a very disagreeable way.

"Now," he said, "the Iroquois are less terrible than in former times. But all Indians were mad for copper kettles, the bigger the better, so large they could not be easily moved, and the possession of a kettle changed their wandering ways. Once they had that copper or iron kettle no longer did they roam the forests and rivers so vigorously. Villages grew up around the kettles. All very well, but someone had to carry those monstrous vessels to them, someone had to toil and haul them up dangerous portage routes." He pointed silently at his breast. "This was below my station in life." And he smote his tree.

"The fur trade moved north and west," he said to the tree as he told of his disenchantment. "The portages. Six, eight miles of rocks with two fur packs the weight of a cow, then back to the canoe and more packs or one of the cursed kettles. Finally, the canoe. You would not believe the enormous loads some of those men carried. One is said to have carried five hundredweight each trip from early morning until darkness." Carrying one of the detested kettles, said Trépagny, his right knee gave way. The injury plagued him still.

"However! The fur company, with the rights the King assigned them, made me a *seigneur* and charged me to gather *habitants* and populate New France. This is the beginning of a great new city in the wilderness."

René asked a question that had bothered him since the first trek through the woods.

"Why do we cut the forest when there are so many fine clearings? Why wouldn't a man build his house in a clearing, one of those meadows that we passed when we walked here? Would it not be easier?"

But Monsieur Trépagny was scandalized. "Easier? Yes, easier, but we are here to clear the forest, to subdue this evil wilderness." He was silent for a minute, thinking, then started in again. "Moreover, here in New France there is a special way of apportioning property. Strips of land that run from a river to the forest give each settler fertile farm soil, high ground safe from floods, and forest trees for timber, fuel and—mushrooms! It is an equitable arrangement not possible with clearings taken up willy-nilly—*bon gré mal gré.*"

René hoped this was the end of the lecture but the man went on. "Men must change this land in order to live in it. In olden times men lived like beasts. In those ancient days men had claws and long teeth, nor could they speak but only growled." He made a sound to show how they growled.

René, chopping trees, felt not the act but the pure motion, the raised ax, the gathering tension in arms and shoulders, buttocks and thighs, the hips pivoting, knees loose and flexed, and then the swing downward as abstract as the shadow of a stone, a kind of forest dance. He had bound a rock to the poll with *babiche* to counterbalance the heavy bit. It increased the accuracy of each stroke.

Monsieur Trépagny launched into a droning sermon on the necessity, the duty of removing the trees, of opening land not just for oneself but for posterity, for what this place would become. "Someday," Monsieur Trépagny said, pointing into the gloom, "someday men will grow cabbages here. To be a man is to clear the forest. I don't see the trees," he said. "I see the cabbages. I see the vineyards."

Monsieur Trépagny said his uncle Jean Trépagny, *dit* Chamailleur for his disputatious nature—Chama for short—would take Duquet's place. He was old but strong, stronger than Duquet. He would arrive soon. Monsieur Trépagny's brothers would also come. Eventually. And he said the time for felling trees was now over. The *bébites* were at their worst, the wet heat dangerous, the trees too full of sap. Indeed, the hellish swarms of biting insects were with them day and night.

"Winter. Winter is the correct time to cut the forest. Today is the time for removing stumps and burning." It was also the time, he added, for René to begin to fulfill his other duties.

"For three days a week your labor is mine. As part of your work," said Monsieur Trépagny, "you are to supply my table with fish." The more immediate work involved preparing the gardens for Mari. The oxen, Roi and Reine, pulled Monsieur Trépagny's old plow sullenly. A savage fly with a green head battened on their blood. Monsieur Trépagny smeared the animals with river clay, which hardened into dusty clots but could do nothing about the clustering gnats. But Mari, the Indian woman, steeped tamarack bark in spring water and twice daily sluiced their burning eyes. In the long afternoons, with many sighs, she planted the despised garden. One day that summer she sent her two young sons to a place called Odanak, where remnants of her people had fled.

"Goose catch learn them. Many traps learn. Good mens there hunting. Here only garden, cut tree learn."

Monsieur Trépagny said acidly that what they would learn would be rebellion against the settlers and warfare.

Mindful of his fishing duties René went to the river. Monsieur Trépagny had given him a knife, fishhooks, a waxed linen line and a large basket for the fish. In the river fish were large and angry and several times the linen line parted and he lost a precious hook. But Mari was scornful. "Small fish," she said. "Good fisherman not Lené. My people make weirs, catch many many. Big many."

To divert her irritation he pointed at a stinging nettle in the garden. "We have those in France," he said.

"Yes. Bad plant grow where step whiteman people—those 'Who is it Coming'—*Wenuj.*"

Mari asked him to leave the fish intact—she would clean them herself. She buried the entrails in the garden and when René asked her if that was the Indian way she gave him a look and said it was a common practice for all fools who grew gardens instead of gathering the riches of the country.

"Eels!" she said. "Eels catch. Eels liking us. We river people."

She wove three eel traps for him and gave him fish scraps for bait, went with him to the river and showed him likely places to try. Almost every day thereafter he brought her fat eels. She said the Mi'kmaq had many ways to catch eels and that the traps were best for him. When her sons came back from the Abenaki village of Odanak they could show him other ways.

In early July the pine trees loosed billows of pollen, yellow plumes like citrine smoke drifting through the forest, mixing with the smoke from burning trees. One morning an old man, his back bent beneath a bundle, his glaring eyes roving left and right, came ricketing out of the pollen clouds from the west trail, which led, as far as René knew, to the end of the world. Above the little mouth stretched a grey mustache like a bit of sheep's wool caught on a twig. The eyes were like Monsieur Trépagny's eyes, black and white and rolling. Chamailleur looked at René, who was preparing to go fishing, and started in at once.

"*Salaud!* You bastard! Why are you not working?"

"I am. It is part of my duty to supply the house with fish for the table."

"What! With a string and a hook? You must use a net. Have the woman make a net. Or a basket trap. Or you must use a spear. Those are the best ways."

"For me the line and hook are best."

"Stupid and obstinate!—*oui, stupide et obstiné!* I know what is best and you do not. It is good I came. I can see you need correction. My nephew is too easy."

René continued stubbornly with his hooks and twisted linen line. But he thought about nets. A net might be better, for the fish were so thick in the river he might get several large ones at the same time. As for Mari's insufferable speechifying on the ways the Mi'kmaq built different kinds of weirs, how they hunted *esturgeon* at night with blazing torches and spears—he ignored all she said. He did use the eel traps she had made, excusing himself on the ground that eels were not fish.

Searching for land to claim when his servitude ended, he discovered Monsieur Trépagny's secret. He had walked far upstream. Recent rains had enlarged the river to a bounding roar over its thousands of rocks. He thought it might be best to choose land not too close to the river, but something with a spring or modest stream. He made his way through an old deadfall where in between the fallen trees millions of saplings grew, as close together as broom straws. Twice he heard a great crashing and saw a swipe of black fur disappear into the underbrush. In early afternoon he came onto a wide but faint trail trending east-west and wondered if it might connect to Monsieur Trépagny's clearing to the east. Instead, with the afternoon before him, he turned west. He saw traces of old ruts that could only have been made by a cart. It was not an Indian trail. Now he was curious.

In midafternoon the trail divided. He followed the wagon ruts. The way became markedly different in character than the usual forest path. Trees had been carefully cleared to create the effect of an *allée,* the ground thinly spread with thousands of broken white shells. He saw this *allée* ran straight, a dark tunnel of trees with a pointed cone of light at the end. He had seen these passageways in France leading to the grand houses of nobles, although he had never ventured into one. And here, in the forests of New France, was the blackest, harshest *allée* of the world, the trees like cruel iron brushes, white shells cracked by deer hooves. The end of the *allée* seemed filled with light, a void at the limit of the tilting earth.

A massive pale thing loomed up, a whitewashed stone house, almost a château, that might have been carried on the sea winds from France and dropped in place. René knew that this was Monsieur Trépagny's *domus,* the center of his secret world. There were three huge chimneys. The windows were of glass, the roof of fine blue slate, and a slate walkway curved around the building, leading to a fenced enclosure. The fence was tall, formed of ornate metal rods. Everything except the stone had come from France, he knew it. It must have cost a fortune, two fortunes, a king's ransom. It was the proof of the *seigneur*'s madness, his mind clotted with old heretic ideas of clan and *domus,* himself the king of an imaginary world.

Disturbed, René cut back to the main trail and followed it east. Dusk was already seeping in. Night came quickly in the forest, even in the long days. As he had guessed, the trail ended in Monsieur Trépagny's clearing. He went straight to the cabin he now shared with Chama, who was rolled up in Duquet's old beaver robe, snoring and mumbling.

The summer months went on. Chama, bossy and cursing, decided where they would cut. They cleared trees, dragging stumps into line to form a bristled root fence. René fished for the table, listened to Mari tell Mi'kmaw stories to Elphège, Theotiste and Jean-Baptiste about beaver bone soup and rainbow clothes and the tiny *wigguladumooch,* and as he absorbed that lore he watched Monsieur Trépagny and wondered about his secret house, which later he learned the *seigneur* had named Le Triomphe. He had the coveted *particule* and could call himself Claude Trépagny du Triomphe.

The heat of summer disappeared abruptly. Overnight a wedge of cold air brought a new scent—the smell of ice, of animal hair, of burning forest and the blood of the hunted.

3

Renardette

Violent maples flared against the black spruce. Rivers of birds on their great autumnal journeys filled the skies—Hudsonian godwits, whole nations of hawks, countless black warblers—*paruline rayée*—looking like tiny men with their black berets, chalky faces and dark mustache streaks, cranes, longspurs, goldeneyes, loons, sparrows, flycatchers, warblers, geese. The first ice storm came one night in October. Then the world pressed flat, snow hissing in the spruce needles, the sun dimmed by a grisaille wash. The forest clenched into itself as though inhaling a breath.

Mari's sons Elphège and Theotiste returned from Odanak carrying traps and snares, whistles and calls to lure game. Mari was intensely interested in these objects, but Monsieur Trépagny called them rubbish and threw Theotiste's beaver funnel trap into the fireplace. René watched the boy's face harden, watched how he kept his eyes lowered, not looking at Monsieur Trépagny. For a moment he saw in Theotiste the cruel Indian.

December brought stone-silent days though a fresh odor came from the heavy sky, the smell of cold purity that was the essence of the boreal forest. So ended René's first year in the New World.

Snow heaped in great drifts smothered the trees so thickly they released avalanches when the wind rose. René learned he had never before in his life experienced extreme cold nor seen the true color of blackness. A burst of ferocious cold screwed down from the circumpolar ice. He woke in darkness to the sound of exploding trees, opened the door against a wall of palpable chill, and his first breath bent him in a spasm of coughing. Jerking with cold he managed to light his candle and, as he knelt to remake the fire, he saw minute snow crystals falling from his exhaled breath.

At breakfast Monsieur Trépagny said it was too cold to cut trees. "On such a day frozen ax blades shatter and one burns the lungs. Soon you cough blood. Then you die. It will be warmer in a few days."

When René mentioned hearing trees explode, the *seigneur* said that in such intense cold even rocks could not bear it and burst asunder. Folding gelid moose bone marrow into a piece of bread he said, "One winter, after such a cold attack, I came upon four deer frozen upright in the forest."

"Ah, ah," said Chama, "one time in the north when the weather was warm and pleasant for ten days, then, in a single breath, a wind of immeasurable cold descended like an ax and the tossing waves in the river instantly froze into cones of ice. We prayed we would not do likewise."

It was during this cold period that Mari's youngest child, Jean-Baptiste, who from infancy had suffered a constant little cough, became seriously ill; the cough deepened into a basso roar. The child lay exhausted and panting.

The moon was a slice of white radish, the shadows of incomparable blackness. The shapes of trees fell sharply on the snow, of blackness so profound they seemed gashes into the underworld. The days were short and the setting sun was snarled in rags of flying storm cloud. The snow turned lurid, hurling away like cast blood. The dark ocean of conifers swallowed the afterglow. René was frightened by the intensity of the cold even in the weak sunlight, and by Jean-Baptiste's sterterous wheezes coming from his pallet near the fire, his weakening calls to Mari and finally the everlasting silence. Monsieur Trépagny said coldly, "All must pay the debt of nature."

The bitter arctic plunge held for a week, then softened to a bright stillness. Mari carried the little body to the mission in Wobik for safekeeping until spring burial. Men went into the forest again. They crossed the frozen river. René learned to walk on snowshoes into the chill world. Tree cutting was easier, and with endless wood supplies they kept a constant fire near the work. Elphège, who had grown taller at Odanak and could help with hauling branches, worked beside him.

"So," said René, "you have learned many hunting skills at that place?"

"*Oui*. Many ways to catch every animal. All different each season. You see over there?" He pointed west into the woods where they had not yet begun to cut. "That heap of snow?"

"Yes," said René.

"What do you observe?"

"Ah. I observe a heap of snow."

"If you go close to it you will see more."

They walked together toward the mound. Elphège pointed to a small hole near the top. A feathery rime surrounded it.

"You see? Frozen breath of a bear." He explained in great detail the ways the bear could be killed and extracted from its den. He continued to talk of ways to lure geese into a deep ditch so they could not open their wings and fly away, explained how to read the age of a moose track, to know the animal's sex, its size and even its condition. René was astonished at the boy's knowledge. He was an Indian hunter, and he was, as Trépagny had prophesied, well versed in trickery and deceit.

René's free days exploring the forest gave him pleasure. Sometimes he went back to the deadfall region near the west trail, where the snow was mounded in fantastic heaps. He did not go near Monsieur Trépagny's elaborate house.

A few days after Mari returned from the mission, Monsieur Bouchard, who, in addition to his duties as government deputy, was captain of the militia, came up from the river, moving easily on snowshoes.

"What brings you here, Captain Bouchard? It's a long way," said Monsieur Trépagny. "Is there a corvée or a militia mustering? Are the Iroquois advancing?"

"On the ship, a letter for you from France. It looked pressing important, red wax seals, a coat of arms. So I bring it to you."

They went up to the house. "The river is a shorter road by half than through the forest," said Monsieur Bouchard as they climbed the slope to the house. "I wonder you don't use your canoe in the pleasant weather."

"Fighting the current is more arduous than walking."

Monsieur Trépagny examined the letter, his sallow skin suddenly scarlet, and put it unopened on the shelf near the door. The men sat at the table drinking hot water with a little whiskey in it.

"We have a sad story in Wobik," said Monsieur Bouchard. "François Poignet—do you know him?"

"By sight only. Tall and with a cast in one eye? A farmer."

"The same, but a good man. He went into the forest on his land during the recent cold to continue clearing. His wife died in childbed the summer past and their only living child is a girl of ten, Léonardette. The unfortunate father's ax glanced off the frozen tree as off a block of granite and cut his left leg to the bone."

"*Zut,*" said Monsieur Trépagny.

"He struggled to get back to his house. The blood trail marked his effort. Perhaps he called out. If so, no one heard him. He exsanguinated and froze. He was lying on his bier of frozen blood, more frozen than the ax, when we found him."

"It is a hard country," said Monsieur Trépagny.

"In addition to bringing you that letter I came to ask if you would take the girl into your household—she is young but strong. You know girls are valuable in this womanless land." He winked.

"Ah," said Monsieur Trépagny. "Now I see why you made such a long trip. Why does not someone in Wobik take this girl? Why not Père Perreault? Why me? What is wrong with the child?"

Monsieur Bouchard lifted his eyes to the smoky ceiling and rolled his head a little.

"It's true that she is not perfect in form." There was a long silence.

"In what way is she not perfect in form?"

"Well, in *form* she is perfect enough, but she has a birthmark—*tache de vin*—on her neck."

"And what does the *tache de vin* signify that it repels the citizens of Wobik and the holy priest?"

"It is, in fact, oh ah"—Monsieur Bouchard was sweating with the heat of the fire and the discomfort of his errand—"it is a perfect little image of a demon—with horns. I thought that as your religious beliefs . . ." And his voice trailed off. He looked yearningly at the door.

"My religious beliefs? You think I would welcome a girl with the mark of the Evil One on her neck?"

"It is said—it is said you have a—respect—not for God but for the devil."

"I do not. Sir, I abhor the demon. You are misinformed. I believe that your Roman Catholic 'God' is the Devil, the Demiurge. You have only to read in the Old Testament to see his cruelty. To me *that* is the Demon. It is you who worship the devil." His squinted eyes caught the light as splinters of ice.

"Perhaps I was misinformed, but my duty is to see the girl in someone's care. The people in the village—" Calling on public opinion was the last card in his hand.

"No, don't speak to me of people in villages."

"Yes, as that may be, but people in the village have seen certain things. For example, they say they have seen you in the flying canoe with the devil and his impious boatmen, plying the clouds and laughing cruelly." He got it out in a tumble.

"What rubbish!" said Monsieur Trépagny. "Who was this sharp-eyed person—witch, I should say—who sees such false wonders?" He had moved closer to the deputy.

"I am not at liberty to name persons," came the smug response of one who protects the innocent.

"Have a care, Monsieur Bouchard."

The old deputy put up his chin. "*You* have a care, Monsieur Claude Trépagny du Triomphe. I have little interest in flying canoes and devil pacts. Nor in you. I want only to find a place for the girl." He added slyly, "She is skilled in brewing excellent beer. She learned well from her mother."

Mari brought more hot water to the table and, eyes downcast, said quietly, "That girl take me. No like make beer me."

"There you go!" cried Monsieur Bouchard. "I'll send her right up. She's just down by the river." Two strides and he was out the door, his long cloak whisking after him.

"Captain Bouchard! Wait!" bellowed Trépagny at the closing door. He whirled around and struck Mari to her knees, then slammed out with his ax in hand.

The skinny, sad child slowly climbed the snowy hill from the river. She was thin with lank hair, dark circles under her small brown eyes and a half-cringing way of carrying herself as though ducking blows before they had been struck. Her fingers were slender and dexterous. Mari, moving slowly, patted her shoulder twice, put a wooden spoon in her hand and set her to stirring mush. When Monsieur Trépagny came in he pulled her to the doorway to examine the demonic birthmark. He saw a small red triangle the size of a thumbnail on the nape of her neck and at its top two tiny triangles the height of a mosquito.

"Hah!" said Monsieur Trépagny. "It's no demon. The stupid town folk have seen only what they wanted to see. The fools. It's a fox. We shall call you Renardette."

Despite her cringing manner the girl was a competent brewer. She began by scouring the brew house and the stone brewing jars. She asked for hop seeds and planted them among the stumps. She picked the ripe hops herself and made very good beer. No one drank more of it than Renardette herself. Though René still preferred *vin rouge*, it had to be imported and was too costly. But if ever the settlers' apple orchards began to bear they could have *cidre*. That would be pleasure.

4

guests from the north

During René's third winter Monsieur Trépagny began to behave erratically. He went off for weeks at a time and when he returned he was rudely commanding, even to Chama.

In early May with snow still on the ground Monsieur Trépagny said he would be gone for a year or perhaps two, as he had pressing business in Kébec and France. He told René that Chama would be in charge of the daily work. He marked out an impossibly large area, more than five arpents (almost five English acres), for them to clear of trees. In France, thought René, the forests were controlled by laws and customs; here there were no forest laws beyond the desires of the *seigneur*. That Trépagny had the right to order the clearing confounded him and he sensed injustice.

Trépagny slapped his gloves on his thigh and mounted his horse. He gave a last order: "Mari, do not neglect the garden." Mari said nothing but her fingers twitched. René knew she disliked gardening, considered it French foolishness. In the garden she felt snared. She neglected it at every chance, she and Renardette going to gather medicine plants. She knew the healing virtues of many tree barks. She kept moldy substances in a box to bind onto infected wounds. Some fungi she worked into salves.

"Of course," Monsieur Trépagny had sneered, as though describing a vicious fault, "all the Indians are physicians and apothecaries. They alone know the secret virtues of many plants. Have you never heard how they cured de Champlain's crew, dying of *scorbut,* with a broth of hemlock needles? Wait, you will hear it a thousand times."

But now he was gone and Chama pranced around like a rooster. And, like that of a rooster, his wet eye fell on the only hens in sight. In the night René heard him slide stealthily out of his beaver robe and ease out the door, his footsteps squeaking in the stiff snow. In minutes rapid running and the slamming door brought him back.

More than two years passed before Monsieur Trépagny returned on a fine sorrel stallion. He sprang off with a flourish like the signature of a state minister. He was decked in a pea-green doublet with paned sleeves, silk breeches in darker green and trimmed with knotted ribbons. His massive belt sported three silver buckles and his boots showed crimson heels. The glory was a low-crowned hat with six red-dyed ostrich plumes wreathed around the brim. He smelled of a cloying perfume that made Elphège sneeze out a gob of snot onto the scalloped cuff of the doublet. Monsieur Trépagny knocked him to the ground and kicked him; Mari threw herself over the boy. Monsieur Trépagny gave her a powerful kick in the ribs as well, remounted his sorrel and rode west, no doubt to revel in his secret house, thought René.

At supper the next night Mari served up stewed eels and dried salmon made into a thick fish pudding. Monsieur Trépagny exploded. Eels were savages' food, he said, and he expected something better as befitted a *seigneur.* They were witnessing Monsieur Trépagny's transformation into a gentleman manifested by his new garments and his dislike for eels, which in the past he had always relished. He expressed his growing disdain for the Indians, calling them lazy and ignorant barbarians. He threw a coin on the table in front of Mari and told her that she must pack up and leave with her children the morrow—he was marrying a French lady in a fortnight. The coin would pay her passage east back to her people, where she might eat all the eels in the world. Mari sat quietly, saying nothing, and René supposed she was unfeeling and submissive.

It was midmorning when they left the house, Mari with her few possessions in a willow basket pack, the children each carrying a bundle. Renardette said to Mari in a low voice that she did not want to go to Wobik, that the people there treated her badly. Mari glanced at Chama, busy sharpening knives but listening attentively.

"Here bad stay you. Come you. Safe that mission."

The little group went down the steps to where Monsieur Trépagny stood in the yard watching, legs spraddled like a colossus. Suddenly he turned to René.

"What are you gaping at? Go with them! And in Wobik arrange with Philippe Bosse to bring out my trunks on his cart. They are by now surely at the deputy's house. Be back in five days' time."

René carried Theotiste across the river, Elphège stumbling behind. Mari, gripping Renardette's reluctant hand, was the first across, moving as though on a firm path beneath the water, then striding eastward along the dim path to Wobik.

"Are your people in Wobik?" René asked her, although everything he had heard indicated otherwise.

"No. No Wobik." She spoke in a low voice.

"Then—where?"

For a long time she said nothing. When they stopped at noon to make tea she said, "Sipekne'katik. River people we. All our life that river, other river. Mi'kma'ki our place. Good rivers. Good food. Eel, fish. Good medicine plant. Better. Here no good." She handed corn cakes spread with *cacamos* to the children.

"How did you come to Monsieur Trépagny's house?" he asked, but she did not answer and they walked in silence until they reached Wobik the next noon. Mari stopped at the edge of the settlement near the path to the mission church. "Here," she said. "Confession,

31

mass. Read, write, talk *French* by Père Perreault." She gave him two corn cakes for his return journey.

"*You* read? *You* write?" said René, astonished and jealous. He had seen no evidence of these skills in Mari.

"*Bientôt*," she said, "soon," and with the silent children she took the path to the mission and the priest's house. Only Elphège turned to look at him. René's glance swept the ground and when he saw a *Sabot de la Vierge* he picked it and pinned it to his shirt with a willow sliver, enjoying the musky perfume.

He went on to the deputy's house. A hundred yards away the river glittered and pranced in the sunlight. Two huge canoes were drawn up on the shore and under the spruce trees a group of men and a few Indian women were making camp—fur traders from the *pays d'en haut* heading for Tadoussac or Kébec. They were a rough-looking lot, great triangles of shoulders, chest, neck and arms balanced on bandy legs, bearded, dark-skinned from smoky fires, their tasseled red hats covering oily hair. One muscular fellow lurching under two heavy packs caught his eye; there was something about him René thought he knew. The man swiveled away and went into the shadow under the trees.

"Ah, Monsieur Sel." Monsieur Bouchard, the deputy, was cordial and smiling, his yellow eyebrows raised in pleasure at seeing the young woodcutter from the forest. René explained that Monsieur Trépagny had renamed Léonardette Renardette because he thought the birthmark resembled a fox face, and he had sent Mari and the children away. He wanted to have his trunks brought out to his house.

"Ah, that is what fine fellows do when a moneyed lady with connections comes in sight. Yes, Philippe Bosse can bring his trunks out—for a consideration which I'm sure the elegant Monsieur Trépagny du Triomphe will be happy to pay, now that he is marrying the wealthy Mélissande du Mouton-Noir. I'll see to it this afternoon so that he may continue to appear as a gentleman. Likely he wants them delivered to his big edifice he calls the 'manor house'?"

"He said nothing of that." As he looked around the room René saw Monsieur Bouchard had a shelf of books with gold letters on the spines. He discerned an *R*.

"Philippe can find him and ask. And you, are you clearing your own land now? Have you built your house? Have you also found someone to marry?"

"Monsieur Trépagny has not yet granted me land." René had lost any sense of years.

"Indeed?" Monsieur Bouchard took down the big ledger and turned the pages. "Well, I believe it is well past the time. You have worked for him five years and four months. He will owe you wages. I will send him a note with Philippe. But have you found land to settle on?"

"I have seen several good places west of Monsieur Trépagny, one in an old Indian clearing about a mile from the river but near a small stream that runs all summer and autumn. Another is in the forest with a clear spring issuing from under a yellow birch. It has a fine mix of hardwoods."

Monsieur Bouchard glanced at the wilted lady's slipper fastened to René's shirt. "Ah, a boutonniere. You know, a young doctor has recently come to Kébec who is much interested in the Indan pharmacognosy. Every day more men of talent arrive. And you shall certainly have your land."

Monsieur Bouchard's haul of long words made René uneasy, but he nodded as one intimate with the Indian pharmacognosy.

"Of course it is best to choose a wooded site and clear it—the more trees we cut down the sooner we'll have fine farms and more settlers. Be sure not to cut down that yellow birch. If you do your spring will dry up. Use the clearing for pasture for your cows." He sighed. "And of course Monsieur Trépagny will continue to be the *seigneur* of those lands. As they say, 'No land without a lord.' He has an extensive holding. When you raise grain you will bring it to his mill to be ground into the fine flour of New France."

"I do not think he has a mill."

"He will certainly build one. It is one of the duties of a *seigneur* to his *habitants.* Presumably he will persuade more people to come to his holding." Monsieur Bouchard put the ledger away and smiled in dismissal.

"Sir," said René. "I have a question."

"Yes?" The deputy's face grew serious.

"Mari the Mi'kmaq woman told me she was learning to read and write from the priest at the mission. Could that be true?"

"Père Perreault tries to teach the Indians their letters, to read a little and write. To what end except to read scripture I do not know, but that is the way of many of the French, especially fur traders, to be cordial to native people. Not all, of course. Most farmers and settlers dislike *les sauvages.*"

"Would he—?"

"What, teach you? You must ask him, but I am almost certain you would have to come to the mission. If you lived nearer Wobik you could easily learn those skills from him. Already almost twenty people are living here. Why not think about choosing land close to Wobik instead of a two-day journey away in the wilderness?" His yellow eyebrows went up and down in conspiratorial inquiry.

René said he would consider all of this. But the deputy knew he would not. He saw the stubborn face of a man with a mind like a stone, a man who preferred to live in the rough forest, the endless forest that amazed and frightened.

On the return trip there was much to think about: Mari, an Indian woman who could—perhaps—read and write; the possibility that he, too, could learn these arts; and the great news that the time for his land grant and freedom from Monsieur Trépagny was at hand. Despite the allure of living near the mission and the settlement, he had a feeling for the woods. As for Wobik, that muddy, tiny scrap of settlement was too much like France.

A little distance past the place where Monsieur Trépagny had killed the porcupine years earlier he began to sense something. He slowed

34

his pace, set each foot with care as silently as he could and listened. Nothing. He went on, but the sense of a menacing entity nearby persisted. Five years of Monsieur Trépagny's talk of supernatural horrors in the forest, the mnemic ethos of the region, had damaged his French rationality. He had come to believe in the *witiku* and its comrades as he believed in the devil and angels. He walked on, the back of his neck exposed and vulnerable, his senses quiveringly alert. The Iroquois were far to the south and west, though he had heard a few raiding parties sometimes slipped through the forests unseen and massacred settlers. He considered what animals might stalk a man: bears, cougars, wolves. Of these, bears had the greatest magical powers. It might be a bear snuffling along his trail, yet he doubted it. At this time of year bears were cramming their bodies with berries and greasy moths, eating, eating. As he paused, looking for blaze marks—for they were weathered and grey, difficult to see in the deepening light—he heard the distinct sound of a breaking twig in the sombrous forest.

From that moment the fleering faces of daemons appeared among the interstices of the branches, among the needles. The fear of Iroquois and their unspeakable tortures flooded his bowels. He might never get back to Monsieur Trépagny's clearing, he might never claim his land.

Away from the trail he saw acres of young dog-hair larch. In there perhaps he could hide, for no one, not even an impassioned Iroquois, would plunge into trees so tightly packed. He burrowed into the larch thicket.

The impression of something alien not far away persisted, and as he rummaged in his pocket for a corn cake he smelled a faint drift of smoke. It was the fire of the Iroquois.

Not daring to light a fire himself, he curled up under the larches and spent a shivering night dozing and listening for their approach. He could make out a pale clump of corpse flowers and other luminous fungi in the gloom. Such sullen smolderings, invisible by day, were the signs of demonic passage.

When the paling east presaged dawn he was on the barely discernible trail, moving swiftly. The feeling of being pursued grew stronger and he half-ran, panting, sure he heard an Iroquois's heaving breath. Then he stopped. Fleeing would not help him. He took up a station behind a spruce a few yards off the trail and waited. He would let the Iroquois appear. He would face their tortures and die as others had died. It was the red thread in the fabric of life in New France.

A short time passed and then he heard not only snapping twigs but a voice, two voices. The few sung words in French—"... you'll find many Iroquois bodies—*plusieurs corps iroquois*"—and then laughter. French! He saw motion through the trees and stepped onto the trail. But stood tense and ready for trouble. They saw him.

"Ah! He has waited for us!" They were short muscular men with black beards, top-heavy with huge shoulders and arms, thick black eyebrows and red lips—*hommes du nord, voyageurs,* men of the north. But he knew them by their large eyes, Monsieur Trépagny eyes, ebon black irises in flashing whites. They were dressed in the mode of *voyageur*–fur traders, one with a red tuque, the other with a neck-erchief tied around his head, both with deerskin leggings and Indian-style breechclouts, oblivious to biting insects. Both wore brilliant sashes knotted around their waists, both wore woolen double shirts. They were drunk and carrying bottles of spirits, which they swigged as they walked. They were Monsieur Trépagny's long-awaited broth-ers from the crowd of boatmen camped at Wobik.

They said their names: Toussaint, whose beard flowed down his breast, and Fernand, with a short bristle of whiskers. *Oui, Taberna-cle!* Of course, by the Holy Tabernacle they were coming to attend Claude's wedding, and yes, they had followed René, but also knew to look for the trail blazes. Some of their comrades would follow, for the chance of a wedding celebration would never be missed by any-one alive in this empty country. Another of their company knew the path, though he preferred not to join the revelry as he said he had a strong dislike of Claude Trépagny. He would stay in Wobik and guard their fur packs. They passed their bottles to René, and soon he was drunk and the brothers grew more boisterous, bragging of their wild and untrammeled lives, singing songs with endless verses.

Toussaint said he knew more than forty songs; Fernand boasted that he had mastered more than fifty and that he would sing all of them this moment commencing with *"Petit Rocher."* He began well but stopped after seven verses. He turned on René.

"You think this is all that we do, sing songs and walk through a forest? No! What they say, we live hard, love hard, sleep hard and eat moose nose!"

Toussaint pressed a dark chunk of food into René's hand, saying it was not moose nose but pemmican. It had a burned, musty flavor and there were hairs in it and nodules of bright fat the color of a chicken's foot. It was chewy stuff and the more he masticated it the more it swelled in his mouth. He took a gulp of whiskey and forced the pemmican down.

René had been thinking of what they said of their companion who would stay in Wobik with the fur packs, thinking of the man he had seen disappear into the spruce shadow, and he knew with sudden surety who it was.

"This one who stays in Wobik, does he have bad teeth?"

"Bad teeth? No. *Chalice!* He has no teeth at all. He dines on mush and broth. He cannot eat pemmican and would be a liability did he not prepare his own repasts."

"Is his name perhaps Duquet? Or something else?"

"Duquet. How do you know?"

"He was an *engagé* with me, on the same ship and hired to the same man—your brother Monsieur Claude Trépagny. He disappeared into the woods one day. Your brother believes he was caught and eaten by the *loup-garou.*"

"Hah! He was not eaten, or if so, only a little around the edges. He is a man of affairs. He knows the important men in the fur trade— even the English. He says he will be a rich man one day."

René had his own idea of why Duquet did not wish to see Monsieur Trépagny.

• • •

The reunion of the brothers and their uncle Chama was noisy and sentimental. They all wept, embraced, cursed, swigged whiskey, slapped each other on the back, looked earnestly at one another, wept again and talked. The brothers disapproved of the clearing. Their own way of life left no scars on the land, they said, denuded no forests. They glided through the waterways and in seconds the wake of their passage vanished in the stream flow and the forests remained as they had been, silent and endless.

"Uncle, you must come back with us to the high country, what good times we'll have again."

But Chama smiled sadly. He had a spine deformity that every year twisted him a little more sideways. He was no longer able to bear the hard *voyageur* life, a statement which motivated the pitiless brothers to describe tremendous paddling feats—twenty hours, thirty hours—without a pause. They named heroes of the water, wept for the memory of a friend who broke his leg so that the bone protruded from the bunched flesh. They had put him up to his neck in the icy water to die.

"Not long enough to sing all of *'J'ai trop grand peur des loups,'* which he asked us to sing. It was his favorite, that song—'I have a great fear of wolves.' And he sang the verses with us with chattering jaws until his heart slowed and he made the mortal change."

This started them off on stories of *coureurs de bois* who suffered untimely ends.

". . . And Médard Baie, who suffered painful stomach cramps and died of the beaver disease?"

"That poison plant that beaver eat with great pleasure, and I have heard the Indians, too, eat of it, but it is death for a Frenchman."

The wedding was four days away as the bride was traveling from Kébec and not expected for at least another three sunrises. A priest, not Père Perreault, but a more important cleric from Kébec, would accompany her. The marriage sacrament would take place in Monsieur Trépagny's big house. Even now, still in his lightly soiled Parisian finery, the *seigneur* was directing two Mi'kmaw men loading a wagon of goods for transport to that elegant structure. Fires burned in the great fireplaces to take away the damp, the floors were strewn with sweet-grass. Those same Indians, with Chama's help, had constructed a long table under the pines. Everything was ready—except the food.

"*Mon Dieu!*" shouted Monsieur Trépagny. He had forgotten the need for a cook when he sent Mari away, and only now realized the great problem.

"What problem?" bawled Toussaint. "Feed them pemmican! We feed twenty-five men a day on the stuff and it does them good."

Monsieur Trépagny turned to René and said, "*Vite! Vite.* Hurry back to Wobik and get Mari. Bring her here. Bring whatever she needs to make a wedding feast. We will procure game and fish while you are gone. *Vite!*"

Mari and Renardette were sitting outside the mission house plucking birds. Mari heard Monsieur Trépagny's demand stoically and kept on pulling feathers, which she dropped to the ground. The light breeze sent them bouncing and rolling. The minutes passed and Mari said nothing.

"So will you come right now? With me? I am to carry any provisions you need. Monsieur Trépagny gave me this for you"—he showed a bright coin. "And this for what you need to make this feast"—and he showed the second coin.

"Elphège shoot good duck with arrow," she said, turning it so he could admire the fat breast. He glanced at Elphège, who grinned and put his head down shyly.

"A very handsome duck," he said. "Finest duck in New France. Maybe Monsieur Trépagny would pay you for that duck."

"It is for Maman," said Elphège, then, overcome with so much social intercourse, he fled to the back of the building.

Renardette stood off to the side, rubbing the dirt with her heel in a semicircular design. "I have good beer back at Monsieur's house."

René understood that Mari preferred to stay where she was and roast Elphège's duck. But she stood up, and he followed her into the mission house.

She put the cleaned duck in a pack basket. She gathered jackets, then said, "Père Pillow not here. Not know. Letter write me." She got a pen and inkwell from the shelf, found a scrap of paper and, sitting at the table, made a parade of marks on it.

"What did you write?" René asked, consumed with curiosity.

"That feather say, 'Cook three suns.' That write me."

He could see with his own eyes that Mari knew writing, though he thought her letters looked like worm casts, nothing like his exquisite *R*.

On the way Mari made several side forays to gather wild onions, mushrooms and green potherbs. She spent a long time searching along the river for something in particular, and when she found it—tall plants with feathery leaves—she stripped off seed heads and put them in a small separate bag. When they arrived at Monsieur Trépagny's clearing, the brothers had butchered six does and Chama was crouched over a large sturgeon, scooping roe into a bucket with his hands. Mari said nothing to any of them but went into the old house and began to haul out pots and kettles to be shifted to the wedding house. From the cupboard she took dried berries and nuts. She found the sourdough crock, neglected in her absence, scraped the contents into a bowl, added flour and water and covered it over, carried it to the cart. She put the seeds she had gathered at the riverside into the cupboard on the top shelf. She spoke to Monsieur Trépagny in a low voice, so quiet in tone only he heard.

"Tomorrow bread bake. Tomorrow all cook. Then mission."

"Eh," said Monsieur Trépagny. "We'll see."

5

the wedding

Philippe Bosse was to bring the bride, her maidservant and the priest to the wedding house in his freshly painted cart. The brothers and their trapper comrades drank and wrestled under the pines. Monsieur Trépagny paced up and down, dashed into the house to adjust something, out again to look into Mari's pots, then to peer into the gloom of the dark *allée*. Elphège had built Mari's cook fire, a long trench where the venison haunches could roast on their green sapling spits and the great sturgeon, pegged to a cedar plank, sizzle. Mari ran back and forth between the fire trench and a small side fire, where she cooked vegetables and herbs. In one pot she simmered a kind of cornmeal pudding with maple syrup and dried apples, a pudding that Monsieur Trépagny loved to the point of gluttony. As it bubbled and popped she sifted in the seeds she had gathered at the streamside.

In clumps and couples the guests from Wobik began to arrive and they sat about drinking Renardette's good beer and talking, admiring Monsieur Trépagny's fine house. They looked into the great bedroom hung with imported tapestries and with inquisitive, work-worn fingers touched the pillows plump with milkweed down.

"It's like old France."

"*Dieu,* maybe too much like . . ."

They heard the bride long before they saw her.

"Hear that!" said Elphège. The company fell silent, listening. Suddenly three deer burst out of the forest, scattered in different directions. They all heard a distant ringing sound that gradually grew louder until it revealed itself as a high-pitched, strident female voice in a passion shrieking, "I refuse! Cheat! Impostor! Skulking savages! Uncivilized! Peasants! Nothing but trees! I have been duped! My uncle has been duped! Someone will pay! I refuse! I will return to Paris! *Je vais retourner à Paris!*" And it was still ten minutes before Philippe Bosse's fur-lined cart turned into the *allée*.

Toussaint said to Fernand, "She is so ugly she must be very, very rich." The bride's face was crimson, enhanced by a liberal application of French red, her orange hair protruding from under her wig. The lady's maid looked as if she might carry a *poignard* in her garter. One bony hand gripping the side of the cart the imported priest, Père Beaulieu, sat stone-faced. The bride's eye fell on Monsieur Trépagny.

"You!" she said. "You will explain this monstrosity"—and she waved disdainfully at Monsieur Trépagny's fine house. "What a shack. *C'est un vrai taudis!* Explain to me how this hut in the forest is a fine manor house and the site of a great rich city as you told my guardian uncle." She sprang from the cart with the elasticity of an Inuit hunter, and the *voyageurs* applauded. She scorched them with a fiery look of disdain and marched into the house with the maid, Monsieur Trépagny and Père Beaulieu following.

Philippe Bosse complained in a low voice to his listeners. "I said, 'Madame, I have contracted to bring you to Monsieur Trépagny's fine house in this fine forest and I will do it. What follows is for him to decide.'"

They expected the bride, her dangerous-looking maid and the bony priest to come out of the house at any instant and get back into the wagon and roll away to France. But none of them appeared. The wedding guests could hear their voices—the bride's hot and savage, upbraiding and sarcastic; Monsieur Trépagny's cajoling, imploring and explaining; the priest's murmuring and calming. As the hour passed the bride's voice softened, Monsieur Trépagny's soared.

Toussaint, Fernand and Chama had listened to it all before, as had

René. Those familiar words! "Rich forests . . . unimaginable hect-ares of land . . . fertile soil . . . fish to feed the world . . . powerful rivers . . . beautiful cities of the future . . . the *domus*."

Twilight fell and Chama, Elphège and Philippe Bosse built a bon-fire. The *voyageurs* sampled the barrel of whiskey. They waited.

"After all, there's the feast," said Toussaint yearning toward the food. He and his comrades moved toward the table where Mari had set out the kettle of stewed eels, the roasted sturgeon, the fat duck in an expensive sugar sauce, platters of corn cakes, moose *cacamos,* the legs of venison done so they were crispy on the outside, tender in the teeth, various porridges and sauces. Down the length of the table paraded bottles of cherry brandy. Before they could touch the savory dishes there was a cry to wait. Monsieur Trépagny stood on the fine stone doorstep, and behind him was Mélissande du Mouton-Noir, her face red and corrugated in the light of the bonfire. Monsieur Trépagny spread out his arms as if he were a wild goose readying for flight.

"Attention!" he cried. "Will the guests please enter."

There was an excited murmur and anticipatory cheers.

Inside the drawing room the guests sat on still-splintery plank benches, taking in the parquet floor, the ornamented *couvre-feu,* gap-ing at the fairy-like chandelier, its crystal prisms shattering the candle flames into a thousand darts that contributed the feeling of a cathe-dral to the marriage ceremony. The Wobik women gazed enviously at the elaborate wrought-iron chimney crane that could hold pots in three positions.

After the ceremony, the celebration began. Elphège built up the bon-fire and the flames threw flaring shadows on the scene. The guests approached the table, the *voyageurs* rushing, stabbing and hacking, the Wobik residents picking at the feast meats with refined airs felt they were in fine society. Monsieur Trépagny produced bottles of many shapes: red wine, rum, brandy, whiskey—even champagne, real French champagne. Two of the *voyageurs* brought out fiddles and began to play while the others clapped and sang. The loud music and the violent stamping of the dancers, their sashes whipping and curling in the firelight as they leapt, drove off any pretensions to gentility. Even the red-faced bride danced, and Monsieur Trépagny was a madman of athletic brilliance. The distorted sound bounced off the forest trees and any nearby evil spirits shrank into the earth until it should be over. Under a bush, covered with a dish towel, waited the cornmeal pudding with its potent water hemlock seeds, Mari's farewell dish for Monsieur Trépagny. She waited for the right moment to present it.

The sky was light when the last dancers rolled up in their blankets under the spruce. Only the *voyageurs* were still awake, sitting around the fire and passing one of the endless bottles. René pumped them for more information on Duquet.

Duquet, they said, was clever. He had friends high in the fur company. He knew important men. He made side deals, keeping all the marten pelts for himself. He brought forbidden whiskey into the north and got the Indians too drunk to strike any but the feeblest and most disadvantageous bargains for their furs. "And Duquet is very strong, the strongest among us. He has great endurance." To be strong was everything. Duquet was becoming a legend of the country.

René thought the *seigneur* had retired with his prize, but he now saw Monsieur Trépagny standing on the other side of the fire, listening. The flames paled in the brightening morning.

"This Duquet," Monsieur Trépagny said, beginning quietly, but speaking in a quickening, sharpening tempo, his eyes bulging and beginning to roll. "Duquet? Would that be Duquet who signed a contract to work for me for three years?" His voice rose to a furious bellow. "Would that be the *Duquet* who ran away like a dog? Is *that* the Duquet of whom you speak?" He looked at his brothers.

Toussaint said nothing, his beard limp and stained, but Fernand rolled his wicked Trépagny eyes at his bridegroom brother and said "*Ouais.* The same. He told us you were cruel."

"Ah," said Monsieur Trépagny. "He does not yet know how cruel I can be. Do you return to Wobik now? I will go with you. I will have the dog's skull. He will serve out his three years and we will see who is cruel."

"Brother," said Toussaint, "you would do well to leave Duquet alone. He is a dangerous man." Monsieur Trépagny, goaded by this apostasy, screamed *"Saddle my horse"* at Elphège.

"Your pudding?" said Mari, holding out the cold pot. But René noticed how the *seigneur* glared at her as he rushed into his house.

In the few minutes it took Monsieur Trépagny to make his excuse to his new wife for his precipitous departure, Toussaint and Fernand ran to the riverbank, leapt into Monsieur Trépagny's canoe and began to paddle like demons, forty-five paddle strokes a minute, downstream toward Wobik. Monsieur Trépagny's horse was slower, and when he galloped into Wobik in late afternoon the traitorous brothers and Duquet were gone. The stolen canoe lay onshore, a marten pelt draped over the thwart—Duquet's mocking signature.

The bridegroom, exhausted and furious, slumped on the deputy's porch until that official returned home from the wedding, then swore out a warrant for Duquet's capture and return.

"I will not rest until I get him and when I do he will suffer."

Monsieur Bouchard was thrilled by this pledge of vengeance, like something in an old ballad, but he had no idea how he could execute the warrant and told Monsieur Trépagny so.

"It will happen," gritted Trépagny through stained teeth.

Mari turned the cornmeal pudding into the embers where at first it gave off a savory smell and then the unpleasant odor of burning grain and sugar; she walked back to the old house. The grey jay that watched everything below waited a day until the ashes were cold and then pecked inquisitively at the burned lump. A few days later Chama discovered the bird's carcass with legs twisted into a sailor's knot, a very strange sight.

Monsieur Trépagny returned to his house in the forest and brooded for some weeks while preparing his expedition into the wilderness to capture Duquet. There was a strange turn in his mind that moved him to delay. He more and more left his new wife to herself and spent much time in his old house with Mari, whom he had forbidden to go back to the mission. Under his direction she cooked handsome dishes and every evening Monsieur Trépagny put on his fine clothes and carried them to Madame Trépagny. There was no cornmeal pudding. The husband and wife dined in silence in the elegant dining room and after dinner, when the maid had cleared the table, when Monsieur Trépagny had drunk a glass of brandy, he said, "Good evening, madame," and returned to Mari. Nothing seemed changed. Mari and her children talked and laughed together in low voices as ever, and their pleasure in each other's company irritated Trépagny, who hissed *"Silence!"* René wondered, too, what she had to say to them in such long ropes of talk, often accompanied by gestures and widened eyes. Months later he understood that she had been telling them the old Mi'kmaw stories, and into the warp of that heritage had interwoven the woof of complicated jokes and language games that gave her people so much pleasure. But Trépagny was sure that he was the butt of their half-smothered laughter, and his red nostrils flared and he demanded silence.

One morning, when René and Chama were cutting in the forest, the Spanish maid appeared and went to the old man. She handed him a letter, telling him Madame Trépagny wished him to carry it to the deputy in Wobik. Chama snorted and shook his head, but when she held up a gold coin he took the letter and put it in his shirt.

His beaver robe was empty for two nights, and it was dusk of the third day before René saw him again, carrying Monsieur Trépagny's captured canoe, his excuse for the trip if his nephew should ask.

"What's afoot?" asked René.

"Nothing good. Monsieur Bouchard turned the color of mud when he read that letter. He said he would come here tomorrow with the priest and consult with Madame and my nephew. It's a bad business."

6

Indian woman

Monsieur Bouchard and Père Perreault entered the clearing riding double on Monsieur Bouchard's old plow horse. René, hauling a basket of fish, straightened up and stared. The visitors passed the storehouse without stopping, heading for Monsieur Trépagny's marriage house. But that elevated gentleman, who had been working at his old forge, saw them through the open door and rushed out. "Where do you go, Monsieur Bouchard? Père Perreault, what do you here?"

The deputy wheeled around, dismounted and glared at Monsieur Trépagny. Père Perreault got down as well and held the reins.

Monsieur Bouchard said, "It is distressing that I find you here and not at your grand house with your lawful wife, Madame Trépagny. I have had a letter from the lady, who complains that you continue to live with the Indian woman, Mari, and are rarely seen at that wedding mansion in which she is lawfully ensconced and where you should be."

Père Perreault spoke in a serious tone: "She wishes to return to her uncle's house in France and demands the return of the rich dowry given you as you have broken your marriage pledge. You have behaved badly and the lady is within her rights. The uncle is a powerful man. He has taken up the matter and it will be a serious thing for you—and your position as *seigneur*. I ask you to accompany us to that house where she now awaits alleviation of her painful and insulting situation."

Monsieur Trépagny followed them silently into the gloom of the west trail.

The day passed slowly. René told Chama and Mari what he had seen and heard. He thought a little smile flickered across Mari's face. When she went inside Chama said, "This nephew should have proceeded in his search for Duquet. He should have stayed with that rich wife. Whenever there is an Indian woman involved there is trouble. His French wife is not the kind to shut her eyes."

Night came and still they did not return. Chama said, "Claude will be begging her, he will grant anything she wishes rather than lose the money and the important position. I know him."

Very early the next morning, as René and Chama were readying for another day of clearing trees, the three men, all in good humor, returned.

"Tell him at once," said Père Perreault. "At once." And they all looked at René.

"What? What is it?" he said. He had still not had a chance to talk to Monsieur Trépagny about his land, and he was afraid now that the *seigneur* had found a way to evade the responsibility.

"You will marry Mari," said Monsieur Trépagny. "Immediately. Père Perreault is on hand to officiate."

"No!" cried René. He whispered, not wishing to be overheard by Mari. "She is old. I do not want to marry her." He had dreamed of a wife from one of the consignment ships with women from France, the King's girls—*les filles du Roi*. A charming and shy young woman with blue eyes. "Also, you and Mari—"

"It was only a country marriage." Père Perreault let the words slide out in his gentle way. "Just a country custom."

"But no," said René.

"You do not yet see reason," said Monsieur Trépagny pleasantly. "She will help you make a house of your own on the land I grant you, and I will be very generous. I will grant you a double portion of land. You will have good workers to aid you—those Indian boys Elphège and Theotiste and that servant girl Renardette. Mari is a clever cook.

48

She will warm you on winter nights. She is adept in curing illness. She has value. What more could you want?"

Mari herself was standing in the doorway, listening without expression. Père Perreault signed to her to come near. René thought furiously in several directions. But to himself he added another reason to Monsieur Trépagny's list: with Mari at his side he could learn to read and write or, even better, depend on her to do whatever reading and writing was needed. The blue-eyed *fille du roi* of his dreams vanished. Again he felt himself caught in the sweeping current of events he was powerless to escape. What could he do against the commands of more important men? He nodded once, yes, he would marry Mari, an old Indian woman. So it was done.

In every life there are events that reshape one's sense of existence. Afterward, all is different and the past is dimmed. For René the great blow had been the loss of Achille, his brother, whom he loved and most dreadfully missed. He came to New France to escape the loss, not realizing he would carry sorrow enclosed within him. The second event was the forced marriage to Mari.

Monsieur Trépagny made a formal assignment of land to René, granting him the old *domus* and workshop and the gardens but not the cow, as well as the clearing to the west that René coveted and the land with clear water springing from under a yellow birch. René was, in one stroke, a man of property. Père Perreault and Monsieur Bouchard left soon after the brief ceremony with Monsieur Trépagny's signature on René's land assignment.

Monsieur Trépagny spoke with casual sarcasm to Mari. "Madame Sel. Cook dinner as you always do and Chama will bring it to my lady wife and myself. After this evening her maid will prepare our food until we find a cook and servant. We will purchase a Pawnee or blackamoor slave or two from Kébec." He walked westward into the forest.

Six woodcock had been hanging for days and had reached the hallucinogenic point of decay that Monsieur Trépagny savored. Mari roasted the birds, put them in a large basket, added a cold leg of venison, four portions of steamed sturgeon. René thought it was a supper the *seigneur* hardly deserved. Chama, who had become attentive to the Spanish maid, carried all of this in the oxcart, the cow tied behind. For their own supper Mari thumped on the table a platter of hot eels graced with the sour-grass sauce. She had baked in the morning and served a loaf of bread with the last of the butter—alas for the loss of the cow.

Mari, walking from fire to table in her deerskin tunic, looked as she had always looked, but she gave René the fattest eel and touched his hand lightly. After the boys went out to the *wikuom* she made up a pallet in front of the fireplace and then pulled off her baggy dress. She stood nude in the firelight—the first naked female he had ever seen—not an old Indian castoff foisted on him, but a strong and well-built woman. She lay on the pallet and waited.

René pulled off his clothes, conscious of his greasy reek. He lay down beside Mari, who rolled toward him. The fabulous shock of warm silky skin against him was powerful in the extreme. Not since he and Achille had intertwined and whispered and tried what they could think to try had he experienced the stunning excitement of another human body naked against his. Mari's elasticity, her hard muscles, her smell of bread, river eels and bitter plants made him wild. She was not Achille, but he thought of his brother as he proceeded.

In the morning Mari said, "Good you," got up, pulled on her deerskin dress with its faded designs and made the fire.

With a shock of insight he understood that Mari's impassive expression was a calm acceptance and knowledge of life's roils and clawing, an attitude that in a way matched his own belief that he flew in the winds of change like a sere leaf. She had answers to the most untoward questions, for the Mi'kmaq had examined the world with boundless imagination for many generations. Over the months and years he learned from her. His relationship with Mari became a marriage of intelligences as well as bodies.

They stood opposed on the nature of the forest. To Mari it was a living entity, as vital as the waterways, filled with the gifts of medicine, food, shelter, tool material, which everyone discovered and remembered. One lived with it in harmony and gratitude. She believed the interminable chopping of every tree for the foolish purpose of "clearing the land" was bad. But that, thought René, was woman's talk. The forest was there, enormous and limitless. The task of men was to subdue its exuberance, to tame the land it grew on—useless land until cleared and planted with wheat and potatoes. It seemed both of them were subject to outside forces, powerless to object in matters of marriage or chopping.

Farther west the manor house resounded with discontent. Monsieur Trépagny tired of his commanding wife, who endlessly harped on how much she wanted to return to Paris, and he began to curse the world he had made. His mind shifted from consolidating the *domus* to vengeance. If only Duquet had been a gentleman he certainly would have tracked him down and challenged him to a duel. Although too much time had passed, he said he would begin his pursuit of Duquet on the next full moon. Elphège, he said, must come with him as his squire. This decision, perhaps, was bolstered by Bouchard's call for a new road-building corvée at that time, an onerous duty that not even one with a *particule* could evade.

At night Mari wept. She said it was right that Monsieur Trépagny pursue Duquet if he wished, but Elphège had no reason to do so.

Before he left, Monsieur Trépagny buried a small metal box beneath the front doorstep, muttering a curse or two. From the hall window upstairs the Spanish maid watched him. Trépagny and Elphège left under the hard dot of the moon and nothing was heard of them nor Duquet nor the bearded brothers until the next spring.

7

bûcheron

Time passed slowly, a long series of days shaped by work. All the second summer, thought René, Mari had been more silent than usual.

"Speak, Mari. What is wrong? You must tell me. Is it Elphège? Are you thinking about Elphège?" he pressed her one night after baby Achille and the newborn twins, Noë and Zoë, were asleep.

She nodded and then bent her head. There was a deep silence, so deep the tumbling flight of a moth drawn to the fire disturbed the air and they heard the puff of vapor as a flame caught it.

"Woman, tell me." He grasped both her hands to show his need to understand.

And the long sad story came out. She was terribly frightened of losing Elphège. Again she spoke of the time when she was a child, when, she said, her people lived on the shore far to the east. One day when they were at their ocean camp a ship came with pale men in it. The newcomers said they were *les Français*. Mari's people showed the *Wenuj* how to gather shellfish and berries, shared food with them. One of the French was Père Perreault—Père Pillow, as she called him. All seemed well for some weeks, but one day the strangers abruptly declared they were returning to France and that some of the Mi'kmaq would come with them. No one wished to go, but the *Wenuj* smiled disarmingly, and then without warning, hairy sailors seized seven of the people, Mari among them, and rushed them to the ship. The anchor was hoisted and the ship away before the people onshore realized. They ran along the coastline gesticulating and shrieking at the ship. The ship sailed on.

"Many days, many days sick us. Then in France come us."

"France? You went to France?"

"Yes. In Palis, ride in wagon, big noise. Weeping all us. Bad food, in box sleep. Long time. Brother sick. Cough, choke he. *Wenuj* away him take. Die. *Maman* die. Sick me. Hot, big sore on me make. All die. Only me, one baby. Ship take us. Père Pillow say home go. Long time. Ocean angry. *Bébé* die. Then our good land. Mi'kmaw people run. Laugh."

But the joy at returning didn't last. Nearly the entire tribe died in the next few months.

"*Wenuj* sickness. Die Mi'kmaq."

"Sick same bad my face make." She pointed at the smallpox scars on her cheeks, then continued. Dozens of the tribe were ravaged by the rotting face disease and the tiny village became a sinkhole of suffering.

He understood that she and other Mi'kmaw had been forced onto a French ship and against their will brought to Paris, where most of them died. Mari fell ill with smallpox but survived and endured the long trip back across the ocean to the homeland. But she had brought sickness with her, and most of her people died.

It was then, she said, Père Pillow brought her to Kébec. She married Lolan, a good Mi'kmaw man, at the mission. Elphège and Theotiste were his children. And Jean-Baptiste.

"Big man but die him. One my baby die. But Elphège, Theotiste, Jean-Baptiste then not die they. Me to Wobik with Père Pillow. That mission know you."

And at the mission Trépagny had found her and hired her as his housekeeper but within days forced himself on her. It was the way things went in New France.

"No him child. No-*bébé* medicine know me. Lené, you me good *bébés*. But now Elphège I say, 'Back come, Elphège, back come!'"

• • •

It was as though he had heard her. The snow was melting away, a hollow circle forming around the base of every tree, a ceaseless piddle of meltwater running over the sopping ground into rills and streams when a man limped into the clearing.

She knew at once. "Elphège!" She ran to him and helped him to the house. The boy was emaciated, covered with the scabs of old cuts and a pattern of bruises. His right ankle was a swollen purple lump. He would not speak. They half-carried him into the house and put him on the pallet. Mari began to stir up the fire and make a sleep potion, to heat a nourishing moose broth. While she took white cedar cones from her storeroom and pounded them to dust, worked them into pounded fern root and leaf for a sprain poultice, René stood gazing at the half-conscious boy.

"Where is the *seigneur*? Where is Monsieur Trépagny?" he asked gently, but Elphège could not answer, not then.

By asking questions to which Elphège would nod or shake his head, Mari learned that Monsieur Trépagny was dead, but when and in what manner he would not say. He lay quiet and half asleep for nine days, then seemed to recover his strength in a great flush. Within a month he joined René in the woods, chopping. He was silent and rarely smiled, his eyes habitually cast down as though the world was too painful to regard.

Chama no longer worked with them. He had gone to Kébec with Madame Trépagny and the Spanish maid, for the bride was again intending France. The Spanish maid was particularly disenchanted with Trépagny's mansion, for she had pried up the front doorstep stone, taken the metal box hidden there. It opened easily enough, despite creeping patterns of rust on the lid, but in it were nothing but human teeth and locks of hair. Even Chama wished to return to the old country to grow onions in root-free soil. They concluded that Monsieur Trépagny was dead. They left by moonlight, and when Mari heard the distant bellowing of the unmilked cow, she went to the manor house and claimed her.

"House. Door much open," she said to René. "Soon inside live *porc-épic* people." Yes, porcupines moved into abandoned houses very soon.

The uncle of Mélissande du Mouton-Noir, now Trépagny's wife, wrote several letters to his niece. Monsieur Bouchard kept them on the corner of his worktable as though the woman would sometime materialize and claim them. But the day came when a peremptory letter addressed directly to Monsieur Bouchard himself demanded information of the lady, who had failed to respond to her uncle's solicitous epistles. Monsieur Bouchard had the unpleasant duty of writing to Mouton-Noir and the Intendant with the sad news that the ship had struck rocks a few miles downstream from Wobik and all aboard had perished. He pretended amazement that news of the disaster had not reached them in Kébec, for it had happened some time ago.

Many months after his return, silent Elphège suddenly spoke at the evening meal, his voice croaking with misuse. He said only that someday he would revenge himself on the Iroquois and their masters, the English. Later that winter during a rest from a long morning of girdling trees Elphège told René that Iroquois women had severed Monsieur Trépagny's leg tendons, then had sewed him up tightly, closed every orifice of his body—ears, eyes, nostrils, mouth, anus and penis—and that after two or three days Monsieur Trépagny had swelled like a thundercloud and burst.

"Don't tell Maman," he said. "She would suffer."

But René thought Mari would not suffer. Still, he could not bring himself to tell her that Trépagny had died so painfully, so distressed in his tender parts.

René paddled one day down to Wobik with Theotiste, who was already old enough to march in the militia and receive Captain Bouchard's harangues on slinking, gliding Indian warfare, although he had learned more at Odanak among the fighting men than Captain Bouchard would ever know. Now he wanted to see the sights of Kébec and Trois-Rivières and would take passage on the next downriver ship. After that, he said, he would throw in with the conglomerate Mi'kmaq, Abenaki, Sokoki, Cowasucks, Penobscots, Androscoggins, Missisquois and a dozen other tribal refugees at Odanak, which the French called St. François. René was sorry to see him go as workmen were scarce and expensive. If he could not do the labor himself it would not be done.

After Theotiste's ship left he went into Captain Bouchard's familiar office. The aging captain had news for René.

"A very good doctor from France now in Kébec and who is already renowned takes an interest in the plants of our forests. He collects information from the savages on their use. He has sent a letter to me asking if Mari would meet with him. If she would show him the curing plants that grow hereabouts he will gladly pay her. How much, I do not know, but he suggested it."

"Who is he?" asked Rene. "Will he come to us?"

Captain Bouchard consulted his letters. "Michel Sarrazine. You understand, Mari's fame in curing the sick and injured has reached as far as Kébec. We are not so pitiful here in Wobik as some think. Although she is only a Micmac Indan."

The doctor was a small man with a high forehead. Wigless, his dark hair receded in front but waved down to his shoulders, his full red lips curled in a dimpled smile. Monsieur Bouchard wondered why he did not wear a wig and tried to bring him into a discussion of books and ideas, to take his measure; was he a deep-dyed conservative, or a pioneer freethinker exploring novel cures? But Dr. Sarrazine, though polite, said his time was limited and he wished to see Mari as soon as possible. He carried a linen bag containing a notebook, cardboard stiffeners and a roll of drying papers. He had a packet of French needles for Mari. Monsieur Bouchard loaned him his only horse and, rather sadly, watched him ride west. Dr. Sarra-zine returned in ten days, humming and smiling, his linen bag bulging with wild vegetable specimens, some of which he would send to the Jardin des Plantes. Bouchard, still longing for bookish conversation, watched the learned man board the ship to Kébec. The doctor turned, smiled his engaging smile and saluted. Bouchard returned the gesture and went back into his office.

The smoke-thickened years passed, and Crown corvée work gangs widened the west trail to a road. More settlers came into the forest. Every morning the sound of distant and near chopping annoyed woodpeckers who imagined rivals, then, feeling outnumbered, fled to wilder parts. The trees groaned and fell, men planted maize between the stumps. The deer and moose retreated, the wolves followed them north. In its own way the forest was swallowing René Sel, its destroyer. The forest was always in front of him. He was powerless to stop chipping at it, but the vigor of multiple sprouts from stumps and still-living roots grew in his face, the rise and fall of his ax almost a continuous circular motion. There seemed always more and more trees on the horizon. He suffered the knowledge that his countless ax blows were nothing against the endless extent of the earth's spiky forest crown.

One spring Mari fell ill, complaining little but too confused to manage the household. She became thin, the round kind face giving way to the shape of the skull beneath; she saw visions and forgot everything said to her, forgot her children, forgot René, had to be tied in a chair to keep her from the river. For a year Renardette cared for her, but one bright May morning Mari answered her long-dead sisters, who called her as owls call.

"Those sister say 'come.'" In two hours she had joined them.

René could not understand it. It was well known that Mi'kmaq lived long, long lives and remained strong until the last, and Mari was not old. It was the bitterest loss.

"It is only fitting," said Renardette to René when a week had passed, "that we should marry." René shook his head, picked up the ax and walked out to the woodlot. Renardette, barely an adult, had become beer-swollen, imperious and hot-tempered, always smarting from imagined insults. She would not forget this one.

Ends come to everyone, even woodcutters. All his life René was a *défricheur, un bûcheron* or, as the ancient book put it, "a woodsman, a forester, a forest owner; an ax owner, a feller of trees, a woodcutter, a user of the ax. He cuts with an ax; he fells trees—cuts them, tops them, strips them, splits them, stacks them." His life was spent in severe toil, stinging sweat running in his eyes, bitten by insects of the hot woods, the callused hands shaping into a permanent curl to fit ax handles, the bruises and blood, the constant smoke of burning trees, the pain of unremitting labor, the awkward saw, treacherous saplings used as pry bars, fitting new handles on broken spades and the everlasting lifting of great vicious tree trunks.

But Achille, his eleven-year-old son, found him dead on his knees in the forest, his knotted hands clenched on the ax handle, the bit sunk into a cedar, René dead at forty from a chop to his neck. A sharp scalping knife had been set above and parallel with his eyebrows and drawn around the circumference of his head, the scalp peeled off and carried away to be redeemed for the bounty. He was, until the end, a skillful woodsman, his life and body shaped to the pleasure of the ax. And so his sons and grandsons after him.

II

"... helplessly they stare at his tracks"

Zhang Ji (768–830)

1693–1727

8

Forgeron

Duquet had escaped Trépagny, but what next? Gripping the sapling he had cut for a stick, his remaining teeth burning in his mouth, coughing and with a stitch in his side, he followed the river west until dark. Before full light he was on his way again, swallowing whole the chunks of fish pudding he had hidden in his jacket the night before. He drank river water and plunged on. He followed the river from the ridge above in case Trépagny and that fool Sel came nosing after him. The higher ground was rough and gullied. He could see crashing water below, trees half in the water, sodden heads thrashing in the current. Hunger drove him back to the bank, where he knotted the neck and sleeves of his shirt and held it sidewise underwater, the open end inviting fish in. He had enough success to get nourishment, sucking the juice from the raw flesh as a spider with an insect. After eight days, scratched and filthy, lost in the wild, but driven by an inchoate need, he reached another river flowing down from the north. To the northwest were rich beaver grounds, the Indians who trapped the beaver and the traders who transported the pelts down the river. He began his long walk.

In the third week of his journey Duquet awoke and opened his left eye, the right stuck shut with hardened pus. In his exhaustion he fell often to the ground and lay with his face against the leaf litter. He was beyond the pain of his abscessed jaw; swathed in veils of mosquitoes he sucked in raw air with its taste of decaying wood. On his hands and arms were five or six suppurating wounds. He had found rib bones with strings of dark meat clinging to them under a serviceberry bush, but when he put one to his mouth something wild came at him, tearing with teeth and claws. It ran with the prize. He was weak from the loss of blood, not only from the biting animal, but from blackflies, from mosquitoes. Then he lost the river. He tried every direction, but it had disappeared. For an entire day he scooped at the dirt with his hands to discover if it was underground. How much easier it was to crawl than to stand and walk. And so he crawled, weeping, mouthing syllables. It rained, the dark grey clouds like unshaven jowls. His horizon was a sawtooth jag of black spruce. He caught a slow duckling, the last in a parade of ducklings on their way to—water! He had found the river again. He thought he might be dying, but it seemed inconsequential. First he would get to the north, to the fur traders, then he would die. As he crept along the rediscovered river he found small frogs and one more duckling that he caught and ate, cowering under the hammering beak and painful wing blows of the mother. Here the riverbank was soft mud, more comfortable for crawling.

An Odaawa hunting party surrounded the creature. They had watched it for two days inching around and around the margin of a small pond, sleeping in mud under the alders, then creeping again on hands and knees.

"He is sick," said one. They all backed away.

"He is wounded," said another.

At the sound of their voices Duquet reared up on his knees. He glowered at them out of his left eye. A pattern of alder twigs indented his cheek. He shaped his mud-crusted fingers into claws and hissed at them. He said something.

"He wishes to attack," said one. The rest laughed and their laughter enraged Duquet.

"He is a French," said one.

"We cannot take him. The French bring sickness."

"He is already sick. He cannot come among us."

"Leave him."

They backed away, disappeared.

Days later a party of French fur traders stopped at the Indians' river-side camp.

"We want peltries," said the old trader. "Look! For you we have axes, hatchets, needles. For you we have guns! Bullets and powder." The others displayed the goods in the bottom of their canoe.

"*Oui, oui,*" said the middlemen hunters, bringing out beaver robes, well worn and of best quality, collected in the north. They had few beaver, but many marten and lynx. Before the traders left, these Odaawa, laughing, mentioned the sick French crawling around and around the little pond.

The traders discovered Duquet. The mud had dried and to get at the man underneath they had to crack and break it away. They carried him to the river and soaked him in the waters until he emerged from his clay armor. They doubted he would live, but the Indian woman with them took his case in hand. In treating him she smelled the foul infection in his mouth. In her medicine bag she had a small wood stick with a leather loop at the end. With this she removed his rotting teeth, gave him an infection-fighting mouthwash and an opiate.

"Not die," she said.

The *voyageurs* put him in their worn canoe and set out for a distant Ojibwa village to the northwest.

It was spring, the rivers almost clear of ice except in early morning, the warm afternoons fragrant and easy. A few mosquitoes flew around them slowly, legs dangling. In the Ojibwa village, where a stream flowed into a small lake, Duquet rested against a log and watched the Indians making canoes, a complex business that involved the whole encampment. The *voyageurs* made themselves useful going with some of the younger men to gather the great sheets of birch bark, twenty feet long. As they brought them into camp they laid them carefully in the stream to keep them supple and weighted them with stones. Some went into the swamp and felled white cedar trees they had girdled the year before, riving the seasoned wood lengthwise. The women went out every day to gather spruce roots and gum. They sat near Duquet, skinning the roots and halving them lengthwise.

The Indians made five canoes for themselves and another five for the *voyageurs*, while Duquet healed. He was up and walking stiffly, eating gargantuan meals of soft foods he could manage with his healing gums. His eyes cleared, his hearing improved, he felt his arms flood with strength, and when the new canoes were finished, the *guide*, an officious imbecile with a burn-scarred face, ordered him to take a seat with the *milieux* and paddle until he dropped. The fragile craft flew down the cold, boulder-studded rivers. There were days of burn and pain in his shoulder blades, wrists and arms before his body accepted the tireless and rapid strokes, and every day he paddled longer. His neck, shoulders, arms began to swell with muscle. Always short in stature he now took on the look of the *voyageur*, almost as wide at the shoulders as he was tall. He learned to read water, to understand currents, recognize eddies, whirlpools, to listen to the old hands, whose expert knowledge of this violent, dangerous water world came from the bitterest kind of experience. In the evening he told his story of being a poor boy from the Paris streets come to make his fortune in New France.

A sinewy man with legs too long for the canoe, Forgeron, a Dutchman turned French by accident, a sailor and fisherman, a surveyor when he could get work and an unhappy *voyageur* when he could not, spoke quietly to Duquet.

"You are ignorant of the *coureur de bois* life. The woods runner's way is no road to wealth. We and the Indians do the dangerous work and the company gets the money. We are all fools."

And in recent years, he went on, the fur trade had become unsettled and insecure. The *coureur de bois* no longer directly approached the trapper Indians to trade for furs—there were Indian specialists, middlemen, who arranged all that. Even now those good Indians were being pushed out by enemy tribes and the decline in beaver numbers. As Duquet learned the intricacies and politics of the fur trade he saw that what Forgeron said was true. Paddling in the *milieux* was no entry to wealth. The best that could come of it would be a short life of striving, of sleeping on riverbanks and looking up through the trees at a narrow slice of darkness stinging with stars like cast handfuls of salt.

Some of the men carried flintlock muzzle-loaders, most the Charleville muskets used by the French army. But for Duquet the loading procedure was impossibly slow—without teeth he could not bite off the end of the cartridge, but had to tear it open with his fingers. Instead, he took as his weapon the French tomahawk, practiced endlessly until he could cleave the tail off a flying bird, gather up the body, have it gutted and half roasted while a comrade was still loading his musket.

Duquet hardened. He saw how the beaver quickly disappeared from hard-trapped areas, where the Indians took every animal, so intent were they on getting European tools and spirits, so harried were they by the acquisitive traders. The beaver country moved always farther north and west. Yet there were white men who gained prodigiously. They were not penniless runaway indentured servants. Duquet set out now to get as much as he could from his lowly position in the fur trade and swore to watch for better opportunities. He had come to New France hoping for quick riches and a return to Old France, but now he wondered if his destiny was not linked to the vast land with its infinite forests and violent rivers. Was not this country his place in the world? Yes, and he would make something of value of it. He went through a rare hour of introspection, seeing that his nature chilled other men. He consciously began to act as a smiling, open fellow of winning address who always had a good story and who, in the tavern, treated with a generous hand. He was sharpening his claws, and in his private center he was an opportunistic tiger—if he had to tear and maul his way to wealth he would do so.

He began to barter privately for furs, offering a drink or two of cheap rum to the naïve red men, hiding his activities from the others, sometimes caching the furs and returning later to pick them up. He bargained ruthlessly with the Indians, smiling guilelessly into the savage faces as he accepted their heavy bundles of furs for a yard of cheap cloth and a cup of adulterated whiskey—a monstrous profit.

Within the year he was sick of the traders who had rescued him.

"Forgeron," he said one day as they struggled up a portage trail. "I do not enjoy these persons, especially the *guide*. I intend to look for another opportunity. Will you come as well?"

"Why not?" said Forgeron. "One canoe is very like another. The *guide* is difficult, perhaps because of his terrible history. The Iroquois threw him into a fire to roast."

"Then why did they not finish the cooking and eat him?"

"Perhaps you will have the chance to ask them that one day."

They worked in harmony, although Forgeron attracted storms and wind. But he had a certain regard for the wild woods. He spoke often to Duquet of the forest and its great untapped wealth.

"If a man could get the logs out, there are a hundred thousand fortunes all around us the like of which the world has not seen since the days of Babylon. It is entirely a question of moving the wood to those who need it." Duquet nodded and began to look at trees with a more acquisitive eye.

They fell in with a flamboyant company of *coureurs de bois,* among whom were the easygoing Trépagny brothers, so unlike the high-minded *seigneur*. They had a reckless style and could outhowl wolves.

Duquet needed every paddling skill he had learned for some of the wild water they ran, between rock ledges that squeezed the canoe through violent chutes, and in one extraordinary place between two towering cliffs that leaned toward each other, narrower than the river so that the sky was a rock-edged slice. When they emerged from the pinching canyon the river hurled itself into a maelstrom. It was necessary to leave the water and edge upward along the Indian trail, little more than a foot width of slippery rock, somehow carrying the canoe over their heads, its weight making their arms quiver. At last they gained the cliff top and could look down on the thrashing water below.

"*Tabernac,*" said Toussaint Trépagny. "I pressed against the cliff face so passionately I left the imprint of my manhood on it." They carried their canoes for many miles that day.

One night, lying under an overturned canoe, Forgeron murmured that he intended to leave.

"My legs are no good for the canoe," he said. It was true that his long arms worked the paddle with great power, but his legs were folded and doubled under him for many hours and when he left the canoe he often had trouble standing upright, so cramped and tightened were his muscles. Many nights he lay groaning from the pain and rubbing his thighs and calves. *Voyageurs* were short-legged and strong-armed. Long legs did not belong in a canoe.

When he finally left, saying he would look for surveying work, Duquet left with him, persuading the Trépagnys to come along. They headed back toward the St. Laurent. Within a month Forgeron found work laying out property lines east of Ville-Marie.

"Our paths will cross again," said Forgeron, "but not in a canoe."

Duquet continued gathering furs with the Trépagny brothers and they became an infamous trio, pouring rum and whiskey for the Indians, red men who gave away their furs in return for terrible and vision-invoking spirits.

9

Les Quatrains de Pibrac

(Guy du Faur, Seigneur de Pibrac)

He prospered during the seasons following a bad year when the settlements were sick with longing for overdue supply ships from France, sick with fear of the Iroquois, who had only ten years earlier surprised and slaughtered the inhabitants of Lachine and might do so again. In spite of ongoing fighting, huge loads of beaver pelts came down the river and kept coming, until the hatters and furriers of France could use no more, until the warehouses were packed full of rodent fur. Again Duquet saw the great weakness of the trade—surplus or scarcity. Beaver might disappear from over-trapping or disease or for no discernible reason. Or the Indians took too many. He watched and considered. He now regarded tales of immense profits in the fur trade as fables. He wanted great and permanent wealth, wealth for a hundred years. He wanted a fortune to pass on to his sons. He wanted his name on buildings. He was surprised to discover in himself a wish for children, a wish to establish a family name. The name Duquet would change from a curse to an honor. But there were difficulties—especially the ugliness of a toothless, collapsed jaw. It might be impossible to find a handsome wife. Unless he had money.

His agile mind ceaselessly worked over the question: what resource existed in this new world that was limitless, that had value, that could build a fortune? He rejected living creatures such as beaver, fish, seals, game or birds, all subject to sudden disappearance and fickle markets. He repeatedly came back to the same conclusion. There was one everlasting commodity that Europe lacked: the forest. Duquet knew, as everyone knew, that the English colonists to the south did well cutting pines for English navy masts. Could the French not do the same? He remembered Forgeron's talk. The forest was unimaginably vast and it replaced itself. It could supply timber and wood for ships, houses, warmth. The profits could come forever. Yes, there were many problems of transport and markets, but it was an unexploited business that could expand and dominate. In France there were men who dealt in forest goods, but few in New France and perhaps not in the colonies to the south. So, he thought, he would get as much money as he could with the furs in the next few years, prepare himself in every way and then change to timber when he was ready. He would not yet give up the lucrative fur trade, a stinking, complicated business for trapper Indians, but with high profits for white traders with market connections.

He briefly sketched his plan to the Trépagny brothers and told them he would be glad if they continued with him as partners when he made his future move to timber and wood. He was surprised that they were not enthusiastic. Their eyes reflected the evening fire like orange beetles. Perhaps, Toussaint said, and Fernand said they would see. They looked away into the trees.

"Well, let it stay as it is." Duquet passed on to another subject and said there was one great obstacle he had to overcome. He could neither read nor write, and it was necessary to gain those skills if he were not to be cheated in dealings with sly merchants. He did not know even a single letter such as that fool Sel had doted on.

"The world cheats men who cannot read. I know this as I have often seen it," Toussaint said. "If you wish to do this, you need one of the Black Robes. The Jesuits all can write countless pages, all can read both silently and aloud until their eyes cross. Let us get one of these fellows and carry him with us. He can convert Indians while we bargain and in quiet moments he will teach you those arts you wish to acquire." And so they kidnapped Père Naufragé, one of several missionaries on the way to the Hurons.

For several days they watched the little group and their Huron guides before acting.

"See," whispered Toussaint from behind their tree, "there are four of them. Choose the one you like. We'll get him when he steps aside to answer the call of nature."

Duquet studied each of the fathers. One seemed quicker and more sprightly than the others. He was first to rise, made the fire with the high technology of a burning glass if the sun shone, packed and unpacked their goods with alacrity, and spent the least time in prayers.

When the missionary stepped into the shadows and hiked up his robe to relieve himself they sprang like savages. Toussaint clapped a leather gag over the priest's mouth, Fernand bound his hands behind him and Duquet frog-marched him into the forest and away to their camp.

"You are French!" exclaimed the priest later when Duquet pulled off the gag. "I thought you were Indians. Why have you taken me from my brothers? We are traveling to the Hurons."

Duquet explained that the Hurons could wait. Père Naufragé would stay with them until Duquet learned to read and write. The Jesuit would be treated well and was advised not to try to escape.

"For if the Iroquois get you, you will become a martyr."

Père Naufragé said he was eager to become a martyr, more eager than to teach illiterates the rudiments of the alphabet. "My friends expect me. I warn you, you will pay dearly for this outrage."

Duquet described the ample opportunities the Jesuit would have to convert savages as they traveled about the country gathering furs.

"What you ask is not even possible. My books of instruction are with my traveling companions." The Jesuit smiled triumphantly.

"That is no problem," said Fernand, opening his possibles bag and rummaging to the bottom. With a vengeful smile he pulled out a stained, worn book and thrust it at Père Naufragé.

"*Icitte!* Here is your instruction book—*Les Quatrains de Pibrac.* It was a gift from my mother and I have never been parted from it. 'First honor God, then Father and Mother—*Dieu tout premier, puis Père et Mère honore,'*" he quoted. "Everything in the world can be found in the pages of Pibrac."

"God knows you will do more good with us than with a thousand Hurons." Père Naufragé, habituated to obedience, nodded acceptance but insisted on daily devotions, a weekly mass and time set aside for disputation on a theological subject which he would select.

The priest had a face like a short sword—thin and sharp. His olive skin stretched over jutting cheekbones and his crenellated hair was as black as that of any Spaniard. Ah, thought Duquet, the fellow looks like a Moor. But it was when he smiled—which he did not do until the third day after his capture—that his face changed entirely. His mouth was very wide and his face seemed to separate into two unrelated parts. And his pointed teeth—*mon Dieu,* thought Duquet, muttering under his breath "how many *is* there"—dazzled with an unnatural whiteness.

As for the lessons, Duquet learned quickly. He scrawled his letters and numbers—arithmetic quickly became part of the curriculum—on hundreds of pieces of birch bark. His hands, heavily muscled by years of paddling, labored with the small muscle coordination necessary to form elegant letters, and his handwriting was coarse. No matter; it was legible. The priest became embedded in the little group and closed his eyes to the whiskey trades and his pupil's disturbing aura of ambitious greed. He was fascinated by Duquet's grasp of information, for he seemed to remember everything, scraps of German, Greek, Latin and English, all that the priest uttered, even prayers. At the end of the first year Pibrac retired to Fernand's bag again as he was suffering wear, but Duquet had memorized the contents and had quatrains to cover every situation in life—should he care to quote doggerel. But he preferred to despise Pibrac.

• • •

In early spring, two years later, Père Naufragé, dressed now like a woodsman as his cassock had shredded in the brush, left them unwillingly.

"But it is time for you to go," said Duquet with a patient smile. "As Pibrac says, 'The steps of man are directed by God.' We will take you now to the Hurons as I must travel to France on business."

"Another year of study and I believe you could have acquired a considerable handiness with Latin, the most important language for men of business such as you intend to become."

But Duquet only twitched his mouth; his thoughts ran in a different direction.

Six days of travel skirting burning fields and woods brought them to the edge of the forest around the Huron mission. Fernand, coughing, said, "Every time I have been in the Huron country the place is afire."

Duquet stood aside while the Trépagnys embraced the priest and wished him good fortune. They watched him make his way toward the clearing. Then he disappeared into the smoke.

10

all the world wishes
to go to China

Duquet could not keep his mind on furs. Again and again he considered the dense problems of the timber trade. First, the trees; the best ones did not always grow near river landings. And who would buy the raw logs when every man could cut what he needed? But sawn planks, ready to carpenter—that was the way. A water-powered sawmill or a sawpit with tools and men was a primary necessity.

He began to note objects made of wood: everything in the world. And it was all around him in quantities inexhaustible and prime. Could the Royal French Navy be persuaded to buy New France timber? England, he knew, badly wanted naval stores as the endless war had disrupted their heavy Baltic trade. Although England was the enemy there were great benefits in trading with them, perhaps possible through a third party. And what of Spain and Portugal? His mind began to weigh the possibilities.

He talked to himself as the Trépagnys did not care for the subject. "Which trees are most desirable? Oak, of course, but oak is scattered and seems to grow only in certain places. Why it is not widespread, as pine and spruce, I do not know." Could English shipbuilders use pine? Hemlock? Beech? How could he move the desirable mast trees from the forest to a ship? Indeed, he needed a ship and a captain if he was to deliver wood products to a land as distant as France.

Thinking of uncommon woods sent his thoughts back to the fur trade, his immediate calling. Why should he concentrate on beaver as everyone else did? There must be those who desired other furs as mink, ermine, otter, muskrat, fox, spotted lynx and marten. He decided to take a season gathering such luxury furs, then go to France with a shipload of rare pelts. He began at once, harrying the Indians for every kind of fur, acting as his own middleman. Sitting at the campfire drinking the harsh whiskey intended for the Indians (fiery with pequin peppers from the Caribe to prove its strength), on his last evening with the Trépagnys he declared that, while he was in France, he would find himself a wife and set her to work bearing children. The Trépagny brothers, in their farewell debauch, said jokingly, while he was at it, to bring back women for them.

Duquet took passage on a ship bound for France commanded by Captain Honoré Deyon, a grey and weathered man with a syphilitic chancre on his upper lip. When the captain invited him to dine Duquet used the opportunity and asked how he might find passage on a China-bound ship.

"I know European ships go there," he said. Captain Deyon brushed the chancre with the knuckle of his right index finger and sighed heavily.

"All the world wants to go to China," he said. "They say, sir, that it is an immensely rich country with many interesting and beautiful objects. On the return one may stop in the islands and purchase the best coffee. And it is known the profits from tea and silks are enormous, and coffee as well, I daresay. But it is not so easy to trade in China. For permission, one must be part of an official delegation as well as prepare great gifts for the emperor and the many officials. This gift, and many others, they take as their just due. And they are not much interested in western goods, only silver. They say they have everything they need or want in their own country. I have no idea what your goods are, but a lone merchant—if you are such, sir— really cannot do business there. It is too difficult."

"My business is fine furs. But even if *I* cannot get there," said Duquet, "how is it others reach China? Who does trade there? Who sends ships to China?"

"The Portuguese were first. Now the Dutch, England, and even France—all are trying to work the eastern trade. But the Dutch are the ones who go there regularly. The Vereenigde Oost-Indische Compagnie—the Dutch East India Company, largest business in the world, controls everything. Perhaps you can find a sympathetic captain who will take you aboard. And I have heard there are a few independent captain traders who are not tied to the VOC. Those are the men you should seek out. But I know none of them."

He swallowed his tumbler of rum and delicately touched the sore on his lip with the long nail of his little finger. "And," he said, "I doubt you speak Chinese."

"Very little," said Duquet. He would learn the most important words as soon as he heard them.

In La Rochelle, unpleasant feelings came over Duquet. The old smells of poverty nearly sent him bending and creeping along close to the walls as he had done in childhood. Relentless hunger and chilblains had been his childhood lot. Of his father he remembered beatings and curses, and at the last, a pair of receding legs.

His eyes burned from the smoke of greasy street fires and he thought of the clear rivers of Kébec, of the forest air, and with these cleansing memories he regained himself. Yet he was mortified that his clothes and person announced him as a country bumpkin in French streets.

In New France he and the Trépagny brothers had been skillful with war hatchets but he saw no hatchets on the streets of La Rochelle. He went to the armorers and purchased a Walloon sword, ambidextrous, flexible. He saw many of these on the street. It was a gentleman's sword. One day, he swore silently, he would order fine garments and a full, rich wig.

. . .

In the area between rue des Petits-Bacs and rue Admyrauld, where the merchants congregated daily, he talked with a sallow wool merchant whose greasy hands trembled; when Duquet casually mentioned China, the merchant said his cousin had been a sailor pressed into three years' service on a Dutch voyage from Hoorn to Guangzhou, that the English called Canton.

"He said it was a very long journey to a horrible place," and the merchant passed back Duquet's brandy bottle. "Very strong stink. Food? *Affreux!* Foreigners not allowed in the city, but penned up in a horrible foreigners' quarter. He prayed to return home. And they despised the ship's cargo, which was horses, the captain having heard the Chinese longed for them horribly. But in Canton the go-between merchant said China now had secured its own horses from the north. So the trip was for nothing. And on the return journey the captain was so angry he pushed all those horrible worthless horses into the sea. They could see them swimming after the ship for a long time."

"Oh, horrible," said Duquet, at once planning to make his way to Amsterdam or Hoorn. How many times had Forgeron told him the men of the Low Countries had a talent for business?

"Stay away from the East India Company ships. They are bound by hard rules and the captains take blood oaths to uphold them. It is a horrible, grasping company that allowed no competition for many years. Only East India ships were allowed to traverse the horrible Strait of Magellan. Now the Cape Horn route has been discovered their grasp is broken, but the old animosities linger. You must choose a captain with care."

II

Dutch sea captain

Without exception every ship captain he approached was exceedingly suspicious, for trade routes and overseas contacts were under constant threat by spies, and Duquet was immediately and repeatedly identified as a French spy. Only after detailed descriptions of the forests of Kébec and the rigors of the fur trade— as well as a flash of the marten skin he had begun to carry as proof of his identity—could he prove his disinterested innocence in matters of trade route secrets.

In the Rock and Shoal, a sailors' tavern on the waterfront, he noticed a group of convivial men who seemed all to be captain mariners. They spoke in a mixture of languages, mostly German, French, Portuguese, Flemish and Dutch, and seemed to be placing bets. One, whom he heard called Captain Verdwijnen, a fair-faced man with a large nose and scarred cheek, wheaten wisps of unshorn hair sticking out from the edges of his ill-seated wig, particularly caught his eye because of his ceaseless motions and apparent sanguine temperament. Duquet edged closer to the group until he was nearly among them, grasping at half-understood words in the Babel of discourse. After a long time Verdwijnen made his excuses to the company and said he had to get back to his ship. Duquet followed him out into the dark street. The captain suddenly spun around and flashed a dagger at Duquet.

"Footpad!" he shouted into the night. "Help! Robbery! Assault! Murther!"

"Captain Verdwijnen," said Duquet. "I am no footpad. I am a friend, I am a fur merchant from New France, begging your favor." And he bowed low, making a clumsy leg. He presented himself as an enterprising businessman. He became the sweet-voiced persuasive Duquet, talked on, explaining and mollifying, opening his pack of furs, which he carried on his back like a peddler. He said that he could pay for his passage—he had enjoyed a good sale of his furs in Montreal, keeping out the best to trade in the east. Moreover, he would supply the captain with cases of the best Schiedam *jenever* for the voyage, the special distillation of gin with a green label showing a large yellow eye, the eye of a furious lion, far superior to the slop the captain had swallowed in the Rock and Shoal. Look, he had a bottle in his coat pocket this very minute, and he swung the garment open to show the luteous eye. The Dutchman thawed a little and told Duquet to follow him aboard his ship, *Steenarend,* the *Golden Eagle,* where they could speak more comfortably. Duquet was surprised to see it was an armed, full-rigged, three-masted frigate, which could accommodate more than a hundred men, the gun room painted red to hide bloodstains.

"There are many pirates in the South China Sea," explained Captain Verdwijnen. Duquet had seen him drink countless glasses of *jenever* in the sailors' tavern, but the man spoke with clarity and decisiveness.

The captain said he was indeed suspicious of foreigners, especially the French and English, most of whom were spies, and it could cost him his livelihood to take Duquet aboard if the ship's German owner heard of it, and of course he *would* hear of it. He glared at Duquet and clenched his fists.

"What you are asking me to do is a grave thing. I cannot do it. Why, sir, it is a thing that was never done before. And never should be done. *Nooit*—never." He wrenched his face through an extraordinary series of grimaces and frowns. Duquet spoke humbly.

"I am only interested in securing a market for my furs. And I am most sensible, dear captain, of the honor you do me by even discussing such a matter." His mouth curved, his eyes winked. He smiled, opened his coat and took out the bottle, uncorked it and handed it to the captain. "Perhaps we can discuss it further," he said softly, "if you do not hold me to be completely odious?" He had marked the captain as one who would do much for a little cup of spirits, not unlike the Indians of the north.

The captain's cabin was a great room, the rear windows giving a vertiginous view of the port. There was a single chair before a mahogany table covered with charts. The captain waved Duquet to a small side bench bolted to the floor; under it lay a huge mastiff that growled at Duquet. The captain sat in his chair, now holding a glass brimming with that best *jenever*. He nodded at the glass.

"Good. We Dutch must drink or die, you know." He swallowed. "Or so they say."

Duquet opened his pack and laid several of the furs atop the charts. The dog looked at the furs with interest.

"Of course I am always happy to buy furs myself to take to Amsterdam," the captain said.

"I shall keep that in mind, but my information is that I can get a great deal of money for them in China. And I wish to establish a trading connection in that place."

Captain Outger Verdwijnen squinted his eyes. Duquet might understand more about business than he showed. Or, indeed Duquet might be a spy, evil thought. But after an hour of serious drinking, when the captain knew Duquet a little better, he abandoned the spy characterization, and when he learned his guest would send ten cases of the green-and-gold-labeled bottles aboard, he told Duquet he might make the journey.

"We sail in two weeks. It is already April, late in the season to begin this voyage. We must catch the southwest monsoon winds that carry ships to India and China between June and September, so make ready and be here on the appointed day. I will show you your quarters, which you will share with Mijnheer Toppunt," he said, and he led Duquet to a pitifully small and rank cubby, though there was a scuttle. His bunk was a wide plank. The other contained a roll of grey blankets and a great leathern bag. On the floor, as though tossed there, were sea boots and heavy gloves, and that constituted Mijnheer Toppunt's presence.

Ashore the next day Duquet ordered three dozen cases of the green-label gin delivered to the ship. At the ship chandler's shop he outfitted himself with a hammock, rough, sturdy clothes and an oiled cape sworn to keep rain out, a bound ledger, quills and ink, an expensive spyglass and a bag of brown sugar.

A week before they sailed, Captain Verdwijnen hailed him. "Monsieur Duquet," he said. "I am going to the coffeehouse to arrange my insurance. As you propose to get into business, perhaps you would like to accompany me for the valuable contacts?" Certainly Duquet would. What a stroke of fortune.

They walked for twenty minutes before they reached the coffeehouse and entered a large room where men sat at tables with papers and account books in front of them. Some scribbled furiously, others talked, pushing their faces forward. At the back of the room five bewigged men laughed as a sixth read from a letter. Near the front a woman handed bowls of hot beverage to serving boys and Captain Verdwijnen called out for two coffees—*"deux cafés"*—and led Duquet to the back table of laughing men, the marine insurance brokers. As they approached, the laughing faded away and six serious and attentive faces turned toward them.

"Ah, Captain Verdwijnen. Here to arrange your insurance, no doubt? Would this gentleman with you be the shipowner?"

Captain Verdwijnen's laugh was a bray. "No, no, he is not the owner of the ship, he is Monsieur Duquet, a gentleman from New France in the timber export business. At the moment he is carrying furs. I thought he might like to meet you gentlemen for future consultations."

The serving boy brought the coffee. Duquet looked suspiciously at the sinister black liquid. It was scalding and bitter, a very dreadful potion, but he drank it. In a quarter of an hour he felt ideas rushing into his head—he memorized the faces before him with newly sharpened senses.

As he looked around he saw a man of about thirty-five with a face that seemed made of some flesh-like material that, once formed, remained set and immobile. A pair of little obsidian eyes looked out at the world as if measuring an antagonist. The unsmiling mouth was pinched and suggested meanness. The ringed fingers and flamboyant crimson sleeves did little to soften the impression of suspicious calculation.

The man's gaze rose from the black sums he was making and fixed on Duquet. The space between them quivered with a discharge of mutual antipathy.

"Who is that man?" Duquet murmured to the captain, letting the words slip out quietly.

"He is a Lübeck trader in wax and metal ores I believe—here and in Bruges. How he does stare! It is as if he knows you."

"He does not know me, nor will he ever know me," said Duquet, but the man's stiff look indicated that he was familiar with the likes of Duquet through and through; it was the stare of a predator encountering another of its kind nosing about in its territory.

12

Steenarend

The ship's crew was polyglot: Spanish, French, Flemish, Greek, German, Genoese, young men from the Malay, from the Canaries, the Isle of Dogs. Duquet thought they looked dangerous, very unlike the rough-cut good-natured *voyageurs* he had known in New France.

Captain Outger Verdwijnen served as his own master and, in this time of dead reckoning and anxious guesswork on the exact location of one's ship, had a reputation for accurate navigation, which Duquet thought might be related to the man's constant study and annotation of charts, but the captain said the charts told nothing of a ship's ever-changing longitudinal position, the bête noire of international trade. But he could recognize the warm black Kuroshio Current, and was often within forty miles of the desired port, by which margin men generally considered him an expert navigator.

The captain's bonhomie evaporated the instant he stepped aboard the *Steenarend,* though he continued his cordiality with Duquet over a glass of the yellow-eyed *jenever* in the evenings. His conversation was lively, of ships and their cargoes, of their short lives and the myth of hundred-year-old ships, of pirates and great storms at sea. He described the Sunda Strait as treacherous, the equatorial Doldrums as maddening, the Guinea Current as a trap and getting caught in the southeasterly trade winds as the sure failure of a voyage.

As they sailed out into the quilted ocean Duquet noticed three or four ships were always in sight. When he remarked on it, Captain Verdwijnen said knowingly, "My friends—*vrienden,*" smiled and shrugged.

The ship stank fearfully though Captain Verdwijnen was proud of the pissdales and the officers' closeted seats of ease with their drains into the sea. The crew perched on an open row of holed seats in the beak, cursing when the icy waves rinsed their salt-raw backsides.

"For we learned from the Portuguese that this is the way to avoid what they called *bicho do cu,* a painful anal infection so burning and biting that seamen went mad with the agony in the olden times," said the captain.

To Duquet the officers looked a rather seedy lot in comparison with the younger crew, though when he made the remark, Captain Verdwijnen laughed and said appearances were deceiving, that while most of the crew looked strong they were riddled with venereal diseases, were laced through with insanities and as stupid as penguins. The officers, on the other hand, were not an attractive lot but each was skilled and experienced in a useful way.

Duquet's cabinmate, François Toppunt, was a pockmarked man whose narrow arms and fleshless face gave him a look of weakness, dispelled by his agility. He dressed smartly in contrast with the crew in their tarry red nap trousers cut high and wide and the caps they knitted themselves. He was as limber as a dancing master, with a knack for making lightning decisions. He thought he had been born in Bourgogne and brought as a young boy to Amsterdam. When his parents both died of the plague he had been adopted by watchmaker Willem Toppunt and his childless wife.

There were similarities between the two men. They both moved at high speeds in body and mind, both were pleased to be able to converse in French, although Toppunt's use of the language was crippled by long neglect and interlarded with Dutch words and phrases. He was also a devotee of the sailors' great pastime, collecting rarities of the natural world. He told Duquet that in his home cabinet of curiosities he had a set of spider teeth and a stuffed bird of paradise, that strange *vogel* born without feet. Then he told Duquet that the captain's mastiff enjoyed climbing into the rigging, where he would bark a warning at the sight of pirates.

A few days after he came on board Duquet confided to François Toppunt that he wanted to order new clothing and a wig that would be ready when they returned from China.

"You will have to pay in advance," said Toppunt, "but I know a good tailor in Paris and there are wigmakers in the same street. There are yet five days before we sail. Let us persuade the captain for leave, take a coach to Paris and visit these worthies, for I, too, would like a wig for special occasions."

The jolting coach nearly liquefied their livers and Duquet chose to get out and run alongside the equipage at every chance. In Paris they found an inn near the street of wigmakers and tailors.

The next sunrise brought one of those blue and spicy days when the wind cleared away noisome odors. It was a fine day for walking and Duquet and Toppunt strode through the streets. Toppunt pointed out a popular coffee shop. They went in and Duquet decided to risk the coffee again. Toppunt smacked his lips over the sugared chocolate and declared it delicious. Despite the tarry flavor of the coffee, Duquet once again felt charged with energy and sharp-minded. Toppunt said that was one of the many virtues of the dark fluid.

"It is good for ailments as well," said the grey-headed coffeehouse server, joining their conversation. "It is the favored drink of merchants and businessmen as it allows them to do great sums in their heads and to work long hours."

At the tailor's shop Duquet selected blue velvet for his coat and accepted the idea of a pair of culottes cut on the bias. The obsequious tailor suggested a fine English cloth, remarking that this fabric was very much preferred. But Duquet chose a striped blue satin, though he couldn't resist the man's suggestion to visit the boot maker next door for a pair of the delicate shoes with rounded toes just coming into vogue.

The wigmaker, his hands shaking with some ague-like affliction or a surfeit of coffee, urged the latest style, smaller, flatter on top and with "pigeon wings" rippling back over the temples, instead of the full-bottomed wigs both men wanted. He stressed greater comfort and ease. Toppunt said yes, but Duquet, his ideas of what a wealthy man looked like set, insisted on the great wig with its expensive mass of curls and frizz.

"Ready when you return, my dear, dear sirs, but only," said the man, "if you pay now, as shipwrecks, pirates, plague and scurvy are not unknown among those who travel to the Far Eastern lands. If you perish, your survivors may call for the hair."

They endured an even more unpleasant journey back to La Rochelle; one of the coach horses fell dead in the traces and then the axle broke on a rough detour. They hired saddle horses and rode more comfortably, but reached the ship with only hours to spare before she sailed. Captain Verdwijnen was in a foul temper and accused Toppunt of neglecting his duty.

"That will be a black mark against you, sir," he said. "You will hear the result of my displeasure shortly." What Toppunt's punishment was Duquet did not know, but he noticed the captain constantly found fault with all the mate did.

So the ship departed, down the Channel, past Brest, past Portugal, then west, well out to sea to avoid Africa's bulge and the Doldrums, down, down through a zone of variable winds until Captain Verdwijnen claimed he could smell Brazil, then swinging southeast for the Cape of Good Hope, keeping well away from the Agulhas Current, and on, ever eastward, until they picked up the southwest monsoon in season that would carry them to the treacherous Sunda Strait and on to China.

Duquet had no love for the sea. Rivers were the thing, ever-changing, muscular waterways that challenged one to decipher their linear characters. In comparison the ocean was a tiresome medium of waves that broke and swelled, sometimes lost their shapes and separated into confusion. Storms and throbbing rollers he endured, and hoped never to see a towering rogue wave as the sailors described, never to hear the awful moaning of a cyclone wind.

Captain Verdwijnen kept a Spartan table and dined alone in his cabin on boiled pork, beer, bread and cheese. At the officers' table, often augmented with fresh-caught dolphin or octopus soup, the dinner talk was conducted in a variety of languages and pointing at the bread or wine was more useful than asking for it. Duquet could understand how Captain Verdwijnen had come to wave his arms and twitch his face in universal sign language. The cook, Li Wen, was Chinese, on his way back to China, said Captain Verdwijnen, after years of study in Amsterdam.

"What did he study?" asked Duquet, suddenly interested.

"Dutch medicine, I believe. He is somewhat important in China, but frugal enough to work his passage by acting as cook."

"So he is a physician?"

"For this voyage he is a surgeon, a master of head injuries. And he is the cook."

"But beyond the voyage is he a physician in China?"

"He is a coroner."

"What is that, a coroner?"

"It is a skilled man who understands the signs of death and who examines bodies to say if they have been the victims of foul play or natural causes. I would rather have him attend me than most ships' doctors, a group given over to drink and devious actions. Coroner is an important profession in China, where jealousies and rivalries are the equal of any at the French court. And one may purchase venoms at numerous shops."

Duquet cornered the coroner and said in his broken Dutch that he would like to learn at least a few phrases of the Chinese language. He showed a coin but Li Wen looked horrified. He expostulated in fluent French.

"Not possible. Chinese government not allow foreigners learn Chinese. Forbidden." Li Wen then recited Chinese poems, translated and explained them to Duquet. There was, he said, no law against declaiming Chinese poetry. Duquet immediately saw himself as the powerful animal in Zhang Ji's poem of a tiger prowling mountain forests, so frightful that an entire village stood rigid, staring at the sight of his tracks. So, too, Duquet thought, he would claim whole forests.

One evening over their postprandial glass, Captain Verdwijnen looked slyly at Duquet and told him that in Guangzhou—Canton—he could order a set of ivory teeth to be carved that would fit his jaws and give him the appearance of a handsome rogue. The work could be done by the very same carver who fashioned dildos for sailors' wives. The carver, he said, was expensive but worth it. And, raising his hands as if in discovery, he said the Hong businessman who acted as his assigned merchant could arrange this and would likely be interested in Duquet's furs. He stroked an especially fine lynx pelt that Duquet had brought into his quarters.

"This was intended as a gift to the emperor of China, but I give it to you." Duquet pressed it into Captain Verdwijnen's hands, adding that perhaps his wife would like it as company for the ivory implement.

"Ha ha," said Captain Verdwijnen, uncorking another *jenever* bottle with his teeth. "Just as well. No foreigner has ever gained an audience with the emperor of China."

It was late October when they and the ships that had kept them company entered the China Sea. The weather had been unusually fine down the west coast of Africa, but then the monsoon winds became dying and fitful. They stopped briefly at the Cape of Good Hope but did not linger as the VOC had a station there with men watching out for independent entrepreneurs. The wind was increasingly unreliable on the east coast. Four stormy days, the sky shuddering, the sea choking on itself, impressed Duquet as very violent, but he was alone in that opinion. Twice threatening sails came over the horizon. Captain Verdwijnen said they were pirates, for through the spyglass he could make out their sinister flags. Duquet asked innocently when the pirate-warning mastiff would climb into the rigging, and only caught on when he heard the crew's smothered laughter.

Listening to the table talk Duquet conjured up a picture of the oceans of the world dotted with ships suspended somehow in fog loom, all unconscious that other ships were near. Those ships carried cargoes of everything in the world.

"What might be the principal cargoes?" asked Duquet one evening at table. The men began to name goods they had known on ships. At first they spoke grudgingly, but a spirit of competition took them and they began excitedly interrupting each other:

"Baskets of truffles, camel wool—bolts of yew, gunpowder, parrots, Potosí silver—yes, silver mined by dying men! tobacco, musk, ocher and indigo, Brazil nuts, do not forget madder, paper, pepper, cinnamon—all noble spices, calicoes, cotton, dyed silks, Brabant cloth, Biscay hatchets, *piñones* from monkey-puzzle trees, horses and elephants, coral teething rings, lacquer, wool, fleeces, woven linen, cowrie shells for slave buying! pounded bark—bales of goats' hair— barrels of Shiraz, oxen, musical instruments, medical instruments. Arab scissors, jewels, shot cannon and precious metals, grain, maize and rice, ivory dominoes, salt, tea, Turkish shoes with curled toes . . ."

Many of the men had served on VOC ships in earlier years and as memories of old cargoes floated up so did recollections of outstanding traders. The crew said ships' surgeons were especially canny traders.

"Whether Good Hope or Batavia, the healthiest ones made their profits."

"There is everything in the world if you only know where to find it and how to get it," said Toppunt, seizing the bread. And the surgeons knew.

But most of these tales ended with the satisfied declaration that the surgeon had not lived long enough to realize his profit, especially if he were bound for Batavia, where the life of a white man was brief. Only the occasional European survived the fetid atmosphere of that port.

"Then, too, they spent much time doctoring the sick, often coming down with the same malady they attempted to cure in another." And so the conversation straggled away from cargoes to the dangers of the east.

13

garden of delightful confusion

Captain Verdwijnen explained China's intricate system of trade to Duquet. All the ship's provisions had to be purchased from licensed provisioners. And everything was licensed. "Ship captains have to deal with licensed Chinese merchants, with licensed translators, we must pay more than sixty separate fees, endure cargo inspections, to trade here. Moreover, all foreigners must stay in the special Factory quarter and may not enter the city."

As they arrived in Guangzhou, Duquet stood on the deck, gazing at the long, long row of warehouses and storerooms that made up the foreign traders' quarter. The flags of different trading countries flying from them looked like a city. He stepped ashore into the novelty and noisy bustle of China.

They settled into the assigned buildings that housed other Dutch traders. Captain Verdwijnen reverted to his established regimen, including Duquet in it: in the morning he made a pot of coffee, roasting the beans in a pan, grinding them in a hand mill, casting the grains into boiling water, counting to fifty and allowing all to settle.

The captain had another vice as well, picked up in the coffeehouses of Amsterdam: he took in smoke from a pipe. That, too, had its ritual. He took out the roll of leather wherein he secreted his tobacco leaves. He chose a likely leaf, then cut it fine and finer. He filled the pipe. He lit a paper spill at the fireplace and sucked in a quantity of smoke, exhaled slowly through pursed lips with a sound like the east wind. At last he was ready for the day's trading, and carrying two heavy satchels, he led Duquet to Wuqua, his Hong merchant contact.

Wuqua was a richly dressed man with a complexion like fresh butter and a black arabesque mustache. The official translator sat between Captain Verdwijnen and Wuqua. Duquet watched the two men bargain, the interpreter going back and forth fluidly, first Mandarin, then Dutch. Captain Verdwijnen wanted special kinds of tea and silks in divers colors and porcelain painted with garden scenes, he wanted lacquer boxes, he wanted unusual plants not too demanding of care as the return voyage was long. Wuqua suggested teas from a bewildering number of remote locations, teas in ropes, boxes, cakes, he named amounts and tempting prices; Captain Verdwijnen flung up his hands and reared back in his chair as though shot. Panting, his hand over his heart, he protested the ghastly prices. He opened one of the heavy bags. Bars of silver gleamed in the darkness of the valise. He countered with an offer. Now it was Wuqua's turn to become pale and wave his ivory fan. He mentioned another set of figures, the same prices but greater amounts of lesser qualities of tea, fewer colors of silks, more modestly painted ceramics and quite ordinary plants. They were at loggerheads. Both men sat stiff and unyielding. After a long silence Wuqua suggested they go into the garden.

The Garden of Delightful Confusion pulled something inside Duquet as a child pulls a toy with a string. He had not known such places existed. They walked slowly along a mosaic path of tiny pebbles arranged in the pattern Wuqua said was "plum blossoms on cracked ice." At every turn there were rare views of flowering shrubs, moon gates; the Cloud-Piercing Tower appeared, then the coarse lacework of Lake Tai rocks in the shape of a mountain. From its highest crag fell a waterfall no wider than three fingers, wrinkling the pool below. On the way to a pavilion called Painted Boat in Spring Snow, they passed between peach tree rows; at the terminus stood black stones like shrouded figures. It was a merchant's garden, and masses of peonies symbolizing wealth, delicate pink with carmine centers, grew in it. Duquet stood on an arched bridge gazing at water flowing over pebbles.

"Many times in New France have I seen water sliding over stones but never considered it especially notable. But this is—different."

Wuqua bowed. "It is assuredly different. In your forest clear streams occur commonly. In a city garden they are precious. I wish you to see the two twisted junipers, undoubtedly rooted in the beginning of the world, that are the secret of this garden. They are hidden from casual view." They followed him along the perimeter paths before crossing a bridge fashioned from a single massive stone. As Duquet looked up from the slightly perilous placement of his foot, the ancient junipers appeared, deformed by centuries of snow burden.

"You see," said Wuqua, "that in addition to rock, water and plant, this garden of reflection and harmony embodies the invisible element of time." He was surprised that this coarse foreigner took pleasure from the garden. He recognized that Duquet was certainly no aesthete, but emanated that irresistible power found in men of strong wills or great wealth. Duquet did not quite see the garden as itself; in his mind he regarded it as though he were suspended some distance above and looking down at himself walking along the mosaic paths. His presence in such a curious place made it notable to him. And it stirred him with an indefinable sensation.

At the edge of a lake they entered a pavilion. A servant brought tea. White flowers seeped a musky perfume. The pale liquid beauty of the garden calmed the negotiators. Duquet watched the way the others held their translucent bowls, inhaled the aroma, sipped, sighed, sipped again. He did the same.

At last Wuqua and Captain Verdwijnen rose, bowed to each other, bowed to the translator and Duquet and they all returned to the business room. The negotiators were gentle with each other now, and each man's offer was presented as a gift, but refused by the other with flowery, elaborate speeches that seemed acceptances. Duquet watched everything intently, memorizing the procedure. Duquet felt he was in a fantastical world, but it was his skill to adapt to strange circumstances, and even to find pleasure in them. As the day drew on, the warm air thickened. At last Wuqua stood up, spoke rapidly to the translator and left the room. Captain Verdwijnen said they all, even the translator, had been invited to a banquet that evening at one of the merchant's private residences.

Back at their rooms Duquet and Captain Verdwijnen washed and changed. They had an hour to wait before Wuqua's servants came for them. Duquet got out the gin.

"Did you work out a fair price for the goods you want?" he asked the captain.

"Not yet, not yet! We have only begun. We shall continue tomorrow and perhaps the next day and the next. Haste is not advisable. Slow, contemplative weighing of loss and gain, of prestige, of honor and much more are involved." Duquet envied this captain who so skillfully played the cards.

Captain Verdwijnen lit his long clay pipe and puffed out smoke. "You are wondering when we will get to your furs, no?" His foot waggled.

"Yes," said Duquet, "I do wonder."

"Eventually. There is no hurry. In any case we cannot leave until we finish conducting our business—next year with the correct wind for our return. So enjoy your time here. What did you think of the garden?"

"Why, very—very—agreeable."

"I also like beautiful gardens and *constich* objects."

This Duquet knew, for he remembered Captain Verdwijnen waking him from a deep sleep one night—"Get up! There is a great sight! Awake!"—and commanding him to come on deck immediately to see a wonder. Swaying in his nightshirt, barefoot and bleary, he clung to the rail and looked down. The water curling back from the rushing ship's prow was a froth of luminescence and behind them the fiery glow marked their recent passage.

"Look! *See there!*" cried Captain Verdwijnen gesturing at the water-riding phosphor and waving his hands. Alongside the ship the bodies of dolphins trailed sparks that twisted and writhed as the fish moved. A sailor hauled up a bucket of quivering light. Captain Verdwijnen plunged his hands into it and held them up, his fingers and palms glowing as the water dripped away. The crests of the waves caught fire, darkened. The ship seemed to be sailing through a burning sea. Duquet yawned, said "remarkable," and returned to his blanket.

Before they stepped into the palanquins, the translator said Wuqua had noticed the foreigners' pleasure in the garden earlier in the day and the dinner invitation included a walk through his personal Garden of Vermilion Dragonflies. But when they arrived, and their host conducted them under the rustling trees, it was dark. There was no moon. The pathway was lighted by a tremble of distant lightning and by paper globes of imprisoned fireflies, which cast a greenish light. Of dragonflies, whether vermilion, amber or blue, there was no sight. But Wuqua took their hands and led them to the darkest shade. "We stand here under a duck-foot tree, the largest in the city. My garden was once part of an ancient temple and this *yin-kuo* tree was old then; they say it lived in the time before Buddha. It is not like any other tree. It is believed to be one of the first trees to live in the world." In the darkness he pulled at the leaves and gave one to Duquet, another to Captain Verdwijnen.

"You must come another time in daylight to see the dragonflies," said Wuqua and led them into a room faced with intricate carved screens. Two dozen lanterns threw a radiant light on the guests and the wine winking in silver bowls. Duquet looked at the *yin-kuo* leaf in his hand; it looked very like a leaf from a maidenhair fern which he had seen a thousand times in the forests of the north. At the back of the room musicians played in the Xinjiang style and a performer sang in a high, strangled voice. The translator said the great dish of the dinner, following many courses, was called Buddha Leaps over the Wall. Duquet enjoyed it while Captain Verdwijnen, longing for herring and headcheese, picked at it fearfully.

On the way back to the Factory quarter, Captain Verdwijnen said, "I offer a wager that wall-jumping concoction will make you ill— perhaps kill you."

"It was worth it," said Duquet.

Weeks passed before Wuqua deigned to consider Duquet's offerings. He seemed to expect a request for ceramics, teas, lacquerware and silks. He seemed to think Duquet's pack contained silver. So when Duquet took out the lustrous furs, one by one, shaking them until they snapped with static electricity, Wuqua's face, trained never to show surprise, showed surprise. He took up a snowy arctic fox fur and caressed it, examined the mink and marten furs, the ice-white ermine and two thick sea otter pelts. At the sight of the velvet-black fur tipped with silver, the world's most desirable luxury, Wuqua sucked in his breath.

"Very pretty. Very, very pretty. We do not too often see furs of such beauty and quality. However, the Russians do bring us furs, so they are not unknown here. And in Guangzhou it is really too warm for furs, but at court and in the north . . . What do you wish for these?"

Instead of the usual list of luxury goods Duquet named a very high price—in silver. Wuqua pretended to faint, his head slumped to one side but watchful eyes glinting from the slitted lids. He revived and named a small sum that would be bolstered by a few rolls of silk and a bale of tea.

Duquet hurled himself to the floor in a fit of shrieking, spasmodic, disbelieving laughter. Even as he fell he realized he had gone too far. He got up, sure he had lost face in the negotiations and that the morning—perhaps the entire trip—was wasted. He sat again in his chair and looked at Wuqua.

The expression on the businessman's face was peculiar. Amazement? Disdain? But Wuqua nodded his head, the slightest nod, but it expressed a kind of calculated admiration, an acceptance of Duquet's behavior as a tolerable and even admirable ploy. Decorum returned. The day progressed, the bargaining continued. They again went to the garden for tea and arranged to meet in two days' time. At the end of the month of bargaining Duquet accepted a princely sum in silver for his furs. He had gained a staggering profit.

"If you come in a future year," said Wuqua, "with furs of equal quality and variety they may excite a greater passion." The servant poured more tea. Wuqua sipped, looked into the distance and then asked offhandedly, "And do you have *this* in your forests of New France?" From his sleeve he withdrew a gnarled root vaguely shaped like a hunchbacked, three-legged man. Duquet had seen this root before, in the hands of the Indian woman who had saved his life.

"Yes, we have this."

"Ah. If you bring me a quantity of these roots I will pay as much as for the furs. Perhaps more, depending on the quality and quantity."

"Very good. And I also have rare woods for fine cabinets," said Duquet, trembling inwardly, knowing he was on the edge of extraordinarily advantageous arrangements.

"Rare woods are of interest. Especially sandalwood. Scented woods are prized."

In a stroke Duquet had become a wealthy man and, he thought, after one or two more trips—if Captain Verdwijnen were willing to take him—his forest enterprise would begin. As they spoke of woods Duquet was emboldened to ask a question.

"Sir, honorable Wuqua, as foreigners may not leave the Factory compound I have wondered many times about the forests of China. I see that men in China make gardens that seem the essence of forest and mountain, but in miniature. But what of the real forests? It is my belief that forests are everlasting and can never disappear, for they replenish themselves, but I have seen in France that they are . . . diminished. And I have noticed that even in New France the forest is drawing back—a little, wherever there are settlements. How far back can a forest withdraw before it replenishes itself?"

Wuqua looked at him as though trying to judge whether or not Duquet had designs on China's woodlands. He glanced at the translator. He hesitated.

"I can only say that China is very large and very old with many people. More than that I cannot say. Perhaps another time?"

Duquet understood that he was dismissed, rose, bowed and backed away.

After some months Duquet yearned to leave. It was irritating to wait for the monsoon to shift. Then one day Wuqua requested his presence in the trading room. It was a clear chill day in springtime and outside the wind cast plum blossom petals on the courtyard tiles. There was a different translator.

"You wished to know about our forests," said Wuqua in a low, hurried voice, pausing impatiently for the translator. "I spoke with an elderly scholar on the subject. He said that our venerated sage Meng-tzu wrote of the people clearing land for crops, pulling grass and weeds, cutting trees ceaselessly, dividing the land and plowing. The people were very numerous even in Meng-tzu's time, and very poor. People must eat or they die. They need fuel to cook rice. They must keep warm. So trees fall." A rod of sunlight touched the toe of Wuqua's black silk slipper. "We are a country of agriculture. You understand of course that land division is the base of all human government."

"The forests then are diminished?"

"It is an arguable point, for men transplant many trees—bamboo, pine, oak and the valuable ones that produce lacquer or rich oils. Bear in mind that if forests and timberlands are diminished, cropland is very much augmented—more food, more money, more people, more contentment."

Duquet nodded though he did not see contentment in this recipe. He knew very well that Wuqua hoped to gain his favor by telling him these secret things.

"But even beyond increasing our agricultural land we cut forests for other reasons. For example, do you know the scholar's four treasures?"

"No. I regret to say I do not."

"This is a country of scholars, poets and calligraphers," said Wuqua, "and the four treasures are brush, paper, ink and inkstone, the necessities of calligraphy. But the source of the ink is the soot from the burning of pine trees. Very many pine trees must burn to supply China's scholars." The sunlight had moved up Wuqua's robe and made a bright band across the embroidery. "And there was war. And metalworkers, potters, brickmakers—all craftsmen's trades demand wood. In some tree-denuded places peasants are forced to gather grass, twist it into hard bundles and burn it as fuel. In other places animal dung." He whispered. "There are wood shortages . . ."

"So the forests of France and China are not everlasting," said Duquet unhappily. "And I have heard that Italy's mountains are stripped."

"Perhaps. But nothing is everlasting. Nothing. Not forests, not mountains."

"But how came the gardens that honor forests and wild country?"

"We do not forget the forests when we have removed the trees. We make gardens to give us the pleasurable illusions of wilderness."

"I myself," said Duquet, "despise the gloomy and unruly forest, even while recognizing that it is a source of wealth and comforts. Yet I would never make a garden alluding to it."

"Of course you would not. You do not understand the saying *'tian ren he yi.'* It refers to a state of harmony between people and nature. You do not feel this. No European does. I cannot explain it to you. It is a kind of personal philosophy for each person, yet it is everything."

Duquet thought it likely that the forests of China and France and Italy had been puny in their beginnings; he believed that the uniquely deep forests of the New World would endure. That was why men came to the unspoiled continent—for the mind-numbing abundance of virgin resources. Only he grasped the opportunity.

• • •

Duquet visited the ivory carver, who took a wax mold of his tooth-less jaws and set to work fashioning teeth. There was a wait of several months until they would be finished. The day came and the carver showed him how to insert the plates of large white teeth hinged with fine gold wires. Duquet looked in a glass for the first time in many years and although the teeth felt monstrous and uncomfortable, they undeniably improved his appearance. The carver told him he would get used to the intrusive feeling, but that the teeth were only for display, not for chewing. "Clean every day with brush, white cloth." In pantomime he showed Duquet that he must expect they would become yellow over time, especially if he let sunshine fall on them. It could not be helped; it was the nature of ivory. Perhaps he should have a second pair made for spares? Yes, nodded Duquet. He wondered if ceramic teeth could be fashioned, then thought of a likely mouthful of broken shards.

Late every afternoon when the day's continuing bargaining was finished Duquet and Captain Verdwijnen enjoyed a glass of *jenever* in the courtyard. The two men had become used to each other. Duquet several times, between panegyrics on the forests of New France, said he wished to arrange another passage as soon as possible, but Captain Verdwijnen always slipped to another subject.

"How do you like this pretty little table I've bought for Margit? That old rogue Wuqua bargained as though I was trying to buy his precious dragonfly garden. At one point he actually fell off the chair and rolled on the floor laughing like a madman. A complete loss of face. But in the end I got it for a good price."

"Hah!" laughed Duquet. Wuqua, the old rogue, had learned a new trick from him.

• • •

Often one or two of the captain's maritime friends, Piet Roos and Jan Goossen, captains of their own ships, dined with them. The face of Piet was like a pale plate set with two round eyes the color of raw sugar. His hair was almost the color of his skin and thus invisible. He dressed in the French mode, black silk culottes and coat set off by a froth of fine lace at the neck. Jan wore an immense sword and coarse workman's fustian trousers. These contrasting men seemed familiar to Duquet and he finally asked about them.

"Of course they are familiar. You saw them in the Rock and Shoal in La Rochelle." Captain Verdwijnen lowered his voice to a whisper. "I told you, they are my partners, my *vrienden*. Piet is my brother-in-law, Jan is my cousin. You didn't think I could defy the Vereenigde Oost-Indische Compagnie and bear the expense of this voyage alone, did you?"

Duquet said, "*I* would like to be a partner with you for the sake of the furs. And for my future lumber enterprise. We could make money together, don't you think?"

After a long silence Captain Outger Verdwijnen spoke slowly. "You know that the Vereenigde Oost-Indische Compagnie for many years tightly controlled Dutch trade with India, China and Japan, the Spice Islands. No private merchant was allowed to do business nor travel through the Strait of Magellan."

"But men *do* try. And succeed," said Duquet.

"If you tried and were caught your goods were seized, your ship taken, and you were punished by the VOC's stony hand. That is what happened to Willem Schouten, who discovered Kaap Hoorn. Now the Company is weaker, but still watchful. My *vrienden* and I made a secret partnership to enter the India-China trade ourselves— and someday even Japan—by banding resources together and sailing together. This is our fourth voyage and it is going well. Of course Piet and Jan own their boats and I am just the captain for Herr Grinz, but I hope to make enough on this trip to buy a good little *fluyt*. I am not altogether sure there is a place in our arrangement for a timber merchant. There may be—I don't know. I fear a *fluyt* could not carry great loads of timber. Our West Indies want lumber, but I prefer to continue the China trade. If I were you I would look into the Indies trade."

But Duquet, with stubborn single-mindedness, began once again to describe the forests of New France. The Dutchman interrupted him.

"My young friend," he said. "Allow someone with knowledge of the world to offer a comment. You speak always as though New France were your country."

"It is. Our fortunes are intertwined. It is a new world, rich and beauteous with massive forests and powerful rivers. It is a place that has earned my respect."

"May I remind you that your New France is not a sovereign country but the colony of a major European power? May I, from long observation of the political machinations of these great powers, introduce a note of caution? The kings of these strong countries do not know their colonies and overseas settlements. They have never been there, nor have their ministers. For them those colonies are colored blotches on maps, they are only counters in the savage games of war, only sources of income. They do not give a fig for anything else. And I might observe that you are not wary enough of France's European enemies, especially England. It might fall out that France trades or otherwise divests itself of New France, as the occasion dictates."

"That could never happen."

"Of course not. But I have heard that France, the mother country, is not particularly enamored of New France, that supply ships are often very late, that she keeps her population at home instead of urging settlement in this northern paradise, that favors and help are conspicuously absent, that she is unwilling to open her markets to what is in a way her own child."

"That is only temporary," said Duquet sullenly, not liking these truths.

"You will see how temporary and remember this conversation if France comes to war with one of the powers and, not doing well, is forced to give up something. How long do you think New France will stay inviolate?"

In the months since they had arrived Captain Verdwijnen arranged to have the ship hauled onto a nearby beach where it could be cleaned, everything removed from the interior. A hundred Chinese men removed the ordure-coated ballast stones from the bilges and laid them in the beating surf, scraped down the bilges, removed the stinking limber ropes and threaded new ones. They laid down a bed of clean sand before replacing the surf-scoured ballast, scraped the exterior bottom free from barnacles and seaweeds (for it was an uncoppered ship), recaulked and repainted the vessel inside and out. The *Steenarend* was refloated and for days long lines of men carrying chests and boxes packed the hold. The reprovisioned ship was fresh and clean, stuffed with the luxury goods of the China trade, and fifty flowering plants. They set off for the Bay of Bengal, with crates of lemons and mangoes to keep them safe from scurvy.

In India, Captain Verdwijnen exchanged some of the ceramics and silks for more cabbages and fruit, spices, especially cloves and pepper, and picked up a chest of Patna opium for medicinal trade in Amsterdam. Duquet's busy mind, once again dense with forest thoughts, took note.

"Such a three-corner trading route could work for a lumber merchant, could it not?"

"Yes, but in my case the profits would be better if I bought the opium going forward, for there is a growing market in China for it. But we were pressed for time. Many foreign traders are taking advantage of the demand. Why should I not as well? But perhaps you were not thinking of opium?"

"But, yes. I was." He was thirty-two and on the way to his fortune.

14

risk

On the home voyage some of the sailors refused to drink the scurvy-preventing lemon juice and threw the mangoes overboard (as they had the oranges and bok choy) when they thought they were unobserved. Those who were caught had the choice of sucking two lemons dry or enduring ten lashes. Most chose the lashes, for they believed that salt meat, hardtack and cheese so stale and granitic they had to be cut with an ax were manly foods suited to sailors. Lemons were not well regarded. Captain Verdwijnen smiled and said he hoped they would enjoy their scurvy. And soon enough those men began to move stiffly, leaving bloodstains on their hardtack, bending double with gut-ripping pains. There was great laughter one day and Toppunt, seeking the cause, found one of the lemon haters staring at his ration of hardtack. He had tried to gnaw it and it came away from his mouth bloodied and with three teeth embedded in it. Now the voyage seemed interminable but Captain Verdwijnen made one more stop.

The ship made port at Ghana, picked up thirty slaves and crowded them into the cargo hold with the crates of porcelain, the rare plants and the chest of Patna. There was not a cat's whisker of free space on the vessel. In the dark hold the slaves got at the contents of the opium chest, a fortuitous find which greatly eased their passage. They found and ate the rare plants, blossom, leaf, stem, root and soil. It was only when they sighted France that the loss was discovered.

Captain Verdwijnen, when he had recovered from his shock, drinking his evening *jenever* put a question to Duquet.

"So, my friend, what think you the value of those slaves now?"

Duquet thought before he answered. The affair had its comic side but he would keep his smiles to himself.

"To you, they must have a very high value, for when you add up the cost of the slaves themselves, then cipher in what you paid for the plants and the opium, they become precious, likely far above the market price for slaves."

"Quite so," said Verdwijnen. "But. It is more complicated than that. For neither the plants nor the opium have fixed prices that are the same everywhere. What amount might I have received for the opium, which is an expensive and desirable medicine? And what if some of the plants soared in value as tulips did in my grandfather's time? Should those estimated future prices be factored into the value of the slaves? And what about the slave buyer? He would see only a slave, not the opium and rare orchids the creatures ingested. To him, the value is the slave-market price."

He thought a moment, then went on. "The slaves, opium and plants were mine. That's all."

"But do you not hold marine insurance for this trip? With the men in the coffeehouse in La Rochelle?"

"That, too, is complicated. Of course Herr Grinz's ship was insured by the coffeehouse men against loss, piracy and wreck, and also his cargo of silk and tea, but the rest . . . no. Piet, Jan and I are self-insured through our *partenrederijen,* so the risks fall equally on all of us. Piet and Jan own their ships—I alone had to hire out to Herr Grinz. They will share my losses and I will share their profits."

Duquet nodded. The motion of the ship was very slight as they were passing through slick water in which long windrows of seaweed made a pattern like a gigantic tweed cloak. He felt slight sympathy for Captain Outger Verdwijnen, who had made a negligible profit from the long, perilous journey, very little to show for all his bargaining and diplomatic skills. Unexpected dangers in business were part of the game. Captain Verdwijnen gave a hard laugh and said, "It's always a risk, such a voyage. We might easily have lost the ship and all its contents, we might have lost our lives, we might have been captured by pirates and sold as slaves ourselves. I look on the pleasant side. We have evaded cyclones and pirates. I still have Margit's little table—and I still have the slaves. I'll get something for them, so in the end it is only the opium and the rare plants that I have lost. In any case we Dutch do not mind taking a risk. If business and enterprise is a fruit, we understand risk is its inner kernel." He stretched his legs and half-smiled. "Besides, I also placed some bets at the coffeehouse before we sailed that the ship would not wreck, that we would dodge pirates, and that I would return very much alive and twice as clever. There is my profit."

And so they returned to France, where the *Steenarend* would stay for three weeks, Duquet chafing to see the new finery which would present him as a person of value and importance.

15

hair

They were late arriving in Paris and rather than go to the tailor's shop in the deepening dusk Toppunt and Duquet spent the night at an inn.

The tailor seemed surprised to see them. Duquet, trying on his finery behind an embroidered screen with the help of Jules, the tailor's assistant, listened while Toppunt and the tailor conversed.

"We have heard so many ships were lost in storms and to pirates that I thought yours was surely among them."

"Not this time," said Toppunt, "though we were severely lashed by typhoons and came close to being driven onto the rocks off the east coast of Africa, a vicious shore. There is more to the sea than water—there is the land that constricts it."

"The sea is the master of all men."

"Not our captain. He is a skilled navigator and of a pleasant nature unlike most ship captains. He is a good man. This was my fourth voyage with him and I will never ship out with another captain."

"And if he dies?" asked the tailor. "Will you accompany him on that voyage as well?"

"Ha ha," said Toppunt, "we'll see. It depends on his port of call."

Duquet, a vision in blue, stepped out from behind the screen and turned about to show the fit of his costume.

"So," said Toppunt. "Even a prince would envy you."

The tailor held both hands up and praised Duquet's legs—"You are certainly a man not in need of calf pads. You, sir, have a well-turned leg."

After this blandishment the tailor tried to wheedle more money from him. "It's for storage. And I gave the costume very much care, dusting the shoulders, airing it outdoors, protecting it from my cat." Duquet took out his smallest coin and spun it on the tailor's table.

The wigmaker's shop was closed, but with loud pounding they raised the proprietor, whose pointed nose gleamed wet. He coughed incessantly.

"The powder on the wigs, you know. It's quite irritating. I have lately changed to a powder made from curious lichens that grow on rocks, and it does not trouble me so severely. I have heard they use it to poison wolves, so rest assured that your fine wig will never be plagued by those ferocious animals."

He brought the wigs out. Toppunt's was black and glossy and very smart. Duquet's was enormous and heavy, of auburn color with countless long ringlets that cascaded down his back and over his shoulders.

"Do you wish it powdered?" asked the wigmaker. He produced a hacking sound.

"No, no," said Duquet, staring at himself in the shop's watery mirror. Between the blue shimmer of the garments, the flash of his ivory teeth and the expensive wig he was transformed into an apparent gentleman—what Toppunt, not altogether kindly, called a *schijn-heer*—an almost-gentleman.

They left the street of shops, heading for a certain eating place. Toppunt had heard the cook came from Bourgogne and was a genius of the kitchen. This inn was in a distant street and the longer they walked the hotter Duquet became until he felt his brains roasting, his shoulders laden with coals. His neck ached with the weight of the wig. The sun glowed as a smelting furnace. They pushed through crowded streets, down alleys that ran at angles. A man carrying a large covered tray on his shoulder came toward them. He brushed past Duquet, who suddenly felt the expensive wig ripped from his head. He spun around in time to see the man with the tray running, and on the tray a ragged child clutching Duquet's new wig. The load was heavy and the man lurched as he ran.

"Au voleur! Au voleur!" shouted Duquet and Toppunt. A passerby stuck out his leg and the man fell, the child, tray and wig hurtling into the mud. The child scampered away at extraordinary speed but the passerby held down the man. A crowd gathered and pinioned the thief.

"It'll be the galleys for him," said Toppunt. "He will join the Huguenots."

Duquet, in an icy rage, retrieved the huge wig that had cost him so much. It looked twice as large as before, quite the armful, as big as a mattress and with clots of mud dangling from its curls; as he shook it he saw it had become entangled with another wig, apparently stolen earlier than his and hidden beneath the cloth.

"It's a good one," said Toppunt, examining the modish second wig critically. "You can sell it." But as he examined it more closely he grimaced.

"It's full of lice and nits." He held it up. "But you could have it fumigated and cleaned. It is a valuable wig." While they were examining the hairy mass the passerby, still holding the thief and craning his neck to better see the wigs, relaxed his grip a little and the miscreant wrenched loose and ran into the faceless multitude. A chase was hopeless.

Duquet had had enough of wigs for the day, and, carrying his own under his arm, he strode away, Toppunt, carrying the lousy wig, running after him, calling, "Slow, slow."

By the time they reached the inn they could laugh at the adventure. Duquet said they should return to the wigmaker and see what he would give for the stranger's wig. It might pay for their dinner. They recklessly ordered dishes with the feeling that someone else would pay—some good French wine. At last, sated and half drunk, they ate a sweet tart, and after that neither could move.

"We need coffee," said Toppunt. The innkeeper told them of a coffeehouse two streets away. They waddled in that direction, passed it twice before seeing it and went in.

When they were finally restored to mobility and mental clarity they returned to the wigmaker's shop, Toppunt carrying the stolen wig. The man recognized it as one he had made himself for a great gentleman. He said he would return it to his client, but Duquet insisted on a reward, naming a sum that covered the cost of their lavish dinner. Moaning, the wigmaker paid it, protesting that his client would hardly pay twice, even for a stolen and returned wig.

In the street Toppunt said the wigmaker would likely cleanse the wig, hide it away and, when the client came to him telling of the theft, the wigmaker would promise him a new one, as like the old as a pea in the pod resembles its neighbor, and charge an even greater sum (for the verisimilitude) than the wig's first sale.

"In truth," he said, "I believe the thieves are in the employ of the wigmakers."

A week later, dressed in his finery and wearing the ivory teeth and stifling wig, Duquet attended a formal return dinner at Captain Verdwijnen's house in Amsterdam. The captain and his wife, Margit, Captains Piet Roos and Jan Goossen, their wives and Piet's two nearly grown daughters, Josina and Cornelia, made up the company. In the entrance hall Duquet noticed the table Captain Verdwijnen had purchased for Margit in Guangzhou.

As Margit looked him over Duquet saw that her right eye was more kindly than the left, which shot out a ray of antipathy. He felt that eye erase his fine clothes, discard the wig, dissolve the ivory teeth and identify him as a scavenging opportunist. He dared not eat anything but soup and gravy as he did not wish to remove his teeth in company. They were inadequate for anything beyond blancmange.

To avoid Madame Verdwijnen's cruel eye, all through the dinner Duquet shot his own glances at young Cornelia. There was a resemblance to Piet and she was passable, though certainly not a beauty. Her eyes were of a blue so pale they seemed white, her nose was broad. She wore a dark brown silk dress with a filmy ruff collar and an embroidered linen cap. Duquet made up his mind that she would be his wife. At the flashing thought of any opposition or denial the inner tiger stirred.

During his time in Amsterdam, at a popular coffeehouse Duquet met a colonial Englishman from Boston, Benton Dred-Peacock, dressed in smart clothes of the best quality but with a face that seemed made from stale bread crusts. Most colonial settlers were of low circumstance; it was obvious Dred-Peacock was a moneyed gentleman. As they talked Duquet learned Dred-Peacock had intimate business dealings with the newly appointed New England royal mast contractor Jonathan Bridger. The man knew very much about the forest business in the colonies, and made it clear that his allegiances lay with the colonists rather than the Crown. And Dred-Peacock recognized in Duquet a man who knew how to get money from turnips if nothing else was at hand. Money was power and Duquet gave off the smell of both. He was one of those men others wished to know, even while they despised him.

Duquet gathered from the conversation the knowledge that many colonials bitterly disliked English rule and the public taxes that went (unfairly, said Dred-Peacock) to support England's reckless wars. Especially did they dislike the restrictive policies of the Royal Board of Trade, which set stringent rules for cutting the dense and dominating forests, rules pressing on amounts and procedures for supplying the Royal Navy with ships' stores—masts, bowsprits and yards, not to mention pitch and tar. The residents were incensed over the Acts of Trade and Navigation, which clamped like vises on colonial trade. And this Bridger fellow was apt to be troublesome about the sale of townships and the cutting of mast trees. But, said Dred-Peacock, "that man is eager to make a name for himself, and I believe he will respond to careful smoothing." And Dred-Peacock knew the Elisha Cookes, both formidable powers in colonial affairs.

Dred-Peacock, his breath heavy with black rum fumes, whispered to Duquet, his eyes casting about for listening spies; "As Dr. Cooke says, we ought to have the rights to trade with the whole world if we have the enterprise to produce the goods and timber, to grow hemp. But these Acts bind us at every turn."

Duquet suggested they move to a more private table near the back, and he ordered a flagon of rum. As the evening wore on he learned there were many sly ways the New Englanders evaded those thousand and one strictures, most generally in collusion with colonial officials, especially the sawmill owners. Dred-Peacock leaned closer, thinking an alliance with this brute could be to his purse's advantage. It was all about money.

"Chief among these exigencies is procuring ownership of great white pine tracts by purchasing old township grants. One must cultivate understandings with men who enjoy political influence and connections. I have done so. The enemy is the King's Surveyor, a dotard in London who makes a big fluster examining the licenses and permits of lumbermen. He is cowardly and dare not come to the colonies lest he suffer an accident. He sends his henchmen, the lowest of men."

"I would know more about acquiring those townships," said Duquet.

Armed with a dozen new names and Dred-Peacock's promise to meet him on his return, Duquet sailed for Boston, reflecting that the great and important advantage of the colonies over New France was the ice-free ports. The St. Laurent was locked in ice for six or even eight months of the year.

He found a small house in the colonial city and for the next year practiced speaking English and cultivating acquaintances with men who could grant him favors, all introduced by Dred-Peacock. Duquet did not quite trust Dred-Peacock, yet the man was a tolerable woodsman, a grand walker with legs cutting distance as springily as sheep-shearing blades. In the early spring Duquet fell ill with cholera, gradually regaining his health. He planned one more trip to China, and then he would buy up old Maine land claims and paper townships. But first he had to go north.

16

"a wicked messenger,
fallen into evil . . ."

(Guy du Faur, Seigneur de Pibrac)

Back in New France Duquet reverted to buckskin and moccasins and set out to find the Trépagny brothers. Everywhere he went there were stump-choked clearings, charcoal kilns and settlers' cabins, for men were cutting maple trees to make charcoal; the English needed it for their glass and gunpowder factories and paid high prices. He could not find Toussaint and Fernand—but that could be explained by the new war. New France, Indians and the English colonies to the south boiled with spies; there were constant ambushes by roving bands of combatants. Duquet was impatient to get the brothers aligned for another season of fur trading. They would dodge the fighting.

Then it was cooler and there was rain in the woods, the smell of leaf mold and mushrooms. The refreshed river hissed. He looked up at a sky that seemed set with rondels of thick glass. He found the brothers tearing out a beaver dam near their old hut on the Rivière des Fourres. Both brothers, muddy and glad to leave the beaver dam for a reunion, were in fair health though Toussaint's beard showed white side streaks and Fernand groaned when he straightened up.

"They call this Queen Anne's War, but it seems the continuance of our old antipathies," Toussaint said. "I blame the Indian factions. One day a tribe is your enemy. The next you are fighting beside them, or they stand back from the battle and smile, like the Iroquois."

"I hope you do not think I came back to fight Indians and English," said Duquet sourly.

"Many do feel an allegiance to New France," said Toussaint.

"I feel an allegiance to gathering furs."

Toussaint poured water into the black kettle and when it boiled Duquet showed them somewhat officiously how to make tea. They sipped it, making wry faces. Duquet said they would develop a taste for it, that it was considered a luxury in Europe. He said he wished he had brought coffee for them but it was extremely dear and doubtless they would not like it as it was very bitter. The rum was more welcome. He apologized for the small amount of fur money he gave them, told a tale of pirate capture and the loss of most of his profits. He was anxious to start trading again and would surely make up the poor showing of this venture. Smoothly he asked for their history. The brothers exchanged a long look.

Toussaint said drily that they had experienced coffee in Ville-Marie, nor was Duquet the only one to see the world. They had traveled on the Mississippi the last several years with Pierre LeMoyne, the son of a man in Ville-Marie who had started his New France life as an indentured servant and become rich.

"Some people now see that there should be French forts all across the land." As Toussaint spoke, Duquet sensed that he was seething with the desire to build forts and fight the English, guessed that they disbelieved his pirate story. But what could they do? Enjoy the rum, that's what.

"We went to find the true mouth of the river. *Sacrebleu!* I swear! Some river—a maze of swamps and black waterways like spiderwebs. LeMoyne explored in a canoe with an Indian and some soldiers. We stayed in the Indian village near the old La Salle fort."

Fernand picked up his brother's story, spoke rapidly, saying that other Indians had stayed in that village—a dozen of them from a Western Ocean tribe who had come to hunt bison. "For they do not have those beasts in their country. The Western Ocean hunters had packs of furs for trade. They came by those furs trading with the North Indians who live near the world of ice."

Toussaint opened a small pack and showed eight rich sea otter furs and four arctic fox.

"Ah!" Duquet stroked the sensual otter pelts. He draped one across his knee and slid his fingers into the caressing warmth. His mouth watered.

"They said the North Indians had so many otter pelts they paved the streets of their villages with them. They said the North Indians traveled with the Russians and all got sick." He stretched out his hand for his otter fur in Duquet's hand and returned it to his pack.

"Did the North Indians with the Russians trade willingly with the Western Ocean Indians?"

Fernand made a deep sound. "At first, yes, then they changed. The Russians were already dead and the North Indians were dying when the Western Ocean Indians came on them. The sick North Indians did not want to trade. The Western Ocean men persuaded them."

"Some of the persuasion was severe? Even fatal?"

Fernand was fumbling with the second pack, Toussaint clearing his throat and frowning at his brother. But Fernand, always a braggart, said, "It is true. Look at this."

He withdrew a rolled skin and opened it out. The brilliant gold and black fur dazzled. "A tiger," he said. "The Russians had it." He stroked the striped pelt. "It is why the sick North Indians did not want to trade." Toussaint turned away.

"Where is the head?" asked Duquet. "The head is valuable."

"The Russians did not have the head. They likely ate it. One must look after oneself in this life, isn't that right?"

"Right," said Duquet, watching Toussaint pull the tiger skin away from his brother and roll it. They would not give up that skin readily. The old easy partnership was gone. In fact, thought Duquet, his feeling for New France was gone. Late in the night, each rolled up in his bison robe, he heard Toussaint's voice, low and rough, oppressing his brother.

• • •

Duquet grew restless during this time with the Trépagny brothers, noting their cramped vocabularies, their repetitive stories, but he drove himself and the brothers into a short but frantic season of gathering furs, letting the Indian middlemen know he especially wanted wildcats. He kept two of the best aside as a present for Cornelia. He had told Piet of his intent to marry her, and although the captain had pursed his lips and shook his head in denial, Duquet thought he would agree when he heard of Duquet's accumulating wealth. The girl had good teeth and looked healthy enough, with broad hips, but each of her features was off-kilter, those colorless eyes too small, the wide nose and heavy cheeks. But it was the father and his business connections, his allegiance with Captain Verdwijnen that Duquet truly wished to marry. Cornelia was to give him the sons he needed to build his business empire. He looked now beyond mere wealth.

The season passed and when the time came for Duquet to return to La Rochelle and China, Toussaint mumbled that he and Fernand would keep their share of the furs unless Duquet would pay a high price for them on the spot.

"We know several traders now," said Toussaint. For months they had built their evening fire apart from Duquet and in the daytime conversed only with each other.

"We cannot wait years for your return, perhaps empty-handed if your pirates strike again. We need ready money," said Fernand, "as we wish to rejoin Pierre LeMoyne. He is in France preparing an expedition to the Caribbean." He stared at the ground as he spoke, unwilling to meet Duquet's eyes, but the tiger was calm. The brothers had no idea what furs brought in China, nor would they ever know. Duquet had learned something about negotiations and after two days of palaver with Toussaint, who spoke for himself and Fernand, Duquet made a wondrous bargain—except for the tiger skin and the white fox furs, which they would not give up.

"I have no doubt there are many adventures in the Caribe attractive to *coureurs de bois*," he said, letting the sarcasm show. Toussaint countered with acerbity: "I understand the Dutch West Indies are a most lucrative market for lumber, and certainly nearer than France or China." Duquet guessed the brothers were waiting for him to renew his offer of a partnership in the timber trade so that they might have the pleasure of refusing him. He said nothing. It was the parting of ways.

He rose near midnight, disappeared as silently as fog. It was many hours later that the brothers discovered the tiger skin, the fox and otter furs were gone. Fernand cursed and said there was no verse in Pibrac to ease the situation, but at least they had got a little hard money.

"Let us drink a toast to that man whose sugar mouth disguises his gall-choked heart." They opened the *jenever* and drank to the riddance of Duquet.

"Perhaps you'd rather have coffee," mocked Toussaint.

"Oh no, it is too bitter for one so backward as I," answered Fernand.

17

"unto a horse
belongeth a whip"

(Guy du Faur, Seigneur de Pibrac)

He could barely waste time sleeping, for his mind was in ferment, his body burned with the intense desire to get on with things. All was occurring as he had hoped. The first morning light was like an armful of dry wood tossed on a fire, and he was choking with energy and ambition as he pulled on his clothes. He despised men who slept until the sun was high—inept laggards who would never be anyone.

In Ville-Marie, before he had found the Trépagny brothers, Duquet had hired *bûcherons* to find and cut white and red cedar, balsam fir and fragrant sumac, others to shape and finish the wood into small boards. These were packed in odorless birch chests to preserve their natural fragrances. Indian women had gathered ginseng roots, bundles of sweetgrass, other plants and roots for him.

He chartered a ship, the *Hendrik,* to take him, his fragrant woods, his magic roots and furs to La Rochelle, where he would meet Captain Verdwijnen. The ship's captain was Gabriel Deyon, the son of Captain Deyon with whom he had first traveled to France years before. The son told Duquet his father had been lost, ship and all hands aboard, in the treacherous Strait of Magellan, whose narrow passageway he had chosen as a safe alternative to Cape Horn.

"One never knows," said Duquet piously. But *he* knew.

Deyon's ship stopped at every settlement along the river. At dusk

117

it moored for the night at Wobik and Duquet went ashore to see what changes had come in the years since he had left.

He could scarcely believe it. Where was the forest? The landscape had been corrupted. The village had swollen by fifty houses, a grain mill, a water-powered sawmill, a large sheep commons. The forest had been pushed out of sight, and in the place of woodlands were rough fields with crops growing between stumps. The muddy trail west that he remembered was now a fair road. For a moment he was frightened; if miles of forest could be removed so quickly by a few men with axes, was the forest then as vulnerable as beaver? No, the forest returned with vigor, resprouted from cut stumps, cast seeds, sent out mother roots from which new trees grew. These forests could not disappear. In New France they were vast and eternal.

One thing had not changed; Monsieur Bouchard still handled the passage money for river travel, still welcomed newcomers.

The old man, looking strong though white-haired, did not recognize him. Duquet asked him to open the ledger where he had made his mark half his lifetime earlier. He pointed.

"There. That is my ignorant mark." A few lines above he saw the pathetically elaborate *R* of René Sel and asked if he was still alive.

"*Certainement.* He has Monsieur Trépagny's old house, where he lives very comfortably with his wife and children. You knew, did you not, that Claude Trépagny met his untimely end seeking you, whom he determined to punish as a runaway?"

"I did not know. He was a vindictive, unforgiving master and I was justified in leaving because of that *maltraitement.* He treated me badly."

"There are some who believe you had him dispatched by the Iroquois."

"What a canard! If the Iroquois killed him it is because they had their own reasons."

And although he did not care, he diverted the conversation. "So, René Sel has become a landowning farmer?"

"He is a woodcutter and keeps a few cows and sheep out in the forest. But there are several farms near his place these days. He cuts firewood and makes potash. There are perhaps six good farms between here and Sel's place. As you can see, Wobik has made tremendous progress in clearing and destroying the wilderness. The only person who laments this labor is that *sauvage* Mari, René's wife. She has become a woman of some importance for her abilities to heal the sick. She mourns the loss of woodland grottoes where certain plants once grew but are no more because of the industry of the settlers. She speaks out more and more against the white settlers. We cannot subdue that streak of vengeance that is part of their character. Her Indan sons have gone to the village of St. Francis, which is crowded with rebellious Indans of every tribe."

"Mari!" cried Duquet. "Married to Mari? But she is much older. Surely a country marriage."

"No. Trépagny forced it years ago so that he would not lose his rich French wife. In the end he lost her and everything else, even his life."

"His brothers do not know this," said Duquet.

"Ah, but they do. I told them myself at the time of the events. By rights they should have inherited at least Claude's big stone house, but they did not wish it. They are wandering men with good hearts and said the house should go to one who was content to be a woodcutter. I expect they are both dead by now, killed by Indans or drowning."

"No doubt," said Duquet, "if they are not in the Caribbean whipping slaves." With that he took his leave and returned to the ship. He felt stifled, he was ready to get away. He had longed to be back in the northern forest but now that he was here he wished for the glittering worlds of La Rochelle, Paris, Amsterdam, even Canton, as the English called Guangzhou. New France had nothing for him now except timber.

"A hard one," murmured Monsieur Bouchard to himself. "Hardened. Very much hardened."

18

reunion

As the ship entered the Bay of Biscay the pale limestone cliffs of La Rochelle gleamed in the first strike of sunlight. Duquet could smell salted cod, the smoke of twisted salt grass from the fires of the poor. Despite the early hour a crowd of fishermen and mariners were on the wharf looking for share employment. Once they had worked the Newfoundland coast, but this was increasingly dangerous and difficult as the English and the New England colonists and even the Spanish and Dutch were pushing in. The La Rochelle boats now fished the offshore Grand Banks, where the *poissons* were larger, stouter and sweeter than those along the coast—and closer to home.

In La Rochelle while he waited for Captain Verdwijnen and his ship, Duquet carried two boxes of his specialty woods one day to the shop of Claude Citron, the merchant who, on his first journey years earlier, had expressed warm interest in unusual cabinet woods. Citron was older now but no less fervent on the subject of woods.

"Ah," he said as if Duquet had been in only the day before instead of long years, "let us see what you have brought from New France— delights, I am sure."

Duquet set his sample boxes of scented cedar and balsam on the table, a few pieces of figured maple. He explained that he was taking most of his stock to China. Citron handled the satiny wood, sniffed and tilted the pieces to catch the light.

"You know I am connected with esteemed cabinetmakers always anxious to buy fine woods. You are taking your fragrant woods to

China? They would find a market here as well, you know, but I suppose the profits will be greater in China, though the cost of shipping and the possibility of loss to pirates and storms greater. You might consider it."

He would make some money selling the cabinet woods to Citron, but it was the fur and growing opium profits of the China trade that made the hazardous journey worthwhile. For this last time, he thought. With the break from the Trépagny brothers he was at the end of his fur-trading days. He was a wealthy man, and although he was strong and hale he felt the pressure of time. He wanted much more; from now on he would concentrate on his forest empire.

He settled on a price for two boxes of his scented woods, said farewell and turned toward the wharves. He passed a patisserie emanating essences of sugared fruit and chocolate, then a small open-air market packed with great luscious lettuces and early onions. It was remarkable how much more interesting the smells of La Rochelle were than those of Boston.

He was staying at the Botte de Mer, the oddly named Sea Boot, a good enough inn with private beds and even private rooms, but the attraction was the extraordinary and ever-changing menu. Night after night an accomplished and inventive cook sent out salpicons, cassoulets and ragouts of sweetbreads or chopped pheasant or chicken, various fish, mushrooms, all savory, all seasoned with the local salt. The cassoulets were especially succulent. Alas, there were only six small tables and two sittings each evening. If you were unfortunate enough to be the seventh diner at the second sitting you would be rejected. Duquet had no intention of being turned away and looked forward keenly to that evening's meal. But first he would store his remaining wood samples.

As he started up the staircase that led to the upper rooms someone spoke at his shoulder in a quiet but familiar voice.

"Duquet. Is it you?"

"*Dieu!* Forgeron! I thought you to be in Nouvelle France?" Lean and dark Forgeron stood at his shoulder.

"Of course I was there for many years, but two years since I have been surveying in the Maine woods. You cannot believe the white pine in Maine." He smiled. "You are looking very well. Clearly you have progressed."

"Forgeron, you, too, look well—healthy and strong. This meeting is fortuitous. I have wished often to speak with you about the Maine forests."

"I have wished often to tell *you* of the opportunities for the timber business in Maine. Have you visited that region?"

"Only a little. Indeed, I am planning to explore further as soon as this, my last journey to China, ends. Let us dine together and tell all that has come our way since last we met. What affairs have brought you to La Rochelle?"

"I was in London to speak with an Englishman who has just won a mast contract for some Crown lands in Maine. He wants me to survey the area and arrange for woodsmen to cut masts. But I foresee difficulties with this fellow. He had other masts cut several years ago and stored them at his property in the West Indies. He was unable to sell them for reasons I do not understand and the masts perished from dry rot. He could not pay the cutting contract and the affair is now in the courts. So I am not eager to accept his offer."

In came their cassoulet of veal and chicken with pink beans and a loaf of still-warm bread as large as a bull's head. They drank good burgundy and when it was gone Forgeron raised his hand for more.

"I have a suggestion," said Duquet. "Why do we not renew our friendship and practice joint business? I shall be two years on this last trip, but perhaps you could survey Maine timberlands for me and purchase townships for Duquet et Fils while I am away?"

"What! You have sons? You have married?"

"No, no, but I hope soon this will come to pass." And he told Forgeron of Cornelia, of his plans for a timber empire and his hope that Forgeron would share in this.

"I do not know if Amsterdam should be the seat of this business, or New France? Or even the English colonies? Should I bring Cornelia to the New World?"

"I would suggest that Boston, with its great and open harbor, its connections to London, and to other colonies by way of the post road, the newspapers which inform, the mail service between Boston and New York and the Connecticut towns, and its nearness to the Maine pineries, is the most advantageous location."

"I had nearly come to that conclusion myself and your opinion settles the matter. Forgeron, if you work with me I will make you a rich man."

"Or will I be the one who makes you the wealthy fellow?"

They laughed and clasped hands.

19

"Exitus in dubio est"

In Amsterdam, Captains Piet Roos and Verdwijnen at a table in their favorite coffeehouse discussed the possibility of the match.

"I do not like the man," said Piet. "Beneath the pleasant manner he is cold and calculating. He is more addicted to his own interests than anything else. There is something in the way that ugly head sits on his shoulders that signals defeat to anyone with whom he converses. He smiles often, yes, but while his lips curve his eyes remain like dried peas. I detect no real fondness for my daughter. His conversation is always about *his* wishes, *his* plans, *his* travels and *his* money. Of the rest of life aside from his personal advantage he knows little."

"Yes, I agree that may be true, his is a rough and masculine view—though I have seen him pleased with a Chinese garden, but he is already wealthy and in a way to command enormous sums."

"Yes, I like money as well, but not as Duquet does. With him it is a sinful greed. Nothing else matters."

Captain Verdwijnen took down his clay pipe from its ceiling hook. He sat again, spilled tobacco leaves on the table and began to cut them fine. "He has a monstrous good head for business and, as you say, a will to dominate. And a rather terrifying lust for work. If Cornelia weds him it would be a familial tie to a great deal of money and credit. You can always make stipulations in the marriage agreement—for example, you can insist that if you give permission for this marriage Cornelia and the children—and children there will be—must

124

remain in Amsterdam until a certain age—say, fourteen or so. He will look after his interests in New France and now, I understand, in the English colonies in some manner, and travel to Amsterdam when business allows, for protracted visits with his wife and family—and business partners. I have no hesitation in doing business with him. And I think if you set it out to him that marriage with Cornelia is an impossibility without these provisions he will accept it, perhaps even welcome it as I see no indications that he would ever be a family man dandling infants on his knee, though I sense that he is lonely."

"He is one of those who cannot be other than lonely. He was born to it. And I dislike the idea of him clambering aboard Cornelia as if she were an Indian canoe." Piet Roos paused for a long moment. "I might do business with him but I do not want him for a son-in-law."

"Some of your feelings are the natural feelings of a father for his daughter. But you need only keep him in check. He is, aside from his raw greed, something of a fool. He is obtuse, has no subtlety and often acts on impulse. He feels his position as a lowborn uneducated man who has had to make his own way. He can be manipulated. He has a respect for older men such as we are. He will listen to you. In this life we meet difficult people. We must take the time to listen and try to understand them. We must never take an adversarial position."

Piet Roos, half convinced, snorted. "I feel he can be dangerous."

"Dear Piet, even a sparrow has a sharp beak. If you set it out that Cornelia and any children must remain here, it is a way you could exercise control over the children at least. You do not yourself have any sons and a sturdy grandson or two might be a real benefit. Or, if the children are girls, carefully chosen sons-in-law could be useful. You might also add business terms that would be to your benefit as well as his; you, after all, have three ships plying the China-Japan trade and he has none and salivates for them. And he has money and will have more. He will make money for us. I know it. So be fatherly. But be watchful."

• • •

It took Duquet another year of cross-Atlantic courtship, not of Cornelia, but of her father, to get his way. But he persisted. He would have her. In Amsterdam in 1711 he spent days with Piet Roos, who pored over Duquet's account books with great thoroughness, listened to his future plans and asked shrewd questions, weighing the answers before he allowed the marriage.

"If I correctly understand what you are proposing, there would be a three-way business partnership working the China trade—Charles Duquet, Piet Roos and Outger Verdwijnen."

"Yes," said Duquet, vibrating internally at the sound of the three linked names.

"Well. In that respect I think we can work an agreeable arrangement. The marriage is perhaps more—delicate. My wife and I do not wish to part with Cornelia. You understand she is our youngest daughter and her mother's pet."

Duquet half-smiled.

"I am not refusing your suit outright, but suggesting certain conditions. We would wish Cornelia to stay in Amsterdam." There was a long silence. Piet rolled and unrolled a corner of the paper on which he was writing. "I would make her a gift of a house I own in the next street, a very pleasant house and close by her parents and sister."

Duquet shifted in his chair. A house, Cornelia's house, *his* house.

"Moreover, we would prefer that any children from the union would live with their mother in Amsterdam. With her family close by she will be well looked after. You can live there, of course, but if you prefer, New France—or, better yet, you may travel between that place and Amsterdam, not only on business, but to spend time with your family." He looked at Duquet, who sat with his face motionless and his mouth slightly open. Duquet looked at the tapestry that hung on the wall behind Piet. He saw only the figure in the border—a hawk stooping on a heron. The heron lay on its back, its claws up to defend itself. But the hawk was fierce and sure. Below ran the words *"Exitus in dubio est,"* which Piet, seeing his puzzled expression, said was Latin meaning "escape is in doubt." Duquet's sympathies lay with the hawk. Piet cast aside the shell of the conversation and came to the kernel.

"The routes are well traveled and others manage this. If you wish I will put a ship and crew at your disposal for that transatlantic passage. How seem these conditions to you?"

Duquet nodded, for this was the connection he needed.

"Yes, yes, my thanks, it is a thing undreamed of." He thought it would be better to have his Dutch wife in Amsterdam, leaving him free from female manipulation and vapors, but still serving as the blood link to Piet Roos and Captain Verdwijnen. He knew that wherever he was, he would be a stranger. It was a price. He would pay it.

The marriage was celebrated with a wedding feast and drinking match that lasted for days. Captain Verdwijnen presented the couple with a splendid present of a set of silver *vorks,* the new eating implements. Margit's left eye bored into Duquet as he regarded the present. Although he expressed loud admiration for the forks, in his private thoughts Duquet took offense at this gift; he knew it was a reproach to his still-coarse table manners. More to his liking was the handsome coffee mill. And the rich tapestry from his father-in-law. It was a week before Cornelia spoke a word, and what she said was known only to her and Duquet.

Within eighteen months he had fathered a daughter and a premature stillborn son. Duquet thought constantly of that lost son, and it seemed everywhere he turned he saw rugged boys. Men his age were accompanied by stout half-grown youths shaped to their fathers' wills and callings. Particularly was he irked by the example of William Wentworth, a growing power in New Hampshire whose wife produced sons as a shingle maker rived the shakes from a bolt of cedar. With nine sons what could Wentworth not do? He,

Duquet, needed sons badly, and said so to Captain Verdwijnen one evening.

"You are in a hurry with sons as in all else," said the captain. "If you cannot wait until God grants your wish you might get some ready-made sons from the *Weeshuis,* that place of orphans, as many as King Priam should you wish. Indeed, I believe Cornelia is on the committee that operates the *Weeshuis.* You might speak of it to her." He lit his pipe and looked at Duquet. "And let her choose the boys. Her affection will then be greater. She can see to their schooling, and you can have them trained in business matters or for the sea."

Duquet was excited by this idea of adopting ready-made sons, and though he did not much wish to leave the choice to Cornelia, he recognized the value of Captain Verdwijnen's diplomatic suggestion.

Cornelia, who was on a committee that oversaw the operation of a home for aged women, not the *Weeshuis,* warmed to the idea of doing orphans a good turn. She said she would be pleased to choose several boys for Duquet's inspection and final decision. And so in 1713 Jan and Nicolaus, both nine years old, became Duquet's sons and immediately began their schooling and a course in manners and correct behavior that Cornelia wished might rub off on Duquet. He had prepared a speech before he saw the children.

"Many boys would give their right hands for the opportunities that are being given to you. You have a chance to help build one of the great fortunes of the world, a chance to remove yourselves from the street mire. I, too, was a boy of the slums, not even so fortunate as to be taken into an orphanage, and you see I have removed myself from the mud."

As sometimes happens after children are adopted, late that year Cornelia gave birth to a healthy, fat boy, little Outger, named for his godfather, Outger Verdwijnen. Duquet was as satisfied as he had ever been but could no longer put off his return to Boston and New France. Then, on the way to La Rochelle, a lightning bolt of an idea came to him: why stop at three sons? In La Rochelle could he not choose a poor but promising boy from the streets, a ragged boy as he himself had been, wild to escape poverty and a dismal future? He would find this boy himself and take him to New France that he might learn something of the forests of the New World.

He wrote to Cornelia and Piet Roos and told them of his find, a clever boy of eleven, Bernard, who was now with him in New France. He would bring him to Amsterdam when next he traveled there—likely in the coming autumn—that he might know his mother, his brothers and sister and be properly schooled.

"You see," said Captain Verdwijnen to Piet Roos. "Perhaps he is developing a kind heart." Piet Roos kept silent.

20

rough deed

Back in New France, which people more and more called Canada after the old Iroquois word *kanata,* Duquet was everywhere, examining, prying, measuring, observing and calculating. He had sent Bernard, the boy he found in La Rochelle, to Cornelia for education and manners. Limbs and low-quality hardwood waste became high-quality firewood and every autumn he packed twenty wagons full for the Kébec market and for Paris when he could charter available ships with the promise of a good return cargo of tea or coffee or textiles, spices or china, but without the sure promise of a rich return cargo, let the Parisians freeze for all he cared. Leasing Piet Roos's ships was well enough, but he needed ships of his own. What fortune if only he could find a competent shipyard in New France. He had heard of some Kébec entrepreneurs' discussion with the French government but it had come to nothing.

"You know," he said to Dred-Peacock at one of their Boston meetings, "it is so without hope I fear I must start my own shipyard."

Dred-Peacock mentioned other possibilities—Boston or Portsmouth on the Piscataqua or even the growing coastal ports in Maine. "You will get a good ship made with local timber at a low price in one of those ports. And do you not know that the colonists build ships especially designed to carry the great pine masts to London? Well, then."

And yet he delayed. The conversation veered from owning his own ships to the business of selling timber to shipyards. Duquet insisted he wanted English customers.

Dred-Peacock shrugged and connected him to an English ship-builder and a new but promising yard on the river Clyde in Scotland, now joined to England by the Act of Union in '07.

"Regard the map, sir," he said, impatient with Duquet's hesitation. "It's the closest point to the colonies—the briefest sailing time. There are signs of success on the Clyde but they need good timbers. They will pay for them. It is an opportunity that cannot be neglected."

Duquet took the plunge and Dred-Peacock took a goodly share of the profits, which increased year by year. There were good precedents in New France for trading with the enemy—Brûlé, Radisson, des Groseilliers had set the pattern—but arrangements with the English and Scots were at first secret, complex, expensive, even dangerous. It took fifty acres of oak to build one seventy-four-gun warship and in the hardwood stands along the rivers of New France the forests began to fall to Duquet's ambitions. But he felt hampered by Kébec's distance from the money pots of the world.

Never did Dred-Peacock present his ill-formed face to Duquet in Kébec; always Duquet made the trip to Boston. As they sat over their papers and receipts in the Sign of the Red Bottle near the wharves, the inn they favored, Dred-Peacock had some advice.

"Duquet, it is past time for you to consider shifting your business operations to Boston, to the colonies." He signaled to the waiter for another plate of oysters.

"Oh, I think on it," said Duquet, swirling the ale in his tankard until it slopped over the rim as if that settled the question. "I think on it often. I am half of a mind to do so, sir." He had observed more hardwoods grew in the south, that great meadows and clearings made both settlement and transportation easier. Massachusetts Bay bustled with shipping. It was the better place for a man of business. And yet.

Dred-Peacock looked at the spilled ale with distaste. Duquet was an ill-bred boor, quite unable to even discern the picturesque, much less appreciate it. It was only his fantastic ability to make money that interested Dred-Peacock. "Damme, sir, it is quite time you acted.

Finish with thinking and act. Every day poxy whoresons of millmen push into the forests and gain control over the land. In Maine there are countless white pine mast trees. You know there is a damned great market for these if you can get them on a ship bound for Scotland, England, or even Spain or Portugal." The dish came, three great succulent oysters gleaming wetly, each as large as a man's hand.

Duquet nodded but his face was sour. Dred-Peacock went on, his voice vibrating. "Where there is a market and money, the businessman must act. And all this will be immeasurably easier if you operate from Boston rather than bloody Kweebeck. And with my help these affairs can be managed." He took up the first oyster.

Still Duquet hesitated. He had valuable connections in New France and a lifetime dislike of the English language. Dred-Peacock babbled on.

"And in any case I understand there are many in New France who are starting to believe that the English will one day prevail, even as a hare senses its pursuer's increasing pace. Nor is it outside the realm of possibility that the colonies will unite, drive out the English and seize New France. Stranger events have occurred. And let me point out that so hungry are the whoreson Scots shipbuilders for the excellent timbers of America that some have removed to the colonies to be close to the supply."

Now he was in partnership with the two Dutchmen, and several ships belonging to Roos, Verdwijnen and Duquet, but flying British flags, ran the seas between Portsmouth and Boston harbors and the ever more numerous Clyde shipyards. It was, they often told one another, like walking on a web of tightropes, but they swam in money as in a school of sardines. They had only to catch it in their nets. And share it with Dred-Peacock.

Over the next year, as his sons grew, fired by the detailed and advice-packed business letters Duquet wrote to each of them every Sunday, with Dred-Peacock's help he began to acquire tracts of woodland in

Maine. Dred-Peacock's genius in the legal procedure of acquiring remote "townships" could not be measured, and his old acquaintance from *voyageur* days, the surveyor, Jacques Forgeron, scouted out the best timberland, Duquet learning the woods looker's judgmental process from him. To outsiders Forgeron was a dour man who overcherished his plagued measuring chains. He could use a chain as a weapon, swinging it around and around until it gained velocity and the free end leapt forward to maim. Duquet knew well that long ago he had used that chain in the Old World and then fled to New France to start anew. Duquet thought there were probably many like Forgeron but he only shrugged. The old days counted for very little. Moreover, he was now a partner in Duquet et Fils, perhaps even a friend if a business tie between two friendless men could be so described.

Duquet and Forgeron landed their canoe one October afternoon on a sandy Maine river shore fronting one of their new white pine properties, twenty thousand acres at a cost of twelve cents an acre. There was a narrow hem of ice along the shaded shoreline. The rich autumn light touched the deciduous trees with xanthene orange and yellow. Their swart shadows fell on the ground like fallen statues. Without speaking the men began to gather firewood. Forgeron held up his hand.

"Listen," he said quietly. They heard the sounds of chopping not far off and began to move cautiously toward the source.

With an acid jolt of fury Duquet saw unknown men in pitch-blackened trousers cutting his pines, others limbing the fallen trees and yet another scoring them. Two men worked with broadaxes to square the logs. Duquet was sure they had a pit sawmill set up nearby. By their bulging pale eyes and doughy faces he knew them to be English colonists. Although Duquet et Fils had no hesitation in cutting big trees wherever they grew, it was intolerable to be the victims of that practice.

"Holà!" Duquet shouted, then, in his clumsy English, "Who say you come my land, cut my tree?" He was so furious his voice strangled in his throat. Forgeron advanced beside him lightly revolving his chain.

The startled woodsmen stared, then, still gripping their tools, they ran on an oblique course toward the river, where they likely had bateaux. But one with a dirty bandage on his right thigh lagged behind.

Duquet did not pause. He drew his tomahawk from his belt and hurled it, striking the runner's left calf. The man fell, crying to his comrades for help in a high childish voice. One of the escaping men turned around and stared at Duquet, called something to the fallen one. The confrontation lasted for only a few seconds but left an unfading impression of a man swelling with hatred. Duquet did not forget the man's mottled slab of face encircled by ginger hair and beard, the yellow animal eyes fixed on him, the sudden turning away and violent run for the river.

"They come from the settlements along the coast," said Forgeron as they ran forward.

They bound their wounded prisoner, a boy not older than fourteen, and dragged him to a pine, tied him against it in a hollow between projecting tree roots.

"You boy, *garçon,* talk up or I cut first your fingers. Then your balls. Who you are? What men you with? How you come here?"

The boy folded his lips in a tight crease, in either pain or defiance. Duquet wrenched the boy's arm and spread his left hand against one of the great humped roots. With a quick slash of his ax he took off a little finger and part of the next.

"Talk or I cut more. You die no head."

Duquet's bloody interrogation gave him the information that the Maine thieves were in the employ of a mill owner, a man named McBogle, an agent of Elisha Cooke. Duquet had heard of Cooke for years; all described him as a passionate opponent of Crown authority. But McBogle's name was new. Although his heart was pounding with anger, Duquet thought Elisha Cooke and perhaps even McBogle sounded like useful men and he fixed their names in his memory. He would learn more from Dred-Peacock.

"Why you come here steal pine?" he said.

"We thought only to cut a few trees. Away from the surveyor's men."

"Show your wounds." When the boy held up his maimed hand Duquet said angrily, "No, not that. Only scratch. Leg wound." He could smell the stink of infection from a distance. With his good hand the boy unwrapped his right leg and disclosed a deep and rotten gash in the thigh. It was a foul injury. A streak of red inflammation ran up toward the groin.

"How happen?" he demanded.

"Uncle Robert felled a big pine. Broke off a branch that gouged my leg."

It was an evil mess. In contrast, the cut in the boy's calf inflicted by Duquet's hawk was clean though it had nearly severed a tendon, and the chopped finger was a trifle. Nothing to be done. They carried the youth to the interlopers' camp half a mile downstream, strewn with abandoned clothing and cook pots, a deer carcass suspended in a tree, and laid him near the still-smoldering fire.

"We will stay here," said Duquet to Forgeron, "as the thieves have prepared a camp for us." He tried to speak calmly, but he was filled with a greater anger than he had ever experienced. After all the injustices he had suffered, after all he had done, crossing to the New World, escaping from Trépagny, learning the hard *voyageur* trade, working out a way to use the forest for his fortune, learning to read and write and cipher, traveling to China, all the business connections he had made, these Maine vermin had come to steal *his timber*.

Forgeron brought their canoe up to the campsite while Duquet searched until he found the trespassers' pit sawmill. They had been there only a few days, but had the clear intention to saw. The stack of limbed and squared logs told him that. He wondered if they had planned to build a fort. It was said the English were plotting to build forts along all the rivers.

"Let us put our mark on them," said Duquet, and he and Forgeron took possession of the logs with two deep hatchet slashes on the butt ends. They talked of ways to move them. In the end it seemed a raft floated to the nearest sawmill might be the best way, getting what they could. While Duquet stayed to guard the timber in case the thieves returned, Forgeron went to Portsmouth to hire raftsmen.

During the early evening the mildness went out of the weather. The sky filled with clouds the color of dark grapes, followed by an hour of rain; behind it the temperature dived into winter. Duquet woke at dawn, shivering. There was not a breath of wind but every twig and branch bristled with spiky hoarfrost. In the distance wolves howled messages to each other, their cries filleting the morning. They had likely scented the boy's blood and infection and would linger out of sight hoping for a chance. Duquet got up and piled more wood on the fire. The wounded boy's eyes were closed, his face feverish and swollen, cheeks wet with melting frost. Duquet thought he would be dead after one more cold night. Or he might not last until nightfall.

With some urgency he prodded the boy awake and fired questions at him: his name, his village, his family's house, how many people. But the boy only croaked for water, which Duquet did not give him, and then went silent. He still lived. Duquet spent the short day estimating the board feet in the felled pines.

The light faded early as the growing storm invaded the sky, the wind and sleety snow rattling and hissing in the pines. While there was still enough light to see clearly, Duquet walked over to the prisoner. The boy lay on his back, the right leg bursting with infection, a yellow froth of pus oozing out from under the bandage, the leg a little splayed as though it were detaching itself. Nothing could be done with this burden except wait for him to die—one more cold night. The boy opened his eyes and stared at something across the river. Duquet followed his gaze, expecting to see Indians or perhaps one of the thieves returning. He saw only a wall of pines until a blink of yellow showed him where to look. A tall grey owl sat on a branch, seeing them. Its eyes were very small and set close together like twin gimlets.

The boy spoke. "Help. Me," he said in English. "Help. Me."

Inside Duquet something like a tightly closed pinecone licked by fire opened abruptly and he exploded with insensate and uncontrollable fury, a life's pent-up rage. "No one helped *me!*" he shrieked. "I did everything myself! I endured! I contended with powerful men. I suffered in the wilderness. I accepted the risk I might die! No one helped me!" The boy's gaze shifted, the fever-boiled eyes following Duquet's rising arm, closing only when the tomahawk split his brain. Duquet struck the hatchet into the loam to clean it.

In the flying snow he dismantled the sawpit scaffolding and threw the boy into the pit hole, piled the scaffolding on top and set it alight. The gibbous moon rose. Hours later when the burning ceased he went to shovel in the half-frozen excavated soil, but before he hurled the first shovelful he glanced down and saw the black arm bones crooked up as if reaching for a helping hand.

"*Foutu!* Done for!"

He shoveled.

Forgeron arrived four days later with six men who began constructing a raft of the cut pines. There was no sign of the wounded boy and although Forgeron opened his mouth as if to speak several times, he did not say anything except that the war was making it very difficult to find able-bodied labor.

21

shifting ground

Again Duquet changed, reinventing himself. In Boston, Duquet et Fils became Duke & Sons and he was Charles Duke. Still he kept his enterprise and some holdings in New France. He sat with Dred-Peacock in the taproom of the Pine Dog, a pleasant tavern with a sign showing an eponymous carved mastiff, now their favored meeting place as the Sign of the Red Bottle had burned in a conflagration that took half the wharves and several ships.

"Do you know aught of that fellow McBogle?" asked Duke, breaking the crust edge from his meat pasty with heavy fingers.

Dred-Peacock, bewigged and togged out, regarded his steaming coffee. "I have not made his acquaintance, but I hear much deleterious talk concerning his ways. Maine is full to the scuppers with woodland entrepreneurs, sawmills, surveyors, armies of tree choppers, potash and turpentine distillers and settlers, every man assaulting the free-to-all timberlands."

"They think as I do," said Duke, "so I cannot fault them. But although they love guns beyond telling, and protect themselves, the woods are dangerous with enemies, not only war foes, but the Crown Surveyor's men. Yet they are only men."

"The settlers are hard men, right enough, but there are others even harder, mostly in New Hampshire. I mean those men of Scots lineage lately removed from Ulster in Ireland."

"Surely they are as other mortal men?"

"No. They are different. They are damned strange, cruel men,

138

clannish and proud to a fault, thirsty for vengeance over imagined slights, hard-drinking and inhumanly tough. The whoresons prefer to sleep outside in storms rather than in the comfort of a house. They know the country as the poxy Indians know it and to live free is their banner. The buggers are impervious to cold and heat and they bear pain as the Indians do, stoically and silently, even with relish. The ridges and watercourses are their highways, the forest their shelter. They choose to live in the most remote places. And they are bloody damned key fighters in the escalating antipathy between the French and the English." He paused and took up his coffee cup, stared into Duke's eyes.

"Dud McBogle, his brothers and his sons are among these men."

Duke threw back his head and laughed. "Well, I have heard bugbear stories aplenty and I would class McBogle tales among them. No doubt he eats children as sweetmeats and wears a red fur cloak bespangled with their bones. What do you say when I tell you I consider taking this man on as a partner?"

For once Dred-Peacock had nothing to say.

The ongoing war and marauding Indians forced Maine's settlements to cluster along the tidewater margins; among them were several small shipyards. But Charles Duke discovered Penobscot Bay, where the great river discharged into the Atlantic and where he built a large house. He thought himself the first white man here, despising a few French-speaking *métis,* fruit of the fornicating priests who had lived earlier among the Indians. The land around the bay, called Norumbega by an unknown explorer, was fancied by credulous souls to be the site of a fabulous city crusted with gold and gems, as Kinkenadon or L'Isle Imaginaire. And here mustachioed Henry Hudson had cut the first mast pine in the New World. For that reason alone he liked the place.

Duke's log house was more like a fort than a dwelling. Half the ground floor was given over to his business room, with its enormous table fashioned from a single slab of pine four feet in width. And it was time to bring his sons, now young men, to the New World and set them to work, although little Outger was still too young to leave his mother.

His Amsterdam sons, Jan and Nicolaus Duke, were fluent in Dutch, French and English with smatterings of German, Frisian and Portuguese. Jan was especially good with numbers and understood the finer points of bookkeeping. He was as forward-looking as a raftsman in a rocky river. Nicolaus, of imposing build, was physically strong and had a ruthless streak that Duke thought would make him feared at the bargaining table. He and Bernard were something of mariners, as both had several times sailed to China on the ships of Piet Roos. Jan and Nicolaus would deal with merchants, contracts and shipping. The French son, Bernard, was on his way from the Baltic, where he had studied the technical details of manufacturing pitch and tar, and where he had picked up a little of the Swedish language and enough Danish to be useful. He would be in charge of naval store production. And he, Charles Duke, the father, would continue to establish contacts, buy up paper townships and arrange for woodsmen and sawmills on the important rivers, to oversee the growing empire. It was time to gather his sons to him. And yet he was not interested in them in any way except an eagerness to recognize proofs of their success. They were the sons he needed. He wrote to Cornelia in English.

Beste Deer Wif.

I hope this liter find you and the childer in good helth I wishd to rite three Dayes pass but found ye Inkwel soe dry no Words in it and by some unhapy chance ye Cup Bord destit of Supply A qart come yester and todaye I take Quil in Hande to rite it is Time my Sons whose Care and Educasun you have fosterd begin Busines Life here with me in Boston and Mane cost New Franc I will rite them eache & mak ye Arangemt firm. I am covincd they will sucede in all our Procedings with ye help of your deer Fater and Unkul They are as capable as I hev ever wish I

regret when I am far from and destite of frend hear and hop join you three
mos. time I prey that you wil not want for hapy Compnee entil I return.
Charles Duke, Penoscot Bay Cost of Mane
Martch 3. 1717

He lodged his sons in Boston, but they came to the Penobscot
Bay house once a month to meet in the business room, to spread out
their papers and books on the great pine table.

He had not been wrong. Already, within a few months, the sons
began to put forth their impressions and ideas. Jan, with his long
bony face and hazel eyes slitted as though squinting into the future,
was perhaps the most long-seeing, but they spoke among themselves
before presenting him with new ideas.

"Father," said Jan. "We have noticed that more and more English
and Scots shipwrights are settling along the New England coast. We
think it would be a sensible move to get a foothold in the shipbuilding industry. It would reduce the necessity of transporting lumber,
masts, bowsprits and yards to English or European ports. It is an
opportunity."

"Yes," said Duke. "I have often felt it would be good to move into
shipbuilding, often and often, but I hesitated. You reassure me."

"Also," said Bernard, who had confounded them all when he
arrived from the Baltic countries with a great horsy wife, Birgit,
"pitch and tar. We have pitch pine here, of course, but the superior
trees are in the Carolinas. And slaves. I would suggest that we purchase and operate a pitch pine plantation in Carolina."

"It shall be done," said the gratified father.

22

disappearance

In Boston one day Dred-Peacock came to him at the Duke warehouse, a cavernous building near the docks, redolent of pine, oak, furs and roots.

"I thought you might wish to know that the man you mentioned some time ago has been asking many people about you. How many sawmills you own, how disgustingly large your fortune may be, what ships you have, what tracts of timber and townships you possess. He himself operates five or six or more sawmills on the Penobscot tributaries and in New Hampshire. He begins to look like a serious rival."

"Who do you mean? Elisha Cooke?" said Duke.

"His damned hard man, McBogle."

"Indeed," said Duke. "I hear this sometimes. He asks questions but we never see him. What is your own perception of this situation?"

"I think as you do, that he should be absorbed. He has the reputation of a dangerous man. I doubt we could buy him out but a partnership may be attractive. He has friendly relations not only with Elisha Cooke and the Wentworths, but with many judges and businessmen here and in New Hampshire. Yet he does not have our contacts across the Atlantic." It was Dred-Peacock who had the invaluable English and European contacts.

"We must talk with him and see what might be arranged. Where do we find him?"

"That may be difficult. He has what they call a 'thunderstorm sawmill'—because the only time it runs properly is when the water is

142

high with rain—on the Moosegut and a house nearby. He keeps very much to himself in this remote place. If we go to him we must bring a few men with us for I hear he has a band of ruffians at his beck. I could accompany you a week today. But no sooner."

"*Bien,*" said Duke. "Good enough."

Then, within the hour, Forgeron, who had led a crew of woodsmen to cut one of Duke's pine-heavy townships, arrived in Boston. His lean face was blotched with a red rash. He hesitated, as though he wished not to speak his news. When he did speak he threw his words down like playing cards.

"We found the best trees taken. The stumps still oozed sap."

"Who?" said Duke.

"*Ne sais pas*—don't know. But there is talk that the man McBogle last week shipped two great loads of masts to Spain. He will have made a fat profit. He is known for tree piracy."

"I plan to find this man in a week's time and see what can be arranged. We will work with him."

"He is not known for compliance."

"Nor am I. Dred-Peacock will accompany us on the Monday. You must come as well." Something had to be done about McBogle and they would do it. "It is necessary we go in a body as we do not know the strength of McBogle's men." But over the last year Duke's eyesight had begun to deteriorate, dimness alternating with flashing light and tiny particles gliding through his field of vision like birds in the sky. He said nothing to Forgeron of this, only "what is wrong with your face that it shows so rough and crimson?" Forgeron shrugged.

The plan was ill-fated. Two days later a packet entered Boston harbor with great sacks of mail. Among Dred-Peacock's mountain of letters was one informing him that his older brother and nephew had both perished in fire, and that he, Dred-Peacock, had succeeded to the title, the great house (now with a somewhat charred east wing) and the family's two-thousand-acre estate, Dred Yew in Wiltshire.

In seconds his talk of colonial liberty and rights evaporated, his self-definition as a man dedicated to New England self-rule shriveled.

"I must go," he said to Duke. "It is my responsibility to my family and to the estate—and the great yew tree now in my care. I cannot evade the title nor the responsibility. I leave at once." In his voice Duke detected a long-suppressed tone of haughtiness. "I will write to you when I have settled my affairs. I believe we can continue our business ventures."

"Yes," said Duke. "I quite see it." Scratch some New England colonists, he thought, and you find Englishmen, as the bark of a tree hides inner rot. "But I cannot believe your chatter about a 'yew tree.' What man would leave a fair and rich land for the sake of a haughty tree?"

"It is an immortal tree, centuries old. It has been on my family estate since a time before Christ, since the time when men worshiped yews and oaks. It is nothing *you* can understand." What could Duke say to that? Nothing. What mattered was the continuance of their business dealings. And as if that were not enough, word came that Forgeron was ill with a fiery skin inflammation and the quinsy, a putrid sore throat that forced him into his bed. Duke said he would not delay. He would seek out McBogle alone.

He ordered a canteen of strong black coffee. He would ration it out, drink it cold, eschewing fires as the forest was sown with skulking Indians and French. A schooner took him to the mouth of the Penobscot and he began his solitary journey.

It was spring, rafts of rotten ice riding the current in company with thousands of logs. Crowds of woodsmen stood on the banks snagging the logs slashed with their outfits' marks of ownership. The work continued all night by the light of enormous bonfires, cat-footed men running out onto the heaving carpet of mixed logs to hook and prod their property to shore. Impossible to put a canoe into that maelstrom. He had ordered his own timber crews to hold back his logs until the river cleared of the floating forest. Now he set out afoot. And noticed two riverbank men turn away from the heaving river and cut obliquely into the forest. He smiled. Did they imagine they were not noticed?

Sometimes he was on dim Indian trails following landmarks almost always obscured by the jagged skyline of conifers, but more often making his way through logging slash and blowdowns. Although timber cutters had worked the area along the river, a mile or so inland was still *terre sauvage,* and like the ocean it breathed wild grandeur. Tree limbs arched over the silent earth like the dark roof of a tomb vault.

He took an entire day to cross an autumn burn, charred trunks of the smaller trees with their own black limbs tangled around their roots like dropped drawers, still-smoldering logs that could not be quenched. The biggest trees stood lightly scorched but unharmed. Winter snow had converted the ash to black muck. On steep slopes it was the ancient wind-felled monsters that caused the greatest hindrance. Some, whose branches interlinked with those of their neighbors, had pulled them to the ground. Often he had to crawl beneath these barriers. It was not possible to get around them as the way was blocked by other recumbents. He could not count all the streams and bogs. The treetops dazzled, the flashing wings of hundreds of thousands of northward migrating birds beat above him. He saw snowy owls drifting silent through the trees, for they had come into the Maine woods in great numbers that winter and with the turn of the season were retreating to the cold lands. His eyes wearied of broken, wind-bent cedar and glinting swamp water. All one afternoon he had the feeling he was being watched, and as twilight thickened he saw a grey owl flutter to a branch stub and grip him with its clenching eyes. Of all birds he most hated this wretch.

After six days he cut back toward the Penobscot following Moosegut brook; McBogle's sawmill could not be very far distant. He listened for the sound of falls. He felt the mill through his feet before he saw it, the metal clank and rasp of the driveshaft gears and pitman arm sending a thumping rhythm into the ground. It was spring, he thought, and the entire forest would soon reverberate with the noise of multiple mills as water ran freely again. His eyes troubled him, tree branches and needles sparked. Abruptly there was the mill, a heavy log structure to take the weight of gang-saw machinery. And there was Dud McBogle standing above him in a razzle of flinching lights.

Recognition was instant. Dud McBogle was the ginger-whiskered timber thief who had long ago turned back and called something to the wounded boy. Duke felt a red cloud of danger envelop him. His blood instantly flowed back on itself. The teeth of the moving saws gnawed and glinted. He saw that he was fatally imperiled. *Exitus in dubio est.*

"Been expecting you," said Dud McBogle in an easy tone. "I went back, you see. I went back and dug up the pit where you burned my boy." The two riverbank men stepped out of the corner and stood beside him. What could not happen began to happen.

"Not yet!" blurted Duke. "I'm not done—"

But at the age of fifty-three with his fortune only half-secured he was done.

III

all these woods once ours

1724–1767

23

dogs and villains

He sat for an hour on a knotty and punishing pine bench before the governor's secretary beckoned him in. As a young missionary Louis-Joseph Crème had first served in New France. Later he had been sent to Port Royal in Acadie, a true wilderness, and among the Mi'kmaq he began to keep a notebook of their rich vocabularies of geological structures, weather and season, plants, animals, mythological creatures, rivers and tides. He saw they were so tightly knitted into the natural world that their language could only reflect the union and that neither could be separated from the other. They seemed to believe they had grown from this place as trees grow from the soil, as new stones emerge aboveground in spring. He thought the central word for this tenet, *weji-sqalia'timk,* deserved an entire dictionary to itself.

Now, with receding hair and arthritic joints although he was only forty, he stood before the governor, shivering, for he felt a coming illness. Sleeping on the ground did not suit him. He was not of this place, he had not sprouted here and so to him the ground was hard.

The governor was a haughty snob, *un bêcheur* with a cleft chin and a bulge of throat fat. He gave off an air of having hung in a silk bag in the adjoining room until it was time for him to emerge and perform the duties of his position. His eyes focused on the wall, never meeting those of Père Crème.

"Surely I do not need to tell you that the English in Hudson Bay press down from the north, they press in from the sea, they squeeze

Acadie, they press east from the Ohio valley. New France is awash in spies, scouts, Englishmen and rangers from New England. The coast fishery is ravaged by English and Boston vessels."

The missionary thought that every sentence the man uttered had a subterranean meaning—if only he could grasp what it was. "Your Excellency, the Mi'kmaq are constantly called to fight for France although they have very few fighting men these days. They were once a vigorous tribe, as many as the hairs on ten men's heads. Today they have but a few hundred warriors. As they die they lose their sensibilities, their knowledge falls away." He hoped he, too, would not fall away. He felt quite dizzy.

"Their sensibilities! These people are masters of inventive cruelties. I mention to you the example of the young sailor captured from a fishing boat. The women, who are even more inhuman than the men, tortured him by fire and knife. They burned his feet with fiery brands, his legs, his privy parts. They cut him until he was pouring blood like an April freshet, then thrust his charred feet into an iron pot of boiling water. So speak not to me of their 'sensibilities.' It is your concern to care only for their souls. And to inculcate in them love and respect for *le Roi notre prince*—the King, our prince. And urge them to fight the English. That is your duty." He spoke as one confident in his position of power.

Père Crème knew that temporal power had its limits, some of them very abrupt if one observed recent history. "I humbly try to do so at every chance," he said, feeling his chills switch suddenly to feverish heat. "And in any case that sailor was an English, a Protestant."

"That is beside the point. You seem to regard the Indians as special persons. They are no more than men, and not very reliable men at that. We are forced to use them as fighters when our territory, when the great fort we are now building at Louisbourg is menaced by the English. It will be the gateway to our North American possessions. You know how important Acadie is to New France. France must retake it. It is vital sea access." Now he was locking his fingers together and stretching them out.

Père Crème forbore to mention that the fort could not protect the seaway; that was the responsibility of the French fleet. But he only said, "Your Excellency, the Indians do suffer. They do have feelings. They love their country, which we are taking, they love their children, whom we are corrupting with our goods and forceful ways. They say France regards them as of little value. And this has long been their land, where untold generations have lived undisturbed."

"Indeed. You know, Père Crème, you seem to me to be lacking in zeal for the cause of France."

"No, no. I only pity them. They have lost so much, so many." Why could the man not grasp that the Mi'kmaq wished only to live their lives as they had for many generations, and that as every day passed that was less possible?

"And France has lost so many. You would do better to think of *them* rather than these libertine heathens who are dogs and villains. They are *not Christians* as you, a designated man of God, might have noticed."

Père Crème, dismissed, tacked for the door, his feet at odds with each other and his neck wry. He prayed silently for the governor to become more observant, more kindly. Or better yet, to fall down in a fit and never rise. He immediately withdrew this cruel wish and requested forgiveness.

Several days later he addressed a letter to his sister Marguerite, one of hundreds of letters never sent, for he had no sister. It eased his mind to have an imaginary confidante, and he was able to work out his sometimes chaotic thoughts this way.

Dear Sister Marguerite.

For a minute he imagined her, slender and pale, sitting in a green chair and opening his letter with a silver knife. She might wear a gold locket with a wisp of her brother's hair in it—or a miniature of their mother, whom Père Crème could scarcely conjure from his faded memories.

They do not have orderly Lives as we do. Their time is fitted to the abundance crests of Animals, Fruits and Fish—that is to say, to the Seasons of the Hunt and ripening Berries. One of the most curious of their attributes is their manner of regarding Trees, Plants, all manner of Fish, the Moose and the Bear and others as their Equals. Many of their tales tell of Women who marry Otters or Birds, or Men who change into Bears until it pleases them to become Men again. In the forest they speak to Toads and Beetles as acquaintances. Sometimes I feel it is they who are teaching me.

He stopped for a long time before continuing with the feeling that he was getting it wrong.

To them Trees are Persons. In vain I tell them that Trees are for the uses of Men to build Houses and Ships. In vain I tell them to give over so much hunting and make Gardens, grow Grains and Food Stuffs, to put order in their Days. They will none of it. Therefore many French people call them lazy because they do not till the Earth.

I have heard a Story that in some earlier time . . .

24

Auguste

The children of Mari—Elphège, Theotiste, Achille, Noë and Zoë—were trying to find their place in a world so different from Mari's stories of the rich Mi'kmaw past. The realities were difficult.

"Dîner!" called Noë without bothering to step outside, slapping down the worn wooden bowls, the old spoons. There was no response, not even from Zoë, who always had a remark. Noë stood in the doorway, listening. The offshore wind had shifted slightly but carried the fading clatter of boots on rock. They were wearing boots instead of moccasins. Noë knew what that meant but denied it. She stepped out onto the path. Auguste clutched her skirt. She saw them far down the shore crossing naked rock. If it were just Elphège and Theotiste—but no, it was all of them. Achille, Theotiste, Elphège and Rouge Emil, all three of her brothers and the cousin, and at the end, half-running to keep up with the striding men, the slight figure of Zoë. Anguish and rage mingled in her like a kind of soup made from nettles and grit. She shouted, "Go on, then!" and pulled Auguste up in front of her so he could see and mark this event.

"That's them," she said through clenched teeth. She picked up a small stone and pressed it into Auguste's hand. "Throw it," she said. "Throw it at the no-goods that has run off." Her voice rose again. "Go on then, you hell brothers and damnation sister," and to the boy, "Throw it, throw your stone at them we'll likely never see again." But even as she said it she knew it was untrue, that she was

153

acting out an imitation of drunken Renardette's angry fits. She did not know why she sounded like someone she detested, nor why she spoke this way once again. She was not behaving as a Mi'kmaw. Why did she even think of Renardette, who was now deep in the past?

The child cast the stone; it fell on the path. As it rolled, the boy saw Zoë, the smallest figure, turn and look back, Zoë who responded to his outstretched arm and waved. The lead figure turned as well and his arm cut an arc in the air, a kind of salute from Achille that made Noë groan. The men should be setting out to hunt moose, but because of the boots she knew they were going to work for the French logger.

"Come, dear Auguste. We'll eat all the dinner, just you and me." Their house was a *wikuom* and although Mi'kmaq sat on the ground to be in contact with the replenishing earth, there was a low single-board table, the nails hammered into the legs from above. Before the stew redolent of duck meat, meadow garlic, wild rice and greens had cooled in the kettle the door flap was pushed aside and Zoë slid in.

"Not what you think," she said before Noë could start in. "They will cut trees on the St. John again. Rouge Emil heard from Eyepatch they should come. Just this winter. Elphège said tell you money is in his good moccasin. You use it for what we need, says he. They come back spring, those cut logs go in the river. Come back a little bit rich, maybe. But not Achille. He goes moose hunting."

Noë nodded. If Zoë stayed it was all right, and if Achille came back from his hunt in ten days or so, they could manage for a winter. It was the idea of abandonment she dreaded. All her life she had been afraid of being left alone while everyone around her vanished. She filled a bowl with stew for Zoë and set it before her. When the bowl was empty Noë filled it again.

"They didn't want to go, thinking what happened before. Rouge Emil's father comes to stay with us so that don't happen another time. He comes soon, I think. Other people see those brothers leave, think just you and me here."

"They think just me—they see you go with them."

Zoë shrugged and made a face. "Maybe. Maybe they see me come back, too."

A little later Rouge Emil's father—Cache Emil—appeared in the doorway. He threw something large and heavy wrapped in blood-stained canvas on the floor.

"*Moinawa*," he said. "Bear meat." He looked at the stew pot. Noë filled a bowl for him.

"Good." He told them he had shot the bear hunting with Achille a few weeks earlier. Not only bear meat, but he had brought his blankets and his flintlock. He would sleep outside in the small *wikuom* that Theotiste and Elphège shared.

"I am here. No male persons will bother you."

Three years before the brothers had made a trip to La Hève to the lumber mill to ask if there was any work for them, but a man with a patch over one eye said the local Indians were sufficient, go away. The cousin, Rouge Emil, was persistent. He stood beside a stack of cut planks.

"You got work for good axmen cut pine?" Everyone knew that the mast pines of Mi'kmaw lands were superior to the trees that grew along the St. Laurent, which were coarse in grain and more liable to snap. Eyepatch nodded. "It's summer, but there's always work for good choppers. Let's see what you can do." He fetched four axes from the mill, then filled his pipe. "See two spruce in front of the rocks? Take them down." His tone was contemptuous, for he knew Indians were lazy and stupid. Eyepatch's pipe was not finished before the spruce lay side by side on the ground, topped and limbed. He reversed his opinion of Indians.

He nodded and they cut mast pines on the St. John River despite the summer heat and biting insects. In a few days they were crusted with black pitch, a kind of woodcutters' armor. When they first had arrived the pine candles had been in bloom, each great tree pulsing out tremendous volumes of pollen until the sky was overcast and the choppers and even ships at sea wondered at the brilliant yellow showering down.

That summer while they were swinging distant axes, Noë, barely fourteen winters old, gathering wild onions, was raped by two boys from the French settlement, one of whom she recognized as Dieudonné, a fisherman's son who returned again and again for his pleasure. She could not evade him. He seemed to live in the underbrush near their *wikuom*. He was only a boy, a fisherman boy, with a red chapped face and eyes flicking as though he feared the priest was near. He was strong from hauling nets and pulling oars. At first she loathed him, but after some weeks he became affectionate and, although he was two years younger, she began to return the sentiment. He said he wished they could marry and would press the matter on his parents when he was older.

When the brothers came back from the St. John her condition was obvious. No one mentioned it. But the next day Elphège looked at her in silence for a long time. He waited. And she told him how it was. By then Dieudonné was weeks dead along with his father and uncle and several other Acadians, for their fishing boats all had been caught in a concentrated snarl of storm that strewed the shore with broken boats. She thought of Dieudonné in the grip of the relentless sea as she had been in his grip. The result of the dead boy's life had been Auguste.

In their childhood days in the forest, Noë thought, none of them had imagined they would come here to the ocean's edge, far from René and Mari's house. But they were here. She had not thought to have a child, but now there was Auguste. All this had happened because Theotiste and Elphège had brought them to Mi'kma'ki, the land of memory.

25

sense of property

Their great change had come about because of Renardette, who caused their lives to become as different as those of strange people. For years at René's old place, heavy drinkers from Wobik lurched out of the trees calling for Renardette. One, "Démon" Meillard, appeared often and Renardette went into the woods with him. The day after René died, Renardette rushed to Wobik, to Meillard, a widower whose taste for spirits matched hers.

Achille, Noë and Zoë stayed on alone at the house in the ever-larger clearing. Achille trapped fish and hunted, cut firewood as had René, and made hardwood potash. He sold this stuff to the traveling merchant who came with his wagon every month or two in the warm season. Noë and Zoë gathered berries, cowslips, fiddlehead ferns in spring, nuts, calamus root, mayapples, sassafras and many barks for the medicines they had learned from their mother. They made maple syrup. They had a garden but it was small and weed-choked for they had adopted Mari's distaste for cultivation. A few pumpkins sometimes matured in the fireweed. Noë made rather awkward willow baskets, which Achille sold to the potash man. Zoë milked and tended the cow. There had been two cows but one died the month after René was killed, perhaps, thought Zoë, out of sympathy so that René's spirit might be comforted by a familiar cow spirit.

Their lives were marred by unwanted visits from swill-wrecked Renardette and her paramour. It was unclear at first why the couple kept returning to René's old house, but they came often, lugging demijohns of spirit, which they urged on Achille. Renardette swaggered into the house looking at each spoon, each wooden cup. Often she would examine a pot or a cloth and say, "Well, that's mine!" Noë would wrest the object from her.

"Nothing in this house is yours. There is nothing here for you."

"This house is mine," said Renardette. "René gave it to me. He said, 'When I am gone, Renardette, you have this house.'"

"What lies!" cried Zoë.

"Go away!" said Noë, swishing the broom.

Achille began to think the drunkards wanted René's house and property and would be pleased to murder all of them to get it. He refused drinks from their jug, which he knew would make him insensible and give them the opportunity to butcher him and his sisters and blame the deaths on bounty killers. He slowly came to the belief that they were the ones who had murdered René. ·

Tales of the alcoholic couple drifted far east to the ears of Elphège and Theotiste along with the rumors that they planned to kill Achille and the twins and seize the property. They heard of Renardette's claim that the house belonged to her.

"They are white people and they think they can seize it," Elphège said to Theotiste.

"They will likely get it."

Elphège was troubled by the idea of inherited property. Was the house René's to give? Was it even Trépagny's? All this was French, French ideas, French ways. English ways, English words, French words. Invaders' ways.

The older brothers had lived for some years at Odanak, the Indian village of Abenaki, Mi'kmaq and mixed tribes, fighting for the French and raiding New England settlements for bounty captives. Once warring enemies, they banded together, lamenting the submergence of their ancestral lands under a flood of white settlers.

At Odanak, Theotiste had married and fathered a son, who died of measles in his third year, two days after the mother succumbed to the same burning illness. Elphège was secretive about women and even wary because of his long infatuation with the youngest wife of Sosep, an elderly *sagmaw*.

Theotiste came to his brother one day. Elphège was sitting near the river shaping a handle for a crooked knife. "Brother," he said, "I have thought much of our younger brother and sisters. Achille, Noë and Zoë. I think we should get them."

"Ho," said Elphège. "Get them? Live with them here as kin? In Odanak? Or make a visit to them?"

"No. I wish for us to be united. I wish them to be with us, wherever we go. They are part of our band. More and more I do not care to stay longer in Odanak."

Elphège said nothing and after a long silence Theotiste said, "Perhaps this is not a very good idea."

Elphège looked at him. "Brother, you have ever put forward good ideas. I will think about what you say." After a little while he said, "Maybe it is good if we go to that place of our mother."

Theotiste said, "Here we are just some Indians. There we will be Mi'kmaw people."

Elphège was silent for a long time. He had no taste for whitemen's "conversation."

"René was a good man," he said at last.

"He was. Do you recall that winter when we gave him a snake and showed him how to play snow snakes and he didn't want to stop at dusk?"

"Yes. Trépagny threw his snake in the fire."

"Small matter, that was only a stick. Maman carved him a better one. It could slide far. I remember that well." He looked at the river. "The children of one mother should be together. We have the same blood." Elphège nodded and bent over his work.

Several days later Theotiste said more. "First it would be good to bring them here to Odanak. And then go with them to our mother's country and make a home there. There are Mi'kmaw here at Odanak who would come with us. Sosep wishes to return. We could find wives. I was happy when my wife was with me."

"Yes, a Mi'kmaw woman. But if our sisters and brother come with us, will they abandon René's house?"

"It is only a white man's house."

"Our mother's thoughts were always in her childhood country. She called it 'the happy land.' It is our place more than Odanak. Even though Sosep says it has changed greatly and there are many troubles."

"It will be good. I dreamed it will be good."

Elphège shifted to his brother's view and said, "Let us go then, first to René's house, then to Mi'kma'ki."

They reached Wobik, much grown, with many paths twisting this way and that. The woodland, which had once wrapped around the village, now began nearly a mile from the most distant house.

They slept in the woods. Elphège woke, staring up at the birds-of-fire stars already folding their wings. It was the time—*wopk*—when dark became grey, quivering night shapes slowly solidifying and returning to their daytime forms. Theotiste rose and stretched his long arms above his head.

"It will be a good day," said Theotiste, ever hopeful.

Smoke coiled from René's roof hole as always. Theotiste pushed in. Noë was making cornmeal porridge and dropped the spoon when he came through the door. "Brother! You terrified me. You know how our father died—I thought . . ."

Zoë came in from the cow carrying a bucket of milk. She shrieked with joy and embraced first Theotiste, then Elphège. Her cry brought Achille up from the river, where he had been mending eel traps.

Achille was almost too handsome a young man to look upon. He was tall but sinewy and as flexible as water, of perfect form. His glossy hair fanned out in the wind, his dark eyes were warm and amused. His mouth, like Mari's, curled at the corners, and all who noticed this curving smile thought of her.

The twins, still children, were more like René with stiff black hair and slanted eyes. They were active as all women were, bending, folding, picking up and reaching, handing out and taking, caressing, scooping good things into bowls, offering their brothers delicacies.

The older brothers looked around, seeing the objects of their childhood—the old table marked with knife cuts. Theotiste remembered Mari wiping it with a piece of damp leather. Those wooden household plates—René had shaped them, Theotiste had smoothed them with a fine-grained stone. Mari's old *wikuom* had sunk back into the earth but they remembered sleeping in it as children, remembered reeds of moonlight shooting through the tiniest holes.

"Brothers," said Achille, "I must tend my potash kettle. Come outside and talk with me." They walked some distance to his potash works. He stirred the kettle's contents with a stick.

"It is our source of cash money—and the firewood I cut."

Money! thought Theotiste with scorn but he said nothing. They talked all day and far into the night. Achille said, "After Renardette left we burned her evil brew house. But men still came out of the woods looking for beer—and her." Theotiste's glance caught something shining on the high shelf against the entry wall. Something like a small snakish eye, he thought.

"None here have married," said Elphège.

"Ah," said Achille, "the Wobik girls are not Mi'kmaw girls. Should I not find a Mi'kmaw woman?"

Theotiste nodded. "We all should do so. Even Elphège."

"Ho," said Elphège.

"Zoë and I never see a good man to marry," said Noë. "We are out here in the woods and the only ones who come by are bad ones."

"So perhaps this place is not so good for you?" asked Theotiste.

"No, no. It is not, even though in childhood it was pleasant, but what else can we do?"

"We want you to come with us," said Elphège, as though it had been his idea. "Theotiste and I are the oldest, but we are of the same blood and we will care for you always." For Elphège this was long oratory.

Theotiste spoke with the assurance of one who knows. "We intend to seek out the land of our mother. Even if it be greatly changed, there must still be a place for us among our people. Mi'kmaq still live there, perhaps even kin. I spoke many times with Mi'kmaq at Odanak. Some of them will come."

Achille nodded.

"I had a vision some time ago that we must do this," said Theotiste very softly. "First we come for you, then all go to Mi'kma'ki. I saw it fair and beautiful as our mother told us."

"But what will we do about Papa's place?" asked Achille, waving his hand, encompassing the house, the river, the weeds, the potash kettle filled with the results of his labor.

With some sadness Elphège thought that Achille might be more French than Mi'kmaw. "If you follow the white man's ways of property you could sell it," said Elphège. "Or, if you are not that way, just leave it and come with us. What are your thoughts?"

It was clear what Achille's thoughts were. He could not just walk away after so much chopping and burning. He was wedded to the idea of ashes as something of value. He had a sense of property. Elphège wondered if all Mi'kmaq were not changing into Frenchmen, wanting money and goods. Few could resist the luxuries, and Achille, Zoë and Noë were *métis*, half French, half Mi'kmaq.

Theotiste nodded. "You maybe sell it. Is that old captain still alive? Bouchard?"

"He was alive last week," said Achille. "He is very old but strong. Yes, he would have ideas."

"Shall you go see him and ask what disposition might be made of this property, all this sad ravaged land? He may be helpful to us."

• • •

The next morning Achille and Theotiste set out to paddle to Wobik in René's canoe, but less than three miles from the house something whistled overhead.

"*Vite!* To the shore!" said Achille through clenched teeth, swerving them under hanging willows. The canoe scraped through tearing branches. Before the willows played out they crept up onto the bank and dragged the canoe behind them.

"The forest is alive with bounty hunters. Let us leave the canoe here and go by foot. But warily."

Theotiste touched Achille's shoulder in assent and they began to weave through the trees.

"What, sell René's house?" said Captain Bouchard. "Yes, such a thing can happen. There is a man, Jean Mague, a farmer from France looking for a property with cleared land and a house. He does not intend to waste the good years of his life chopping trees. I think he would pay a fair price. He will soon be here." Jean Mague, he remarked, had two brothers, three grown sons, their wives, two nephews and their wives to farm with him. They were a strong group and handy with firearms. As the old man spoke, Jean Mague himself came through the door, a lipless face, legs and arms as long as *wikuom* poles.

Mague was interested to hear about René Sel's place and wondered how it had come in the possession of these Indians. He liked the sound of a sturdy French house, a potash kettle, cleared land. He looked Achille and Theotiste up and down rather insolently but agreed to walk back with them to see René's property.

"I'll tell you something," he said when they mentioned René's death. "Bounty hunters will never molest *my* family." And because he was who he was he wished he had brought some beads and cheap whiskey to trade. He carried his gun and followed.

Before the house came in sight Theotiste ran ahead. He dug quickly in a certain place and put what he found in his pack basket, then rushed to the house to tell Elphège and his sisters that Jean

Mague was coming. Noë ran into the back room and rummaged for the small birch-bark box decorated with colorful quillwork, a box from Mari's childhood and precious to Noë. Inside the door Theotiste reached up to the high shelf. His hand grasped René's old snow snake. They went out where Achille was already talking with Jean Mague, the newcomer looking around the property with narrowed eyes to show no one could put anything over on him. His squared shoulders and long heavy steps showed he already felt himself the possessor.

"Will we give him the potash I made?" Achille asked Elphège in a low voice.

"Yes."

Before the talk of price even began, they were interrupted by Renardette and Démon Meillard, who came out of the trees riding tandem on a black horse. They were sober and grim. Démon, his rum-red face shaped like a hazelnut, the modest chin augmented by a pointed black beard, spoke only to Jean Mague and said that the previous owner, René Sel, who had held the notarized title to the property, had bequeathed it to Renardette, his adopted daughter. René and Renardette, he said knowingly, were both pure French. Renardette owned it, not the half-breed Indian squatters who claimed it, who said they were René's children. Demonstrably a falsehood. What Indian knew his true parentage? None!

Démon spoke directly to Jean Mague. "Renardette will sell this good property to you. We will record the sale in Captain Bouchard's great ledger and all will be legal and binding. This is white man's business. These Indians have no claims, they are nothing at all. Nothing."

Achille whispered to Theotiste. "But is it not recorded in the ledger that the house belonged to René? And that René married Mari, our mother, following the whiteman law?"

Theotiste whispered back: "Perhaps it was, but when I asked Captain Bouchard he went in the back room with the ledger, came out a moment later and showed me there was nothing. But I could see rough bits of torn paper in the cleft of that book."

In the end Jean Mague, Démon and Renardette Meillard stood apart under the trees and made their arrangement. They shook hands, turned and faced Elphège, Theotiste, Achille, Zoë and Noë. Jean Mague said, "I have agreed to buy the property from the owners. You must now leave." He raised his gun, ready primed and loaded, to his shoulder.

Achille stood stiff with rage but Elphège touched his arm and said in a low voice, "Brother, it is only a whiteman house. You do not wish to be tied down to a potash kettle like such a one. Let us go. We will hunt and fight. We will not burn trees into dirty ashes."

Achille's voice was tight. He felt his blood curdling with poison. "It is clear that Captain Bouchard informed them, that he removed René's claim from the ledger. He was friendly to our father—for our father was a white *Wenuj*. But to our mother and to us his friendship was false."

"What does it matter? Before you there lie many good years of hunting. That is a better life for you."

Achille stood silent for many heartbeats, then said, "We will come with you to our mother's country."

"Good. First we go to Odanak."

26

Mi'kma'ki

At Odanak, Zoë, Noë and Achille turned shy, unused to such a moil. The village, with its *wikuoms,* and even some log cabins, frothed with people working, cooking, softening hides, splitting canoe ribs, lifting a tangle of gaudy roots from a dye kettle. Two men played *waltes,* the bone dice leaping up when they slapped down the wooden bowl. Jen, a round-faced Mi'kmaw woman with three children, looked at Zoë and Noë, at their soiled whiteman dresses.

"Sit down. Eat," she said. "You are good strong girls who will make a journey to Mi'kma'ki." Zoë and Noë, starved of female company for years, began to thaw. Noë had brought three of her baskets, which she presented to them, but these were not admired. In Odanak there were basket makers of great skill and the women brought out several to show her: an oval birch-bark container sewn with spruce root and worked with such intricate designs the eye could not hold them. Noë touched a basket with a decorative rim of artfully twisted black root. Some baskets were tiny, woven of sweet-grass, some were splendid with red- and green-dyed root strips.

"I wish to learn how to make such beautiful baskets," said Noë, kicking at her own poor efforts.

"We will show you," said a young and heavy woman with callused hands who told the story of Ai'ip, the lazy woman who split and twisted roots around her fingers and somehow made the first basket. "No person could name this object. And they had to call it 'that root thing.'"

166

"I am choking with new thoughts," said Zoë. "We know nothing," for they had only ten winters.

Theotiste, Elphège and Achille wanted to start at once for Mi'kma'ki, but Sosep, an old trapper *sagmaw,* took them aside and spoke at length.

"I am going with you. But it is not good to go now when winter is advancing. There is nothing to eat at that place in the winter. People go up the river. We better wait until spring."

Achille itched to go.

"What does he mean, there is no food at Mi'kma'ki? Mari our mother told us it was a place of great richness, fish, lobsters, clams and oysters, birds by the thousand, succulent plants." Sosep over-heard this and laughed. "Mi'kma'ki is a summer place. Winter very hard there unless you cached ten moose and sixteen bears."

For more than four cycles of the moon the Sels waited at Odanak. Theotiste, Elphège and Achille hunted and fished, talked with the men about the best route to Mi'kma'ki. The women helped Noë and Zoë dry and smoke venison and eel for their journey. Noë, deter-mined to become a maker of fine baskets, worked at it until her fin-gers blistered.

The approaching journey with their older brothers to their mother's country filled their thoughts. From Mari they had heard of the parts of their homeland: Wild Potato Place, Skin Dresser's Terri-tory and Land of Fog. They were discarding memories of their forest childhood. Would spring never come?

Theotiste told Zoë one day that Mari's spirit would surely be there in the trees and wild plants, perhaps in the rocks, in the fish and ani-mals. It would be a reconnection.

"I wish we had brought Maman's bones," said Zoë.

Theotiste nodded. "I have brought them," he said.

"That is good!" Then a moment later she said, "I wish I had brought the little wall basket she made to hold René's comb."

"Noë will make one. It will hold new combs."

When at last they set out, the woman friend of Theotiste's dead

wife came with them as well as old Sosep, who had the solid reputation of an important trapper-hunter, the wavering reputation of a
sagmaw and the faded reputation of a local chief. His scarred face was
serious. He had a grave manner that indicated character and wisdom.
His teeth were large and yellow, his black eyes squinted, for his sight
was failing. "It is good you waited. Even now it may be too early.
But we can advance. My trapping run is still in Mi'kmaw country—
if those French have not built their square houses on it. I wish to
return. I wanted to see what Odanak was like—but even here there
were whitemen. The worst is this Odanak priest, Father Lacet." He
imitated the priest's sly expression, his dabbling hands. "He is boring holes in all the *waltes* bowls so they cannot hold water and give
us divinations. I will help you. I know your father's favored trapping
places, for his brother told me."

"His *brother*!" said Theotiste. "Do we then have an uncle? Living?"

"Very alive. Cache Emil. He will show you that place and others.
But these days whitemen want those places, too. And they take them
without courtesy or talk. They *take* them."

For Theotiste and Elphège this was earth-shaking news. They had
believed their father, whom they did not remember, and all of their
father's kin were dead. This magical uncle was a proof that they had
made a correct decision.

Sosep said, "We will be pressing through the end season of snow.
We must make snowshoes as you did not bring any from that place
you were before you came here." And he sat with Elphège and Theotiste and Achille making the ash-wood frames while the woman
friend of Theotiste's dead wife, Zoë and Noë wove the caribou raw-
hide webbing in a close mesh to better support the weight of their
loads.

They began to walk toward the ocean, which none of the Sels had
ever seen except in imagination. The journey was rough underfoot and circuitous in their minds. They lived on their dried meat

and sacks of maize, for at this time of year wild creatures were still deep in the forest, plants had not broken through the ground. Every morning the streams were edged in ice. But in the second week Theotiste got two fat beaver.

Winter returned with a snowstorm, a giddy flying mass, heaping drifts behind logs, covering all. When the storm cleared and night became as day with reflected moonlight the cold increased. In the next weeks they twice had to build temporary *wikuoms* and take shelter from the snows.

"Oh, what a late spring. If it snows more," said Sosep, "we will have to construct a toboggan."

"Perhaps it will not snow," said Theotiste.

"Perhaps the sun will not rise tomorrow," muttered Sosep.

"I am hungry," said Nöe.

Sosep laughed. "Mi'kmaw persons can stand hunger for a long time without dying."

In the waiting days inside the *wikuoms* Noë and Zoë plagued Theotiste and Elphège to retell their mother's stories about Mi'kma'ki. They never tired of hearing about the blueberry patches, the elderberries with their drooping umbels, serviceberries, chokecherry trees, the succulent crayfish, roasted beaver, the fattest eels, even oily walrus, all part of the rich Mi'kma'ki life where one had only to step outside the *wikuom* and take a plump turkey. Later Elphège wondered if it had been a mistake to fill their heads with stories of a summer world, so different from what they found when they reached their destination. Others told stories about Kluskap when life for the Mi'kmaq was good.

"Listen to me," said Sosep. "This is a bad time to return to our country, not only because of this untimely weather. Do you not know that the French king gave our lands to the British?"

Theotiste looked at him. "How can that be? It is not the land of the French king to give. It is ours."

"This happened some winters ago. Surely you heard the talk of it in Odanak?"

"I thought it was only foolish talk. I heard the British seized Port Royal, but you say 'our lands.'"

"Yes. It is our land but we suffer advances from both French and English. The French see us as soldiers to fight for them, our women good only for fucking. The priests see us as bounty for their God as we might see beaver skins. They do not see us as a worthy people. The French use us for their protection. They do not understand that we are allies of the French king, but not his subjects. We are not obliged to him. That is why he gives us presents—to buy our favor. Now the British greedily claim even more land than the French king gave that was not his to give." He stopped, raised his chin. "And the British give no presents."

"But Mi'kmaq are going back there. As we are. And I have heard that French and Mi'kmaq often marry. As our father René married our mother, Mari."

"Yes, it is true. And that is good because there are so few of us left. Now that the beaver are so few we must marry someone, *ha ha!* I fear we will soon find the English putting their houses on our trapping grounds."

"I heard some French families live near us Mi'kmaw and they are not unfriendly."

"That maybe is so, the French have long been our friends—somewhat—but now the English think they possess everything. Their settlers move in. The English king pays good money for Mi'kmaw scalps. So we make a war against the English. Many Mi'kmaq are fighting in canoes. We are good fighters and capture many English boats. But we are so few. We are so often ill."

They reached the Mi'kmaw country in late March with spring trembling behind the wind. Bird migration flights had started. In a small stream they saw numerous small fish surging up against the current.

Sosep pointed out a dozen French families living along the shore. He spoke of the woodlands and fruitful edges that had supplied so many generations with berries and edible roots but warned that now much land had been plowed up and given over to maize fields and turnips. These French Acadians had drained many of the salt marshes to grow salt hay for their livestock. The larger game animals, moose, caribou and bear, had all retreated. The beaver were greatly reduced in number so severely had they been taken, for their skins could be turned into guns and metal pots. Yes, the beaver had become a kind of whiteman money and the custom of placing a beaver skin on a grave had fallen away.

"Still," said Theotiste, "we can trade meat for maize and pumpkins. Will not the Acadians be glad of venison as they always are? As we are glad of bread. And I think the sky and land must be the same as they forever were, for not the *Plets-mun* nor the English have the power to level cliffs, they have not the power to drain the sea nor eat the sky. Can we not live side by side?"

"We have little choice," said Sosep with a puckered expression. And soon there were so many birds the sky rattled, so many fish the bay boiled like a pot. There was enough for all.

Despite the old man's complaints that all was spoiled, the Sels were astounded at the unfolding bounty of Mi'kma'ki. The great bay with its powerful tides, its estuaries and islands, its freshwater rivers and the nurturing ocean supplied everything. The newcomers stared at the ocean beating in ceaselessly, stared agape as the tide went out exposing miles of mudflats riddled with tiny holes from which came the hissing noise of mud shrimp below. Equally fascinating was the swift return of the ocean, the saline water coming in stealthily.

They had to learn this new country, its red cliffs, the changing tides, the seasons for herring, for shad, a different pattern of weather and storms than they had ever known. At first the ocean seemed all-powerful, but they came to understand that the true richness of Mi'kma'ki was in its rivers. They had to learn the names of unfamiliar fish. Farther out from shore there swam several kinds of great whales, porpoises and dolphins. There were varieties of seals, lobsters as big as women. The Sel men, as hunters and trappers, had to learn their ways quickly.

They saw that the foolish Acadians were diligent gardeners and because of this they felt themselves superior. The local surviving Mi'kmaq lived on the edges of old trapping areas, somewhat away from the French settlers.

"But we newcomers have no *wikuom*. We have no shelter," said Noë, who longed for the stability of a *wikuom* or even a house. A whiteman house was impossible. She knew that. There were several of those geometric structures at Odanak, but here people despised them and there was the example of the young Mi'kmaw hunter a few years earlier who had been to a white settlement and there he had seen English drinking brown water from a saucer. The saucer was very beautiful with a deep blue rim. Somehow he had gained possession of this saucer—or one like it—and brought it back to Mi'kma'ki. His scandalized and outraged neighbors saw him drinking from it and killed him for a traitor to traditional ways. The repulsive object was smashed on a stone.

"But," said old grandmother Loze, "two families have saucers now and no one has killed them. Everything does change."

27

blood kin

With some ceremony Sosep brought Cache Emil, Elphège and Theotiste's uncle, to them. Cache Emil, a tall, powerful old man with hulking shoulders and a deeply lined face as though flint-gouged, stepped forward and put both hands on Elphège's shoulders.

"Yes," he said. "I know you, the children of my brother. Often my life has been heavy with loss and sadness, but today I feel so much joy that I have no good words for it." He grasped first Elphège, then Theotiste; his cheeks were wet. For Elphège and Theotiste in that moment Cache Emil became the center of life. They had longed for a father without knowing it. Cache Emil said he had a son, Rouge Emil. Their own blood, their cousin.

"You," he said to Achille, who had only fourteen winters. "You are the son of Mari, long-ago wife of my brother Lolan before he ceased his existence. I welcome you. When Rouge Emil returns we will have a feast. But come with me, Elphège, I will take you to some old places where my brother who was your father often got his quarry, fur or flesh. And good places at the river mouths for fish weirs. Sosep and I will speak together of choice trapping lines for Theotiste—and Achille." Sosep pompously and formally assigned Elphège their father's old trapping territory and told Theotiste and Achille they would have productive areas adjoining his own. No priest could do that!

But Rouge Emil made a face; neither his father nor Sosep understood that the old custom of assigning trapping and fishing territories was no longer in the power of Mi'kmaw men; white men and their rules of land division had taken over. Such territories were house sites, garden plots and cow pastures.

Achille respected Cache Emil but gravitated to old Sosep, not Sosep as a *sagmaw,* but Sosep the renowned hunter. Achille had been a natural hunter from childhood; René had been a wood chopper who hunted only when pressed by necessity. Now Achille became passionate. It was his new identity in this new world that had enclosed him. He preferred to hunt and stalk on land—and let others concern themselves with the life of rivers and the ocean.

At the welcoming feast Theotiste, who believed drink was an evil spirit's brew, saw Cache Emil drank only one small cup of brandy, but Rouge Emil swallowed cup after cup.

"Will you not drink, Cousin?" asked Rouge Emil, but Theotiste turned his face away.

"I have ever disliked the white man's whiskey," he mumbled. Rouge Emil drank on until he surrendered to the weight of the spirit and fell senseless.

A few days later many Mi'kmaq came to help put up a big *wikuom,* large enough for all of them, on the edge of the forest overlooking the sea where a path bent down to the shore. Here they buried Mari's bones. After a long search Achille killed a beaver and put its skin on the burial place as they did in the old times, but a few days later it was gone. Someone had taken it to sell.

Achille and Theotiste said they would later make small *wikuoms* in suitable places, but for now it was better if they all stayed together. Zoë laughed to see a band of Mi'kmaw seamstresses sewing their house as one would sew a garment, until they put her to work painting the moose-hide door in whirls and double curves of black, purple and red.

"Sister, there was never a more beautiful entrance," said Elphège. Inside the *wikuom* was floored with reed mats, a central stone circle for fire. Inside was quiet. Inside was their haven.

"A fine *wikuom*," said Cache Emil. "The French brag of their great tall houses in their home villages, but why does one need such a tall house? Men are not so high in stature. Perhaps they have giants for visitors? Nor can those houses be moved, they say. And if those houses and those villages are so fine, as we often hear, why did they leave them, leave their friends and wives and come here? Truly these must be the rejected ones from their own people so stupid, so hairy and grasping."

The elderly Mi'kmaw grandmother Loze, who had been at Odanak, bossed the sewing. "But everything is changed," she said, as she always said. "Because our fathers killed so many beaver to trade with the Europeans the beaver are angry and have left the country, and now strike us with illnesses." She pointed at Alit Spot, who had ulcers on his neck and hands that refused to heal. Many of the old beaver hunters had suffered those sores, and when the disease went inside the body they had died coughing blood. "But you know well," she said, "after eel, beaver meat is the best meat for the Mi'kmaq. We destroyed our best food to trade their furs to the white men. Now these people from far away try to push us off the shore, push us into the interior, where the biting insects live. Here, near the ocean, the breeze teaches insects kind ways." She said enviously that she had heard a true story that at one place the Mi'kmaq had shot the settlers' cows, but French soldiers came and arrested the hunters. "They should have arrested the cows." She said that as a child she had been shown the place where the rattling plant—*mededeskooï*—grew, that magic plant that could cure many illnesses and even grant wishes. Even in the old days it had been elusive. Her accounts always ended "that was a long time ago." Yes, that was the old life.

When the weather warmed she came with the Sels at low tide, showing them how to dig clams, their feet sinking into the rich mud, shorebirds running before them and crying out warnings to each other. Loze told Noë that the dog whelks made the beautiful purple dye the Mi'kmaw people liked.

"I will show you how to do it one day," the old woman said, and she urged them to gather armfuls of seaweed to flavor the clams they would steam on hot rocks.

The summer and autumn passed. It was time to reinforce the *wikuoms* with skins and weighty poles. The loons called in their storm-coming voices, a sign that otherworld being without legs, Coolpujot, would soon send winter gales. For the men the cold and deepening snow made easier hunting. Achille went into the woods on snowshoes, sleeping out many nights. In January he hunted seals on the ice with Rouge Emil. Achille preferred to hunt with Sosep, whom he called *Nikskamich*—grandfather. He did not smoke the pipe as it dulled the senses. He shuddered to think that he had once stood over a reeking potash kettle. Although January and February were the best months to hunt moose, for dogs could drive the animals into the deep snow, where they floundered and made easy targets for men on snowshoes, Achille hunted them in every season. Before a summer hunt he took a steam bath and then rubbed himself with earth and leaves to dampen his human odor. Unlike other hunters he did not use dogs to find moose except in winter; he could smell them from a great distance and he knew their minds and habits. Old Sosep told Cache Emil that Achille was such a hunter as only emerges every few generations, almost a *megumoowesoo,* one of those fortunate Mi'kmaq whom Kluskap honored with extraordinary abilities. But to Achille he said jokingly, "Now you must marry and have a woman to bring home the meat you catch. Now you must learn to play the flute to attract such a one."

In spring Achille went with Rouge Emil to an island where *Apagtuey,* the great white auk, nested. They took two each, for the birds were good eating and their gullets made the finest arrow quivers. But the next year when they went to that same island there were no birds, only a litter of feathers and bones, for English and Boston whalers had come before them.

Gradually people began to say that Achille did not care about

Mi'kmaw girls because he must be married to *team,* a moose, as he knew moose ways so well. He traveled into the interior and one time went far northwest. When he returned from one long journey he spoke privately to Elphège and said that Captain Bouchard would betray no more Mi'kmaw people, for his tongue had come loose and fallen to the ground.

Elphège nodded and said, "My brother, it is good."

Mi'kma'ki was richer in birds than the forests of New France, but when the annual migrations began, the volume of birds, as many as the snowflakes in a blizzard, the smell of their hot bodies intensified by millions of pulsing wings, stunned them. It seemed every bird on earth was here—especially sandpipers, so many they covered the shore like a monstrous twitching grey blanket, gorging on mud shrimp. They poured out of the south sky like froth-crested waves. It was the time of birds roasted and steamed, broiled and boiled. The wood pigeons, which they had seen in childhood in Kébec, darkened the world. Predatory birds arrived, too, pierce-eyed ospreys, eagles, hawks, falcons. Old Sosep commented that Europeans would soon be arriving in numbers rivaling the birds. His listeners shuddered. The *sagmaw* seemed to ricochet between two thoughts: he foresaw billows of overseas white people arriving in countless ships—but he spoke and acted as if the old traditions still governed their world.

Theotiste and Elphège went out at night in their canoes with others during the migrations. They lay quietly in the bottoms of their canoes and let them drift like logs into great flocks of sleeping ducks. Then Cache Emil and old Sosep lit birch torches and held them high over their heads in the darkness. The ducks awoke, shrieking, and flew confusedly around the torches while the younger men knocked them down with poles. In this way they filled five canoes with fat ducks in one night.

"Now, Brothers," called Elphège, "you will see how well we eat. We do not go for long solitary journeys to get one tough old moose, we go together and quickly get an abundance of delicious fat greasy ducks."

Theotiste and Elphège sat in fog-softened sunlight making ax handles, for the new white settlers coming into Mi'kma'ki thought of nothing else until they had taken down enough trees to build their heavy square huts. It was not interesting work to make the same shape of wood over and again, but they left the hunting to Achille, who was so quiet and stealthy he could creep close to a fever-eyed ruffed grouse on a hollow log rolling out his crescendos of wingbeats, and slip the leather noose at the end of a long stick over the bird's head. Making ax handles for a little money helped, for there were many things that now must be purchased, things that had never been known in the old times. They had to have metal pots and utensils, nails, wire, tools and weapons.

As they scraped and whittled the ash handles, a group of men and women came down the slope. One of the women—Talis—stopped. She was tall, with smiling eyes that crinkled at the corners, her flawless teeth bright.

"Why do you not put away those sticks and come help us mend the weir?"

"Why indeed," said Theotiste, getting up and setting aside the handle he had begun to shape. "I will go with you."

The rivers of Mi'kma'ki were not solitary currents of water but strands in a great net of liquid motion that defined the land and mingled with the sea in outward flow and inward rush of tide. Each tiny runnel, each roaring raceway, torrent and trickle, cascade and flood had its own habits and ways, and Mi'kmaq had to know those ways. This was the water world that Theotiste and Elphège began to learn.

"My head is swollen with all this fish lore," said Elphège.

"Yes," said a sinewy old fellow with long earlobes, "as long as there are Mi'kmaw people there will be knowledge of fishing."

• • •

The French king sent money to build roads to the interior (where they wished to push the Mi'kmaq, said Sosep), and now, when time allowed, many men, including Theotiste and Elphège, took temporary work as chainmen for surveyors and as laborers on the new road for hard cash. Chopping trees was another thing that had to be done, said the new people.

When a whiteman lumber outfit set up a sawmill and began cutting trees in the interior country, there was more work for money that could be used at the trading post. The missionary, Père Crème, urged them to put aside trapping and fishing for a time in favor of this occupation. With the money, he said, they could buy salt pork and flour. Although salt pork was a disgusting food, flour made bread and the people had come to like bread. Elphège, Theotiste and Achille had all labored long hours with René clearing the forest, they were skilled with the ax and found work with the French company Duquet et Fils. Rouge Emil was less skilled, but he joined them. It was not the Mi'kmaw way, but it seemed necessary.

One who was not pleased with the newcomers from Odanak was Père Crème. He was disturbed that old Joseph, the one the Mi'kmaq called Sosep, had returned. And the Sel family, what a calamity! All of them could speak French, and it was best that Indians did not learn French. The two older brothers could read and write, using the Roman alphabet, a serious error on the part of some mission cleric decades earlier. They were capable of doing much harm and stirring up trouble. And they resisted farming, the men preferring to work in the woods, on the rivers or at odd jobs for some of the year, reserving the autumn and winter for trapping and hunting. He wrote,

Dear Sister Marguerite.

While I have great Sympathy for the Indians, they are difficult. The sorest Point is their Refusal to grasp the Fact that Land belongs to the Man who improves it as Scriptures show. They only fish (an idler's

occupation) and wander through the Forest taking Animals and Plants for Sustenance, but when a White Man comes and cuts the oppressive encroaching Forest, builds a House for his Family and Shelter for his Beasts, the Indians complain that he takes their Land, Land they have done nothing to improve, but rather have allowed to ever thicken with more and more Trees. They do not understand that the White Man who struggles and strives to reduce the Forest's grip has exerted his God-given Right to claim the cleared Land as his own. By virtue of the suffering of Indian Attack and severe Labor as well as the adversities of removing from their Homelands to take up a Place in the Wilderness it is the Destiny of the French to hold this Land as they have earned moral Title to it from God.

Nor did Sosep like what he saw. He immediately counted harmful changes. One of the French settlers, Philippe Null, had inherited a sum of money from an uncle in France, and with this windfall he bought three cows, a bull and two horses. The huge animals roamed freely and within days had consumed all the nutritious and medicinal plants within a day's walk.

"Those animals must have been very sick," said old grandmother Loze, "for they have eaten herbs to cure headache, lingering cough, prolapsed uterus, fevers, broken bones and sore throats." Sosep added that once butchered and cooked, the cows, though not as tasty as moose or caribou, looked the same in the pot. But one had to be very private about it.

Other Acadians, sharpened with envy of Null's increasing livestock herd, bought pigs. No pasture nor pen was necessary as the animals grew fat on forest forage and very quickly learned to dig clams. Now the Mi'kmaw women had difficulty getting clams, for the hogs were on the sands as soon as the tide ebbed, rooting and gobbling. There was a tragic loss when a hog attacked and killed a lagging Mi'kmaw toddler who was trying to imitate the clam diggers. The child was dead and partially eaten when the others finally saw.

It took hours, even days, to find many once-common things. But of uncommon weeds there was no lack—mallows, dock, stinging nettles, sow thistle, knotgrass and adder's-tongue, aggressive clovers. Sosep filled his lobster-claw pipe with dried wild tobacco and spoke out one evening.

"We are sharing our land with the *Wenuj* and they take more and more. You see how their beasts destroy our food, how their boats and nets take our fish. They bring plants that vanquish our plants. Most do not mean to hurt us, but they are many and we are few. I believe they will become as a great wave sweeping over us." His deep voice became charged with intensity, a conduit of spiritual power. "All these woods once ours," he said, "and we went anywhere we wished without hindrance. That time has passed. But I wish to tell you that if we Mi'kmaw people are to survive we must constantly hold to the thought of Mi'kmaw ways in our minds. We will live in two worlds. We must keep our Mi'kmaw world—where we, the plants, animals and birds are all persons together who help each other—fresh in our thoughts and lives. We must renew and revere the vision in our minds so it can stand against this outside force that encroaches. Otherwise we could not bear it."

Noë muttered to Zoë, "Does he mean we must give up metal pots and go back to boiling food with hot rocks in a hollow wood pot as Loze said they did in the old days?"

Sosep had not heard this and continued. "If we had not harmed so many animal beings they would fight with us against the outsiders. Especially the beaver. But no longer. I know that some of you love the French, and that is unavoidable lest we die out, but remember that you are Mi'kmaw, remember."

Achille told himself he would live the Mi'kmaw way, imagining all was well. He would take a wife and he would tell his children that they, too, must imagine that they lived in a Mi'kmaw world though it was ceasing to exist. They must remember how that life had been, not how it now had become.

But even as old Sosep spoke he knew very well that many Mi'kmaq welcomed the ways of the Acadian French—their clothing, their stout boats, their vegetables and pork roasts, the metal tools, glass ornaments and bolts of fabric, their intoxicating spirits and bright flags and even their hot bare bodies, so pale. Already the Mi'kmaw language was awash in French words with remnants of Portuguese and Basque from the days of those earlier European fishermen on their shores. And he himself, as a connection to the spiritual, as a former *sagmaw,* saw that the priests had already replaced him and the wise old men of former times.

28

the secret of green leaves

The years went by and the white settlers, many from La Rochelle in France, doubled and redoubled in number. Familiar with the arts of drainage dike and ditch, they were demons to reshape the great grassy marshes into farm fields, and where there was forest they felled the trees. They set their immovable houses in rows along mud-thick streets where hogs wallowed and domestic fowl strutted. They encased themselves in thick woolen clothes so that bodily odors were never wafted away in the wind. The Mi'kmaq tolerated and even befriended them, although they did not understand the newcomers' zeal for surplus—clams, berries, fish, logs, hay, moose hides—which they sold or exchanged for more cows and horses, more chickens and pigs.

The Sels married: Noë to Zephirin Desautels, an Acadian fisherman who was a cousin of the dead boy who had fathered Auguste; Zoë to Paul, an older Mi'kmaw man whose left shoulder in childhood had been grievously hurt by an enraged moose, an injury that damaged his hunting abilities. But he became a superior eeler and their *wikuom* was never empty of food. Achille married a Mi'kmaw beauty named Isobel, already well known for her strong fingers and skill in making the new kind of basket, not of roots but of thin cedar and ash splints—always she had a splint, *ligpete'gnapi,* in her hand. Elphège had found and courted Delima, the widow of a man killed in an ambush, and Theotiste at last married Anne-Marie, the woman who had been his first wife's friend. They settled into a way of living away from the white settlers, though more and more men went to cut pine in the winter camps.

Achille grew proud of his hunting skill and he imagined there was no beast he could not understand and kill.

"To be sure, on the land," said Rouge Emil, "but you avoid the creatures of the sea. You are no fish hunter," and he laughed.

This remark smarted and Achille kept thinking of the stories of old times, when the Mi'kmaq had hunted whales in their bark canoes. Everyone said canoes were best in rivers and along the seashore; in deep water they could be dangerous when certain bad fish attacked. Achille did not believe that a fish could harm a canoe; this was a story to frighten children. He said he would go far out in the bay and fish alone in a canoe, and twice he did so and caught cod half his own length each time. He carried a fish spear—in case of English attackers, he said. But one hour's experience changed his opinion of fish.

He persuaded two others, his friends Barth Nocout and Alit Spot, to paddle their canoes out with him. They could see the people onshore as small as their little fingers. From the corner of his eye Achille saw something briefly rise from the water farther out. The fishing was good; they made jokes. Then his canoe lurched. He peered into the water but could see nothing. A few moments later Nocout's canoe rose high out of the water and they saw the enormous black and white orca that had lifted it up on its back. The whale sank and Nocout's canoe tipped and rocked but did not go over.

"Do not paddle!" called Nocout, whose father had told the stories of dangerous fish. "Take up your spears! When it comes near again strike it hard." For long tense minutes they waited and then, ten canoe lengths from Nocout, they saw a dorsal fin like a monstrous pine stump rise from the water and slowly sink again. They gripped their spears. Achille saw the gleaming white oval patch behind the invisible eye as the creature rose below him. He stabbed the spear with force into the sleek side as it came up. The animal rolled away and dived at once, wrenching the spear from his hands and carrying it away. Before the animal disappeared it spoke to Achille in a familiar voice.

"You are not," it said in Sosep's deep voice. Then it was gone.

"It may leave us now," said Nocout. "I pray there are no others." They waited, motionless, terrified. Then Nocout whispered, "Let us paddle to shore."

As they paddled, they constantly searched the distant water for the great fin, the near water for the black and white giant.

"We were protected by spirits," Nocout said, panting, as they reached the shallows.

"Did you hear them speak?" asked Achille.

"I felt their presence."

Nocout and Spot told their story many times that evening and Nocout's father shook his head and said that in the old days when Mi'kmaq had to make sea journeys in frail canoes they would put many leafy branches in the prow and stern.

"Those evil fish smell the leaves and they think the canoe is a little island and they are in danger of being stranded on its shore. So they veer away. You were fortunate there was only one. Had there been a pack they would have toppled your canoes and thrown you in the water. They have eaten many of our people. They know the trick of tipping canoes from their way of bumping ice floes. The seals fall in the water and they are caught. Perhaps they think men are seals."

Nocout's father went to a storage basket where he kept curiosities and brought out a single tooth the length of a man's hand. "They have a hundred such teeth," he said, passing the heavy ivory around.

Achille saw that he had been a fool. He looked across the fire at Sosep. He wanted to ask him what the fish meant when it said "You are not" in Sosep's voice. Had it truly spoken? What was the meaning of those words? The old man was staring at him, and as their glances met Sosep raised his eyebrows. But Achille was unable to find a way to ask.

29

roast moose head

Sosep died suddenly after a hard day's moose hunt. The old man sat by the fire with a piece of meat in his hand. Achille saw he had fallen asleep. He could not be roused. Perhaps an easy death for an old man tired from a successful hunt, enjoying the warmth of a fire and rich moose meat, thought Achille. But Sosep had long been planning his death song, a great recounting of his hunting feats, journeys, his children, wonderful things he had seen in his time as when, during a long battle, an enemy had transformed himself into a bear. Now he had fallen silently into the world of the departed with no death song at all.

Achille went down to the sea and looked out. The water was nearly flat, a dull color under a dull sky. The sky seemed gone, there never had been sky and Sosep was down there, under the water. A gull floated, quietly asleep.

"Grandfather," called Achille. "I wish you a good journey under the sea even though you told me 'you are not.'" At the sound of his voice the gull awoke and, after some effort, lifted into the air.

He had thirty-three winters entering his middle years now. Because game was scarce he was away for many days on each hunt. He had somehow lost the respect of the animal persons. His wife, Isobel, sighed at his frequent absences.

"Why can you not work in the forest cutting *lo'gs* as do others?"

186

"I cut *lo'gs* after good hunt if we got plenty food." His children and wife wore French clothing as he did, and rumors flew that this time the English settlers were coming in truly large numbers to seize the land. *You are not,* he said to himself. The thought never left his mind.

No one knew if they were at war, or with whom. Bloodthirsty woods rangers came from Boston in armed ships and killed indiscriminately. The English dug up their graveyards and threw Mi'kmaw corpses into fires. *Aloosool,* the black measles, killed so many there were few left to bury them and in one place they had to put the bodies in a pond to keep them from the whitemen's devouring hogs.

Although the Mi'kmaq resented their Acadian neighbors' incursions, they married some of them, taught them their language and beliefs and absorbed many of their ways, moving ever more deeply into their double lives, the interior reality warring with the external world in a kind of teetering madness. For their part, the Acadians, conservative and serious agriculturists, passionate marsh drainers, wished to be left alone and resented the priest's exhortations to take arms against the English. Père Crème occasionally thought that a new kind of people, part Mi'kmaq, part Acadian, seemed to be forming. Then the English king urged volunteer English on retirement from the army or navy, and colonial New Englanders, to take up free land in Nova Scotia. Thousands upon thousands came.

Achille, once again beset by the spring urge to travel north, planned a hunting trip of two or three moons with his oldest son, Kuntaw, named for a powerful stone with bright copper specks, and his nephew Auguste, light-eyed and brown-haired like an overseas person, *Alman'tiew.* Years before, when Kuntaw had passed three winters and it seemed he would survive, Achille had made him a tiny bow and miniature blunt-ended arrows.

"Now you shall hunt," he said.

The child imitated Auguste, who was older and already knew how to kill birds and frogs. He notched the arrow, drew the little bow and released the string. The arrow traveled only the length of his shadow. Late in summer he was successful. At a distance the length of a *wikuom* pole, a large grasshopper rested on a stalk of tall grass. Kuntaw, eyes narrowed, aimed and shot. The grasshopper flailed in midair, fell to the ground and lay on its side, legs drawn up. Kuntaw picked up his kill and rushed to Achille. He might have bagged a moose for all the congratulations. The grasshopper was displayed on a piece of birch bark. They celebrated with a feast and a grasshopper dance. In this way the family welcomed a new hunter.

Kuntaw reached eleven winters and looked longingly at a certain girl, Malaan. He wanted to marry but this could not happen until he killed his first moose. Auguste, who had already killed his moose two winters past, suggested Kuntaw seek out a giant grasshopper instead. But Achille drew the boys close and said they would go with him to the land of little sticks in the far north, the taiga where the black spruce grew, wind-stripped of branches on their weather side, wind-forced to lean aslant, giving way to the rolling tundra studded with lakes and boulders, a land of birds that stretched to the horizon.

"After eight or ten days we will be in a forest of *masgwi*—birch—and spruce. Here we stop to hunt and fish, to smoke meat, make our canoe, for farther north than this place the birch does not grow. When we find good game country we hunt."

Each made up his pack of necessary things. Achille brought flint and a supply of the black fire-starting fungus, but, he said, they would also carry fire with them. The morning they left he put a hot coal from the home fire in each of three clay-lined clamshells, tied them tightly closed with strips of hide.

"We will be able to make a fire quickly," he said. "Every morning that we travel we will do this. Each will carry a fresh fire coal. We will hunt with bow and arrows. Bring your spears. We will not use European firearms. We will be Mi'kmaw men."

Jenny, one of Noë's daughters, watched all this. One evening in the *wikuom* she whispered to a friend. "You know those whiteman pigs get our *e's*—our clams?"

"I do. A big grandmother pig is the leader."

"Yes. I have a plan." She reached behind her and took up a skin sack filled with empty clamshells. She whispered to her friend and the other girl laughed.

"I will help you," she said.

They were up before the tide turned. From the banked night fire Jenny and her friend took hot coals and put them in the clamshells, joined the halves together with clay so the clams seemed their usual unshucked selves. They placed the shells temptingly just above the waterline, then sprinkled a little sand over them. They waited, high up on the shore. A great sow and six lesser beasts came down to ravage the clams. The first clam was rooted up and as it fell open the old sow seized the hot coal. The watching girls were gratified at the terrific squealing and roaring and rolled on the sand in laughter. The old sow rushed away to the village emitting unearthly squalls. The other hogs rooted up the rest of the burning clams and in a short while the Acadian village trembled with porcine uproar. For the women it was a wonderful day.

The hunting journey began well. Auguste and Kuntaw were excited by the new territory and the chance for a real hunt as Mi'kmaw men had made in the old days. On the third day Auguste shot a swimming beaver, then dived into the water to retrieve it and his arrow. Before he was back onshore another beaver came up out of the depths and Kuntaw shot it. Auguste brought both to land. They ate well that night. Achille had picked willow and kinnikinnick leaves on the way and tied the stems to his pack basket; as he walked they cured. At night they smoked their pipes before bed and told stories.

The new territory refreshed their eyes, everything infused with the spirit of *mntu*. They camped beside waters so crowded with hungry lake trout it was the work of a few breaths to net six. They saw bears at the rotten logs, noticed the small creatures that made their livings in cavity-riddled snags and the many owls who lived on this bounty. This was a world *Wenuj* never noticed, even when walking through it.

After a rainy night they woke to a spider's world of spangled webs. Heavy mist silenced footfalls and the sound of movement through brush. It was a good morning for hunting and many more good mornings followed. Kuntaw saw that Achille was very strong in his body and in his understanding of the unseen forces that bound all into one—animals, spirits, people, fish, trees, ocean, winter, clouds.

"We got not much food now," said Achille, sharing out two small woodcock. "We hunt today, go a little east." They walked toward the sun all morning and while resting at noon near a small lake, their prize came to them. Out of a tangle of small spruce a lustrous black bear ambled onto a grassy bank. The bear was so fat his belly trembled with each step. Achille shot first, Kuntaw and Auguste simultaneously, then Achille again. The bear lay still.

"How we get him back to camp?" said Auguste. "He's too big."

"Ho, you will see. Come," said Achille. "First we gut this bear, leave for wolves." They eviscerated the huge animal and Achille dragged it to the edge of the bank. "Watch. I show you." Achille took sinew cords he always carried and bound the bear's hind feet to the front feet. He jumped down off the bank, turned his back to the bear, slid his arms into the loops formed by the bound paws, leaned forward and with a heave and lurch stood almost upright, the bear like a monstrous knapsack on his back. He alone carried it to their camp, his feet making deep impressions with every step. After he let the burden down he made them examine his footprints. "You see how deep when a man carries a heavy burden? Sometimes that person is carrying supplies, sometimes fur packs. And sometimes a bear."

A full moon passed before they neared the end of the birch forest. Here the hunting party stopped early one evening on the shore of a small lake. Achille looked about. "The *masgwi*—white birch—of this forest is good. And I see trees encumbered with knots of the fire-starting tinder. We make two canoes with this bark," he said, "even though it is not the correct moon." Auguste, who had brought his crooked knife, would fashion the paddles. They made camp in the dying light. Auguste, who had a way with naming, called it Canoe-Making Place.

While Auguste resoled his worn moccasins, Kuntaw and Achille set out for the east end of the lake in the wavering darkness of early morning, frost crackling beneath their feet. From the distance of an English mile they could see a moose-shaped dot at the end of the lake. As they came closer Kuntaw could see it was a young female moose in the shallows; the rising sun caught the glittering water dripping from her muzzle. They left the shore lest she see them and backed into the woods, circling closer, each step painfully slow and carefully placed. Long before they were near, the moose raised her head and stared in their direction. She had heard them. Kuntaw was shocked by the acuteness of hearing that let her sense their distant approach. A cloud of steam swelled into the bitter dawn with each of her exhalations and Achille thought that these puffs were like the lives of men and animals, brief, then swallowed up in the air. Kuntaw had no room in his mind for thoughts; he was so tense his jaw ached. "Wait, now," whispered Achille. "Let her become sure there is no one." After a long time the moose splashed closer to them. "She will feed along the shore, she will come to you," signed Achille in pantomime. Closer she came until they could hear the tearing of the water plants. When she clambered onto solid ground again Achille motioned and Kuntaw raised his bow, drew back the string and released it. The moose bled and fell.

"Now you are a man," said Achille. "I show you how we get this moose back to our camp." He tied his useful sinew cords around its neck, plunged into the water as did Kuntaw, and together they towed the cow along the shore.

Auguste said, "We now may call you Moose Killer instead of Grasshopper Slayer."

They dragged the heavy animal onto the sloping shore and gutted it. Kuntaw and Auguste carried the head up to the cooking fire and Achille followed with the heart, liver, a handful of fat and several choice cuts.

"So," said Achille, "do you make up the fire now and broil liver slices, and cook the heart slices in moose fat. And heat many small stones. I will prepare the head for baking."

They ate the liver slices half-raw. While Achille split the moose skull, removed the eyes and washed the head in the lake, Kuntaw set a flat rock in the fire. When the rock was hot he dropped moose fat on it, then laid the slices of heart in the sizzling grease. Achille half-filled their biggest birch container with water and dropped hot rocks into it. The water boiled and he put the moose head in. It was too large and he had to keep turning it end on end. He kept it boiling for several hours, and while they waited they feasted on the fine-grained heart meat. After many hours of boiling Achille could twist the jawbone loose from the steaming head. While he pulled out the bones Kuntaw and Auguste dug a deep hole and made a strong fire in it. They continued to eat the heart slices and to throw fuel into the roasting pit while Achille gathered the herbs he needed. He scooped out half the coals, wrapped the moose head in cattail leaves, wild onions and other flavorsome greens, put the head in the pit, raked coals on top, covered all with soil.

As they finished two Cree stepped out of the trees. They said they and their families had a fishing camp on the far side of the lake. Achille invited them all to the moose head feast of the next morning.

"I have heard of this food," said one of the Cree, "but never enjoyed the taste."

"In the morning you will have the best food of your lives," said Achille.

The Cree came in the morning with all their bundles and dried salmon trout, for they were moving on that day to another good fishing lake. The group included two passably pretty girls and some small, noisy boys. Achille put the cooked head on a large slab of birch bark and they all leaned forward to appreciate the enticing aroma. Kuntaw and Auguste sat beside the Cree girls, eating. In the following days, as they built their canoes, they fed on moose and more moose until the Cree returned to their fishing camp.

"Moosehead Lake," said Auguste.

Achille, Kuntaw and Auguste, laden with smoked moose meat, went on, hard traveling by labyrinthine waterways interrupted by beaver dams that forced them to portage packs and canoe overland. The birch became scanty, submitting to white spruce. And finally even those trees fell away and they entered the land of little sticks, the meager black spruce and dwarf birch, and beyond them the endless tundra. They saw a vast expanse filled with feathery puffs of arctic cotton grass. Auguste called this Walking-in-White-Things Place. Here, too, was the hairy-stem mastodon flower catching the low sun so that thousands of plants glowed with unearthly light.

The bird millions that had passed through Mi'kma'ki earlier were in this north country, every kind of duck and goose, loons, ptarmigan, ravens, owls and jaegers. Herds of caribou drifted across the tundra. There were broken eggshells and unripe berries without number; sometimes they saw heavy grizzly bears in the distance. The expanse of tundra trembled in the distorting heat waves; in the distance lay great grey rocks, their surfaces brilliant with orange, black, green and ocher lichens. On many days it was breathlessly hot, and the biting flies were a savage danger.

"Truly, Father," said Kuntaw, "this is the country of insatiable biting flies. No one could live here. Only birds."

"We are here. We are alive," said Achille. "But did we not rub ourselves with grease and ashes we would not last long." The ground quivered, dark water welled up around their feet when they stepped on land. Their canoe angled through the twisting waterways and at every turn they saw strange new sights. At last early frosts that turned the willow stems red warned them to turn back. So ended the summer of their great hunting journey, which would last in their memories as long as they lived, but tinctured with irremediable rage and grief.

Achille carried a moose quarter for the feast that would mark their return. As they approached their home place, Achille's *wikuom,* they heard a terrific hubbub of tree chopping and voices calling in a fractured language. And then they walked into two hundred English settlers cutting trees and building log houses where Achille's *wikuom* had stood. They did not speak French. Thirty armed English soldiers stood ready. The remnants of Achille's *wikuom* smoked on the ground.

"Where is my wife? My children?" Achille demanded, his eyes swollen with anger, and the soldiers pointed their guns at him. Six of them rushed forward and seized the moose meat, hitting and kicking. One fired, and the ball gouged a furrow in the side of Achille's head above his ear. More than pain he felt the heat of his own blood streaming down his neck. As he fell he saw on the edge of a debris pile that once had been the furnishings of his *wikuom* a still-shapely hand and blackened forearm, the skin burned away, exposing the heat-spasmed muscles. He knew the hand well, for he had caressed it, many times seen it preparing his food. Isobel. His wife.

Everything in his memory emptied out and refilled with the smell of burned *wikuom* bark, scorched bearskin beds, the caressing hand metamorphosed to charred meat, the corpse-white face of a soldier and his black oily hair, the groan of a falling spruce and English laughter.

Kuntaw seized his arm, pulling with reckless, frightened strength. "Father, get up," he screamed. He, too, had recognized his mother's severed arm and hand. "Run! They will kill us."

Achille knew this was true and he longed for death, but Kuntaw and Auguste dragged him on and, shot whizzing above their crouching runs, they arrived at Elphège's *wikuom.* And so Elphège learned the English had killed Achille's wife and his younger children, their bones incinerated in the burning *wikuom*. When Elphège's wife tried to treat his wound Achille thrust her away; he preferred the wound. Kuntaw wept while Achille went outside and reeled up and down, silent but with hard, lurching footfall. Numb and disconnected, he tried to think of small things such as weather clouds to rid himself of what he had seen. Useless. The scene burned his mind as though he still stood before his ruined life. Everything smashed. He went back inside and sat speechless beside his brother. The day passed and twilight softened the interior of the *wikuom* before Achille spoke, his voice rough in his constricted throat.

"The English have taken my wife, my children," he said. "There are hundreds of them and armed soldiers. It is what Sosep foretold." The brothers sat in silence. Achille shuddered, his heart and entrails knotted with pain, spoke in a trembling unnatural voice.

"This place, Mi'kma'ki, is indeed rich and beautiful, and because of its richness now they will take it, as Sosep told us. I hunt no more. My life here is finished. *I am not.* I leave this land of our mother. I will go south, do lumbering in Maine. I will despoil *their* land."

"They will not notice. They believe despoiling is the correct way."

"You are right, but I will do it anyway."

"Brother," said Elphège, "we may follow you if more English come."

"They will come."

"Father! I am going with you," said Kuntaw passionately. And Auguste, outside the *wikuom,* heard this and called that he, too, would be with them. But several days passed taken up with funerals, mourning and serious talking before Achille left, a great scabby welt above his left ear, the ruined ear, which now heard nothing but a roaring sound. He said Kuntaw and Auguste would stay with Elphège until he sent word for them to come. He must find a safe place first. He had to be alone to bury the memory of what had fallen on him. Elphège would help Kuntaw and Auguste. But no one could help Achille.

30

losing ground

Achille went into the disputed border region between Maine, New Hampshire and New Brunswick. He found Georges Fraude, a middle-aged Frenchman with a great bald dome to the apex of his head from which line of demarcation his hair flared back in thick silver waves.

"I got a woods crew two days south. Pay choppers good wages. I got some Indans—you all go together down to the camp. Right away." He snorted and spat on the ground. "Got to be fast. Everywhere there's falls there's a sawmill nowdays. We'll cut pine all the winter." He spat again and hitched at his drooping trousers. "I want men to work the rafts when the ice goes." Achille signed up.

Men were chopping pine in hundreds of places. The big softwoods fell. New seedlings burst up on cutover ground, but now there was a break in the density of the woodland, and as new trees sprouted, the species succession shifted a little in each cutover tract. The forest began to alter in small ways. It still lived but it was not what it had been. Few noticed. The forest was a grand resource and it was both the enemy and wealth. Achille felt it was the same with the Mi'kmaq; the white settlers used them and took them down.

Four of them walked to the camp, all Mi'kmaq. There was a little snow on the ground. As they walked, the *kookoogwes* called and called—René's name for this little owl had been *chouette*—and the

English bent it into *saw-whet*. The youngest of them, Perrine, was making his first attempt at a paid job. He was not more than eighteen winters, thought Achille. Watching over him was his uncle, Toosh, also from Cape Breton.

They reached Fraude's camp boss, Alois LaGrange, in late afternoon. The man was a block of muscle, with a knife-scarred face and whiskers like pinfeathers. He gave them a sour look, pointed in the direction of the camp.

They found a clearing full of stumps and two rough and windowless hovels built by the loggers; one had a stick chimney in the roof and a fire pit in the single room below. Achille put his head inside the door, but the insufferable whiteman stink made him reel.

"I rather sleep with wolves than whitemen," said Toosh. They would build their own *wikuom* and keep to themselves.

In the greying daylight they quickly cut sapling poles and slabs of spruce bark, made a large but rough A-frame *wikuom* some distance from the reeking hovel of the whitemen. They weighted the slanting sides with poles. It was shelter. In a few weeks it would be half-covered with insulating snow.

When he saw the new lodging Alois LaGrange said, "*Bien!* Less trouble that way, keepin men separate." He was thinking of the inevitable fights and lost days of work. "Got two other Indans, Passamaquoddy, in the crew, better they move in with you." LaGrange said this would keep all the chickens in the same coop, so to speak. Achille nodded. At least the Passamaquoddy were Algonkian relatives of the Mi'kmaq.

There were three groups: Maine men, French-Canadas and Indians. The Maine men, crouched around their indoor fire pit, put their various fixings in one gigantic frying pan and, cursing and blowing on their burned fingers, ate directly out of the hot utensil. The French buried a cast-iron Dutch oven filled with beans in the hot ashes of the central fire pit to cook overnight. When they had pork they added it to the beans. These beans smelled very delicious and when the Maine men could stand it no longer they stole the cast-iron pot, carried it into the woods and ate the contents. The empty Dutch oven was found a mile from the camp, near where they were cutting, and there was a tremendous fight with ax handles, rocks, knives, one man dead and the iron pot recovered by the supperless French. Most of the Maine men left the camp the next day. When a new crew came in from Bangor, they brought a Dutch oven and a bushel of dried beans.

The Indians cooked meat outdoors on the coals on the lee side of their *wikuom,* protected from the wind. They had no iron kettle, but the Passamaquoddy shared two good bark baskets so they could heat water for spruce tea. The Passamaquoddy had a little bag of China tea but the Mi'kmaq preferred spruce tips and black birch bark. During the daylight hours while chopping Achille kept an eye open for game, or even put down his ax for an hour or two and hunted the ridges. When at last he found a bear's den under the snow they spent their free Sunday killing it. The frozen meat lasted a month, and the pelt went on the *wikuom* floor, the best place to sit. None of them had more than a few words of English, but Achille began to learn the tongue-twisting talk.

He had several axes, including an old one that had belonged to René. Hard use had worn away much of the cutting-edge metal and the thick remnant dulled quickly. He wanted an American falling ax with a heavy poll and, if he had enough money, a good goose-wing hewing ax. He planned to buy these when Fraude paid him for the winter's work. He thought of René and his inimitable chopping style. At this moment in among the big pines he missed him and wished they were cutting together again. Every chopper had his own way of doing the work, but René had been notable for quick light strokes with his very sharp ax; he could go on chopping for hours without tiring. As a boy Achille had found it difficult to chop in rhythm with him.

As spring began its slow crawl up from the south, Georges Fraude arrived on a heavily breathing horse one morning and said they had to get the logs into the river immediately. The ice was going, and with one more warm day the snowmelt freshets would pour into the heavier water. But they still had hundreds of logs to drag out of the woods.

"Forget them! Roll what we got in the water." The man's haste seemed desperate and Achille remarked on it to the swamper.

Leon LaFlèche, one of the French choppers, said, "Did you not know that we are in the New England colonies and that we have cut their forbidden mast pines all the winter long?"

"Know nothing that. Thought we was in—what they call it?—Brunsick."

Leon laughed. "That is why Fraude is in a hurry. The owner of this forest tract must be sendin his men to seize the logs and Fraude heard of it. The owners always know where we cuttin and let us do the work. Then they take the logs the last minute before we get them into the river."

Getting the logs in the water was the trick. The river flowed north into New Brunswick, where they would be pulled out by Georges Fraude's sawmill men and metamorphosed from the English king's mast pines into New Brunswick planks. Fraude shouted and ran back and forth, urging the men to roll the logs faster. But before thirty timbers were in the drink a gang of woodsmen and Bangor toughs armed with ax handles and chains burst out of the forest and the fight was on. The militant ox teamster led Fraude's troops in joyous resistance; the Maine men enjoyed fights above all else. They were grossly outnumbered, for the landowner had rounded up scores of men from the saloons with the promise of pay and an exciting fight. Those of Fraude's men who could swim plunged in and made for the far shore.

The logs were captured by the landowner. Fraude paid no one. Most of the Mi'kmaq headed north, but Achille, who had meant to go back to Elphège and fetch Kuntaw and Auguste, could not return empty-handed. He drifted south looking for work.

31

follow me

Elphège, now sixty-six winters, was half-blind but sat outside in fair weather. The smell of autumn, the tick of waxy leaves hitting one another on their descent to earth let him remember the fierce colors. The leaves fell, the first winter winds swept them into hollows, rain and new snow pressed them flat. Then the woods went silent.

Winters he huddled next to the fire, buried in thoughts of colors and fog, of hunts and journeys, of the terrible day six years earlier when scorching tears burned his cheeks as he knelt beside Theotiste's headless corpse. Despite his fifty-nine years Theotiste had become a warrior. In August 1749, when Cornwallis, ignoring Mi'kmaq territorial rights, declared Halifax an English settlement, Theotiste's band attacked some English tree-choppers. He escaped the avenging rangers, but fell the next week to an unknown assassin, his head a prize to a bounty hunter.

Elphège was now composing his death song. Noë's daughter Febe, after the death of her mother, had moved in to care for him. Sometimes they guessed at what might have befallen Achille, the youngest brother, who went to Maine to chop trees years before.

"Kuntaw," said Febe. "Kuntaw will find him," for Kuntaw, after much trouble with his wife, Malaan, left her and their boy, Tonny, and went south to search.

"If he lives," said Elphège. "If he lives. Many evils could befall Kuntaw as he is headstrong."

"Not so headstrong as Auguste." Auguste spent much time with the English; he broke many English laws, drank whiskey, stole, he was imprisoned and beaten but remained defiant. The English called him a bad Indian and he took pleasure in the epithet.

"One day they will kill you," warned Elphège.

"No. I kill them," said Auguste. It was true that occasionally some villager was found drowned in the lake behind the town, or washed up on the shore, the white puckered body lacerated with knife wounds. Children had wandered into the forest and never emerged, their bones found years later with great crunched holes in the skulls. No one knew how these things had happened but Elphège had thoughts he did not wish to explore.

It was amusing to Elphège that with age he was presumed to be a wise man, even a *sagmaw*. Many people came to him to ask what they should do when an English housewife threw scalding water on a Mi'kmaw child begging food, or when another asked for magic help. It was a punishment to see his people half starved, skulking around the English and asking for employment or food. There were not many Mi'kmaw people left in the world, and each of them seemed plagued by sickness, hunger and sadness. They died easily, for they wished to die.

Years went by and Achille did not go north to his people. He kept to himself. He had the reputation of a skilled axman. The camp toughs stayed away from him. He fought with intensity and cold malice, and a man who had come up behind him in the woods and tried to club him at the base of the neck was spouting blood from the stump of his forearm—his severed hand hit the ground before he could strike. Another who crept up in the night with a firebrand to burn Achille's *wikuom* was himself roasted though no one knew quite how it had happened. The man's charred body was dumped in front of the shanty. Newcomers to the logging camp were warned to stay shy of the killer Indian, the reincarnation of the bloodthirsty savages who had massacred settlers in earlier times.

Kuntaw heard some of these stories as he made his way from camp to camp after leaving Malaan and Tonny in Mi'kma'ki. He hired on as a swamper for Duquet et Fils. It was becoming difficult to find good chances of pine on fair-size streams, so the swampers worked summers, constructing dams on the smallest rills. And the forest was dangerous; the fighting, ambushes and skirmishes continued. Men were in a killing mood.

There were more Indians in the Maine camps, and occasionally he heard some news of one named Sheely. He thought it might be Achille. This Sheely was a very good hunter, a good axman. All Kuntaw could find out was that Sheely was working in York state, cutting pine on the Raquette River. He made up his mind to go there in spring. It would take two weeks of walking, he thought. Maybe he would join Achille's crew. How surprised his father would be. Maybe they would go to Mi'kma'ki together after they drove the logs down to Montreal. He would have his wages and they could arrange passage in a trade canoe until the river forced them to walk.

The spring of 1758 came on uncommonly fast; one day the shrinking snow was frozen and he could make good time, the next it was mush and mud. The forest gurgled and slopped. It was slow going and when he reached the river Frenchmen rolling logs into the black water said Sheely had gone with the first logs.

"Hey, Indan, you look him Montreal," they said. "Maybe Nouveau Brunswick. Maybe Terre-Neuve. Maybe *l'enfer*." Suddenly the long chase seemed foolish. He turned back and headed for Maine. There was still time to hire on a spring drive. It wasn't meant for him to find Achille.

A month later he was on the west shore of Penobscot Bay in Catawamkeag, where crews were loading timber onto ships for export. There were several shipyards and a straggle of whiteman houses, one great log house and a tiny settlement of the few surviving Penobscots. He walked along the street fronting the bay following five or six other lumberjacks headed for the loggers' bar where most of the rivermen would drink, wake up the next day penniless and amnesiac.

Kuntaw felt very well. He was strong, his muscular body hard. He was relieved to have given up the search for Achille. Maybe someday they would find each other, but now he would enjoy being alive and vigorous. He strode along, his eyes flashing left and right as he took in the sights. After six months in the woods even the poor settlement of Catawamkeag looked like a city.

"You!" called a strident voice in English. "You there, you Indian!"

He turned and looked behind him. There was a young woman on a brown horse and she was pointing at him. He guessed correctly that she had only eighteen winters, a double-handful less than he.

"Come here." Her voice was firm.

He hesitated, then shrugged and walked toward the horse. It was a valuable horse, nothing like the big scarred beasts that drew logs to the landings. He stood a few yards back from the horse and looked at the girl. She was elegant, wearing a black cloak edged in red. Something about her dark-ivory face said she was part Indian.

"You like to make some money?" she asked, moving close. She lifted her head and inhaled his odor of smoke, meat and pine pitch.

He shrugged. "What do?"

"Split wood, of course." She enunciated very carefully. "You carry an ax. Do you not know how to split firewood?"

He nodded. "I know."

"I need you, Indian man. Follow." Beatrix Duquet turned her horse and trotted gracefully toward the big house; he had to run to keep up with her. Watching her long crinkled hair sway, the bright heels of her boots, he felt a wave of enchantment strike him like warm rain. So, in his thirtieth spring, began the strangest part of his life as he seemed to stumble out of the knotted forest and onto a shining path.

Were not René Sel's children and grandchildren as he had been, like leaves that fall on moving water, to be carried where the stream takes them?

IV

the severed snake

1756–1766

32

a funeral

On the day of old Forgeron's funeral, unusually warm for mid-November Boston, the sky was covered with mild cloud. A dozen elderly men sat in the front pews to remember the surveyor who had made them fortunes with timberland. At last the three Duke brothers, Jan, Nicolaus and Bernard, aided by the company bookkeeper, Henk Steen, carried the clear-pine casket, lacquered and rubbed to a glass-like glare, an elegant burial case for a man who had spent almost forty years taking the measure of *Pinus strobus.* Jan silently willed Bernard not to stumble, not to fall. Outger, the youngest brother, should have been there but he refused to leave the house on Penobscot Bay, refused to give up the great table, a single board from the largest pine Duquet had ever cut. This icon belonged in the company's Boston council room.

"I need it for my work," Outger had said with passion.

"What sort of work would that be?" Bernard had asked of the ceiling; he thought Outger an imbecile. It was said that Indians visited him often. He could not be depended on for anything except to receive his annual stipend. Still, he should have been there.

The sermon had gone on for two hours, but at the graveside things began to move briskly. A rising wind wrinkled the milky sky. Nicolaus shifted from foot to foot, his boots gleaming like oiled hooves. All warmth leaked from the day as the wind hauled to the north. The brothers looked knowingly at each other. It was the Forgeron weather curse. The sudden chill urged the minister on. They lowered the coffin into the dark hole, and at last came the words "rest in peace."

The brothers and the skeleton-thin Henk Steen, one of the many Dutch orphan protégés who came to Duke & Sons as apprentices over the years, walked away from the graveside. In a body the fittest mourners walked to Nicolaus Duke's house, treading in the center of the street, where it was smoothest.

"Do come along, Henk," Nicolaus said to the bookkeeper, who hovered at the edge of the crowd. "Join us in farewell to the old fellow." Nicolaus was the best diplomat among the brothers and had learned the art of persuasion from his grandfather Piet Roos, with whom he had made voyages to China and Japan. Now his dark hair, when not covered with a wig, was ragged grey. His face and neck had swollen with fat though he still moved easily, unlike Jan and Bernard.

Deceived by the mild forenoon, none of them was warmly dressed. They hurried on past a wooded lot, a large garden stiffened by the last week's frosts, until they saw the candlelight glowing enticingly in Nicolaus's front windows. Through the wavery glass they could see his wife, Mercy; Bernard's wife, Birgit; and the Panis slave girls passing to and fro with tureens and pitchers, for Bernard had brought Panis—Pawnee—Indian slaves down from Ville-Marie.

The door to the best parlor stood invitingly open with Mercy welcoming them. In the center of the room a long table covered with a fine turkey carpet presented the collation of covered dishes, an array of silver and twist-stem glasses. Some fragrant wood burned in the fireplace; Steen thought it might be a few pieces of sandalwood to perfume the room, a scrap of Charles Duquet's oriental plunder. Beeswax candles in brass sconces lit the room, their trembling light reflected in a large pier-glass mirror. Henk Steen gaped at the dozen black walnut chairs with cushions—so many, so rich.

"Please enter, dear guests, come in," said Mercy, guiding them into the warmth. She wore a loose grey silk *saque* pleated at the shoulders over a scarlet bodice and underskirt, her wig low and neat. She often suffered from crushing headaches that sent her to a quiet room and she now silently prayed to get through the evening without an attack. Their children, Patience, Piet and Sedley, lived nearby, the two sons well settled into the family lumber business. Patience had married a boatbuilder, Jeremiah Deckbolt.

Henk Steen hung back in the entryway staring at the luxuries and rich clothing of the guests. He felt out of place, and longed for his cold little room, but Nicolaus urged him to take a tankard of steaming cider laced with rum. Mercy led him to the cold sliced meats and Birgit's famous horseradish sauce, so stinging, she said, it would make the devil gasp. "Hardly an inducement to try it," Steen muttered to himself and his hand veered away. He took a small marzipan cake. The fireplace crackled and spoke to itself. Yes, thought Steen, Nicolaus Duke lived very well. And why not, with Duke & Sons' swelling sales to the timber traders whose millmen converted logs into planks, barrel staves and clapboards, hogshead staves, shingles, masts, spars and bowsprits, dike timbers. All the Duke brothers lived gallant lives, except perhaps the strange one, Outger, who kept to the disappeared father's house in Penobscot Bay and whom Steen had never seen and imagined as a crabbed hermit clutching a blackthorn stick. The marzipan cake surged in his gut and he thought he might have to rush outside.

Mercy glanced over the room to see if everyone had a cup of comfort, a chair, someone with whom to converse. In truth she wished the company were different. These old men with their timber holdings! She wished very much to entertain (and be entertained by) the wealthy Boston families connected with commercial shipping, quite different from the fishing boat owners who had thought themselves the crème de la crème in her parents' day. The merchant shipping families had replaced them and built magnificent houses. She and Jan's wife, Sarah, gossiped enviously of their social doings. But never had any member of the Duke families been invited to their collations or soirees. Mercy told Nicolaus that she longed to give a grand party and invite these worthies, but Nicolaus said, "My dear, better not. You do not wish us to be regarded as jump-ups"—that most odious word.

Bernard and his lanky Danish or Norwegian wife, Birgit, stood in a corner talking with Joab Hitchbone, who was even older than old Forgeron. Birgit spoke in her odd accent, smiling and nodding.

What a jolt they all had felt when Bernard returned with Birgit from one of the Baltic or Scandinavian countries, precisely which one was never clear. She once told Mercy she had been born near the great *Kongeegen* tree in Denmark. It was a shock, for Bernard had been a remarkably attractive youth with wavy hair and cobalt-blue eyes. His habitual expression indicated he was about to smile and a mole on his left cheek encouraged that impression. Cornelia, his adoptive mother, had imagined that he was the by-blow of some French aristocrat and a pretty seamstress. He was still handsome though the dark hair had disappeared and the fine jawline had been replaced with a jowl; he limped. No one understood what had drawn him to Birgit. But their marriage, though childless, had lasted nearly thirty years. Birgit kept an orderly house and a rich table. She spent much time in the kitchen, not content to leave cookery to the slaves. Despite hoopskirts she preferred to mix and singe and roast herself. Her flummeries were renowned.

Sarah, the only daughter of the wealthy molasses and sugar importer James Pickering, had been a beauty with dark oiled hair and melting hazel eyes. She rejected hoops in favor of stiff petticoats that swelled out her skirts at the ankle, showing pink silk stockings, an unseemly mode for a woman in her fifties. Their oldest son, George Pickering Duke, had recently returned from reading law at the Inns of Court in London. For years he had struggled against being pushed into this profession, saying he wished to go to sea, not as an officer but as a common sailor, to visit other lands.

"George," said Jan, "it is necessary to the business to have a trained legal mind among us. You will have a good income and in later years you can see the world in a more comfortable manner than you would before the mast. Only ask Bernard what that life is like."

He had, in fact, talked with Uncle Bernard, who froze his bone marrow with stories of typhoons, men overboard, the paralyzing Doldrums, the boredom, the eternal work, the noisome ports, the capricious cruelty of captains. George Pickering Duke was dissuaded and took his adventure in books.

Bernard spoke to Joab Hitchbone, young Piet standing with them. "Old Forgeron would have taken joy in knowing the day started with good weather." Hitchbone sucked at his cup of syllabub. "And how goes your pitch production? Do you still travel down to the pine-woods in the Carolinas?"

Bernard made a wry face. "Oh no. I have ever preferred the Québec end of the business. We still operate logging enterprises in the north. As for Carolina, young Piet here"—Bernard touched his nephew's shoulder—"took on that responsibility. He works two hundred black slaves and our pitch and tar are best quality. We've done well despite England's punitive laws."

"I return to the plantation in several days' time," said young Piet. The older men ignored him.

"Forgeron," said old Hitchbone, "a good man, but you know— he had some strange ideas. His outlook remained both French and English, surely an uncomfortable mixture."

Bernard's eyebrows rose. "Perhaps you do not know that Forgeron was born in Ostende, not France. He encouraged our father to deal with the Low Countries. Father always said that Hollanders had an innate sense of landforms. That was a talent, he said, that made good timberland lookers such as Forgeron."

But old Hitchbone went on. "He deplored wholesale cutting, those who felled trees but took only the trunks and burned the rest. He had a frugal mind."

"Oh, he was ever a leading spirit in controversies," Bernard said. "I well remember his sentiments. He believed that men, when confronted with a vast plenitude of anything, feel an irresistible urge to take it all, then to smash and destroy what they cannot use."

Old Hitchbone peered at him. "Hah! As we might descend on our host's table, gobble the dainties, then shiver the cups and plates on the hearth?"

"Few of us feel that urge, I trust," said Bernard.

"I meant it as an example of Forgeron's thinking. Better you remember your Bible: 'And God said replenish the earth, and subdue it, and have dominion over the fish of the sea and every living thing that moveth, and every green tree and herb.' Of course, here in New England there is such bounty of every wild resource that there is no limit to the assets, whether fish or furs or land or forests."

Bernard did not correct Hitchbone's misquotes; the old man was known for twisting scripture to suit his intent.

"Then perhaps, with all this bounty, you will explain the shortage of firewood in Boston and its ever-rising price? A good thing for Duke and Sons, but driving some inhabitants away from the city."

Old Hitchbone refused to be drawn; he examined the low level of syllabub in his cup. "The Indans. That is our problem. The Indans do not use land correctly because of their raw roaming and hunting. As the Bible tells us, it is a duty to *use* land. And there is so much here that one can do what one wishes and then move on. You cannot make the Indans understand that the correct use is to clear, till, plant and harvest, to raise domestic stock, to mine or make timber. In a nutshell, they are uncivilized. And un-Christian."

Bernard dipped his head, not wishing a quarrel, but thought to himself that King Philip's War had not come about through some vague whim of the Indians. They had fought like rabid dogs to keep their lands and they had lost. Why was hunting and plucking berries not considered as use of the land? But he kept this question to himself. "Well, sir, although Forgeron scalped Indians for the bounty, he also had Indian friends. And he once or twice remarked that the reason New France did not prosper was because of the fur trade, which pulled all the able men away from the settlements and thereby cost a great deal in enterprise and development."

"There may be something in that," said old Hitchbone. "But I might advance popishness being their great pitfall. And their low population for all that they breed like mice."

Bernard ignored this and went on. "He was ever a man of contradictions. He urged Duquet et Fils to keep a hand in the fur trade—which we have done in a small way. He thought that if a certain military triumph occurred, trade could revive."

"They say the Ohio valley is stuffed with beavers. If the English are successful in seizing New France—the inevitable triumph you avoid naming—that trade might become lucrative once more."

"Yes, Forgeron said much on various points which did not always make him agreeable company. One felt extremely nervous near him, not only because he attracted lightning and high winds. And yet he himself did more to drive down the forest and the Indans than anyone else."

"And so in him we see the double nature of man quite revealed."

"He profited in many ways," said Hitchbone, who had himself profited in those ways.

"I only saw our father angry with him one time. They were speaking of the Wentworths and Forgeron had the temerity to tell Father that he—Father—could never hope to become one of the merchant aristocracy. That the Wentworths had connections with the English peerage and knew well how to move in those exalted circles. By my God, Father flew into a fury."

Hitchbone smiled, returned to the Wentworths. "I remember what your father used to say about old Wentworth. 'His foot shall slide in due time.' Deuteronomy."

Bernard laughed. "It ain't yet slid. A wily and unscrupulous man."

"Forgeron amassed considerable wealth, but I was always surprised that he lived as a wild Indan on game and maize. His was a lonely life." He lowered his voice. "I wonder who will inherit his properties."

Bernard's eyebrows rose. He ignored the question. No doubt everyone in the room was squirming with curiosity to know Forgeron's bequests, not the usual tiresome accounts of linens, laying hens and chairs, but his timberland holdings. "Perhaps not so lonely. I have heard he had a dozen Indian consorts. May I fetch you another dollop of syllabub?"

"My dears," said Birgit, striding up to them, "the syllabub is quite finished. Do try the maple cream cakes. Piet, dear boy, come with me instead of standing here like a fence listening to these old fogies mumble. There is a gentleman I think you would like to know." Joab Hitchbone thought once more that she had an especially sweet and gentle voice, the voice of an innocent girl, not the tough old matron she looked.

While the Indian slaves cleared the table the women followed Mercy into the second parlor, where there were turkey-work chairs with the look of wooden animals, four or five small tables scattered among them like waterholes. The women sat in front of the fire sipping China tea and laughing over rumors that the pope worshiper Duc de Richelieu had invited dinner guests to dine in the nude. "And," said Birgit, "we have heard that after his spring 'success'—if we may call it that—over the English at Port Mahon, his chef invented a sumptuous dressing of olive oil and egg yolk. The duke called it '*mahonnaise.*'" They made some wordplay over the juxtaposition of nude diners and dressed viands.

"The table looked brilliantly handsome tonight, dear Mercy," said Birgit.

"Oh, pshaw! Nothing compared to your exquisite collations— those blue dishes with gold rims."

"You really are too kind, my dear. But, you know, four of them slid to a smash in that untoward earthquake a year past. We nearly fell out of the bed. I told Bernard that if this is one of the delights of New England I would prefer Chimborazo. I still do not understand how, if the tremor was located at Cape Ann as they say, it damaged so much in Boston."

Mercy sighed and said, "I expect there will be more such grief in our days as human depravity continues to irk the Omnipotent."

The evening wore on, Mercy several times raising her hand to her temple and sighing. At last she admitted what they all knew.

"My dear guests, what I dreaded has come to pass." She called the slave girl to bring cold water and her headache powder.

"I must retire," she said and went to a back room scented with orris root and reserved for headache recovery, murmuring general farewells.

"Poor Mercy," said Sarah. "Those headaches are truly her cross. A pity after such an evening."

"Yes, but a great deal of work. Mother is not really strong enough for this," Patience said and waved her hand at the room and all that was in it.

The guests, taking the hostess's retreat as a signal, began to leave by ones and twos. Nicolaus pressed their hands, made apologies for Mercy and begged them to come again soon on a happier occasion. Henk Steen the bookkeeper bowed, bowed and grinned as he backed toward the door. Nicolaus half-expected him to tug his forelock.

"Peace be with you and your syllabub," murmured Joab Hitchbone, doddering down the steps.

33

an interesting case

Then the outsiders were gone except for Jan's hollow-chested father-in-law, James Pickering, once a notorious molasses smuggler, and the judge, Louis Bluzzard. The judge's trousers were too thin and emphasized the manly bulge, the more disturbing as he was elderly.

"Judge, do show my brothers that paper," said Jan, his long fingers tapping the side of his rum glass. Jan was the one who clinched deals with merchants and arranged contracts; he worked out complex shipping arrangements. He had the duty of smoothing the ruffled feelings of men who were aggrieved by Duke & Sons' business proceedings, in part because he had the dispassionate nature of one who cares for nothing, too often mistaken for neutrality. In his private mind he wished the ax for all royalists.

The judge passed around a rather grubby newspaper, the *Pennsylvania Gazette*. The page showed an illustration of a snake cut into many parts, each segment with the label of one of the colonies and the motto below, JOIN OR DIE.

"There are so many papers these days," George said, rolling his eyes.

"Ha!" said Nicolaus. "That's that fellow Franklin. I knew his brother James. A family distinguished for their seditious bosoms. Ben is back here or in Connecticut now and I can tell you that this joined colonial snake he calls for can never happen. There are too many here who are English to the bone, for all they were born here.

216

And the tobacco colonies are markedly different from the fish and forest colonies." For decades Duke & Sons had managed a precarious balance between their French allegiances and the new ambitious generation of American-born men. A separation of opinions was beginning to surface.

Young Piet ventured a comment. "The forest legislation the Crown has imposed on us has driven a wedge between colonists and England, has it not?" The older men ignored his dim-witted observation.

James Pickering, showing a violet silk waistcoat, spoke. "Let me remind you, dear friends, that this city harbored two of the regicide judges a century back. There are loyalists sprinkled about but the colonial heart desires independence and cherishes a distaste for kings and their men. It is nothing new. And is not forest legislation despised by all American businessmen?" He turned and spat gracefully into the fire.

Jan said, "The tangled situation grows more tangled every day. Louis, tell them what you told me."

"Ah. That. I ventured to say that England's plans of attack increase the danger to your forest property in Québec. When they take Québec they will take your woodlands." The judge flicked a glance at Bernard. He considered him a little too fond of French Canada.

"Perhaps," said Bernard, "but remember that New France has a strong militia. The regional troops are excellent and we have good aid from our Indians. Governor-General Pierre de Rigaud de Vaudreuil, I think, is intelligent and knows the country. I have heard that this Montcalm prefers to fight in European style, sieges and rigid opposing lines—Braddock's great fault. But in New France we have developed the stealthy woodcraft style of the Indians."

"That is the situation here as well," said the judge, sneering a little. "Your French half-breeds are hardly singular in their fighting abilities. But beware—there are many houses in Boston where your opinions would sound as treason."

Bernard ignored this dart. "I have heard also that Montcalm and Vaudreuil loath each other and show it openly." He sighed. "When the French defeated and killed Braddock I thought that would be the end of it."

The judge shook his head and gave a hard barking laugh. He stared at Bernard. "I think not. I thoroughly believe England will seize New France using colonial troops however long it takes. The battle on Lake George last September shows their perseverance." His tone was combative.

Jan thought it time to raise the question. He looked at his son. "George, after your study of the law, what is your opinion on this difficult matter? Where should Duke and Sons bestow its allegiance? France or England?"

"Would it were that simple," muttered Bernard.

"In our law readings this particular situation never arose, but there were several of us from the colonies who discussed it privately among ourselves." George puffed himself up a little.

"And what did you think?" Bernard suspected that there in the heart of London studying English law, George would have been and probably still was an advocate for eternal obeisance to England.

"We thought that in terms of law and jurisdictions the colonies were drawing ever more distant from England. The veer became sharply evident in 1686, when the British government, concerned that we were growing too independent and too wealthy on our own abilities, sent Governor Andros to us and revoked our colonial charter." Well, thought Bernard, so much for obeisance.

Nicolaus said, "After two generations of colonial self-government this was a gross error on their part. Nor did getting rid of Andros repair the situation."

George boldly put in his oar. "And what do we have today! Englishmen in positions of power who make the decisions that affect us, who rarely know anything of the colonies, have no real experience here nor do they wish to have. They put forth their ukases and rules based on ignorance and self-interest. What matters to them is how much they can squeeze from the colony into their personal strongboxes."

"It seems not so different in the example of France and New France," said Bernard, rather surprised at lethargic George's impassioned tone. "It may be the misfortune of all colonies."

"If the rancorous discontent continues—well, I can point out a legal example that is particularly telling for Duke and Sons as it concerned cutting the forest." George felt his importance.

"I wonder if I know your reference," said Nicolaus, squinting his eyes. "Do you mean the Dregg case of about ten years ago?"

"No, I had in mind the Frost case—somewhat earlier than Dregg. In our private discussions we student colonials thought it an important case. It came up only once with the faculty. A lawyer at Inns of Court saw it as evidence of the sly and impudent colonial character."

Bernard looked at young George. "Will you relieve us of our ignorance? What was this 'case'?"

"On the face of it, Uncle Bernard, it could have been construed as yet another example of the common tendency of Massachusetts court judgments in favor of colonial lumber millmen accused of trespassing on private land and cutting what they found there."

"Yes," said Nicolaus. "Those liberal courts were one of the attractions of the region for our father. And we have endured Surveyors General of His Majesty's Woods, those damnable wretches, for more than sixty-five years. It is right that they suffer in the courts." He gave a small whinny.

"And how does this dispute you mention differ?"

George looked at Judge Bluzzard.

The judge refilled his glass of rum. "It started, as many of our problems do, in London—think of the massive land grants to Mason and Gorges." He swallowed.

"To the point, in 1730 the Crown granted a five-year mast procurement license to Ralph Gulston, a Turkey merchant, one of those swarthy fellows who trade with the Levant. The license allowed him to enter any Maine lands belonging to the Crown in 1691—*id est,* public land—and cut mast pines for the Royal Navy." He nodded at George.

George set out the case of trespass, which hinged on the date of 1691, when the land in question belonged to the Crown. "After some delay, Gulston hired a colonial logger, William Leighton, to cut the pines for him. And through the winter of 1733–34 Leighton cut them and dragged them out. No one objected. However, in the passage of years since 1691, title to the land had passed to an American, John Frost, of Berwick, Maine. The Royal Surveyor General chose to ignore Frost's title. When spring came in 1734, John Frost, waving his legal title, sued Leighton for trespass."

"I think I know how this must end," said Bernard. "But continue."

"Yes. The court—no surprise—found for Frost."

"By God, I now recall the hubbub," said Jan. "Leighton stupidly paid the judgment, did he not?"

"He did," said George, "but—" He extended his hand as though announcing the kingpin fact on which all turned. "On the other side of the ocean when Gulston heard, he began to turn his monstrous wheels. He had the King's ear. In due time a royal order arrived in Boston."

Judge Bluzzard, smiling like a wolf, took up the tale.

"It was not until June of 1738 that the hearing on the motion came before the court. Everyone was astonished when the court declared it had no authority to execute that royal order. The court's attitude was that its authority was to set out laws and hold courts for events that occurred *only within the province.* They claimed they had no power to enforce what they referred to as 'a foreign judgment.' It was the same as if they had declared an intention to disobey that royal order. Do you see? It was the same as if they had said, 'The King is a foreigner and he is nothing to do with us.' It was a triumph for the independent American spirit."

"Sir!" cried Jan, as if to warn of agents who might have heard this traitorous remark.

Bernard closed the discussion by bringing them back to the simpler question of how they should choose sides—England or France. "We may ask ourselves what Father would do."

"Hardly difficult. He threw in his lot with the English when he left New France."

"Father did not reckon on the growing discontent of the colonies with each other *and* with England as Franklin's severed snake shows. Today our situation is rather different."

"I agree," said Jan. "There is increasing murmuration that the colonies should join together and flout England. We already do so flout when it comes to timber and shipbuilding, to smuggling and molasses. The constant promulgation of punitive acts and taxes do threaten our region's livelihood. If we were not the creature of England we would thrive greatly."

Bernard smiled. "As businessmen must we not maintain cordial relations with all parties? The French, the English and the colonials both south and north—and the Wentworths?"

"Yea," said Jan. "We must remain cordial with all factions, including the English, and often test the direction of the wind. And stay aware of new Acts. The Crown seems as determined to shackle us as we are to evade the bonds."

"Hear, hear," said Pickering. The rum bottle made its rounds.

Bernard came up to them holding his wife's blue woolen cloak. "It is time," he said gently, and they slid out the door.

Young Piet was wrapping up in his own cloak when his cousin George came over to him. He spoke sotto voce. "Cousin, shall we meet again? I must leave for Carolina in three days' time. I wish us to be friends as one day we will work together for the company. I feel we—and Sedley—represent the young blood of the family. Do you know the Wolf's Den tavern?" George was twenty-six and Piet a year younger.

"Well enough. Do you prefer it to the Bear Tavern or the Turkie Cock?"

"I do—quiet and less chance of a drunken hubbub. Let us meet there tomorrow evening." They touched hands and young Piet went out into the fresh night with its sweet odor of woodsmoke and the not-distant evergreen forest.

34

the thing in the trunk

The Wolf's Den was a quiet and pleasant tavern with half a dozen small tables, and a commodious fireplace at one end of the room. The place was empty except for the pockmarked innkeeper, busy decanting a keg into bottles. The two cousins went to the smallest table near the fireplace. Both ordered hot peppered rum, for it was a cold and windless night that promised a hard frost. Piet stretched out his hands to the dying fire.

"I relish a good fire. In Europe and England I am always cold with their stingy little twig arrangements in fireplaces the size of soup bowls. Only here do we drive the cold away with a proper blaze. This one needs replenishing."

The innkeeper, overhearing, said, "We were to lay a new back log this morning, but one of the men was detained. He is here now." He held up a finger indicating a short wait. Within minutes four men, one of them a colossus crowned with dirty white hair, all redolent of fresh air and tree bark, came into the room. The innkeeper came to their table. "You gentlemen may wish to move to a more distant table to avoid the commotion. Robert Kemball, who is necessary to the task, has only now arrived." That would be the big man, thought Piet.

The door opened and through it came a bolt of cold air and the men lurching under the weight of a monstrous green beech log eight feet long and two feet in diameter. They got it into the great fireplace with grunts and swaying and shoving, with remarks on its hundredweights. The innkeeper rushed forward with an iron bar to lever the great log to the back. Then came a hemlock forestick of considerable dimension, and the innkeeper heaped ashes onto the fresh wood to slow combustion. A boy brought in a basket of pitch pine splinters and in a minute or two a young blaze filled the room with heat and dancing light. The innkeeper gave each of the men a glass of rum and a coin, slapped Robert Kemball on a shoulder like an ox rump. He looked at Piet and George, asking if they would return to their original table with a questioning gesture of his arm. But now the fire was too hot to sit near and they stayed where they were.

"Ah," said George Pickering Duke, swigging his toddy and patting his red lips. Piet, as angular as tree branches, nodded and smiled. They were quiet for a long time, enjoying the fire's warmth and the hot spirit.

"I wonder we have not met like this before," said George, who saw his cousins rarely. "Neither you nor Sedley. But one day, not too distant, you and I will make the decisions for the company of what should be done and what not done."

"Yes. We should meet more often. Of course, you are sometimes in Carolina."

"Unfortunately. But I do find reasons to return to Boston." They sat in comfortable silence. George cleared his throat. "I assume, following last night's discussion, that you would side with the colonists rather than England or France."

"Yes, I would. And I think Uncle Bernard would support New France rather than France itself. Although he has lived in Boston so long he may be on the side of the colonies."

"So much of the news we get is conjecture."

"Indeed. And much is, I suspect, deliberately misleading."

George stretched out his legs and broke into their meditations. "Dear cousin, I have a somewhat private question for you."

"Ah?"

"Have you ever clapped eyes on our uncle Outger?"

"Yes. But only once. The same day that you saw him."

"I? I have never seen him. He is a mysterious and unknown figure to me."

"No, no. You saw him. Surely you remember that day when we gave the birds great happiness? It was springtime and we must have been seven or eight years old. Not older."

"That occasion of the birds' rejoicing is fixed forever in my memory. But what of Uncle Outger?"

"Do you not remember a thin little man with wild eyes spreading bedsheets over a table and telling us to get away from him?"

"I do. I remember his violent expostulations and the way he swung the sheets around as though he were raising sails. Surely that wasn't—"

"That was Uncle Outger. He is said to have many connections abroad, men of science to whom he writes and sends specimens of plants and weeds."

"That mad old——? That man is our famous uncle Outger? He sends weeds to men of science?"

"Indeed. To them the weeds of New England are novel."

"So that was Uncle Outger. I am horrified." He called for two more hot rum flips. "My truest memory is of the birds and what we found in that old trunk."

The innkeeper brought the hot drinks, the cousins held up their glasses and remembered.

Their parents had been closeted with the mad uncle in what they called the "old assembly room." The boys had explored the house, crept up the creaking narrow stairs to an attic. A small and filthy window let in the only light. There was a desiccated owl carcass in one corner, which gave them a pleasant frisson. A leathern trunk stood against a low wall and they were drawn to it, worked at the rusty hasp, trying to guess what might be inside, then leapt back as the lid flew up with a crash and showered them with dust and owl feathers. They waited. George then walked boldly up to the trunk and looked inside. With a scream he bolted for the stairs crying, "It's alive!" Young Piet galloped beside him. "What? What was it? A wolf?"

"Maybe a wolf! Maybe a Indan! It was a horrible hairy thing. It looked at me. It moved!"

It took long minutes for them to creep up the stairs again. All was quiet. The trunk stood open, the owl lay in its corner.

They approached the trunk, looked inside. The thing, all twists and tangles, did not move very much, but it gave off a sense of suppressed liveliness. Piet reached inside very slowly and touched it, then sprang back.

"Very hairy," he said. "Nasty."

It was George's turn to touch it. He did so and even, to show his boldness, closed his fingers on the mass for a few seconds before backing away. In truth they both knew what it was but it served their mood to pretend it was an incarnation of evil. Piet wrenched at the begrimed attic window and raised it to admit light.

At last they lifted the mass and for the first time in more than thirty years Duquet's wig resurfaced. They hauled it around the attic, draped it like a shroud over the owl, tried to throw it at each other though it was heavy. At last George dragged it over to the window and stuffed it through the opening. It fell on the ground below with the whoosh of a gassy cow.

"George Pickering! Young Piet!" called Patience from below. "What antic gambols are you practicing up there? You are making more noise than the militia. Go out into the garden at once."

In the fresh air their prize looked less interesting. Piet got a strip of leather from the stable and tied it onto the wig. They ran with it, the hairy mass bounding and gathering twigs. When Piet's mother Mercy called them to come and have a dish of apple slump, they left it in the brambles. Later the adults returned to the assembly room, ever talking, and the cousins drifted outside once more. A marvelous sight! Birds were wrenching hairs from the wig.

"They're building their nests with it," said Piet. "They are very well pleased," said George. They watched for a long time and even as their carriage drove away in late afternoon they saw birds flying in the direction of the garden. In this adventure a childhood friendship formed.

• • •

"Yes," said George, who knew nothing of his grandfather Charles Duquet, "it was the memorable day of mad Uncle Outger's wig. Had he seen us he would have become madder."

Young Piet got up and unnecessarily prodded the fire, driven by masculine instinct. Fresh sparks roared up the chimney and heat pulsed out.

"That's the way," said George as the warmth licked his face. "And what of your brother, Sedley? He was not at the funeral or the gathering."

"No, Eugenia is near her time and Dr. Perry advised complete bedrest. Sedley felt he should stay with her as she is very delicate— and may not survive."

Into George's mind leapt a cruel sentence he had read somewhere in his London days, the comment about colonial American women by a Mr. Ward: "the Women, like Early Fruit, are soon ripe and soon Rotten."

Piet talked on. "Moreover, Sedley always disliked old Forgeron so Father excused him." He sat down again and looked into his toddy mug; still plenty in it. "Do you ever return to London since your studies?"

"No. Though I very much like voyages. You know, I wanted to follow the sea but Father insisted I read law. Our fathers seem to think only on business. Business and business again." Everyone in the family knew of George's fondness for sea adventure tales, stories of shipwreck and castaways, ships that disintegrated in violent storms, wild men with spears on remote islands who captured sailors and ate them raw, rogue waves that swallowed entire fleets. When the London bookseller sent a copy of Defoe's *The Life and Strange Surprizing Adventures of Robinson Crusoe,* George was enamored for weeks and read the book over and over.

"I am glad to hear you like voyages, as we may be making one. Father recently had a letter from Uncle Outger, that uncle you have utterly forgotten. He plans a trip to Amsterdam next year to see his aged mother and sister, Doortje. Father says we must all go as Grandmother Cornelia is very old and infirm. And we cousins have never seen Auntie Doortje."

They talked for a while about the ongoing wars, Major Rogers and his bands of ruffians, putting off the moment of going out into the night. But it was late. Piet looked at the handsome watch pinned to his waistcoat. "I dream that the colonies will unite. At the moment there is jealousy and business competition among them. For Duke and Sons there is much that should be changed, beginning with certain difficulties in North Carolina. I hope we may meet and work out ways to improve the company's income when you and I and Sedley are in a position to do so."

"And improve the Duke social standing. At present, ignored as we are, it is damned difficult to meet girls of interest and with good connections." Piet got up, paid the innkeeper, put on his heavy cloak and moved toward the door. "Are you coming?" he said to George.

"Yes, as far as the church. The fresh air will do us good and dissipate the fumes of rum."

They stepped out of the Wolf's Den into a blaze of stars so flagrant and shuddering the sky seemed to emit sounds like plucked wires.

"Cold!" said Piet.

"Very cold," said George. "Very, very cold." They breathed the tingling piney air. Yet there was the sense of an implacable, even malevolent, force bending the meteorite-streaked night.

35

Etdidu

Bernard Duke, fifty-five, had two great problems. His mind gnawed at them constantly. The first worry was his successor. There was no one in the family who could take on the crucial land-looker's job of assessing the valuable timber on Duke & Sons' vast acreages after he was gone. He himself had learned from Charles Duquet before the man's unexplained disappearance, then from old Forgeron, but among the nephews he had found no one remotely interested in judging trees, estimating cubic volumes and board feet.

Nicolaus's son Sedley had come out with him several times. But even explaining the difference between linear and piece measurements made Sedley's eyes glaze, and working out the cubic volume of a tapering eighty-foot log was beyond him. When they were moving through an area of standing timber, Bernard making notes and calculations and then, moving to another plot, Sedley stumbled behind.

"Uncle, is it not possible just to hire a surveyor who can say whether or nay there are big trees worth cutting?"

"It's a business," said Bernard one noon after a repast of scorched stale bread and hot tea, sitting on a stump and lighting his pipe. "We need to know what timber we've got and what board feet it will make. Finding a good surveyor is difficult. It is arduous work, and inaccurate estimates and outright lies abound. Surveyors we have tried have sometimes submitted false maps and false reports to save themselves trouble. They have sworn that trees were sound, trees that proved rotten or with hollow centers."

He sucked on the pipe, knocked out the dottle and refilled it. "It smokes hot," he said. "I must get a new one." He took a burning stick from their noon fire and lit the tobacco.

"Those surveyors accepted bribes from the Wentworths and others to wrongly value a stand of timber as sound. One time our cutters arrived with their axes and found a thousand stumps left by timber thieves. The stumps were grey with age; *id est,* the surveyor had never been there. Another sent a report of a thick-forested township—we were confronted with ashes." He made a face, emptied his half-smoked pipe again and put it in his pocket.

Sedley, on an adjacent stump, waggled his feet, slapped at mosquitoes. He saw a fine tendril of smoke coiling up from the duff where Bernard had knocked out his pipe. The lecture continued.

"It takes an experienced man more than a week to determine the timber value of only five hundred acres. An honest surveyor is crucial to our business. A member of the family must take the responsibility. Otherwise, when I am gone you will be cheated." But Sedley would not take this bait.

"Uncle, I fear we must make a great effort to find someone outside the family who will work for a good income and nurture him. My attraction is to the expansion of the business. I am interested in going obliquely beyond trees and lumber."

"You consider potash the crown of the future?" His tone was disparaging, as though Sedley had announced an interest in growing lettuces. Bernard rose.

"Come. We can be back at the inn by nightfall if we ride at once." Behind them the pipe dottle glowed in the pine duff, waxed and grew into a small licking fire. In Boston the next day Bernard saw the distant smoke and reckoned it was in Duke & Sons' forestland; but fire could not be helped. Forests burned, according to God's will. The end of summer was always smoky.

Bernard felt himself getting old; he had no time to lose. He would have to look outside the family for his surveyor. He would inquire of sawmill operators, the latter themselves no slouches at board foot estimations—once they had the logs before their eyes. Yet estimating the lumber in a standing tree was more difficult by far. There might be a bright lad or two out there who could be trained. If only he could find them.

As for the other problem, it was insoluble, it was all up to God. If he saw the problem approaching he could do something. But if he was dead he could not and fate would have its way.

In 1758 the French were losing their territories in Africa and America to England. It was a dangerous time to travel, but when was travel ever safe? The Duke party of six—Bernard, Nicolaus, Jan, Outger, Piet and George Pickering—would take passage on a new Dutch merchant frigate, *Bladwesp,* carrying Duke & Sons cargo (dike timbers) from Boston to Amsterdam. Bernard wished to stop at La Rochelle for business meetings, but because of the war it was out of the question; they would do well to slide up the coast of France without harm and go straight to Amsterdam. Sedley would remain in Boston as Eugenia, delivered of a son, was weak and sinking. Dr. Perry thought she could not last long. The child was strong—it was as though he had drained all of the mother's vitality into himself. Eugenia whispered that they should name him James; Sedley promised, but already harbored a hatred against the murdering infant.

For Bernard it would be a quick trip. He planned to return after a month. The others could stay as long as they wished; indeed, George Pickering talked of a European tour—excluding France because of the war—which Jan and Bernard encouraged. But Nicolaus said no to Piet, who wished to join his cousin. George Pickering was well enough pleased to travel alone as he planned a private adventure in whoring and drinking and preferred not to have a witness, no matter how congenial. It was too bad to miss France, which he had always heard was the apogee of depravity.

"You, Piet, have the responsibility of the pitch plantation," said Nicolaus. "You cannot attempt such a tour. I had thought we might send Henk Steen to oversee the plantation if you wished to travel for a few months, but he made a scene. He said he was unsuited for the responsibility. Apparently he has moral scruples on slavery. On my return I plan to replace Steen with a harder-headed man. He may take his moral scruples elsewhere."

There was but one day until they sailed and still Outger had not arrived. It was unthinkable to sail without him—the voyage had been at his urging. Bernard talked with Captain Strik, a dour old Dutchman who disliked passengers no matter how well they paid. He was pleased when they died at sea and had to be pitched overboard. Now he said he would sail at the appointed time, Outger Duquet or no. He already had the passenger's money and if that passenger chose not to arrive in a timely fashion, why then he could walk to Amsterdam. He wheezed out a laugh.

Piet and George Pickering hung over the rail keeping watch for the infamous uncle. Their patience was rewarded. Piet clattered down to Bernard's quarters and found him writing in his red leather business book.

"Uncle! He is here. In a coach. Followed by three wagons of trunks and boxes."

Bernard followed his nephew up on deck and saw Outger. He resembled Charles Duquet though he lacked his father's muscle mass and shrunken jaw. Limp yellow hair stuck out from under his tie wig, but the pale eyes had the piercing Duquet focus. He was thin and very white, obviously one who lived indoors.

Outger ignored Bernard and rushed to the captain's cabin, where he yammered and jawed for a quarter of an hour. When he came out again six sailors followed him off the ship to carry his boxes and trunks on board, stowing them in the extra quarters Outger had engaged. A fourth wagon holding a massive packing crate arrived at the dock. It took twelve sailors to move it up onto the deck, where it stayed, covered with a tarpaulin and lashed down. The sailors, laughing and biting Outger's coins, returned to their duties. Outger examined Bernard, displeased at what he saw—a heavy, aging man, somewhat gimpy.

"Welkom, broeder," said Bernard. Outger pursed his lips.

"Please to remember, Bernard, that we are not brothers. My parents may have adopted you and the others, but we are, most emphatically, not blood brothers."

"I am in no danger of forgetting that. Yet we were ever closer to your father than you yourself."

He was surprised when Outger laughed. "Yes, yes. But that's hardly an enviable distinction. The man was a brute."

"He was also a very good businessman, to our mutual advantage—yours as well as mine. A great pity for Duke and Sons when he vanished."

"Quite. But amidst all the fanciful imaginings put forward I wonder you have never suspected that he was sickening for the smallpox, which was very prevalent in those days, and went into the forest alone and died of it? It is logical, I think."

"You may be right."

"Yes. And now that we've got the spleenishness out of the way shall we try for civility as we must travel in each other's pockets for the next six weeks?"

"That would please me inordinately. And I *am* glad to see you." They were like two terriers sniffing and circling.

"And I to see you, though I know you doubt it. But tell me, who are those goggling monkeys staring at me?" He gestured toward the ship's rail.

"That one with the watch chain on his vest is young Piet, one of Nicolaus's sons. Piet oversees our pitch production plantation in Carolina. The other is George Pickering Duke, Jan's son, recently returned from London, where he read law at the Inns of Court. Missing is Sedley, Piet's brother. He has just become a father and is staying in Boston with his wife." He took a breath and turned to his nephews.

"Gentlemen—this is Outger Duquet, of whom you have heard."

They had also heard Outger's disclaimer of kinship with Bernard and were rather at a loss how to address him. Outger saw their confusion and said, "You may call me Uncle as long as we all understand it to be an address of respect for an elder rather than a claim to a nonexistent kinship." He spoke as though he were a prince of the blood.

"Thank you, Uncle," said Piet; George mumbled the same.

"We will meet again at the captain's table," said Outger haughtily and went below to arrange his belongings.

The dinner was reasonably pleasant, even Captain Strik twisting a half smile out of his crusty features now and then. When pressed for his opinion about danger from French warships he said, "I heard this very morning that the British have captured more than two hundred French ships. The French are concerned for their West Indies trade, and for Nova Scotia. I doubt the few of their ships under way will waste time chasing a Dutch merchant."

When the pudding had come and gone a good port arrived and the older men took out their smoking paraphernalia. Uncle Outger flourished a yellow tobacco pouch with horrid claws.

"It is made from the foot of an albatross. All the bones were drawn out and the leather well tanned. Many parts of the albatross have uses—the beak makes an admirable clip to keep papers from flying apart. And the flesh is as tasty as any pheasant."

"And where did you happen to capture an albatross?" asked Jan.

Outger waved his hand eastward.

Jan peppered him with questions. "Will you spend considerable time in Amsterdam?"

"Not at all. I'll have a few days with my mother and sister, Doortje. Then away to the University of Leiden to meet with scholars of natural history. I have been in correspondence with some of these learned men for decades, and although I feel I know them well, we have never met." He swigged the port. "Nor would they know me if we were to be introduced this very moment. As a caution I have ever used a disguised name in my correspondence with them." He went on to say that he had derived that mysterious name by writing the alphabet in a circle and choosing the letters opposite those of his last name. As an added precaution he then reversed the order of those letters and came up with his secret correspondence name—Etdidu.

"Very clever," said Nicolaus, humoring him. He forbore to ask why Outger felt such a pressing need for anonymity. Bernard was both gratified and disconcerted that he had been correct about Outger. The man, penned up in Charles Duquet's Penobscot Bay house for decades, had developed into a full-blown crank—a code name, worthless plants and who knew what else?

"What is your subject of interest if I may ask?" he asked.

"Various. The flora of the New World. Indian artifacts and descriptions of their strange rites. Weather manifestations peculiar to Penobscot Bay. Mathematical conundrums. And my invention, now situated on the ship's deck with the kind compliance of Captain Strik."

The captain bobbed his head.

"My invention, which I prefer not to discuss. And very much more." Outger, smoking his pipe fiercely, helped himself to a final ladle of pease and another boiled potato.

"It sounds as though you may be there for some months, if not years." Bernard watched Outger swish his potato through the greenish pond of pease.

"At least a year. I shall make my home in Amsterdam or Leiden, depending which I find more salubrious. I might live with Doortje; her letters show she has many of the same interests in natural history as I. Or I might stay with the men of science in Leiden—if my invention captures their approval. However, I am aware they may see me as a hopelessly ignorant colonial and bid me adieu. Though I do not think so. I know any number of things of which they do not dream.

We shall see, eh?" And he puffed out a forceful cloud of smoke and
a few flecks of pease.

Jan hoped Outger would remain in Holland for the rest of his
life. Then Duke & Sons could finally get possession of the great pine
table in the Penobscot house.

But Nicolaus, who spent much time with the company's contract tree cutters, saw Outger had some similarity with the half-
unbalanced men who came in from the isolation of the woods. The
forest had made them strange—"woods-queer"—as some called it.
They leapt with fright at any loud noise, they took their pay and
then stormed back into the office an hour later demanding to be
compensated—and were flustered when Henk Steen showed them
their Xs or signatures on the receipts. But Nicolaus understood. The
moment of payment had been too matter-of-fact; there had been no
ceremony, no release from the tensions of solitude and dangerous
work. He invited the overwrought barkskins to a nearby tavern for a
drink. He urged them to tell him of the perils of the recent job—the
catface growth that caused a tree to twist and fall badly, illnesses and
other afflictions, unseen tree limbs that hurtled down, food shortages, troublesome men. An hour or so of putting the past into the
past restored their hearts. It was the same, he thought, with Outger.
He would take the man aside and urge him to talk of his invention
and the difficulties he had suffered in creating it—whatever it was.

It was at dinner that Etdidu shone most brightly. He ate rapidly,
like a dog, hunching and gulping so he then could command the
conversation. He dominated the talk with a succession of bizarre
tales, all recounted as though he had experienced them himself, an
impossibility, thought Bernard, unless he possessed the power of
ubiquity. It was difficult to grasp the tendrils of these stories, which
emerged from intertwined sentences spangled with English, French,
Dutch and fragments of some Algonkian tongue. The rest of the diners were forced into a zone of silence.

He spoke of hurricanes that sought out Papist churches, of man-
drakes, rains of blood, burial vaults where unseen forces shifted

coffins from their positions and disgorged their contents onto the floor. He knew of birds that built their nests of cinnamon sticks, and others that used only the entrails of sea lions for the purpose. He described cities of ice floating in the polar ocean, leaps of death from high places and persons who could leave their earthly bodies at night, transmute into mosquitoes and annoy their neighbors. As proof of this he advanced a description of a Paris baker who, in mosquito guise, feasted on the blood of a handsome mademoiselle, was slapped by the bitee for his impudence and died on the windowsill as he sought to escape, in his human shape, but horribly squashed.

Bernard grew irritated with Outger's monopoly of talk. "Surely you do not expect us to believe that you yourself actually went to the isle of Cagayan Sulu and saw cannibal vampires at their fell banquets?"

"*Non, non,* not I personally. But my good friend E. Skertchley of Dublin wrote me the full description as he witnessed it. As I read his letter, terror palsied my limbs."

"As it has mine. Excuse me, gentlemen. I must retire while my mental abilities are still intact."

George Pickering and Piet were delighted. If one had to have a mad uncle, Outger was tremendous. They especially liked the mosquito story. It was a new comprehension of insect pests. Who knew if it might not be Genghis Khan plunging his proboscis into one's flesh?

Captain Strik kept a lookout in the crow's nest from dawn until full dark scanning the sea for possible French sails pricking the horizon. There were French ships faster than a laden merchant, and many evenings he stayed on deck, taking his meal standing until some distant speck of white was identified. In the third week of the voyage the weather showed storm signs: swells that the captain called "dogs running before their master," heavier seas, increasingly overcast sky, and the wind moaning in the rigging. George Pickering strode about the deck sucking in the salty wind, leaning over the rail to stare at the leaping froth. The sailors all had huge misshapen hands and their faces seemed baked by the sun into corroded metal. Since the first day of the voyage he had pestered the crew with questions, particularly Wigglesworth, the heavily muscled ruffian with a beard like a wheat field whom they had seen in the tavern dancing a hornpipe two nights before they embarked. Bernard noticed Wigglesworth tried to dodge George Pickering, who was always asking for a rollicking chantey, not understanding that the songs were tailored to certain kinds of work as hauling at halyards, at the pumps, at stamp and go. Captain Strik frowned at this quizzing of his crew but gnawed his lower lip and said nothing.

Outger daily inspected the lashings holding his invention in place on the deck. "She's sound, she's bound, she can't shift around," he said. When he said it at the dinner table before launching into another fable, the captain shook his head.

Said Outger/Etdidu, "My old friend Captain Pearfowle of Iceland escaped a severe storm in a singular manner. His ship was off Cape Circumcision's rocky coast when a storm forced them nearer the jagged cliffs. He had fitted out with eighteen huge anchors and nine large barrels, one for himself and each of the eight crewmen. The storm made foundering their likely fate, but he dropped the anchors, pulled the wood stopper in the bilges and took refuge under his barrel as did each of the sailors. The ship sank, and they with it, but in their upended barrels they had enough air to breathe until the storm passed."

Captain Strik listened to this with a curious expression. *"And then?"* he asked menacingly.

"Why then—they plugged the hole, bailed away and emptied the water out, and continued on their way."

"*Stilte!* Silence! This is a foc's'le yarn that tests my temper, sir. I'll have no more of these blatherings. Kindly take your dinner in your stateroom for the remainder of the voyage." He found Outger Duquet a source of irritation and discontent; it was best to dampen his squibs. And he intended to have a word with George Pickering. Outger and George Pickering had greatly reinforced Captain Strik's hatred of passengers.

But if Captain Luther Pearfowle's storm was imaginary, the tempest that caught *Bladwesp* was terrifyingly real. Great seas rose and fell on them with shuddering crashes. The bare masts groaned and the rigging ropes howled. A black monster swelled on the horizon, raced toward them, then sprang on the *Bladwesp* with terrible weight, and the topgallant section of the foremast broke in a tangle of ropes and torn canvas. There was a grinding noise; the ship rolled, listed. As quick as an eel grasping its prey Captain Strik himself ran onto the deck with an ax, slashed the ropes holding down Outger's invention and leapt back. The *Bladwesp* shrugged off the heavy case, which smashed through the rail and sank like the original rock. The ship, relieved of this weight, rose up ripped and leaking but afloat.

For the next two days the ship's carpenters worked on the damaged mast, cutting away the splinters and ruined wood and replacing it with a new top section stored in the hold.

Outger locked himself in his cabin. They could hear him expostulating and excoriating the captain for hours. He emerged the next day haggard and morose, eyes blazing in a sore countenance, his fingers crooked into claws.

Nicolaus, fearing for Captain Strik, tried to calm the situation. "I am truly sorry about your lost invention," he said.

Outger/Etdidu glared at him with red eyes. "I do not know what you mean. There is no invention. There never was an invention. It was simply a box to pique fools."

"But the weight!"

"*Steenen.* Stones. New England granite." And Etdidu turned away.

Captain Strik liked to put on a smart appearance when entering port, and when they were a week away he gave the order to shift sails, a difficult procedure demanding intense concentration and extraordinary effort for two days. George Pickering Duke, his mouth open, watched three men to a yardarm struggling to unbend the old sails from their spars from the topgallants down. One of the men on the yardarm above was Wigglesworth, the hornpipe dancer whom George Pickering admired.

From the deck George Pickering bellowed, "Wigglesworth! Give us a chantey, Wigglesworth!" The sailor twisted his head around at the sound of his name, just as a sudden burst of wind puffed the sail and broke the temporary slender rope yarns securing it. The sail jerked away from Wigglesworth's hand and its convulsive twitch knocked the sailor loose and sent him cartwheeling down.

"Ah, God!" said George Pickering. Wigglesworth clutched, fell, hit a yardarm below and bounced off into the sea. George Pickering rushed to the side. Wigglesworth floated faceup in the center of a spreading wash of blood. Before George Pickering could think what to do two sailors had thrown lines over the side and were down in the water, rigging a bowline around the injured man's chest.

"Haul away!" shouted one of the swimmers. "Haul!"

Captain Strik emerged from his cabin with a threaded needle, a pair of scissors and a swab. He snipped away the bloody hair, wiped Wigglesworth's head, already well rinsed in salt water, and quickly stitched him up. He ordered two sailors to take him to his hammock and keep an eye on him.

"He'll come through. Head hard as a quahog shell. Maybe more confused than usual for a bit. We'll watch how he goes." He turned to George Pickering, who was watching with great interest.

"You are not to speak to any member of this ship's crew for the duration of the voyage. You would do well to keep out of sight or there might be an accident. The crew regards you as a Jonah."

"They are just jealous of my friendship with Wigglesworth," smiled George Pickering.

"It is Wigglesworth would give you the push, Mr. GEORGE PICKERING Duke."

36

clouds

Before they left Boston, Bernard had arranged the hire of a private carriage to take them around Amsterdam as he was not sure if Cornelia and Doortje had a stable and conveyances. Outger had made his own arrangements. A wealthy merchant to whom he had sent crates of sassafras over the years had offered him the use of his berlin, horses and coachman.

It was a bright blue January morning when they came off the *Bladwesp*. Outger's borrowed equipage stood at the end of the wharf. The travelers looked it over. The berlin was an exquisite thing, deep marine-blue enamel, glass windows, the merchant's initials coiling like golden snakes on the doors. The body of the carriage was slung on steel springs, the apex of travel comfort. The coachman's livery was a strong yellow and from a distance, Bernard said the ensemble resembled a blue teapot with a canary sitting on the spout. Outger ordered the *Bladwesp* sailors to load his trunks onto a waiting dray and in minutes the merchant's cream-colored horses bore him away.

Amsterdam had grown so large it shocked Jan, Bernard and Nicolaus, so bustling, its port jammed with ships of every nation, the streets—the streets of their childhood—thick with people speaking twenty tongues. Jan found he could barely understand the street slang, yet it shot tendrils of painful nostalgia through him. The travelers recovered their legs by walking to their inn, then hired a laundress to wash their linen in fresh water. Jan strolled about the streets; Nicolaus bought an old book, Erasmus's *De civilitate morum puerilium,* a book of manners for children, but useful to adults, especially in uncouth New England, where force and boldness defied efforts at politesse. He opened the book and immediately read that wild eyes implied a violent character, and fixed stares were proofs of effrontery. Outger, he reflected, had both wild eyes and a fixed stare, depending on his disposition.

Back at the inn a messenger presented Bernard with a letter from Doortje telling them that in the morning they should go to Piet Roos's old house, which was now Cornelia's home. She, Doortje, was living in their parents' house attended by her servant, Mieke. She would meet them at Cornelia's and wished them Godspeed. She added a postscript: "Outger is here already one day."

Amsterdam had swollen like a cracker in hot milk, but Bernard remembered the stale odor of the canals, the wet cobbled streets and sky milky with overhead cloud. After so many years in the dark forests at the top of the world, where trees rejected the puny efforts of men, he found pollarded willows ridiculous. He and his adopted brothers had changed very much, the world had changed. He felt he belonged neither here nor there. The next day when he entered his assigned room in Cornelia's house he was pleased to see a half-remembered painting of a hunting scene, a huntsman raising a horn to his lips. This painting stirred some subterranean image of lost familiarity and it was a good omen that it still pleased him.

As for Jan, the return to his homeland affected him deeply—the light, the long, long horizon and the opalescent subtleties of clouds—the clouds!—made him long to toss away his present life, to remain here in the few short years left him, for he was fifty-four. He did not want to see Cornelia or Doortje; he only wanted to gaze at clouds. In their shifting forms and vaporous mutations they seemed uncanny manifestations of what he felt inside his private self.

• • •

The next morning they walked to the old Piet Roos house. Inside the entry hall the first thing Jan saw was a painting of horizon and endless sky filled with clouds of unraveling lace, clouds pulling up the dark of the sea into their nether regions. Why had he never seen this painting when he was young? How different his life might have been. But no, had he not been rescued from the *Weeshuis* orphanage he would likely have been apprenticed to some farrier or chimney sweep. But perhaps . . .

Nicolaus, too, was shuddering with recognition, with awakened recollections as ribboned as the shifting light. The bridges delighted him, bridges of many shapes and lengths, of stone and wood, the latter very likely of timbers from the forest properties of Duke & Sons. Arched bridges shaped the diffuse light so correctly he felt a flare of joy. He remembered cold winter ice and sliding along on his shoes under one of those very bridges. On one of his walks he saw the skinny bridge—*Magere Brug*—over the Amstel and he grinned like a fool as he crossed it.

Outger was in residence. He had to be first; he was the real son, and he was gratified when Cornelia said "my own dear boy," and squeezed his hands in her buttery paws. He sat on the floor with his head leaning against her knee—a pose he had seen in a painting— and poured out his (expurgated) life history in the English colony which he had decided to renounce.

"I might live with Doortje, if you do not have room for me here, dear Mother. I do need several rooms and a very large table for my Work."

Doortje looked at Outger, then at the plaster cherubs on the ceiling, back again at Outger. Cornelia was slightly alarmed. She began to talk of his childhood ways and of the great changes in the world since he had left. She did not mention Charles Duquet. But as soon as the others arrived she shifted Outger to the fringes of her affection, or so he felt. They all came at once, tall strong men filling the room, everyone pressing forward.

Age and plumpness had ironed out Cornelia. Her quite smooth

face and broad nose seemed almost flat and one eye sat noticeably higher than the other. Her brows were invisible and the white-blue eyes seemed they might be sightless. Her thin hair was covered by a finely embroidered linen cap. She wore a grey silk dress and, as the day was chilly, a little cape of marten fur. One by one the sons approached, bent low and kissed her. The grandsons George Pickering Duke and Young Piet came forward in their turn and pecked at her hand. She tried to feel a stir of affection for these young sons of her adopted boys.

Doortje's face had the same sharp features as Charles Duquet's and Outger's, but her body was obese. She wore a dress of fine blue wool. Her small eyes flashed around, taking in every detail of the colonial company, and she showed a slight, almost pitying smile. Bernard thought she looked intelligent and likely was sharp-tempered.

Cornelia had ordered a welcoming dinner and many relatives poured into the house, laughing and smiling, beseeching information on the New World and its rigors. Before they went to table there were drinks and delicacies. Jan had not tasted North Sea herrings since he was a boy—there was nothing better on earth. Bernard was enjoying good *jenever* and smoked eel. At dinner the main dish was *waterzooi,* a rich stew of freshwater fish.

Bernard was interested in some of the cousins. Jaap Akkerman he remembered as a small, black-haired boy picking fleas off a spotted dog. Now he showed a drooping face topped with heavy eyes, the lids like ivory covers on pillboxes. He was involved in some business with eelgrass, once used to procure salt, but now, said Akkerman, a very good material for packing fragile items.

"*Zeegras*—sea grass or eelgrass—has many virtues. You know of course, that in olden times they used it to help bind the dikes together?"

"I did not know," said Bernard. He could not imagine how eelgrass could be made to hold back the sea, but by the end of the meal he was stuffed full of *waterzooi* and eelgrass particulars.

Bernard tired of the tales Outger told at every meal. Doortje bore it for two nights and then told her mother, "I will take dinner at home. I am needed there." Some years earlier Doortje had married Roelof Vogel, a learned antiquarian who died before their son, Lennart, was three. Doortje said Lennart was ill at home. As for the idea that Outger might live there with them—impossible.

After dinner Cornelia announced that as this visit was a rare occasion she wished to have a painting of the family. The portrait of Piet Roos which hung in her bedroom would serve as the necessary paterfamilias. It would take center position and the rest of them would be grouped below. Two serving men took the portrait from its nail and brought it downstairs.

"There," said Cornelia. "You see my father. It is true we no longer have the great painters of the last century, but Cornelis Ploos van Amstel is a fine portrait painter. I shall send a message to him at once."

The next morning the painter arrived, a long-bodied chap with an arrogant expression on his florid face. He enjoyed coffee and cakes, heard Cornelia's plan to have the portrait of Piet Roos included in the work. Ploos van Amstel sauntered around the room looking at the chairs, selected the two largest, heavily carved and gilded, ordered the servants to set them side by side in front of a faded tapestry. He put the portrait of Piet Roos in one and Cornelia in the other. Of Charles Duquet there was nothing except Outger and Doortje. His life had come and gone, and even here among the people he had imagined as a family he was forgotten.

Ploos van Amstel placed them around Cornelia and asked them to do something with their hands. Doortje folded hers primly. Bernard took out a little pocketknife and began to pare his nails. George Pickering Duke had spent the morning trolling the book stalls and had come back with a prize, an old quarto edition of Willem Bontekoe's *Gedenkwaardige Beschrijving Van de Achtjarige en zeer Avontuurlyke Rise Niewe Hoorne,* and he held it in his hands opened to a woodcut of an exploding ship, pieces of human anatomy flung into the sky.

Jan and Nicolaus folded their arms across their chests. Outger threw himself at Cornelia's feet as though beseeching her for something. Two mornings dragged by. Then Ploos van Amstel took himself, his canvas, charcoal pencils and easel away to begin the painting, for, he said, the sketches were done.

It was happy news for everyone except Cornelia when, after a week, Outger left for Leiden with a trunk of papers. Nicolaus had many meetings with businessmen, even the eelgrass cousin. One morning he told Bernard that there were splendid opportunities just waiting to be picked up. They were sitting in a little smoking room. Nicolaus had sheets of paper under his hand, papers that described business ventures he found tempting. One by one Bernard dismissed them. He told Nicolaus it was better exercise to worry about their own market. For two decades Duke & Sons had supplied heavy timbers for the dikes, but in recent years the destructive *Teredo navalis* had come to Holland in bottom-gnawed cargo ships and attacked the dikes. The dike builders were now importing stone. Duke & Sons had lost several municipal contracts. And unless shipbuilding picked up in Boston they would suffer more losses. Nicolaus continued to describe bargain investments. It was good, thought Bernard, that they would soon leave.

At the end of a month Bernard was ready to go. He was concerned about Jan, who spent too much time wandering around in polders and along dikes staring at the sky. He had looked at small houses in the company of purchase agents. And Bernard saw him go into a shop specializing in pigments and canvas. What was the fellow thinking? He followed Jan on one of his daily rambles.

"Jan," he called. "Have a cup of warmth with me." He guided him to a coffee shop. They sat near a window.

He spoke kindly; he understood how affected Jan had been by their return, but what else drew him? They had to think of going home. Soon.

"Brother," said Jan. "This may sound strange to you but I have always longed to be a painter. And here is the place I wish to paint." He pointed upward. "The clouds."

"Clouds? Jan, you are a mature man, you are—you are *old*! You cannot abandon the company and take up painting. Duke and Sons needs your services."

"Bernard, I must try. Let me stay on for another six months to see if I can paint. I have so many pictures in my head. Brother, have you not ever wanted to do something that was—how can I say it—out of the ordinary?"

Bernard laughed bitterly. "Oh God, I have. I entirely understand the feeling." He went quiet while Jan drank his mixture of hot sweetened chocolate and coffee. When his cup was empty Bernard sighed.

"So do that, stay here and paint clouds for six months. But give me your word that you will return at the end of that time."

"I will," said Jan. "I'll bring you my best painting."

"That is what I need, Jan, more than anything—a painting of Dutch clouds. But take care not to get windmills in your mind."

"I will leave that to Outger," said Jan.

They both smiled tightly. Bernard was ready to embark, his passage already arranged. He had only one or two last things to do; he had ordered a pair of bucket-top boots from a boot maker reputed to be an artist with leather and they must be ready. They would look well with his wraprascal coachman's cloak. He stopped first at a lace maker's shop and selected a present for Birgit, a needlepoint flounce, point de France, in something the shopkeeper called the *candélabre* pattern. His boots were not quite ready and the leather artist asked him to come back in two hours; only a few nails had yet to go into the soles. He waited.

The boots were ready, black and gleaming, lacking only a pair of silver spurs. Impatient to wear them Bernard put them on in the shop and walked back to old Piet Roos's house. After some minutes he felt a painful sharp object digging into his left foot. As he could hardly take the boot off in the street, he went back to the boot maker's shop, favoring his foot to avoid driving the sharp object further into his flesh.

The boot maker was surprised. "What, sir, back so soon? Not to your liking?"

"There is something sharp in this one," said Bernard, sitting in the customer's chair and tugging at the boot. There was blood on his stocking. He didn't bother to look inside, but tossed the thing at the boot maker, who caught it deftly and plunged his hand into it.

"Ah," he said. "A nail went awry. Haste made waste, ha-ha. I'll have it right in a moment." With pincers he drew the nail, threw it into a bin and set another with a few sharp taps of his hammer, plunged his hand in again and felt around vigorously. "There you are, quite sound. I am sorry for the nail." He gave Bernard an oiled chamois cloth as a make-peace gift. Bernard pulled the boot back on and tested it. He left, heels ringing on the floor.

As he came through the door of the old Piet Roos house the servant girl was there. She curtsied and said, "Mevrouw wishes you to join her and the others in the library." He expected Cornelia had arranged some sort of farewell party and was not surprised to see Doortje, Nicolaus, Jan, Piet and George Pickering Duke when he came into the library. On a side table there was a steaming coffeepot and cups.

"I have asked you all to be here," said Cornelia, "because I have had a letter from Outger this past hour. He encloses a private envelope for Bernard. In the letter to me he says that he has been invited to join the Leiden faculty. He will send for his possessions once he has found a furnished and well-staffed house." She passed the other envelope to Bernard, who opened it and drew out a single sheet.

"Oh," he said. "Oh God damn his eyes—forgive my language, Mother. I must read this aloud since it is of importance to all of us.

Dear Almost-Brothers. This is to notify you that I will not be returning to the Colonies nor the House on Penobscot Bay. But do not think you can have the Large Table. It, and all the other Contents of the House, are now the Property of my Daughter, Beatrix Duquet. Her Mother was a Passamaquoddy Indian, a kind and gentle Woman who helped Me with My studies of Indian ways and beliefs. She died and I had the charge of my Daughter who has benefited from a Good Education. From Me. She is in Residence at My House on Penobscot Bay as I write this. I have told her all that I am telling you. Perhaps she will eventually join me in Leiden. I will endeavor to return occasionally in order to pay Her a visit. On such Trips I will not stop in Boston. Yours, quite sincerely, Outger Duquet."

Cornelia put her hand over her heart and leaned back in her chair with her eyes closed. The servant ran for smelling salts.

"Daughter?" shouted Nicolaus. "That fool has a daughter? Who else but an Indian would take up with Outger? We must go back and get her out of our house. It was never Outger's to own, it was always the property of the company. We only let him remain in it to keep him from troubling the business. How soon can you be ready to leave, Bernard? We must see to this immediately."

Doortje helped Cornelia up to bed, then rejoined the men. The talk went on for hours with a hundred bold and impractical plans to oust the "daughter," to punish Outger, to cut off his company stipend, to get the large table, to claim the house. In the end they decided that Nicolaus and Bernard would go up to Penobscot Bay as soon as they were back in the colonies and see the situation for themselves.

The first available ship sailing for Boston was a tired old East Indiaman—*De bloem.* The captain's small pointed face, a narrow pointed nose that led to a pointed chin embellished with a pointed wisp of beard, did little to inspire confidence. His cheeks were red, whether from drink or eczema Bernard did not know, but the man promised all speed.

"She looks tired but she moves smart over the waves," he said. The ship was, in fact, going to be broken up in Boston.

• • •

The ship bucked and sidled in the North Sea. Nicolaus and Bernard put their shared stateroom in order. Bernard's bucket-top boots took up a surprising amount of space and he finally folded them over and stowed them in his trunk. He would wear them when he was back in Boston.

Nicolaus noticed that Bernard was limping. He had limped for years with his old injury but now he also seemed unwarrantedly slow, as though dazed. Perhaps the news of Outger's daughter had affected him.

"What is it?" asked Nicolaus. "Aside from our hitherto unknown niece?"

"Nothing, really. My new boot had a nail in it and it cut my foot before we left. Where it pierced seems very sore. I am not so worried about the girl, although we do not know how old she is. We may be able to talk sense with her."

"If she is half Indian and half Outger I think there is a poor chance of talking sense with her. But we'll find out. Now let me see your foot," said Nicolaus. Bernard drew off his stocking and showed a swollen foot.

"I will ask for a basin of hot water," said Nicolaus. "And perhaps some ointment—if there is any on board."

The ship's surgeon, an elderly man with bleared eyes, sent in the cabin boy with a basin of tepid grey water and himself brought the "ointment," a thick, tarry substance they used on ropes to keep them from chafing. By afternoon Bernard said he felt better but the next morning he was unable to walk. His foot and lower leg were badly swollen. The old surgeon came in and looked at it.

"Keep it elevated," he said to Nicolaus. "Soak in hot water. Drink rum, as much as you can stand."

"It is my brother who is ill, not I," said Nicolaus.

• • •

Nicolaus tried to brighten the fetid cabin by propping the painting of a woodland hunt Bernard had brought from Cornelia's house. Perhaps he could find surcease from the pain of his leg in contemplating the vivid scene.

The hot water soaks did not help. Daily the leg—his bad leg, of course—swelled. Sores and ulcers appeared and festered from foot to groin. Bernard was unable to leave his bunk and lay in a half swoon, breathing stertorously. The surgeon came in one last time huffing fumes of *jenever.*

"That leg needs to be amputated," he said. "Look for my saw." He went out and did not return. When Nicolaus found him the old man was insensible with drink. The great medical chest stood against the wall, top flung back, the interior gaping. Nicolaus picked up a dried carrot among broken pieces of deer antler. The amputation saw lay on the cabin floor, its teeth crusted with old blood.

He went at once to the captain and told him of the empty medical chest. The little man twisted his pointed beard into a spike and bared his teeth.

"That hyena-headed flea has sold the medicines for *jenever.* Now his hour has come!" he declared and he rushed away toward the lair of the so-called practitioner of the medical arts.

Nicolaus went back to Bernard, who lay comatose and radiating heat like a birch fire. Bernard stared unseeing at the beams above his head, black and wormholed. The painting stood on a chair near the bunk. One of the huntsmen was raising a horn to his lips. Nicolaus almost thought he heard the sound of the horn and it came to him that his brother was not going to get home.

They buried Bernard at sea three weeks out from Amsterdam.

In Boston port Nicolaus felt fortunate to find a ship only days away from embarking for Amsterdam and sent a message by its captain to Jan, Piet and George Pickering Duke telling of Bernard's death and demanding their immediate return.

"This is a Crisis beyond the Loss of dear Bernard," he wrote.

It is not just a Question of the Penobscot Bay hous and the Dautter, but of our Company itself. Timber and lumber orders stacked hie but Henk Steen not to be fond. He is gone—no leter no word. the Retch. There is no Body to serve as our Book Keeper. No one to serve as Looker of Woodland. Sedley in Grief over loss of his Wife lies ill abed. Your Wifes upset and caling your return. Bernard's Wife Birgit tears her hair with Soro. Return quick we may marshal our Forces in Business. Charter a ship ere all is lost.

Your loving Brother and Uncle, Nicolaus Duke.

37

change

In later years Piet Duke thought sometimes of Nicolaus's night-mare letter and the hurried arrangements and great expense of taking passage back to Boston. Outger had not returned with them. Since then he and George and Sedley had suffered under the controlling leadership of Jan and Nicolaus, who allowed no innovation except closing down portions of the business. So the Carolina plantation was sold and Piet assigned the task of handling the New England logging jobbers, the Québec holdings diminished. Jan managed what remained of those forestlands. Nicolaus served as the company president at the Boston headquarters. But as Jan and Nicolaus doddered on they gradually allowed Piet and George a greater say in business decisions, though still watching from the sidelines. And today the cousins had a chance to make an important change.

Piet combed at his thinning hair with his fingers, adjusted his stock and moved his shoulders inside his coat. He called Oliver Wedge, his secretary, a rural youth with aspirations beyond maize and cows, the first secretary Duke & Sons had ever hired and now indispensable.

"Are the papers ready?" he asked Wedge, who pointed to a squared-up stack of pages.

Wedge loved his job passionately, loved being in Boston and away from the farm and its futile, never-ending work, away from his father's anger at marauding wild animals, anger that Wedge and his six hard-worked brothers shared: huge flocks of birds pulled up the sprouted seeds, especially corn, beloved by turkeys, squirrels, crows, red-winged blackbirds and a thousand other avian robbers, raccoons and bears. The raccoons got the eggs the hens laid and the fox, hawks, falcons, skunks, wolves and weasels killed the hens. Bears took the pigs and calves and once a full-grown cow. Sheep were impossible as long as wolves and catamounts and lynx and bobcats could get their scent. But he thought squirrels were the worst as there were thousands upon thousands of them, the forest and woodlot alive with the furry devils—red, black, gray squirrels and he knew for a fact that two squirrels could make six, seven, even nine more squirrels every year and each of these was soon mature. He tried to work out how many squirrels one pair created over, say, ten years, but the sums became so large they frightened him. The earth might be carpeted with squirrels in his lifetime. And woodchucks ate salads, cabbage, turnips, onions and beans. The house swarmed with mice, more than one cat could ever catch. He would never go back.

"You are sure that the papers are ready?" Piet could not stop asking.

"Yes, Mr. Duke. Everything is ready." Wedge's long knobby fingers, early trained to pull thistles, now flew among papers, creating order. Although he had been employed as a secretary for only a year he had learned much of Boston life from a dirty manuscript folded in the back of an account book, a furious, rambling critique by a man who signed himself Henk Steen. Steen was aggrieved at the cruelties beyond slavery that he saw in the colonies: husbands who beat their wives with iron pokers until ribs crackled, an overbearing bully who pushed a road through an elderly widow's property, thieving servants branded with B for burglary, the many who fornicated before marriage, trespassing swine, barrels of rotten fish sold as sound, breaches of peace, drunkenness and swearing—it was a wonderfully wicked place.

Silence and late-afternoon spring sunlight filled the second-floor conference room. Four stacks of paper, glittering inkwells and sharpened quills rested on the company's long maple table, constructed from four planks after the humiliating failure to wrest Duquet's old single-board pine table away from Outger's daughter. Piet checked his watch again and again. He feared this coming meeting but it seemed the only way to get ahead. For years the King's men had robbed both Crown and colony by granting lands—while securing for themselves the adjoining five-hundred-acre corners of those grants until they had amassed thousands of the richest, most heavily timbered acres. They and the important landholders clubbed together. That was how the Wentworth brothers and brothers-in-law, the Elisha Cookes and their cronies had made their fortunes—by stealth and holding.

Duke & Sons, perpetual outsiders, had never gotten involved in politics. If the younger men had not been forced by Bernard's death to assume junior positions in the company they might have moved into rich political offices. It would have been useful to have a Duke as the governor of Massachusetts or Maine or even New York. Now that England had New France entirely within her claws everything was very different.

This time Duke & Sons had the upper hand, thought Piet. The entrenched political landholders with their great swathes of coastal pine had suffered tremendous losses a year earlier when an epic wildfire strode out of New Hampshire and incinerated fifty miles of seacoast forest, eating deep miles inland until beneficent rain fell. Duke & Sons' chief holdings were along the interior rivers, a long distance from the fire. Even before the ashes cooled men whose timber had been destroyed looked covetously on the Duke timberlands.

He consulted his new waistcoat watch; half an hour to wait. Half an hour to stare out the north window. Once illimitable forest filled the horizon. Now there were dozens of streets and the forest was a distant smudge.

While the nephews waited, Jan, at his home a mile away, was sorting through personal papers. He also thought of a fire several years back after their hasty return from Amsterdam, a different and smaller fire only a dozen miles from Outger's Penobscot Bay house. He and Nicolaus had used this fire as their excuse to rescue the great pine table—fear of future incineration. They journeyed to the house.

The daughter, Beatrix, was no beauty, but striking. She was young, perhaps fifteen or sixteen, and rather lissome, quiet-spoken. Her black, undressed hair hung loose, and this gave her a wild look that suited her brown Indian skin. But she greeted them in pleasant English and asked them into the house. They sat before the fire in the familiar room where the great table gleamed with waxy luster. She left them to admire it while she went to the kitchen. They heard the busy roar of the coffee grinder. Jan trailed his fingers over the deep amber wood, darkening with age.

"We must persuade her," he whispered.

Over the steaming coffee mixed with Dutch chocolate and cinnamon, no doubt supplied by Outger, Jan enlarged on their fears for the table should another fire break out, and Nicolaus expressed his certainty that their father, Charles Duquet, had intended it for the company office. She listened attentively. They waited. In the firelight Nicolaus saw that Outger's daughter might be called exotically attractive. Finally she spoke.

"That fire was distant, and the table," she said smoothly, "is, as you say, too large for any practical use. If you would send me a handsome small table you may have this large one." She rapped her knuckles on the pine. She said she did not know why Outger was so passionate about it. He asked after it in every letter and would undoubtedly be angry when she told him it was gone. She did not seem troubled by the promise of Outger's rage. Nor did she seem interested in knowing these stranger "uncles" who came so suddenly, who spoke dismissively of Outger as though he were a castoff from the body of society. She retreated from the conversation and said nothing more while they talked eagerly on, telling her of the family history, of Duke & Sons' many successes. Jan was sure she had heard a garbled and erroneous account from Outger, who had likely described the "uncles" as orphans with evil intentions who had cornered all power in the company. They invited her confidences, which were not forthcoming, and at last Jan and Nicolaus had no more to say. But the matter of the large table was settled. Despite this prize the two aging men were discomfited. They left in an uncomfortable silence. Something was wrong.

"Like Outger in cold disposition," said Nicolaus.

"Like an Indian in conversation," said Jan. "We were too easy. She is only a chit of a bastard girl."

"It would be justice to send the cramped oaken table we use in the anteroom," said Jan. "The one with the mended leg."

"No, let us send a fine table, however diminutive, so she need have no complaint—one of exotic wood and with well-carved legs."

"We'll send Piet now that he's available, as well as a skilled carpenter and long-bed wagon to fetch it to Boston."

But it fell out differently. A month later Piet, followed by a wagon, approached the gate of Duquet's old house with a ready smile; he was greeted by a growling mastiff. Afraid to open the gate and enter he called out.

"Hallo the house! Hallo. Mademoiselle Duquet! Are you at home?"

The door flew open and the girl stood on the great granite stone that served as top step. Her oval face was olive-toned and her hair blacker than soot.

"Who are you and what do you here, sir?" she asked with the warmth of a January midnight.

"I am your cousin Piet Duke. My uncles Jan and Nicolaus Duke spoke with you in recent weeks past about Duke and Sons' large business table in this house. I have come for it. And look, I have brought you this smaller mahogany table as you requested."

"I know nothing of this," she said. "There is no large business table here, and you may take your mahogany object away. Pray do not trouble me again, sir." She closed the door with a hard swinging crash.

Piet swore undying enmity for Beatrix and Outger and the table all the way to Boston. Nicolaus said only "You must have spoken in a way that angered her." Useless to protest.

Boston's population swelled to more than 150,000 people. England had seized New France and driven away the Acadians. Yet New France must be a disappointment compared to the extraordinarily rich income, more than four thousand times greater than any timberland investment, from sugar and molasses in the West Indies. People felt time rushing past ever since England had adopted the Gregorian calendar and forced the colonies to do the same, robbing everyone of eleven days of life. And who could count the new inventions and occupations? Colleges emerged from raw ideas; daring men invented river flatboats to penetrate the wilderness; shipmasters, not content with trade or passengers, began to pursue whales for the costly and fine oil; teacups suddenly had handles, an effete fad that Nicolaus thought would soon die out. And that fellow Franklin's inventions: the lightning rods, which had saved hundreds of churches and houses from destruction, and the stove, which encased fire safely. It was an exciting time to live.

There had been changes in Duke & Sons after Bernard's death. Sedley had remarried, and his new wife, Elizabeth, was a pretty young widow who had family connections to the second cousin of a Wentworth aunt. And after nearly a year of grieving, Birgit, Bernard's old wife, had died. Then Nicolaus began his series of bouts with pneumonia. They had had to scramble to find a competent timber surveyor, but Sedley, who had at least some idea of what was needed, found two: Wolfgang Breitsprecher, a German forester newly arrived; and a French, Jacques Nadeau, who had worked with old Forgeron for a season in New France. These men were antagonists. There was a new bookkeeper to replace Henk Steen, Thomas

Ashbridge, one of the first graduates of the College of New Jersey. With Wedge, Breitsprecher, Nadeau and Ashbridge, Duke & Sons had let in the first outsiders.

Piet had been engaged for a year to Silence Gibben, but she changed her mind. It seemed he might stay a bachelor. George had married Margery Buttolph and already had fathered two boys, Edward and Freegrace. There had been other events, one darkly mysterious. None of the cousins had ever understood the details of Birgit's death, only that it was, in some unknown way, unspeakable. She had been buried at sea "to be with Bernard," as Piet's mother, Mercy, lamely explained. So, Piet thought, Aunt Birgit likely had had some deadly disease. He shuddered. He looked at his watch. Once more he called out to Wedge asking if the papers were ready. The political men would arrive soon. He heard a sound in the anteroom. Now!

But it was only George Pickering Duke, red face shining, who came in with a handful of additional papers.

"All ready, Piet?"

"Of course."

"This is important. This can make us if we handle it correctly. I see it as our chance."

"And I. With God's grace it will go to our advantage. Pray that Uncle Jan does not make an appearance." They were safe from Nicolaus, who was ill.

Sedley came in, stiff-faced and silent but sending out a feeling of discontent and rancor. He was just getting over a cold and his long thin nose was still red with chafed, sore-looking nostrils. He and Piet were barely civil to one another.

Under a goose-down comforter Nicolaus was thinking about that meeting. If Jan was there he could prevent Piet's rash and headlong decisions. George Pickering Duke was as hopeless as Piet. He looked the part of a distinguished businessman, but the exterior masked a rather dim and credulous being. Best would be Sedley, who was more like Charles Duquet than any of the sons or grandsons—embittered, sharp, willful, full of purpose and drive. But Sedley held himself separate from the others. Nicolaus was sure that he would eventually dominate Piet and George Pickering Duke. If only, he thought, Bernard had fathered children and those children had inherited some of Bernard's equitable, quiet character. If only hams and cakes could fly. If only it were always summer. Poor Bernard. And the shock he gave all of them. The memory of Birgit's extraordinary departure from the world forced its way into his mind.

She sank rather quickly. One day she was well and busy, the next she was unable to rise from the bed. She complained of a headache, a twisting pain in her gut, her mind wandered, her thin arms thrust up toward the ceiling. She called for Bernard, forgetting he was in Davy Jones's locker. Mercy and Sarah and Patience attended her bedside, fetching cold compresses, urging the sick woman to sup a little broth—which she promptly vomited up.

"You will be well again in a day or so," said Mercy. "It is an indisposition, nothing more." But as the day wore on the patient became more silent, concentrated on drawing ragged, bubbled breaths. She confounded them by dying in the late afternoon. One moment she seemed no worse, the next she stopped breathing.

Mercy came out of the sickroom and put the kettle on. "She has just left us," she said. "She is with God."

"How can that be?" asked Jan, who sat with Nicolaus at the table. "I thought it was a fleeting illness."

"Apparently not. We never know when He will take us." She sighed, lowered her eyes, then looked at Nicolaus. "If you could order the coffin from Mr. Kent, Sarah and I will prepare her body. I think that rose silk dress she liked so well." She did not cry; death was too familiar and demanded its rituals. Older women were deeply familiar with the events of passage. She took the basin of warm water and dry cloths into the death room. She might have preferred to wait some time before this task but Sarah and Patience had already stripped away the comforter and top sheet. To avoid handling the body more than was necessary Sarah suggested they cut her night-gown off. It was soiled with dark vomit in any case. Mercy thought this a criminal idea—it was a good nightgown and, once washed and bleached, someone could use it. So they unbuttoned the high-necked gown and drew it upward over the thin shoulders, over the head, pulling the stick-like arms from the sleeves, and tugging the garment higher over the knees, up the thin thighs, and—

Nicolaus would never forget the way the door of the sickroom flew open with the two women jammed in the opening. He and Jan had been sitting in mourning quiet, watching the flames in the fire-place.

"Nicolaus! Jan! Come into this room." Nicolaus had never heard his wife speak in that shocked tone. The scarlet-faced women half-ran into the kitchen and let the men go in alone.

The thin and wasted body of an elderly man lay on the still sweat-damp sheet. It was Birgit, certainly it was Birgit, but Birgit was a man. Indubitably. The wispy hairs on the narrow chest and the male sexual organs, shrunken and withered but quite real, confounded them. Nicolaus's mind seethed. He thought not of Birgit but of Ber-nard. Why? Why? For forty years! And none of them had known.

He now wrenched his mind away from the still-shocking image engraved in his memory. It was in the past. Instead he thought of what was happening this very hour while he lay sick abed—Piet, Sedley and George Pickering Duke trying to bargain with some of the shrewdest, most ruthless men in the colonies, men noted for their rapacious ways. There was no help for it; if it killed him he had to go there.

Coughing, he called Mercy. "My clothes. I must go to that meet-ing."

"You cannot. I forbid it. You are ill, dangerously ill."

"Let me alone, Mercy. I must go, I tell you. Help me if you wish me to live. Bar me from this and I'll die of spite."

She thought he could do that; the Dukes were nothing if not stubborn and willful. He caught Jan descending from his carriage in front of the Duke building.

Piet, George Pickering, Sedley and their invited guests sat around the oval mahogany table. The Wentworth brother-in-law's heavy mouth twitched and twitched with a small smile. The proposition was unusual: they would shower the Duke brothers and nephews with social invitations, they would encourage useful connections. They would make the Duke family known, not only in Boston society, but in England. In return they wanted free access to the Duke pineland holdings in the north country, for which, of course, they would pay a fair price. They would share equally the costs of getting the logs out of the forest and to the mills. George Pickering Duke thought it a good agreement as everyone knew that the way to gain advantages was through political and social connections, connections Duke & Sons had never enjoyed. Piet was a little concerned over the "free access" phrase. How free did these political men imagine such access might be? Sedley was in a cold sweat with visions of a thousand choppers cutting their pine, perhaps these very men presenting false accounts or smoothly saying that other men, unknown, had stolen the logs. Worse yet, once given this opening, they were in a position to tamper with the law and seize Duke forestlands. But before Piet could say "Done," the door opened and the two aged Duke brothers, Jan and Nicolaus, came in. Nicolaus looked half dead, pasty-faced except for burning fever spots on his cheeks. He threw his black cane on the table, looked at the Wentworth brother-in-law and his cronies.

Piet explained the offer. The Wentworth brother-in-law, not liking the look of the old men, softened the offer a little by saying that they would only cut on mutually agreed-upon plots. The words "free access" were not spoken this time.

Nicolaus said, "Out."

"Out," repeated Jan. "Out now. The meeting is finished. We agree to nothing."

"Thank God," murmured Sedley, emboldened to pick up Nicolaus's cane as if he would use it on the political men if they made an intention to stay.

But as the men left they treated the elderly Dukes to looks of pure malevolence. The Dukes would never be invited to even the meanest dogfight after this.

It took an hour and more for them to convince Piet and George Pickering Duke that they had been saved from a perilous fate that would have ruined Duke & Sons.

Nicolaus said, "Piet, I know that your mother, Mercy, has long wanted to put us into a brighter social light, but Jan and I feel it would be best if this company now cultivated a quiet presence. We should be more stealthy in our operations and avoid partnership entanglements—try to keep everything in the family as much as we can—use straw men for land purchases. We do not want Duke and Sons trumpeted about as a great power or even as important. If we remain quiet, grey and invisible, we will have advantages over our competitors." In fact, they were afraid that details of Birgit's death would leak into Boston gossip if the Duke women consorted with society in drawing rooms. Under the influence of a glass of sherry anything might be said.

Piet and George looked sulky, like chastised schoolboys. Sedley's red mouth was fixed in a wolfish grin. The old uncles left the room and went down the stairs. At the bottom Jan said, "We may have trouble from Piet and George."

Nicolaus coughed. "I love my son Piet, but I put my money on Sedley."

Nicolaus said, "We can't die now. We have to get Sedley in position." But he began to cough again as though his end was at hand. Jan saw him home, where Mercy prodded him to the bed; she and the servant girls brought mustard plasters, syrups, hot bricks, cups of boiling chamomile tea and a beaker of imported malmsey. He *would* recover.

In the weeks that followed Sedley came every day to sit by his father's bedside and encourage his health. Jan came often and the three parleyed. Sedley's ideas, which he had long nurtured in secret, were expansive. He talked, the strong, highly colored face animated, his dark eyes glittering; a businessman's face, thought Nicolaus. High praise.

"We are too narrow in our holdings, Father, though it was a good move to get out of Carolina. We are concentrated in New England, which has become a hotbed of grasping men with shipping interests and many in their hire. But I believe the future in New England—in Boston—to be very constrained as long as England controls our destinies. We need banks, we need insurance, we need regulated markets, we need a set currency—skilled workmen are moving to Portsmouth, to Salem and other towns as business languishes in Boston. The population is dropping. England's hand squeezes us."

"What would you have us do?" The sick man lay aslant stiff pillows.

"For the long plan I would wish us to look into the timber of the Ohio valley and north and west of there. There is a group of men in Virginia who are taking up much of that land. They have their eyes on the future. Forestland can be had for almost nothing. We should explore the region and see what might be valuable. We must, I feel, be more adventurous. Forests need consideration many years before they become money in the pocket."

"You have the right attitude. Better than falling back on cozy local contacts with important men who will be unimportant tomorrow. What other ideas have you? I know you have been considering ways to strengthen the business."

"I have. And you know, ever since I was a child I have heard that Duke and Sons thought it advantageous to own a shipyard. And yet when Grandfather Duquet disappeared so did the idea. I think the time has long passed for a bargain shipyard but I still feel we should act as soon as possible and acquire. That is my second idea. Think, one ship with a load of sawed planks to the French West Indies would pay for the vessel. And if that ship should return with a load of molasses or sugar—"

"Ah," said Jan. "But who would manage this shipyard?"

"Uncle, I think George Pickering could make a success of it. He has often regretted that he was not able to go to sea as you two did when you were young. A maritime interest is there. His knowledge of English law might be an advantage. And he needs a controlling position of some sort."

"And what of Piet?"

"I suggest he head Duke and Sons here in Boston. He will remain as the company figurehead. And I think Duke and Sons should consider shifting out of Boston. All is so muddled here, so lackadaisical and awry. Boston seems to me always in a lunatic mood, always suspicious that some entity is usurping its rights."

"That may be a well-founded suspicion," said Jan.

"Perhaps. But I think we will need a place with more vigorous businessmen, with less interference from England. Boston has ever been England's spaniel."

Nicolaus coughed phlegmily and said, "Even spaniels will bite if provoked. And something I find extremely trying is the masts on British ships, masts that we cut from our forestlands. The vaunted English navy is constructed from New England timbers. Our pines and oaks come back to us, eh?" But he thought it would be better to leave Boston to its aloof cliques and fulminating gossip.

Jan nodded but did not want to get into this uneasy topic. "What place are you thinking of, Sedley?" Privately he thought it would be difficult. They had been in Boston for decades.

"New York. Or Philadelphia. Men there are inclined to take the longer sight of possibilities."

Jan thought Sedley had considered well, up to a point.

"You have mentioned the advantages of a boy going to sea to build character and confidence. You have given thought to the future. And yet you do not mention the possibility of sending your own son, James, to sea. He is of an age when he might be enrolled as a midshipman."

Sedley frowned. He habitually avoided the boy, who had been sent away to school as early as possible.

"You surprise me, Uncle. You, who forbade George to go to sea."

"George Pickering was beguiled by hornpipes and wharf swagger. He wished to go as a sailor before the mast. I propose an aim rather higher. James is a bright and quick youngster who might well advance in a naval career before taking up his place in the business. It is important to bring on the young sons. And it will set an example for the other boys of the family. I have no doubt that we can make use of our maritime connections to secure him a midshipman's place on board a good ship."

"I will think about it," Sedley said, but he was already considering that to place James as a Royal Navy midshipman would be a step to the enemy's side, with the colonial feeling against England stronger every year. He would look into placing the boy on an American privateer.

"Do," said Nicolaus.

V

in the lumber camps

1754–1804

38

the house on Penobscot Bay

A month after Kuntaw's leaving in the year 1754, his wife, Malaan, sat in the weak autumn sunlight outside the English trading post when a whiteman they called Simon kicked her leg lightly and gestured for her to follow him. He said nothing and she said nothing, but he kept her in his room all winter. In the spring the man returned to England and she went with Richard Tarbox. Her son, Tonny Sel, grew up around the post running with the omnipresent dogs and scruffy knot of untended children. They made themselves a kind of wild den under the old canoes. Malaan showed only a fitful interest in Tonny or in the women from the Mi'kmaw village who came several times to coax her from the current white man who kept her, but she was furious when they tried to take Tonny away.

"He should be brought up by Mi'kmaw people," said the women.

"And am I not a Mi'kmaw person? I will keep him here at the post. He will learn whiteman ways. Mi'kmaw ways not good now." Too deep in private despair to bother with the child who did well enough on his own, she existed on a narrow ledge of life that was neither Mi'kmaw nor white, going with whichever man nodded at her or gave her food. She grew fat. She slept prodigiously, night and day, difficult to arouse, as though it was too painful to rise from submergence.

"Ah," said one of the old women, "I remember when she was a girl, she was clever. She made fine quill embroidery." No one knew what had changed her into the somnolent, distant woman. Some said she was sick with the whiteman whiskey disease, others said it was for love of Kuntaw and shame at his abandonment. They had all heard that Kuntaw was living with a whiteman woman in Maine. He had not come back and no one had gone to talk him back. Some said Malaan had divorced Kuntaw.

They had married as children, soon after Kuntaw, Auguste and Achille had returned from their moose hunt to find ruin. In sorrow Achille had left his lonely and grieving son, a boy so sore in heart he could not accept that he and Malaan were too young for marriage. Elphège had forbidden it, but Kuntaw argued that he had killed his moose, now he was a man, he would marry! Elphège was not his father and could not deny him. They married and Malaan bore their son, Tonny. She had only thirteen winters and her labor was long and painful. Before the child was three Kuntaw left for the lumber camps and Malaan discovered whiteman's whiskey. The boy ran with a pack of orphaned and abandoned children.

From the older women who sometimes coaxed Tonny into their *wikuoms* to feed him good moose meat, to tell him that he could always come to them for food and shelter, he heard stories about his father, Grasshopper Slayer, and his skill with bow and arrow at a time when Mi'kmaw men preferred whiteman guns. It embarrassed him to have a father called Grasshopper Slayer. Now only a few feeble oldsters still kept their unstrung bows and time-warped arrows. Every Mi'kmaw man had a gun and it was possible even for an inept hunter to kill five or six geese from a distance. Food was easier to get and there was little reason to spend long hours tracking and stalking keen-witted prey.

Tonny was a sly thief and beggar; he had neither bow nor gun and depended on his wits for food and shelter. He ran errands for whitemen, slept under an upturned canoe or in a sapling lean-to he had scuffled together in the broken woods. At fourteen he and Hanah, a girl whose mother also hung around the post, began to sleep together under old canoes and while still very young they made three children, Elise, Amboise and Jinot, who all managed to live, scrabbling around the post like young turkeys. Then Hanah, too, who liked rum and the free wild feeling it gave, began to go with whitemen and when she was twenty she was beaten to death by Henry Clefford, a jealous and bellicose trader who kept two other Mi'kmaw women. It was early spring, windy cold days mixed with sleet and intermittent sunlight.

"Here I leave," said Tonny to his mother, Malaan, smarting with hatred and sorrow. He despised her; why should he tell her anything? "I am grown. I am a father. I go, my children go with me."

"You leave here," she said flat-toned. "Always I know this." She nodded and turned away, yawning one of her deep, deep gaping yawns. He could say nothing else; her wretched life was with the post. He was now grown, strong but without hunting skills or weapons, ignorant of animal behavior, which was men's correct interest and work. He no longer belonged here, if ever he had. He woke one morning, his eyes fixed on the underside of the broken canoe, the children wedged under his arm, and turned away from this life. He would no longer be part of the tattered Mi'kmaw people, whose customs had fallen off like flakes of dead skin. But he still believed that his children should live with blood kin. He felt a bitter sadness for them, nearly orphans with a dead mother and a worthless father. He could not leave them at the pernicious post. He knew only that his father was in a place called Penobscot Bay. Unannounced, paddling a stolen canoe and walking for weeks in mud and old snow, often carrying Jinot, the youngest, he found the house, the house of Kuntaw and the whiteman woman.

Year after year the logs of the old house had darkened almost to black. It seemed to be settling into the earth, but new cedar shingles shone like precious metal in the sunrise. The paint on the door and shutters had faded to a moss-grey color, something that made Beatrix think they must be repainted. Kuntaw paid no attention to house chores beyond getting in the winter wood and hunting.

"Enter you," Beatrix Duquet called when she heard the scratching on the door. Tonny and the children stepped inside, ragged and travel-worn. They stood on the polished boards smelling the strange odors of the household, seeing the slant light dropped through glass windows, reflecting from mirrors.

Beatrix, grey-black hair streaming down her back like water, drew in a quick breath.

"Who are you?" She stared at them. "Who are you?" But Tonny thought she must know.

"I Tonny. Kuntaw Sel my father. These my children, Kuntaw their grandfather. Their mother dead. Names Elise, Amboise, Jinot." As he turned them toward her he touched each child on the forehead. "No good live Mi'kmaw place now. I grown man but no good. I pretty bad man. I come my father Kuntaw, you. Help them."

"Ah," said Beatrix. She looked at the children; Elise at nine the oldest, withdrawn and shy; seven-year-old Amboise, also shy but with a winning smile; and Jinot, almost five, with a plump merry face.

"Sit at the table. I will give you food." The chairs were strange and high, the table like the goods counter in the post. Jinot struggled to get on a chair until Beatrix lifted him up, found him warm and heavy, gave him a small squeeze.

"There you are, *snoezepoes*—sweetie pie," she said, then turned to Tonny. "Oh poor Tonny, you must tell me everything, everything that has happened. Kuntaw is out hunting with our sons, Francis-Outger and Josime. They are close to the ages of your children. I know Kuntaw will weep with happiness to see you. He has spoken to me many times of his son, Tonny, and wondered if he still lived and how things were with him." She felt a flash of compassion for this young man who resembled the handsome Indian striding into her life years past. "And now you are here. How happy he will be. But you, you are so young to be the father of three such big children." She looked at them.

"Elise, Amboise, can you read or write?" They bent their faces low.

"Jinot, what do you like best?"

"Get sugar stick at post."

"Ah, well, I have no sugar sticks, but I think you will like pancakes and some Dutch cocoa."

"You good," said Tonny. "I dream it you good." He and Beatrix exchanged looks, Beatrix's steady eyes a promise that the children were safe. Tonny's returned gaze showed a distance that could not be traversed.

They were licking their plates for the last drops of maple syrup when Kuntaw came in with Francis-Outger and Josime. Tonny's children threw quick shy glances at their uncles, their black eyebrows and hair; their pale eyes. Josime carried a tom turkey by its feet, the bloody beak dragging along the floor.

When Kuntaw grasped who the strangers were his face swelled, his hands trembled. He could barely speak, but croaked, "Stay, stay, we all live here." He looked at Beatrix, his eyebrows drawn together beseechingly.

So that is how it is, Tonny thought coldly; Kuntaw likely had to plead for favors from this tall woman who looked Indian when she stood in the shadowed corner of the room. He thought she was not one to stand in shadowy corners and in full hard light she showed her whiteman blood in those water-clear eyes. But she spoke the Mi'kmaw language better than Tonny or the children, who got along with a rough scramble of Mi'kmaw, French and English words.

While Kuntaw, Francis-Outger, Josime and Tonny went upstairs, she took the children around the big house, explaining the use of each room to them, especially the room with a vast table. This, she said, was the schoolroom, the *schoollokaal*, where they would learn to read and write. She would teach them. She sat at the table and took Jinot on her lap, whispered to him that on the morrow she would make him a little toy horse, drew Elise and Amboise close. She spoke to them in a low intimate voice, confiding her reasons. "Our people had special ones among them, those who remembered old stories—old ways. My mother died when I was a baby and she told me nothing. But from my father, even though he was a Dutchman, I learned that

Indian people must take whatever is useful from the whitemen. It is just, because they have taken everything from us. Many of our people died with secrets locked in their heads. Now it is good for us to learn how to read and write so we may know how we make useful things, how our grandfathers lived. That is why we learn to read—so we can remember."

Jinot was afraid of the tall staircase, for he had never seen more than three steps, and sniveled until Beatrix took his hand and led him up very many, counting *"zeven, acht, negen . . . dertien."* Up in the attic they found Kuntaw and big Josime pushing ancient trunks, broken furniture, boxes of books and Kuntaw's worn-out bows and old quivers against the wall to make room for pallets.

"You will have this for your sleeping place," Beatrix said. Jinot saw Josime roll his eyes as though she had said she was going to give roast moose to a pack of wolves. He smiled at Josime as only Jinot could smile and Josime twitched his lips in amusement. Jinot wanted to please—this woman; his father, Tonny; his grandfather Kuntaw; even Josime and Francis-Outger, who were ready to dislike their new kinfolk.

Tonny and the children were awkward eating at a table, but Beatrix signed they should not sit on the floor. They were cowed by the many dishes of meat and bread, unknown pottage and something that looked like a fish. Francis-Outger and Josime whispered and laughed together, took up their bowls and headed outside to eat far from the newcomers. Kuntaw called them back.

"In your places." They ate in silence.

After dinner Beatrix put Tonny's children to bed. Josime leaned against the doorframe, listening.

"I will tell you two stories," said Beatrix in a low, slow voice. "Listen. Here is the first one. Long ago in the old days three children were lost in the forest, and in that forest they saw a tree, a very strong big tree so tall its leaves tickled the clouds. The tree was old, old, so

old all the other trees called it Old Woman Tree, except the clouds, who said it was Old Foolish Tree. It was big"—she stretched her arms wide apart to show its girth—"and for many years it grew in the forest. It was so big it had a great hollow at the bottom and in there lived two bear-people . . ."

As they went down the stairs, hearing Beatrix's murmuring voice above, Kuntaw put his hand on Tonny's shoulder.

"Come outside with me and walk to the river. The recent rain fattened the river and disturbed the weir. While we mend it I want you to tell me of Malaan and Mi'kma'ki. Do not spare me."

They waded in, shifted stones. Tonny watched Kuntaw to see how it was done, replacing those the current had dislodged. The sky was overcast, a leaden dreary day of biting damp. The water numbed their feet and legs. Tonny talked haltingly, then furiously, told of Malaan's lethargy, her withdrawal into a silent world, the whitemen who pulled her about. He told of Hanah and how her wildness with the same whitemen had brought about her death. "Henly Clawfoot. I would kill him if I stayed there. Many times I want kill all."

"You did well, my son, to bring your children here. I will care for them as I should have cared for you. I will pay for my neglect of Malaan and our people. I know well my earlier life was one of wrong behavior and loss. I did not teach you the things you need to know." They came out of the water, pulled on their *mkisn* and began to walk back to the house in silence, Kuntaw opening his mouth several times until at last he began.

"It is not winter, but I will tell you the old stories of our people and the great ones in our lineage." He did not wait for Tonny's reply but began to speak of warriors and hunters, of ancestors, but could not tell of the horror of seeing his mother's severed arm, of Achille's disappearance, his own years searching for that missing father. All the time he spoke he felt he was talking to the sky. The sky, as unmoved as Tonny, responded with a chill fine mist that thickened into steady

rain. Kuntaw said, "I went from one tree to another, unthinking, never reflecting on you, my first son. But now I see I was not a good man. I should not have looked for Achille. I should have stayed with you and Malaan. So I say you should not leave your children."

Tonny shrugged. The more Kuntaw spoke the colder grew his feeling for this father. He called him by name.

"Kuntaw. I do not belong here. I do not belong in Mi'kma'ki—Nova Scotia, they say it now. I am apart from every person, English, Mi'kmaq, French, American. I have *no place.* Many Mi'kmaw people in the village pretend all is well, but the animals are scarce and no one knows the correct way to live. White people take the berries, the clams, the fish and sell them. I cannot pretend. I have told you how things are at the English post. You, you have this woman. I have no one. I not belong. No place good for me. I go away. Maybe somebody kill me soon. Then I be done." So he said, with rain trickling from his hair, soaking his shoulders.

The rain became a deluge. Kuntaw felt needles of fear in his throat when he heard these words. Was this his son or a malignant spirit in his shape? It was true that Tonny appeared different—not as two-spirit people are different, but more . . . white. Bad white. He was nicked everywhere with old scars, his features bunched in a scowl, he spoke in a hoarse voice. He was dirty and ill-clothed. Kuntaw wondered what he truly was, this isolate and unknowable young man. But he smiled numbly and said, "Foolish words. You still young. You have a place here. You did a good thing to bring the children here. Do not inflict the wrong that I did you on them. Stay here with me. Stay."

He was afraid the whitemen had broken this abandoned son.

It rained all night and a heavy fog made the world impenetrable, yet Tonny said he would go, he would try New Brunswick for work.

"I hope to come back for you," he mumbled to Elise, Amboise and Jinot. He met Kuntaw's censorious eyes boldly. Had he not done the same? Yes, Kuntaw wordlessly agreed, he had done the same.

• • •

There was little work. The lumber camps were the only places that would hire Indians, considered disposable labor—good enough, as long as they lasted, and for water work the best, while they stayed among the living. From a lumber camp, Tonny thought, he could always move deeper into the forest though he had no gun. He thought about trying to live in the forest without a gun. Without knowing the ways of animals. Would he go to a city? To Boston? Would he find something or someone? He had to find a new way. He would try the lumber camps first. And so he went to a chaotic world of groaning trees that ripped holes in the canopy, felled other trees, snapped off halfway, exploded into splinters. Some trees refused to come down, locking their branches into nearby neighbors, teetering on half-gnawed stumps. A few, on the edge of a new clearing and unprotected by the fallen hundreds, waited for the windstorms that would sweep them flat in great waves, uprooted, clods of dirt dropping with small sounds. He worked through the winter limbing felled pine and in the spring drive the boss ordered him into a bateau: he was an Indian and by birth skilled with the paddle. But Tonny's knowledge of bateaux was that they were shelters, roofs that had protected him from the rain in his childhood. He was no riverman. Before he could collect his season's pay, he drowned below Wolf Falls and, like countless other fathers, slipped into the past.

At the house on Penobscot Bay, Kuntaw's failure to make Tonny into an instant Mi'kmaw wrenched his heart; he withdrew a little from Beatrix. He spoke to Amboise, too young to understand. "I am shamed I left Mi'kma'ki, my people and my son." He saw himself without pity as one who was witlessly destroying the ancient ways. Although he reflected that the larch loses its needles, the maple and beech their leaves, standing bare until gleaming new leaves open again, Mi'kmaw people were putting out very few fresh leaves. And he, none at all.

A thousand times Kuntaw had heard Beatrix say, "I need you, Indian man," as she had the day she rode up to him on her horse. At first he thought she meant she needed him to split wood for her. As the weeks passed he thought she meant she needed him for sex. But one day he understood. She needed him because she was a half-Indian woman who had been brought up as a whiteman girl. She needed him to make her an Indian. She had been leading him into books. But now that he knew he pushed the books aside.

"Woman," he said, "now I will teach *you* to read," and he led her into the forest, patiently explaining, as he should have done with Tonny, how to understand and decipher the tracks of animals, the seasonal signs of plants and trees, the odors of bears and coming rain, of frost-leathered leaves, the changing surface of water, intimating how it all fitted together. "These are things every Mi'kmaw person knows," he said. "And now do you understand that the forest and the ocean shore are tied together with countless strings as fine as spiderweb silks? Do you begin to glimpse Indian ways and learning? I would not wish an ignorant wife."

"Yes," Beatrix said. "But it is too much to remember."

"Not to remember like a lesson," he said, "but to know, to feel." He knew this was hopeless.

She soon begged off these excursions. "I have told you my Passamaquoddy mother died when I was very young, before she could teach me anything. It is a pity. What I know I learned from my father. I had to learn the medicinal plants. He often wrote to me from Leiden and asked to have certain pungent leaves sent to him." But this father, Outger, who never returned yet bombarded Beatrix with letters and advice, with packets of books and outmoded European garments, died abroad a year before Kuntaw came out of the woods to her. He thought of Beatrix's father, if he thought of him at all, as a whiteman, all fiery will and command but with many affectations. He was glad that an ocean and death lay between them.

Beatrix taught the children their letters and numbers, gave them books to read, and Kuntaw, who had failed to teach Tonny, now showed his grandchildren what Francis-Outger and Josime already knew—how to hunt, to paddle a canoe. The boys stuck to him like burrs, and together they prowled the shrinking woodlands, carved and whittled, mended garments, stewed eels, coaxed fish into their hands. "You must learn these things," said Kuntaw, "you who are more unconscious of the world than stones. You are Mi'kmaw blood but you know nothing." He showed them animals, plants and yes, grasshoppers as prey. He fashioned child-size bows for Amboise and Jinot. Let them hunt grasshoppers, even as he had! Let them not be ignorant of Mi'kmaw ways. Yet he found it impossible to teach them everything he knew unless all could live inside the Mi'kmaw life; it was more than knowing how to use certain tools or recognize plants. What he taught was not a real life; it was only a kind of play, he thought gloomily. That world he wanted them to know had vanished as smoke deserts the dying embers that made it.

All around the Penobscot settlement the trees fell, tracks inched through the forests, only one or two, then seven, then webs of trails that over the decades widened into roads. The roads were muddy, sometimes like batter, sometimes thick and clutching until late summer, when they metamorphosed into choking dust so fine it hung in the air long after a horse and carriage passed, settling on the grass as the English people settled on the land.

The years passed and logging companies and settlers stripped the banks of the bay and moved up the Penobscot. Fields of wheat and hay took the land, these fields enclosed by linked stumps, the root wads of the forest that had once stood there turned on their edges to bar the whiteman's cows and sheep. Along the shore settlers' houses were stitched into tight rows by paling fences. The old Charles Duquet house sat alone in its acreage, surrounded by forest that had never been cut, a relic of the wooden world.

A day came when Beatrix noticed her son Josime giving Elise glances that were not brotherly and said to Kuntaw that perhaps it was time she was married. Elise was fifteen, rather old to be single. Kuntaw's advice was to send her to Nova Scotia to stay with his sister, Aledonia; there she might find a Mi'kmaw husband. There she might live a Mi'kmaw life. He had forgotten what Tonny had said of the place, remembered only the good days before the moose hunt of his childhood.

Everyone noticed how the little girls of the settlement, whether Indian, French, *métis* or English, wanted to be with Jinot. They ran to meet him, told him their small secrets and swore him not to tell—he never did—brought him pieces of ginger cake stolen from the home pantries. Beatrix, who watched them whispering, asked, "What do they tell you, Jinot?"

"Tell me worms, funny frogs. Just nothing." The conversations were loaded with giggles. Few girls, or later, women, could resist Jinot's impish, smiling ways.

"Stay that way, dear child," murmured Beatrix, who was not immune to his charm.

Kuntaw also watched Jinot and noticed he was different as some Mi'kmaw of the old days were different. The name for the difference escaped him.

The wooden world extended out into the bay in the shape of water-craft. Amboise and Jinot Sel played with the village boys on the wharves, ran, balanced and jumped on the floating logs in the saw-mill ponds, pretending they were on a log drive. The heroes of all were the rivermen riding the logs down the surly Penobscot. The boys around the bay paddled canoes and rowed skiffs; as they grew, they worked with fishermen, learned to mend and cast nets and haul lines, and the sons of the fishermen pulled for deeper water when they, too, joined the maritime trade. Day after day the children watched men loading mast ships with the great pine spars, stacking plank lumber on decks. The Sel children went with Kuntaw to mend the weirs, to help drive and catch eels—their dependable and favored food. For the town boys the ideal future was to chop great pines and ride the boiling waters of the spring freshets. For Jinot and Amboise Sel it was an irresistible pull.

The children grew up too rapidly, Beatrix thought. One day they were children, still full of questions and innocent enthusiasms, and the next day they were grown men with tempers and ideas who pre-ferred Kuntaw's company to hers. When Francis-Outger turned twenty-one and married a half-French, half-Mi'kmaw girl, he and the girl's father built a small cabin for the young couple. Then Josime left home, going to the New Brunswick lumber camps. A month later it was Amboise's turn to go to the woods. For Jinot Sel, the only one left, time passed very slowly. For him the year dragged on, spring arrived and he watched the acres of logs that escaped the mills float down the river and into the bay, envied the jaunty rivermen who prod-ded and corraled the dumb timber. After the drive Amboise, broader and stronger, came home with tremendous stories. And money, too. Summer came and faded. Amboise left again to work as a swamper for a New Brunswick outfit. For weeks the cries of geese rang like blacksmiths hammering lofty anvils. The moon waxed full, lunatic clouds racing across its face. Jinot suffered from a restless urge to go somewhere. One morning, his decision made, he went to Kuntaw.

"Grandfather, I am old enough and I want to go to the forest camps to cut trees," he said. Kuntaw nodded. "I know you think of starting a man's life," he said, "although there are many girls who maybe think you better stay. You have been warm with these girls. Is it not possible many children here will call you father?"

Jinot, shocked, said no, no. "Grandfather, the girls only talk to me. Girls like to talk to somebody. We are friends." Kuntaw looked at his grandson with an assessing, weighing eye, putting wispy thoughts together.

"Yes, I see. I see you. I am old, Jinot, but do not take me for a fool.

If you were among Mi'kmaw people they would see no wrong in a man who has a double spirit. But whitemen call it bad. And those church men."

There was nothing to say to this. In a moment Kuntaw continued. "When will you go?"

"Today. I have warm clothes in a hide bag. Shall I take an ax?"

"Have an ax if you wish, but the lumber camp will give you as many as you need. They provide the tools. This I know, for I, too, worked in those camps chopping trees, even as my father, Achille, did, and his father, the Frenchman René Sel, before him."

"I did not know of the Frenchman René. He is our ancestor?"

"He was my grandfather, murdered, they said, by a girl he adopted. So you see we have French blood in us. But René Sel did not work in lumber camps. He cut trees for himself. Jinot, before you go into the forest I want you to travel with Amboise to Mi'kma'ki and see Elise, see if she is well, if she has children. We have heard nothing. And I want you to inquire if my cousin Auguste, son of my deceased aunt Noë, is still alive. He was a person always in trouble so he may be dead. Though I have noticed that many people who cause trouble live long lives. If he is alive I want him to come here and stay with us. And take care. The woods and rivers are full of English and Americans fighting. Stay distant if you hear firearms."

Amboise, who was very strong and heavy-shouldered, and Jinot, waving farewell to a bouquet of girls on the wharf who called his name, went by ship up the coast to Halifax, made a foot journey to the post.

"I do not have a good feeling for Elise," said Amboise. "I remember Tonny said Mi'kma'ki was a bad place." In his pocket he had a small wooden turkey he had carved long ago, an object that amused Elise when she was young.

"If she has children," he said, "I thought maybe they like to play with this."

"Amboise, that is a good idea. I wish I had brought something—even a pinecone."

Kuntaw's sister, Aledonia, thin and with many teeth missing, made much of them, pointed out certain people with the patronym Sel, and told them that yes, Auguste still lived. "That one! He is too bad to die!"

But Amboise and Jinot saw the Mi'kmaw village was a hungry sad place, a mix of *wikuoms* and whiteman cabins. The eel weirs were in disrepair and rarely did the men make an effort to put them in order. It was easier to eat bread and pork from the agency than catch eels. Luçon Brassua, Elise's husband, lay drunk in the mud beside their *wikuom,* whose torn bark covering needed repairs. They were sorry for Elise, who cried and said she had lost a baby girl whom she had called Bee after Beatrix.

"I thought married would be like Beatrix and Grandfather Kuntaw, nice, laughing, you know?" She wept women's tears.

While they were in the chopped lands of what once had been Mi'kma'ki they heard stories of Kuntaw's father, Achille the Great Hunter. For some reason these stories made Amboise resentful. "Everything yesterday! Everything good happens long ago! Now—oh now . . ." His eyes narrowed. "Elise, if Brassua is not good to you, you must come with us." They knew that Brassua was not good to her. Guilty and uneasy, they wanted to get away.

Old Auguste had succumbed to drink. They found him at the *wikuom* of one of his granddaughters, bleary and nodding, sitting outside squinting at whatever happened there. When they told him they were Kuntaw's grandsons he roused a little, huffing out rum breath, gave a bitter smile and said Kuntaw had had a fortunate life, unlike him. He spoke in an old man voice, then clamped his mouth shut. They sat together and watched the dozen idle Mi'kmaw men who hung around the post like flies on meat. Amboise was surprised to see tears running down wicked old Auguste's face as he watched them.

"They have nothing to do. When Kuntaw and I were of those

years," he said, "we were always ready for a hunt or go for eels, fish or seals or sturgeon. We made our bows and arrows, we made crooked knives and good canoes, we fashioned the paddles. We had good war games then, not like fighting foreigners with guns. The young men—yes, even I—committed brave deeds and there were feasts and dances such as are no longer performed. But you see what we have become," he said and he pointed first at the idlers, then at himself. His hand groped beneath his thigh for the flat bottle.

"Elise," said Amboise. "Come away now." She threw her few possessions into a turnip sack and outstripped them running for the boat landing. Luçon Brassua was not there to hold her back.

"He is drunk with his friends," said Elise. "We go now, now!"

"Wait. We must get Auguste. Kuntaw wants him to live in the Penobscot house." The old man got up, trembling when he heard he was to come with them. He looked around. The idlers stood near the post doorway, a dog scratched its fleas. He sat down again, smiling slyly.

"No. Too late. You go. I stay."

No matter what they said he refused. "Someone must stay. I will be the One Who Remains."

He was always good at naming.

Amboise used the money Kuntaw had given them to buy passages on a vessel going from Halifax to Boston, then persuaded the owner of a fishing boat bound for Georges Bank to detour and drop them at Penobscot Bay. Elise said very little to them on the return journey, but when the boat sailed into their home port she sucked in a great deep breath and exhaled. Beatrix, who saw them coming up from the wharf, threw the front door open. She looked at Elise, saw the fading bruises and brimming eyes and understood everything. She stretched out her arms.

"Oh, thank God, my poor Elise, you are with us again. You are safe at home now."

"Mother," Elise cried. Beatrix embraced her and both women began to sob. Amboise and Jinot looked at each other; they had never seen Beatrix cry.

"This is a woman thing," muttered Amboise, his eyes stinging. "Let us go out."

Though Jinot wanted to be with Elise and Beatrix, he followed Amboise.

39

Dr. Mukhtar

"What is *wrong* with me?" demanded Beatrix of Elise's dog, Ami, a wolfish creature who could not ignore porcupines. The dog, flinching from her angry tone, looked at the floor. For months a pain had been twisting in the woman's belly, came like a crab in the night to pinch at her gut. She had days when she rushed about as usual, teaching a boy from the village to read and write, concocting elaborate meals for Kuntaw, who turned away. He only wanted the spare foods of his childhood.

A new path had opened to Kuntaw—guiding whitemen to hunt and fish. It started when a Boston man, Mr. Williams, came to him and said he wanted to go in the Maine woods and hunt, and he needed a guide; he would pay. Kuntaw knew the forest, streams and lakes from his years in the logging camps. And they went north together on the train, then by buckboard, then by canoe. Mr. Williams returned to Boston dirty, scratched up, his eyes red from campfire smoke, thinner and more agile; he felt himself a tough woodsman. He had caught more than fifty trout in a single day and described his taciturn Mi'kmaw guide to envious friends. Not only that. The war for independence had linked the idea of freedom to a country of wild forests. Americans saw themselves as *homines sylvestris*—men of the forest.

Kuntaw worked tirelessly at this odd business; he carried the packs and canoe, hacked trails through young spruce thickets, and at the campsite he built the lean-to, chopped firewood and got a fire going, cooked samp, trout, wild meat, seasoned only with shreds of wild ginger and garlic. Soon he had regular customers who wanted to hunt moose or caribou, whitemen who wove these trips into tales of manly adventures.

It seemed to Kuntaw he had blundered into the strangest occupation in the world, helping men have a "holiday," men ignorant of the tattered forests, ignorant of canoes and paddling, ignorant of weather signs and plants, of fire building. They angered him sometimes. Judge James, whom the others treated with deference, said, "You Indians have a nice life. Just hunt and fish all the time, let the women do the work." He laughed. Kuntaw said nothing then but later, smoking a pipe with Ti-Sabatis, another guide he saw sometimes at the boat landing, he said, "Whitemen never see it was our *work*. For them hunt and fish is only to play. They think we lazy because we only 'play.'"

Ti-Sabatis smiled a little. "These men don't know nothing about the woods, but they pay good money and I don't know how they get that money, so they do somethin pretty smart."

"It was our life and we lived it, but it was not easy like those whitemen think." Yet he enjoyed these excursions.

The illness had made Beatrix a different person from the energetic long-haired beauty on a sorrel horse. They had had many happy years, but she was old now, as was he. She was ill and the illness frightened him. Kuntaw wanted to turn it back, to return her to the old Beatrix. He brought her cups of tea. She drank slowly, slowly, smiled at him and then vomited. It was now, when she most needed him, that he veered away from her. He could not help it. His feelings had begun to change years earlier, when Tonny arrived with his three children, bringing the old Mi'kmaw life with him. In his shame at his neglect of Tonny and Malaan, Kuntaw began to regard Beatrix as Other. The feeling was always there, even when they were glad to be together and with their children. Like a faraway drumbeat something inside him said, *She is not Mi'kmaq.* He had not made her into an Indian. He had betrayed his people by leaving Malaan and Tonny for her. He had betrayed Beatrix by failing to fullfill her wish. Every spring when he readied to take a Boston man on a fishing trip he was a little more pleased to be away from Beatrix's house, to be back in the forest.

Beatrix's good days became fewer; the pain always returned as though refreshed by its holiday and bit into its victim with greater force. If Elise brought cod broth to her she would sip a few drops from the spoon and then vomit. Her bowels became untrustworthy, her face gaunt and drawn, arms and legs like reeds, but the treacherous stomach swelled and grew enormous. The pain was the size of a beaver and gnawing with a beaver's yellow chisel teeth.

Elise washed Beatrix's soiled linens and hung them out to be sweetened by the chill wind off the bay. She cooked for herself and Kuntaw, kept broth simmering for Beatrix, who often could not swallow it. Elise knew little of herbal medicines and came to Kuntaw.

"Grandfather Kuntaw. Beatrix has been ill for six moons and I do not know how to ease the pain. It grows. She won't eat nothin. Do you not know a healer who understands this sickness?"

But Kuntaw shook his head. "Maybe still in Mi'kma'ki, but here, no. She will want a whiteman doctor."

"If he will come," said Elise. "I have heard that he is haughty and says he will only treat white people."

"Well," said Kuntaw. "Beatrix's father was whiteman. He had doctor friends. Maybe all dead now."

He spent an uncomfortable quarter hour with the sick woman and prized the names of two medical men from her. The first, elderly Dr. Woodrit, sent a message that he had a full list of patients and could not come. The second, Dr. Hallagher, an Irish fellow new to Penobscot Bay, visited Beatrix, examined and talked with her for some time. When he came out of the sickroom he sat beside Elise and shook his head.

"She knows many big words, this Ind—this lady. I think she has a bad sickness, and I advise to call in a certain learned doctor from Boston—Dr. Mukhtar—if he will come. He has much experience with—with stomach ailments. Of this kind."

Elise wanted to ask what "this kind" was, but only stared at him with pleading dark eyes.

Hallagher continued, studying the tense woman. "He is a foreigner, and his ways are not our—your—usual ways, but he is very learned in medicine. If anyone can do anything . . ." He promised he would write to Dr. Mukhtar himself and see if he could be persuaded to make the trip to the Penobscot Bay house. Elise's face changed for a moment and she smiled at him, the roguish Sel smile.

When Kuntaw heard all this he exhaled between his teeth, a hissing sound like that of an angry animal, furious to feel so helpless, and went outside. He could not bear to see her suffering.

Dr. Hallagher returned on a weekday afternoon ten days later, shining with cleanliness and fresh linen, hoping to find Elise alone. But Kuntaw was also there, repairing his guide equipment for another Maine trip.

Kuntaw nodded and nodded when Dr. Hallagher said that the Boston doctor—Mukhtar—would arrive any day and examine Beatrix. He was making the arduous trip. But, said the Irishman, Kuntaw should not get his hopes up expecting a cure. Beatrix's illness was profound. Kuntaw nodded, then asked a brutal question.

"How long she live?"

Hallagher stuttered out that he did not know, that God would decide, that Dr. Mukhtar could perhaps say, but he—no, he could not say. He left without a chance for a few private minutes with Elise.

• • •

It was a cool autumn afternoon when Dr. Mukhtar arrived on a black Arabian mare that had turned heads all the way from Boston. As he was removing his saddlebags, Elise came out and said that if he liked he could turn the mare in to the horse pasture or put her in the stable, as he preferred. He chose the pasture with its shady maples and rattling brook. He was a small, wiry man with a foreign face, wet black eyes and a nose like a falcon's beak. Elise thought his dark face was frightening, even devilish, his voice somewhat rough but kind. A little reluctantly she led him into the house.

As soon as he stepped into the hall he sniffed the fetid air and knew what he would find. Elise took him first into the schoolroom, where Beatrix always served visitors and brought him a cup of tea. He put his saddlebags on the great pine table. He asked Elise many questions, demanded she show him Beatrix's soiled sheets, examined them closely. He looked at Elise with his glittering foreign eyes.

"Is there another person who can help *you*? You are thin and very tired. Nursing someone with an advanced stomach cancer is exhausting. We must get you some help." Elise was shocked to hear Beatrix's sickness named and knew at once there must be a fatal conclusion. Then came his questions; never had she been asked so many. He wanted to know everything about Beatrix, about Elise, Kuntaw and the family, their circumstances, how they came to be in this house; he even asked about the foods they ate and nodded as if he already knew when Elise told him Beatrix was uncommonly fond of meats smoked in the chimney. It was unnerving how many questions the man could ask. She saw how he looked around the schoolroom. Their two porcelain cups looked small and frail on the table's wood expanse.

The house on Penobscot Bay had always been the great possession of Outger and Beatrix. But Outger had left and she had stayed. New people were building bigger houses with clapboarded painted sides all around the bay now. Charles Duquet's great log house had become a decaying eyesore derided by the white settlers as "the wood wigwam." When at last she sold the woodlot stumpage, the house, black with age, stood naked and decrepit.

With the trees gone Beatrix saw the decaying house. The roof and sills could not wait and just as she fell ill Beatrix sold the last big pines in her woodlot to pay for the repairs. Kuntaw simply did not notice such defects; it was a house, a big immovable house.

Elise showed Dr. Mukhtar to the sick woman's room. Under the single window was a table piled with books Beatrix had been reading before they became too heavy for her to hold. He looked at the titles, then sat beside the bed in a rosewood chair with a cracked leg. The woman lay in an uneasy sleep of shallow rapid breaths, febrile and wasted. He looked at her steadily. Suddenly she moaned and her eyes flew open.

"Am I in hell now?" she whispered as her eyes took his measure.

Dr. Mukhtar, who quite understood that the pain had awakened her and that she thought he was the devil, said, "No, madam, you are not, although it may seem that way. Allow me to introduce myself and let us work together to see how I may help you. But at the moment I believe you are in too much pain to carry on a rational conversation, so I will just fetch a sedative that will allow you some ease for a while."

He went to his saddlebags and came back with a black vial and a teaspoon.

"Please open and swallow."

"I will vomit," she said.

"No, you will not. You will be calmed and the pain will back away. For a while. Open." He watched her swallow painfully, half-retching. He held her up until the easing began.

In a few minutes Beatrix, panting with relief, looked at Dr. Mukhtar. "Oh," she said, "oh, oh. Oh how good. Thank you."

"The pain will return but we shall fight it in every way we can."

He examined her legs, palpated the great lump of stomach, asked her if she was able to eat anything, how long it had been difficult to swallow, did she vomit blood, was there blood in her stool, black and grainy, was she often breathless? In the midst of a reply she fell asleep again, but breathed deeply.

The next time she woke the light in the room was dim. Dr. Mukhtar still sat in the chair, his dark face hidden in shadow, his black clothing blending in to the chair's indigo shadow. Beatrix's pain was still at bay and this pleased him.

"I know my death is approaching," said Beatrix. "What is wrong with me, is the pain returning soon, how long . . ." Her voice fell away.

"You have a stomach cancer but also much fluid in your stomach, which I can relieve, though it, like the pain, will return. It is a battle, Mistress Beatrix, a battle that at this stage you cannot win. Perhaps another month, perhaps two. I will do all I can to smother the pain. Will you allow me to stay here? Your daughter, Elise, needs rest and I must be on hand to attend you. Do not worry, I have brought enough elixir to soothe elephants for a decade."

"I want to die," she said. "I want to be done with the pain, done with this life." But this was not entirely true. Over the next six weeks Beatrix developed deep feelings for Dr. Mukhtar as they spoke of books and ideas, of places imagined but never seen, of peace and quiet, of horses, for Mukhtar knew much about these animals. It pleased Beatrix to think of galloping horses, fluttering silky manes. At first it was the doctor who spoke while she listened, half asleep, half dead. The pain elixir became less effective and he tried another. Kuntaw came in now and then, but Beatrix could not look lovingly at him nor he at her.

To Dr. Mukhtar she said, "My father told me once that swallowing Guatemalan lizards was a cure for this illness."

"Never can this be. It is the rarity of Guatemalan lizards in Boston and its environs that earns them the reputation of a great cure. One might also name unicorn milk as a cure. There is no cure. When it becomes resistant to all I have, I will give you a sleeping draft that never fails to bring the final relief."

He came in every morning, opened the window, which shrieked in its warped frame, and gave her the blesséd elixir. From the bed Beatrix looked at the sky and saw a thin cloud like a ribbon of spilled cream on blue satin. In the hours of respite from pain she began to talk to him in her hoarse voice, sometimes whispering when her throat was too painful for speaking.

She told of her lonely childhood, Outger's obsessive teaching, books and books, his declaration that when she was sixteen he would send her to Europe for "finishing," likely to Switzerland, which was fashionable, something that never happened, the usual way of Outger's promises. She spoke of the enmity of the Dukes, who did not acknowledge her existence after their failed efforts to wrest Outger's big pine table from her. She told him of Kuntaw and their happy years, her children, Francis-Outger and Josime, spoke of Tonny and the grandchildren, now grown, but always she circled back to Outger and his hours drilling her in Latin and Greek, assigning books for her to read, his discussions of theories and inventions.

"I can see now," she said, "that all his pedagogy was an experiment." The books and instruction had been his attempt to make her into something like a learned whiteman, like himself. After he left for Leiden the instruction continued in the form of boxes of books, papers, long letters of advice and orders, but she gradually understood that she herself was not wanted—she was nothing to Outger but a subject on which to practice his ideas of intellectual development. She had failed in some way to become an Enlightened Savage, and so remained alone in the house on Penobscot Bay. When the solitude became a monstrous frustration she began to look for one who could help her become an Indian. Kuntaw had come with her to split wood and had stayed for many years. They had made children together.

"But," she said sadly, "I could not become an Indian."

"Of course not," said Dr. Mukhtar. "There is a whole world of signs, symbols and spirits which all must be absorbed from birth. You could not hope to grasp the meanings except by living the entire life."

She could not, she explained to Dr. Mukhtar, express affection except by teaching, holding out books as tokens of love. When at last light the doctor, exhausted from listening, stood to go to his room above for the night and pinched out the candle, she begged him to leave the curtains and the window open. The door closed gently and she could look at the moon, a blood-streaked egg yolk rolling in the shell of sky.

In the last week of her life Beatrix had the illusion she was suspended in an immense bowl of water. At first the water was as easy to breathe as air, but gradually as the mass in her stomach pressed on her lungs it became viscous as old honey. The bowl was similar to the yellow crockery bowl in which she had mixed bread dough. Occasionally she surfaced and in the distance could see its pale rim. Some days the water was limpid and yielding, others, shot through with strong orange currents of pain. Underwater storms raged, and then she had tried to draw up her legs to protect her throbbing gut from the lightning strikes.

Dr. Mukhtar tried many ways to make Beatrix's fading existence more bearable. Francis-Outger, whose house was only a mile distant, came every day with balsam boughs for the sickroom so the spicy scent of the forest could cleanse the air. He brought juniper berries and Dr. Mukhtar crushed these and their dry bitter perfume made Beatrix smile, a smile more like a grimace, but all she could manage. She died in this cordial of fragrance. Fifty-two strange years and then to fall in love on her deathbed.

Elise stood weeping at the window. Francis-Outger said to her, "I will go to Josime's camp and tell him. Maybe he knows where Amboise works now, maybe he knows where Jinot is. Did they not tell you their camps?"

"Jinot sent a letter asking if we all were well, but I have not found a moment to answer. He said he was working for a Canada man— Marchand. Up north. Amboise I don't know."

•   •   •

Kuntaw had hardened himself to resist the pain of losing Beatrix. He had lost Tonny, he had lost Malaan. He had lost Beatrix. He had lost himself. He turned his painful feelings into rejection, told himself his years with Beatrix had been wasted. She was not an Indian but an overeducated white woman in an Indian body. In those years with her he had become weak and powerless. Yet he knew he could regain his lost strength, for he felt young, though perhaps not young enough to dance and drive his feet deep into the earth up to the knee with each crashing step.

He would go to the north, where there was still half-wild forest. He thought of the way his people had lived in it when they were not on the coast, thought of Achille, his father, standing up with the great dead bear on his back; it must have weighed four hundred pounds. He, Kuntaw, could not carry full-grown bears, but he could live in the old way, even though the trees of the forest were now mere stuff, whiteman stuff. Whitemen looked at trees and saw they were good only to build flat-sided cage-houses or ships. Kuntaw wanted to know trees again as the old people knew them.

The year before Beatrix was ill he had killed a moose—for there were still a few moose for men who knew how to find them—and made himself a proper Mi'kmaw jacket. He had never given up greased *mkisn* for whiteman shoes. He had his beaver cloak and deer-hide leggings, pliable and silent when he moved through brush. And now, with Beatrix dead, he would go to the northern forest and he would build a camp as if for two, just as he did for his clients, but there would be no client. He would have everything for two— clothing, bed robes; he would have no whiteman's metal pots for they would spoil the magic of his camp. He would cook for two people, setting out the dish for the One Who Would Come. He had once believed Beatrix was that One, and surely she herself had believed it of him.

He mended his bows and made new arrows. He would live among trees until the One Who Would Come appeared, and he knew it would be like the shadows of moving leaves at first, gradually becoming more solid until the day the One accepted the extra set of clothes and appeared before him as firm and real as a tree. They would hunt together, deep companions, and he, Kuntaw, would share his new friend's magic power. He would be strong again. He would be a Mi'kmaw man again.

40

choppers and rivermen

At seventeen Jinot Sel's smiling face had been at once amusing and dissolute with full cheeks, heavy-lidded eyes. His hair was thick and springy as a bear's pelt, his mouth thin and curled, a face with something of a mink's eager expression. He was quick of movement like Grandfather Kuntaw. Not only girls and women wanted to sit with him, mature men also looked at him, and in a certain way.

After a year as a swamper-limber in a decrepit Penobscot camp, he hired on as a chopper and riverman with Simon Marchand. The camp lay on a feeder branch of the big Penobscot. Marchand, a subcontractor, had taken on a tract of aged monster trees judged by most lumbermen as too big, too awkwardly placed on a gullied ridge to be worth getting.

"Nah," said Marchand, "what I say is this is a long route—take two seasons cut up to them old trees. Then we might get them big boys, *if* we cut good track for a ice road. Biggest log in the world comes along sweet on a ice road. It's a pretty good show."

Marchand seemed to have started life as an ash tree, barked, scraped and whittled down to sinewy fiber. His hooded eyes glinted. His neck was encircled by coarse hair foaming up from his chest. He was a hard-nosed Maine man who had kicked his way up and was still kicking.

God-fearing Marchand did not allow holy names to be used as curses in the camp. "You know the man that oaths like that, will be a judgment on him." He cited scores of examples of men who had cursed and without fail they had been mashed, drowned, frozen, quartered, speared and fried. Every logger knew of such things. And so Marchand's camps were fueled by imprecations of "all-fired tarnal dickie bird," "by dang," "dern," "by gar!" Jinot kept a holy silence.

Like most camps Marchand's looked impermanent; the cookhouse was crowded into the north end of the shanty. Downslope stood a slipshod ox hovel. A constant stream of red-shirted choppers came and went, men from the north and coastal fishermen—Irish, Bluenoses, Province men, a few French Canadians, St. Francis Indians, Passamaquoddy and Mi'kmaq, and P. I.s—men from Prince Edward Island—and sometimes a man from foreign shores. There were always two or three Québécois running from the impoverished *habitant* life. The border between Maine and Québec was so twisted by the waterways that men passed freely over the unknown line—a place that could be what you wanted it to be.

In the lumber camp they were a brotherhood of the ax. A kind of pride in excess and risky work knitted them. Up before daylight to gnaw on cold salt pork and gulp boiled tea, they walked to the cut carrying their sharpened axes and private thoughts. They walked back to the shanty in near dark to more pork and watery bean porridge, then fell into stunned sleep until the bull cook's wordless catamount shrieks woke them—too dark to see, too dark to cut until the faintest light arrived. They stood in the still and merciless cold, ax heads beneath their jackets thrust up into their armpits to keep the steel from freezing, waiting for the light, so cold they could feel the arcs of their eyebrows, ice-stiffened nostril hairs.

There were no bunks, only the dirt floor, moist with tobacco juice and tramped-in food scraps; along one wall lay a greasy blanket to cover a row of louse-infested men. At night they heard wood borers rasping through the logs. If rain slanted in and soaked the blanket it took a week of multiple body heat to dry it out again.

After the spring drive most blew their wages in the log-shanty bars and whorehouses of the nearest town, bummed around until some contract logger came looking for raw labor. This calling of destruction was suited to them: no chance for other work, nothing to lose but their lives—but they were young and immortal, and you were safe if you were fast. A few worked for Marchand all year, chopping in the winter, driving in the spring, sawing in his mills through the summer. Jinot chopped and worked the drive that first year, tried the sawmill but after a few days of wood dust and noise he went home to the big house to gorge on eel and fresh garden truck, luxuriate in the attention of Beatrix and Kuntaw, then back to the camp with the autumn frosts.

Like most woods bosses Marchand tagged Indians and *métis* for river work. Indians were the best rivermen for the long-log drives. Their quick reactions and inborn sense of balance, he said, made them agile on moving logs. "Them sons a porcupines born in a canoe," Marchand said, and described himself as half French, half Malecite, half Penobscot and half Scots and, as a 200 percent man, was naturally more than a little skillful in a bateau. Every spring drive most of the choppers went back to their farms, leaving Marchand and the Indians in charge of the river and its blanket of hurtling, jackstraw-prone logs.

From his first season Jinot fit into the life. At the north end of the shanty Peter the cook and his helper Panette produced pork, fried cornmeal mush and yellow-eye beans, potatoes, bread, boiled beef and mashed turnip; Jinot relished it all. In late afternoon before the men came in the cook set out a bowl of water with a dipper in it. Every man chewed tobacco and after drinking put the dipper back in the bowl. A thin film of tobacco-flavored spit spread over the water surface. Jinot tried the dipper once and then whittled out a wood canister, which he filled with clean brook water.

"What," said Panette menacingly, "common water ain't good enough for a dirty Indan? You got a have your own special water?"

"Don't drink tobacco flavorin."

"Hell you don't," snapped Panette, "keeps ye from gettin worms," and then shut up, but a half-chewed plug of tobacco showed up on

Jinot's morning plate of beans and the coffee tasted of tobacco—and worse. He left his plate standing and beckoned the bull cook outside.

"What you think you can do about it, Indan?" said Panette, bouncing on his toes to remind Jinot that he was a well-known fighter of the saloon alleys. Only one reply to that: Jinot limbered his knees, then from a standstill leapt high, driving his heels into Panette's chest, and when the bull cook went down, kicked and trampled him from forehead to toenail.

It had all happened too quietly and the loggers felt cheated of seeing a good fight, but the head cook gave details and Jinot found himself with elbow room. He slept with his ax under the rolled-up marten pelt he and his friend, Franceway, used for a pillow.

Evenings the men sat on the deacon's bench staring into the flames, arms resting on thighs, hands dangling; they chewed and smoked, they talked and their lives crept out of the stories as moths out of chrysalises. The first night with a new crew in a shanty was cautious, men measuring the others; where they came from, who had brought a fiddle or a harmonica, who was the insufferable fool, did anyone carry new songs in his head, who were the storytellers, who was comical, what rivers had the others worked, what had each seen in his time in the woods? There were five or six fair singers and a whipcord little Montagnais known only as Franceway with a skinny kid's neck, who brought them all to attention with his true-pitched mournful voice. Franceway and Jinot had been together from the first day they saw each other. Franceway knew songs most had never heard before, as "The Randy Shanty Boy," and when he sang his version of "Roy's Wife," he gave a little twist to the words that expressed lechery and wounded pride. Those who could only croak and bellow listened. He was a limber and a riverman, dexterous and elastic. His dark eyes glowed with concentration as he filed his ax. He often sang as he worked—old songs and now and then made new songs himself, celebrating river heroism or describing accidents—

even the cook's more inventive dishes, as the cherry pie made from dried prunes.

In late November the winter set in hard. After their silent supper some men threw themselves down and slept, but most sat looking into the fire.

An ex-sailor in his late forties, one eyebrow missing, was one of four men in the camp who knew how to sign their names. He claimed to have sailed distant oceans on fifty ships in his younger life, told of seeing elephants and chained slaves before he took up the ax.

Sash was the shortest man; he always talked in a monotone about his homeplace and large numbers of dead kin, mostly drowned. "Then next spring Sis slipped on the riverbank and drowned," said Sash. "Drownin's in our family."

"You'll be next," said someone, sotto voce, and Jinot shuddered. Now it would happen.

Sam Keyo and his sons, Ted and Stinking Tom, left their farm and came to the woods every winter for the hard cash. Sam left the laborious agricultural work to the sons while he scoured the woods with his dogs, and claimed the first year on his land he had shot ninety-five deer and eighteen bears, trapped eleven wolves, six cata-mounts and a "tremenjous large sortment of varmints." He was one of several Indian haters in the camp and Jinot stayed clear of him.

His son Ted spent his Sundays hunting for spruce gum and knurls. A crazy-grained knurl brought fifty cents in town and made a superior maul head that would never split. Brother Tom had enough energy after a hard week's work to set traps in the dark on Saturday night and run the line the next afternoon. He stank more than any-one in the camp, a kind of bitter animal musk from his traps.

One who worked silently was Op den Ool, who kept to himself in the back of the ox hovel, where he had a straw bed. The oxen were his company. At the end of the day he picked ice from their hairy legs then massaged them with a liniment he mixed himself of heal-ing herbs, bear grease and crushed ocher-red pigment. Anyone could recognize his red-legged animals from half a mile away.

• • •

They all knew that river work was the most dangerous; there were countless wooden crosses along the banks. That was why the boss gave the water work to the Indians. "Walk the river after ever drive and you'll find Indans floatin in the backwaters. They drown just as good as white men."

Hernias, sprains, broken arms and legs, smashed patellas were part of the work, and the possibility of a mangling death rode on all the men's shoulders even as they defied death with flourishes. The young men had style and they knew it, swaggering about in their pants chopped off below the knee, red shirts and jaunty hats. "A short life and a grieving song," said Byers after Sash's foot was caught between logs rolling off the landing and into the river, where he followed the rest of his family into the water. They recovered his body the next day, fitted him into two flour barrels and buried him.

"Guess he's got enough biscuit dust now," said Byers, for Sash had been famous for polishing off the biscuits, and when they thrust his legs into the first barrel a floury rain fell from the staves onto the wet pants, mixing with the blood seeping from his crushed legs. Franceway sang a grieving song and the lonely fall of his voice was as much for all of them as for Sash.

After the cut Marchand sorted his rivermen. The most important were the dead-water men, who worked the logs like fractious cows with twenty-foot-long pike poles. Most men wrangled hung-up sticks with a swinging bitch, a handle with an irritatingly movable dog on the business end that gave enough leverage to shift the log. All day they were running and jumping, riding the bucking logs, moving so quickly they seemed to dance on river foam, shifting to keep their balance, even in fast water. "You," said Marchand, pointing at Jinot and jabbing his thumb in the direction of the bateaux.

The dark river was flecked with rotten ice, rocks studding its course glistening like fresh-mined coal. The current frothed and boiled, standing waves at the head of a rock and a quiet lozenge of still water at the tail, where, in the old days before the rivers carried millions of bobbing, colliding logs, big salmon would lie.

All day and into the night, their legs festooned with bloodsuckers, the watermen fended off logs trying for the shore, a shore as deep in mire as a hog yard, mud that gave no purchase to a straining man. Days in the icy water caused chilblains, swollen and redly itching legs that swelled and blistered; some men could not bear to sit by the fire for the pain.

Yet twice, despite their labor, the river logs knitted together, bobbing and rising, a huge wooden knot forming to block the river, which began to back up and flood the land. Farmers ran down to the shore shouting that their hay meadows were ruined. Twenty men attacked the first jam, prying and separating logs that seemed to grow into each other. Minutes changed to hours and suddenly a quiver trembled through the mass and the men ran like squirrels for the shore, turned and looked back at what they had escaped: thousands of logs shooting downstream, picking up speed, riding up on each other, hissing with the speed of the current, acres of pine forest on the ride. But the second jam was a killer and they all saw it.

The day was overcast and dark grey. Marchand hoped for rain, a good hard rain that would lift the water level. The rain held off and the difficulty came right where they knew it would. A granite ledge like the backbone of the world ran halfway across the river, plunged underground leaving an opening of two or three rods, then rose again on the other side of the river. The logs had to go through the central channel. The ledge was no problem at high water; logs glided over it with grace. In low water the trick was to have good men standing on each side ready with their pike poles, and more men in the bateaux to guide logs into the narrow passage. Jinot Sel was in one of the three bateaux. Downriver he saw James Ketchum and Franceway standing up to their knees in water herding strays. The orderly procession of logs slowed and almost stopped as tenders upstream jabbed at bunching troublemakers. Onshore, Tom Keyo saw one slightly crooked log, a good forty-footer, elbow its way into a crowd.

"Lookit, that's a bad one, you see it?" he said.

As he spoke the men upstream shoved scores of hustling logs out into the faster current and these swallowed up the troublemaker.

"Goddamn!" yelled Tom Keyo, with no regard for Marchand's rule about swearing. A great batch of logs reached the ledge all at once, and among them was the crooked stick, which hung itself on the ledge. The rest of the logs began to pile up on Old Crooked, as they were already calling it, like sheep struggling through brush to escape a pack of wolves.

"All hands and the cook!" someone screamed.

Higher and higher the logs rose on each other's backs, a vast sheaf of wheat for giants, covering the ledge and forcing Franceway and James Ketchum toward the shore. So high did the logs stack that a few top ones began, of their own volition, to roll down into the central current.

Marchand was dancing with frustration. "From the top, roll 'em in from the top," he shouted, unaware of the crooked key log at the bottom holding the main bunch in place. A dozen men scrambled high and began rolling logs down into the current. But the central jam did not move and new sticks continued to build up. Franceway put down his pike pole and ran for his ax. He shouted at Marchand, who didn't hear him, "There's a key down there, crooked ol son of a goddamn jeezly bitch key!" Gripping his ax he ran out onto the ledge toward the jam, got into the hung-up bunch at the bottom and spied the ill-shaped jam maker. It was crisscrossed by half a dozen big stems and he beckoned to James Ketchum to come help him chop down to the problem.

"Marchand!" screamed Byers over the roar of water, "you got a key hung on the ledge." Marchand nodded. A few of the men on top came to the lower level and began prying at logs. Franceway and Ketchum chopped their way down to the bad log and began to cut into its crooked bend. Crackling sounds came from it and Ketchum shouted "Run!" suiting his action to the words. But Franceway lifted his arms and smote the bent devil a final blow. It broke, the jam quivered and immediately began to haul. Logs gushed over the edge. Jinot, in his bateau above the jam, saw a thirty-foot log rear up at the top of the releasing pile and plunge down like a falling arrow, striking Franceway square in the center of his back. Men onshore heard the crack. Franceway folded backward like a sheet of paper, his heels came past his ears and now a butcher's package of meat, he went under the grind. Jinot opened his jaws to scream but his throat was paralyzed. In that moment his childhood ended.

The workday lasted until after sunset, the long summer light slowly giving way to darkness, and Jinot bereft, weeping in rasps and chokes, crept under the bateau to lie beside Franceway's empty place. He did not sleep but wept and rolled back and forth. It was the first of many sleepless nights. Trying to get past the misery he worked. He cut trees with a surety and rapidity that made him difficult as a chopping partner. He always volunteered for the spring drives and people up and down the rivers recognized his fluid, quick-footed style. "Jinot!" they called. "Jinot Sel." And waved.

He worked for Marchand again for two years, then, like his brothers, moved on to different camps, different rivers. He went home in the summers and chopped the winter's firewood for Beatrix and Kuntaw—eighty cords to keep the old house warm, sometimes also for Francis-Outger, who lived nearby. It was good when Josime or Amboise was there and they sawed, chopped and split in comradely fashion. He went fishing with Kuntaw and Francis-Outger's young son, Édouard-Outger. Once Beatrix made a picnic with roast chicken and potatoes cooked in hot coals. Another year Kuntaw and Beatrix went to the mudflats and came back with a bushel basket of clams, which Kuntaw cooked Mi'kmaw style smothered in seaweed. Jinot helped Elise by lifting great boiling kettles off the fire when she put up vegetables and fruit for the winter, gleaming purple beets in their glass prisons on the cellar shelves alongside varicolored jars of blueberries, peas, beans, applesauce, pickled eggs, and pear halves. Then came the morning when he'd had enough of domesticity, packed his turkey and set off for Bangor and the hiring bosses. If Josime or Amboise was at home, this itch to leave was infectious and they went the distance together. Sometimes they hired out together and hiring bosses fought to get them; it was well known the Sel brothers were the best in the woods.

The years slid by distinguished only by accidents, injuries, wildfire and strange events. Then, around the time of the new century, for some unclear reason, they again began to work at different camps. Once more Jinot joined Marchand, by mistake, as he had come late to Bangor and the best camps already had their quotas of men. Marchand's camp was as rough and primitive as in the old days, but he was cutting in the Allagash watershed, where Jinot had not been. The trees were some of the best remaining white pine, and he wondered how Marchand had come by such a choice woodlot. He slept under a bateau rather than in the bunkhouse, thinking of Franceway in their young days. How would it have been now, with both of them close to thirty winters? He would always think of Franceway when he slept under a boat.

Someone called his name in a hoarse voice.

"Jinot! Jinot! Wake!" His heart leapt. He had been dreaming of him. It was not Franceway, it never would be Franceway again, but his half brother Francis-Outger, holding a lantern in his left hand and shaking Jinot's knee with the other.

"Get up! Come. Now."

"What? What?"

"Mother is dead. Kuntaw wants you to come. I told Marchand. He cursed me hell to breakfast—a bad-swearin man. Josime rode to tell Amboise. You come. Now!"

●　●　●

Beatrix was buried in the plot that Outger had laid out behind the house. The judge read the will directly after the funeral as the family was at hand. Beatrix had left the house, furniture and property to Elise in gratitude for her care and in atonement for sending her to a miserable marriage when she was a girl. All her books she left to Dr. Mukhtar. The secret pine woodlot she owned in northern Maine, a property of forty thousand acres, went to her sons, Francis-Outger and Josime. To Kuntaw she left two of the five horses they kept, a red English wool blanket he had always liked and a letter. He opened and read the letter of only a few sentences, gave a short laugh and turned silent. Beatrix had made him laugh once again, and once again she had puzzled him. He said he would go back to Canada. Jinot and Amboise each received a small package. Amboise pulled away the paper and found a small watercolor Beatrix had painted depicting Elise, himself and Jinot sitting on a bench under the apple tree. He had a very faint memory that long ago she had sat them in a row and made a drawing in her red sketchbook. He had never seen this painting. There was a small deerskin sock containing five gold pieces. Mopping his eyes and putting his inheritance carefully in his breast pocket he said he would go to New Brunswick for the drive that was barely under way. Jinot opened his own package—it was a familiar stuffed toy horse, four inches tall, that Beatrix had made for him the day after Tonny brought them there. And he, too, had a deerskin pouch of coins. A folded paper written in her unsteady hand said, "Remember me." How could it be otherwise?

That evening Amboise said to Jinot, "You come my camp end of July and we talk where to go. I got some ideas. But first go find Marchand and git your pay. I can tell you got some trouble, not just Mother's death—better come work."

Marchand said, "I shouldn't give you nothin. You left me in the lurch, just walk off like that middle of the night." But he paid him and Jinot found himself with nearly two hundred dollars in his pocket as well as Beatrix's coins. Yet his heart was sore with the loss of Beatrix. He had loved her since the day she lifted him onto the chair and called him *snoezepoes*. He had loved the little stuffed horse with its yarn mane and painted eyes; it had been lost, and it seemed he was holding his childhood again. He put it with his other precious memento—Franceway's tiny songbook, two or three reminder words for many songs. He could feel Beatrix's warm closeness, could hear Franceway's beloved voice.

This last day at the Penobscot house he stuffed his pack basket with clothing, a crooked knife, flint, extra moccasins as if he were going on a long journey. He came into the kitchen for the last time. Elise was sitting at the table writing a list of chores. She looked up at him.

"When will you come again?" she said.

"I do not know. I can't tell. I will work awhile, maybe find Amboise, maybe go back up north. Maybe find Grandfather Kuntaw? I don't know."

Taking down the trees was his anodyne. The forests of New England vibrated with chopping. Swarms of men limbed and hauled the windfall to the rivers. Mills sawed day and night and the great glut of lumber brought new settlers and encouraged an unprecedented construction boom.

Another year passed and another and Jinot counted his more than thirty winters. It was time he found Amboise, if he was still in that New Brunswick camp.

41

Gatineau camps

The New Brunswick camp was deserted except for a mournful ex-logger with a bandaged head and scabbed face sitting on the cookhouse steps peeling potatoes. "Wal, they tell me I am lucky. They tell me I am lucky I can peel taters. Lost half my teeth, see?" He exposed empty purple gums. "On the drive, log took half my face, bled like a busted dam. They give me a job of cookee but I spect by fall I'll be good agin."

"Looking for my brother, Amboise Sel?"

"Yah, I see it—you got a Indan phiz like Amboise. I seen him come out the bunkhouse with that old Indan pack basket and known he was goin his own way. He talked about makin a shack in the woods, out by our cut. Liked it out there, but I don't know what there was to like—just swamp. Say, have some tea! I take some this time a day. Name's Mikla. Joe Mikla." Like many who spend time alone he could not stop talking. They went into the cookhouse. Jinot noticed shrouded mounds of rising bread, raised his eyebrows at the cookee.

"Yeah, there's a crew a swampers workin, but no choppers. Here, show you where we *was* cuttin." Dipping his finger in his tea he drew a wet map on the table marking the old cut where Amboise might be found. "Can't miss a cut like that. Guess Amboise'd pick a good spot next to the swamp, get the full benefit a the mosquitoes. I was glad to get out a there."

• • •

309

He found Amboise at the end of three days of swamp slash, bent over and whittling on something. To one side Jinot saw a row of dressed tree roots.

"I'm gettin these," said Amboise, gesturing at the row of roots. "It's old Perley Palmer's show. He don't care if I take the knees—all stumps to him anyways."

Maybe, thought Jinot, Amboise had lost his mind. He shifted the subject and asked about Kuntaw.

"Grandfather Kuntaw? After her buryin he rolled up and went north. Back to Canada. Back to where he come from. Last I heard. Maybe he writes to Elise?"

"She's in Boston with that doctor husband, Hallagher."

"Who is livin in the house?"

"I don't know. Francis-Outger looks after it now. Maybe Elise sold it? Nobody told me."

There was silence while they thought about Kuntaw, an old man heading into the north woods. Their thoughts were envious.

"Brother," said Amboise. "I have work we can do together."

"What work? Not swampin out roads. Told Marchand I'd be back in November. If I could."

"Not swampin; I talked with some fellers down in Portsmouth shipyard after—after the drive. I heard they'd pay good for them things." He waved at his root assembly. "Workin this cut I seen the swamp full a hackmatack. They want ship timber, knees—knees for ships. They say 'ships get built in the woods.'"

Jinot looked at the root knees lined out in a row. Hackmatack, hard as iron, prized for its tough and twisted root fibers.

"We just do it for a while, eh? You go with Marchand when he starts. Winter, I chop again."

"Guess we can. This a good hackmatack-juniper swamp?"

Amboise said that it was better to get the knees late in the year, when the sap stopped running. In summer it was a sticky business. "But it's dryin up pretty good now. I figured work on them until frost. And then go back in the camps."

They dug around the roots of likely hackmatacks. When they found one with a good bend, they cleared away the soil, cut the end two feet out from the tree and went after the taproot. The tree teetered, went down and they bucked off the root stump a good five feet up.

"Now we got a knee," said Amboise, and he showed Jinot how to measure and mark the line and hew to make a ninety-degree angle at the heel, a smooth throat on the inner curve, the back and bottom smooth and flat.

Jinot didn't much like grubbing in the swamp for knees and he did not want to go back to Marchand. He felt as Kuntaw, that he had to get away.

"Brother," he said to Amboise. "Let us go west. I have heard there are great forests west. I do not want to get these hackmatack knees."

Amboise looked upward at the treetops. "Yes," he said.

It was dark when Jinot came awake. There was something—someone—outside the shack. He reached over and touched Amboise and knew by his rigid shoulder that he had heard it and was awake. Slowly, soundlessly, Jinot sat up. His ax was near the door flap. He began to stretch toward it when a voice said, "Long ago in the old days three children were lost in the forest—"

"Josime!" yelled Amboise. "You fool! Could of shot you."

"If you had a firearm," said Jinot, groping for the candle. Josime built up the fire outside, Amboise filled the kettle. They sat in front of the fire, brothers in stained shirts, spark-holed hats. In the first light their uncle-brother Josime saw the hackmatack knees.

"Is this man's work?"

"No, we are now travelers and hunters. Go to that west forest, Pennsylvany, Ohio, we don't know how far. Kuntaw said that forest goes to end of the world. We go there," said Jinot. Amboise nodded. "That is our plan."

Josime laughed. "That is not your plan. That is *my* plan. I care nothing for that woodland I was to share with Francis-Outger. He was happy to hear me say, 'Brother, you can have it all.' I think about you, my nephew-brothers. You better come with me, but I am going. Today. It is my plan."

The decision began a welding of their lives and work as they angled north through the forest, leaving behind them a world of chopped and broken trees, woodland changed to cornfields and pasture. They yearned to go to a place where the trees still stood thick and wild. Josime said he had heard of a timber operation in the Gatineau country to the north.

"There is a man from Boston went there. He got three camps, sendin log rafts down to Montreal. I say go north."

The important word for them was *north*. They were of the north and they would go north.

In ten days they walked to Three Rivers—Trois-Rivières—where they found some Omamiwinini downriver people preparing to go beyond Montreal up the Kichisìpi. These travelers, many women and children, in the care of a tall man with a dark and serious face, were happy to have three more strong men to help on the portages, to move along before the hard cold. Already there were morning frosts.

When they stopped for the first night a knot of girls enclosed Jinot. Some of them were exceptionally pretty. The Omamiwinini told Josime that some of them were Odaawa people on their way to Manitoulin Island, where other Odaawa people lived. Once, long ago, they had all lived on that big island, but whiteman's diseases had come and the survivors set their villages afire; some moved to Trois-Rivières. Now they were returning home, for the diseases had disappeared. They would break their journey for a few days at First

Meeting Place—Montréal. Josime, in another canoe, stared at one girl for a long time before he turned away and asked the men questions about the Gatineau. Yes, said the man with the serious face, it was true, whitemen cut pine up that river. They were making round logs to be flat on all sides. Very strange.

Jinot disliked the Ottawa River, deceptively smooth for many miles, then bursting into tumbling, roiling falls. He sensed its malevolent character. The onshore thickets of old wooden crosses below the falls indicated a death river. He bent to the paddle.

At First Meeting Place one of the loveliest Odaawa girls gave Jinot a fern frond, hastily plucked as the canoe passed close to a verdant rock face. The paddlers did not linger but called farewell, farewell and pushed on up the Ottawa with the Sels.

They stopped below the Chaudière Falls and the serious-faced man told Josime the lumber camps were a two-day walk upstream. Or come with them to Manitoulin and lead a good life away from the whiteman's doings. They themselves, he said, would now double back, pick up the Trois-Rivières Odaawa party and continue up the river, portage to Lake Nipissing, down La Rivière de Français and on to Manitoulin. "Two, three more week," he said.

"You are good people," said Josime, his eyes following their canoe. "Now, brothers, we walk."

On the path around the falls they passed two parties of whitemen talking about starting log businesses. The leader of one party was white-haired and stout with a crimson face.

"Why? England needs timber," he said to Josime, who had asked him why he ventured far from home. The man turned away, adding that he had no time to waste on idle talk with savages. A second group was friendlier and the leader said, "Do you not know that England is hungry for timber? The pine most gone in New England so lumbermen comin into this Ottawa country. Still fresh country with big pines. Make a fortune here."

It was in these encounters with whitemen they learned that they were not Indians but *métis* or, as one Anglo entrepreneur pejora-

tively called them, "half-breeds." In Maine their white-settler neighbors knew confidently that they were fading from the earth; yes, said
Josime to his brothers, they were disappearing, not by disease and
wasting away in sorrow as the whites supposed, but through absorp-
tion into the white population—only look at their sister, Elise. "Her
children are almost whitemen already," for she had married Dr. Hallagher, the Irishman who had first examined Beatrix. Here on the
Gatineau the Sels were a different kind of people, neither Mi'kmaq
nor the other, and certainly not both.

"What we are," said Josime, "is tree choppers."

Sawmill site prospectors and timber lookers, men seeking good pine
stands, had pounded the trail into a broad pathway; pine remained
the ideal. Small entrepreneurs from the east hurried along, buying
tracts of land and stumpage, damming the small streams to power
their sawmills. The big money went to men with good credit and
connections who could quickly get out the most squared timber for
the British market. The most important was William Scugog, a Massachusetts man who had fought against the British in the Revolution
and now claimed he repented of it.

"Lot of camps," said Josime. They heard of logging outfits along
the Ottawa itself, on its tributaries; to the north the Black, Dumoine,
Coulonge, the Gatineau, Rouge and the Lièvre, on the south the
Rideau, Madawaska, Petawawa, Mattawa, the Bonnechère, powerful
streams that swelled the huge rush of forest water flowing into the
mighty St. Laurent; all the valleys were packed with big pine.

The Sel brothers hired on with William Scugog. He sent them to
a camp up on the Gatineau. Before the Sels got there they set their
minds against the camp, against the men in the camp and against
Scugog. But Scugog had hired an outstanding cook, Diamond Bob,
so called for a tattoo on his neck and a flashing ring on his finger. He

did elegant things with a caribou haunch, but understood that the logger was strengthened by beans and biscuits and supplied them in plenty.

Scugog and his oldest son, Cato, traveled between their houses on the Gatineau, in Montréal and Québec, cajoling promises of money from timber-shipping merchants for pinewood still uncut and in most cases unseen.

The Gatineau forest was noisy, echoing with ax blows and the rushing crackle of falling timber, with shouted warnings and orders. The axmen cut the great pines, but only a few in each plot were suitable for squaring. The rest were left to rot on the ground. Jinot did not like to bend over for hours scoring trees for the hewer; he preferred to chop down trees. Amboise, whose arms were longer, did not mind scoring and Josime was a fine hewer with the weighty broadax, trimming the log smooth and flat within a fraction of the chalk line. The waste was terrific—twenty-five percent of each squared tree lost; unwanted trees lay prostrate, severed branches everywhere, heaps of bark and mountains of chips. But squared timber made up into rafts more easily and would not roll when packed into ships for transport to England. There were so many trees, what did it matter? Maine men were used to waste—it was usual—but this was beyond anything even they had seen. The slash and chips from the hewers' axes was knee-high.

The Scugogs had enough squared timber for two rafts at the end of the winter. The bigger raft, made up of fifty cribs, belonged to old William, and the smaller raft to son Cato. The rafts traveled well enough on smooth water but broke apart at the falls. There was nothing for it but to disassemble them and send the cribs through, one by one, then put all together again. Jinot often thought of free logs surging through the boisterous spring freshet of the Penobscot. But of course rafts did not get into killing jams.

When the rafts arrived in Montréal they could not find a place to moor. Scugog had made no arrangements for the unwieldy mass of timbers. And it seemed to the choppers and rivermen that they were paid off grudgingly, that Scugog's fingers lingered over the money. The tavern word was that he was having difficulty selling his timber.

A second son, Blade Scugog, was running a shanty farther up the Gatineau. The Sels shifted to this son's shanty, glad to work with round logs. It was too bad to leave Diamond Bob's grub, but the regret faded when they heard the famous cook had abandoned Scugog *père* in midseason in favor of Montréal, where he opened an oyster house. This younger Scugog, whose deep scratched-up voice was familiar to the river's lumbermen, despised not only the uncertain rafting enterprise but his father's stupidity in cutting without permits and permissions. He quickly got a cutting permit for himself after declaring he intended to make lumber for domestic enterprises, not for export.

"What do you imagine you are doing?" shouted the older man at his contrary offspring.

"After the war ends there will be thousands of settlers coming into this country. They will need boards and shingles to build houses." To himself he added, "Not bloody squared warship timbers that the Crown can seize without remuneration."

"You are, sir, a reckless fool. There will always be wars, always a need for squared timbers. You will fail with your trust in chimerical men who will never come to settle such rude lands. Do not ask me for aid when poverty brings you down."

"And do you not come to me with your square timbers hoping for an introduction to purchasers," said the son in his rough voice.

Blade Scugog's sawmill ran through the summer, but at the end of dry September it was caught in a fast-moving wildfire and burned to the ground. The ambitious son refused to see he was ruined, rushed to Québec and leveraged money to rebuild. "I may not know much about square timbers," he said, "but I know how to make money."

• • •

The settlers did come and with them came bridges, lightning-fast clearing, plans for crib-size timber slides around the worst falls, canals to bypass rough water, large new settlements, cemeteries, flour mills and postal service. They pushed back the wildwood. Civilization rushed into the trees.

The Sels moved on to other camps after Scugog's fire. Pine choppers from Maine arrived every season, now and then someone they knew. On Jinot's first day on the Fischer-Helden cut, walking to the marked trees behind a knot of choppers he recognized the familiar jaunty stride of Joe Martel from Marchand's long-ago Penobscot camp at the time of Franceway.

"Joe!" he called. "Joe Martel, what you do here?"

Martel turned around, his black beard ruffed out like a grouse's breast, a gleam of teeth, a happy exclamation.

"Jinot Sel, Jinot. You are here?" He waited until Jinot came up to him and they walked together.

"I seen four, five Penobscots up here in the Canada trees. It's bad in Maine now, you know. The white pine give out. Cuttin spruce and hardwood now. But this here"—he waved his arm at the riches of the Gatineau—"looks like a pretty good chance, eh?" He said Marchand had gone broke and was swinging an ax like the rest of them somewhere on the Gatineau. Tom Keyo was dead, decapitated by a flying log. That night after supper they talked on about the old days when they were Penobscot rivermen running on bubbles, the best in the world. "We made our mark, by gaw."

The next winter was windy and bad for accidents. One man's ax head flew off its handle, sailed twenty feet and sheared a young chopper's face away; widow-makers caught three, killing two outright and breaking the third so badly he never worked again. Two buckers cut their feet to the bone and night after night the men talked about the need for stouter boots. Most of them still wore heavy elk-hide mid-calf moccasins. An ax cut through one as if it were a syrup-soaked pancake.

The Sel brothers and Martel made the Saturday night trek to the near settlement "to drink and watch the fools" as Amboise put it, "to talk with the girls" as Jinot said. He only came for drink and company. So he said. In the settlement's two whorehouses the girls made much of Jinot, and if Amboise or Josime came in alone always asked, "Where is Jinot?"

"What is it they see in him?" Martel said. Jinot was only Jinot—a good riverman, easygoing in character, but off a log nothing special. He couldn't sing, did not play the fiddle, wasn't much of a step dancer. It had to be his smile and chaffing banter, for Jinot was always good-natured when others were gloomy and he listened to the girls' complaints with real interest.

"By now he knows more bout women than anybody in the world," Josime told Martel. "He been listenin to them jabber long, long years now. I guess half the brats in Maine come from Jinot." Martel, thinking of Franceway, raised his eyebrows but said nothing.

A few winters later in the Ottawa drainage they were again squaring timbers, this time at Harold Honey's camp. The shanty was crowded with dirty, lousy men who were strong beyond modern comprehension. The interior was always drafty and smoky. At night, exhausted by the constant swing of the ax against the living tree, they thought the rough accommodations of bare ground luxurious.

The days were longer and the taste of spring was in their mouths. The drive was only a few weeks away. At the end of one day Honey came to them in the shanty.

"Well, boys, I guess I got some bad news. The log market's fell out the bottom. Scugog's got all the Canada business. I can't sell them logs we got on the rollway. I am broke and will have to go back to Maine and hire out again. I can't pay nobody, but you are welcome to the logs if you can move 'em." His smile was painful. There was nothing to do but pack up and head downriver with the rest of the crew.

Jinot was the only one with any money. The Sels agreed to spend it on a blowout in Montréal and then decide whether to go back to Maine or stay in the Ottawa valley.

"They still cut trees in Maine—water pine is gone but there's red pine and spruce and hardwood. There's work. Plenty work on the booms. There's still some long log drives."

"Let's go west," mumbled Amboise. "Not go back to the Penobscot and that—all that." They knew what he meant: Beatrix's grave, the old house, the choppers they knew, scabby woods and stump forests, the ghosts of dead men. Martel said that if they went west he would go with them.

In Montréal they hit the Golden Pine, the dingiest whorehouse, but good enough for woodsmen and fur traders—even *métis* and "savages." They agreed to meet up afterward at the Wing King saloon, where the proprietor not only sold liquor but rented beds for the night in the big storeroom.

The focal point of the Golden Pine was an upright log carved like a *membrum virile* and painted "golden" yellow supporting the ceiling. No food was served, but a fierce kind of fermented apple cider Madam Georgine called "calvados" or "Napoleon brandy" or just "spirits" depending on the customer. The room was crowded when they went in. A long row of chairs ranged against one wall and on the chairs sat the merchandise. There were stout Irish girls with flaming cheeks, some blue-eyed milk-skinned English blondes, one sultry Jewess, a smattering of French-speaking farm girls and, in the bargain corner, a few native women. Martel made his little joke, asking Jinot if he would like a chair with the girls, then began talking with one from Kébec, asking her foolish questions about her family. Madam Georgine, who knew Jinot, tugged at his jacket sleeve.

"Come over here," she said and led him to a murky alcove. "Here, try this." She poured liquor from a black bottle into a tiny glass and handed it to him. "Go on, drink it. It's the real thing. Brandy. Napoleon brandy. We had a swell in here and he left it behind." Jinot swallowed the fiery stuff and thought that if that was what Napoleon drank his death was imminent. He smiled, pinched Madam Georgine's encarmined cheek and turned back to the line.

"Jinot! Look." It was Josime, pointing with his pursed lips at a woman bent over her lap, avoiding the stares of the men. "See who that is?"

"No. Who is it?"

"It's that girl in the canoe when we come here. Long time ago. The Odaawa. The one give you that fern."

He studied the figure. Who could tell, the way she was slouched over? Fern, what fern? Who could remember after six or eight years what a girl in a canoe had looked like? Josime, Josime could remember. Jinot walked over to her, said, "Heyo, pretty girl." She looked up. She said, *"Jinot?"* Her eyes gleamed with tears. She was thin, half-starved, he reckoned. He didn't remember her but she remembered him. "It'll get better by and by, don't cry." He went back to Josime, who was breathing hard.

"Don't remember," he said.

"How that gal git here?" he asked Madam Georgine.

"How you think? Some men brought her in and left her. Traders, fur traders. Bad-trouble girl, her, a no-good. Scratch and bite. I get rid her pret' soon."

When he looked again Josime had led the girl to one of the tables and was talking earnestly, asking questions in the way he had of stretching his head forward as if to catch the faintest whisper. Suddenly Jinot was sick of the place. He could feel the rotgut wrenching his innards.

At the door he looked back again. The girl was looking beyond Josime to Jinot with a pleading expression. Josime's head was close to hers and he was still talking.

"She don't hear a word he's sayin," Jinot murmured. Then he remembered he had all the money. Once more he went to Madam Georgine and stuffed the money into her hands.

"I'm payin for my brothers and our friend Martel. They sposed to come to the Wing King later. They know it, but tell 'em anyway."

He walked along the plank sidewalks. He thought of Josime, he thought of the girl. He still did not recollect her. What he remembered about the time in the canoe was Josime's hard bright stare, he had assumed it was aimed at all of the girls, a fixed gaze that went on and on. But it must have been for only that one. He felt a little sorry for Josime.

In the morning Amboise and Martel were waiting for him outside the Wing King.

"Where's Josime?" He had a headache and saw they, too, were suffering.

Amboise shook his head. There was a long silence. "Got to make tea," he said at last.

"Where's Josime?"

"He took that girl off. Old Madam screamed like wild cat she can't go, he's got to pay her money, so he didn't have any money but he give her somethin, maybe he found some money he forgot in his pocket, and she shut up. Josime said tell you he's gone Manitoulin with that girl, says we better wait—he comes back."

"Wait where? No place here we can wait. We got no money."

"Get work—plenty sawmills here. You know, move the logs up into the mill. Sort logs in the millpond. Other jobs. Plenty work, if you know logs and water, hey?"

He was right. They all found jobs at sawmills and the cross-eyed toothless owner of the Wing King, once a logger and riverman, said they could stay on as long as they could pay. They could, but Amboise and Martel began to drink their money up. Amboise said he didn't care, he liked to drink whiskey. Jinot, who also liked to drink whiskey and who didn't know how far it was to Manitoulin, hoped Josime would come back soon so they could get away from the city, back to the sober life of the camps.

More than two months later Jinot came into the Wing King storeroom and Josime was there, lying on his bed, his eyes closed. He sat up.

"What took you so long time come back?" said Jinot.

"Brother, my life has changed greatly. I chop trees no more. I stay always with that girl on Manitoulin Island and give up whiteman ways, whiteman work. That girl my wife. I come tell you I go back to her now."

"You are like Kuntaw," said Jinot, "slaved to a woman. And you talk different. Much time with that Manitoulin girl."

"It is right for me to be with her in the forest, away from stinking men and the wounding of the land. It is—what I want."

Jinot thought he looked very much like Beatrix, especially his pale eyes. "I know," he said.

"It is a joy that you do not know," said Josime stiffly. They sat silent for a long time, then Josime spoke again.

"I wish you come with me. I know you will not but I wish it. We are not so young now. You would feel a happiness to eat whitefish, see those people living good lives, not false whiteman lives like we do in lumber camp. One day you come to Manitoulin and learn what I say is true."

"I sure to come, Josime, come visit, see you, your children. But you doin this makes me afraid. Maybe I wish I was the one do it."

Josime laughed. "You! You leave the ax? No, I do not think so. But I want to tell you something I have seen a day's paddle south from that country. Brother, I have seen with my own eyes the largest white pines that ever grew in the world. The Manitoulin people told me that pine tree forest is very big, maybe a thousand English people's miles. It is their forest and they move through it, their rivers and they travel on them for they are traders and have been traders for many generations. They are good people who have not forgotten the old ways. You must never tell any white man about this pine forest for they will come in numbers like *ples*—passenger pigeons—and cut it down. Never speak of it to anyone. Never."

He would not speak of it but they would come anyway.

A few weeks later Jinot, Amboise and Martel drifted back to Maine. Before they went to Bangor to look for work they returned to Penobscot Bay. Josime had a too-small shirt that he wanted to give to his nephew, Francis-Outger's son, Édouard-Outger. He must be near-grown by now.

VI

"fortune's a right whore"

1808–1826

42

inlaid table

Captain James Duke, in his early fifties, was complicated, dark-haired, and somewhat handsome. He took a hard-headed and hard-handed stance to disguise an inner recognition of worthlessness. Quixotic, he swung from morbid self-pity to rigid authority over his crews and himself. The future flickered before him as a likely series of disappointments.

On the annual occasion of an all-day drunk (his ill-starred birthday) he dragged out the piteous litany that he had been pitched onto a British ship as a midshipman in his tenth year "as an unwanted pup-dog is tied to a sapling in the woods and left to be torn apart by wild beasts." Even his appointment had come about only because his grandfather, old Nicolaus Duke, wrote to the more ancient Dred-Peacock and begged the favor of a recommendation. The favor granted, Nicolaus Duke and the antique peer died within weeks of each other and could be depended on no more. But James Duke lasted; repeatedly passed over for promotion in favor of candidates from influential landed families or members of the peerage, he lasted.

He had done moderately well on the examination, then stalled for years as a "passed midshipman." But the Napoleonic Wars had lofted him swiftly over a lieutenancy to post captain. And there he stayed until, in his fifty-first year, a letter arrived from his Boston cousin Freegrace Duke, asking if he would consider a director's seat on the Board of Duke & Sons to fill the vacancy left by the death of his father, Sedley.

That his father had died was a shock to James. He had heard no news from him nor of him for many years. He had never had a letter, nor a remembrance, never a visit. He thought that if Sedley had left him anything in his will it would be an insultingly paltry sum, as a single shilling, or a savage castigation for causing the death of his first wife, James's mother; he had always known why his father hated him.

As the days passed he considered the idea of sitting on the Board of the family timber company. Little had ever come to James from the Dukes beyond a yearly allowance of fifty pounds. If he accepted, he would have to make concessions, would have to revert to being an American. He would bring a touch of English distinction to the no doubt squalid Board meetings of Duke & Sons—likely the reason they invited him to join them. He could imagine those meetings, a scarred oaken table with half a dozen backwoodsmen slouched around it on pine benches, tankards of rum-laced home-brewed beer, tipsy ribaldries, for he had no illusions that the Dukes were models of moral behavior.

Before he could draft his cool note of refusal, a letter arrived from a Boston law office signed by the attorney Hugh Trumbull. It was late December, the days short and dark, the worst of the English year. Advocate Trumbull begged James's attendance at Trumbull & Tendrill as soon as he might manage the journey in order to hear something to his advantage; enclosed was a draft for one hundred pounds (drawn on Duke & Sons) for his passage to Boston. So rarely had the words "something to your advantage" come to him that he decided on the minute to accept Freegrace's offer and remove permanently to Boston. "Advantage" meant more than a single shilling! He made his arrangements and booked passage for Boston.

The *Western Blessing* was crowded with German immigrants journeying to Pennsylvania to found a utopia and these people quarreled incessantly with each other about the details of the earthly paradise to come. To keep free of them James Duke stayed in his cabin during the day, coming out only to take the wintery air or to dine and drink with Captain Euclid Gunn, who was even older than himself but of an equal rank. Over a roast chicken they raked through sea acquaintances held in common. They spoke of retired and disabled friends as the level sank in the decanter. "Captain Richard Moore, one of the most ablest seamen I ever knew, is forced to open a herring stall in Bristol. You are a fortunate man, Captain Duke, to be connected to a wealthy family. Some of us depart from the sea to live out sad lives ashore selling fish or driving a goods cart. I myself have no expectations of a rich sinecure but hope I will go to Davy Jones afore I wheel a barrow of mussels."

"Shocked to hear that Dick Moore has come to such a pass. But, Captain Gunn, I am sure that a happier future awaits you than clam mongering. Do you not have a reputation for fashioning small attractive tables?"

"It is only my amusement, you know, never to make a living from it."

"You might try—everyone admires small tables—as that one," he said and he pointed to an example of the captain's handiwork, an ebon side table inlaid with a ship in full sail cut from walrus-tusk ivory. "Any mariner's family would be happy to possess such a handsome article of furnishing."

"You must have it when you disembark! I will make another, but you shall take this one as a memento of your years at sea and this voyage. I insist. Look, it has a secret drawer where you may keep your love letters, *heh*."

Once a week other choice guests joined the captain's table, and once a female, Mistress Posey Brandon, a dark-haired lady of considerable stature, quite overtopping the gentlemen at the table, but sitting silent for the most part unless pressed to speak. She was traveling home after a long visit with a relative, to rejoin her husband, Winthrop Brandon, a Presbyterian preacher who had made his name with a book of virtuous precepts. Another passenger, Thomas Gort, showed her excessive attention. James understood why Gort fawned; she had great onyx-dark eyes fringed by thick lashes. But Gort made too much of her. When Mrs. Brandon said she had visited Madame Tussaud's exhibition, at the Lyceum Theatre, of wax curiosities of crime Gort begged for repulsive details. The lady demurred, saying she had averted her eyes before many of the exhibits.

"I do not see how a member of the gentler sex, even a German or French lady, could have fastened on such an unpleasant mode of expression," she said and cut at her meat. "I understand she first gained her skill in making wax flowers for family funeral wreaths." After that she said nothing more.

The days of tilting horizon passed slowly. As they neared the continent they saw increasing dozens of ships, wooden leviathans rope-strung like musical instruments, shimmering with raw salt. Boston harbor was so jammed they anchored a twenty-minute row from the docks.

James located his trunk, a scuffed brown affair, on the deck. He did not see the promised inlaid table with the boxes and bundles to go ashore and found Captain Gunn on the bridge.

"I thought I would thank you again for the table," he said.

It seemed to him Captain Gunn showed a coolness. "Ah," he remarked.

"Sir, I look forward to enjoying it in my new quarters."

"Ah."

"Shall I fetch it on deck myself?"

"Ha! You, Woodrow!" He bellowed at a sailor. "Fetch the small table in my cabin to the deck for this gentleman." There was undoubtedly a sneer embedded in the word *gentleman*. James Duke guessed that Captain Gunn was in his true self a parsimonious man made momentarily generous by Madeira.

• • •

He was crowded into the tender with two dozen passengers, Bostonians from their accents. In their anxiety to get on shore they were very restive, passing bundles back and forth. A portly matron stood up to receive a small trunk. The weight surprised her and she swayed, tried to hold it, then fell with a shriek into the wintery harbor. Gasping, she clutched at the gunwale, and her weight dislodged two more passengers. Captain Duke stretched out his hand to a terrified man and in slow but inexorable motion the tender rose on its side and sent ten or twelve more people bellowing and clawing over the side. Gasping (for he could not swim), James Duke thrashed his arms, trying for the gunwale. His hand touched it, though he could barely feel it, then he went under again as the heavy woman wrapped one arm around him. He escaped his captor and with an atavistic swimming motion burst upward into the sweet air. Something clenched his hair and dragged him to the side of the tender, something got hold of the back of his coat collar and hauled relentlessly. He came up over the gunwale, crashed into the bottom of the boat and looked up at his savior—a woman wearing a black bonnet and staring at him with lustrous, intensely black eyes—Mistress Brandon, who had exhibited the strength of two men.

Chattering thanks and promises to call on his rescuer in a few days, James Duke returned to his homeland on this first day of February. In a sopping freeze he managed a cab to take him to the Pine Tree Inn. Waiting for his trunk to arrive he stood as close as he could to the fire drinking boiling tea. At last the trunk was hauled up to his room and trembling, he pulled on his warmest clothes—wool, wool, good English wool.

It was exceedingly cold in Boston; snow fell an inch or two every day for a week until all was muffled and silent, roofs, carriages, and still the snow came. Two days after his arrival, and with a drumbeat headache, James Duke walked to the offices of Trumbull & Tendrill slipping on icy cobblestones.

The clerk who let him in and took his hat gave him two swift startled looks before his habitual air of indifference returned, an empty expression that classified the people he met as side chairs or pen wipers. It was the same with the advocate Hugh Trumbull, whose mouth fell open and then closed. His wrinkled face suddenly creaked into a smile. He might have been English, thought James, taking in the fashionable double-breasted coat with notable lapels. Half-laughing in welcome, Trumbull made James comfortable in a chair near the snapping fire. The clerk brought in tumblers of hot rum toddy.

"You quite shook me! It's uncanny how you resemble your late father." Trumbull drank off half his glass of rum and waved his hand at the window, where the flying snow half-obliterated the street and the buildings across the way. "Would you believe that I have killed deer from this window?" he asked. "Of course it was many years ago and deer are now scarce. Now, sir," he said, "to business," and over the next hour laid out the details of Sedley Duke's will.

Elated and confused James Duke returned to the Pine Tree with a weight of keys in his pocket. In essence, Sedley Duke had regretted his long hatred and left half of his rich estate to James, including his dwelling house north of Tremont Street complete with six acres of garden land, a fruit orchard, twenty acres of fresh meadow, a twelve-stall stable, two carriages and six matched pair of horses, nearly two million acres of forest in Maine (passed to Sedley from Charles Duke's old partner, Forgeron), a collection of Indian relics, a stuffed crocodile, eight silver platters, four and twenty pewter plates, a turtle-shell hafted knife, a library of eighty-four books, two hogsheads of Portuguese *vinho,* eight barrels of rum, two waistcoats embroidered with bucolic scenes, five turkey carpets, six warehouses of lumber, twenty-seven acres of salt marsh, part interests in several ships, potash manufactories, a shingle factory, Ohio timberlands, bank accounts and stocks. And more that he could not remember.

Trumbull had enjoyed detailing the provisions of the will. "The servants are staying on at the house and hope that you will retain them. You may remember that your father called the property Black Swan and populated his pond with those birds. Sixty-odd years ago it was all rough, gloomy forest, and now we see handsome estates. I would advise you to keep the servants as they understand the peculiarities and virtues of the place and will make the transition to Boston pleasanter for you."

James sat with his mouth open, hardly believing what he was hearing.

"Mrs. Trumbull and I hope you will do us the favor of dinner with us a week hence? Some of your cousins will be in attendance and we thought you might wish to meet them away from the offices."

"Sir," said James, "sir . . ."

His head aching fiercely and his throat a raw ribbon of fire, he took to his bed at the Pine Tree for the next four days and lay swooning and dreaming of the delights that lay before him. He would move to the house as soon as he was well, and then pay a call on the Winthrop Brandons and thank Mistress Brandon properly with a gift. But he was embarrassed to have been pulled from the water by a woman. *He* should have saved *her*. And should he wait until the Trumbulls' dinner party or immediately pay a call on Cousin Freegrace Duke, who certainly knew of James's unexpected fortune? No doubt he would try to wheedle it away to himself and the other Dukes or at least to the failing business coffers, for the gang of backwoodsmen had likely put the company in disarray. Perhaps Sedley Duke had been the white sheep in a black flock.

• • •

He directed the hired coachman to his father's—now his—house. They rolled up a curved drive to a house of rosy brick with a black lacquer door set off by pedimented windows. He counted eight smoking chimneys. A grey-haired woman wearing a grey linsey-woolsey dress opened the door and her eyes widened as she took him in. She curtsied and said, in a welcome English voice, that she was Mrs. Tubjoy, "Mr. Sedley's housekeeper, sir. And now in your service. We all welcome you."

As he stepped into the entrance hall he was dashed into his childhood as though seated on a swing that someone had suddenly given a great shove. He knew every inch of this place. There was the complex mahogany staircase rising into the dim upper hall, there a gleaming carpet rod and there—there—the terrible hall stand, ten feet high, intensely authoritarian. This piece of furniture with its blotched looking glass, its hat hooks and cloak holders was the ceremonial guard of the house. Every day when Sedley came home he had placed his umbrella in the crooked holder, hung his tall black hat on the hook, his greatcoat on another and, divested of his city exterior, passed into the world of "home." He went into his library and drank whiskey until the housemaid rang the bell for dinner. Young James and Sedley sat at opposite ends of the sixteen-foot table with never a word spoken. He shook the memory loose.

In the hall behind Mrs. Tubjoy stood half a dozen servants. He caught vainly at their names; the beardless grinning boy was Tom, the cook, Louisa. Two men brought his trunk and Captain Gunn's small table into the hall. Mrs. Tubjoy said, "I am sure you wish to see the house, and after a little refreshment, rest until dinner? Follow me, sir, if you please.

"Perhaps you will wish to take your late father's room, Mr. James?" she asked, opening a heavy mahogany door. The room was large, the windows were large and gave a view of great-trunked oaks.

Mrs. Tubjoy said, "Forgive my familiarity, Mr. James, but you strongly resemble my late employer."

"Yes, Mr. Trumbull said so as well. But I cannot help it. I never saw the late Mr. Duke—my father—from the time I was a boy. So I did not know of the resemblance." The monstrous bed was mahogany with a fringed green canopy, the posts carved into dolphins and mermaids. He detected a faded scent of cigar smoke, wool, leather polish and horsiness. As he leaned over the bed to examine the monogram on the pillow slip, another smell, altogether rancid and disgusting, rose from the mattress.

"Those coiled hair mattresses must be changed every few years," said Mrs. Tubjoy, seeing his flared nostrils.

"I am happy you mention this, Mrs. Tubjoy," he said. "Shall we not have all the old mattresses burned and replace them with best new?"

On the third floor they entered a room he liked immediately. It was moderate in size but with a large fireplace. In front of the fireplace stood two companionable wing chairs upholstered in faded red brocade. He admired the sun-softened color and suddenly remembered the table with the ivory inlaid ship that Captain Gunn had grudged him.

"Mrs. Tubjoy, could the boy bring my small table in the entryway up at once?"

"Of course. I'll see to it," she said and she glided from the room and down the stairs, grey and silent.

Alone, he examined the room. The furnishings were of rosewood rather than mahogany, and the bed had plain posts; there was neither canopy nor carved dolphins. He liked the brilliant turkey carpets on the floor and opened a small cabinet—it was empty, and he liked the emptiness. Above the washstand hung a large and slightly clouded mirror and he saw himself in it, the dimmed image of a man who appeared resolute, strong, with no sign that he was unworthy. The windows looked out over the oaks toward a shining strip of sea invisible from his father's room.

He heard them on the stairs. Mrs. Tubjoy came in, followed by the grinning Tom lugging the table and seeming somewhat strained although the table was small. Of course ebony was heavy, ivory was heavy.

"Put it there," said James to the boy, who stood breathing heavily and gripping the table with white fingers. He pointed to the space before the fireplace and between the wing chairs. The table was correct. This would be his room.

43

error of judgment

A visit to the stables was a heady experience. He had his choice of
a barouche or a sporty gig, and Billy, the fat-cheeked stableboy,
said there were four other vehicles in the carriage house including
a green sleigh and a very pretty coach. It was a sunny day; he chose
the barouche, finished in grey enamel with silver fittings. Billy said,
"Mr. Sedley bought the greys special for this carriage," and began to
harness them. The coachman, Will Thing, came in, stuffing his arms
into his livery jacket. He was garrulous and obsequious, sprinkling
yes sirs around as though casting handfuls of seed on new-raked soil.

Out on the high road he pointed out landmarks and distinguished
points, the establishments and houses of leading merchants and men
of account. He moved on to the likes and dislikes of Mr. Sedley, and
so James came to know his father through the impressions of his
coachman.

The Winthrop Brandons lived in a small cottage in Williams Court
near two taverns and a devotional bookshop. There was no room for
the barouche to stand and Will Thing said he would wait in the yard
of the Liberty Cod across the way.

As James walked up the tramped earth path to the door, in his
hands his present of a silver dish (wrapped in a length of muslin) for
Mistress Brandon, he heard unlikely sounds inside the house: meaty
thumps and a shrill cry.

"Kind Jesus, he is beating her!" He stopped on the bottom step and stood irresolute: should he leave and come another time, or knock on the door and perhaps engage with an enraged husband in the flower of fury? Was it not his responsibility to save the woman who had saved him? It was, and he knocked very briskly. There was a hoarse shriek. He knocked again. The house went silent. After long minutes, just as he was turning away, the door opened and Mistress Brandon stood on the sill, somewhat breathless and with heaving bosom.

"Mr. Duke! What a pleasure. Come in, do come in, please."

He looked at her but could see no signs of ill use beyond her rapid breathing and a disarranged black curl in front of one ear. The pupils of her beautiful eyes were dilated. He followed her into a disheveled sitting room, where opened books covered an octagonal table. There was a sideboard choked with pewter, five doors and a row of sunny windows.

"Mr. Duke, will you not take tea?"

"I would very much like to do so," he said, resting his gift on a pine chair with a broken rung.

"I will just be a moment. We keep no servant so I prepare everything myself." She strode out of the room and he sat looking about him. The bookcase, behind its glass-fronted doors, carried the collected expository discourses of many scribbling preachers. He looked at several of the open pages of the books heaped on the octagonal table. All were sermons, and a half-filled sheet of foolscap, pen and ink indicated that the master of the house, Reverend Brandon, was cribbing up filler for his coming sermon. James heard faint sounds in the distance: the rattling of a stove lid, a clinking sound and nearby, a very discreet low moan. He went to the window and looked out, was about to sit down again when there was a slithering sound behind one of the doors. He turned. The door was ajar and through the gap he saw the raw, wet face of a man of about forty, fair hair matted and sweaty, who muttered something between bleeding lips, then, at the jangle of the approaching tea tray, darted away.

"Here we are!" cried Mistress Brandon merrily, coming into the room with the tray. She looked about, but there was no place to put it.

"Just hold this a moment, will you?" she said, thrusting the tray at him. He held it, his mind whirring with curiosity. She swept the octagonal table free of the books of sermons with a strong arm, sent them crashing to the floor. She took the tray from his astonished hands.

"There. Don't mind all the old books—just Mr. Brandon's work. He has a perfectly good study but prefers to spraddle his books on the tea table. He *says* the light is better, but I think he does it to annoy. He was struck by lightning two summers ago and has been somewhat difficult since that day." The great dark eyes gazed on him so intently he began to stammer and blurt.

"I have known men—mariners—others—struck by, by lightning bolts myself, others, you understand, and when it does not kill them, hurt them, outright, it disorders their minds—often—to a marked degree. Some recover, some never. Some." And he went on, describing several cases of lightning-induced mental derangement.

"I fear that is the case with Mr. Brandon. I live in expectation that he will do himself a mortal injury so disordered are his mental faculties. He has great trouble preaching. He wanders about the streets at night." She held out a plate of walnut cakes and he took one. She said, in an aggrieved tone, "These walnuts I gathered with my father last season. I picked out hundreds of nut meats and stored them for winter use. If Mr. Brandon made a better living we might have money to employ a gardener and kitchen help who would gather the nuts. It is *very* trying to scrimp along. I was not brought up to live in this manner. I was quite spoiled on my visit to my mother's aunt in England. Her husband is a cloth merchant and everything in their country house is of the best quality. They have a city house as well, in London, and I wish you could see it. A veritable treasure." Again the dark gaze.

"Mr.—Parson—Minister—Brandon was unable? To accompany you?"

"Quite unable. He has a little flock of parishioners and feels the responsibility. Also, his behavior is somewhat unpredictable and I thought it better not to bring him into polite society. A neighbor woman looked after him while I was away."

He took the bull by the horns. "While you were preparing tea I thought I saw—Mr. Brandon, I assumed. He peed—no, *peeped* in that door," James said and he pointed in an agony of embarrassment. "He looked somewhat—out of order?" In fact, he thought Mr. Brandon had looked swinishly drunk.

"I have no doubt," she said. "He is always out of order. It is best to take no notice of his high jinks when he is in his fits."

There seemed nothing to say to this. She cast her eyes down. A long silence fell. He sensed she was listening for noises in the back of the house. He studied her face, trying to combat the power of the black eyes by finding faults with her nose—too long—and her mouth—thin and wide.

Unable to think of more conversation—after the disclosures of the damaged husband it was too late to introduce the topic of weather—James Duke, suddenly glib, began to rattle off details of his good fortune, his surprise and delight at receiving a large inheritance from his long-estranged father.

"You see," he said, "I was sent away from home at a young age to become a maritime officer, and over the years we never corresponded. My mother died at my birth and my father always blamed me for it. Still, I have survived and now come into a good situation."

Mistress Brandon, turning her attention wholly on him, said, "But what a fortunate outcome! We all dream that a rich relative will shower us with gold and manses, but you are the first one I have ever known who has experienced such a turnover. What will you now do, live happily ever after? Is your wife ecstatic?"

"I will participate in the affairs of the family company, Duke and Sons, in what capacity I am not yet secure. And as to the other, I have no wife. I have ever been single."

"Indeed!" cried Mistress Brandon. "Did you say Duke and Sons? The great timber company?" Her eyes were forest pools.

"Yes. It is the family business and I am joining it. I have been asked to serve on the Board—as my father did. But the truth is that I am somewhat nervous as I know very little about the timber trade."

"My dear Mr. Duke! Perhaps I may be of help to you. I am the daughter of Phineas Breeley of the Breeley Lumber Contractors in New Brunswick. He has had many dealings in Maine. As a girl I assisted my father in his paperwork. I know something of the business and all that I know I shall impart to you. And then we must find you a wife."

James visited the Brandons again the next week. Mrs. Brandon let him in.

Mr. Brandon was nowhere in sight—"closeted with another fit," said Mistress Brandon, whose first name, he learned, was Posey. She smiled, she looked at his lips when he spoke, questioned him about his cousins and the Duke business, asked his advice on the choice between a deep blue shawl and one of rose cashmere, and then, from the corner cupboard, she pulled out a sheaf of closely inscribed pages held together by a dressmaker's pin detailing the structure and proceedings of her father's timber contracting business—his work as timber looker, the cheapest kinds of lumber camps, where to find the best men (Penobscot men, found in Bangor). He thought he had never met so intelligent and fine a woman and told her so. To himself he thought that not only were her eyes beautiful, but she had the grace of a swan, the voice of a dove. Batting those beautiful eyes and blushing from cleavage to hairline, she begged him to call on her again the next week, when he should have digested all the workings of her timber business scrawls. She would answer his questions and even quiz him if he thought it beneficial. But before then came the dinner at the Trumbulls'—seven the next evening. He would at last meet the Duke cousins.

• • •

It was a bitter cold and blowy evening spitting snow. Would spring never come? He arrived at the Trumbull house one minute before seven, and in the near dark saw the loom of a brick building. A black man in black livery opened the door for him. At the same moment the cousins and their wives arrived in their coach. They exchanged names and greetings in the vestibule while Mr. Trumbull urged them into the parlor, where a snapping fire spread out billows of heat. A bald-domed giant in an exquisite French-embroidered waist-coat stood near the fire holding a glass. This was the law partner, Josiah Tendrill, and he crushed James's hand saying, in a blast of brandy, "Very like, very like indeed."

Cousin Freegrace Duke was plump and short, breathing with asthmatic stertor. Freegrace's brother, Edward, was a large heavy man like his father, George Pickering Duke. Neither resembled the backwoodsmen of James's imagination. Freegrace's wife, Lenore, was a pale beauty with smoky eyes and a flaxen chignon, who would attract attention in any gathering. James was astonished. How had such a fat little man got such a beautiful wife? Edward's wife, Lydia, was of a more common type, brown braids wound around her head, and a habit of clearing her throat before she spoke.

They all kept glancing at James, and Freegrace finally said, "Forgive the scrutiny, but you are uncommon similar in appearance to Sedley. It is as if he went away for six months to the fountain of youth and tonight has rejoined us."

James did not like the constant references to his father as the shaper of his appearance, however true they might be. A maid brought hot toddies for the gentlemen and glasses of sherry for the ladies. They spoke of the unseasonable weather and the cold.

"Truly unusual the way this winter hangs on," said Mrs. Trumbull.

"Ah, James," said Lenore, "you will harden up in Boston. The dulcet climate of England is in your distant past. Here we must wrap in furs to keep alive. Going out in the winter or a spring like this one is always a dangerous adventure."

Josiah Tendrill told of a great snowstorm that had come in his childhood. "The snow fell for five days and when it ceased the drifts were up to the eaves of three-story houses. It took fifteen men three days to shovel us out."

The dinner was long, but not a single word was spoken about the business, Duke & Sons.

At last an English pudding streaked with blue brandy fire came in, and when it was reduced to a rubble of crumbs the ladies retired to Mrs. Trumbull's sitting room and the men to the library for cigars and imported cognac.

"I beg you tell me more of the family," said James. "I remember a large number of cousins. Are not some of them involved in the family business?"

Edward sighed. "Time has not been kind to the family. We lost almost an entire generation. Your uncle Piet on a visit to Virginia took the cholera in the very warm summer of—what—years ago now, and did not survive the attack. He is buried there. Aunt Patience Deckbolt suffered mental exhaustion and finally passed away in her sleep. Three of her daughters still live in the city with their husbands and families and you shall meet them at a future gathering. None of their husbands—well, I shall forbear to describe the husbands. Patience's grandson Cyrus is a clever young man and shows some promise for the company. We employed him. In time he will ascend the ladder of success. You will meet him when we have our meeting in June. Your half siblings, Sedley's second family, have all repaired to Philadelphia. Maury, the eldest, who is Sedley's only other son, your half brother I suppose we might say, works for a banking firm and I wish he had remained in Boston as he is certainly good timber."

"And are there no other cousins and relatives I should know?"

"Your great-uncle Old Outger Duquet returned to Amsterdam or Leiden and lived there. He continued to draw his stipend from the business to the end. But now he is gone. His half-breed daughter lived in flagrant concubinage with an Indian in Outger's house on Penobscot Bay. They produced an army of Indian brats. They are quite unknown to us. I have mentioned Cyrus Hempstead. And we have Lennart Vogel, the only son of your great-aunt Doortje Duquet. So, you see, it comes down to you to help replenish our ideas and fortune."

Weeks passed and James often called on Mrs. Brandon. They had become great friends. It was foolish to pretend he was calling on both husband and wife. Mr. Brandon was always in his fits and James had never actually seen him save for the glimpse of wild eyes on his first visit.

He had read attentively through Mrs. Brandon's notes on her father's timber business. "There is still much I do not understand," he said. "For example, I hear everywhere that Maine is the place for the best pine, but I know little or nothing of Maine."

"What could be easier? Maine is not yet a state, but sure to be very soon. It is a large territory heavy with forests, especially the valuable white pine. Maine is spotted with a thousand lakes and ponds like a slice of yeasty bread is riddled with holes, has great rivers, each with a hundred branches. I can name some of them for you and next time you come I will have a map of sorts showing the best waterways—the Androscoggin, Kennebec, St. George, St. John and the Allagash, and the best, the Penobscot. All the rivers of Maine have countless streams feeding them, but you can only get logs down them with dams in the time of the spring freshets." He could hardly think when she looked at him so intensely and struggled to find sensible questions.

One afternoon he came into the now-familiar parlor and found her sitting at the table with a stack of bills and accounts. Her face showed traces of tears, and wiping them away and throwing down her pen she rushed into the kitchen to make the tea. He glanced over the accounts; ye gods, what was she living on? The Brandons had no money at all. And was it right that such an intelligent and handsome woman had to scratch up the tea herself in some back kitchen? Although he had never been in any of the other rooms of the house, he set out for the kitchen. He would help her. Damme, he would help her!

She was stuffing kindling into the stove. The kitchen smelled of bad drains and the disagreeable odor of the wet soapstone sink, old ashes and a sour dishclout. She turned, frowning horribly when she heard his footstep, but the frown transformed into a tear-wet dimpled smile when she saw it was James.

"Ah! I thought—"

He knew what she thought; she thought it was the fit-prone Mr. Brandon blundering in on her, perhaps twitching and spewing, pissing in his filthy pants.

"My dear," he said and took her hand. "You shall not endure this another day. I shall hire a woman to come in and do for you at once. Let us now forget the tea, go into the parlor and have a little talk about what must be done," for he intended to pay up those nagging past-due accounts, intended to have Mr. Brandon put in an asylum, intended much more. He had money and he would put it to use. He could get what he wanted and he wanted Posey Brandon.

She confessed that she had pawned the silver dish he had brought her to pay some of the bills and to buy food. He was deeply shocked and deeply pleased that he could set matters right. When he left the house two hours later he had set changes in motion.

"Come in, sir," said Mrs. Deere, the new cook, who also served as housemaid, opening the door. The parlor table gleamed with waxy luster and there was a jar of pussy willows on the windowsill. He could smell something pleasant in the distant kitchen, something Mrs. Deere said was "a rhubarb roly-poly, first rhubarb of the year." And, as was now his right, he went to that delicious room where Mrs. Deere had performed miracles. The new stove glowed, the soapstone sink no longer reeked.

"Very good, Mrs. Deere. Have you had any trouble with—with Mr. Brandon?"

"No sir. I make him bread and butter and hot milk, which Dr. Hudson says is good for deranged people. Missus Brandon takes it to him and brings back the dishes." She came closer and whispered: "But I have to lock away the leftover joint as he strives for meat."

"I hope we will have a solution to the problem before long. I met with Dr. Hudson myself this morning. Would you be so good as to bring tea into the parlor while I discuss the doctor's findings with Mistress Brandon?"

"And dried apple pie?" she said, pointing with her chin. "Or roly-poly?"

"And pie," he agreed, for rhubarb could be sour.

"My dear," he said to Posey Brandon, waving his hand over his saucer of steaming pie. "I spoke with Dr. Hudson this morning for some time. He is of two opinions. He thinks it possible that Mr. Brandon may someday come to his senses. He thinks fresh air would be very good for him, and a place to walk and exercise. To that end he suggests that you send Mr. Brandon to the care of a farm family. They would be glad of the extra money and would keep him clean and expose him to much fresh air. He has a farmer in mind, a Jeremiah Taunton, who lives about five miles out of town, a man of calm ways. His wife is a generous woman, very pleasant and quiet. They have two or three children. They would welcome Mr. Brandon and house him comfortably. Does that not sound a good solution?"

"Oh yes, yes. But you said Dr. Hudson had two opinions."

"I did. And he does. He said, should by any chance Mr. Brandon not thrive in the farmer's care or should he become wild and phrenetic, it might be possible to arrange for him to be housed in Williamsburg, in Virginia, at the Public Hospital for Persons of Insane and Disordered Minds, a unique institution that Boston absolutely must emulate. Here we see the mad and incompetent wandering the countryside, but in Williamsburg they are kept in a special place and treated. The caretakers effect many cures with plunge baths, various drugs, bleeding and certain salves. There are exercise yards."

"It sounds very well. But first let us send him to the farmer. Should we not send his books of sermons as well? He might resume reading and writing. It meant much to him in earlier times before that lightning strike."

"I will ask Dr. Hudson. He did mention 'complete rest and quiet,' but perhaps books would be allowed. This pie is delicious, is it not? Are you pleased with Mrs. Deere?"

"I am most pleased. And with Mrs. Blitter, who is a fair enough housekeeper. You are very good to me and I am grateful." She looked at him with her great dark eyes.

But the next day he called again to say that books would not be allowed; books could cause brain fever even in people who had not been struck by lightning. The doctor himself would take Mr. Brandon to the farm on the coming Monday. In his breast pocket James heard the doctor's bill crackle a little. A small price to get rid of the wretched Brandon.

44

keepsake

Spring came at last in early June, a rushing spate of warm days, the gutters streaming with meltwater, people smiling and walking about as though their legs were new-made. Birds raced through the branches, the smell of earth dizzied the senses. Posey Brandon opened the windows of her renovated and refurnished house before James Duke arrived for his afternoon tea. But he was late. She went to the window a hundred times and peered down the street, hoping to see the gig bowling along. On the tea table lay a tiny packet wrapped in blue paper, the minuscule label bearing the words "James Duke a Keepesake." Would he not find it presumptuous? He would surely take his leave immediately, leaving it exposed on the table. He would withdraw Mrs. Deere and Mrs. Blitter. The bills would pile up.

Why did he not come? Was her benefactor ill or had he met with an accident? Surely he would have sent a messenger for any ordinary delay. Had he somehow found out about—it—the keepsake? She paced. The sunlight color began to deepen and late-afternoon chill flowed into the room. She closed the window and called for Mrs. Blitter.

"I am worrit that Mr. Duke is delayed for some reason. And it grows chill. I think we need a small fire in this room. If he does not come soon I must send a messenger to inquire."

"We can send Mrs. Deere's boy—that slow coach is still in the kitchen—he has been at it *all day*—taking out the old flour and molasses barrels." Her voice was scornful.

"Yes, let us send him. Here, I will write a brief note."

But before the fire was burning well Mrs. Deere's boy was back.

"He was at the corner. I give him your note but he's right at the gate. Hear his horse?"

"I am extremely sorry to be late," said James Duke. "I was delayed by Dr. Hudson, who called on me only moments before I left. To be brief about it, he says that Mr. Brandon has become ill from some other source than his derangement. He coughs continuously and cannot keep any food down. He is very thin and weak. To spare the farmer's wife extra work I have hired a day nurse to assist, for he is in bed in his room and cannot rise from it. Dr. Hudson has ordered two fresh eggs a day beaten into warm milk with a spoonful of rum and says he may recover with the warm days but he may not. We can only wait."

Her entire body flooded with relief. That Mr. Brandon would make a generous exit was her deepest wish. It changed the afternoon. They both sat silent and pensive, both thinking of Mr. Brandon. She could not now give James Duke the gift. It would not be apropos. At first opportunity she slid the little packet up her sleeve unobserved. So they sat drinking tea and saying very little until the twilight deepened.

"I must go, I fear," said James Duke, rising. "I wish—" But what he wished was not spoken.

"Of course I would like to see Mr. Brandon if there comes any—crisis," she murmured.

"Dr. Hudson said he would come straight to you if, if, if the illness took a grave turn." As he spoke the doctor's gig turned in to the street and drew up before the house.

"Oh heavens," said Mrs. Brandon. James stood waiting, exultation seizing him.

"Dr. Hudson, ma'am," said Mrs. Blitter, opening the parlor door to show him in.

"Bring more tea, Blitter," said Mrs. Brandon. She looked at the doctor. His face was expressionless, noncommittal.

"Dr. Hudson, do take tea with us," she said although her bladder was bursting with tea. "I will just see to it," and she strode briskly out of the room.

James Duke looked at him. "Is there a change?" he asked in a low voice.

"There is a change," the doctor answered and said nothing more, waiting for Mrs. Brandon to return. The lady returned, skirts swishing with the violence of her stride.

"Please tell us, Doctor, how Mr. Brandon does." Her voice was calm and steady.

"I am happy to say that he has rallied, rallied enough to eat heartily and drink like a camel. His derangement seems rather more settled as well. I think he must have passed some sort of crisis. He recognized me, inquired after your health, praised the farmer and his wife. He still objects to milk and bread but in a week or so we may try him with breast of chicken. I feel he might be able to come home soon. Certainly the day nurse is no longer needed," he said with a nod at James indicating his release from that expense.

Posey was stunned into silence for a long, long beat. "Ah! But can I care for him here? The space is so limited, and the air is not the bracing country air. And certainly not if his derangement persists." The fresh tea tray and a dish of seedcake arrived; Posey Brandon poured with a steady hand. "Sugar? Yes, lemon?" She passed a cup to the doctor.

"We will wait and see if he continues to improve. I allowed that tonight he may sleep on the farmhouse porch for the benefits of fresh air. In a week if he has grown stronger I think he will be little trouble. I can always send the nurse with him if there is any doubt. It's rather an interesting case and it would be far easier for me to follow his progress if he were here instead of out in the country. Wouldn't you agree, Mr. Duke?"

"Of course," said James Duke in a grudging voice. "Who could disagree?"

When the clock struck the half hour the men rose, made their good-byes and went out together. James sent Mrs. Brandon a scorching look she quite understood. She smiled and nodded and as soon as the door closed ran to her room muttering sailors' curses and threw herself into the pillows.

In the street gloaming it was difficult to see the doctor's expression when James asked him if he might call on Mr. Brandon.

"Perhaps, in a day or two you might, but I fear that the appearance of a stranger alone might startle him into a relapse. I equally do not yet approve a visit from Mrs. Brandon. It is one of his crotchets that he has developed a fear of her and claims—ridiculous as it sounds—that she somehow harms him. But that will likely pass as he recovers his reason. Shall we go out to the farm together in the morning?"

"If I find I have no other appointments that would be agreeable," said James Duke. But later, when the moon rose, he went to the stable, saddled his horse and in the gathering darkness took the high road out of the city toward the farm where Mr. Brandon lay dreaming of rib roast.

45

error compounded

The quiet morning broke into noisy pieces when Farmer Taunton's youngest son, William, a grimy boy with a common face, pounded into the town bareback on a black plow horse. He went panting to the house of his married sister, Charlotte, and she roused her husband, Saul Fleet, who ran to magistrate Jonas Gildart's house and blurted out the tale, his voice leaping a high whinny and sinking back with the gravity of the news. The magistrate set his full coffee cup down. He pushed it away, sloshing the table.

Saul Fleet blurted, "Charlotte's brother! He come in from the old place, brought word the old man been found dead. Layin on the porch floor. Strangled or choked looks like. Said his neck all crooked, color a rhubarb stalk."

Mrs. Gildart brought her husband a new bowl of coffee and the magistrate continued his questions. Saul answered eagerly: No, he didn't think the old man was given to falling down. No, his mother-in-law slept in the house. Had done so for many years, after a dispute over Mr. Taunton's snoring, which shook the house timbers. Mr. Taunton slept on the porch in good weather and on the kitchen day-bed in winter. He, Saul Fleet, had no idea why anyone would harm Mr. Taunton, a hardworking inoffensive man who did some black-smithing on the side, was a regular churchgoer and neither drank nor smoked. His turnips were much prized.

The magistrate sent for Charlotte Fleet and her young brother William, who had brought the news. Charlotte knew nothing except what she had heard from William, and the magistrate turned to him.

"Well, boy, I have a few questions. You are William Taunton, the son of Jeremiah Taunton, is that not correct? Good, good. Now, what family members were sleeping in the house last night?"

"My mother, sir. My sister Abigail, me, and T-T-Tom." He stuttered and mumbled.

"Who is Tom?"

"He is my big brother."

"Were there any servants in the house?"

"Only Sarah Whitwell. She helps Mother with the washin and comes after prayers Sunday night to be at hand early on Mondays. She sleeps in the little bed in Mother's room."

"Did your father allow any vagrants or strangers to sleep in the barn last night?"

"No sir, he never lets them sleep in the barn. Unless they pay. In New England money."

"And were there any of these paying strangers present last night?"

"Only Mr. Brandon, sir."

"And who is Mr. Brandon?"

"He is a preacher sir, but is funny in the head from lightnin. He shows a gret big scar on his face. Mother cared for him and Mr. Duke paid Father. He stayed with us since two months or more. Father give him the good front room."

"Who is Mr. Duke?"

"I don't know, sir, but Father said he was a rich man. He drives a gig with two greys. Very good horses. I thought I heard them horses last night but it was a patridge in the woods."

"And was Mr. Brandon in the house last night?"

"Yessir. Dr. Hudson said he was some better and could go home soon. He felt very well yesterday and wanted to sleep on the back porch for the fresh air. Pa said he wished Mr. Brandon could stay on as he was a good boarder and the money helped us."

"And did Mr. Brandon sleep on the back porch last night?"

"No sir, he did not. Father's bed is there and he said he would not be turned out of it for any man."

"Did Mr. Brandon like your father?"

"Most times. But then he said he was sick and tired of bread and milk, which was what we fed him. Pa said, 'Eat it or go hungry.' And Mr. Brandon squinched up his eyes very fierce."

"And where is Mr. Brandon now?"

"He is helpin Mother and Tom lay Father out. He's mighty heavy, is Pa."

The magistrate exchanged significant glances with two men who had come in with Dr. Hudson and dismissed the boy.

"It may be—" said the magistrate, "it may be that we must look at this fellow Brandon. Doctor, what can you tell us about him? Is he sick or well, what is the nature of his illness, is he strong, what is his disposition, does he have a grudge against Mr. Taunton?"

"He has been suffering from the effects of a lightning strike he sustained two years past and has certainly been much disturbed in his mind, babbling and confused and plagued by suspicions. But yesterday he appeared to be a little better and said he wished soon to go home."

"In your opinion, Doctor, is it possible that this preacher nourished a hatred of Mr. Taunton on account of the bread and milk or whatever reason, and gripped by a mad fit in the night crept in and strangled him?"

"He was given to fears, that is true, but I never heard him say anything against Mr. Taunton. Except the bread and milk, which was being fed him on my orders. Of course he may have been overcome with jealousy over the porch bed. I gave him leave to sleep there but the boy says Mr. Taunton denied permission."

"Could he not, in his disturbed mind, have laid the blame for the repetitive comestibles on Mr. Taunton? And the sequestering of the porch bed?"

"Yeee-es," said the doctor reluctantly. "Of course it could have fallen out that way. But I do not think he is strong enough to strangle a man."

"But it has been known, has it not, for insane persons to exhibit great strength in their fits?"

"It has been *known,* certainly. There are many mysteries associated with insanity."

"So you knew him to be insane?"

"I knew him to have been deranged by a lightning bolt. He did have fits and temper tantrums. But I was quite sure he was mending well and soon would be as sane as you or I."

" 'Soon would be' is not the same as 'was.' And if there was no one there but the family and this Mr. Brandon, subject to fits of insanity, I put it to you that it was he who strangled Mr. Taunton. Gentlemen, I ask you to go out and return with Mr. Brandon, who must be examined and stand trial."

Mr. Brandon was incarcerated and relapsed into fulminating babble of his innocence. His loyal flock stood in vigil outside the gaol singing hymns, and later, outside the court, when, after a speedy trial he was found guilty and a date set for his hanging.

46

business meeting

All through a hot damp Boston summer James Duke courted Posey Breeley Brandon. He knew that no one could ever grasp what she meant to him. He had been sent away as a boy, passed over for promotion, he had been poor and crushed. And then how everything had changed. The crown of joy was Posey. He knew also that his cousins would be scandalized by the age difference between them, for he was now fifty-five and Posey twenty years younger. She was his constant visitor. In the evenings, when a cooling sea breeze moved inshore, they walked in the rose garden, around and around the sundial, talking of lumber and true love's knot, her silk skirt rustling, her great dark eyes cast low. They walked from the first leaves on the roses to pink buds, to opened petals, to drowsy full-blown lush blooms, to faded blossoms, frost-nipped browning leaves. He would do anything for her, had already done so without regret. She asked him for nothing except his company and his conversation. She paid rapt attention to everything he said, he who all his life had been ignored. But the getting of Posey was hard, and as long as Mr. Brandon lived (he had escaped hanging) she was not gettable. Not only did the minister's congregation include two members connected to important Boston families but Brandon himself was the nephew of Judge Archibald Brandon, who moved silently behind the closest circles of power. The judge would not see his unfortunate relative, a man whom he believed had been the innocent victim of an evil marriage and a lightning bolt, hanged as a murderer.

"I almost understand why God laid this affliction on him," said the judge to Dr. Hudson, whom he had discovered after a short search. "The city has become a stinking mire of corruption and evildoing. I see this as a sign of God's punishing vengeance. And yet I cannot feel my nephew was guilty of strangling this farmer over disagreeable suppers. He was ever a gentle man."

"There may be a way for him to avoid that—that end," said the doctor. "I think we must appeal to the Williamsburg authorities at the Public Hospital for Persons of Insane and Disordered Minds. There was some indication earlier that he might be harbored there." The weight of the judge's name, the pleas of Mr. Brandon's flock and Dr. Hudson's carefully composed essay on the felon's gentleness secured him a room at the Virginia retreat. In the company of others with disordered minds Mr. Brandon shone out as a model inmate.

Freegrace called the October business meeting of Duke & Sons. As always James felt the significance of being a voting Board member. He dressed carefully: tan wool pantaloons with a narrow fall and instep straps, tan vest piped in black, single-breasted cutaway coat. He carried Sedley's gold watch, and to its chain he had attached Posey Breeley Brandon's gift, a gold-wreathed fob that enclosed a miniature painting of her beautiful left eye, for intimate eye paintings were all the rage. Beautiful the subject was, but it had a certain fixing quality not altogether pleasant. Beside him Freegrace and Edward seemed drab in their old-fashioned knee breeches and pale silk stockings, the backs spotted with mud.

Freegrace introduced a cadaverous man with eyes like candles in a cave as Lennart Vogel, who had missed the last two meetings as he was traveling. He was Doortje Duquet's only child, and so a cousin of Sedley Duke, James Duke's hard-hearted father. After a cosseted and overeducated life, Lennart eventually came to Boston and made the acquaintance of his Duke relatives. No one was more fastidious in his dress and on this day he wore pearl-grey pantaloons buttoned four inches above the ankle over white silk stockings, his shoes the merest slippers, replaced every fortnight. He had made himself into an indispensable walking encyclopedia of figures, trends and innovations affecting the timber trade. His greatest value, Edward whispered to James, lay in his fluent command of seven languages. Lennart had another side. For two months every year he put away his town clothes, donned heavy bush pants and logging boots and went into the woods, sometimes with an Indian guide. He said he was fishing and visiting subcontractors' logging camps. He seemed unusually cheerful when he returned to Boston.

The meeting room was warm with a fire to spite the autumn chill. Freegrace said, "Let us begin." There was a great scraping of chair legs and a rustle of paper.

"This year the Maine drives got under way late, all was delayed, with the contractors hoping for rain to raise the rivers," said Freegrace. "We hear from those jobbers that it was only a fair winter, not at all like the snows we had here. Meager snow forced the men to resort to dams to get the sticks down feeder streams and into the river—much labor and time. The jobber is demanding recompense. He won't get it. I do have some figures for the previous year, which should cheer."

James interrupted in a low voice. "Excuse my ignorance—how many men do we employ in the woods?"

Lennart Vogel answered, the figures ready in his mouth. "Better than one thousand this year for six to eight months. At ten dollars a month and their bed, board and tools. Ridiculous as it may seem, we've increasingly had to hire well-known cooks as other camps will get the better men by dishing up fancy vittles. Vittles!" He clearly relished the slangy American word and thought of himself as an adept slang slinger. "We figure twenty cents a day to board each man, which is a great deal of provision. We are forced to hire cooks who might command the kitchens of elegant restaurants save for personality blemishes."

Edward spoke up. "But victualing is not the greatest expense. Corn and hay for the oxen. Hay is almost twenty dollars a ton and we last year used more than five thousand tons. Corn is a dollar a bushel and the oxen will gorge on four thousand bushels the season. The oxen are dear and so are the drivers—twenty thousand dollars in costs. Then there are timberland purchases and palms to be greased, especially in procuring the so-called Indian lands that the idiot Congress strives to keep from us with its 'Nonintercourse Act.'"

Freegrace muttered, "In what other country must businessmen trouble with murderous barbarians coddled by the government?"

Edward continued on his set path. "We have high survey expenses, and though we have been cutting most on our own lands and have our own mills and so have few stumpage or mill rent costs, there are a hundred other expenses—axes and tools, grindstones, oil, iron, blacksmiths and their forges, log boomage and lockage." The clerk's pen scratched violently as he tried to keep up with Edward's rapid speaking.

Cyrus thought James looked puzzled and said, "Sir, boomage is the cost for making booms to hold the logs in a body and lockage—" But Edward disliked being interrupted and said curtly, "Cyrus, you may please save your explanations for later. I am sure James understands the terms. What we need to discuss today is first, the precipitous decline in large, first-rate white pine, and second, the persistent problem of timber thieves plundering our holdings and other cheatings and malfeasances. And among the thieves those who manufacture shingles and clapboards are the most terrible dishonest. The thieves are worse on the public lands, but they show no hesitation in cutting Duke trees. New Brunswick loggers are the bane of the forest. Wherever they see it they cut it and then run with it. New Brunswick has no thriving farms nor vigorous towns. Its residents are the locusts of the forest. We regard New Brunswickers as our enemies." He stopped to draw breath, reviewed what he had said and allowed that "the problem might be somewhat ameliorated if ever the boundary lines with Canada were clearly drawn." He was stuttering a bit, uneasy with James Duke's presence—the man too closely resembled his dictatorial father, Sedley, who had made Edward's life miserable with harping and picking. And James's awful watch fob flashing its censorious stare rattled him.

James leaned back. He had planned to tell his cousins over the evening dinner that the widow Posey Brandon had accepted his proposal of marriage and that they had set the wedding date for May. After news of Mr. Brandon's death from pneumonia in Virginia he had waited a decent interval—twenty-four hours—before proposing to her. She had accepted on the spot and he had embraced her and tried to seal the betrothal with a tender kiss. How surprised he had been by the fierce and spitty ardor with which she returned his dry kiss. Later, much later, he was to think back on it and interpret it as a warning, a warning he did not—could not—heed. But now his brain whirred with alarming scenarios of how his cousins would take the news that he was marrying the daughter of David Breeley, *a New Brunswick logging contractor.* He had not yet met his future father-in-law, but from what Posey told him he had no doubt that Mr. Breeley flourished a free hand with the ax, damnation to any damned border.

James, gazing out the window, saw a distant smudge in the sky that he had learned to recognize as a body of passenger pigeons.

Cyrus spoke up. "I thought we were to hear today of new markets—was I mistaken in this apprehension?"

"Not at all," said Lennart, speaking out of turn to judge by Edward's glare. James guessed that Lennart too often put himself forward. "We are shipping more and more lumber every year, and not from Boston, but out of Bangor. We have heard that Cuba wants sugar boxes. Freegrace is in correspondence with a Cuban dignitary on this possibility. The West Indies are hungry for everything—boards, shingles, clapboards, pickets and lath, hemlock bark, even some hardwood. Even some hackmatack knees. We cannot send enough shiploads to the West Indies, and of course we bring back rum, sugar and molasses. Many European cities have discovered the utility of wood paving blocks, and such a market allows us to dispose of wood otherwise wasted. And not only Europe, but Charleston, Buenos Aires, yes, even Australia. I have not mentioned the growing coast trade."

"We are straying from the subject," said Freegrace.

"Quite, and thank you, Freegrace, for hauling us back so smartly," said Edward. "Well, then, Armenius Breitsprecher, our timberland looker since his father passed on, was gulled with a false map and a false report for the lands on the White Moose branch and we have just now discovered the fraud. The surveyor's map showed that the timber grew thick along a watercourse, the north branch of the Moose, but the reality proved the stream lay miles distant from the pine. Breitsprecher says he went to see the timber at the time, now four years past, but it was winter and deep snow. The surveyor insisted the frozen stream lay under the snow beneath their feet. And because of the waist-deep snow Armenius could not thoroughly investigate the trees. He admits it. So the report on which we based our purchase indicated a good stream and a hundred million of pine. In fact, there were only fourteen million. And a distant stream. We had great expenses in road building and drawing the timber out with hired ox teams. The question now is whether or not we should continue to retain Breitsprecher as our land looker. He made an expensive error. He relied overly on a thieving surveyor."

Freegrace sighed. "Yes, we could discharge Breitsprecher but he is an experienced and able land looker and has served us for many years and made Duke and Sons a great deal of money. This is almost the only instance of bad judgment on his part. I know he regrets it. I suggest we speak sternly to him but retain his services."

"I agree," said Lennart Vogel. "Judgment of the costs and profit to be obtained from a standing forest is difficult and takes many years of experienced looking." He, too, had noticed the unwinking watch fob and felt the presence of the unknown original.

"What do you think, Cyrus?"

"Why, how difficult can it be to find good timberland judges? Surely Breitsprecher is not the only fellow who can look at trees. Are there not legions of such men trooping through the forest?" He leaned back carelessly in his chair, crossed one leg over the other and dandled his right foot.

Edward spoke again. "There are indeed, most of them crooked scalawags who tender false reports about the quality of the pine, all sound trees, of course, which turn into core-rotted hulks when the ax smites. James, what do you think?"

"If he has been an honest employee all these years—how long has he worked for us?"

"Since he was a boy under the tutelage of his father, say thirty-odd years now."

"After thirty years of faithful service and only one misjudgment of a lying surveyor, it seems to me extreme to let the man go. I argue to keep him on."

"All in favor," droned Freegrace. "Now, let us pass on to the problems of trespass and plundering, which grow apace. We have put out warning notices that trespassing on our woodlands will lead to prosecution. We only hope the notices are noticed!"

He flourished a paper and read aloud:

This gives notice that the Timber marked D&S stacked on Distress Brook Lot 17 is the property of Duke & Sons, Boston. All persons are hereby warned not to meddle with same or drive it from where it now lays or risk prosecution. Measures will be taken to detect persons evading this notice.

"A hollow threat," said Edward. "Maine juries are utterly corrupt. They find for the criminals—their relatives and associates—every time."

James said, "Who are these lawless men who cut your—our—timber?"

"Every man!" Edward said angrily, spit flying. "They are mostly small, mean men seeking to make some money. But there are so many of them. They are often savage hungry fellows who stop at nothing. They fight the owners until blood flows and heads are cracked. Even when we catch and prosecute them, they and their friends slip back at night and continue cutting. Settlers, failed businessmen, shingle makers and clapboard sawyers, those are the thieves. And moonlight nights see many good pines fall."

"It is more than just the stealage," said Edward. "Their campfires do great harm and burn much timber. Some of these men will deliberately set fires on the edge of good timber, then connive to purchase the entire valuable woods as burned wasteland for a meager cost. And in any case the damned poxy settlers clear their wretched plots with fire when they will, and in the dry season the fire escapes and devours our wood."

Cyrus pulled at his cravat and tried to sum up the situation. "The truth is, gentlemen, that Maine—and New Brunswick—forests are swarming with lawless men. What we long for is virgin woodland without these human locusts. As Maine used to be."

James asked if the Ohio lands his father had visited were not just such a virgin Eden.

"No, it is good timber, but there is not that much. A few years' worth. We must think far ahead into the future. We *hear* of great forests farther west, and this may be the time to investigate the reports. I have several times proposed we meet with Armenius Breitsprecher and ask him to make the journey westward. Would he not be eager to reclaim his honor after the mishap on the north branch of the White Moose?"

"Sensible if one of us went with him," said Lennart Vogel. "For an unbiased report. It could be a valuable expedition."

"Easy for you to say, Lennart—you are a world traveler, but most of us prefer to stay put in Boston and deal with the accounts and contracts. Perhaps *you* should go." Vogel shook his head.

"Might we not look closer to home? I have heard that there is a vast kingdom of white pine along the Susquehanna and Allegheny Rivers in Pennsylvania. Some say that *this* is the finest white pine that ever grew," said Cyrus.

"Ah, they said the same about Maine pine, the same of New

Brunswick pine. We should start buying with an eye to fifty years hence," said Freegrace.

"God knows why. Take what we can get as soon as we can get it is what I say. I am not interested in fifty years hence as there is no need for concern. The forests are infinite and permanent," said Edward.

The dinner, at an inn on Rowes Wharf, was simple—baked golden plovers, salmon and succotash, fresh pease. They talked freely, loosened from the fetters of the formal meeting. Cyrus explained boomage and lockage at length to James, then moved on to fire.

"You know, talk of fire could well have included our own depredations. One of our contractors, on Edward's orders, set fire to several haystacks the thieves had brought to one of our pineries to feed their oxen. The fire got away and burned not only the haystacks but the pines they were trying to steal. So you see, we can give as good as we get." James found the logic of this summation impaired, but said nothing. He began to wonder if Cyrus Hempstead was not a dunce.

"James," said Lennart Vogel, "by now you know that timber profits are almost entirely based on transportation costs. Steamboats can change the way we move our logs."

Edward spoke up as soon as he had swallowed his mouthful of pandowdy. "We know the English are using steam locomotives in collieries. Why shouldn't steam engines succeed? In a few years, Freegrace, we might be building a railway into our dryland pineries, where no rivers flow. Right now every penny we gain still depends on the rivers. The steam engine could have a profound effect on our business."

"Edward, you are right," said Lennart. "There is certainly a mood of great things in the air, days of glorious prosperity ahead."

The rum went around the table and around until the Board members were speaking so loudly at one another that a florid man at a distant table asked the proprietor if they might be put out in the street.

"That's Saltonstall," said Cyrus, "the old barnacle. He believes himself the most important man in Boston. If he wants quiet let him stay home in his mausoleum."

At midnight James lurched out to his coach, where Will Thing sat waiting in the darkness. In half an hour he was in his library, where the embers still glowed. Here he had a final glass of brandy. And so, his head spinning, James Duke went to bed.

It seemed only minutes before the maid Lily woke him.

"Sir, sir, Mistress Brandon is downstairs and wishes to breakfast with you."

"Oh my heart and soul," said James, "tell her I will be down in a few minutes. Do give her some tea or coffee or—"

"Yessir."

It was close to forty minutes before he came into the breakfast room, bathed, freshly shaven, in clean linen and a black cashmere suit, for the day was chilly.

"My dear," he said. "What brings you here so very early?"

"Why, James, I am eager to hear every detail of the business meeting. You know my great interest in your business affairs. You must tell me all about your cousins, who said what, the problems, the decisions, the plans for the future."

He buttered a hot biscuit and dipped it in a dish of honey, leaned over his plate, bit it and avoided dripping on his waistcoat. He began to talk. It was exhilarating to have someone pay such close attention to his descriptions. She asked intelligent questions and quizzed him on the Board members' mannerisms.

Mrs. Brandon, back at her house, went to a little walnut escritoire James had had made for her, withdrew a brown leather-bound book half-filled with misspelled notes in her sprawling hand. She began to set down the salient points of the business meeting. She made special note of Lennart Vogel's recommendations that Duke & Sons make investments outside the timber industry, especially in the booming textile mills, or cane sugar production.

47

needles and pins, needles and pins

James Duke's oft-postponed wedding day—he feared his cousins' reaction to his connection with a New Brunswick lumberman—began with a shock like a snapped fiddle string. His future father-in-law arrived in midmorning astride a limping, rolling-gaited woods horse of indifferent color. And who had ever seen such a physiognomy as that possessed by Phineas Breeley? His head looked as though it had been lopped off with a broadax just above the eyebrows and then squeezed back together leaving a great horizontal scar. Below the scar sat two anthracite-black eyes, a much-broken nose (a sure sign of coarseness) and a lipless mouth opening. His left ear was missing, only a hairy hole remained. The man let himself carefully down to the ground and advanced on Posey. He gripped her in a mighty hug, plastered her face with kisses that sounded like popping corn and turned to James.

"Well," he said. "Here I be. Ready for the shivaree and our *Grand Trip.*" Posey had invited her father to accompany them on their honeymoon to New York. She had wanted James to invite Freegrace and Edward Duke and their wives to the ceremony and the celebratory dinner, but he found excuses—Edward was traveling, Freegrace's wife was abed with pleurisy—and he presented very excellent reasons for not asking the others. Indeed, he had not told them of his impending marriage. Not yet, not yet, he temporized.

"I know you'll love my papa," she had said, "and he's always wanted to see that New York. It will be company for us in a place

367

we don't know no one." Now the moment had arrived. James and Posey would be getting into a hired coach with this man in a few hours. Unsure how to greet the fellow, James looked covertly at the horse's hooves, which showed founder rings. No wonder the wretched beast limped.

"Let us turn out your horse in the pasture," he said. "I see he is sore-footed. He may have a holiday while we tour New York."

"Now, fellows, don't spend too much time talkin," said Posey, looking at the brass mantel clock. "We are to be at the magistrate's eleven sharp. It lacks only half an hour to that time."

"Sore foot or not, all the same to me," said Phineas Breeley. "They are all jades and nags. I have *No Love for Horses.*"

I can see that, thought James, somewhat put off by the fellow's odd emphases.

The ceremony was brief and, as James had hoped, unknown to his cousins. Father and daughter chattered animatedly on the long coach trip while James, across from them but huddled into the corner, tried to doze. The father's arm encircled Posey and occasionally he peppered her with his clicking kisses. The day waned and twilight darkened the coach interior and they talked on of people born and dead, accidents, departures from the scene, violent weather, amusing happenings, the faults of the men who worked for Breeley. All night they talked, a great telling of names and antics. The coach stopped for a change of horses just after dawn and Breeley, who seemed quite lively, obligingly ran into the hostelry and came back with a pan of weak coffee and six cold boiled eggs. He swallowed half the contents of the coffee pan and four of the eggs, tossing the shells out the window. Refreshed by this repast he addressed his first remarks to James.

"I guess you and me will have many a good old *Woods Talk.* I always knowed I'd hook up to a *Big Outfit,* and a course Duke Sons is one of the *Biggest.* Got some of the *Best Pineries* in Maine. We can sure enough make *Some Pile a Boards,* eh?" And he gave a frightful wink that implied he knew Duke timberlands very intimately. James was horrified. How to disabuse the man? He seemed to assume that the marriage meant that he, Phineas Breeley, was now a partner in Duke & Sons. If Edward and Freegrace ever discovered this scarred New Brunswicker imagined himself one with them they would perish from shock.

It was nearly two when they arrived at their inn, a handsome Georgian building fronted by graceful wineglass *Ulmus americana,* favored by red men for council meetings in ancient days. It was set far enough back that the roar of iron-shod hooves and rattling wheels did not drown out conversation.

James was relieved that Phineas Breeley's room was some distance down the hall from the handsome suite he had reserved, for Breeley had followed them upstairs, trailing the men carrying the trunks. He had inspected their room as though he were going to occupy it with them. Finally, oh finally, thought James, he went to his own room, calling out that they must meet in an hour's time under the elms and begin their exploration of New York.

"At last I have you to myself," he murmured to Posey, embracing her lightly.

"Yes! Isn't Father grand company? He has a thousand stories."

"What caused that great scar on his head?"

"You must ask him. He rarely refers to it."

James knew he never would ask, and reconciled himself to a week in the man's company. Somehow he had to explain to Breeley that a marriage to Posey did not automatically enlist her father as a partner in Duke & Sons. How to put it without offending the man occupied his waking thoughts for the rest of the day. In their long perambulation down the busy streets ankle-deep in horse manure, they dodged scores of pigs, passed a platform said to be the site of the slave market, hurried past the stench of cattle pens and slaughterhouses, the vacant lots piled high with animal manure. James prayed it would not rain, would spare them the ordeal of wading through liquid shit. There was a constant moil of people harnessing horses, loading and unloading carts. Horses crowded the streets—omnibus horses, butcher horses, bakery cart horses, milk delivery horses, express horses—and lying alongside the curbs they saw dead and dying horses. These inhumane sights did not crush their appetites. They dined at the famous Red Cow Tavern on roast bear (*very* like pork) and mashed turnips. The waiter said they had a rare treat— pineapples from the Bahamas had just arrived, would they not wish to try one? They would. Swarms of flies hung like living chandeliers over the tables but the attentive waiters stood near waving fly whisks and they managed.

The pineapple, pared and sliced and served on pale blue dishes, was prime, ripe and fragrant. They fought the flies for the treat, but it was almost impossible to avoid the nasty sensation of a frantic buzz- ing insect in the mouth. When the pineapple was gone and the bill paid they started back to the Four Elms. On the way they passed sev- eral rowdy taverns where singing and the thumping of drums and female shrieks signaled some kind of coarse entertainment. At the door of their hotel Phineas Breeley stopped. "Reckon I'll just *Walk About* for nother hour—that *Pineapple* made me restless. See you on the *Morrow*." He saluted and turned down a side street.

The wedding night was an extreme experience for James Duke. He knew what was expected of him and even looked forward to it, but in no way was he prepared for the flying tigress who leapt on him, tore open the falls of his trousers and seized his penis, in no way was he prepared for her biting and scratching, thrusting and wriggling, tearing at his and her own clothes, nor for the wrestling and pant- ing. All night long Posey kept him going. Just before dawn he fell into a near-delirious sleep, his body shockingly embroidered with the experiences of the previous hours.

With daylight he woke and slid gingerly out of bed. Posey lay a-sprawl, breathing stertorously. James washed gingerly, dressed and went down to the small parlor, where coffee, tea and hot chocolate sat on a sideboard. He helped himself to a plate of still-warm biscuits dabbed with butter and strawberry jam, took his cup and plate to a table near the window and gazed out at the waving elm branches.

"There You Are!" cried Phineas Breeley, entering the quiet room, striding to the coffeepot and pouring himself an overfull cup. He sat opposite James, looked at him searchingly. He saw the welts, the black and blue bite marks, the scratches on the backs of his hands, his swollen lips and earlobes.

"Give you *Quite a Ride,* didn't she? She's *Pretty Feisty,* ain't she? I taught her *Everything* she knows and she turned out *Good.* She's a chip off the *Old Stump.* Guess you can take it better than *Old Preacher Man Brandon."* He winked and leered.

James felt the blood in his veins turn to mud. What in the name of God did Phineas Breeley mean? That he had tutored his daughter in the sexual arts? Cold horror flooded his mind at the thought. That a father would—! James felt his gorge rising, although he knew that such things happened, mostly to backwoods people deprived of diverse company. He could say nothing, and was relieved when Breeley launched into a monologue detailing the sights he had seen after he parted from them the evening before, the plump blond "patridge" he had found and *"Give a Good Fuck,"* the drinks he had swallowed. At last James got up and excused himself saying he would bring Posey a cup of morning coffee.

"Oh yas, I know about the mornin *'Cup a Coffee.'"* Breeley smirked, licking his lips and winking.

James Duke would have been happy to forgo sex for the next thirty years, but he was trapped. Indeed, Posey interpreted the morning cup of coffee much as her father had and pulled at James's waistcoat, trying to get him back on the bed. He looked at her. He was repulsed by the thought that the old scar-faced troll had had her and turned away. She seized his wrist with her hard grip and yanked. He fell onto the bed and she swarmed over him like ants on honeycomb. He tried, but could not keep down the image of the scar-laced head of Phineas Breeley pressed between his daughter's legs.

"No!" he shouted and leapt from the bed. Posey came after him, arms swinging, gorilla teeth bared. She beat him to blancmange consistency and left him in the corner.

"You had better come to some sense," she gritted between those strong white teeth. "I won't have another milksop husband."

"And *I* will not have a violent wife," said James, summoning his quarterdeck persona. "We must talk all of this out." He believed in reason, though it was unreasonable to do so.

James and Posey Duke walked out alone, leaving Phineas Breeley behind at James's impassioned request. "We must talk *alone, we must.*" After three and a half hours of questions, halting answers, temper fits, tears, scorn and expressions of sad disappointment they came to a compromise: Posey would have her own suite of rooms; she and James would agree beforehand on the times he would visit the matrimonial bed; he would not ask questions if she invited another (unspecified); she would not use violence to get her way; they would try to live happily ever after even though it might take great effort; one week after their return to Boston, Phineas Breeley must find his own quarters or return to New Brunswick. On this last point James had been diamond hard, and pledged a sum toward the purchase of a Breeley house. He said, in an almost threatening voice, that the alternative was divorce. But he had not asked the question of Posey's childhood relations with old Breeley. And she had not asked the question about his late-night visit to the Taunton farm.

Breeley seemed pleased with the idea of his own place and set off at once to look at houses in the neighborhood, for he did not wish to return to New Brunswick.

"It's *Lively* down here. I enjoy the *Lively*. Maunderville's quiet as a dead horse. Quieter. Your dead horse passes gas."

In four days he discovered a small stone cottage with a garden and two-horse stable half a mile distant. James cheerfully paid the owner for the place, and Breeley, he thought, would no longer annoy.

A few weeks later, at the breakfast table, Posey said, in an agreeable and placatory tone, "I am givin a dinner party Friday week for your cousins and other relatives. I made up a menu and will sit down with Mrs. Tubjoy and the cook and see if they can deal with my selections and if we must get in an extra girl for the evening. Time we got into some society. And I wish an occasion to wear my red silk that I had fitted in New York. It come by post yesterday—fits to perfection." She smiled and touched his hand very lightly as if to say, "See how chastely I behave."

James felt a shiver of fear. He had not yet told the cousins of his marriage and had no idea how they would take it. Thank God that old lecher would be in his stone house. He thought rapidly. He would not present Freegrace and Edward with a surprise, but would pen lighthearted little notes to each letting them know he had embarked on the matrimonial state.

"I suppose we must do so sooner or later. By all means proceed."

Posey whisked from the room, all purpose and plan.

48

James is surprised

The house was caught up in a hurricane of preparation. Mrs. Tub-joy hired two extra girls. They polished the silver, washed the best plates in vinegar water and dried them with linen cloths, wiped the glassware free of thumbprints. The cook's helper roasted and ground the best green coffee, pounded loaf sugar into heaps of crystals. Mrs. Tubjoy set one of the girls to seeding raisins and the other to winkling butternut meats from their chambering shells. James and Will Thing made an excursion to the distant woods to gather green pine boughs for decoration, for it was December. Posey engaged a string quartet to play—something high-toned. Two days before the all-important Friday, men arrived at the kitchen door with tubs of thrushes, pigeons and ducks, six wild turkeys, two venison hams. The cook's helpers were up until very late plucking the birds and storing them in the cold pantry. The grocer delivered gingerroot, lemons, nutmeg, allspice, hothouse Belgian endive. On the day itself came lobsters and sweet oysters, both in favor as they were growing scarce.

"Dear heaven," said James, "there is enough food for a militia."

"We do not wish to appear *poor,* do we?" said Posey. "Will you take Jason"—the new butler—"and see that there is sufficient of drink?"

"It is done," said James, who had been overseeing jeroboams, magnums, bottles and decanters all the week. "Our guests shall reel—with spirits if not amazement."

• • •

The hour arrived and Jason ushered in the first guests, the solicitor Hugh Trumbull and Mrs. Trumbull.

"My God, James, what a handsome wife you have caught, and how well you have done for yourself," murmured Mr. Trumbull, looking around the warm room, taking in Posey's red silk, the decanters on the sideboard, the hundred blazing beeswax candles, the platter of smoking hot lobster pasties fresh from the kitchen, "and how well everything looks, far more festive than when your esteemed father held court. Of course he was not a one for society. I am glad you are venturing forth." James fetched Mrs. Trumbull a glass of aged *jerez* and saw her seated near the fire. Posey, in her New York dress, drew up a chair beside her and flattered her by asking her opinion on the mushroom-colored velvet curtains—should they not be changed for some of wine color? Or ocean blue?

There was a rush at the door as the other guests arrived: Freegrace and Lenore advanced, smiling, toward the new bride, but Posey put on a strained social smile as she took in the flaxen-haired Lenore's simple Empire dress of silvery grey enhanced with a string of large pearls around her creamy neck.

"That is a beautiful dress," said Posey. "Is it from New York?"

"Oh no. Paris. I go every autumn for the new fashions."

Edward and Lydia came in with Lennart Vogel and Cyrus Hempstead, neither of whom had married, though it was rumored Cyrus kept a mistress of color. But they were not without dinner partners as Cyrus had brought a fresh-faced second cousin, Sarah Close, and Lennart the widow of his accountant, Martha Scoot. James glimpsed someone else behind Cyrus and with horror saw it was his father-in-law dressed in creased and spotted garments, his striped pants of the awful thousand-pleats style, so baggy they concealed a heavy abdomen and could accommodate a forked tail, the coat also striped and with a high collar. As he was wondering how to introduce them, Edward turned to the man and said, with familiarity, "Mr. Breeley, let me fetch you a glass of rum that we may continue our talk." They had apparently met and performed mutual introductions on the walkway.

The two sat together much of evening, drinking, eating and talking as though they were the closest friends. James suspected Mr. Breeley had not disclosed his New Brunswick affiliations. It must be done at once, however unpleasant the result might be, and he watched for his chance, filled with rage at the old impostor busily pulling a thick fleece over Edward's eyes. At the dinner table the two sat side by side, drawing diagrams on the damask cloth with fingers dipped in red wine. Edward sat on Posey's right and between earnest conversation with her father, he talked gaily with her, staring into her lustrous eyes like a lovesick youth, thought James with some distaste. He had never seen Edward so outgoing, so full of smiles and charm.

"Well, Edward," said James loudly, "I see you and Mr. Breeley have subjects of mutual interest."

"Indeed, we do," said Edward. "I must say I was surprised and delighted to find a gentleman so knowledgeable on the timber trade here this evening. It is especially interesting to me to have a New Brunswick lumberman's point of view." Smiles all around, especially on Posey's full red lips. James saw her hand slip below the table, saw Edward's startled face, which immediately blushed rose-red. Free-grace noticed as well and tapped his spoon against his front teeth.

"Beautiful autumn weather," bleated Edward to the old lecher by his side—who winked at the error and said it was indeed.

Later, when the ladies had gone upstairs to Posey's parlor for China tea and cream cakes, Edward drew James aside. "I think it would be a very good move if we asked Mr. Breeley to come on the Board. He could be of inestimable value to us as he is very practical and takes a hard line against timber thieves. I like him. And he is more or less connected with the family now. And Posey, an enchanting woman who also knows and understands the business. An extraordinary parent and child."

Ah, thought James, you may well guess how extraordinary! But Edward clutched his hand and said, "Thank you, James, for bringing us all together." And a vile picture floated before James.

In the weeks that followed the dinner Edward came more and

more to the house to take tea with Posey, to ask if she would not like to go and see the curious object dug up by some road builders, to wonder if she would give him advice on a present he wished to buy for Lydia. It seemed they were together every afternoon either in her parlor or out riding. Often Phineas Breeley was with them. More than that James did not care to know.

Over the next decade Posey remade herself into a high-toned dashing hostess of the sort that money creates, and the Duke galas became famous for exotic dishes, rare blooms, the finest silver and crystal and entertainments of string quartets or celebrated singers—and only once a man in a turban, his torso enwrapped by a boa constrictor. "What next?" roared James, who despised low culture, "an Italian with a hurdy-gurdy? A trained bear with gilded ears? You show your New Brunswick origin with these jinks." But temper was unusual as the husband and wife had reached a kind of equilibrium free from harangues and rages except for extreme provocation, such as turbaned men with boa constrictors.

In 1825 something close to a miracle—Posey thought it a miracle for she was fifty-one—came into their lives. Connubial peace deepened with the birth of Lavinia, their only child where no child had been expected. James was enthralled by his daughter. One look at her thick black hair and his own features, the features of the baby's grandfather Sedley, and he was assured that this was his little child, whom he was free to love.

Motherhood also awakened some deep feeling in Posey and she objected to the idea of a hired nurse, saying she would care for the infant herself. She threw over the endless dinner parties and lively social life that had been everything and became a goddess mother, even going to the kitchen to smear jam on bread for the little girl. Lavinia was bright and sweet-tempered, someone both parents could love without the intrusive need to love each other. The cordial atmosphere of the house brought the old cousins and their wives for frequent visits, but Phineas Breeley was forbidden to come near the child. "There are reasons," said Posey, and after several months of rejection he went back to New Brunswick in very ill humor.

When Lavinia was five Posey consented to an imported governess, Miss Chess, a stout Englishwoman with a clear bell-like voice and gold hair plaited and coiled in a shining little tower on the apex of her head. That same year James bought his little girl a docile pony, something he had ardently wished for in his own warped childhood.

VII

broken sticks

1825–1840

49

stupendous conflagration

In the years since the Sels had worked on the Gatineau, Maine had been freed from Massachusetts, although there were many people who expected all-out war with the Bay State; a meteor dashing its bloody sparks through the sky had foretold it. But nothing happened and Maine swelled with men, not only rough lumbermen on a three-day guzzle, but jobbers and land agents and Boston men eager to buy pieces of the dwindled pine forest, talking also of spruce and hack-matack, hemlock bark and hardwood. The remaining pineries were scarce and remote, but there were growing markets for other woods. The push was to clear the beetle-browed forest and a profit. Every-where the great mantle of forest had been torn into small pieces, hundreds of thousands of acres converted to stumps and stubs. The lumber cuts bared once-shaded stream banks, exposing the water to harsh sunlight. Silted pools and gravel bars discouraged trout. Towns were noisy with saloons, eateries, hotels and palaces of plea-sure, with the spring and summer rumble of logs. The sawmills ran day and night, the saws constantly under repair, the danger of fire omnipresent. Countless wagons hauled cut lumber to the wharf. Bangor bragged of being the world center of lumber shipping.

A crazy taste for invention and improvement blew through the state like a dust storm. Shingle mills used small circular saws and men swore the time was just around the corner when round saws would replace the old up-and-down and even gang saws. Already there was a forty-eight-inch circular saw in a mill on the Kenduskeag, and another in Waterville that was rumored to cut an amazing four thousand board feet an hour. Steam engines were taking over the world. In Boston the new gaslights burned as brightly as high noon. It was too much progress to swallow in a lump. Amboise and Jinot Sel—Josime was still in far Manitoulin—did not like it and after one season on the much-cut Penobscot among crews of griping farmer-loggers they went north to New Brunswick, to the monkish silence of the old-fashioned woods camps where they found other broad-cheeked Mi'kmaq living the hybrid lives of woodsmen. Their people could no longer live without whiteman goods and food; instead of hunting and making the things they needed they worked for pay.

Jinot could fall a little six-inch pine in less than a minute. Down they went, the small pines. The brothers, pressed between the white world and their own half-known and disappearing culture, settled back into the woodsman's life. Amboise was highly susceptible to rum. In the camp he was sober and thoughtful, but when they went south for a blowout he became a Drunken Indan, lying sodden in the muddy street, where boys thought it funny to thrust burning splinters into the toes of his boots.

One year Jinot, like a man visiting his old homestead, went back to Penobscot Bay. He walked down to the Duquet house, just to look. He felt nothing. It was run-down and dilapidated, the roofline sagged, two damaged wagons stood in the yard. But someone lived in it—he could see dogs under the porch. There were sheets hanging limp on a line. Was Elise still there? He walked past the house several times, unable to go to the door. But there were two shops now in the settlement and he went into one to buy tobacco.

"Them that live in that old log place down by the water? Doc Hallagher, years ago?"

The old shopkeeper, walnut-stained color, long thin fingers, looked up.

"They did live there. Move to Boston five, six year past. Bay folks too healthy for the doc to make a livin. Kids to feed."

"Lot a kids?"

"Course *she* was Indan, so what can—" He broke off, recognizing that the man he was talking with might take offense at what he almost had said. He had some not too distant Indian ancestors himself. He squinted at Jinot. "You related?"

"Yah. She's my sister. I didn't see her long time."

"You go down Boston way you might find her. Don't know who's in that house now. I think Elise sold it or give it to Francis Sel, rich stuck-up bastid. Ask him. He owns it, leases it out. He lives in that house next the sawmill. Sawmill owner. If he's feelin good he might tell you." He thought a moment, then said, "But if Elise is your sister, then Francis is your brother? You better go ask him yourself."

But Jinot did not care to see Francis-Outger. If young Édouard-Outger was at home it might have been a temptation, but the storekeeper said the nephew was working in the camps somewhere. Jinot wasn't going to Boston. He went back into the Miramichi woods. But not back to Mi'kma'ki. Better to be in the lumber camps.

It was a dry winter, cold enough, but no amount of snow compared to the old days. It made woods work easier except for getting the logs to the stream. They ran the water wagon at night to make a slick runway. While the choppers ate breakfast the driver ate his dinner, told of seeing lynx and once a black catamount, its eyes catching the yellow moonlight for a moment and then gone like pinched-out candles.

They rolled the logs into the scanty freshet. Logs grounded on gravel bars and it was hot, hard work prying them off. Sun glint off the river made them half blind and when they walked into the woods the shade throbbed with green blaze.

"Crimes, it's like hayin season. Hot!"

With half the drive stranded along the river until heavy rain or the next spring drive the farmers went back to their homesteads, complaining, "'Tis only June, but I never see it so unseasonable hot. And dry." Few seeds sprouted. Those that managed to send up shoots withered when no rain came. The wells quit. Women scraped water from inch-deep brooks for their gardens but as the long hot August blazed on, the plants remained stunted and starved. By September potato plants prostrate, maize stalks like faded paper foretold a hungry winter. Even impious men prayed, staring up at the monotone sky.

The only farmwork that could be done was more clearing. Work was the cure for every trouble. And it was thirsty work. The tough French and English farmers came from generations who had burned fallow fields and they saw no reason to change. Burning was part of farming—piles of slash from months of clearing, heaps of deadwood and dry rushes from drained swamps. The easiest way to clear woodland was to set it on fire and later grub out the black stumps. In that crackling dry autumn when dead weeds shattered into dust and brittle grasses crunched underfoot hundreds of settlers set their clearance fires as usual.

In the camps swampers were building roads for the winter cut. Most smoked pipes and now knocking the glowing dottle onto the ground started a swift little fire. The habit was to let fires burn. Fires were inevitable. It cheered settlers to know a little more of the forest was going down.

By early October the air was smoke-hazed violet, thick with heat, so humid that sweat-soaked shirts could not dry. Everyone moved slowly, cranky with rash and sweat sores. The choppers drank gallons of water from the shriveled brooks and their steaming hair hung lank. No evening breezes cooled and people lay in their smelly beds praying for the heat to break.

On the seventh of October the prayer began to be answered. Dry air from the west crossed an invisible frontal boundary, encountering the stagnant wet air. The winds began to mix with ferocious results, blasting oxygen like myriad bellows into the many small fires.

Amboise and Joe Martel, their old friend from the Penobscot, had hired on with a jobber on the Nepisiguit. Amboise seemed to land in Bartibog jail every time he left the camp. Miles south on the Miramichi, Jinot, another half Mi'kmaw named Joe Wax and Swanee, a bullnecked limber, were cutting for one-armed old Lew Green.

Jinot's crew was two miles upstream from the shanty, just starting the show on a marked-out plot. The terrain was level enough where they were cutting, but to the west and southwest steep hills and inaccessible ravines were packed with big timber, deadfalls and heavy underbrush. That morning Swanee had laid his pipe down on an old stump and it had smoldered on sullenly after he took his pipe up. There were little smoke spirals in every direction, always fire somewhere. They let the stump burn; whenever they wanted to light a new pipe they could put a dry splinter into the smolder and have an instant light, but a sudden rush of wind out of the southwest set the stump ablaze in seconds and they stood amazed, watching it rise into a towering column of fire. They heard the sound then—faraway thunder, then a roar like the rumble of logs coming off a rollway. It went on and on and grew louder.

"Hell *is* that?" said Swanee. The wind increased and it bent the stump's tower of flame to the ground. Immediately fire spread out like spilled water. They could see bulging black smoke to the southwest. Cinders and ash flew overhead. Joe Wax pointed south and Jinot saw a sight he could never forget. Behind the pine ridge billowed a mountain-scape of smoke and a brightness grew behind the ridge, silhouetting the jagged crest of pines. The roaring sound was tremendous, and with fear they now grasped that it was the wind and fire in a concert of combustion. With a harsh snarl like an exhalation from hell, the entire five-mile-long ridge burst into orange streamers that ran up the pines. Great slabs of flame broke free from the main

385

fire and sprang at the sky. A hail of burning twigs and coals came down on the men. Rivulets of fire snaked up trees they had planned to cut. A nearby pine exploded. The noise from the approaching holocaust and the hurricane wind deafened them. Trees burst open. Nothing could exist in that massive furnace.

"The river!" someone shouted. "Run!" The river lay half a mile beyond the shanty. It was a long journey and the fire raced with them, bellowing and booming, jumping its hot sparks over them and getting a head start each time. It was like being pursued by a ravening, demonic beast and Jinot was terrified. He saw Joe Wax's hair on fire, the man oblivious to the pain, running, running. Now stumbling and falling, they passed the shanty, its smoking roof. The cook, Victor Goochey, stood in the doorway holding a long fork.

"The river!" screamed Swanee and ran on. The cook stood rigid and unmoving, his eyes fixed on the lusty springing flames behind the men. Jinot saw that the man could not move, swerved and ran to him, wrenching the cook from the doorway and shouting, "Run! Run! Run! Run!"

They leapt into the pool where the cook had often fished. The water was warm but deep enough to let them submerge, rise, submerge again. The teamster was in the pool with his oxen, sharing it with several deer, a wildcat and a black bear cub. The cook arrived, still clutching his long fork, his greasy apron smoking.

"Shanty's afire," he yelled and jumped in.

Joe Wax put his hand to his head, which was badly charred and blistered. Soot-stained river water ran down his face and neck. He was sobbing with pain. "Got me, most got me."

The fire jumped over the heated river and the shallows quivered. The wind veered, fire greedily gobbled the landscape. Night fell and the pool was lighted by the lurid flames of the great fire. Near morning the wind lessened and in the first terrible day's light Jinot saw ash swirl and ruffle. The pool was choked with dead fish. The cook, still holding his long fork, crouched in the shallows near the bear cub and was saying something to the animal in a low voice. Joe Wax floated facedown, the top of his head a massive red blister like a satin cushion. Swanee was nowhere. Jinot tried to call, but his throat was swollen shut and no sound came out. He sucked in a little of the river water, noticing with detachment that his hands and arms were deeply wrinkled from long immersion, and marked with welts and burns. Although his legs seemed strangely stiff he waded toward Joe Wax and shook his shoulder. No good, he was dead. The bear cub suddenly climbed out of the pool and, bawling, began moving over the burned ground, ashes accumulating on his wet fur, running toward a horrible shambling shape coming down the slope, a half-blind sow bear with most of her fur burned off and showing great raw swatches of roasted skin. She passed the cub and lumbered on toward the river, where she fell in, half-stood and began to drink and drink and drink.

The teamster, Jinot and Victor Goochey came out of the river and began the long walk to Fredericton. They had only shuffled half a mile when Jinot understood his legs had been burned. His charred pants had mostly disappeared and in places the wool cloth baked into the flesh. In the river he had hardly felt the pain, but in the open air and with gritty ash blowing against the open wounds the pain rose up in great waves. His endurance had burned down to a clinker and he fell.

He was lying naked on a rush mat. Above, birch bark slanted upward to a cluster of pole ends and a blackened smoke hole. He thought about it a long time. The realization came very slowly as he drifted in and out of consciousness; for the first time in his life he was in a *wikuom*. He was alone. His eyes were sore but he could see. He could smell something sweet and faintly familiar that attached to memories of pond edges. His legs itched and hurt intolerably and his thinking wavered and blinked out. When he woke again the light was very soft. It was twilight. He could smell honey, even taste it. He tried to put his hand to his mouth, but his arm was weak. It fell back and lay inert. His legs itched and he was violently thirsty. He slept again, half-woke when something sweet and wonderful dripped into his sore mouth.

The sound of wind woke him. It was grey dawn light. Slowly he remembered pieces of the fire, the burning, his legs, Victor Goochey holding his fork, the swollen red dome of Joe Wax's head. He tried to move his legs but they were somehow stuck together. He smelled the honey. And the sweet swamp-edge fragrance.

A voice spoke, but he couldn't understand the words. He thought it was Mi'kmaq but he had forgotten too many words to be sure. An arm half-lifted him up; a cup pressed against his mouth. The liquid was fresh with the taste of pine resin and soothing and after he swallowed it a deep lassitude overcame him and he drifted into the dark again, but not so soon that he couldn't smell and almost feel that someone was dripping honey on his legs.

A long time later, days or weeks, he knew not which, he came out of his medicinal torpor and saw the broad face of a Mi'kmaw man of middle years, perhaps a few years older than himself. His hooded eyes had the protective coolness of a man deeply acquainted with suffering.

"Where am I? Who?" he whispered.

"*Inui'sit? Parlez Mi'kmaw?*" the man said.

"No, few words."

"*Français?*"

"*Un, deux, trois, quatre—c'est tout.*"

"So." The man said nothing for a long time, then, in a resigned and sad voice he continued in English. "This Indiantown. By Shubenacadie. Men bring you here tie like turkey. Leg burn. Name my Jim Sillyboy. Help burn people. I burn one time, *enfant* fall in fire. Know pain. Now burn people here come, Mi'kmaq, Iroquois, even whitemen. Some better. Some die. Burn is very bad, die. You little bad. I think walk one day."

Jinot had heard the name Shubenacadie before and knew it was in Nova Scotia, part of old Mi'kmaw territory. How had he come here from New Brunswick? Who brought him here? Was it that cook, Vic Goochey? What did he mean "walk one day"? Of course he would walk, he would dance on the logs again as soon as he had his strength. He had been hurt many times and always he had healed quickly. He wanted to know about the fire.

"Big fire . . ." was all he could say.

"Ver, ver grand *incendie*. New Brunswick place. All burn up." There was another long silence, then Jim Sillyboy sighed.

"Tomorrow maybe we start clean leg, both him. See you move leg. Now drink medicine. Sleep. Sleep good for burn."

Over the next days Jinot learned that Jim Sillyboy was a renowned burn healer, that people came to him from far distances, bringing children scalded with hot oil, drunks pulled from fireplaces, woodsmen trapped in burning shanties, farmers half-roasted in flaming barns, and now he tended five from the Miramichi fire. This *wikuom*, and three others like it, were special healing places. Jim Sillyboy's son Beeto helped him with the burned people.

"Long time burn pain. Long time."

His two other sons, he said, spent much time roaming in search of bee trees, for honey was essential for treating burns. "Use much honey." He took no pay for his services though he was poor.

"Kji-Niskam say one, spirit place. Black robe say brothers, help, do good." His unease in speaking English showed in his rough sentences.

Slowly Jinot learned that many of the people in Indiantown were poor and miserable, so poor that there was not enough food. The old hunting places and the game had been destroyed, the salmon rivers clogged with logs, bark and sawdust from mills. Now, said Sillyboy, his people talked of changing Mi'kmaw ways, of growing gardens like the whites so at least there would be food.

"Our chief go London, speak king. Ask how make *jardin*. We never know this. We try."

Were the Mi'kmaq now embracing even more doings of the white men? Jinot thought suddenly of Amboise, his embittered brother who liked saloons best in the white man's culture if he had to like anything. And Martel, what of their comrade Joe Martel? Did the fire reach Bartibog? When Jim Sillyboy came in the evening Jinot asked him for information.

"Can no one tell me about the fire? You say it burned up New Brunswick? Could not burn up all New Brunswick. *Très* big place, many *rivières*," he said, hauling out a few French words.

"I hear all burn. I look somebody. For tell you. Maybe find that man you bring."

The next day Sillyboy gently cleaned the honey from his legs. He rolled Jinot on his side, said the back of the right leg was the worst.

"Big scar come you, I think."

This meant nothing to Jinot. Scars were common, scars didn't kill you. Scars were the proofs of survival. But as the weeks and months went on he discovered their cruelty. The cicatrices made him a walking dead man, for the scarred back of his right leg contracted painfully and made it almost impossible for him to walk. When he tried, it was to hobble with tremendous pain and he could manage only a few steps. The scar froze his leg in an unnatural position.

All through the winter he lay in the *wikuom*. Early in his recovery, when Jim Sillyboy examined the itchy healing wounds, he explained in words and gestures that the scar was "too *enfant*" for his special massage that would make it a little softer and more flexible. Beeto would do this—it was his skill. He would use a special salve Jim Sillyboy compounded of the *mila-l'uiknek*, the seven kinds of healing herbs, roots, bark and needles. He made another good salve of beaver fat and the gum of *kjimuatkw*, the white spruce. And there were useful decoctions and teas which he would teach Jinot to make himself from the good ingredients. For the scar was now his master and it would demand a lifetime of care. The fire had been the salient point of his life. He had an absolute knowledge that nothing—nothing—would ever be as it had been.

• • •

One day, sitting outside the healing *wikuom* in a special chair, he had a visitor. A lanky whiteman came striding down the path. Jinot didn't know who he was but hated him for his good legs. The man stopped in front of him.

"Member me? Vic Goochey? Borned Gautier but they all call me Goochey. We was in the fire and the river? Brung ya here with Lew Green? Dragged a damn wagon with a old black horse. He got burned up, y'know. Most a the crew got it. But Lew heered about this Indan, Jim Sillybub, he's a burn healer. I had to get away from New Brunswick anyhow, place is all black and stinkin, so we brung you here. Lew Green had his right ear burned off and Sillybub fixed him up good. Course his ear is gone, just a little bit a skin left, but he's up and around. Figured he might do the same for you. Seein you got me to run down to the river. I was goin a stay in the shanty, figured the fire would never take it, but when you come runnin and half on fire yellin 'run! run!' I change my mind. So I'm alive and hardly got scorched. Remember that sow bear on fire? She died right there and the cub just kept on tryin to suck. It was a bad fire."

"God save me," said Jinot. "I want to know about that fire. How big, what they say. I got a brother, Amboise, workin up on the Big Bartibogue."

"Ver bad, that place. Fire come in, burned her up. They say three million acres a good timber burned. Towns, houses, jails, lumber camps, sawmills. Half a Fredericton got it."

"Amboise and Joe Martel," said Jinot. "Oh my brother, my friend. It can't be the fire killed them."

"Must of. More'n a hundred people got it."

Jinot could not speak for choking. Goochey waited. He sighed to express sorrow for Jinot's people, then he spoke softly. "We was lucky we made it, specially me. How your legs comin along?"

Jinot snuffled a little, then spoke in the hard and angry voice of someone who puts bad news behind him and gets on. "Slow. Sillyboy says it takes a long time. The scar draws up my leg, so I can't walk good. Can't do much." He slapped the side of his right leg to indicate that it was the most damaged limb.

"Well, I come to ask if you want to go back out west, work the Gatineau?"

Jinot, unable to stop thinking about Amboise, shook his head. "I just told you I can't do nothin now. And I got no clothes cept what Sillyboy got from the priest, can't do no work. Not a chance I can do woods work now."

"Hell, y'can cook, can't ya? That's the law, people get hurt in the woods, they cook."

"I can't cook nothin but fish. Can't stand up for long, just two, three minutes. I tell ya, the burn pulls my leg up hard. I don't know how I'll get along. I want to get away from here. Sillyboys, all of 'em, been good but this is a hard place, hungry, poor, no money, no job, no huntin, nothin. I don't belong here no more. If I ever did. If I could maybe get to my other brother on Manitoulin, let him know what happened, I might work out some things."

"Hell, Jinot, I'll take you out a here, Manitoulin if that's where you want a go. You save my life. I ain't forgettin that."

"I got to get healed up, first. Sillyboy says couple more months, this fall, maybe, I might be walkin. Some. I got to get so I can move around better. I'm just cripple this way."

"Say what, you get Sillabub fix you up some more and I'll come git you. Lessee, it is now just about June, drives are on, what say I come back October, see how ya go? Maybe you be better and we'll see what."

He left, and Jinot thought Goochey was a good man, though he'd never paid him any attention before the fire. He cried again for Amboise, his older brother, a drinker, a dreamer of past days he never knew, now lost to him forever. Amboise, who hated cutting the forest but did it because when they went into new woods he felt he was entering a past world. Amboise, who drank whiskey to get away from the present.

• • •

The son, Beeto Sillyboy, showed him there was something more that could be done besides the gentle massage and softening salves. He coaxed the stiff, scar-bound leg into positions that hurt, very gradually stretching the clenching scar, moving the leg carefully, carefully, not to tear the stiff tissue. So by September, almost a year after the fire, Jinot could limp slowly. The leg was dreadfully painful, a kind of pain like no other, tedious and biting, angry and gripping, and he could see how the scar held his leg under tension. He said one day to Jim Sillyboy, "If you was to cut right here—seems to me it would let the leg stretch more. That scar is like a rope tyin me up. Just a little cut where that thick place binds, eh?" But Jim Sillyboy did not want to make such a cut. So Jinot was no good for the woods, or other heavy work. He had no money, everything lost in the fire, and when Goochey came back he would have to say he could not go with him. He would have to stay in Indiantown until he died, poor, hungry and crippled. He saw that life in front of him. But he tried once more with Beeto Sillyboy, saying that one little cut might make the scar easier. Beeto thought he was right.

"We do it. I get good knife, old kind, black stone she ver sharp." And he came the next day with a wicked little slant of fresh-flaked obsidian and made the cut, put on healing salve and an eel skin binding to hold the leg in a more open position. In a week Jinot was hobbling around and Jim Sillyboy admitted the cut had been useful. "But some it don't work. You lucky."

"Oh, yes, I am lucky," said Jinot.

When Vic Goochey came in October, Jinot told him he wanted to go to Boston and find Elise, to see his nieces and nephews. He wanted next to find Josime on Manitoulin Island and count up more nieces and nephews. He had come out of the year of trial by fire wanting children.

Goochey looked at him and drew down his lips. "You want kids? Way most folks git 'em is git married and do that thing. Find you a woman-girl and git married. Hell, I been married twice and got some kids in Bangor, two more in Waterville. Why I keep workin—send them all the money I make. You know plenty women—I seen you jabberin with 'em four at a whack. Snatch one out."

Jinot knew a trip to Boston was stupid. He had no money, he would not know where to begin the search for Elise in a city squirming with people. And Goochey said he had maybe promised too much when he said he could get Jinot to Manitoulin. He was grateful for having his life saved, but he wanted some time to live it.

"Your talk about kiddos made me itch to see the ones I got, turn over a new leaf. But I'll keep my eyes open, see if I find any work you kin do. I know you kin learn cookin and git took on with a lumber camp. It's all beans and pork, anyway. Easy. Hell, I done it for years. Nobody never died from beans and pork."

Jinot did not want to cook. To hobble around the shanty cook stove while strong men cut and limbed in the fragrant forest— no. He borrowed a dollar from Vic Goochey, shook his hand and thanked him for his trouble, said he would send him back the dollar when he found work.

He went with the dollar to the first saloon he could find.

"Whiskey." Though he preferred rum, whiskey was the cheapest drink. For twenty cents he bought a bottle of the cheapest. This was his first binge since the fire. The pain faded and faded as he drank and he suddenly felt very well, even happy. He smiled to himself and poured more in his glass.

"Spare some a that?" said the man next to him, a heavyset fellow in wool pants with callused hands and a long grey face. He was a lumberman from his looks.

"Hold on," said Jinot. "Here she comes," and he poured liberally. He discovered the man was Resolve Smith, part Passamaquoddy, and had worked the Penobscot as a master driver, knew the river country well. He, too, had crippled legs, both broken in a rollway accident. "Whole damn pile knocked me flat, come down on my legs and I could see ever one a them logs comin before it hit me. Broke my legs into pieces like a stick and they set crooked. Awful when it rains."

Jinot told him about the fire on the Miramichi that swept New Brunswick and how Amboise and Martel had perished in the fire, and he himself had been crippled. The next hour was devoted to stories of woods fires, Amboise, Martel, injuries. They finished the bottle together and Jinot bought another. After a long time they fell silent, then Smith said, "You lookin for work?"

"*Lookin* for work but I can't do woods work no more."

"Me neither, but there's something I heerd. These fellers in Massachusetts or somewhere are startin up a ax factory, make the heads in numerous numbers. They lookin for men know axes. So I heerd. You been a axman a long time, you know axes."

"Like I know a tree," Jinot said. "All kind of ax. All my life since I was a kid I live with a ax in my hand."

"Let's go up there, see can we get us a job. Hell, we'll have good drinkin and good times." They agreed to meet the next noon in front of the saloon.

50

a twisted life

Mr. Albert Bone pushed his baby face forward, the whitest face Jinot had ever seen, ice-blue eyes set deep and mouth fixed in a knot. He resembled a wizened child but spoke in a voice that was asymmetrically large. He fitted two fingers of his right hand into his watch pocket, gazed at Jinot, who shifted his weight, uncomfortable in the confines of the office.

"What can you tell me of the ax? Have you made axes?" The questions rumbled.

"Never made one. Wore out a good many fallin pine on Penobscot and Gatineau. Twenty years a-choppin. Know a bad ax, used quite a few." He was exhausted by all this talk.

"So, Mr. Jinot Sel, would you say this was a good ax or a bad ax?" and Baby Face turned and grasped a fresh-faced ax that lay on his desk, gave it helve first to Jinot, who, after the shock of being addressed as Mister, hefted it, turned it every which way, sighted down the handle, peered closely, looking for the weld (which he did not see), ran his thumb carefully along the bit edge. He took an attenuated swing. "You got a tree or a log?" he said. "Better try it before I say nothin," for he knew this was a test.

They went out into the fresh morning, mist lifting from the river. Two crows cawed amiably from the invisible far side. Mr. Bone pointed at a chestnut tree, perhaps ten inches through, on the bank. Jinot limped over to it, took his stance, swung the ax; it bit and the chips flew. It was a young tree and did not deserve to be cut. It was

396

not as yielding as soft pine but he had it on the ground in minutes and thought that if he had had any half-submerged thought of chopping for a living again he could drown it; he was slow now and each stroke shot a pang through his scarred leg.

"Good ax," he said. "Quality."

"Yes. I and the men I have trained are dedicated to making the best axes. Quality is everything, and a man who works for me must swear to uphold the growing reputation of these axes. This is the Penobscot model. Let me ask you a question. You are an Indian, I suppose?" A tiny *ding* came from his vest pocket.

Ah, thought Jinot, he only hires whitemen. "I am Mi'kmaw. From Nova Scotia. They say there's a Frenchman way back there. Great-great-*grand-père* Sel." He half-turned to go. There was still time to find Resolve Smith in one of the saloons and tie one on. But he added, "I lived in Maine most a my life."

Bone talked, his words flowing into the mist. "I have a particular regard for Indians. I know English newcomers practiced great injustices on them and in my life I have tried to make up for those malfeasances. I have ever believed that if your people had resisted the first explorers you would still be living in the forest gathering nuts. I have, in my own way, sought to repair injustices when I can." As he talked he strolled back to his office, limiting his stride to accommodate Jinot's limp. "To that end I hire some Indians. I find Indians have an instinctive ability for mechanical improvements and invention. My foreman, Mr. Joseph Dogg, for example." The little mouth twitched.

Jinot stood speechless. He had never heard a whiteman make such talk. He didn't like it.

When they reached the door Mr. Bone drew a gold watch from his pocket and pressed a button; it sang sweetly, telling the nearest hour. The sun found a hole in the thinning mist and the watch glittered. "Mr. Jinot Sel, you will learn the processes of forging and tempering. I need good men in those skills. And grinding and filing—we will try you there. It would be to our mutual advantage if you learned every facet of ax manufacture. What do you say? Yes? All right. I will take you on and may you do good work, for I know I will lose money until you grasp the essentials. Go with that man there, my foreman, Mr. Dogg. He'll show you the ropes, as mariners say." He nodded at a hunchbacked *métis* who stood inside the hallway, grinning, not more than thirty years old.

Jinot nodded, but trembled inside. He was hired. It had been so easy.

"Iroquois-Seneca," said Joe Dogg to his unasked question. "Come on." And they rushed back out the door and through the yard, Dogg pointing out Mr. Bone's array of buildings. "He's a fair man," said Dogg, "no matter what you hear." They walked into the forge shop, a room of fire and hammering where men cut hot iron stock. "You think I'd ever git hired by somebody else? Nossir. Ha-ha, Mr. Bone says I am his Hephaestus, though I have not yet forged any thunderbolts."

"And do you have two comely maidens to help you?" asked Jinot, dredging up Beatrix's accounts of the Greek gods. Joe Dogg laughed with delight. "Hah, y'are an educated Injun, ain't you? And it don't do you no good at all, hey? Tell you, there's more than Jinot Sel can read books," he declared, indicating himself. Jinot watched a mope-faced man take up a metal bar and lay it on an anvil. While he held it in place another man scored it with hammer and cold chisel, and broke the bar. "Them patterns is the start, they make up into axes," said Dogg. "A man—if he's any good—makes eight axes a day. If he's no good he can make ten or twelve."

They walked on into the din. Jinot had never seen a trip-hammer before and here were six of the pounding things, tireless in their idiot strength. The stone floor trembled.

"Ever one a them bastids got its own waterwheel for power," bellowed Dogg.

At the grinding shop they stepped into an oppressive roar punctuated by the soft coughing of men who inhaled steel dust all day long.

A row of stone wheels six to eight feet in diameter stood along one wall, their rotation making a hoarse wet whisper; men grasping the new axes bent over the speeding stones.

"Now," said Dogg in a normal voice when they stepped outside, "over there is workers' lodgin. Y'go there and they'll give y'own room. Anything y'want to know, y'ask me."

Jinot began to learn the skills and subtle judgments of ax makers. In the forge house his old river-drive reactions to the quixotries of moving water and rolling logs translated into recognition of gradations of the shapes and colors of hot metals, quickly, delicately turning the ax under the descending hammer blows, all motion in the deafening heat like running dream-like through a chamber of the inferno; it was the Miramichi fire compressed into a bed of coals, the hurricane wind blowing only at the command of the bellows. Those dark wraiths in the room were not men of nerve and skill but demons, beckoning him to their damned society.

Dogg, his tutor, talked about himself. "How I come to leave that Iroquois country in upstate York, why, smart whitemen they get our property. Iroquois don't think that way. Sell it but we so foolish think it still ours. Whiteman give whiskey, give little presents—and get our huntin land. That land be theirs. They say, 'Indan, give up them ways you people, Indan, get civilize.' So I come here to get civilize, get job. That blacksmith, Mr. Bone, pretty nice to me—he see me down by river, I try catch frog—hungry—he fix me up, learn me to be smith. You maybe never think Mr. Bone can find end of his thing but he make a good ax. Good smith. He make a good ax."

This was difficult to believe, Mr. Bone looked so small and childlike. Later, covertly, Jinot began to study the small frame beneath the black suit, the small hands. He had been deceived by the baby face. The body was small but steely, the little hands callused and hard.

• • •

He was drawn to the trip-hammers. The hammerman had to be something of an artist, shifting the position of the glowing ax clamped in his tongs for the perfect shape, and he had to be fast. Most wracking was the tempering process, which demanded experience and a good eye. Hugh Boss, in his fifties, tall and lopsided from spine-twisting scoliosis, heated a new-shaped ax, then dropped it into a vat of water.

"Makes it so damn brittle the bit will break first time you use it," said Boss. "So—you got to draw the temper, eh?" He winked at Jinot and again the ax went to the forge, where it was reheated; he worked a file over it. "Watch the colors edge down to the bit." Jinot saw the color parade from pale yellow to orange, to dark orange to brown. It went again into the water.

"It'll go all the way to blue, but brown is where we want a ax. There. She's fixed, now."

The months slid into years before Mr. Bone was satisfied that the tools Jinot made could withstand thousands of heavy strikes.

It was the richest and strangest part of his life, for he felt he was no longer Jinot Sel, but someone else, a hybrid creature in a contrived space. Mr. Bone took an interest in him. There were many good Indian men in the factory but he had fastened on Jinot, who, with his fresh, smiling face, looked younger than he was.

One day, when Mr. Bone had to make a trip to Boston, he told Jinot to come with him.

Alone in the coach neither spoke for an hour until Mr. Bone said earnestly, "I want you to understand all the intricacies of the ax business. I have undertaken to educate Indans such as yourself in the mechanic and manufacturing arts. But there is more to a business than that. The sooner your people leave the forests and adopt useful trades, the sooner the woodlands will become civilized and productive. That is not to say that it will be goose pie all the way—no. I wish you to know the business end of ax making. You must learn how to consort with men of quality." He took out his repeater and pressed the knob; the watch chimed.

"There are problems and troubles that keep me awake at night—competitors who make an inferior product painted up to look like a Bone ax, workmen who complain they are not paid enough, some who agitate, some who are spies for other ax makers. Now it is time you learn how to conduct yourself and speak with businessmen." Jinot wanted to say that he did not want to speak with businessmen—he preferred the company of the forge, where, under the blanket of noise, men communicated with hand gestures as did workers in saw-mills. He preferred—he didn't know what he preferred except to be more distant from Mr. Bone's solicitous interest.

But Mr. Bone's vaunted enthusiasm for native people did not extend to the forests and shorelines they had inhabited. For Mr. Bone, only when the trees were gone, when houses crowded together and the soil was cultivated to grow European crops was it a real place.

On the return journey he said abruptly, as though he had been long arranging the words in his mind, "I came from Scotland to Philadelphia with my father. My mother died when I was but an infant. And two days after we arrived in this country Father also perished, a victim of some shipboard pestilence. So I was orphaned and thrown on my own resources." He said nothing more.

Months later they were again alone in a coach that stank of stale urine on the way to Bangor, and Mr. Bone, who seemed unable to speak of his past unless in jolting motion, continued his history. "Relative to the events of my youth, after I found myself alone in a strange city, at first I begged bread and then coins from passersby, then I fell in with some boys who, like myself, were homeless. We contrived a society of cooperative thievery, taking chickens, garden plunder. For amuse-ment we loitered near the stage stop, the farrier and blacksmith shops, places of interest to all boys. One day I happened to be alone watching one of the smiths and the man looked at me and said, 'Pump the bellows, boy, my helper run off.' I pumped that bellows. At day's end he told me I was employed. I filled the tempering baths, pumped the bellows, ran errands and learned the best uses of the hardies, swages, bicks, holdfasts and mandrels, the twenty kinds of hammers, the fifty kinds of tongs, the punches and chisels. When Mr. Judah Bitter, the smith, saw I was interested he undertook to tutor me in the arcane lore of the forge and anvil. Even blacksmithing has its heroes and Mr. Bitter was such a one. He inculcated in me a love for the black metal. Well do I remember the day I made my first adze."

Embedded in this strew of words Jinot scented a clue; Mr. Bone favored him because he glimpsed something that made him equate Jinot's situation with that of the poor orphan emigrant. Jinot could understand that for Joe Dogg, but not for himself. Or did Mr. Bone see him as a lump of raw iron that needed heating and pounding to be made into a tool? His employer drew his gold watch from its pocket and smiled at it. "My family treasure."

The coach stopped and three more travelers boarded, but Mr. Bone was wrought up and he continued, in a hissing whisper he imagined reached only Jinot's ear. His breath reeked of strong peppermint from the candy he kept in his pocket.

"Mr. Bitter favored me with an invitation to join him as partner in his smithy. There would be a new sign—'Bitter and Bone'—it sounds well, does it not?" He noticed then that the entire population of the coach was staring at him agog. And shut up.

But when they were at the rough inn, Mr. Bone returned to his subject. "As I said, Mr. Bitter offered me a partnership. I accepted. But before the arrangements were complete, Mr. Bitter, on his way home from the smithy, was run down by a profligate jehu swilled to the gills. The smithy went by inheritance law to an idiot nephew who could not tell an anvil from an anthill, and once more I was bereft and alone and without resources.

"I looked about me to discover what I might do. I saw the vast forests, saw the great need of thousands of people to build houses and barns, and so I decided on the ax. I recognized the opportunity and vowed my axes would be the best."

Emboldened by the toddy Jinot had to ask. "Why favor me, Mr. Bone? I do wonder." There was a long silence, then Mr. Bone stirred, sighed and spoke.

"When I saw the great injustices that my race visited on the native population I took a private vow to encourage young Indian men to take up a trade. It is the Christian way. Had I not become a smith I might have been drawn to the missionary life among the heathen. It is my hope that you may become the first Indian businessman, a part of the society in which you now live. Do you visit your people often? If not, you should, for there may be excellent business opportunities to be discovered. I think I have shown you how to see those opportunities." Jinot shuddered inwardly.

Hugh Boss, the hammerman, became a friend, and Jinot began to spend Saturday evenings at the family household playing checkers. The Boss family lived in a large cabin a mile from the factory. Mrs. Boss, a pretty woman with wheat-colored hair and wide hips, was usually swollen with pregnancy. She hovered constantly over the cast-iron cooking range and was a notable cook. But what Jinot liked were the children, for the Boss family was large, from Minnie, at sixteen the oldest, to Baby, barely a year old, and eight more in between.

Minnie, petite, dark-haired and dark-eyed, had inherited Hugh Boss's scoliosis and once a month had to visit Dr. Mallard for cruel stretching exercises. In the doctor's "stretching room" she removed all her clothing above the waist, for the doctor had to observe her spine; stepped under an enormous tripod, where he fitted her into a complicated system of straps and pads that was his own invention. She was mightily stretched, almost hoisted into the air while Dr. Mallard adjusted the tension to force her spine into a straighter position. She told Jinot that at first she had been ashamed to stand half naked before the doctor but he was indifferent to anything but the curve of her spine and she no longer went crimson with embarrassment. After each treatment Minnie was carried home exhausted by the ordeal. Jinot, who understood the pain of stretching recalcitrant muscles and tissues, sometimes read aloud to her while she lay on the kitchen daybed with the coverlet drawn up under her small chin. She was not a pretty girl, but kind-natured despite the pain of her infirmity, and she responded to Jinot's sympathy with growing love which did not escape Hugh Boss's eye. For a long time nothing was said and he got used to the idea of Minnie and Jinot together, despite the years between them.

When Dr. Mallard said Minnie was much improved and he would allow two months between stretching sessions, the family declared a celebration. Hugh Boss gave her money for dress fabric. That Sunday she appeared in the new dress and Jinot's eyes went wide. The dress was the marvelous blue of Beatrix's old dressing gown and it was silk.

Hugh Boss took Jinot out to the cow barn, where he kept his jugs of hard cider.

"See here, Jinot, you know Minnie likes you a terrible lot."

"I like her, too." He fidgeted.

"Well, there's nothing to it then—we'll get the hitchin post set up." A month later they were married in the front room of the Boss house. Minnie wore her blue silk dress and through the brief ceremony they could all hear the oaths and struggles of the men heaving up logs for the bridal couple's cabin in the back corner of Hugh Boss's pasture. Minnie thought of the flower game she played as a girl pulling petals off a daisy to discover who she would marry: rich man, poor man, beggar man, thief, doctor, lawyer, Indian chief. Well, he wasn't a chief.

With the birth of his and Minnie's first children—twin boys Amboise and Aaron, who resembled Kuntaw more than Hugh Boss—it seemed to Jinot that now he was like other men and could nearly understand once-mysterious truths. It could not last.

• • •

Minnie was a nervous mother, daily inspecting the posture of the boys to see if there were signs of scoliosis. She took Amboise and Aaron to Dr. Mallard as soon as they began walking, but he saw no sign of the deformity. "Of course, my dear, it can always appear later in life, often not visible even to the expert eye"—he blinked modestly—"until well under way. We shall keep a close watch on the children. Bring them in for consultation every six months, and we shall hope to catch it early if in fact it appears and correct any malformation. As for yourself, I had hopes that childbearing would help augment the stretching sessions you so bravely endured, but it seems it is not so. It has come to endurance rather than cure." It was so; Minnie bent more and more to the left, her posture at table a decided lean. The left shoulder of her old jacket hanging on the wooden hook near the door hung low. She worried, worried about everything—that her father would catch a hand under the relentless hammer, that Jinot would disappear (for he often enough went away with Mr. Bone on business), that disease or pestilence would take them all. Many nights she woke shuddering from dreams of her children being torn apart by hydrophobic dogs, stretching out imploring little hands to her and she, straining every muscle but bound by her twisted back, unable to reach them but forced to hear their piteous cries.

Hugh Boss made play objects for the children, one winter, a glass-smooth birch plank with strips of polished steel embedded in the underside for snow sliding, a kind of toboggan. There was a stand of young spruce at the bottom of their sloping land, a favorite resort for the neighborhood children in summer as the narrow passages between the trees were a twisted maze, greenish and shadowy tunnels ideal for I Spy and the noisy intricacies of Sheep and Wolf. Jinot sometimes joined them in this game, they the sheep scampering through the tunnels, Jinot the ferocious howling wolf. In winter the snowy slope was the neighborhood sliding place. The winter Amboise and Aaron were six, a freakish rain storm gave Sam Withers, a prankish neighbor boy, the idea of sprinkling even more water on the already icy slide that it might freeze. A sharp temperature plunge converted the slope to a trackless icy pitch. Sam Withers, claiming responsibility for the ice, took the first ride. The plank swerved and curveted at speed, Sam screeching with excitement at his brilliant success. "Me! Me next!" Three boys squeezed together on the plank for the second ride, Sam in the back, then Aaron and in the front, Amboise. The greater weight gave the object more speed and a less wavering track. The toboggan could not be steered and remorselessly curved toward the spruce bosque, the metal strips on the underside of the ride setting up a whine, and every tiny ridge in the ice producing a clatter that gave proof of great speed. There was no avoiding the spiky trees and the conveyance plunged into the naked lower branches like a meteorite.

Minnie heard Aaron's shriek and Sam Withers's bawling roar for the whipping he knew he would get. She ran out in her apron, one shoe lost in the snow. On the icy slope she saw the boys entangled in the spruce, saw bloody-faced Aaron on hands and knees crawling toward her, saw Sam Withers stumble deeper into the trees, saw Amboise inert. She slipped and fell and had to creep to reach him.

Amboise lay on his right side, pierced through the neck by a dry stick-spear one of the children had left in the trees during the days of summer games; the pulsing fountain of blood was already down to a trickle, and she gave a cry that shook the limbs of the forest.

Jinot became grave and serious after the death of young Amboise. Away with Mr. Bone, he had not found out until late that evening, when their coach returned. By then Minnie and Aaron had fallen into a fatalistic calm. The three-year old twins, Lewie and Lancey, slept, unknowing, uncaring. Jinot went outside and walked the night with spasmodic spells of choking cries, returning to the house a little before dawn.

When he came in, cold and exhausted, Minnie, driven by habit, was making tea. They sat together at the blue-painted kitchen table, their hands locked as though all that could not be said could be understood through gripping fingers. The firelight shone from the grate and colored red the tears on their cheeks. The house was somber for days until Lewie and Lancey began to laugh and run again.

The loss of Amboise reawakened Jinot's hunger for relatives and he decided to find Elise and Josime. He began by constructing a careful and painful letter to Francis-Outger, for at least he knew he lived on Penobscot Bay and he was sure the half brother would know where Elise and Dr. Hallagher were. He sent off his letter with trepidation and doubted he would ever receive a reply. It was almost comical how quickly a letter came.

Dear Jinot.

I was inexpressibly delighted to have your missive. How glad I am that mother's lessons were not forgot. We have long wondered what adventures you have undergone, and your description of the terrible Miramichi fire, your injuries and the loss of our brother Amboise and your little son was painful to read. But it seems you have fallen on good times from your benefactor, Mr. Albert Bone. You have been fortunate too in choosing a wife and in your wealth of children.

I can grant your wish to know the whereabouts of Elise. She and Dr. Hallagher have a domicile in Boston. The address is below. Their youngest son, Humphrey, has an unusual medical condition where the muscles of the body somehow convert to bone. Learned doctors come to the house to examine and prescribe, but nothing really makes the ailment better. The poor child likely has not long to live before he is solid bone. I am sure Elise would skreech with joy if you were to pay a call on her. Boston is not so far distant from you. (Nor is Penobscot, and you are ever welcome here.)

As for Josime, your account of parting with him in Montreal is the most recent news. I have felt rather pained that he has never seen fit to

write me as we are full blood brothers. I suffer bouts of pleurisy and debil-
itating headaches but suppose one must expect such ailments as one ages.

I will close now as I wish to get this off in the next post. I hope we
may soon meet again and exchange news, at the very least, that we may
continue to correspond.

Your affectionate half brother, Francis-Outger Sel
Penobscot Bay, Maine

Now Elise was on Jinot's mind constantly. A fortnight later, on a
brilliant April day so enriched with untimely summer warmth that the
horses took pleasure in being alive, tossed their heads and looked at the
azure sky, he took the stage to Boston and began his search on foot.
He had not written, thinking a surprise visit would be better, a bit of
drama for Elise. He took half a day asking directions before he found
the Hallaghers' plain brick two-story house. There was a clapboard
addition on the south side and a sign reading: DR. HALLAGHER, M.D.

Elise herself opened the red front door. She had become a middle-
aged woman with a knot of black-grey hair. But she had the same
impish sparkle in her eyes, the same curling smile and pointed teeth
as all the Sels.

She knew him at once. "Jinot. You are my brother Jinot." They
embraced in a mighty hug and Elise began to cry. "Oh, how long I
have waited to hear something of you. Francis-Outger wrote and
told me he had a letter from you asking news of us. Come with me,
dear brother, come with me for a moment. And then we shall go in."
She drew him to a side yard, removed six fragrant loaves of wheaten
bread from an old clay oven, wrapped them in a piece of muslin and
carried them to the kitchen.

"Now, Jinot, you must tell me everything." He followed her down
a dim hall, the plaster walls hung with likenesses of stags drinking
from mountain pools, into a stuffy parlor, where his own reflection
in a tall mottled mirror frightened him. A pale, listless boy of ten
or twelve lay dozing on a daybed with a closed book resting on his
breastbone.

"This is my boy Humphrey," said Elise, bending over the child and kissing his hair. The boy opened his eyes and looked at Jinot.

"This is your uncle Jinot," said Elise.

"Ahhhh," said the boy and closed his eyes.

"Come into the kitchen, Jinot, I will make us a pot of tea," said Elise. "Or coffee, if you like. It is almost time for the doctor to come in for his pick-me-up. He will be very pleased to see you."

But when Dr. Hallagher came in he was less than delighted, gave a brusque handshake then sat at the table blowing on his tea.

"So, you've found us out," he said in the tone of a captured criminal.

"I thought that as so many years have passed, for the sake of our children it would be good to be in touch with each other again." He told them of the great Miramichi fire, of Amboise's death in that fire, without mentioning the town jail or drunkenness. He told them of Minnie, of his children, of little Amboise's accident. It was only when he described the kindness of Mr. Bone and his favors over the years that Dr. Hallagher relaxed. Jinot guessed that he had been expecting to be asked for a loan and that he was relieved to hear Jinot was independent enough to support a wife and four—no, three—children. When he returned to his surgery the visit became jollier with Elise and Jinot trading old stories and "do you remembers," plans for a family gathering on the Fourth of July, and bits of gossip about distant Mi'kmaw relatives, for there were countless Sels in Nova Scotia, all descended from René Sel, the little-known Frenchman who had started their history. Elise remembered a few of them, but Jinot knew none.

"We even heard something of our grandfather Kuntaw, can you believe that? He went back to the old place, all English settlers now except a part they call Frenchtown, and another part they call the Diggins. That is where the Mi'kmaw people live, the ones that are left. Not many, now, not even a hundred they say. So he married a Mi'kmaw woman and had more children. Yes, that old man, can you believe it!"

They laughed, the talk shifted to their children. Elise's oldest boy,

Skerry (a Hallagher name), was clever, a great reader and had a powerful inquiring mind. "He wants to go to that Dartmouth school," she said, "as he is, y'know, at least part Mi'kmaw, and they are said to take an interest in Indian scholars, so it could come to pass. I don't know if it *will,* but Doctor wants it. Don't it seem strange, from how we lived at the post when we was—were—little? We've had big changes in our lives, Jinot. And maybe Josime? If Amboise had lived . . ."

Jinot thought that if Amboise had lived he would have been run over by a freight wagon as he lay stuporous in the roadway. But he did not say it.

The brief hours of family affection began to fade and by the time the stage left, the sky had clouded over. The coach traveled through a storm that came in repetitive squalls with a few tremendous claps of thunder, minutes of hard rain followed by a breathless silence until the next wave caught them. The cleansed air chilled and he thought it would clear, but the interludes of rain turned to sleet and then to snow, a strange end to the summery day. And Jinot, recollecting the visit and the wasted boy lying on the daybed, thought of his own little Amboise, who could never be twelve, and the barely healed old wrenching began afresh.

51

dense thickets

Minnie had vowed there would be no more children. They were too fragile, too precious. She could not bear to have her heart torn so savagely again. How true, she said, was the often heard, and now proven, old adage that life was a vale of tears. Of all Jinot's children Amboise had been especially beloved, a kind of resurrection of Amboise, his burned brother. Jinot knew, guiltily, that he had granted Aaron less affection. Now he vowed to make up for this, and from that moment he and Minnie favored Aaron with love and gifts.

Jinot, indifferent to Minnie's long speech telling him she would never again sleep with him—somehow he felt she blamed him for Amboise's death—put a worn bison robe he had used on the Gatineau on the back porch and slept there summer and winter. The children could come to him any time they wished but he was not the old affectionate silly father. So remote was his stare, so remote was he, except with Aaron, that he did not see Minnie's slow decline, how she grew smaller inside the fine-striped dress, did not hear her constant wet cough. In the two years since Amboise had died she became gaunt as her spine twisted. She suffered and pulled at her hair to shift the pain. The cooking deteriorated, the children grew out of their ragged and dirty clothes. Jinot made a great kettle of pease porridge once a week and the children were to help themselves until he discovered Lewie laughing as he threw handfuls of—something or other,

411

assuredly filthy—into the pot. Then he hired a neighbor widow, Mrs. Joyful Woodlawn, to feed the boys and look after Minnie.

"Of course I'd be glad to look after poor Minnie and the boys. I'll make soups to build Minnie up and beef and taters for the lads. And will bring over some water from our well, as it is known to be the best water in the town. There is no better thirst quencher than good water. Mr. Woodlawn was always proud of our well water."

That winter ended like a snapped cable with days of sudden heat and flooding brooks, thrusting skunk cabbage growing three inches a day. The crows began to take their seasonal places, the males stretching their wings to show the long primaries, fanning their tail feathers, their dark eyes aglitter, the lady crows watching coolly from nearby perches, measuring the presentation of every point with critical eyes. Hugh Boss, stumping along on his canes, came over on a Saturday morning and spent several hours sitting beside his daughter's bed. When Jinot came in from the factory Minnie was sleeping. Hugh Boss got up from his chair and jerked Jinot into the parlor.

"Jinot, Minnie is sick, very sick. Have you had the doctor in?"

"I didn't— No, I did not know it was so bad. I thought she was just poorly but—I did get Mrs. Woodlawn to care for her betimes."

"Betimes! To me she seems not long for this world. *I* will send the doctor." And he stalked out, no friend to Jinot.

The doctor, not Dr. Mallard but a mealy-faced old gent with a silk cravat spotted with pork drippings, said it was consumption. Advanced consumption. Nothing to be done though they could try raw eggs and brandy alternating with hot beef broth. He offered to bleed the woman but Jinot would not have it. He wished he knew of a Mi'kmaw healer such as they said his great-great-*grand-mère* had been.

• • •

He thought he had scraped dry the dish of deep sorrow, but time brought a helping of worse. Mrs. Woodlawn bustled into the Sel kitchen one morning with her famous jug of well water, swigging a large glass of it herself, bringing some to Minnie. When Jinot came in at noon he found the widow had gone a ghastly blue and was braced against the table, her hands clenching the edge. She looked at him with a terrible expression and then doubled over in dual spasms of explosive diarrhea and violent vomiting. There was no doubt of the cause—the cholera had been rampant in New York and was now encroaching on smaller towns.

"Save us all!" said Jinot, running into Minnie's room. But the galloping disease had got there first and Minnie was sinking, fingers and toes clenched with spasm. The twins, Lewie and Lancey, still clung to life, but died while their father stood gaping down at them. It could happen so quickly.

"Aaron. Aaron!" he called, but the boy was not in the house. He found him in the woodshed with a book of tales. He said he had been there since early morning, had breakfasted on a piece of ham fat left over from supper. No, he had not taken Mrs. Woodlawn's water. He felt well, he said, and he looked well.

They walked together to Hugh Boss's house. "Hugh, it's the cholera," said Jinot. "It took them. Just me and Aaron's left." The big man cursed them both, broke down, buried his face in his hands. He was not well. Mrs. Boss, pregnant again, was abed with an illness that resembled cholera and the youngest children were ill. Mrs. Woodlawn had brought them some of her delicious water before she went to Minnie. Hugh Boss lived, but Mrs. Boss and the three youngest children all died on the same day.

After the funerals weeks passed, dragging their crippled hours like chains. Hugh Boss and Jinot hated each other for months until they met in the cemetery to put up the seven fresh-cut stones and were reconciled in grief. The memorials bore only the names and dates and the word *cholera*.

They agreed that Jinot and Aaron would live with Hugh Boss, sleeping in the haymow and helping with the surviving children until Mrs. Boss's sister could come from Danbury, Connecticut. Jinot swore he would keep Aaron with him, keep him safe until he became a man. Yet there was something new to worry about as Aaron several times said that he wanted to go to Nova Scotia and know his Mi'kmaw relatives. He wanted to be an Indian. By the time young birds were crowding the crows' nests the cholera plague had eased and Jinot and Aaron returned to their silent house.

For Jinot the palliative was work and he spent much time with Mr. Bone, now shrunken and stooped, but still making great plans and filled with energy unseemly for an old man. He spoke of starting a handsaw manufacturing factory. He talked of setting up a rolling mill and making his own steel. Anything could excite his fertile imagination.

Though axes remained Mr. Bone's true love, he wanted new lands to conquer. He sat up nights roving over the world through the pages of his swollen atlas (for it had been dropped in the bath and dried page by page over the stove) and reading foreign newspapers.

"I think," said Mr. Bone, after a year of consideration, "that the best course is to set up an ax manufactory abroad. Trees grow all over the world and everywhere men need houses and buildings, they need axes. My life has ever been dedicated to the removal of the forest for the good of men. I have studied countries where there is a burgeoning population, plenty of trees and a need for axes. The list is not a long one, but I would value your opinion before I take any steps."

Jinot laid his hand on the atlas and waited. Mr. Bone's peculiar list named Norway, Russia, Java, New Zealand and Brazil. Jinot said, "Why not go to the western forests of this country? They say there are forests that cannot be measured from Ohio westward to the end of the land." Mr. Bone ignored this.

"It will be simpler for a swift establishment of the factory if the inhabitants speak English; that removes four of the countries from the list and leaves us with New Zealand."

"They speak English in New Zealand?"

"Those in government and control do so. The country is allied to England, where they *do* speak English. The New Zealand natives speak some gibberish of their own, but many have learned English."

"But do they have trees there?" asked Jinot, who fancied New Zealand was mostly desert and salt flats. He had only a vague idea of the country's location—perhaps near India.

Mr. Bone leaned back in his chair. He smiled the smile of a man who knows a great secret.

"Yes. They have trees. Especially do they have certain 'kauri' trees, which experts describe as the most perfect trees on the earth, truly enormous trees that rise high with all the branches clustered conveniently at the top. The wood of these trees is without blemish, light, odorless, of a delightful golden color, easy to carve and work, strong and long-wearing. I have learned that a nascent trade in poor-quality axes is in progress through the efforts of a bumptious Australian entrepreneur who was once a convict now working in New Zealand. Before I make my decision I have decided to go to New Zealand and see these forests for myself. They are said by men who know timber to be one of the wonders of the world. You must accompany me. I have arranged passage. We leave in a fortnight, Mr. Joseph Dogg will manage the factory while we are away. He is thoroughly competent to do so."

Jinot opened his mouth to say something, then consulted the atlas. It was far, far—a long skinny wasp-waisted country at the bottom of the world.

"I— Mr. Bone, I have sworn to keep Aaron close to me until he attains manhood. You know my sad history, sir. He is all I have left."

"Quite simple. Tell him to pack his trunk. He shall come with us. A husky lad is useful when traveling."

• • •

But Aaron only shook his head and went into one of his long, silent spells. For days he did not respond to Jinot's badgering and pleading. He smiled distantly as if his thoughts were too lofty to share.

"Father, I do not wish to go on the ocean. It is my desire to go to Nova Scotia and find our family, whatever Sel relatives may be there. I wish to know that life."

"Then you would do better to go west to Manitoulin Island and seek out your uncle Josime. He returned to the old ways."

"But not Mi'kmaq!"

"No, because Mi'kmaw old ways no longer exist. And because he loved that Odaawa girl I have told you about many times. If you wish to know the old forest life of our people you must find Josime. But you are too young to make that journey alone. Come with us to this New Zealand and on our return I will go with you to Manitoulin Island and together we will find Josime." But secretly he thought the shadow of whitemen ways might have lengthened far across the land to touch even Manitoulin Island and the Odaawa.

Aaron listened to all of this; it did seem best to find Josime, a person with a name and a place. But he would not go over the ocean. He wrote a short letter and pinned it to Jinot's black coat.

Dear Father. I do not go to Newzeelum. I go Nova Scohsia then I go find uncle Josime. When I return you hear my good stories.

He believed the old Mi'kmaw ways—whatever they were—could not be utterly lost, and started walking north, hopeful.

Jinot wrote to Elise that he was going with Mr. Bone across the ocean. Anything might happen to him, for he was crippled and not young, and he wanted her to know where he was. Aaron, he wrote, had refused to come with him. "I will write to you," he promised. Two days before he left he had a long answer from Elise, who was unhappy with his news of New Zealand. "It seems everyone is going far away Aaron is repeated here with Skerry i fear we must allow these boys their desires even know how cruel the world may treat them." She described the upsetting scene between Skerry and Dr. Hallagher.

Skerry come home from that dartmouth college very sad What is wrong with you Skerry are you not pleased to be at home again among those who love you you are unnatural quiet said the doctor dear Jinot I fetched a venison pasty from the pantry Skerry's favorite food I thought sad because he was morning Humphrey we all morn him you know but doctor told us many times that the end was come we try to make his hour on earth with us as happy Skerry said i have known that for years as you then what is the matter is it the school Doctor spoke very loud but Skerry would not say nothing doctor said it is the school something has happen is that not so Skerry made a sore face and said they want us who came there because we have Indian blood they want us to be missionaries All are to be missionaries, return to our tribe and preach gospel I was never in a tribe I have no body to preach to I want study law but they said the onli study for Indans was thology and preachin so it is useless for me to go to that school Instead Skerry said papa I wish you let me read law with judge foster I wish you to ask him I can do this Jinot to Doctor this was unwelcome request as he once treat judge fosters daughter lauraRose for consumption and she die he explain to the judge that disease was far gone nothing save her but the judge turned his grieve into hate for Doctor So he could not ask that And Skerry left home he said he would go to canada and find his tribe he was very angry and he left

Ps forgive I forget writing like Beatrix showed us

52

kauri

Jinot felt as a fallen pine must feel, hurled into another world. London was not the larger Boston he had expected but a sweating, boiling turmoil of thieves, cloudy-eyed horses with bad legs, miry streets, each with its equine corpse, the stink of excrement and coal smoke and burned cabbage and extraordinary glimpses of silk and exotic feather where crossing sweepers with brooms cleared a way for pedestrians. Mr. Bone had leased quarters for a month in a shabby-genteel neighborhood a mile from the great wharves and bustle of shipping. The ax maker's rooms were pleasant with a sitting room and a bedroom featuring a carved mahogany bedstead enclosed by only slightly moldy bed curtains. Jinot's adjoining room was small and dark, but Mr. Bone graciously invited him to share the sitting room.

"Come, Mr. Jinot Sel," said Mr. Bone on the first morning ashore. "Let us walk about in this greatest city in the world. I will show you the wonders of the place. Let us go down to the wharves."

They left the avenue of decaying Georgian residences for a street of ironmongers, red piles of metal and dumps of coal. Jinot flinched at the sight of a family of ragged adults and their swarm of filthy, emaciated children—"likely refugees forced off rural lands by enclosure," Mr. Bone remarked. Hundreds of workers rushed about, navvies and dockworkers, cobble setters laying stones, scavengers, sooty sweeps emptying their buckets into the river. They heard cheers and shouts nearby.

"What is that hullie-balloo?" said Mr. Bone. "Let us see." Rounding the corner they came on a pair of fighting men circled by forty or more shouting onlookers. Jinot remarked that the English seemed to enjoy fisticuffs as much as drunken barkskins.

"We are a fighting race," said Mr. Bone with relish as they walked on. Newspaper hawkers thrust their wares in the men's faces, and among a dozen bills pasted on the side of a warehouse one shouted in swollen letters: EMIGRATION TO NEW ZEALAND.

"Ah, Mr. Edward Wakefield, the gentleman behind the New Zealand Company, is an immensely clever Englishman," said Mr. Bone. "He has very sound ideas on colonization. He has a sense of feeling for the solid English workingman and small businessman as well as the gentry. He understands that random settlement, as happened in the American colonies, is contrary to clear reason and scientific method. His plan of systematic colonization is admirable, for then society is stratified from the beginning with correct classes. Had England done this with the American colonies and Canada, those countries would not be ruled by the pigheaded creatures of today." He looked at his watch and said, "Enough sightseeing. Let us hurry. I have a meeting."

Mr. Bone's chief adviser was a missionary of obscure Protestant denomination, the Reverend Mr. Edward Torrents Rainburrow, possessed of a thick jaw blue with crowding whiskers, a mouth as wide as his face and inside it a set of pale green teeth. His basso completed the picture of an overbearing bully, but he had tamed his voice to a quiet pitch, and he smiled.

There were a dozen travelers at the meeting. A tall-headed fellow speculated how long the voyage from London to New Zealand might take. "Depending on weather and the favor of God it might be as swift as five months—or considerably more," said a jowly missionary who repeatedly filled his wineglass. "First port of call will be Port Jackson, the convict colony which will also be the departure point for New Zealand. The convict transports go on to that island and pick up a load of masts before returning to England. The trees are of high quality."

One of Mr. Bone's correspondents had sent him a letter saying the Maori inhabitants, embroiled in constant wars with one another, were the most ferocious savages on the planet, bloodthirsty cannibals. Their faces were scarified in hideous whorls and dots. As for clothing, they dressed in vegetable matter.

Another missionary—there were seven in the group—Mr. Boxall, with a young girlish face, spoke directly to Mr. Bone. "I have heard differently—that the Maori are an intelligent and even spiritual people held under the sway of the Prince of Darkness. They are hungry for messages of peace." Mr. Rainburrow resented this incursion into his own friendship with Mr. Bone, and, after their dinner of pork cheek and withered potatoes prepared by one of the missionary wives, he put his lips close to the factory man's ear. "Dear Mr. Bone, *I* will let you know about passage from Australia to New Zealand, accommodation I am trying to secure even as we speak." From the other side of the table Jinot begged his attention: "Sir, Mr. Bone, I wish to return to Boston. I have no desire to meet those wild people." But Mr. Bone was enthusiastic about visiting the cannibals. "Thank you, Reverend Rainburrow," he said, then turned to Jinot and said in a low, severe voice, "I sincerely doubt that they are truly eaters of human flesh. It is one of those sailors' tales. And you, of all people, are being unjust. I can well believe they are only protecting their land from men who would seize it unfairly. With kind treatment, in time they will come to see how pleasant their lives would become with some of the whiteman's inventions."

Frugal missionaries often took passage on convict transport, and though Jinot objected he found himself swept aboard the *Doublehail* with Mr. Bone. Seasickness doubled most of the passengers, but not Mr. Rainburrow, who continued to enjoy his morning bacon. Jinot had never seen such a busy man, for the missionary rushed about from first light to lanterns-out. Mr. Boxall, his friend again, followed in his wake with his little yellow notebook.

Belowdecks the dangerous felons crouched in chains and cramping cubbies, the convicts England was pleased to remove from her finer population.

Jinot was wearied by pitching decks, the missionaries' zeal, the ocean's monotonous view of a horizon as flat as a sawed plank. Everywhere the spread of ocean showed it was not the Atlantic, which had given Jinot the odor of life forever. Even deep in the Maine lumber camps certain weatherly days would bring the salt taste of it to him a hundred miles distant. Stern, cold, inimical, resentful of men, rock-girt and often flashing with cruel storms, for him, for all Mi'kmaq, it was the only true ocean, and like a salmon he longed to go back to it.

When Australia finally came in sight as a great recumbent sausage at the edge of the world, he wondered how he could bear to sail still farther on to New Zealand. Only the thought of the interminable return voyage to Boston and a lack of passage money—for Mr. Bone had paid him no wages since they left Boston—kept him silent. He was fated to continue with the ax maker.

Port Jackson smelled different and unfamiliar, a somewhat dry roasty odor like parched coffee and burning twigs.

Through the strange trees flew birds of shocking colors, iridescent and violently noisy, birds with headdresses and wings like burning angels, flying apparitions from dreams. But in the month the travelers lingered in the colony awaiting passage, whenever they walked out they saw creatures that surpassed any nightmare, springing fur-covered beasts with rudder-like tails, lizards swelling out their throats in gruesome puffs, assorted spiders said to be fatally poisonous.

In Port Jackson the missionary arranged with a Maori who had come to sell New Zealand flax, that he should give lessons in his language to himself and Mr. Bone. Soon Mr. Bone was flinging such words as *tapu, waka, wahine, iti, ihu* about, and imagining himself a fluent speaker of this Polynesian language.

Jinot was disheartened to see that the same detestable *Doublehail* that had carried them from England would now take them to New Zealand. There were several Maoris on board and Mr. Bone spoke to them in what he imagined was their language. The energetic Mr. Rainburrow had better luck and began proselytizing whenever he caught one of the Maoris gazing out to sea. Jinot was surprised to see that they listened with interest and asked questions. As for Jinot, the natives immediately classed him as an inferior servant to Mr. Bone and ignored him.

They sailed up a river past gullied stumpland and the voyage ended in a busy settlement. The dominant building was near the wharf, a trader's huge *whare hoka*. Next to this warehouse stood a chandler's shop ornamented with an old anchor for a sign. Two shacks leaned off to one side. The larger bore a sign that said NEW ZEALAND COMPANY. The houses of the *pakeha* traders and government men ranged along streets terracing the hillside. Behind a screen of distant trees was the Maori village—*pa*—fenced round with poles; farther back loomed a fantastic tangle of ferns, trees, creepers and exotic fragrances, a fresh world.

"A translator will soon join you, Mr. Bone. You must excuse me as I am going to see the site chosen for our mission," said Mr. Rainburrow.

Mr. Bone and Jinot waited for the translator, a Scotsman, John Grapple, whom they could see descending the steep path. Grapple walked gingerly and Jinot guessed he was wary of falling on the precipitous way. He reached them at the same time a Maori canoe drew up on the beach and a muscular native man jumped out and walked toward them. They came together under a motte of trees.

"Well, then," said Grapple, showing his crimson face and fiery nose. "This chief speaks no English, so I will translate for you." The moment Mr. Bone heard John Grapple's Scots burr he loved him and the two talked for a quarter hour working out a remote kinship before they turned to the Maori who stood waiting, his heavy arms folded across his chest. Mr. Bone showed off some of his Maori words and amazingly, this man, his brown face a map of curled and dotted tattoos and clad in a sinuous flaxen cloak that tickled his ankles, understood some of the compromised phrases. At first the two men seemed pleased with each other. The chief wondered if Mr. Bone had come to buy flax. No? Sealskins? No? Spars? No? What then?

Mr. Bone, casting his limited vocabulary aside, looked at John Grapple to translate as he tried to describe ax making and his plan for a factory. With a stick he drew figures on the ground that represented an ax on a forge and a looming trip-hammer. To further illustrate Mr. Bone removed a Penobscot model ax he carried in his valise and handed it to the chief.

The chief's eyes widened with pleasure as he examined the quality and beauty of the ax. Too late Mr. Bone realized that the man believed it was a gift rather than a demonstration of goods.

"Well, no matter, I have others," he muttered to himself.

"You got others?" asked the chief in fluent if rather sudden English.

"Let me congratulate you on your rapid command of our language. As to the axes, yes, I have others but they are only to show. I hope to manufacture them here as soon as we establish a source of good iron ore in New Zealand. I am the owner of an ax factory in the United States. I hope to construct one here." A crowd had gathered around them, stretching their necks to see the ax.

"What is wrong with these people?" said Mr. Bone to John Grapple sotto voce. "One would think they had never seen an ax before."

"I think that may be the case," said Grapple.

The chief smiled delightedly.

"Oh my friend," he said to Mr. Bone. "That is good. Good, good.

Come with me. We wish to make a *powhiri* and *hakari* feast for you and your *whekere,*" he said, glancing at Jinot.

"I think, sir," whispered Jinot, "that he believes *I* am the factory. He sees a factory as a kind of servant. Or slave." For he reckoned that the Maori had slaves.

"Oh, what bosh! You do not understand the situation, Mr. Jinot Sel. He is in complete accord with me. He understands everything." Mr. Bone, as was his usual habit, withdrew his repeating watch from his pocket. Before he had completed the motion the crowd sucked in its breath as one and stepped back, horrified expressions on their faces. They murmured *"atua"* at each other. Mr. Bone looked to John Grapple for an explanation.

"Hum hum," said Grapple, with a twisted expression, putting aside his Scots speech in favor of plain English. "They fancy your watch is a demon, they say they can hear its heart beating." Mr. Bone smiled to hear such simple suppositions and added to the tension by pressing the button that activated the chiming mechanism. A soft *ding-ding* came from the watch. A man in the crowd shouted something.

"What did he say?" asked Mr. Bone.

"He said the demon wishes to escape from his prison," said Grapple. "I suggest you put your watch away, sir, as the Maori have strong feelings about such instruments. Some years ago a whaler stopped here to rewater and gather spars. The clumsy captain managed to drop his watch in the harbor and a number of fatal illnesses and calamities fell on the people in the following weeks. They ascribed those troubles to the evil spirit that was lurking beneath their harbor."

But Mr. Bone decided to display his whiteman power. Frowning, he shook his watch and then spoke to it harshly as though to a disobedient child before putting it back in his pocket, where once again it seemed to call impetuously to its master to be released. The crowd breathed and drew back a little further.

When Mr. Bone asked Grapple sotto voce where the chief had learned his English, Grapple said it was likely he had served as a sailor on an American whaler or sealer and was of a secretive nature that led him to hide his knowledge in order to gain advantages. Mr. Bone smiled at the chief. He took note of the tattoo pattern that he might recognize him again.

"So, sir," he said, "do you mostly fish, or make war?"

"Sometime fish, sometime war."

"Ha. And what do you suppose I do with my life?"

"You travel about?"

Mr. Bone spoke slowly and loudly as one did with foreigners, and also because the birds in the branches above them overwhelmed their voices. "No, I rarely travel about. I live in America and, as I said, I make the best axes. Like that one." He pointed to the Penobscot ax the chief still held in his hand. Mr. Bone extended his hand and waggled the fingers with a beckoning motion to show he wanted the ax returned to him. The Maori looked at Mr. Bone, his eye darkened and he fled with the ax.

"Here!" cried Mr. Bone. "You ruffian! Bring that back at once." But the man had disappeared into the ferns.

"You are impetuous, Mr. Bone," said John Grapple. "Metal tools are highly prized here." He smiled and his voice wheedled, the Scots accent thickened. "He believes ye gae at tae him as a gift. Why do ye not come tae ma hoose and we'll hae a wee dram and gab eh? Let us move awa frae thes bickerin blaitherskites." Indeed, the birds were fiery in their declamations.

Jinot and Mr. Bone ate and slept in a hut in one of the established missionaries' enclaves. Gourd plants grew up the sides, extending their tendrils to the roof peak, and jeweled geckos hunting insects rustled through them. "When Mr. Rainburrow's mission buildings are in place we will shift houses, or when I find a factory site and put up our first dwellings. But for the time being we must accept this small guesthouse under the trees as our temporary home," said Mr. Bone.

"Do I hear my name mentioned?" called the missionary's voice as he came into the twilight hut smiling and humming a hymn. "I am well pleased with the site for our mission. It lies on a moderate bluff overlooking the harbor and has a brisk stream of excellent water running through it. We have already begun the construction. Before I left fifty or more Maoris were cutting great poles and lashing them together with vines, a curious but effective way of construction."

At the end of the second week the missionary had become a partner with the trader Orion Palmer, a Maine man who had come to New Zealand years before in a sealer and had no intention of returning to the pine tree lands, where trees burst with cold in the winter nights.

Jinot rose before dawn to the sound of intertwining birdcalls, haunting organ-like notes, slow and deliberate as if the bird was deeply considering the composition. Low notes and harmonics seemed to express both sadness and resignation. A distant bird answered from far in the forest and the somber voices laced together. He twisted his head this way and that trying to find the feathered creature that made such a poignant song. And he saw it, a large blue-grey bird opening and closing its wings, fanning its tail. It showed a black mask and under its chin hung two blue wattles. The bird arched its neck, opened its strong curved beak and called lingeringly: . . . *ing* . . . *ong* . . . *ang ang* . . . *cleet!* . . . *ing.*

Outside Jinot climbed up to the ridge through a forest so unlike the pine forests of Maine, New Brunswick and Ontario, or any other he had ever seen, he never could have imagined it. He sensed antiquity in the place but could not know that he was walking through the oldest living forest on earth, part of a world never scoured by encroaching glaciers, never overrun with grazing mammals. With the industrial ugliness of London fresh in his mind, New Zealand's beauty moved him powerfully. It was a fresh world pulsing with life and color, the trees dripping vines, epiphytes, scarlet flowers and dizzying perfumes spilling from cascades of tiny orchids, supplejack knitting the forest together, red-fluffed rata—a place hidden from the coarser world by its remoteness. He had the feeling he should not be here; perhaps it was one of the *tapu* places the missionaries had joked about. The ground was cut with wooded ravines. At the bottom of each ran a clear stream. Threads of water twisted through tree roots. Birds crowded the tree branches like fruits and the crowns twitched with their movements. He would come to know many of them and the trees—totara, beech, kahikatea, rimu, matai and miro, manuka and kanuka, the great kauri and nikau palms. When he came on a secluded stand of kauri, their great grey trunks like monster elephant legs, he touched bark, looked up into the bunched limbs at the tops of the sheer and monstrous stems. He imagined he felt the tree flinch and drew back his hand.

In his desire to see every part of this new forest he left the trail and descended into a ravine. It was like a somewhat nightmarish dream when he ignorantly touched a glistening leaf and received a burning jolt of pain. Looking closely at the leaves of this small tree, the stinging nettle tree, he could see silvery hairs. Alas, not a true paradise. And there were mosquitoes. A wave of anxiety suddenly washed over him and he felt he had to get out of the ravine quickly. His feet tangled in creepers and rough vines, in the maze of supplejack. An extraordinary jumble of plants, grasses, vines, trees, shrubs were crowded together in huge knots. His clothes, decayed by long exposure to sun and salt, began to tear as he climbed up again, slipping on the muddy slope, hoping to find the trail again, his pants in ribbons from cutty grass.

Above him, at the head of the ravine, lay an old kumara field which in recent years had reverted to bracken. Eight or ten women and girls, their *ko* sticks laid aside, were resting from their labor of digging aruhe—fern root. The roots, many of them ten and twelve inches long, fat and heavy, were piled in great heaps. "What is that sound?" asked a small girl, cocking her head, alert to everything out of the ordinary. They all listened; yes, breaking branches and scrabbling slide of soil, a kind of thrashing in the ravine below. They half-rose in trepidation, ready to flee. The noise came closer and then a frightful creature came up over the rim and ran straight at them.

Jinot, stained with mud, panting and itchy, clawed up out of the ravine. His bloodied clothing hung in shreds, his hair was spiky with sweat. To his delight he saw the women surrounded by their piles of fern roots. He could not resist. All his life girls had welcomed his company. But this time as he ran toward them smiling and stretching out his arms, waiting to be welcomed, they fled as if from an indescribable terror, some crying in fear. He shouted at them, "Come back, I mean no harm!" They were already out of sight. And the old, smiling, merry Jinot evaporated, in his place an aging man who had known sorrow and difficulty and now, painful rejection.

Mr. Bone had spread a mat on the ground and was sitting cross-legged on it drinking tea and eating baked yam and fruits. Jinot returned his greeting with a peevish grunt.

"How I wish we had possessed the foresight to bring sacks of coffee. Tea is all very well, but it is not coffee." Jinot said nothing, but he knew Mr. Bone's Scots "cousin," John Grapple, had a store of coffee. He had smelled it on the path out of the forest that ran behind the *pakeha* houses.

Several days later while Jinot was mending his torn clothing with a borrowed needle, and Mr. Bone scratching in his Idea book, the chief with the many-colored flax cape reappeared.

"Oh, Mr. Captain Sir," he said in a wheedling tone, "you have many ax?"

"I have fifty in a crate," said Mr. Bone, putting down his pen and waving at the hut where the crate stood, "for *demonstration only*. As I explained, it is my hope to establish an ax factory here. It is my hope to teach the Maori how to make axes of quality. I feel there is a great need here."

"You want see good deck for *whekere*? You walk me." He gestured to an oblique trail leading into the bush.

"Is it a place with a stream of running water?"

"Oh yes. Too many water."

Mr. Bone smiled, turned to Jinot and said, "You see, it was very easy to interest this man in my idea. I'll warrant he knows of a good location for the factory."

"Mr. Bone, it is not possible. The trader says there is no iron ore in the entire country and laughs at you. You cannot make axes without metal."

"I think I know better than you, Mr. Jinot Sel, what I can and cannot do. It is not that there is no ore, it is only that it has not yet been found." The cloaked Maori stood outside the hut stepping backward along on the trail and beckoning to Mr. Bone.

"I would not go with him," said Jinot in a low voice. "He may be planning mischief."

"Bosh! I'll be perfectly safe. He is friendly. For a savage, Mr. Jinot Sel, you are timid. Nor do you understand these people any more than you understand establishing yourself in a new place," he went on, for he had heard how the women had fled from the awful stranger lurching out of the ravine. It was the talk of the missionary enclave. "This is why whitemen get ahead. They know how to command. He will be my first recruit. In a year he will be running the trip-hammer. I take no satisfaction in saying that after all these years you prove a sad disappointment to me." Mr. Bone left the hut and followed his eager guide up the trail.

After a mile and a little more the trail became faint and disappeared, but the chief pushed on, following a way marked with ponga ferns turned silver side up (invisible to Mr. Bone). Two more Maori fell silently in behind the ax entrepreneur, who was so absorbed in looking at the massive tree trunks that he did not notice. Huge, huge trees, giants of the earth, the pale grey columns as wide as European houses. Who could believe such immensity? Was it possible an ax could take such monstrous trees down? Could they be—?

Much moved, he called to the chief, "Tell me, are these kauri trees?"

"Kauri," said the man, turning around and flashing his eyes at someone behind Mr. Bone. But so stunned was Mr. Bone by the impossible trees that he was not aware of the descending club that burst his brain. His last shattered thought was that a great kauri had fallen on him.

"Quick!" said the chief to one of his comrades, pulling out a fresh-edged obsidian knife. "Do you run back and get the axes. Then return here and help me carry the meat." Before he severed the limbs he gingerly withdrew the Quare watch from Mr. Bone's pocket. The demon's heart was pounding, pounding!

"We know how to deal with you," said the chief, placing the evil thing on a large leaf and covering it with another protective magic leaf while he got on with the cutting up. He spoke true words for that night he cast the watch into the fire and with satisfaction all the sated assembly saw the demon fling his wiry arms out as he cried aloud, then perished.

Two days later when Mr. Bone had not returned, Jinot felt mildly uneasy but the headstrong old man had had his way as always and would likely make some kind of a success of his venture. No doubt he was looking for iron ore. Jinot, his captive, now wanted to find a ship going to Boston and work his way home, although the mariner's trade was unfamiliar to him. He would quit Mr. Bone, for he knew a South Sea ax factory was an improbable dream; there was no metal ore in New Zealand from all he had heard—miners and explorers aplenty, but no mines. Even if there were grand mines he was finished with ax making. He wanted only to go back to whatever was left of the places he knew. The wild New Zealand forest had moved him in incomprehensible ways, yet it repulsed him with its violent tangle of vegetable exuberance, its unfamiliarity and ancient aloofness. To escape he would have to get to Port Jackson first unless an American whaler put in to a Hokianga port. Mr. Bone could not hold him. He would leave with or without the old man. He was planning his escape when Mr. Rainburrow marched into the hut, breathing heavily, his eyes slitted.

"Where is Mr. Bone?" His voice was penetratingly loud and Jinot saw people standing outside the hut, listening and watching.

"I do not know. He set off several days ago with a native man wearing a grass cloak. Against my advice."

"Your advice! Who are you, a servant, to give advice to Mr. Bone! Which native man did he go with?"

"I do not know, sir, only that it was a native man, much tattooed, and wearing a cloak."

"I beg to inform you, *sir*"—there was a sneer in his voice—"that there is much apprehension as to his whereabouts. It is thought he has come to harm and the one under suspicion is not some mysterious native in a grass cloak, but you, his servant, who have prowled the ravines of the locale with an eye to disposing of your master's body."

"Untrue!" said Jinot. "You have only to ask Mr. Grapple. He knows the native man and first introduced Mr. Bone to him."

"What a pity. John Grapple is in Port Jackson for a month on business. You must be confined to this hut until he returns. I will arrange for food to be brought to you, but you, Sel, are our prisoner, pending verification of your statements. We shall mount guards against any attempted escape."

Back in his mission Mr. Rainburrow put fresh ink in the inkwell, selected a steel nib and composed a letter.

Reverend Rainburrow To Mr. Joseph Dogg, Bone Ax Company, Massachusetts

Sir.

I am prompted to get in touch with you re circumstances relating to your employer, Mr. Albert Bone whom I had the pleasure of traveling with these past eight months. We esteemed each other greatly, indeed, I may say we became close friends. Within the last few days a worrisome circumstance has arisen which I feel I must impart to you. Mr. Bone was accompanied by his servant, Jinot Sel a dark-skinned man much given to exploration of the forest and who has frightened some of the natives by suddenly appearing from behind a bush and screeching at them. It is with concern that I write that his forays into the forest may have a sinister motive. Mr. Bone disappeared entirely from our enclave three days ago and has not been seen since. Within this hour I have quizzed Mr. Sel on his knowledge of Mr. Bone's whereabouts. He insists that his employer went away with a native wearing a grass cloak. As many do wear grass cloaks there is no way to discern the truth of this statement except, as Sel claims, by a witness, that is the respected interpreter in these parts, Mr. John Grapple, who is unfortunately away on business for some weeks and therefore cannot vouch for Sel's statements. I have taken the liberty of confining Sel to his quarters until Mr. Grapple returns and we can get at the truth of this matter. I have also taken Mr. Bone's money box into care as I suspect it is the motive for Mr. Bone's disappearance and for Sel's forays into the trees. His claim that Mr. Bone owed him money lends weight to my suspicions.

Should Mr. Bone have come to harm I can assure you that I can act for him as his friend <u>and spiritual adviser</u> in every way. I have considerable influence in the country and can arrange to have his possessions returned to Boston and see to it that the servant Sel receives British justice—for New Zealand has recently been annexed by the Mother Country. I can oversee any legal matters that may arise. To my knowledge he has made no will in the colony but perhaps you know more than I of such a document if it exists at all.

I will inform you at once if we learn anything in the matter.

I am, &c.,

The Rev. Edward Torrents Rainburrow, Church Missionary, New Zealand.

Confined to the hut Jinot's days passed slowly. One of the missionary wives brought him roasted yams and fish. She never spoke to him and if he asked a question she scuttled away. He thought about this often, that here in New Zealand every woman he had seen ran from him, shunned him. The four powerful Maori guards lounged around outside waiting for his escape, two of them scratching at pieces of dark green stone, the other two talking and laughing with each other. He stood in the doorway on some days, sat on the veranda on others, listening for the kokako, but always watching the harbor. From the doorway he could see a rock outcrop in the near distance crowned with half a dozen old pohutukawa trees setting the world on fire with their crimson blossoms. He would rather have seen a ship. If an American ship put in he would risk everything to get to it. But only English ships arrived to take on kauri spars. Every day he looked out past the pohutukawa trees to scan the sea for vessels. One morning he saw that the oldest tree at the end was down. As he stared he caught the flash of an ax and made out two whitemen attacking the trees. As the trees fell each sent up a puff of red blossoms like an exclamation. By late afternoon they were all down and he looked no more in that direction.

It was more than a month before Grapple climbed up the hill to his house again, followed almost immediately by several of the missionaries. The reverend men started back down the greasy steep slope a quarter of an hour later. But it was not until dusk that Mr. Rainburrow and his crony, Boxall, came to the guesthouse, both looking sour.

"It is my duty to say that John Grapple has returned from Port Jackson. He does corroborate your tale of the native in the grass cloak, but he says he did not know the man. He is a chief from other parts who somehow heard of Mr. Bone and wanted to know him. He may have been one of the rare bad Maori. There is no way to tell as his name and place are unknown here."

Boxall said in a rush, "So there is no reason to hold you. You may leave."

"That is very well," said Jinot Sel. "I would like to return to my country. I ask you to pay me my wages from Mr. Bone's money box. He has not paid me since we left Boston more than a year ago."

Mr. Rainburrow wriggled his shoulders as if his coat was out of order. He cast his eyes around the hut as if looking for the money box. "Sir, you must know I—we—cannot do such a thing. The money in Mr. Bone's strongbox belongs to him, and if he does not return it will go to his heirs and family—I doubt you are among that number. In any case I shall take it for safekeeping lest you be tempted to help yourself."

"But I have no money for my passage."

"I suggest that you take up the ax again. Mr. Bone said you were once a good woodsman. You can earn your way back to where you came from. And to show there are no hard feelings I will tell you that after discussion with Mr. Palmer I understand there is suitable work for you felling trees. Mr. Palmer owns several shore stations with allied timber camps in the kauri bush. You shall leave tomorrow."

Yes, it seemed he must do that and save his wages until he could buy passage; he was old now but his scarred leg had improved over the years and he felt he could swing an ax. What else could he do? And he would be away from the swarm of missionaries and their ukases.

53

in the bush

At the Bunder shore station Jinot was disturbed to see some Maoris selling tattooed enemy heads to eager whiteman sailors as curiosities. He thought suddenly of Kuntaw and imagined him laughing at the gruesome sight—Kuntaw always laughed at horrors as though they were nothing much. Jinot walked away for fear he might see Mr. Bone's old grey head among the wares. He went into the trader's *whare hoka* to see the show of goods—brilliant bolts of cotton, wooden flutes, tambourines, buttons and spools of thread in twelve magical colors. This was the place to find precious needles, choose from an array of hats—and yes, axes of poor quality. A Maori would come in timidly for the first time and stand in the center of the *whare hoka,* then turn slowly, slowly to see everything, dazzled and made to desire many strange objects of unknown use. Imprisoned in the hut Jinot had overheard the missionaries say that Sydney merchants were filling all the good harbors of the Northland with shore stations—in the Hokianga, on the Coromandel, anywhere there was deep water and handy timber. "Opening the country right up," they said with approval.

Miles apart, the stations were not only logging camps but trading posts dealing in flax, spars and lumber. Separate enterprises—chandlers, warehouses, sawmills and small shipyards—drew Europeans to them. They skimmed off the cream of the shore forest and moved the camps on to the next good show leaving behind smoldering stumps and shoulder-deep waste. The intense assault fell first on kahikatea, then on the kauri, cutting and cutting. In some places men could walk for days on the downed timber that carpeted the ground. Then the great mass was set alight, the fastest way to clear the forest, brush, vines, birds, insects, fruit, bats, epiphytes, twigs, ferns and forest litter. The newcomers did not care to understand the strange new country beyond taking whatever turned a profit. They knew only what they knew. The forest was there for them.

Trader Palmer had two logging camps, Little Yam and Big Yam, named for nearby Maori plantations of sweet potatoes. Many of his warehouses and camps stood on land that had once belonged to members of his wife's clan. Smart and wily, a fluent and persuasive talker, he moved people to his advantage as a cook moves gobbets of meat around in the hot pan.

Temporary or not, Jinot had never seen a camp so flimsy and ragtail-bob as the Little Yam. The quarters that passed for a bunkhouse were nothing more than ridgepole tents with fly openings, thatched with great hairy masses of nikau leaves from the cabbage palm.

Almost every small mixed-race child that Jinot saw in New Zealand looked like Waddy Baker, the bush-boss, swart, pale-eyed, jugeared and quick-handed whether catching something or striking someone with his *wadi*. The bush gang at the Little Yam was small, not more than twenty choppers—ex-sailors, ex-convicts, Irish, British settlers, Maori. Half of them had never worked in the woods before.

The evening meal was a "Captain Cooker" stew from descendants of the pigs Cook had released, and a loaf of bread for each man. Jinot hoped to find a partner who knew woods work; if luck was with him a partner who knew the ways of big kauri cutting, for he reckoned there was something to learn about taking down these giants beyond the swinging of an ax. The young rickers they would cut first would be easy, but when he thought about it he did not see how they could do more than nibble around the circumference of the grey-bark giants. They were just too massive. He had heard that the Maori got them down by cutting into them and then making and tending a fire in the cut until the tree burned through. It was a poor method as the burning hardened the wood so that no sawmill could get through such a log. As for getting the logs to the sawmills on the shore, he hoped there was a better way than what he had seen while standing in the doorway of the missionary hut in detention.

One morning, smoking his pipe and regarding an offshore pod of spouting whales, he heard a distant rhythmic chant, a call and response chant such as a ship crew's capstan shanty stamp-and-go used when weighing anchor. At least eighty Maori men emerged from the forest hauling on a hawser bound around an immense kauri spar. A muscular headman stood on the log, which was decorated with flowers and feathers, and it was he who called out the urging chant, and the pullers who drew deep breaths, opened their mouths and roared a response as they heaved. The great spar moved forward a few feet on the roller roadway. Again and again the pullers answered the caller and the giant mast moved down to the ship.

Jinot worked one day with a half Maori named Arana Palmer who spoke English with what sounded like his own familiar Maine accent. He was young, not more than twenty, and strong, said, "I worked in the kauri since I was a boy." When Jinot told him he was a Penobscot man from Maine, Arana laughed. "Orion Palmer, the trader, is my father. He come here from Maine years ago after seals. Them times not many *pakeha*. So I say I am part Maine. He talks once a while about his old life there. You come talk with him some-time. He likes talkin Maine, goes down to the ships, says, 'Anybody from Maine here?' Sometimes there is and he'll keep 'em up all night guzzlin rum and talk, talk, talk, get jeezalum drunk."

Jinot had not heard anyone say *jeezalum* in years and was glad to hear it now, in Arana's inherited accent. Arana showed Jinot how to stuff a large sack with bracken fern for a mattress. Better, said his new partner, was to get a wool fleece—nothing more comfortable.

They agreed to work together and share one of the thatched tents. Before he fell asleep Jinot looked forward to replacing the ferns with a fleece.

He was no longer the man he had been the last time he chopped trees. His scarred leg would carry him in the mornings; by the end of the workday it burned and ached intolerably and could barely take his weight. He was too old for logging.

"What troubles your leg?" asked Arana, and Jinot told him of the Miramichi fire that had nearly caught him, that had burned his brother Amboise. It was a great ease to have conversation with someone he liked. It had been a long, long time since he had had the pleasure of friendship. He went with Arana to meet his father, Orion Palmer, the trader from Maine. The white-haired old ruffian launched into a flood of reminiscence about his early days in Maine and a long involved story of why he could never go back, something to do with killing a rich man's horse.

The labor of axing down a tree with the girth of a village church was monstrous. The bushmen tried every way, whittling around the sides for weeks until the trunk began to resemble a pencil, chipping and chopping until a saw could finish the cut. Or chopping out a commodious room within the living tree, room enough to swing an ax, a great waste of good timber. They built platforms to lift them above the stack of debris at the base of every kauri. It took weeks to bring down a single giant. The ax alone was not enough and the trader ordered ten-foot felling saws—double-tooth rakers every four teeth—onto the job. When the saws arrived the kauri began to come down by the hundreds. "*Now* we're doin it," said Shutter-cock, one of the choppers. On the shore near the wharves Palmer's roaring steam-powered sawmill, specially equipped to handle kauri, spat out the most desirable lumber in the world day after day. Hundreds of Maori hauled vast logs to these mills, inching them up out of the ravines, easing them down the steep slope below the ridge. They could not bring them in fast enough to suit Palmer, who began to talk of getting bullocks from Australia. "Queensland," he said. "Where there's good timber-broke beasts to be had."

On Saturday nights Arana went home to his father's house to exchange his filthy work clothes for fresh, sink into his mother's large family clan again and eat his favorite dishes, to be Maori once more. Jinot stayed in the camp, washed and mended his single garment, a pair of canvas trousers torn off at the knee.

Arana came back one Sunday evening with a home delicacy, a basket of eels that had been wrapped in leaves of green flax and roasted over the coals. "We worked all day fixin our eel weirs. Some settlers pulled up all the manuka stakes that show the eel the way into the *hinaki*." Between mouthfuls of the juicy meat they talked about weirs and nets and eel pots, the different ways to make good weirs. "Mi'kmaq make weirs with river stones," said Jinot, arranging pebbles on the ground. "Takes a lot of attention, the river shifts them." Arana explained how brush and ferns could be worked in between the manuka stakes to make a good fence, and spoke eloquently on the importance of a strong and beautiful *hinaki* net that did the eels honor.

For Jinot, cutting his first big kauri was pain. He had to clear away a mountain of debris around the tree with ax and brush hook, with hoe and mattock. Then it had taken three days to chop out a large enough "room" so he could climb up and get inside the tree and, in a twisted half crouch, swing his ax. At last the true assault began. He managed the first hour, but the pain in his leg was bad, very bad. At noon he moved like a crab to the edge of his chopping hole to get down to the ground and some cold tea. He was not hungry. He jumped and felt something give way in his knee. When he tried to stand upright the bad leg folded. He could not straighten it and fell again, the knee hitting the mattock point. Arana saw him down, loped over and looked at blood seeping through Jinot's pants. "We'll get it fixed," he said, "we'll get you right." He cut a forked sapling and made a makeshift crutch, helped the injured man up. Jinot, standing because he could not sit, drank a quart of tepid tea, leaned against the maimed kauri and panted. He put his head against the old tree's grey bark and whispered, "You got me this time."

"You can't work," said Arana and helped him back to the bunkhouse, pulled off his trousers and looked at the knee still oozing blood from the blue and swelling cut. The knee looked strangely flat. He got water from the cook and tore a bit of rag from his extra shirt, mopped the wound and left Jinot to lie there all afternoon trying to find a position that would ease the pain.

There was no doctor. Palmer did any necessary doctoring or burying. Arana brought him in the next day and the trader looked at Jinot's knee, deformed when the ligament had torn and the patella moved up into the thigh; the mattock wound was red and swollen. "Christ," he said. "You better lay up. Maine men heals pretty quick so we'll see." He noticed Jinot's graying hair—the man had aged in New Zealand. He went up to the store himself and got two bottles of opium-heavy patent medicines—Sydenham's laudanum and Dover's powder. "Course he's not no chicken now—older feller, you don't heal so good." While he was gone Arana put his hand on Jinot's burning cheek, leaned over and said into his ear, "Rest, rest."

Jinot slid in and out of narcotic dreams in the bunkhouse for a week while the infected wound broke free from restraint, galloping headlong toward victory. Bright with fever, panting, he did not recognize Arana, called out to Franceway. Arana and Palmer regarded the leg, one vast black blister. Arana sighed.

Arana and Shuttercock buried Jinot near the river at the edge of the hay field where they had cut rickers two years earlier. Before the last shovelful of earth topped the grave it began to rain. They

walked back up the steep tree-bare slope sloughing off muddy soil
as the rain increased. It was the beginning of a great lopping storm
that loosed unreasonable torrents. The mountain streams, joined by
other runaway water, raced flashing down the hills carrying rocks,
ricker slash, logs, gravel, soil, the old cookhouse, and, disinterring
Jinot Sel, swept his carcass out into the Pacific.

The old year ended trembling in storms of wind after a wild winter,
but once again a fresh spring morning, pastel and calm, gave Mr.
Rainburrow pleasure as he sucked in the sweet air. He left the door
open and hoped for no interruptions. If he finished all his correspondence within the hour he would have the afternoon free to count and
arrange the flax bales in his storeroom, but before he had written half
a page he heard tramping on the earthen path and a figure loomed,
entered his sunny workroom. Another followed. He thought that
he had rarely seen uglier customers than the two men who stood
with folded arms staring at him. One was hoop-backed and swart, an
aging hunchback with obsidian eyes in a flat American Indian face.
The other had even more marked Indian features and a wiry body.
His inward-drawn mouth showed that he cared for neither Englishmen nor missionaries. To Mr. Rainburrow the pressed-in lips and
knotted eyebrows indicated a particularly disagreeable nature.

"Yes?" said the missionary in the brusque voice he used to dust
off time wasters.

"Joe Dogg," said the crooked man, fishing in his pocket, then
extending Mr. Rainburrow's own letter written several years earlier. It was stained and tattered, one corner quite torn away. "I am
Mr. Bone's foreman and acting manager of the ax works. Your letter came to me. Has Mr. Bone now returned? My inquiries have
remained unanswered."

"Oh, he—no, he—he has never returned. We are quite satisfied
that he was decoyed and killed by a renegade Maori—it is quite sure
that poor Mr. Bone is dead. Quite sure."

"What basis have you for that surety?"

"Well," blustered Mr. Rainburrow, "well, because it is *known* by some—I am not at liberty to say whom—that he was—killed. Killed and likely"—his voice dropped—"in the custom of some of these heathens, eaten."

Dogg grimaced, shook his head as if driving off an irritating sweat bee. "We will have proof of your assertion, sir. People do not just 'disappear,' people are not just 'eaten.'"

"In New Zealand it can happen. Mr. Bone was headstrong and showed no reticence in going into the forest with a native he did not know. Guile is part of the Maori nature."

"I ask you to produce those people who 'know,'" said Joseph Dogg. "A great deal depends on being sure. And what of his money box, do you have it?"

"I keep it in a safe place, it is in my cupboard in my sleeping room. I will get it directly." The words tripped over each other like a too-often-repeated prayer.

The hard-faced Indian clenching and unclenching his fists spoke loudly and angrily. "Where is Jinot Sel? I wish to see Jinot."

Mr. Rainburrow also had a wish—that he might be instantly transported to a desert isle. If he had never written that letter these men would have remained forever in their wretched land of rebels and upstarts.

"He—he, too, is dead."

Dogg, the hunchback, who had been looking out at the harbor, spun around, spoke in a tigerish voice. "What! Jinot dead? Not possible. Never. How? When?"

"Last year, in, in— I have forgotten the month."

"He died how? Or did he also 'disappear'?"

"He died of illness. Of blood poison. He worked as a bushman and hurt his foot. Or leg. His friend, Arana Palmer, was with him and no doubt can tell you all the particulars."

Joseph Dogg said in a low voice, "Perhaps you do not know that Jinot Sel was not Mr. Bone's 'servant' as you surmise, but was greatly favored by him as a friend and business associate and it is to him that Mr. Bone has willed all his works and possessions, which include the ax factory in Massachusetts. And if truly he is dead, and if Jinot is also dead, then likely Mr. Bone's holdings will shift into Jinot's estate and go to his son, Aaron. I have the responsibility to bring all details back to Aaron Sel, who could not make the interminable journey."

"I am also Sel," said the dark Indian. "Etienne Sel, an uncle of Jinot Sel although he was older than me by many years. We came to reclaim him and take him back to his home country. If what you say is true we must have his bones that he may be returned to the land where he began. This is important."

"I cannot speak to the whereabouts of his grave," said Mr. Rainburrow, seeing an escape route. "I can only advise you to search out Arana Palmer, one of the sons of the trader here, Mr. Orion Palmer. He was a friend of Jinot Sel—and, I think, did bury him—where I do not know. So, I wish you good day, gentlemen, and good fortune with discovering what you wish to know."

"The money box, sir," said Joseph Dogg. "I will take it in hand before we leave this place. I trust you have not availed yourself of any of the funds?" A cloud passed over the sun, briefly dimming the flood of light through the open door.

"How dare you, sir, imply that I am a thief?" Mr. Rainburrow swelled up. The word *sir* hissed through his teeth.

"Why, Mr. Rainbillow, I see that you are a clergyman of sorts, and it has been my experience that pastors, ministers, clergymen and church officials of all kinds feel entitled to use any stray funds that come their way to further their influence and control of local affairs—as well as building new churches, adding wings to existing churches, gilding the altar and such so-called good works, especially improving the parsonage or the wine cellar."

"I will have you know that I have not touched a ha'pence," lied the missionary, who had, in fact, used more than a hundred pounds of Mr. Bone's money to build the storeroom where he cached his bales of flax.

"It will be a simple matter to judge," said Joe Dogg, "as I know to the last penny what Mr. Bone had in that box. I have his monthly accounts up until three years ago, when correspondence ceased. He was meticulous in noting his expenditures. Before we depart I will conduct my examination of the contents of the money box and any papers he may have left. Also, you will present that proof of his demise."

They left the missionary biting at his thumbnail. Sunlight washed the room as before.

Orion Palmer leaned on his counter near the open door, his narrow temples surmounted by a wave of cresting auburn hair, his hard blue eyes wide open. Etienne stared at his odd face, for below the earlobes the jaws swelled out, fleshy and full, carried down to a thick neck. "My son? Which one? I have more than a dozen, all fine fellows, but I certainly do not know the whereabouts of each. Most with their mother's people." The trader, in an easy mood and pleased with the fine day and the flock of sheep-like clouds marching overhead, sized up the two men.

"Your son Arana Palmer, sir," said Etienne in the weighty voice he used with assertive whitemen. "We have heard that he knew my nephew Jinot Sel."

"Ayuh, he did." The trader sighed and thought for a long moment. "Pret' sure Arana is workin the kauri yet." He picked his teeth with a long fingernail. "Yep, he did know Jinot, we all known him. He frighted the women wicked when he first come here. So some took a dislike to him. He died of a poisoned wound—nothin we could do. Too late for amputation and no white man doctor here—just me, and I don't go in for cuttin men's limbs off." As he warmed up he became more voluble, his limber mouth stretched in the smirk of a self-regarding man. "I say he was not young or strong enough in the first place to work cuttin kauri, but the missionary put him to it so's he could earn his passage back home. He tried. Choppin kauri

calls for strong young men," he said. "He was not so young, pret'
lame though he knew well how to handle the ax. You could see that.
He said he was a Penobscot man, and maybe he was a long time ago.
Them days is gone, y'see—we got circle saws and trained bullocks.
Now bullocks—"

He was ready to tell them his brilliant innovation of importing
bullocks to New Zealand, for the trader had to get some indication
of his importance into every conversation, but something in their
intent leaning postures, their serious eyes following his lips as he
spoke deterred him. He told them instead to take the steamer two
harbors north and, following the map he sketched out on a broken
packing-case slat, to walk the track to the Big Yam camp, where the
choppers and sawyers were laying the kauri down. He wished them
luck. "And I guess you want to finish your business here pretty quick
as the *Vigor* is leaving for Port Jackson next week. We don't get that
many ships these days since the whales is all gone. Catch the *Vigor*
and return to your own place."

Etienne spoke. "We only just come here. Long long trip. We see
something of this new land, not leave so soon. Country pretty different to K'taqmkuk." He stared out at the bulging forest line beyond
the cutover slope hardly believing the size of the stumps.

"Arana can show you—his mother is Maori. The Maori got a good
many *tapu* places you best not disturb." And the trader drew the edge
of his hand across his throat.

The calm morning had changed; intermittent clouds now cast their
stuttering shadows over the landscape. Arana, when they found him
at work, was, like many Maori, handsome and strongly built with
great leg muscles. There was little of the trader Orion Palmer in his
appearance beyond a slightly oversize jaw. His hair hung long and
snaggled. He listened to them, then said, "Come with me," and led
them through the stumps to an awkward place—a huge kauri stump
surrounded by slash and the great pale arms of its severed limbs.

He jumped on the flat top, the size of a barn floor, and beckoned to them to join him. "This is the very stump of the kauri Jinot was cuttin when his bad leg give way. There's the cuts he made," he said and pointed to the ax marks on the outer rings. Etienne touched the greying wood, old ax marks all that remained here to show that Jinot had walked the earth.

He diverted the conversation to the peculiarities of these curious tree giants that tempted woodsmen with their perfectly knotless bodies, for he, too, had chopped trees in Maine and Nova Scotia and had never seen anything like them. Arana said they were a kind of pine.

"Many men say," said Arana, "that kauri is the best wood in the world." They smoked their pipes in silence for some time. Etienne said, "What can you tell us of Jinot here?"

"He wanted to return to you but could not. He had no money. What else could he do? Become a trader? My father would not allow that. A cook? Perhaps. But he knew the ax, he knew how to bring a tree down even if it were the biggest tree of the world. He was very skilled with axes. He made a chair one Sunday, all with his ax. I think he was lonely here, nobody talk with but me and some of the choppers. He said he never meant to come here but that man, Mr. Bone, made him do it. He did not want to cut kauri—he said they were trees of power, and we also believe this. I do not think he ever told me of his uncle." He squinted at Etienne as if he had just jumped down from the sky.

"He could not, for he did not know me, ha? His grandfather—my father—Kuntaw, left Penobscot a long time ago and returned to his Mi'kmaw people near Sipekne'katik river. Kuntaw got two wives after that whiteman woman, and one of them, my mother. Settlers pressed on us, the Scotlands, destroyed our eel weirs, burned our *wikuoms*." Arana nodded at the mention of eels; they were his bond with Jinot. "The government give our reserve to those Scotland people with burning hair color, so Kuntaw led us across the water to K'taqmkuk—as the whitemen say, Newfoundland, where there were good eel rivers, good fish, and some Mi'kmaw people. For us it was good because the whites did not go into the rough parts of this place. But we did and now we live well. We come to bring Jinot back with us. Aaron was there for two years. He went to Boston. We look, we can't find him to come here with us."

Joseph Dogg, who had been silent during this recitation, asked softly if whitemen were not pushing into such a bountiful country. "Yes," said Etienne, "but it is rich only for us Mi'kmaw. For white-men who want something that makes money it is not promising. They come not to make houses, but only hunt caribou and get fish. These whitemen come to Kuntaw and ask him to take them to good fishing places. No harm can come from that."

Joe Dogg rolled his eyes and said emphatically, "It is dangerous to bring whitemen into your country. However rough the trail, they remember it and soon begin to want it."

Etienne said, "We live our Mi'kmaw life. That is what we want give to Jinot." Looking at Arana, he shifted the talk. "The trader said you were a friend to Jinot. Maybe you will tell us about this place that he came to. Maybe you will show us how you and your mother's people live. We like to know this."

Arana was silent for long minutes, then said, "We will go in the bush with my sister Kahu—*he kanohi komiromiro*—she has the eye-sight of that little bird that finds invisible insects. She knows the for-est with all her senses."

Their excursion fell on a day of days, clear and bright at sunrise in the time of nesting birds. They were five in number, for not only did Arana's elder sister Kahu come with her pet parrot on her shoulder, but also their young cousin Aihe, muscular and as quick of motion as the dolphin in her name. Aihe's crinkly hair seemed alive and mov-ing, as though each strand was a tendril reaching for a hold. Kahu's pet kaka flashed his red underwings and shouted whenever he felt like it, which was frequently, a call that sounded to Joe Dogg like someone ripping boards off the side of a barn.

Arana and Kahu tried to explain their country (despairingly, because it could not be explained but only lived), saying all land was owned by Maori tribes and clans, who kept forests intact for birds and only cut trees judiciously. Aihe interrupted, saying hotly that some tribal chiefs were greedy and sold their relatives' land to whitemen of the New Zealand Company. As they walked Kahu pointed at some gnarled pohutukawa trees and said they were sacred. Springs of purest water bubbled out of the ground. In the distance they could see the swell of the forest like a great wave.

They entered what Kahu called "the forest of Tane," and the air became still and heavy. Above them the westerly wind stirred the treetops and always some birds rose crying out. They went silently as Kahu pointed out the tallest trees making a top roof over the forest, the lesser trees below. Joe Dogg was scandalized by the way of the rata, which began life in the high branches of other trees and, as it grew, sucking the life force from its host, sent roots downward until they reached the earth and twisted together into a distorted trunk until the host tree became part of the rata.

Late in the morning the small pieces of visible sky clouded over and Kahu said they might have a little fast-moving storm. Before she finished speaking they could hear the rain pelting down above them, beating on the leaves, though so interlaced were the treetops that no drops reached them.

They came out of the trees as the storm pulled away, and from a lookout rock they saw pillars of mist exhaled from the folded hills. Aihe said it was Papatuanuku, the earth mother, sighing for Ranginui, the sky father, and that in the Beginning they had been glued tightly to each other in amorous conjunction, making great darkness for their god children. The children decided to separate their parents and let in light, she said, and Tane, the forest god, held them apart with trees. She asked Etienne for Mi'kmaw stories. He remembered several imperfectly, but stayed silent as he thought they would show empty against her accounts of a Maori world teeming with so many gods. The Mi'kmaq had lost their spirit world to the missionaries' God.

When they passed near an ongaonga Aihe pulled at Joe Dogg's sleeve, pointed and told him it was a dangerous plant with a poison sting. "They tell of a whiteman sailor who ran away from his ship in the night. He ran into a forest where there were many ongaonga plants and he fell in them in the darkness, crying out. But the onga-onga did not spare him and he died of its stings." A little later she caught something and passed it to Etienne—"here is a *pepekemataru-wai* for you, we call it 'insect with a silly face.'" He flung it from him, laughing.

Etienne was impressed that everything they saw or heard or smelled was linked to Maori gods and their feverish vengeful lives. He prom-ised himself that when he returned to K'taqmkuk he would find old people and ask for stories of ancestors. He stared at the ocean below, glinting through the trees, and thought it looked back at him. Never in K'taqmkuk had the Atlantic Ocean fixed him with its watery eye. Was this a sign?

At the new moon Joe Dogg and Etienne Sel worked their passage to Port Jackson and after a long wait signed on to a London-bound ship and on to Boston. "We must find Aaron," said Etienne.

VIII

glory days

1836–1870

54

vegetable wealth

James had spent the early August morning hour combing very carefully through the monthly household accounts and totaling up Posey's expenditures. Since their marriage he had kept her on a liberal but strict allowance; in their early days it was his only ascendancy over her. She had found him rigorous—a single penny beyond the allowance and the next month's amount was halved. But now he cared less and since the birth of Lavinia (long after they resumed subdued marital relations), Posey had changed, all her tigerish flauntings behind her. The waves of her affectionate care washed beyond Lavinia and over James, his cousins and their wives, the house staff—all except Phineas Breeley, who had been banished to New Brunswick, far, far from infant Lavinia. Posey read stories and poems from *Tales of the Robin* to the child every night; Lavinia developed a tender regard for "the pious bird with the scarlet breast."

James closed the account book. Posey had become almost frugal in her expenditures. For himself, beyond his cigars, presents for Lavinia, decent port and a very occasional waistcoat, he spent little money—except for new horseflesh. He had just purchased Throstle, a handsome chestnut Hanoverian saddle mount, and decided now on a half hour of manly horse talk with Will Thing, his aged coachman. As he rose to go down to the stables the new butler came in and said, "Mr. Vogel requesting to see you, sir."

"Let him come in, let him in," said James, for Lennart Vogel had become a particular friend. "Lennart, you must be just now returned from your annual jaunt?" He was slightly shocked. There was no sign of Lennart the elegant. He wore dark fustian workman's trousers, a grey wool vest and heavy boots. The boot heels were crusted with mud.

"I am. And very interesting it was, James," said Lennart. "Forgive my appearance. I am so charged with information I came straight here. Apropos of my journey I wonder if you have a little time to talk with me. This last week I have been forced to consider the future of the company. I see pitfalls ahead that must be avoided. But also a chance to enlarge our scope if we exert ourselves. No use talking to Edward or the others just yet."

"Would you like to walk about the grounds while we converse? The day's heat is not yet intolerable."

"Better to walk about outside," said Lennart, "I am so disheveled."

They strolled through the grounds, under the grape arbor with its clusters of unripe fruit, past the gaudy geometries of bedding plants. Posey was delighted with the strident colors of pelargonium, salvias, petunias and calceolarias, but James preferred roses, which at least had some height and perfume; the bedding gardens, very much the new thing, were like cheap oriental carpets.

Lennart walked too quickly for James's taste; James finally sat on a stone bench near the roses and said, "Lennart, stop a bit and tell me what troubles you."

Lennart did not sit but walked back and forth, the words tumbling out. "James, I believe we now must urgently consider the future and our forest holdings. We have had several rather lean years and you know as well as I that we do not have many good patches left in New England or York state. The pine is cut out. I know, you are going to say, 'What about the forest lands in Ohio' that your father bought some years back. That purchase is the catalyst to my visit here today. In my woodland journey this year I went to that Ohio property and what I saw utterly dismayed me. It was no longer the pine forest that your father persuaded us to purchase. In his day there were only Indians and fur traders passing through great stands of white pine, but now settlers, mostly from northern Europe, have come there in number. Thousands arrived en masse eighteen months ago and they have burned and cut almost all of those trees and replaced them with farms. Can you imagine? The finest white pine heaped up to burn. There is nothing left. And they keep coming."

"My God," said James. "It was several thousands of acres."

"Yes, we should have had a trespass agent in attendance. But the forest stood empty of all but trees and the inrushing people believed it was free for the taking. They took it. It is gone."

"I thought Armenius Breitsprecher was supposed to make yearly inspections of those holdings."

"We settled on every two years as it was a long and arduous trip and he has other duties. When your father went there he had to traverse the Great Black Swamp, one of the most horrific barriers to travel on the continent. Now with new roads and the Erie Canal it is all greatly improved. Breitsprecher planned to go this year—too late. These settlers are so many that they have taken those thousands of acres to the ground in little more than a single year."

"That is difficult to believe."

"James, you have seen birds of prey pick a fallen deer to the bone in one or two days?"

"Of course."

"Consider settlers as human birds of prey," said Lennart. "Birds of prey with the weapon of fire. They burned great swathes of our trees. You have certainly read in the papers of wilderness glades that become towns of more than a hundred houses in two months?"

James could feel the old pain starting to grip his stomach, reminiscent of the days when Posey threw her temper fits. "But surely there is still a glut of forest in other places. We can find other forests. I have heard it said that this continent has unequaled vastness of forests, the most in the world."

"Quite true. There are still untouched and unknown forests. And that brings me to my point. We need to find these forests and get our woods crews on them as soon as we may. Else all of Europe will come in and burn and cut everything. In some European countries there are laws and prohibitions against free cutting of trees, and the more rebellious peasants who chafed under those rules now are here, and released from those ukases, they go mad with the power of destruction. They are like no people seen on the face of the earth before now. They are like tigers who have tasted blood. And like tigers they pass on their lustful craving for land to their children and grandchildren, who continue to believe it is their *right* to take whatever is there in this land of plenty." He threw his cigar stub down. "I propose that you and I make a reconnaissance to find new forest. We are not young, James, but both hale and strong. On my journey I went no farther than those properties in Ohio, but while there I heard that to the north in Michigan Territory there are pines. Very many white pines."

James sat smoking and thinking. "Yes, I suppose our usual way of buying land or stumpage in New England or York state and then cutting it with no idea of where new timber will be found could undo the company in future. There are more competitors than ever and we have learned our near forests are not eternal. Trees grow too slowly. This is not a fresh idea; we have gnawed on it several times at meetings. But Edward and Freegrace balk at exploration, they delay and counsel waiting, for what I do not know. I recall that at a gathering several years ago Cyrus spoke of excellent chances in Pennsylvania, but Edward said, 'Not now, not now!' and our competitors gobbled them up."

"It is time for action, it is our turn to be first. If we can convince Cyrus, we can outvote Edward and Freegrace. It has come to that. They are timid. Since Lydia died Edward exchanges ideas only with his housekeeper and the cats." This was patently untrue, for Edward was a passionate Trinitarian and Freegrace a seduced Unitarian dabbling in the new Higher Criticism and the two brothers had fiery discussions that flamed into shouting matches.

James considered that Lennart and he were not many years behind those brothers; they were all old, he thought, though he didn't feel it.

And Lennart was spry enough. No doubt Edward and Freegrace felt able to run a business. The Duke blood promised longevity.

"James, they hold the company back. What do you say, are you willing to undertake a journey to Michigan Territory with me? Or even farther if we choose. I am intrigued by occasional remarks by mariners who have worked the otter fur trade on the west coast—sightings of heavy forests. I would like to see for myself, for what do sailors know of trees?"

"That is very distant. Almost Japan."

"We are speaking of the future, James, the future! We must not let these chances pass us by."

"What about Breitsprecher? Would he come with us?" James wondered why childless Lennart was so emphatic about the future.

"I think Breitsprecher is essential. It is he who can best judge the board feet of standing timber."

"Lennart, I will go with you. And Breitsprecher. When do you think of leaving?"

"I have several important things to attend at once. First, I must see Cyrus. Then an immediate Board meeting. I must enlist Breitsprecher and persuade Edward and Freegrace that this exploration is vital. With luck I think we might leave in two weeks' time." He stopped talking, paced around the fragrant damask La Ville de Bruxelles, turned and flicked his finger at a Maiden's Blush. "The first part of this journey by coach and rail I know well. The most tiresome is the canal boat to Oswego. Bring a large book to read on the canal boat. It is the greatest boredom known. Rail to Buffalo and the last leg to Detroit by steamboat. Progress has eased the traveler's lot. When I think of poor Sedley in the grip of knee-deep mud . . ."

James was interested not in his father's travail in that hundred miles of infested swampland but in what he should pack for the journey. Cigars, he thought, were of first importance. The Indians were in love with Cuban tobacco—as was he—and they rarely got it, so he planned to carefully wrap hundreds of cigars and fill two saddlebags. "But is there any transport beyond Detroit? I would be surprised."

They strolled toward the end of the property marked by aged oaks filled with quarreling squirrels.

"No, though steamboats, roads and trails extend travel every week. From Detroit it will all be terra incognita. Bring sturdy clothes for rough weeks of living off the land. And guns and ammunition. Only one thing I am sure of—we must go beyond Ohio."

Near the oaks James picked up a fallen stick and pointed it like a gun; the squirrels fled. The friends shook hands. Both had a sense of urgency, a feeling that the North American forests were going up in clearance fires and fireplaces, that armies of immigrant settlers were seizing everything. Lennart Vogel, thought James, had looked into the treeless future and decided to act. It would be dangerous, but he recalled Lewis and Clark, who, three decades earlier, had safely made their way to the far Pacific and back.

When they met the next day Lennart Vogel had spruced up and looked pleased. "I had good fortune of a sort since Cyrus now lives in Boston. We talked and he will side with us against Edward and Freegrace if it reaches that point. Also, there is a Post Office map for Michigan Territory and I have procured a somewhat worn copy. It shows post roads and stage roads, but the intelligence is twenty years past. More useful I think is word of a well-traveled Indian path suitable for horse travel from Detroit to that mudhole Chicago. The westward Sauk Trail has many branches and I think that if we can discover one northbound we will find the reputed forests by horse and shank's mare. Indian guides and paddlers are easy to come by everywhere along those great lakes where the fur trade flourished so long ago. The natives will do anything for a bottle of spirits."

"Would that Freegrace and Edward were so easily managed."

"Give Edward a present of catnip for his beasts and he will smile on us." It was true. Since his wife, Lydia, died of a profound asthma aggravated by the inescapable brown manure dust in the streets, Edward doted on Casimir and Vaughn, her two pampered striped felines.

• • •

And so, on an early September morning of drizzling rain Lennart Vogel, James Duke and Armenius Breitsprecher (accompanied by his *kurzhaar* hunting dog, Hans Carl von Carlowitz) got into their hired coach and headed northwest. Lennart set a hamper of roast chickens and beer on the floor. Hans Carl von Carlowitz ran beside the coach. "He may become footsore," said Lennart. The dog heard this and ran faster.

They bought horses in Detroit and rode into the hardwood forest. As they left Detroit behind Lennart said, "I have heard that a hundred years ago old Sieur de la Mothe Cadillac thought La Ville d'Étroit and its environs 'so beautiful that it may justly be called the earthly paradise of North America.'"

They were in unpopulated country and James was disturbed by the green gloom. There were no landmarks, only trees, no open sky, only wind-rustled canopy. He felt as he sometimes had felt at sea, that glittering, hallucinatory sense of trackless immensity. But unlike wind-fated ocean travel the Sauk pathway was obvious, an ancient trail made by weighty mastodons and already very old when men from the steppes of Asia found it.

At a ravine they looked down on a sinuous course of dry stones.

"A sign that settlers are nearby," said Breitsprecher, pointing at the desiccated watercourse. Another quarter mile took them past an eroded cutover slope. They could hear ax blows and smell smoke as they came to a stumpy clearing of twenty acres where three men were cutting trees in a windrow for a winter burn. An adjacent field already fired showed incinerated soil and cracked rocks.

The settler—James judged him somewhere between forty and sixty years old—came toward them swinging sinewy arms. His hair hung to his shoulders, pale expressionless eyes gazed at them.

"Where ye headed?"

"West. Going west," answered Lennart. "I'm Lennart Vogel."

The settler looked them up and down. The ropy sons came near and stared at the strangers, jaws relaxed.

"You, Moony, Kelmar. Git back t' choppin, *schnell,*" the father said fast and hard. He turned his eyes on James, on his horse, looked at his boots, squinted up to see his face better. "Look like you might be some kind a govmint man?"

James said nothing. The father gave Armenius Breitsprecher one of his lingering looks, opened his mouth, closed it when Breitsprecher treated him to a similar examination. "We'll be getting along," said Armenius to Lennart and James with some emphasis. Without another word they clucked at their horses and moved out.

They had ridden half a mile in silence when Armenius suddenly motioned them into the woods and down an incline to a swamp. At the end of a beaver dam, willows, brush and saplings had all been clear-cut by the rodents, making open ground with good views over the pond and their back trail.

"Stay with the horses, keep quiet and no smoke," he whispered. "That old man means trouble and I'm going up to see if he and the imbeciles are creeping along the trail. Hans Carl von Carlowitz, *komm!*" In a minute man and dog were out of sight. James and Lennart waited, the pond surface, the beaver house, the horses, their faces honey-glazed by the setting sun. The day began to close in and the mosquitoes thickened. "I got to have a cigar," said James in a low voice. "Better not," whispered Lennart. "Some settlers been known to kill travelers, take their money and goods, their horses. You see how the old man looked us over? How he marked us with his eye?"

"Suppose they got Armenius? Suppose he don't come back," whispered James.

"Cross that bridge when we get on it."

James took out his vial of pennyroyal and slathered it on to repel mosquitoes, fell asleep leaning against a mossy but damp spruce log. Something, a noise, woke him. He was more wide awake than he had ever been in his life. Something—someone—was there, near them, not moving carefully but letting branches swish, footsteps squelch.

"Armenius?" said James very quietly. "Is that you?"

"Hunh!" said something that clumbered off into the swamp, and for the rest of the night they could hear dripping water as the moose pulled up weed. James dozed against Lennart's comforting snore. In the cold fog of dawn they both woke violently alert when the yellow horse nickered quietly.

"Someone coming," whispered Lennart. The horses had their ears cocked in the same direction, then placidly began to pull at some blueberry bushes. "Breitsprecher. They know his tread." They waited. The swamp mist took on a tender color showing it would be a clear day. James fished in his saddlebag, found his Boston cheddar and cut it in half. As he was putting it to his lips a terrific splash startled him and he dropped it in the muck, cried, "Damnation!" A beaver, galvanized at the sight of Armenius Breitsprecher and his dog whipping along its dam, had signaled danger. Hans Carl von Carlowitz took a pose, pointing at the expanding rings of water. Beaver far down the pond slapped their tails. Breitsprecher stepped off the dam and walked up to the horses, patting each on the nose. He smiled broadly at Lennart and James and opened his coat to show a cotton sack. From the sack he drew a flitch of bacon, half a dozen eggs, striped apples and warm biscuits.

"*Guter Mann,*" he said. "Name was Anton Heinrich. He *was* on the trail, not following us with evil intent but to bring us to their *Klotzhaus* for the night. I did not have time to return for you before the woods went *dunkel*—so I went on with him. He was *ein Deutscher,* once a *Bauer* in Maine. We only talk *Deutsch*—you would not like it. No English. They give me a big supper and sleep in a hay bed in the barn. Here is breakfast that the wife, Kristina, gives to us. Maybe eight *Kinder,* sets a good table, *ja, es gab reichlich zu essen und zu trinken. Gute Menschen.*"

"Do not forget how to speak English," said James.

"*Ja,* sorry. He bought that farm from the *Witwe*—widow Kristina— when the first owner died from a fever. Anton used to have a farm in Maine but *die Erde,* the soil, didn't last. It couldn't, the way they burn the ground dead and then try to grow crops in the ashes year after year. Four, five years it's done. *Erde* that the forest took *tausend* years to make." He bit into an apple and continued. "But you cannot be too careful. There are settlers—and there are settlers."

Lennart said to himself, "There's travelers—and there's travelers," for he saw blood on Armenius's trouser leg. He wasn't going to ask.

The trail took them through a clearing thick with bracken fern edged by red pine and hemlock and occasional white pine. By late afternoon they were again in forest, and in a mix of deciduous and conifer, frond and lichen, Breitsprecher pointed out white birch and aspen groves and more scattered white pine, taller than other trees. The next morning as they scrambled up a south-facing ridge Breitsprecher scraped up a handful of the dry sandy soil and said, "Now we come where white pine rules." Yet on the other side there were more hemlocks than white pine and the trail betrayed them with a knot of intersecting pathways. Which was the Sauk Trail, which the unknown way to thick growths of white pine?

"We have to try the different ways," said Breitsprecher. "Let us start with this north branch." As they hiked along, young hemlocks and hardwoods fighting for space slapped at them, and even smaller pathways cut in—game trails, said Lennart. James wondered if any might lead them to what they were seeking. By noon the next day they were confused by the multiplicity of unknown trails.

"I find it strange that we have not seen any Indians," said Breitsprecher. "If we meet Indians we can ask them where to find the white pine. I think we must go back to the main trail and wait until a party of Indians comes by."

They camped and waited, and after two days a hunting party of six Chippewa stopped and asked in English for "bacco" when they saw James smoking his morning cigar. "Give bacco," said the youngest Chippewa, a boy of about ten. The others repeated the magic phrase, and Breitsprecher, speaking to them in some all-purpose linguistic mix, said James would give them tobacco if they showed the correct trail to many big white pines. He pointed to a handy example fifty feet off the trail, a large tree with exposed roots spread out like monstrous fingers. They all spoke at once and pointed in the same direction—back toward Detroit. An older man in the party broke a twig and drew a map in the soft soil. "Him d'Étroit," he said. He drew five trails coming out of Detroit. "Sauk," he said, pointing at a southwest way. "San Joe," he said, pointing to the trail they were on. Breitsprecher's choice of the right-hand trail at the intersection had taken them off the Sauk, which was wrong in any case. "Saginaw," he said, pointing at a line that ran northwest. "Shiawassee," he said prodding another. "Mackinac." The Shiawassee and the Saginaw connected to the Mackinac and two other important trails. They should have taken the Shiawassee or the Saginaw trail from Detroit, not the Sauk.

"Do we have to go back to Detroit?" said Lennart. Armenius put the question and the Chippewa talked excitedly.

"He says there is a side trail that will take us onto the Shiawassee. The Mackinac crosses the Shiawassee. But we do not go on the Mackinac but continue straight on a trail that follows the shore of Huron. He calls it Along-the-Shore Trail." The Chippewa volunteered to show them the side trail that would take them to the Shiawassee and without waiting for more talk set off at a fast lope.

"I'll just go with them, mark the trail and return for you," Breitsprecher said. Before they were out of sight the Indians stopped suddenly and spoke among themselves, then the youngest one looked back at James. "Bacco! Bacco now!" James plunged his hands into his pack and pulled out twelve Cuban cigars, two for each man. He was about to present them to the Chippewa with a bit of a flourish when Breitsprecher said, "They will want to stay and smoke with us, so give them to me and when they have pointed out the connecting trail I will give them the tobacco and return for you." He explained this to the Indians and they set off again, Breitsprecher stretching his legs to keep up. Once again James and Lennart and the horses waited. And waited.

"Suppose they killed Armenius?" said James in the afternoon. "They could do so and take the cigars. It's a long time he's gone."

"Backtracking can take time. Did not Armenius say about eight miles? I warrant it is at least eight miles. But I do not understand why we could not all have gone with them. There's less danger in numbers. And it would have saved time since we must go there anyway. I'll smoke one of your remaining cigars with you while we wait."

"To be sure. Cigars are useful when hunting white pine, eh?"

Breitsprecher was back before dusk. Before he could say anything, Lennart, who had been coming to a slow boil, said, "We should all have gone with you. We would be on that trail now if we had. We lost time. From now on we do not sit and wait while you run ahead. Do you understand me, Herr Breitsprecher?"

"I do. Of course you are right, but I was afraid it might be a ruse and that the proximity of James's cigars would have incited them to bad actions. In fact they were very agreeable, very pleased with the Cuban tobacco. They sat down at once to smoke at the trail junction."

"How far is it?" said James, stiff from the long wait.

"Not above nine miles, less than two hours horseback. Then they said maybe five, six days' walk, which I think we may do in three as we have horses. The connecting trail looked not so bad. A bit overgrown. We can go there now if you like or rest until morning. You decide," he said to Lennart Vogel.

"Immediately. The wait was very tiring. I, for one, am anxious to find these pines."

Breitsprecher's assessment of the trail was inadequate. The first mile was relatively open but then they were on low ground forcing their way through such choking rampant growth they had to dismount and lead their suffering animals. "Not so many Indians use this trail," said Breitsprecher. "Nature is taking it back."

When they finally stopped for the night and had rubbed grease on the horses' cut legs he said, "The Chippewa told me when they go up to those pines they go by water in canoes. That is good news for us as it means the forests are on a river or the lakeshore. Michigan is all lakes and rivers. It is country made for the lumber business."

There was no mistaking the Shiawassee when they reached it, a fair trail well beaten by many travelers. Their path climbed ever higher, ever clearer into forest. And what forest. Big white pine were everywhere, thicker and thicker. As they curved northeast the Saginaw Trail came in on their right and they were in the most choice pine forest any of them had ever seen. A pure stand of huge trees four and five feet in diameter, the tiered branches resembling great green pagodas a hundred and fifty feet tall, two hundred feet and more of the prized fine-grained wood, easy to float downriver or hold in bays and pounds.

They made an early camp and Breitsprecher spent the daylight hours walking, looking, measuring, computing, marking, marking. He came back and sat on a log beside the fire. He was trembling a little and ate the last of the near-rancid venison.

"Well?" said Lennart. "What do you think?"

"I walked off ten acres square and did some computing." He jerked his thumb at the trees. "This right where we are measures out to about twenty-five thousand board feet each acre."

"That cannot be correct," said James. "You must have made an error."

"I did not believe it myself, so I surveyed twice. That is a modest estimate. I have never seen a forest like this in my life, did not know such a thing existed. This must be the greatest stand of white pine in the world. Now we must try and grasp the extent. It may be just a few hundred acres of these extraordinary trees. It may be more."

It was more. Mile after dense mile after mile of the largest and straightest pines. "God," said Lennart looking up at the clouds, "we thank Thee for this glorious treasure."

None of them could sleep that night and Breitsprecher was up before first light, making a fire, boiling coffee, dropping things. They drank the scalding black stuff, packed up and set out as soon as there was light enough to see. Day after day they walked and rode through the magic forest. They reached a great bay on Huron's shore, but of the pines there was no end.

"This is so far beyond anything we expected," said Lennart. "Here is what we must do. First, we must get to the land office and start buying up as much of this forest as we possibly can. We must establish a headquarters, whether Detroit or where I do not know. We must rush back to Boston and explain to the Board what we have found. Armenius must continue looking, continue surveying and grading. There are centuries of timberwork here. But we have so many things that must be done we will not be able to start cutting for at least a year, perhaps two, while we lay the groundwork. We shall have to hire you some assistants," he said to Breitsprecher. "And someone must deal with the land office. Cyrus has to help. We must contact our markets. Albany may well be a good shipping point as it has the canal terminus. This is our future for generations, right here," he said, and he stamped his boot on the pine duff. "This is the making of Duke and Sons. There can never be anything better than what we have found." He was babbling.

"Great gods," said James. "A thousand men could not cut all this in a thousand years. We'll get them. We'll get a thousand men."

Armenius Breitsprecher gazed into the fire and said nothing. Not for the first time he saw the acquisitive hunger of Duke & Sons was so great they intended to clear the continent. And he was helping them. He hated the American clear-cut despoliation, the insane wastage of sound valuable wood, the destruction of the soil, the gullying and erosion, the ruin of the forest world with no thought for the future—the choppers considered the supply to be endless—there was always another forest. Rapine had been a force in the affairs of Duke & Sons since its beginnings, but with this find it would likely become the company's engine.

He himself did not stand to become wealthy from his percentage of the glorious treasure. In the years he had worked for the Dukes he had only received a little pinch of the forestland he cruised—twenty acres here, a section there, two acres on a mountaintop, fifty acres of tamarack swamp. Small pieces too widely separated that were difficult to sell, a meager return for his work. If he wanted any of the big Michigan pine he would have to connive to get it. The thought troubled him.

As they always did James Duke and Lennart Vogel smoked a cigar before they unrolled their blankets, and as he always did Armenius gathered an armful of wood, called Hans Carl von Carlowitz to him, ruffled his ears and lay down beside the fire. It was his task to keep it stoked through the night.

Lennart spoke in a near whisper. "James, I wish to ask you a delicate question. I would value your frank answer."

"Yes. What is it?"

"Do you—please answer frankly—do you—do you entirely trust Armenius?" James considered for a long time. Despite the excitement of the day and the gravity of the question Lennart was nearly asleep when James said, "I have no reason to distrust Armenius."

"Nor I," said Lennart. "It is just that this vast richness of pine breeds suspicion and worry. It is so great it can hardly be encompassed by my mind."

55

never enough

It was a clear October dawn when they reached Boston, the autumn leaves in their fiery coats. James went straight to his house. On his way out again in clean linen, and a butternut-brown frock coat, he looked in at Posey and said, "My dear, I am returned."

"Well, James. Did you find what you hoped for?"

"We certainly found good timber. The difficulty will be in getting it out."

"Isn't that always the same problem? Well do I remember the stratagems of log extraction in New Brunswick and Maine."

"This is a somewhat different proposition. How does Lavinia do? When does she leave for England?" Lavinia had been sent to a school for girls in London the past year.

"Thank you for your interest, sir," said Posey acidly. "Very much appreciated, I'm sure. In truth we are having a tussle over this. She does not wish to go back to that school—why I cannot say beyond her stubborn character. She finds no fault with the school except to denigrate the mathematics teacher, whom she calls 'an ignoramus.'"

"No doubt. She has always been very quick at figures and abstract notions."

"At first I was opposed to these vapors, but this morning I have been considering if it may not be for the best to keep her here and hire private tutors."

"I quite agree," said James. "She is too impressionable for school in England." He thought of his own unhappy childhood in that place.

"She is young but it is in her and our interests to see she meets young men of the best families. In England I worry that she might become the prey of impoverished fortune hunters."

"Likely enough. The place swarms with old families who have nothing but their names and crumbling houses. A wealthy American girl is a plum to them. I saw it often. Really, it would be better to keep her here."

"Good, we agree. Should I begin a search for a proper girls' school in Boston? Or a tutor?"

But James was already cantering down the stairs and into the New England morning.

"Always the selfish ruffian," said Posey.

Lennart and James tried to set the Board afire with descriptions of the mighty pines of Michigan, the great rivers and streams all connected to Lakes Huron, Michigan or Superior, the strategic placement of Detroit on the narrows between Huron and Erie, road expansions, the Erie Canal connection to Albany and on to New York City. Edward and Freegrace sat stone-faced. Cyrus Hempstead was nodding yes, yes, yes.

Lennart said, "We all know that getting the logs out of the forests and to the mills is the key to timber profits." James got up and opened a window, letting in the bright air.

"Ah," said Edward sourly. "A very rosy picture. But where are the lumbermen to come from? You are speaking of an unpopulated region. Or do you intend to teach Indians how to use the ax?"

"Some of our best axmen began life in a wigwam. But that is beside the point. White men are coming into the southern part of Michigan like spring geese heading north. The population is in spate. Have you not heard the expression 'Michigan Fever,' which denotes the rush? I am confident we can attract men to work in the woods. Many of the newcomers are Maine men—they smell the trees. We'll put out advertisements. Where there are trees such as we saw, men will come for them. But first we *must* procure the land and build our sawmills. James is returning to the Detroit land office immediately to buy up sections—if the Board agrees. The government cost is one hundred dollars for an eighty, eight hundred for a section."

"You say 'we' but James does not have authority to loose Duke and Sons' purse strings."

James spoke up. "Because Lennart and I feel immediate action is vital I have agreed to use my own money to secure the lands. I will then sell them to the company for an additional twenty-five cents an acre."

Edward, who as elder and Board president did hold the purse strings (Freegrace was nominally the treasurer), scribbled and said, "That is nine hundred sixty dollars a section. A tidy little profit for James."

"I think it fair as I have the ready funds and, if I am not mistaken, Duke and Sons do not. Is it not true that we would have to liquidate some of the New York and New England holdings in order to make large purchases?"

"Of course, but I cannot see what the all-fired hurry is about," snapped Edward.

When Freegrace made a disgreeable sound, Lennart, though he felt like shouting in the old men's faces, said in a calm pleasant voice, "Breitsprecher gave a conservative figure of twenty-five thousand board feet per acre. With lumber at four dollars a thousand the company would net one hundred dollars per acre or sixty-four thousand a section. Duke and Sons will take in sixty-four thousand dollars on each section, for which they will have paid only nine hundred and sixty dollars."

"I have never heard of such a high per acre yield," said Edward, drumming his fingers on the table. "It cannot be correct." He glared at the open window as though he would shut out the azure day.

"Breitsprecher took his tally and measurements over and over to be sure. It is unprecedented. Yet the trees are there. We saw them, touched them, walked through them for two and a half weeks. You cannot envision the vast extent of this monstrous fine pinery." Lennart spoke as though to dangerous idiots.

"The competition is no doubt rushing in."

"They have not yet begun rushing. We are the first," said Lennart, barely subduing the triumph in his voice. "It was a tiresome journey and not many would wish to undertake it."

"Then there is no reason for haste," said Edward.

"Remember Pennsylvania," said Cyrus, who had watched the company lose a rich chance.

The meeting lasted longer than any meeting in Duke & Sons' history and continued the next day as they wrangled over the advantages and difficulties of setting up a new headquarters in Detroit, the impossibility of running an expanded company with only family members sitting in Boston. The good weather held and it became a punishment to be shut up in meeting after meeting.

"We will certainly have to hire outsiders," said Freegrace. "Outsiders! Against Duke and Sons' policy."

"That is the case," said Lennart. "And we must start this hiring at once. We need more landlookers. There is too much forest for Breitsprecher and we must get all the experienced men we can. Other timbermen will soon smell the perfume of those Michigan pines. There will be a scramble."

"And more employees in the office here, and in Detroit to keep track of the land purchases, the maps, the subcontractors, our markets, the shifting tides of lumber prices, boats and transport—everything. Everything. We must build an office building and houses in Detroit as soon as ever we can."

"Let us not rush ahead so quickly," moaned Freegrace.

"James," said Lennart, who somehow during the course of the meeting had moved into a primary position to order the company's affairs, "how soon can you return to Detroit and commence buying up of the lands Breitsprecher surveyed on our exploratory journey?"

"Fairly soon. In ten days perhaps. I have some affairs to set in order and need to make arrangements for certificates of deposit and surety for the payments."

"I have nightmares of interlopers getting those lands before we do. It is urgent that we buy now. We can always buy on credit—that would hasten acquisition."

"Duke and Sons have never bought on credit," said Edward stiffly. "We pay cash and that is why our custom is favored. It is our signature."

"If we commence buying townships, with such large purchases we may need to proceed with buying on credit," said Lennart. "The day will come."

A week later James went west again. In Detroit he took rooms near the government land office. In three days of intense work with the clerk, a cold-syrup sort of man he thought, Duke & Sons owned all the timberlands Breitsprecher had surveyed on their exploratory trip, a hundred thousand acres. He bought three city lots and hired carpenters to begin putting up an office building and three houses. He returned to Boston to await the land patent certificates. Breitsprecher stayed in Michigan surveying, marking sections and whole townships.

"We should buy up the townships sight unseen," said Lennart. "We know the trees are there. It is not essential to send a landlooker to comb through every acre before purchase."

Edward and Freegrace recoiled. "What, take a flyer on getting worthless swampland or cliffs and sinkholes? Or nothing but grass or spindly trees?"

"It is not in the nature of these Michigan lands to deviate from pine. It would save a great deal of anxiety if we bought sight unseen straight from the land office map." Lennart's voice was hoarse with talking. But the two oldest Dukes flamed up with such passion, and Cyrus Hempstead unaccountably sided with them, that he dropped the idea.

• • •

In December, Breitsprecher returned. It was a cold day. He went up the cramped stairs of the old Duke building and into the board-room to make his report. As he heard the first figures Cyrus sucked in his breath. The board foot estimates were so enormous they could barely be grasped.

"It is all standing timber. I saw no sign of other landlookers but I did see a government surveyor and his chainman on the trail. He said there are many such surveyors at work in Michigan Territory now, those in the south doing section work, the men to the north in the timberlands roughing out townships. He said some of the early surveyors were far from expert and because of their inexperience Michigan has two base lines. I do not know how much Mr. James has procured of the timberland that we saw on our first journey. I have heard of connivance and foul play at the land offices, though I think the men in Detroit are reasonably honest."

Cyrus spoke up. "Mr. James Duke procured most, if not all, of those lands you examined earlier. And now we must acquire these you have just marked for us. We cannot move quickly enough. No reflection on your excellent work, Armenius, but we need more land-lookers. If you have any names to put forward this is the time to do it."

He had no ready names.

As they left the meeting room Lennart drew Cyrus aside and said, "We need you to help James make the purchases. There is another Michigan land office in Monroe, and I think it would be best to use it and allay possible competitors' suspicions that Duke and Sons are taking all of Michigan. We have liquidated some of the New England holdings now and there is money for this. I wish you to think how important it may be to buy on credit if we want to secure large hold-ings. The immediate investment is small compared to the future income. So far we have only begun. There are many millions of acres of pineland in Michigan, and perhaps contiguous areas to the west and south. You can take the coordinates Breitsprecher has just given us, go to Monroe and start buying. Come with me now and I will give you the bonds. Buy as fast as ever you can."

Armenius Breitsprecher left the overheated office, walked home enjoying the smell of a coming storm. At his small house Frau Stern welcomed him back with his favorite, a lemon posset. There was a great sack of accumulated mail on the kitchen floor. He swallowed the posset and four roast pigeons and slept for sixteen hours.

The next morning he got at the mail. The Christmas season was at hand and the homeland Breitsprechers flooded their relative with affectionate greetings and presents—cakes and *Blutwurst,* a small keg of best sauerkraut, tins of nuts and candied fruits, and his grandmother Fredda had written out a description of the geese that were to be roasted. The *Blutwurst* delighted him and before he opened the rest of the letters he sent Frau Stern for some good dark bread.

With the plate of sliced *Blutwurst* and bread and a thumb-size blob of Flower of Mustard beside him he read the letters one by one. The *Blutwurst* was gone, the bread gone and only a smear of mustard left by the time he reached the pages from his cousin Dieter Breitsprecher. Dieter had suffered in his childhood—both his parents on a holiday in the Jura had been caught in an unseasonable snowstorm and avalanche. The orphan was brought up by his severe maternal grandmother. Armenius could almost see Dieter before him, tall and with gooseberry eyes. He had studied privately with Heinrich von Cotta in Saxony and now was working as a forester on the estate of Graf Ernst-August von Rotstein. The estate's most distinguished feature, he wrote, was a large forest. Armenius moaned with envy at Dieter's description of his catalog of the forest's insects and how they affected the different species of trees, temperature diaries and rainfall measurements, boundary plantings, a coppice experiment. Yet Armenius had seen enough wild American forest to slightly dampen his enthusiasm for management. How could one possibly control the fantastic complexity of the New World forests?

Several days passed before he could begin to answer his cousin's letter and so filled with discontent were his paragraphs that he crumpled and threw down page after page. Hopeless, hopeless to try to describe the situation in North America, where people spurned the age-old craft of forestry, a craft he knew only partially from books, his father's lectures and his own observations. He had to get Dieter to come and see for himself the Michigan forest, a massive but innocent forest standing complete before the slaughter began. What discussions they would have! He scribbled rapidly and posted the result without rereading it.

An answer came in March. Dieter was making the journey. Armenius worked it out that his cousin was at that moment on the high seas and with fair weather would arrive within two weeks.

With his dog, Hans Carl von Carlowitz, beside him he stood on the wharf staring, as he had for the last half hour, at the docked *Hansa*. Passengers lined the rails, eager to get off. He looked for Dieter's head, which should be among the highest, but did not see him. Nor did he see him in the flood of passengers. He was startled when a hand closed on his shoulder and the familiar voice said, *"Wie geht's, Menius?"*

"Ach. You startled me. I was looking for you."

"Yes, I saw you staring. I tipped my hat. *Sehr kalt hier."*

"It is. *Amerikanischer Frühling. Komm, komm,* we'll be at my house very soon."

"You have your own house? And is this your *Hund?"* He patted Hans Carl's head.

"Ja, this is Hans Carl von Carlowitz, who goes everywhere with me, and as for the house, it was my parents' and I am not often in it as I spend most of my time in the forest making computations of board feet. As I mentioned in my letters."

"Ideal name. So the observant one is always at your side, *nicht wahr?"*

"*Ja, ja.* Always. And on cold nights— *Ach*, Dieter, I can't say how glad I am you have come, and with time enough for me to show you everything."

"I have always wanted to see the famous forests of North America, and the Graf, who is a second cousin, though reluctant to see me go, was generous with the time—because of your letter, which I showed him. 'See everything,' he said, 'and if you find good timber investments for me write at once.'"

"Ah, he is just like the Dukes. Just like the Americans."

"I think not," said Dieter, laughing, his pronounced Adam's apple rising and falling, his gooseberry eyes trying to see everything at once. "He suffered a great deal from the Peasants' Uprising a few years ago. They reject his control of the forest, the laws, they hate the managed plantations."

"As soon as you have rested from your voyage we will start for Michigan. But first I will introduce you to the Dukes and Lennart Vogel. We will go to the Duke office tomorrow morning."

"Dear cousin, while I get warm with some hot spirit and water you will tell me all about the Dukes, their plan to seize the forests of the earth, their fiendish little ways."

In half an hour the two cousins had finished Frau Stern's boiled pigs' feet and kraut and settled in front of the Franklin stove with their pipes and the port decanter to talk about the Dukes and forestry while the wind shrieked around the corner of the house.

Edward Duke did not take to Dieter Breitsprecher. Later he complained to Freegrace. "Why, he looks like Ichabod Crane, a great thin tall gawk. And how he stares!"

"Yes, but Armenius says he is a forester on a great estate in Germany. He manages a large forest. He might be useful to us."

"God's sake, how on earth does he 'manage' a forest?" snorted Edward. "Cut 'em down! That's forest managing. Tell Ichabod to take his managing back to Germany. No use to us."

• • •

James sat at the breakfast table with his plate of toast and the honey jar. He smiled when Lavinia came in. She had changed from a child with a sullen expression to a young woman whose greatest charm was the bloom of youth. Her mustard-colored wool dress caught the stream of sunlight as she passed the window.

"My dear Lavinia," he said. "How very well you look. Well kempt and soigné. Will you join me at breakfast this morning and tell me all your secrets?"

"I have no secrets," said Lavinia, turning scarlet, tears suddenly brimming over and running down her cheeks.

"Good lord, girl, I do not mean to pry. I only wanted to be agreeable. I have seen so little of you since I came back and I cherish each hour in your company."

But Lavinia was weeping loudly into her napkin. It seemed a long time until she stopped and James felt it was rude for him to attack his toast while his daughter wept. So he waited.

"Papa," she said, mopping the tears. "I do have—" She wept again.

"For God's sake, child, what is it? Tell me. And here, have a piece of toast." He buttered a now-cold slice and dabbed on honey, handed it dripping to Lavinia. She took it and held it at arm's length as though it were a poison snake, then put it on the edge of his plate.

"It drips honey," she said and unaccountably began to laugh at James with his tower of cold toast when the whole world knew he liked it hot and crunchy.

"Yes, that is a known property of honey—it drips. Would you care for toast without honey?"

"Yes." She took the toast, put it on a plate, went to the sideboard and slid a poached egg onto the toast, brought the plate back to the table and began to cut up her breakfast. James observed that the egg also dripped, perhaps more fluidly than honey. They sat in companionable understanding while they ate.

"Papa," said Lavinia. "I do have a secret."

477

"Yes, I thought you might. We all have 'em. What's yours?"

"I think I might shock you."

"Oh try, dear girl, do try. It has been years since I was shocked and I am keen to know the sensation again."

"You are too silly." She was a trifle fat, with dimpled hands and a plump chin.

"Not in the least. Silliness finished. I am your adoring papa and wish to know if there is any wish, no matter how picayune, I might grant you. You have only to speak."

"Very well. It is this: I do not want to be 'finished.' Nor do I want to 'come out' nor catch a beau nor marry." She took a breath. "I want to learn the timber trade."

His hand lurched and coffee spilled. If she had said she wished to learn how to slaughter pigs she could not have startled him more.

"But my dear girl, there simply are no women in the timber trade. It is a man's affair from ax to beeswax. If you were a boy we might place you in one of the lumber camps for a season so you could know the work, but I can't imagine what role a girl—a woman—could have in the timber trade. I just cannot! Have you considered what you might do as a 'timberwoman'?" He smiled at the preposterous image the word raised. She did not return the smile but scowled.

"Mother helped *her* father in his timber business. She learned a great deal and was considerable use in all those affairs. She said she even helped *you* when you came from commanding ships. Papa, I know I would be good at it. I am very good with mathematics. I could work out problems with board feet and measurements. I am good at compiling papers and sorting them into categories. I am interested in finance, in banks and loans, in credit and assets, in prices and factors that change them. I know I could do something of value. And I will not get married. Mama is harping on marriage day and night and I shall run away rather than marry. I am quite, quite serious about this. I think of nothing else. Why cannot I do something in the office of Duke and Sons? I know you have clerks—I could be a clerk. I would learn much that way. You say the company is going to open new

478

offices in Detroit. I will be a part of this. I will!" Now she resembled Posey, eyes flashing dangerously, bosom heaving.

For a very brief second James considered how a lumber buyer might respond to such a display. Ye gods, he thought, ye gods, what can I do, what say? He ate the last piece of toast, very poor toast now, cold and somewhat sodden from spilled coffee.

"Lavinia. Give me several days to think about your surprising request. I will seriously consider how something might be arranged."

The chance came sooner than he imagined. Lennart stopped by one May morning and begged James to go with him to the offices. "We have several applicants for clerical positions in Detroit and even two landlookers from New Hampshire. One of them has been as far west as Ohio. Clerks are another matter. Most of them are barely able to read, and as for ciphering—you might whistle."

"I have a rather unusual applicant for a clerk," said James. "Let me find my hat and I will tell you on the way."

Armenius thought his cousin Dieter Breitsprecher was, aside from Hans Carl von Carlowitz, the best traveling companion he had ever known. Their large knapsacks were packed, they were ready for the wild forests. Armenius brought tobacco, not Cuban cigars but dark and tarry twists. Dieter carried his heavy .60 caliber *jaeger* rifle, and Armenius a new .50 caliber plains rifle with a beaver tail cheek piece—Dieter slavered over this gun and before they left he ordered one from the Missouri gunsmith.

"It will be my memento of this journey," he said.

"You will have other mementos."

The journey, familiar to Armenius, was full of shocks and wonders for Dieter. The Erie Canal boat was insufferably tiresome at four miles an hour. On fine days they ran along the towpath, sometimes ranging out to see the countryside. They had time for talk.

"The thing is," said Armenius, "there is here a complete lack of knowledge of forest management. Americans do not understand shelter belts, they have never heard of thinning trees nor pruning them, they cannot believe that soil has anything to do with forests, nor water. Hedgerows? What an idea! They do not believe in hedgerows. Nor coppices. The most elemental precepts of forestry are as Chinese."

"Surely they have some sense of soil erosion, so painfully obvious when it appears?"

"Not at all. They accept it as the natural order of the world. And although they choke in the fumes of the city they do not make a connection with the purer air in the forest. 'Why is the air clean and fresh near the forest but not in the city?' one can ask. The answer is 'Because God made it thus.' So extensive are the forests here that Americans cannot see an end to them. Therefore, they have no interest in preserving them."

"Do not your employers see the economic advantages of maintained forests? Is there no reforestation at all?"

"None. They do not even leave seed trees in their vast cutover lands. One hard rain or a deep snow comes and the soil begins to run downhill like molten gold. If I say anything to the Dukes about commonsense ways to protect and repair their cut forestlands for the future they look at me as if I were mad. Well, perhaps I am mad. I hate aiding them in their quest to destroy every forest in North America."

"This is quite sad. What are the most pressing uses here for cut timber? Houses, I suppose."

"Railroad ties. I think that the railroads should manage private forests where they might grow trees for ties. But it is not done. They take down wild forests and transport the timber at high cost. Charcoal furnaces for smelting use uncountable numbers of trees. Moreover, every household consumes almost one hundred cords of wood during the long cold winters. The fireplaces here are large enough to roast an entire ox. But stoves are making an advance. And speaking of fires! *Mein Gott,* the forests are constantly on fire, but not controlled fire—the settlers set vast acreages ablaze to clear the way for farms and houses. Then, disappointed that the soil is poor, they move on west, always west, and do the same elsewhere. Not one in a hundred American farmers can tell you the characteristics of soils. The Indians were better managers of the forest than these settlers. They were very good observers of water, weather, all animals and growing things. And they forbore to cut lavishly. They used many parts of many trees for different tools and medicines, not unlike the old German peasantry."

"I wonder you do not return to Germany," said Dieter.

"Dieter, through no doing of my own I was born in this country. It is a population where each settler vies to be more of a *Nichtswisser* than his neighbor—learning is considered shameful—but I am used to it. It would be difficult to change. Besides, Germany now is not the Germany I have in my mind."

"I wonder," said Dieter.

"I want to see what happens next. Always this is my interest."

In Detroit they spent a day walking about, passed a small plank-sided building with a sign that read GENERAL LAND OFFICE MICHIGAN.

"Let us go in," said Dieter. "I want to see what sort of man the recorder is."

He was tall and pale from lack of sunlight, his eyes colorless and expressionless. He greeted them with a jerk of a smile. "What can I do for you? Land purchase today? A few town lots?" He stared at Armenius.

"No, not today. In a few weeks, perhaps. We are just getting our bearings," he said.

"I think I have seen you here before," said the man, "in the company of Mr. James Duke?"

"It is possible."

"Yes, I believe he said you were his landlooker."

"I was," said Armenius.

"And you are no longer?" asked the man almost happily.

"No, I am yet, but I am on leave of absence just now. This is my cousin Dieter Breitsprecher, who is visiting. He is a forester from Germany. We are going to look at the timberland."

"Right," said the man. "This is the place for timber, yes it is." There was a silence and the man, now gazing out the window, said almost dreamily that one of the federal surveyors and his chainman had stopped in the day before. "Dozens of surveyors measuring Michigan these days. And some like you coming to get hold of timberland."

"Where are those surveyors working now?"

"Marking out townships. Northwest of where Mr. Duke purchased. They said the prospects for a timberman are even richer up north. I think to myself that I might buy a forty, could I ever have the money. Clerks make very little, you know, though the employment is steady."

"May your wish be granted," said Armenius, smiling like the famous cat who caught the mouse. He spoke kindly to this man remembering that James Duke had treated him as a servant, saying "Come, fellow, we haven't all day," and ordering him to copy the papers out in a fair hand "instead of black claw marks as an ink-foot crow might make."

"Are they surveying along the shore?" asked Dieter, looking at the map on the counter. The man nodded. "Along the shore, inland, along the rivers, almost to Mackinac—a huge amount of territory— all pinelands." Armenius would have asked more questions but a man came to complain about the old French long lots in Detroit. "Like damn noodles," he said. "Long, long skinny noodles. I want my money back."

"Many thanks," said Armenius to the clerk. "We may come back tomorrow and speak a little with you."

"I look forward to that."

They left and returned to their boardinghouse. "I could not follow all that was said," said Dieter. "What is a 'forty'? Is he giving us important information about the surveying?"

"A 'forty' is a quarter of a quarter section—forty acres. And he was certainly giving us important information—and, I believe, asking for a bribe. We might modify our trip a little. I would like to see that northern region."

"I would also like to see it. Perhaps you will not always be a land-looker for Duke and Sons. Let us find some dinner in this rough place. And talk with the clerk again tomorrow, then set out to find those wondrous pines."

A day later they started their journey on two hired horses, one the yellow horse from Armenius's former trip. "At the junction we will bypass the trail to the Duke purchases and go north. Cousin, I mention that we will pass a stump farm that belongs to an incompetent farmer, Anton Heinrich. He has worn out two farms already and is quickly ruining the third. He has a quite pretty daughter. You have heard all the old stories about farmers' daughters? Yes, they are true. I lay with this girl but it was rather—I can't say. Maybe we stop there again."

So Dieter discovered an unknown side of his cousin. Nor had he suspected he could speak so casually of bribes, for the clerk had made it clear when they returned the next day that information about the pines farther north should be rewarded. Armenius told him that if they found heavy timber to be there they would certainly stop in on their return and make an arrangement. His cousin had become an American.

The Heinrich log house came in sight. Moony, one of the dumm-kopf sons, was splitting stove wood, Kelmar, the other, stacking it on the listing porch. As they came nearer Moony slammed his ax into the chopping block and ran inside, calling, "Ma! Ma!" A woman with two small children clutching her skirts came out. Dieter thought she looked like a barn cat. She had been at her washtub and her hands were like wet roots.

"Hullo, Mistress Kristina," said Armenius cheerfully. "Is Anton at home today?"

The woman gave a howl, threw her apron up over her face and lurched inside. Armenius and Dieter looked at each other. Moony edged closer and stood clenching and unclenching his hands.

"What is wrong? Where is your father? Anton. Is he here?" Armenius saw the daughter holding the hands of two more children. He stepped toward her and she stepped back.

Moony opened his mouth to speak, as though he had something to tell but didn't know how to go about it. Armenius looked at Kelmar.

"*Was ist los?* Tell me!" He remembered the two fools had a few words of English, a few words of *Deutsch*.

"*Vater—*" said Kelmar forcefully. And again, "*Vater.*"

"*Ja?*" encouraged Armenius.

"*Kaput,*" said Moony.

It was the girl who, keeping at a distance, told them a bizarre story. She looked only at Dieter and spoke to him in a low voice. If Armenius made a step in her direction she moved back. She said the father had been chopping trees with Moony and Kelmar. Father was not so quick. A big tree had fallen and pinned him to the ground. He cried for help. Moony and Kelmar came to him. They were strong. They seized the butt end of the tree and began to pull. They dragged the entire tree across Vater's body as he shrieked. At this point Moony, who had been listening and grinning, gave an imitation of Vater's agonizing cries.

"And where is he now?" asked Armenius.

"He did not live. That tree's branches tore his belly and his inside came outside when they pulled."

"*Kaput,*" said Moony.

"Fucked," said Kelmar in clear English.

"Let us get away from this place," said Dieter sotto voce. He did not like Moony and Kelmar and it was clear the girl was avoiding Armenius. The whole family seemed deranged. The thought came to him that his cousin might be something of a scoundrel. So?

• • •

They said nothing until dark fell and Armenius had a fire going.

He said, "I have never heard anything as stupid as that. Never. They could have trimmed the limbs and lifted it off him. They could have chopped away the crown and butt to small size. One could have pried it up while the other pulled the man out. They could have rigged a hoist."

Dieter murmured, "Sometimes one must get tired of chopping trees endlessly."

For the next ten days they walked through the great pines and Dieter became very quiet. Occasionally he scraped away the needles and examined the soil beneath the duff.

"You see?" said Armenius as they stood tiny and amazed in the kingdom of the pines.

"I do," said Dieter as though pledging a marriage vow.

A decanter of brandy stood on a side table in Edward Duke's mahogany office. Edward was turning the pages of a thick sheaf of survey pages and locating them on a crisp, new-drawn map of Saginaw Bay's shoreline with the Duke & Sons sections neatly crosshatched in sepia ink. He had come to believe the exploration and discovery had all come about at his urging.

"Hullo, Cyrus. Ready for the great move?" Cyrus would head up the new offices in Detroit. A wagonload of desks and chairs, boxes of papers, ink bottles, pens and other office impedimenta had headed west two weeks before, three fresh-hired clerks to oversee the journey and unpacking. A fourth clerk, Lavinia Duke, would remain at the Boston office and work for Edward, Freegrace and James for a year arranging markets for their Michigan lumber. Edward had not been scandalized—Lavinia was blood kin. She was cleverer than any clerk Edward remembered. She brought order to chaos.

"I have something you need to see," said Cyrus. He unfurled another map, laid it over Edward's desk and handed him a new wad of survey information.

Edward stared at it without seeing anything remarkable.

"What is this supposed to be?" he said. "It looks like land parcels farther north—has James been enlarging the scope of the purchases? I do not feel we are ready to do this. We are quite overextended and need to see income before any more goes out—" He had finally noticed a name on the top survey page.

"What is this? Graf Ernst-August von Rotstein? A competitor?"

"Indeed. Look more closely."

Edward peered. The purchaser of these northern timber lots was the RBB Timber Company. "Who are they? Maine men? How did they learn about this?"

"RBB stands for Rotstein, Breitsprecher and Breitsprecher. Our old landlooker has become our formidable competitor. You may remember his cousin, the manager of an estate forest in Prussia?"

"Ichabod Crane. I remember him perfectly. Dreadful fellow."

"The dreadful fellow is related to Graf Ernst-August von Rotstein. He is enormously wealthy and already their holdings almost equal ours."

"I knew it! I knew it! I never trusted Breitsprecher. The snake, the damnable cursèd python."

"It is too bad Lennart chose this time to be away. But I will go to James's house and let him know." Lavinia, behind the door, heard it all and ran home, getting to James before Cyrus arrived.

"Papa! Treachery!" she shouted. "Breitsprecher and his cousin and a rich man have bought a quarter million acres of Michigan pine. They are now our enemies." And so a rivalry began.

56

Lavinia

Edward, fat ancient Edward, who had become a great gourmand in the years since his wife Lydia's death, called for a dinner party to celebrate the rich returns of the first Michigan cut.

"Everyone must come, though of course Cyrus and James cannot, for they are in Detroit. We'll have those hearty lobsters, though how they shall be prepared I will leave to the chef, thrushes *à la Liègeoise,* and one of the black turkeys from Newport sweetened on acorns, *la surprise* and then an English *rosbif* with Russian salad. And whatever else the chef wishes to give us. The wines I will discuss with Freegrace." He laughed his old man's reedy *heyheyhey* as Lavinia wrote out the invitations. It was a Duke & Sons business affair, and without a doubt the company could afford to scrape the Boston Market stalls empty, stalls always heaped with the bounteous harvests of market hunters at pennies for a brace—pigeons, turkeys, wood thrushes and robins, pipits, countless ducks, swans and geese, even owls, reputed to taste like chicken.

Lavinia begged off attendance. The thrushes were sure to be robins and she could not bear to see them lying roasted on a platter. "You know, Uncle Edward, that I cannot be in a house where cats live. My eyes swell and burn, I can barely breathe. And I get dizzy. It has been so since I was a child and Mama allowed no cats in our house for which I thank her."

"Oh pish," said Edward. "Mrs. Trame will put them out in the garden and you will not be troubled." It was useless to explain to him that cats did not need to be present; a house with cats was permeated with the invisible poison residue of their breath, their hairs. "Do you not remember the last time I tried to dine at your house? How I fell ill and had to be carried home?" It was an unpleasant memory, the gripping choke in her chest, the painful wheeze.

But Edward said stiffly, "I regret you do not show the same regard for cats that you exhibit for birds."

The conflagration spared four—two cats; the household cook, Mrs. Trame; and Chef Laliberte, who had been hired for the dinner. The scullions escaped early by chance and were sitting in the garden over a wooden platter of orts. In the half-cleaned kitchen, enjoying the leftover birds and a glass of steely hock with Chef Laliberte, Mrs. Trame heard a roaring in the adjacent dining room. She got up and opened the door. A sheet of flame leapt out, scorching her from hem to cap. The chef, no stranger to fire, seized her by the arm and rushed her outside, where they joined the servants. The opening of the kitchen door allowed a blast of oxygen to surge through the house and they could hear the shrieks upstairs, where the dinner party had retired with the port and walnuts. A figure appeared in the upstairs window briefly—Mrs. Trame thought it was Lennart Vogel—then fell back into the rosy light.

Afterward, when her injured throat allowed her to speak, she whispered she had twice chased the cats off the vacated dining room table that evening. She intended to clear it after she and Chef Laliberte had their own dinner and a restorative glass. She surmised the cats had knocked over the candle on the sideboard. They often romped on the furniture.

"When Mrs. Duke was alive the cats were not permitted in the dining room," she said and wept. "But after she passed on Mr. Duke doted so on Casimir and Vaughn that he allowed anything, even letting them sleep on his bed though it be well known that cats will suck your breath at night."

●　●　●

James Duke and Cyrus Hempstead left for Boston as soon as word of the fatal dinner party reached them. Edward and Freegrace had been very old, both into their nineties, but Posey and Lennart had been still in strong life.

James, speaking slowly so as not to jostle his headache, found Lavinia in Posey's room sorting out her clothes, packing them into a great wicker hamper.

"Papa! I am so glad you have come," said Lavinia. "It has been dreadful, just dreadful. People call at all hours to express their regrets. Many think you were in the fire as well as Mama. I have had to repeat endlessly that you were away. I don't know what I would have done without Mrs. Trame."

"Poor, poor child. What a trial. And tell me what you intend with that clothing. Is any of use to you?" He doubted this as Posey had been stout and busty. His head pounded.

"The church ladies will send someone for the garments. They are to be distributed to the needy. I will keep Mama's jewelry and winter cloaks." James thought that very few needy women would feel comfortable in Posey's silks, but what did he know? It might be a tonic for them. His hand fell on a kingfisher-blue dressing gown Posey had often worn. Marabou feathers, fur muffs, satin slippers with tiny glass beads on the toes . . . he could imagine some slattern stuffing her horny feet into them.

"I saved out the crimson ball gown that she loved so well—for her funeral dress." James shuddered inwardly at the thought of his wife's charred corpse in red satin, but dredged up a painful smile for Lavinia. "You have a strength of character far beyond your years, and I salute you." He needed to lie down with a cold compress on his forehead later.

James breathed in and out gently, straightened up. "Come, dear daughter, let us go down to the library and make a list of what must be done. We will have our plate of toast and decide on the future. We must work together, you and I, to make a life."

He staggered a little with the force of the tightening vise.

"Papa, are you all right?"

"Yes, yes, it's just one of my headaches—my grandmother Mercy was prone to headaches."

"Shall I send for Dr. Cunningham?"

"No. I shall be well after a good night's sleep." How he longed for that deep draft of laudanum.

But as they entered the library Lavinia said, "Papa, I think Mama's clothes are too fine to give to the poor. I have an idea I might sell them. Do I have your permission to try?"

"Sell them to whom? I agree that they are of too high quality to just give to those who will not appreciate their value. But who would buy them? I hope you do not think of approaching her friends on this?" He heard his voice meanly snappish.

"No. I think I may go to her dressmakers, Madame Aiglet in New York and Mrs. Brawn in Boston. Both know her wardrobe—indeed, many of the dresses originated with one or the other—and they have a select list of customers, some of whom may appreciate and purchase these beautiful garments. Mama kept them clean, protected from moths in the cedar closet, safe in drawers and chests away from the destroying sunlight. They are like new."

James, impressed by both his daughter's business acumen and her cool and unsentimental regard for the wardrobe, said she had his approval. He would have approved if she had said she wanted to boil cabbages. He wanted only to lie down.

"I'll go to New York in a few days and speak with Madame Aiglet."

"Dear Lavinia," said the dressmaker, a tall woman with coiled black hair, her square face very heavily powdered, "I am sorry for your loss." She allowed ten or twelve seconds for grieving. "Your mother dressed very well in the most fashionable garments and although this is a somewhat provocative situation I think I can place a number of the dresses. One of my clients, married to a rising politician and of Mrs. Duke's size—perhaps an inch shorter—has many evening dinner demands. She is ever asking for dresses 'a *leetle* less expensive'—and of course I never have such a thing. It takes time to construct an elaborate dress. This situation may answer the purpose very well. Now, let me ask, what of her furs and capes? She had an exquisite yellow satin evening cape with glass bugles at the hem. Very desirable."

Mrs. Brawn in Boston was even more eager to have the finery, the hats and gloves, boas, even the silk undergarments from Paris and the least worn of the shoes.

Some weeks later at the breakfast table James read his paper while Lavinia opened her letters. "Papa! Here is a bit of cheer which I badly need. It is from Mrs. Brawn. We have cleared two thousand dollars on Mama's dresses. Should we invest it in Michigan pinelands? It will gain us a few more sections."

For the hundredth time James thought that his daughter had an unusually canny eye for business. She was—always had been—a go-ahead type. If she had been a man she would have been in the thick of every business fray, following the go-ahead method, accelerating, progressive! He remembered her childhood horse. Posey gave her a small amount of pocket money each week, but she had to "earn" it by taking instruction in sewing, cookery, music (piano); she had to make her own bed and run errands for Posey.

"But the cook's boy can do that, and the housekeeper can make the bed," said spoiled Lavinia.

"Yes, but I want *you* to do it. If you know from experience what others must do to earn a living you will be a better person with deeper knowledge of others. I have no use for the weak and helpless woman. You may need independence in your life, for women are too often taken advantage of—no one knows this better than I." But when Lavinia pressed her for those details she said, "Never mind, you need not know. It is only that I do not want you to be helpless if your expectations are dashed. You will thank me someday."

One August morning that summer young Lavinia had come to the breakfast table with a bulging red purse. She opened it and poured out twenty-seven dollars in coins. "I have saved this money from Mama's weekly gifts and my birthday gift. I wish to buy a horse."

James's eyes had flooded with tears of pride. He had looked at Posey and shaken his head in wonderment. "Dear child, I will take you to the horse fair this coming Friday that you may see what manner of horse goes for twenty-seven dollars."

The Friday horse fair was not crowded at the early hour James and Lavinia arrived. They walked around, examining horses, James naming good features and warning Lavinia not to choose solely by the color of the coat or a bright eye.

"We look for a strong short back, a nice muscled croup, straight legs, oh, a hundred little things. And the teeth. It takes some years to know a good horse—it's like learning the ropes on a ship. And I warn you now that for your twenty-seven dollars you will not be able to afford a Thoroughbred."

James suggested two animals, a gray Tennessee Walker with white on its face and a handsome black three-year-old Morgan mare. Lavinia loved both of them and could not decide. The owner of the Walker wanted fifty dollars firm; the owner of the Morgan, Mr. Robinson, an elderly farmer with silvery whiskers and red-apple cheeks, asked thirty-five, but he winked at Lavinia and they went over to the fence together to bargain, for James was determined not to step in.

Lavinia rushed back, seized his hand. "Papa, she was born in Vermont. They call her Blackie, but I will call her Black Robin. We have an agreement—if we can go straight back home now and get Greengage, my parakeet, and his cage and dishes, Mr. Robinson will take him in addition to the twenty-seven dollars." James could tell she put a high value on the man's name—the son of a robin could only be a good man, and, allied to birds by his name he would be kind to Greengage, the most valuable parakeet in New England. Silently he thanked Posey for Lavinia's character. And now that Posey was dead and all her faults forgotten he thanked the lucky day he fell into Boston harbor. But all he said as Lavinia mounted her new mare was "I doubt Greengage will enjoy the Vermont winters."

"Mr. Robinson said he will live in the kitchen near the stove and Mrs. Robinson will knit him a wool vest and leggins if it's a terrible cold winter."

Several weeks after the mass funeral a letter of condolence reached them in Boston from Armenius Breitsprecher with the postscript that if James and Cyrus needed aid he and Dieter would be pleased to help in any way. Lavinia was inclined to think it presumptuous, but James took it in good heart and said Duke & Sons were in no position to offend other timber companies. "We cannot tell what the future will bring. In fact, other timbermen are beginning to buy parcels of Michigan pinelands. Many of them are from Maine. Now, Lavinia, I think it is finally time to shift all our operations west," he said, dipping a crust in his cocoa.

"Is there any decent society in Detroit? Or is it still a captive of the wilderness?"

"Oh, Detroit is very well, it is not Boston but it has a growing population and is convenient for our current business. We have a good solid establishment there and the lakes provide transport, though they are difficult and dangerous waters, quite as perilous as the oceans, yet not saline—one drowns more quickly they say. But as for society—there is not much of that. It is, as you say, yet a captive of the wilderness."

"Papa, have we a great deal of money?"

"The truth is that indeed we do have a great deal of money despite the timberland purchases of recent years. Why do you ask? Is there some great expense you contemplate?"

"Yes. I would wish for this house"—she waved her arm over her head in a compassing sweep—"to be replicated in Detroit to the last roof slate. Perhaps it would be the first mansion in Detroit. Would it not be soothingly familiar if we had our old rooms? I can make lists of the linens and Mrs. Trame may enumerate the kitchen goods, the plates and silver. We can order those."

James felt a frisson of fear—it would take many thousands to replicate Sedley's Boston house. But he could afford the expense, and what better way to use the money now coming in from the Michigan pines? And there were the legacies from Edward and Freegrace, even from Lennart. He did not hesitate. "Yes. We can do this. I will contact an architect. We might even have a few embellishments added, as bathing tubs. Bigger stables and new equipages. A chapel dedicated to your mother. But I put my foot down on one thing—that monstrous mahogany hall stand will not come to Detroit."

"We must have something where people can hang their hats and put their umbrellas."

"We will get another, something elegant and simple rather than carved elks and hunting horns." For a week they talked of this new house. Mrs. Trame entered the sport with an eager list of improvements—a bigger pantry, a butler's room for cleaning silver, a larger staff that included two housemaids, a wine decanting room with a private staircase to the cellar, piped-in water instead of a kitchen cistern.

But old Will Thing would have none of it. "No Detroit for me. I was born in Boston, I will stay in Boston. I worked all my life for your father and you right in this stable and here I will stay."

"But as soon as may be we intend to sell it all," said James. "You would have a new family in residence. Suppose you do not like them?"

"It is not my place to like or dislike, I shall get along," said the old fellow and there the conversation ended. James was disappointed and still hoped to prevail. Perhaps Will did not realize the horses were going to Detroit.

Planning the new house became a postprandial exercise for Lavinia. After dinner a stack of paper, sharp pencils and samples of wallpaper littered the mahogany. James had years before chosen a hilltop site in Detroit with a sweeping view south to Lake Saint Clair, that extra lake too small to be Great. He made a sketch for his daughter, outlining the back and sides of the lot as an encircling arm of forest opened to frame the bluest lake and distant smudgy Ontario.

"This house will eclipse Black Swan," said Lavinia.

"Oh, we will have no black swans," said James. "In any case let us leave the water feature to the landscape designer, whom we must still discover. We might send to England, where these fellows abound. This country is too young to have acquired such glossy professions. It will take several years to construct this house as we wish, so we must put up with something simpler now. The company houses I had built two years past will do." He felt his headache creeping in, a tiny pain in his neck that would, he knew, grow into a throbbing agony. He resolved to find another doctor who might help him.

But if this was the amusement of evenings, for Lavinia the daytimes were packed with study and reading of newspapers and government bulletins that came in the mail coach, writing letters and quizzing visitors for news of new inventions and technical advances. Most of the news concerned the exploratory claims of various would-be railroad promoters; short local lines were springing up all over the eastern cities like weeds after rain and there was no doubt that a transcontinental railroad would be built sooner or later but the fights over the central-northern route or the southern route were ferocious. Both James and Lavinia were in favor of a northern route. "It will be another twenty years before they lay the first rail," said James. His thoughts were on another invention. "Have you read anything of the telegraph experiments? No? They say the electric telegraph will allow people to send messages over great distances as long as there is a copper wire to carry the impulses. Imagine. If the process comes to pass and if the wire comes to Detroit I can send an immediate message to someone in Boston, a message that can be read within minutes. But so far it is only on trial in England."

Lavinia was charmed by the idea of words traveling along coppery wires like ducks swimming across a river inlet. It seemed close to a fictional tale. James lit his cigar and puffed, immediately put it out as it urged the headache to reappear, then said, "What do you think of a rotunda with a stained-glass ceiling for the entrance?" But his heart wasn't in rotunda discussions. A new doctor, a neurologist, was coming at eight with a curative contraption.

James, wearing Putnam's Head Electrode on his cranium and hoping static electricity would finally overcome his headaches, was overwhelmed with work; the design of the new house caught only fitfully at his imagination. With the loss of Lennart the work of handling jobbers, the new-hired landlookers and scalers, their lumber volume reports, the lumber camps and their expected yield, the actual yield, their sawmills and the requests for new equipment as well as technological developments in milling, commissioning shipyards to build lumber barges to deliver the milled lumber to brokers in Albany all fell on him. Nor could Cyrus do Lennart's work as he was busy with the complex order department. He personally knew every naval buyer, every lumber dealer. No, Cyrus could not take on Lennart's work and no one could replace that head full of company history and lumber knowledge. But someone could try.

"Lavinia," he called, "will you come here a moment?" He explained that someone had to handle the details of the current production work. They could hire an outsider, and likely would in time, but immediate attention was vital. If she could temporarily take on some of Lennart's work—well, not the exploration, but the day-today affairs. He knew it would be very difficult for her—she was only a woman and there would be resistance to her from every logging contractor. Duke & Sons had two jobbers at work in Michigan now, both more than a day's ride from Detroit. Five more applying for winter work had to be interviewed. Lennart had been able to saunter into a camp, eat pork and beans, josh with the men, discover how the cut was going. But James would not ask Lavinia to go to the individual camps. Instead he would request the jobbers to come to Detroit and make a report to her.

"Why should I not go?" she said.

"Because you are a girl—a woman. It isn't done. It is impossible."

"Papa, it is not impossible. It is not customary, perhaps, but I will make it so. I insist. If I do not know the jobbers and see how the camps operate there is no way I can judge their worth—or the cut. You and Lennart told me I am doing well learning the business. This is a necessary step. If I could I would hire on to cut trees, the better to know the work. I will visit the camps starting as soon as we can get ourselves removed to Detroit."

"Lavinia, this is only temporary. I am searching for a permanent replacement for Lennart."

It was time to go. Sixteen wagons of household goods and linens had been crated and shipped. Lavinia leaned far out of the coach looking at her childhood home. I go into a new life, she thought. I will succeed.

In Detroit, Cyrus and his wife, Clara, welcomed them with a heavy pork and potatoes family dinner. Clara's pride was the elaborate dining room chandelier with a thousand crystal prisms. James ate little. He had come down with intermittent fever on the journey and after the roast pork dinner took to his bed for five days. Clara and Lavinia instinctively disliked each other. Clara, from an important Boston family—Judge Spottiswood was her father—was the Ideal Woman with a simpering way, averted gaze and subservient fealty to Cyrus,

who sprawled about in a lordly manner. She was known for her collection of silk scarves and shawls. The children were automatons,
chirping "yes, Mama," "yes, Papa," curtsying and very quiet. After
dinner the company had to go to the music room and endure an
hour on narrow chairs while Clara played the parlor organ and entertained them with mournful songs of lost dear ones.

Duke & Sons' three company houses in Detroit were a great step
down from the Black Swan estate. Cyrus and his family had the center house with two wind-whipped rosebushes in the front yard: they
called it Rose Cottage. James, with a manservant and cook, settled in
the one to the east. Lavinia had the west house, which she thought
extremely rustic, but the rooms on the second floor had a view of the
lake and its marine traffic. "I shall learn every ship," she said. "I shall
get a spyglass and study them."

On the ground floor there were servants' rooms, kitchen, dining room and parlor. The Boston house maid, Ruby Smythe, rather
sniffy about the situation, had one room and Mrs. Trame settled
into the other and her new kitchen with a bare minimum of cookery
equipment. She had no complaints with the great cast-iron stove, its
hot water reservoir and the brimming woodbox filled every morning
by Robert Kneebone, an all-purpose Duke employee. The plan was
to live very simply for several years until the new mansion was ready.
It was only the promise of the great new house that kept the snobbish
maid in service. James had found a New York architect, Lyford L.
Lundy, who studied Black Swan until he knew every feature to be
replicated in the Detroit house. He had ideas for improvements and
set them out in letters that arrived daily and irked James.

"We must get the business established here," said James, "and let
Mr. Lundy and his assistants deal with the new house. I have given
him all the suggestions we discussed, which he is to work into the
design. Let him do it. He has carte blanche with the money and as
much fine Michigan pine from our Arrow Mill as he can use." As

soon as he thought of the mill James decided a tour would instruct Lavinia.

"Tomorrow I'll take you to our sawmills. You must understand every part of the business, and the mills are at the heart of it. Arrow Mill, the closest, is not as I would wish—we have ordered new saws and equipment."

To Lavinia the mill seemed a wandering, ramshackle affair spread over acres of yard with narrow passages between stacks of drying lumber. The mill was on a good stream and the dammed pond produced enough power to run an overshot wheel and two heavy up-and-down saws in the same frame. But the place was silent when they arrived, and a boy came out and said his father was picking up a replacement saw from a shipper near the wharf. "The old one bust out most the teeth."

"Then let us go on and look at the other mill," said James. The Push Mill, called after its foreman, Joe Bouchard, sawyer and mill-wright, better known as Joe Push, lay a mile upstream. When Lavinia stepped through the doorway into the roar Push shut off the saws—a single muley saw and a two-blade gang. He came bustling up to James, looking at Lavinia from the corner of his eye. "Mr. Duke, I never know you was comin."

"That's how it is, Joe—surprises now and then. I'm taking my daughter around to see the parts of our operation. Go ahead, turn 'em back on—she wants to become acquainted with milling. She has a position in the company."

The millman threw the lever and with a wet clatter water dumped onto the wheel outside and the muley saw began to gnaw slowly through the log with a steely nasal sound. A rain of sawdust fell below, the air thickened with the smell of pine, earth and hot metal. Lavinia saw how the log carriage was pulled forward by a cable and at the end of the log another small wheel gigged the carriage back. Two edger men put the fresh-cut boards on top of the log, Joe Push reset for the next cut and the saws began to bite again, removing the bark edges from the passenger planks. Men carried them outside to a stack. The pondman sent another log up the ramp.

"Slow, but she gets it done," Joe Push said, pointing to the great ziggurats of boards outside, temples of wood boards. They walked about in the noise and dust, watching the men in the millpond harry the logs to the bottom of the ramp. In the yard a dozen men were buck-sawing small and crooked logs into firewood chunks, stacking them in drying sheds.

"A nice bit of extra income from waste wood," said James. He pointed at a mountainous stack, said, "Lavinia, note the bottom front crosspiece. It ensures the pile slopes and allows rain and snow to run off. There's an art to building a proper pile."

"How long does it dry?"

The stacker spoke up. "For this here pine? Say a year for your one-inch boards, better two-three years or more for thick stuff."

"Yes," said James, "of course we want to get it onto the market as soon as we can, so drying sheds such as the men here are using for firewood are helpful to get your market lumber ready sooner rather than later. One of our problems with drying lumber on site is that when the cut is finished and the men move to another area the mill is usually dismantled and transported as well. Lumber thieves come and help themselves to untended drying stacks so we usually hire one of the shanty boys, an injured or older man not as strong as he was, to stay behind until we move the lumber ourselves."

The stacker grunted.

"This is why some timbermen—not I—say it is better to move the logs to a permanent mill that is always guarded."

They walked to the back of the mill and Lavinia glanced at a pile of something—shrieked and put her hands over her eyes.

"Great gods! Mr. Bouchard, come out here and explain this—this horror," shouted James.

Joe Push hurried out, not knowing what they had found, a corpse or a ruined board, and then laughed. "That's all them snakes the boys got last week. Had a big parade of frogs and ever snake for ten mile around showed up to eat on 'em." There were thousands of huge muscular snakes in a six-foot pile, now beginning to rot and give off a memorable stench.

"Better pitch them into the river, Joe, or you'll have a dozen bears on your hands."

"Already shot two, but sure, we'll give 'em the heave-ho."

On the way back Lavinia asked James why they did not have circular saws in the mill. "I have read or heard that circular saws cut much more quickly as they are continuous and do not have to be reset."

"Why, you are quite right, and we have them on order, but it is not so easy to do everything at once. This mill was already in operation and we bought it from Joe Push, whom we now employ. There will soon be hundreds of sawmills in the Michigan woods if it is anything like Maine. This old gang rig will be sold and replaced with circular blades as soon as they arrive. I would like to put turbines in place for the extra power and really cut some wood. This rig can only produce about three thousand board feet a day right now and the shanty boys cut trees so fast the mill can't keep up—the weak link in the chain is the milling. I want to put a portable mill at every cut where it is convenient and transport lumber, not just logs. There is no reason why the mills cannot follow the lumber camps, cutting on site as we go. But a permanent mill near a town or city has several advantages beyond foiling thieves. Lennart and I once discussed someday adding a finishing mill to our operations that could sand planks smooth and even a wood-steaming oven to form stair balusters and such."

Cyrus objected strongly to Lavinia's plan to visit the lumber camps, and when she persisted in writing to the jobbers—Hobble Peterson and Vernon Roby—announcing her coming inspection he said that although he was terrible busy he would put his work aside and go with her as her protector. "You cannot go alone," he said. "You are too young and too—too womanly beauteous. You simply cannot go alone."

Lavinia blushed scarlet. "Uncle Cyrus, I am no such thing. And I will go. I will ride Black Robin. She will see me through safely. I know I can do this."

But James agreed with Cyrus. "It is not just the trails. There are roughnecks in the woods everywhere. There are men who would— harm you, renegades and low fellows as well as stray Indians. You must have someone—a man—with you. You must. I mean it, Lavinia. It may be different when you are older but now it is not. No argument. The travel is arduous. You do not know the way, you cannot build a fire in the wilderness, you cannot defend yourself against wild beasts or human beasts. Cyrus is needed here so I will find a steady woods-wise man to go with you."

He inquired of the Detroit hostler Paul Roque about a suitable travel companion and protector. On the next afternoon Roque suggested his oldest son, Andre Roque, a competent hunter who knew the ways of the forest and who had worked in both of the camps Lavinia proposed to visit. He could speak French and some Indian. James met the young man, taller than his father, very bashful and shy. But he answered all of James's questions easily. Yes, the best way to make this journey was on horseback. His father, the hostler, could provide the best horses in the stable. They were used to the forest trails and so would be better than a Boston horse, however highly esteemed. He would cook all their food and serve it, groom and feed the horses, prepare the bedrolls and blankets, point out whatever local landmarks they passed. He would protect Lavinia with his life. He would do his best.

It was early October and the first inches of snow lay in the cold woods. The horses' breath, their own breath steamed. The endless procession of huge trees aroused a new sensation in Lavinia—a powerful sense of ownership; they were her trees, she could cause these giants to fall and be devoured by the saws. She regarded their monolithic forms with scorn. Her trees—well, her trees with James and

Cyrus. And the birds that rested in them, her birds, her squirrels and porcupines; all of it.

At the end of the day Andre built a lean-to shelter with the fire in front of it, their separate blankets at each end and the impedimenta and saddles stacked between them. She was asleep before he finished rubbing the legs of the horses. But she woke in the night to feel the youth embracing her from behind, his breath on her nape, one hand over her left breast.

"What are you doing?" she said fiercely.

Andre Roque was silent, breathing slowly and regularly. Stiff with outrage she lay still and gradually realized that he was asleep, not plotting rape, but deeply asleep. Did he fancy he was protecting her, or was this how he slept with all his siblings in the home bed? She would explain in the morning that proper people of opposite sexes did not lie together unless they were married. And fell asleep herself. In the morning Andre was some distance away making a fire, fetching water for tea, cutting hunks of bread from the loaf, feeding the horses. He seemed his shy, quiet self and handed her a cup of hot black pekoe. He said nothing about his presence under her blanket and although she opened her mouth to begin, somehow she said nothing. The most troubling part of the experience was the depth of his sleep; when she spoke he should have awakened. Suppose hostiles or predatory beasts had been creeping toward them?—he would have slept blissfully on while wolves gnawed her arm. And what if the fire had gone out in the small hours—such a deep sleeper as he could not replenish it. Perhaps he was even feigning sleep. These possibilities were marks against him. Still, in a few nights it seemed quite the ordinary way to sleep and she was glad of his warmth and closeness when branches cracked in the darkness and the owl called, and he was always up and at work by dawn.

They reached Vernon Roby's camp in midmorning, the sun very bright in a cloudless sky, the river so brilliantly reflective the sun glint was painful. They came into a clearing surrounded by forest except along the shore, a landscape of stumps as far as Lavinia could see. There was no one around. They went to a shack with a sign saying OFFICE over the door; it was empty.

"Hey-o," called Andre and got a jay's call for answer. There was smoke coming out of a stovepipe from a log building. A door was ajar and Lavinia pushed in. A man slinging tin plates along an endless table was making such a clatter he did not hear her speak. She tried again.

"Sir. *Sir!*"

He turned and saw them, gave a high shriek and dropped the armful of plates. Lavinia rushed to help pick them up but the man motioned her away. "What you want? Who you are!"

"I want to see Mr. Roby. I am Lavinia Duke and I sent him a letter telling him I was coming to look at the cut."

"Oh Christ! He's out with the boys." He gestured at the stumps. "Bout two mile up the lake. Jesus Christ! He don't know you comin here."

"I wrote a letter."

"He don't read. He don't get no letter."

Lavinia was annoyed. This was a charade. "Please go and fetch him. Right now."

"Can't! I'm cook. Soon they come eat. Be mad if ain't on table."

"Go now. *Now!* Or I will fire you from your job."

The unfortunate man went out.

"We might as well sit while we wait," said Lavinia to Andre. "Perhaps I had better see what he is cooking." It was a great pot of stew. Biscuits rising but not quite ready to go in the oven stood on a table half-covered with a forest of sauce bottles. Lavinia, unable to sit and wait, stirred the stew, just beginning to catch to the bottom of the pot. She put a few sticks in the fire and opened the oven door to gauge the temperature. Hot enough for biscuits. They waited. The biscuits rose. Lavinia put the pan in the oven and noted the time on her little watch. Just as she was taking out the browned biscuits the cook came rushing in, his chest heaving with anxiety. He saw the hot biscuits, turned to the stew, which Lavinia had pushed to the back of the stove, where the heat was less. "I stirred it," she said.

"Okay, okay. Good."

Vern Roby came in a few minutes later. He was a short, heavyset man with an eye patch and thin scars on his face. He said nothing, just stared at her, then turned to Andre.

"What she doin here?"

"Mr. Duke sent her. She's his daughter. She come to see you, look over the cut."

"A woman! This ain't woman's business." He turned to Lavinia. "You better pack up your kit, miss, and skedaddle. Where's Mr. Vogel? Lennart Vogel, he's the one we work with for Duke."

"I sent you a letter, Mr. Roby, explaining that my uncle Lennart Vogel died in a fire last year. I am assuming some of his duties. Knowing the men cutting for Duke and Sons is one of those duties. This gentleman is Mr. Andre Roque, who is accompanying me. Uncle Lennart is gone and whatever you may think of the arrangement I am taking his place. You may find me ignorant at first, but I hope we will get to know one another and be able to speak frankly and honestly. Perhaps you will tell me the situation. It looks like an extensive cut. I would like to see the landings and hear your plan for the spring drive. I would like to hear of any problems you have or anticipate, problems of any kind whatsoever. I am not here to interfere but to see what we may expect in the spring—precisely what Uncle Lennart would wish to know from you. And I have the authority to fire or retain you according to what I may find."

Roby took a deep breath. Another. "Yes, ma'am," he said, standing like a trained bear. He looked at Andre, tried to regain his command. "I remember you—worked horses for me last year, yah?"

"Yah," said Andre in an insolent tone. No help for Roby there.

She wanted to see the choppers at work. Roby shook his head in disapproval but they walked along the edge of the icy skid road to a hillside where men chopped and the echoes flew back at them. A tree fell, axmen went at it, slashing the limbs, severing the top. The men glanced covertly at Lavinia. Hot breath puffed from their mouths. The air tingled with pine. The men hitched a chain around the log butt and jockeyed it onto a sled. Someone's foot slid, she heard a muffled curse.

Out of the corner of his mouth a man wearing a red tuque said to his fellows, "See that woman? That's the rich man's daughter of privilege there come to see the workin stiffs like a zoo, old Duke owns everything you see. He got it free from the govmint, the big giveaway, stealin public forest land, cut it down and get rich."

"Save it for later."

"Don't you worry, I will. Tell you how they get the power and legal rights, fix the laws, them takin everything got value—trees, copper, everything—for their selves. Workin man don't get nothin but older."

Lavinia did not hear what he said but after her year in the English girls' school she was sensitive to the most subtle of oblique sneers, the hunched shoulder and lifted chin, and she felt his antipathy. Two could play at this game, she thought, and looked often in his direction, always finding his hard little eyes.

"One more question, Mr. Roby, who is the man, the chopper, in the red tuque?" He knew instantly who she meant.

"Heh. Rattle is what he calls himself."

"I would like you to dismiss him."

"Miss Duke, he is a bit of a talker but a good axman."

"Dismiss him, Mr. Roby. Today."

Horses drew the logs from the cut to a landing where Lavinia was startled to see a young woman, younger than she, a girl, come forward with a branding hammer and strike the D&S mark into the end of the log.

"That girl?" she asked Mr. Roby.

"That's Angélique, the cook's daughter."

"Is he not concerned for her safety among so many rough men?"

Vernon Roby laughed for the first time that day, a great roaring hearty laugh. "No! She got seven brothers choppin here. See? Him, him over there, that one—" He pointed. "Nobody bother her they want to live. She most strong as a man anyway. She got that hammer. She break his arm."

That was something new to think about as she made counts of the number and sizes of the logs. Lavinia determined to learn scaling; it was useless to say that you had five hundred logs with an average diameter of thirty-seven inches. How many feet of inch-thick boards would come out of that log? How did you allow for the bark, for the saw kerf, for the taper of the log? She wanted to learn the mathematics of scaling. She knew there were log rules that took all of these variances into account and let the scaler make at least an estimate of the number of boards in a single tree. How to learn the skill? She wished that Breitsprecher still worked for them—he had been a good scaler. Once Lennart had spoken of a minister turned schoolmaster at a female seminary somewhere in Ohio who was working out a detailed mathematical guide to estimate board feet in standing trees. One thing she knew from life was that nothing could be known precisely; no one could make a perfect rule to accommodate every tree, no one could know when a cat would knock over a candle. She had determined as a young child on her way to England not to be taken aback by the most untoward events. She might arrange a visit to that minister and beg him to show her the art of scaling, though a ladies' seminary seemed far from the right place for such instruction. But perhaps not—and because of Angélique and her hammer Lavinia entertained an image of an army of young women advancing into the forests with their scale sticks. In the afternoon, the light beginning to draw in like the neck of a sack, they left Vern Roby. Lavinia shook his hand, promised—threatened?—to come again in the spring for the drive, the log drive, *her* logs running to the mill. Roby caught her casual expressions of ownership. He knew which side was up, smiled, said he would look for her in spring. As they disappeared into the trees he beckoned to the man in the red tuque. He did not know

507

how Lavinia had picked the one troublemaker in the crew, but she was right, somehow she could judge men. Rattle constantly stirred the boys up for higher wages, better hours, special food. "You, Rattle," he called. "Pack your turkey and hit the road. Here's your time. The lady don't like your looks."

The visit to the Hobble Peterson camp did not go as well. Peterson disliked women, whom he considered brainless and backward, refused to talk to her and addressed sarcastic replies to her questions only to Andre Roque. His camp was dirty, the ground littered with wood chips, torn rags, a ragged ox hide, several broken barrels surrounded by circling flies, broken ax handles, rusted wire and worn-out saw blades, discarded boots. The drying lumber stacks looked ragged and the ends sagged. As they rode away from the camp Andre, who had been silent until now, followed her glance and said, "Them boards won't dry even." Lavinia noted all of this in her little red book, a book that became infamous in the logging camps, for a bad report from Lavinia meant the jobber would not work for Duke & Sons again, as Peterson discovered when the spring drive ended.

On the return trip there was one night when Andre was thoroughly awake. A storm had been hovering on the horizon all afternoon. They made camp early and dinner was the inadequate New England "nookick," parched corn ground to a powder and mixed with hot water, filling but tasteless, and as dark fell the storm arrived. Lightning cracked without interval and violent rain doused the fire. While Andre sat near, Lavinia tried to sleep but the mad winds tore their lean-to apart. They could hear trees falling in the forest and even see them in the stuttering blue flashes. With the shelter gone they were soaked through in minutes. When lightning cleaved a great pine a short distance away Andre wrapped his wet arms around Lavinia as if to take the brunt of any falling tree. Two hours passed before the rain slackened and suddenly stopped, pushed southeast by an icy wind. Andre got up, groping in the dark for a log he had set aside earlier and with his ax laid the dry interior open. He spent the next half hour with the tinderbox and char cloth, and when that was not successful put a little gunpowder on the log. The spark ignited, the log surface showed a tiny flame, which he fed with a feather stick and twiglets, then pulled out the dry branches he had cached under their bags. Only then Lavinia remembered the little box of Congreves her father had pressed on her before they left. The next morning she dug out the box, opened it and tried rubbing one of the little strips on a piece of wood and was utterly surprised when it flared up brilliantly. She held the box out to Andre, who examined the matches, frowned and handed them back. He preferred steel and spark. And a week later, back in the Detroit house, she learned that matches were dangerous.

She was copying out her notes from the trip while Ruby unpacked her bags. She heard a slight noise and a smothered word, then a shriek from the unfortunate maid, who had dropped the Congreves box and stepped on one of the spilled strips, which immediately ignited her cotton dress. Lavinia seized the pitcher in the washbasin and sloshed the contents on the fiery dress, shouted for Mrs. Trame to bring a bucketful, pushed the maid to the floor and stamped on the still-burning cloth, singeing her own wool skirt hem.

"Butter," said Mrs. Trame. "Butter will calm the pain," and she ran back down to the kitchen. Ruby's burns on her hands and neck were painful despite the butter. James called in a physician who pooh-poohed the butter and substituted a salve of his own making and prescribed generous doses of opium for the pain. The burns healed but Ruby's attachment to opium increased and after several months James sent the scarred and addicted maid back to Boston with a generous allowance. Lavinia replaced her with a local girl.

It was not necessary to go to Ohio to learn scaling. Lavinia swallowed her pride and wrote to Armenius Breitsprecher, explaining what she wanted and asking how to gain the knowledge. Both Breitsprechers were in their Monroe office, just back from surveying heavy river sections. Armenius was amused; laughing, he showed the letter to Dieter.

"Duke and Sons are our chief rival—it seems they may have to change their name to Duke and Daughter, as there are no sons except the young children of Cyrus Hempstead. James is old and it looks rather as though this Lavinia, a chit of a girl, will have a position in the company. I think we may quickly swallow them up."

But Dieter thought it must have taken courage to write that letter. "She has spirit. Does she have brains? Do you know her?"

"I never met her. I just knew she existed. It's *lächerlich,* a woman wanting to learn how to scale logs. A rich girl's passing fancy, something she heard about but hasn't any idea of the reasons or procedures." He crumpled and tossed the letter into the woodbox near the fireplace. It was Dieter who plucked it from the woodbox the next day and answered the letter himself, offering his personal instruction if she could manage to come to Monroe for a week.

"I hope you have some knowledge of mathematics," he wrote. "Few women do, but familiarity with numbers is quite essential in estimating log volumes. I would be pleased to tutor you in the rudiments of the art and if it is to your liking you may advance to more difficult problems." He thought she would not reply; he made the work sound disagreeable and difficult. She wrote back with a list of dates she could be in Monroe and assured him she had no fear of arithmetic nor mathematics and particularly enjoyed calculus above all things—not quite the truth.

57

a cure for headache

For James there was one highly annoying disadvantage to living in Detroit—his wine cellar remained in the Boston house and in Detroit there were rivers of whiskey but no wineshop. It had always been his intent to have his cellar shipped, but he shuddered when he thought how many good bottles would suffer from stirred-up sediments and take years to settle down. The longer it took to arrange for the packing and shipping the more he pined for the dark dusty bottles of choice Madeiras and clarets in their silent racks. His mouth watered. Dinner without wine was insipid. There was no pleasanter end to a day than a glass of port and a cigar by the fire.

James and Lavinia made a point of dining together at each other's table in turn. This night it was James's house. After dinner—venison roast with baked apples, potato soufflé and small business talk—in the library, each with a glass of whiskey, he said, "Lavinia, I am determined to return to Boston and arrange to have my wine crated and shipped here. While I am gone—I will be about six weeks away—I'm having a carpenter put bottle racks in this cellar. Of course I shall stay at Black Swan, though likely eat out, visit my tailor and bankers. Where did I put my—there they are." He hung the cord of his pince-nez around his neck. "I've spoken to Cyrus and he said that while I am away anything you wish he will help you procure." Cyrus was becoming hard of hearing and it meant strenuous shouting to explain anything to him.

"I shall do very well, Papa, and look forward to your return and perhaps a glass of champagne?"

"Oh, we will have a champagne gala," said James. "You and I and Cyrus and Clara. I shall bring all the news of Boston with me as well as wine. If there is anything I may fetch for you give me a little list. Why not let me choose a new dress for you—something colorful?"

"Books, Papa, I would have some new books. That is all I want." And, thought Lavinia, when you return I will know how to scale logs.

But two days before his departure he came storming to Lavinia's house in a froth. She invited him into the little parlor with the deep green velvet curtains making a dusky forest-like gloom; the gilt tassels glinted dully. She sat on a chair, ankles crossed; he strode up and down. "Daughter, I have just made an unpleasant discovery. I am sorry to say this but that rascal, Andre Roque, cannot accompany you again on any trips whatsoever."

"May I ask why not?" said Lavinia. "I have always found him to be most accommodating."

"I daresay," sneered James, continuing to stamp across the carpet.

"Oh do sit down, Papa, sit down. And tell me calmly, what has he done? What is wrong? Why?"

James sat on the edge of a large, throne-like chair. "Why! Never mind, it is not something for a young girl to hear."

She sat straight, both feet flat on the floor, a combative attitude. "Let me remind you I am no longer a 'young girl' but almost a woman grown—and with a masculine mind as you have several times remarked. I am immune from vapors and fainting. I demand to know why you are forbidding me his company and protection." Her dark eyes glinted and the red mouth pressed into a knot.

Now he was really irritated. "Very well, since you fancy yourself so advanced in worldly experience I'll tell you that Andre Roque has got his *sister* with child. He cannot be trusted with females. Some men are that way." He thought of his lascivious old father-in-law. "I do not want him to travel with you again." He waited for her shocked exclamation.

Lavinia said coolly, "I suppose it comes from all the children sleeping in the same bed."

"How would you know that!" He was back on his feet.

"I surmise it, that is all."

"A piece of advice, Miss Lavinia. Surmising is the way to the greatest error. Never surmise, never." But what he really feared was that Lavinia might have a streak of Posey's abandoned ways and the hostler's son would sniff it out and give him an illegitimate grandchild.

"I quite agree that surety is preferable to the most advanced surmising," said Lavinia, "I will do as you say," and she offered him tea.

Back at the old house in Boston, James was struck by its shabby condition. The familiar interior was musty and chill with an air of fatigue, the furniture, especially the hall stand, seemed cruelly old-fashioned. The rooms looked rather mean. He thought they should not copy every detail in the new house but simply sell Black Swan as it stood and start anew in Detroit. He would have a talk with the architect while he was in Boston and cancel the copycat plans—present Lavinia with a fait accompli when he returned to the lake country.

Mr. Prentiss, his wine merchant for many years, was excited to see his second-best customer again. His wattled red face contrasted with his pink turkey neck stretching naked above the new style of low collar and bow tie, and James thought he should have kept to a high stock that would keep him decently covered. The merchant flapped his hands open as though inviting James to dance and said, "I am delighted to see you again, Mr. Duke. Are you returning? Oh, just a visit, *tsk*. How may I help you? Would you like to know of the new wines? I have some really good German hock. At your service, sir," and he made a body movement very like a bow. Nothing had changed in the wineshop, the same dusty musty smell, Mr. Prentiss clucking and nodding.

"Mr. Prentiss, you look well and I trust you do well. Indeed, just a visit. And as much as I would like to explore the hock I have come on a different errand. I wish to have my cellar crated and shipped to new quarters in Detroit. But I fear breakage and disturbance will wreak havoc on the contents unless the job is carefully undertaken. Can you advise me of the best way we may do this?"

"Mr. Duke, to disturb those hundreds of bottles, to crate and jostle them halfway across the continent would ruin a great portion. It would be a true sin. Why not trade with me—a move from your cellar to my shop is not a great journey. In exchange I will give you a greater measure of aged Madeira or whatever else you like in casks and barrels that can stand the trip without damage."

"That seems a logical course of action. Let us do it." They spoke for a while and then the merchant asked offhandedly if Freegrace's cellar had been sold or passed to a family member.

"It passed to me," said James. "Freegrace's will left it to Edward, but Edward's possessions have become mine. I haven't thought of Freegrace's cellar though I always heard it was very good." His eyes kept straying to the bottles. He looked forward to an excellent dinner—with wine and more wine.

"Very good! I should say it was very good! Among the best in Boston." He coughed. "If you think of disposing of it I would be interested in buying. I would never consider moving those rare bottles any distance."

"Well," said James. "I do not know the extent of what he had. But I have a set of keys at my house. Shall we meet tomorrow morning and examine what is there?"

"Nothing would delight me more," said Mr. Prentiss, suddenly sneezing.

"Shall we meet here at ten?"

"Excellent. Now, Mr. Duke, will you take a glass of amontillado with me?"

"I will," said James. "It will set me right. I keep having bouts of malaise."

"Are you sure you would not rather have a hot toddy?"

"No, no, amontillado is what I crave. And please send a half dozen of the hock you mentioned round to Black Swan—I must have something to drink while I am here, though I can certainly make inroads on my cellar."

"I advise it," said Mr. Prentiss. "If you have special wines this visit would be the very best time to enjoy them. Now, just step into the tasting room."

James felt it was good to be back in Boston. And tonight, he said to himself, a very good dinner.

He had a headache the next morning and sent it on its way with a large glass of champagne and the most savorous coffee he'd had in a year, taken at Bliss's Coffee House, where not even the waiter had changed—old Henry with the great wen on his chin, who greeted him by name. The morning was sharp with frost, the hired horse lively. He drove up to the wineshop, where Mr. Prentiss's florid smiling face floated in the window. The door opened and the wine merchant skipped out carrying an abacus and a notebook.

"I heard that Mr. Freegrace Duke kept a cellar book and I thought I would count bottles with this"—he held the instrument aloft—"and take a few notes." He was in high humor.

It seemed to James he had never left Boston so familiar was this street, the clopping of the horse. "Brisk day," he said. The headache was quite gone. He felt very well; sea air was certainly healthier than lake vapors. "He-up!"

"Brisker to come. The almanac promises a hard winter. I suppose the winters are pleasanter in Michigan?"

"I would not say that," said James, "never would I say that."

Inside Freegrace's house everything was coated with dust. There were a great many tracks on the floor. No sheets protected the furniture. The house was bitterly cold.

"Only a few months ago, I paid his butler a year's salary to stay on and look after the place until we could make arrangements," said

James. "It looks as though he left as soon as I did. What was the fellow's name—Eccles, I think. I will look into this. Damn, I will have him taken up! Well, never mind. Let us find a lantern and some candles and go down into the cellar."

The door to the cellar was ajar and as they went down the broad stairs James noticed chunks of plaster and mud on the stairs and gouge marks on the wall.

"I don't like the look of this," he said, pointing at the plaster dust with his toe. Mr. Prentiss made a clucking sound. He knew what they would find; he had seen it once before.

The bottle racks were empty, the cask cradles empty, shelves tipped over. Broken glass glinted in the light of their lantern and the air had a winy stench. Freegrace's wine cellar had been stripped.

They turned to each other and spoke as one: "the butler!" And James was impressed to see tears in Prentiss's little eyes. The Adam's apple bobbed in his turkey neck.

James drove Prentiss back, then went to the new-formed police office, and told of Freegrace's missing wine. Two men James thought rather thick-minded came with him and looked at the shambles in the cellar. They pointed out circles in the dust on the sideboards where silver chafing dishes and other ornaments had once stood. In five minutes they concluded that a criminal gang of immigrants must have done the deed. "Comin in Boston by the t'ousand," said one, likely an immigrant himself, thought James.

"But the butler—" he said to no response. They went out. He went into the library, for what he did not know, picked up the several old copies of *Burton's Gentleman's Magazine* on the table—something to read at least.

He returned to Mr. Prentiss and made the arrangements to exchange most of his bottles for casks of Madeira to travel by cart to Albany, then by canal and lake steamer to Detroit.

"At least we can do that much." But he saw the wine merchant was still grieving the loss of Freegrace's cellar and shifting James's wines would be little consolation.

"The terrible sin of that theft. I'll warrant the swine did not know what they had. I have heard for years that Mr. Freegrace possessed Château d'Yquem sauternes from Thomas Jefferson's private cellar—the 1784 vintage. And I heard of a 1792 vintage Madeira. Madeira is truly the prince of old wines, at its best after half a century. The 1792 would just now be coming into maturity. Open a fine old bottle and it fills the room with such rich deep aromatics—" He broke off and turned away from the light.

The actual taking up of the Black Swan bottles, and Mr. Prentiss's excruciatingly slow methods of packing and transferring the bottles to his shop delayed James's return by nearly ten days. The blazing autumn faded and November rain began the morning after Guy Fawkes Day, which Bostonians still called Pope Day, drowning the last smoldering bonfires. A day or two later the first line storm to screech off the Atlantic shook the oak outside his old bedroom window and brought down the dead leaves.

The house agent called. He had sent a letter saying that he represented a leading Bostonian and wished to discuss a real estate purchase with Mr. Duke. James knew the man was the son of one of the shareholders in the New England Mississippi Land Company, which a few decades earlier had enjoyed a controversial congressional appropriation of more than a million dollars. Now the son, who had inherited the windfall, offered $90,000 for Black Swan and its grounds. James pretended reluctance and was finally persuaded to part with the property, house and all its contents (save his small inlaid table, which would travel with him to Detroit) for a rather larger sum. The next day he put Edward's place, Freegrace's rifled mansion and even Lennart Vogel's handsome brick Federal-style house in the agent's hands. A week before Thanksgiving he began his own return passage. The wine would follow.

• • •

517

In his stateroom on the steamer *Liberty Tree* he read the last *Burton's Gentleman's Magazine* and was disturbed by a story, "The Fall of the House of Usher," the opening paragraphs unpleasantly reminiscent of his cousin's ravaged house. He had a sore throat. He was coming down with a cold. The worst place to have a cold was on a steamer on Lake Erie in winter. In his valise he had a copy of *Nicholas Nickleby* for Lavinia. He would read this. So the last leg of the tedious and cold journey began with James wincing at the antics of Mr. Squeers, who certainly would not have balked at stealing a cellarful of wine.

He felt it before he knew what he felt. His own marine experience lay in the days of sail on the Atlantic but he sensed the change in the beat of the inland sea, the increasingly labored response of the steamer. He knew that the Great Lakes and especially Erie were among the most treacherous waters of the earth and that the winter storms wrecked ships as men trod wildflowers. Duke & Sons had lost two lumber boats the last winter, delighting settlers along the shore with planks that floated to them with no labor but to bend over and pick them up. He read on but felt the cold. When he got up to search for his heavy coat he nearly fell with the ship's violent pitch. He could hear it groaning now, every timber twisting as the vessel gyred through mountainous waves. He put on his coat, a hat, heavy gloves and went out on deck.

A savage wind blew spume off the tops of the waves. It was a fresh gale and God, God it was cold! His first breath of the sharp air wakened his old headache, which struck like a hurled rock. Ice formed as he watched—along the rail, on the deck, on every rope, the hatch covers, heavy deep blue ice, tons of it. With fascination he watched it glaze the front of his coat. He felt his eyebrows weighted. The footing was treacherous. Passengers coming out of their cabins to see how the ship did gasped in the searing cold and one heavy man immediately fell and slid across the deck, but was able to cling to the bottom rail. He could not get up again and at each lurch of the ship his feet swung outward over the abyss. James saw ice forming on the man's legs. Could James reach him? He could not. He looked for rope, saw a coil, but it was frozen in a great lump of ice. Passengers were clinging to anything they could reach. James wondered if he could get back to his cabin and tried a step without relinquishing his hold on the rail. His foot skidded and he gave it up. People were shrieking now, calling, "Help, help." Never in his life had he felt such cold. Two icicles hung from his snotty nostrils. The fallen man suddenly shot away under the rail and into Erie. The entire ship was sealed in a casket of ice a foot thick, and it labored and wallowed in the troughs of the waves—slower, lower. Why had no crewmen chipped ice as soon as it started to form, James wanted to ask, but his mouth could not shape the words. Through the sheeting spray he thought he saw land nearby, less than a mile distant. They were making for a local harbor or at least the lee of an island, and he felt cheered. He would last—he'd been through worse. The wind pushed the helpless *Liberty Tree* on and a quarter mile from a desolate stump-choked shore she smashed onto the foaming rocks; he knew he would never drink that damn Madeira, but with a bizarre sense of victory he felt his headache become a dwindling spicule.

Cyrus had the news first from the steamship owner and came for Lavinia.

"We must go there," she said. "We cannot wait. It is my *father*. We must go to him." It took them two days to reach the shore near the wreck through some of the coldest weather of the century. Cyrus was exhausted by Lavinia's agitation, her restless head-tossing and weeping. The bitter temperatures persisted until the entire Erie shore humped up in crystalline domes of ice. Among the stumps, converted to glittering ice cylinders, they found thirty-odd frozen bodies where loggers, summoned from their chopping work a mile distant, had laid them. The passengers were frozen in angular postures just as they had been when the blood solidified in their veins. Many had hands crooked in their last grasp of rope or rail, and the faces fixed in final expressions of struggle or resignation. The captain in his ice uniform held an ice watch in his solid hand. They found

James, congealed eyes glaring up at the sky, his tight lips narrow as a crack. Lavinia touched his marble cheek. She looked at Cyrus. He made a hopeless gesture and said, "We shall meet him in heaven." Some of the shanty men were trying to salvage the last bits of rigging and spars still tumbling in the heavy surf. Lavinia called to a man whose rounded back and sloping shoulders she somehow knew.

"Mr. Roby? Oh, oh it really is you, Mr. Roby. You can do me a very great favor and I will pay you for it. My father, James Duke, lies among those bodies. I must have him brought to Detroit so we may bury him. Will you help me?" The man looked in her face white as dirty old snow, tracked with frozen tears.

"What! Mr. James Duke? Your father? Oh Jesus and Mary, Miss Duke, I will. We'll take him out soon as we may. And I'll take no pay for it."

"I'll never forget this kindness," she said.

Now she was alone, except for Cyrus and Clara, who did not count. She had encountered aloneness in the hated English school. And now with James buried in the Mount Elliot Cemetery and Posey buried in Boston, the uncles all dead, it was the same. She lay on her bed and tried to breathe slowly. She breathed, breathed and then almost heard the saddest sound in the world, the far notes of a piano played in an empty room . . . *re mi fa sol* . . . "Mama. *Mama!*"

Hours later in the dark she woke, her heart galloping, her salty face stuck to the silk pillow slip. Why had she not thought of this before? She was not alone. There was someone who would protect her, care for her. Although he was a common man she sensed he had a noble character no matter what they said. She got out of bed, lit the oil lamp and began to write. Her pen gouged into the paper page after page, ink sputtering, and when she stopped it was milky dawn. She folded the pages, wrapped, sealed and addressed the packet. She felt a sense of completion, knew she had saved herself. Very tired she crept back into the chilled bed and slept.

She rose at noon, dined on a poached chicken breast. She carried her letter to the post office and saw it on its way. Now she could only wait. She was not anxious. He would not fail her.

The days passed and Lavinia began to fret. After ten days there was still no response. She threw herself at the office work but it was hourly apparent that she could not run Duke & Sons by herself.

She arranged a meeting with Mr. Edward Pye. James had brought Pye, the company's accountant, treasurer and paymaster, to Detroit and settled him in a house near the Duke offices. Mr. Pye, pale-faced with dark curling hair and beard, was reticent and responsible, the ideal employee. But he had a way of pointing out Duke & Sons' deficiencies that Lavinia could not quite like. He introduced her to a Chicago lawyer visiting Detroit on business, Clayton Jasper Flense. Within two weeks Flense had become indispensable. He advised her to shift the company to Chicago—Chicago had a far better geograph-ical location than Detroit, it was central to the entire country, it was becoming an important city. He advised her to incorporate and name a board of directors.

"Very many businesses do incorporate. For then, anything the company may choose to do, if some action excites litigation, why, such an attack does not fall on you nor on any individual director, but on the corporation, which is a thing, and not a person. It is a legal protection, you see. And this is a way you can raise capital to purchase extensive woodlands. Your investors enjoy limited liability, that is, they face no losses greater than their invested moneys. Incor-poration is one of the great benefits to business in this country—incorporation lies with the states not the central government—and if you are not content in one state and the opportunities look better in another, why you may go there. It is the lifeblood of our Ameri-can spirit of enterprise. We do not have tyrannical kings and despots squeezing us into poverty. We can invent and make and work and do and keep the fruits of our labor."

"But my father said that corporations were often monopolies, and that they would prove fatal to partnerships and sole proprietor situations. He cited the East India Company as an example."

"That was hardly an American institution. Remember, too, that it was a royal charter, under the 'protection' of the British government—and under its thumb. The thing American people fear about corporations is that they might achieve too much power. We have an antipathy to power even as we admire it. And I believe competition among corporations will make that concern null and void."

She did see, she thought she understood the situation. It was time to reshape Duke & Sons. And every day she waited for the answer to that painful letter written in the night.

Flense and Pye were valuable but she needed an assistant, someone who could act as secretary, handle the paperwork and office supplies, oversee other employees, manage visitors and business callers. She put a small advertisement in *The Democratic Free Press and Michigan Intelligencer* for a responsible woman with a sense of order.

The advertisement brought only two responses. The first was a bony eighteen-year-old girl wild to get away from her father's stump farm. She was alternatively doubled over with shyness and forthright. She picked nervously at bleeding cuticles and seemed to have only a few qualifications beyond her desire to escape farm life. "I can read. I can write. I can learn!" she said when Lavinia asked what skills she had.

"I admire your spirit, but that may not be enough, Miss Heinrich. I will keep your name in my book and let you know if we have a suitable opening in future."

The second applicant was a middle-aged rusty-haired widow, Annag Duncan, thin, with long spider-leg fingers. She had a low easy voice.

"I worked in the office of a hat manufacturer in Glasgow before I met my husband, Alasdair Duncan. Then I stayed to home. We married and he wanted to come to the New World and make a living as a purveyor of fine woods. He knew what was desirable. We went to New York. But his cough—he had a little cough for years, nothing much—this cough became very constant and brought blood. A doctor said he had consumption and should go to a dry mountain climate. But before the mountains, said the man he worked for, he must go to Detroit and examine some beautiful clear pinewood, so we came and he died two weeks after we come ashore. He never got to the mountains."

She was homely, had no money, indeed she wore threadbare garments. But her office experience with the hat manufacturer gave her value and Lavinia hired her. She sent again for the stump farmer's daughter to help Annag. "I will put your avowal of wanting to learn to the test. You are hired. You will be paid five dollars a month with a chance of more if you do well. We will be shifting to Chicago in coming months. Report to Mrs. Duncan at seven tomorrow morning—she will assign your tasks. I expect hard and accurate work from you."

Now, she thought, I must deal with Cyrus, for she longed to get him out of the company. His fussy, overbearing ways, his dulled hearing, were unwanted. She had every confidence in her own abilities aided and abetted by Flense and Pye. And still there was no reply to that letter.

The answer when it came was so contrary to her expectations she could hardly grasp what she was reading. She plowed through it again and again, sure she had made a mistake. But right enough, it was a refusal: ". . . your generous but unusual offer . . . prefer to keep my own name . . . choose my own helpmeet . . . earn my own way in the world." Mr. Andre Roque had the effrontery to wish her good fortune.

She fell apart, she raved and shrieked, hurled clothes, furniture, smashed books through the window, screamed obscene words she didn't know she knew and finally crashed sobbing onto the torn-apart bed.

Downstairs Mrs. Trame and the new maid, Alberta Snow, heard the uproar.

"Whatever ails her!" said Alberta.

"I expect she is grieving for her father," said Mrs. Trame.

"That is no grieving. That is fury, that is a fiery rage. That is a mad-dog rage."

"Grieving occurs in different ways," said Mrs. Trame.

The next morning, dressed in black, Lavinia came down to break-fast table very quietly, drank three cups of coffee and ate toast and an apple.

"Mrs. Trame, I shall be going to the Duke offices today. I will be home at noon and would like something simple for lunch—whatever you have on hand. And please ask Mr. Kneebone to repair the lights in my bedroom window. I had a bit of difficulty yesterday but am quite all right today." That moment, she told herself, had been her last emotional expression; from now on she would reject sympathy and condolences as evidence of weakness. She would feel nothing for anyone.

Cyrus came into the office smoking one of James's cigars (he had taken the box from James's desk after the funeral) and stood gazing at Mrs. Duncan, who sat at her desk, pin-neat in a black woolen dress with a modest collar.

"Who might you be?" His tone was offensive.

"Mrs. Annag Duncan. Miss Duke took me on as office manager. And you are—?"

"Hah? Hah?" At last he understood. "Office manager! I was not consulted. Where is she?"

Mrs. Duncan nodded at Lavinia's door. "May I announce you, sir?"

"What! Hah! Foolishness!"

Cyrus began at once. "Who gave you leave to hire that woman?"

She shouted in his half-deaf ear, "Every member of the Board save you and me has passed on. I need permission from no one. I am the head of Duke and Sons, the heir to James Duke's estate and business interests, and I shall do as I feel necessary."

"Well that is blunt enough, ma'am."

"Now, about your own place in this company. It is better if you leave." Cyrus would bluster, make a scene—but he surprised her.

"Lavinia, I, too, think it is a time for a change. I have wanted my own lumber brokerage for some years. I have contacts with several logging companies, not just Duke and Sons. And every day sees a dozen new logging concerns at work in the woods. Of course I would hope Duke and Sons would be my prize client." Annag Duncan in the outer room heard every word.

Lavinia smiled. "Cyrus, I congratulate you. I intend to shift this company to Chicago. And rename it Duke Logging and Lumber as there are no extant sons." Cyrus started to say something but she put her finger to her lips and pointed at the door to the outer office. She took up her pen and wrote: "Company outgrown Detroit. Center shifting. Chicago ideal. Double population in 2 yrs, forest, lakes, rivers easy transport logs. Gal. & Chi. Railroad and more building. Ill & Mich Canal connect Miss." She waited until he had read this and then shrieked into his hairy ear, "The flow of business is shifting from north-south to east-west with the railroads going where no rivers flow. Chicago the center. No business can ignore this."

"Hah!" said Cyrus, impressed by this rounding out of Chicago's situation. "Gad, it's true." Men all over the country, all over the world had caught the arousing scent of Chicago, the city of the century, already a central hub, everyone coming to it with a common hunger, coming to take and take and take again. Chicago was raw greed and action, and would perhaps become the most important business city in the world. He decided to shift his own enterprise to Chicago immediately.

Lavinia wrote again: "Board meeting, you formally step away. Please remain on Board of Duke Logging. Likely we incorporate."

He read this, gave her a sharp, surprised look and said, "In many states the legislatures hamper the activities of corporations."

"Duke Logging is in a favorable situation as far as the Michigan legislature is concerned." Cyrus said nothing and she took his silence for understanding. "I want you to start your new venture without acrimony. Are Breitsprechers one of your clients?"

"That is for me to know, not to say. Ha ha." He might as well have written it on the wall.

In another year she was settled in Chicago in a lakefront house topped by a glassed-in copper-roofed cupola, but Mrs. Trame was gone, a victim of dropsy that made her legs swell to the size, shape and color of Boston harbor seals. She had suddenly fallen dead on the floor while kneading bread dough. The new cook, Mrs. Agnes Balclop, was proficient enough. And old Kneebone kept things in repair, tended the horses and yard, got drunk and roared on Saturday night. Lavinia had a companion, Goosey Breeley, a distant New Brunswick cousin of Posey, who had found her way to Chicago. She looked somewhat like Posey and her voice and accent were very like. She became official sympathizer, consulting physician, favoring critic and errand runner. She managed the household, everyone in fear of her wicked New Brunswicker tongue. And she explained freely and often that nothing in Chicago could compare with the virtues of New Brunswick.

Lavinia, Lawyer Flense and Accountant Pye met in the new boardroom, a perfect square of white plaster walls with seven windows looking onto Lake Michigan, for a discussion of suitable candidates for the company's positions. Annag Duncan put a steaming coffeepot and a plate of cookies and cakes on the long table under the windows. Although James had hired four new landlookers and their assistants before his fated trip east, they needed more; the Breitsprechers were buying vast tracts of land on credit—they were pulling ahead. Someone had to take on Lennart's old job.

"In my current situation I cannot serve as company head and still manage the landlookers, jobbers and mills." Lavinia tapped on a stack of papers. Flense bit into a crisp lemon cookie. Mr. Pye made a note. "You want a production manager," he said, and she nodded. "Let me suggest Noah Ludlum—a Maine man familiar with everything from beans to boomage. He is subject to occasional fits of epilepsy so cannot work in the woods as a logging contractor, but he has great knowledge of all operations and a talent for working well with men and choosing good ones to carry out what he cannot."

"Can I meet with him next week? Is he in the region?"

"He is currently working for the Breitsprechers, but I know he is not happy with their odd ways. Shall I contact him?"

"Yes, do so. And transport—do we not need someone responsible to oversee all our transport means whether rafts, barges, wagonloads or railcars? And ships? Should we build our own lumber barges?"

"Miss Duke," said Flense, "wherever you can cut out the middleman you will profit. Reduce the number of hands through which your product must pass before it brings you income. Your company would do well to build its own ships and barges in its own shipyards." Lavinia made a note but an idea was stirring. Flense got up and went to the cookie plate. He took two with lemon icing.

Pye spoke again. "And even small actions will make a difference in your bottom line. A question: do you have stores at the jobbers' camps? Places where the axmen can purchase clothing, tobacco and other necessaries?"

"No. Is that not the business of the jobber?"

Flense leapt in. "Ah, precisely my point. You must directly employ camp overseers and run your own crews. Pass over the jobbers."

Pye again, "Yes, pass over the jobbers, operate Duke Logging crews under strong-minded salaried overseers. Hire the best camp cooks at the lowest wage. At each camp introduce stores stocked with trousers, boots and socks, knives and axes, galluses and candy, tobacco, maybe even papers and candles, combs and such. Get these things at the lowest price. I can take on a buyer's duty if you wish. Then charge a little higher than the merchants in town and you will get back a considerable part of what you lay out in wages."

She nodded. She interpreted these suggestions to mean "pay as little as you can in wages and sell your goods to the workers for as much as they can stand." Shanty men in remote locations would think it a benefit to have a camp store. Ideas were boiling in her mind. She said, "I have read of a Pennsylvania logging company with a short-line railroad from the cut to the mill, a small steam engine hauling the cars. We could look into doing the same. It would be an escape from the tyranny of rivers, for we now cut only trees close to waterways. Some of the most desirable timber is distant from water and deemed too much trouble to cut. Though of course a railroad would be frightfully expensive."

"You have to spend money to make money. Do not fear innovation—that is where money grows." Flense had demolished the lemon cookies and was starting on the molasses drops.

"I read also that same company milled on site and then sent the seasoned lumber to market by rail. We need to build our own railroads." She hesitated a little then said, "Mentioning Maine made me think. I believe we still need someone reliable in Maine to handle our interests. My father planned to dispose of our forestland there since the white pine is almost completely cut, but he died before it could be sold and now I wonder if there might be a market for other kinds of wood than pine? There is spruce, hemlock, but also much hardwood—beech, maple, walnut, oak. These might have values we do not yet recognize. I think we should hold on to it and look into possible markets for other woods. The Michigan land also has many more kinds of trees than pine."

"Miss Duke," said Lawyer Flense. "You have business acumen beyond that of most men."

"I learned from my father. And Uncle Lennart."

"But one more suggestion." He whisked crumbs from his vest.

He squinted at her with great seriousness. She felt it—this was not a game, not fancy nor whim; he took her as an equal intelligence.

"Yes?"

"Buy as much Chicago city property as you can and sit on it. You need do nothing with it and as time passes it will swell and double, triple, turn pennies into thousands. When first I came here you could buy a central acre for a dollar or two. Now a quarter acre of downtown urban land goes for fifteen hundred dollars. This happened in New York and it is happening here in Chicago. It will be the source of tremendous wealth to those who have land and sit on it, hold it. Yes, yes, I know what you are going to say, that you have most of the company's money tied up in forestland. Very well. When the wood is off, sell that land to settlers. But the big money, made with no effort nor outlay beyond the original purchase price, is right under your feet. City land. Mark my words."

"I mark them well."

Mr. Pye straightened up from his notes and suggested that after so much talk they go to the Tremont for a dinner. On the way out Lawyer Flense stopped at Annag Duncan's desk. "You are a wonderful woman, Mrs. Duncan," he said. "A remarkable office manager *and* a fine pastry cook." Annag blushed and put her head down. Lavinia thought she was a bit of a fool to be flattered by the lawyer's attentions.

Over chops and roasted potatoes they talked of properties, city lots and blocks, and Flense said he would introduce Lavinia to a knowing and shrewd real estate agent. She nodded, but her mind was still swarming with ideas for extending her kingdom and she said musingly, "We may look abroad as well—oh, I do not mean Europe with its worn-out old lands—Europe is not our source but our market— yet there are other countries, places we do not know about. Not now, but in future years. What fabulous kinds of wood may not grow in distant places?" Far to the east, deep under leaf mold and black forest soil, the bones of Charles Duquet relaxed.

• • •

She knew something now; the only true safety was money. Very well, Lavinia Duke, a wealthy and able businesswoman, would build a protective wall of money. And within ten years Duke Logging and Lumber had a general manager and assistants, a sales manager, dozens of landlookers, thirty logging camps, a few miles of forest rail and a steam locomotive named James; it had barges and ships and their crews, sawmills and finishing mills, two furniture mills that used hardwoods, as well as blocks and lots of choice downtown Chicago land; it had Flense's roster of lawyers, who played legislatures, senators and congressmen like they were banjos. Chicago's ten railroads covered the city like the spread-out fingers of two hands. Two lots Lavinia had bought in the summer for twelve thousand dollars each were valued at more than twenty thousand six months later. She bought as much land as she could. She knew Lawyer Flense was buying whatever he could for himself. The Chicago population exploded from twenty thousand to almost one hundred thousand in those few years.

She often watched the ship traffic on Lake Michigan, noticed fewer sails each month and more steamboats. She cultivated newspapermen who praised Duke Logging and Lumber as a philanthropic, job-giving business of impeccable moral distinction and Lavinia as a rare and progressive businesswoman. An occasional small municipal gift such as a bandstand or a contribution to Fourth of July fireworks set off yards of enthusiastic prose. She urged editors to praise the manliness and toughness of shanty men, inculcating axmen with the belief that they could take extreme risks and withstand the most desperate conditions because they were heroic rugged fellows; the same sauce served settlers unto the third generation, who believed they were "pioneers" and could outlast perils and adversities. Loggers and frontier settlers, she thought, would live on pride and belief in their own invulnerability instead of money. She learned that small gestures secured tremendous goodwill. When she heard that the shanty boys at one camp had played three old cat on a Sunday she decreed that work should stop at Saturday noon in Duke camps and the afternoon be given over to pastimes such as baseball, but that no amusements would occur on Sunday, the holy day of rest. For this she was held up as a devout but modern sportswoman and invited to Hoboken to attend a Knickerbockers' game.

After these dinners she often sat at her rosewood desk and, in a habit she had taken from Posey, wrote down as much of the conversation as she could remember in a book bound in green leather. She outlined her plan to cheaply buy up schooners, strip them of masts and rigging and make them into lumber barges.

But dinners with political men and lawyers were even more interesting and the hot questions of the day—slavery, "free soil" and territorial expansion—never burned more fiercely. A well-known senator, a champion of democracy much inclined to oratory, used her table as a platform. "The people who live in whatever states or territories they live in have the right to make their own decisions. It is none of the government's business to decide if a territory may permit slavery inside its borders or no." He did not mention that his wife owned a cotton plantation with a hundred slaves and he himself received income as its manager. The phrase "will of the people" was always in his mouth; he meant the will of white people, for another of his banners was that "the Constitution was made by whites *for* whites." After all, who else was there?

"Hear, hear," echoed down the table.

People streamed into the country—almost a million Irish in twenty years, half a million Germans. They came from all over the world, Germans, Canadians, English, Irish, French, Norwegians, Swedes. The world had heard of the rich continent with its inexhaustible coverlet of forests, its earth streaked as a moldy cheese with veins of valuable metals, fish and game in numbers too great to be compassed, hundreds of millions of acres of empty land waiting to be taken and a beckoning, generous government too enchanted with its own democratic image to deal with shrewd men whose people had lived by their wits for centuries. Everything was there for the taking—it was the chance of a lifetime and it would never come again.

For some it did not come at all: a logger whose cheap boots fell apart during the spring drive, another who did not regard a slice of raw pork dipped in molasses as the acme of dining, the man laid up for six months by a woods accident immobile in bed while his wife took in "boarders" who stayed in the house less than twenty minutes, a drought-ruined Kansas family eating coyotes to stay alive. And in Chicago fast-growing slums, hovels built from scrap wood and rotted leather clustered around the stockyards, lumber mills and tanneries encircled by poisonous water.

58

locked room

Lavinia was corseted and dressed for the day in green silk, an elaborately draped skirt over a bustle. There was a lace frill at her throat. Out on the open deck of the cupola the wind was like a clawing, rolling wildcat trapped between lake and sky. She saw two distant ships on the trembling horizon, but looking south over the city with her opera glasses, she saw no slums. She turned again to the north and squinted at the ships. The wind pulled at her black hair piled on top of her head. There would always be the poor, hordes who had no ambition to better themselves. The world swarmed with terrible problems but they were not her affair. She strained to make out details of the faraway steamers. A telescope was needed. Despite her superior position she had her own difficulties: the gnawing aloneness (for Goosey Breeley was more like a chest of drawers than a companion), tiresome business negotiations, spiteful rivals—and succession. It was legal now for women to own property and she had to decide who would inherit Duke Logging and Lumber, the great timberland holdings, the mills and railroad stocks. The wind pulled at her hair. Smoothing the loose strands she went inside and laid the opera glasses on the marble-topped table just inside the door. The thought would not leave her. An heir had to be someone of the Duke bloodline. It would *not* be Goosey. She had a swiftly dissolving thought of the human flotsam that came to cut trees, their lives nothing beyond a few sweaty years with an ax. Despite their winters in the forests they all seemed to produce large families. They had no worries about succession, nor about credit or character.

"My God," she said to her silver-framed dressing room mirror, "how do they stand it?" Her hair was a fright wig. But who they were and what it was they had to stand was unclear. People spoke of happiness, but what was that? What was anything? Posey had had no such doubts, nor James, who fretted over nothing except the most banal irritants. But she was different. She had terrible wrathy feelings directed everywhere. She was short-tempered with people who did not respond to her requests speedily. If they could not keep up with the pace of development, let them stand aside! James had taught her that getting ahead was the important thing. Of course the problems and impediments were endless, the brain-wracking decisions of which men she could extend credit to, and she almost envied women like Clara, who simply let a husband guide them. Honor and promise had ruled in James's day, but now there were so many rogues about that money and contracts were the only safe way to proceed. Thank God for Tappan's Mercantile Agency, with its reports on the worth of individual businessmen. She relied on their astute judgments. Bad creditors could bring the largest businesses down. And children: was not that the root of her discontent? Perhaps not, for she disliked the sight of pregnant women, who seemed everywhere, especially along the rural roads. Farm women were like sawmills. She shuddered and went downstairs for tea with Goosey.

"Your hair!" cried Goosey, clasping her large pale hands. "Shall I get a little lavender oil to smooth the flyaways in place?"

"Thank you, Goosey, that is what I need, but I would prefer the damask oil. Lavender is too reminiscent of bedsheets."

Goosey was back in a minute with a vial of scented oil and a feather. "You should always wear a head scarf when you go to the cupola," she said in a flat voice, knowing Lavinia would not bother.

The question of heirs began to disturb Lavinia's sleep when Cyrus and his family, as well as many Chicago people high and low, fell

ill with typhoid. Cyrus perished in great pain with intestinal perfo-
rations. The children went one by one and finally Clara, demented
with grief and helplessness, fashioned a knotted loop in a heavy shell-
pink silk scarf, stepped off a chair set on the dining room table and
hanged herself from the chandelier.

That winter Lavinia herself had many illnesses, intestinal gripes
and skin eruptions. She had not liked Clara but missed her, missed
poor old Cyrus. Under the pressure of these afflictions she began to
examine the Duke family papers for possible heirs and consult with
foreign-born genealogists; she found few Americans interested in
ancestral searches, as they took pride in being unshackled by the past—
unless they had a distinguished early family member and then they
waved him like a flag. She reviewed her relatives. Sedley Duke's children by his second marriage had all died without issue. Lennart Vogel
had never married. Edward and Freegrace had no known children.

"You know," she said to Mr. Flense, "it is unpleasantly clear that I
am the last surviving Duke."

"Nonsense, Lavinia. There must be heirs out there. You must
employ someone to search for them." His tone was impatient as
if there were undiscovered cousins stacked like cordwood in some
nearby cave. But she had doubts; could genealogists discover any
heirs, whether in the still-United States or in the Netherlands? The
two savants she discovered—Sextus Bollard of Boston and R. R.
Tetrazinni in Philadelphia—both presided over bookshops where
tracing family lines eased long hours between customers.

Lavinia invited each to Chicago for an interview. The first to arrive
at the house for dinner and the interview was Sextus Bollard. He was
at least sixty, Lavinia thought, looking at his old-fashioned checked
trousers. But he did carry a fine stick with a gold knob in the likeness
of a gorgon's head.

Goosey and Mr. Flense dined with them and they made small talk
about Mr. Bollard's journey (difficult) and the tale the conductor told
him of the horrors of crossing the plains to the west. He said sparks
from the engines often ignited the dry grass, and that passengers cow-

ered in their seats as the train made its way through a sea of flame. He said that during one unfortunate traverse flames had seized the train and roasted the passengers like pigeons. "Indians came and ate them as we would a turnspit ox. I counted myself fortunate to have had no worse adventure than encounters with the uncouth inhabitants of Ohio and Indiana Territory."

"A very disturbing tale if true," said Mr. Flense, "but I fear the conductor was pulling your leg, Mr. Bollocks."

"Bollard, sir, is the name," snapped the guest. "And I believe he told the truth as he showed me the clipped illustration and account from *Harper's,* which he kept in his breast pocket to entertain travelers." He narrowed his eyes at Flense, to whom he had taken a dislike.

After dinner Goosey went upstairs and Lavinia, Lawyer Flense and Mr. Bollard went into the library to give him copies of the Duke family papers and discuss the terms of the genealogist's employment.

"Of course Holland, but not France?" Bollard asked. "My cursory examination of your papers indicates your ancestor Charles Duquet came from France. Indeed, from Paris. Is that not correct?"

Lavinia felt a burning itch on her neck, one of the unpleasant blotches that came so often. "Yes, of course, France. It slipped my mind. Though we always have thought of Holland as our point of origin—Uncle Lennart Vogel fostered that idea. Our ancestor Charles Duquet has always been something of a mystery. It has been my understanding that he vanished in the wilderness. But do search in Paris. Who knows what you may find? I am thinking you might begin with a six-month search. Of course we will pay your travel expenses, and provide a purse. And if necessary to make more trips we can discuss it when the time arrives."

"And do keep receipts for even the smallest purchases," said Lawyer Flense. "That is the correct way." And so Bollard, who considered Lavinia a paler, older, homelier and more modern imitation of the learned female characters in Thomas Amory's *The Life and Opinions of John Buncle, Esq.,* closed his bookshop and sailed for France on the trail of Duquet relatives, his valises packed with scratch paper, grammars and dictionaries; he read French but did not speak it and planned to write out his questions.

Tetrazinni, younger and with a wild red beard and spectacles in pot-metal frames, came a week later. He was more modishly attired than old Bollard—a pleated shirtfront with a turndown collar and a wide silk tie drawn through a heavy signet ring, velvet waistcoat and—were they?—yes, they were, black velvet trousers. The dinner was mutton and boiled potatoes. Tetrazinni stared musingly at his plate and looked several times toward the kitchen door, but no larded capons nor Pacific oysters came. Goosey was ill with a catarrh and sipped a little veal broth in her room. Lawyer Flense sawed at his mutton, listened to Tetrazinni's verbose and excited account of his journey—by some stroke of coincidence he had been regaled by the same tale of the burning prairie as Bollard. Over the dried peach pie Lawyer Flense caught Lavinia's eye, nodded and made his excuses.

"I fear I must run. I have a court appearance tomorrow and wish to be fresh for argument. Delighted to meet you, Mr. Tetrazinni, and wish you good fortune in your search," he said, bowing and backing.

Lavinia and Tetrazinni went to the library for port and she gave him the bulky packet of family papers, most copied out by Annag Duncan and Miss Heinrich. Tetrazinni's fingers flew through the pages for a few minutes but he did not stop talking. He had too many questions to suit Lavinia. They had hired him, why could he not do his job without harassing her for names? Surely the old family records and letters were enough—if he would shut up and read them instead of gabbling on.

"I cannot tell you," she said for the fourth time when he asked for a list of Amsterdam relatives and all ancestors, their current addresses and business interests. "I suppose they all may be dead. It is for you to discover." She was tired of him.

"Yes, but names will lead me to *today's* generations. That is how we do it. I must have a place to start," he said, jutting his chin out. She pointed at the wad of copied family papers in his hands. In the end Tetrazinni read aloud for two hours, culling dozens of names from Vogel's Dutch correspondence. A month later he sailed with his list and Lavinia's letter of introduction to whom it might concern for information on any living connection to Charles Duquet and Cornelia Roos.

Tetrazinni made an inner note to particularly examine the history of Charles Duquet's son Outger, who had been something of a learned authority on American Indians. Scholar or no, he likely had cohabited with someone in Leiden and his other haunts. And had he not lived in America for some years? Where that might have been he had no idea. Although in the papers Lavinia had supplied there was frequent mention of a "large pine table" that Duquet possessed and Duke & Sons claimed, there was no mention of the location of either table or man. Tetrazinni assumed both had once been somewhere in Boston, but the old city directories had no Outger Duquet listed. As he read again through the meager family history on three faded pages held together with a tailor's pin and signed Bernard Duke, two short sentences on the ancestor's voyages to China caught Tetrazinni's attention. "Well, well," he said to himself, "if no one turns up in Amsterdam there may be Duquets in Peking, though perhaps rather difficult to sort out from Yees and Yongs." He imagined the risible possibility of telling Miss Duke that her only living relative and heir was a Chinese noodle seller.

For the Dukes and the Breitsprechers and lesser timbermen business was good. Insatiable markets along the Mississippi and Missouri Rivers squalling for lumber unmade Albany and Buffalo. A tide of agricultural-minded immigrants—sinewy men, their swollen wives and bruised children—streamed onto the prairies, all needing houses and barns, silos and stables, needing furniture and shingles, lathes and pickets, rails and posts. New railroads to and from the prairies delivered them lumber and brought beef cattle and hogs back to Chicago, where the war and fulfillment of the Indian treaties guaranteeing annual livestock distributions meant acres of stock-yards. There was a fierce need for planks and poles, fencing and pens. And if it all burned down every two or three years, there were more trees in the woods—endless trees.

During the war with the south the Duke Board of Directors included Lawyer Flense; Accountant Mr. Pye; David Neale, owner of the newspaper *Chicago Progress;* Annag Duncan, the office manager; Noah Ludlum, who oversaw the logging sites and sawmills; another Maine man, Glafford Jones, responsible for log and lumber transport; two wealthy logging kings, Theodore Jinks and Axel Cowes, both large shareholders in Duke Logging. Jinks and Cowes built mansions on properties adjoining Lavinia's grounds. The three shared a park—thirty acres of woodland area on the lakeside of their abutting proper-ties. It was Lavinia's habit to walk on the silent paths in early evening, when she sometimes met Axel Cowes and his spaniels.

"Evening, Lavinia," Cowes would say, half-bowing. "A fine day."

"Yes, very fine, Axel."

Cowes was in his sixties, white-haired and with a soft rosy face. It was he who had suggested the park. He collected paintings and had an artistic bent. He saw beauty in the forest as well as wealth, some-thing Lavinia found as inexplicable as her pleasure walking the shad-owed paths. As for art, he liked pictures that showed stags drinking from forest pools, lone Indians paddling canoes across mirrored lakes. Lavinia favored large canvases showing the triumph of the hunt and engravings with panoramic city views and lines of statistics enclosed in ornate scrolls. Cowes, despite his years and differing ways, had suggested marriage to Lavinia as some men did. They wanted her money and holdings, she knew this. Theodore Jinks, who was a rougher type and slightly tainted with gossip of a gambling habit, had done the same. Yet she did not hold the proposals against them. She liked both men, both were dependable Board members with solid knowledge of the logging business. When Cowes suggested the park it was easy to agree, though she noticed Jinks's expression when Cowes talked of "sequestering" the valuable pines.

"Those pines would bring a good dollar," Jinks said.

"Oh yes, but it is good to leave a few to remind us of our early days of fortune. No one wishes to live next to a stump field." Cowes had an elevated way of saying such things that made Jinks shuffle his feet and curse under his breath. "Except agriculturists," he said lamely. It was no use; Lavinia and Cowes only tolerated him. He found ease in the knowledge that one day those pines would come down as all pines must.

Pye, Flense and Lavinia made up the inner circle of Duke Logging and Lumber. None of them had any small talk; conversation was always business. The arrival of the telegraph some years earlier had been like a kettle of water dashed into a cauldron of boiling oil for the business world and the railroads. Giveaway Congress guaranteed the Union Pacific and Central Pacific railroads sixteen thousand dollars for every mile of track laid on level ground, and double that through mountainous terrain and included a forty-mile-wide corridor across the entire continent. Now *there* was real money, great *great* fortunes of which the Dukes could not even dream. But there were consolations. The center of the country exploded in hysterical expansion. Duke's lumber shipments quadrupled as the Union Army hammered up forts and prison camps. Chicago businessmen joyously mulcted the government with shoddy war goods from canned beef to forage caps at high prices, and not Lavinia, Cowes nor Jinks scrupled to hold back warped and knotty lumber billed at the price of clear.

"Why pay more when you can get it for less?" said Flense, who cared little for archaic idealism and who despised James Duke's timberland purchases when he could have got the same land for nothing. "The government can't prove land claims weren't made in good faith." They used the General Land Office's preemption acts, which allowed settlers to take up and then purchase land at the giveaway price of $1.25 for a quarter section—180 acres. Duke sent out its landlookers, chose the best woods tracts and used dummy men who went through the motions of settling and then handed over the deeds to Flense. An army of preemption brokers greased the nefarious skids. Nor was it any great feat to bribe the federal land agents. The Homestead Acts of the 1860s were sweet gifts to Duke, which hired perjurous "settlers," who camped on the land for a few days, nailed up a feeble shack of a few boards—the "house"—shoved two empty whiskey bottles between the boards for windows, ground a heel in the dirt to indicate a well and claimed a homestead. Others toted around a dollhouse with windows, roof and floors, put it on the site and at the Land Office declared a house "fourteen by sixteen," not mentioning that the measurements were in inches rather than feet. Still others had the smallest allowable "house" on skids that was hauled around to the various claims and designated a livable shanty. Duke bought up huge blocks of land in these ways, rushed in, cut the timber and then gave up the homestead rights. No one objected; they were smart American businessmen going ahead, doing what businessmen did. No one got rich by walking seven miles to return a penny. And there were hundreds of small loggers anxious to sell out to Duke after a few hard lessons—being shot at by unknown persons, suffering frequent sawmill fires and large-scale log stealage that made the game not worth the candle.

None of these affairs were discussed at Board meetings—it was business. Tappan's Mercantile report had called James Duke "A-one. Wealthy family, sound business practices. Good as gold." Duke's Board was more concerned with such nagging subjects as continuing to outfit all their mills with steam-powered circular saws and what to do with encroaching piles of sawdust. Noah Ludlum, smooth-shaven except for a pointy little goatee, said, "Them big circle saws cut damn fast—beg pardon—but they don't stay firm. There is a wobble. You can't hardly see it but that jeezly wobble costs the comp'ny money as it makes a big wide kerf. I know for a fact every thousand board feet cut we lose more than three hundred in sawdust. Thing is, the steel in them saws is not good. So much steel goes into rails and guns we can't git good saws. And you got sawdust piles higher than Katahdin. Course we burn it to power the boilers but—"

Lavinia interrupted. "Lose no sleep over the sawdust, Mr. Ludlum. There is nothing we can do about it at the moment except burn it or throw it in the rivers. The trees of Michigan are so plentiful we need not be frugal."

"Wal," said Mr. Ludlum, who was determined to have the last word, "we have to leave the biggest trees out in the woods. Them saws can't cut nothin a hair more than half their diameter. Bigger saws needed, but the bigger they are the more they wobble."

Lavinia looked down at her papers, glanced at Annag Duncan, who had compiled the figures, and said, "All the same, our Avery Mill alone will cut three million board feet this year, well ahead of last year. We still have a few old water-powered mills with up-and-down saws and the sooner we get circular saws and steam engines into them the better. That is our goal right now, whatever the wobble. And I would suggest we look at the new double circular saws that can accommodate larger logs."

"Good work, Annag," said Lawyer Flense in his stage whisper voice, smiling at the office manager.

There was no wobble in the government's need for lumber and Duke Logging profited through the rich years of the war. Mr. Pye seemed almost sad when it ended in the spring, followed by Lincoln's assassination. But the south needed to rebuild, and the cry for lumber had never been louder.

"There are rich forests in the south," said Theodore Jinks, "closer to the need. I suggest we buy up some southern woodland and get our cutting crews to work. If the Board agrees, I can make a reconnaissance." The idea was good and Jinks and Mr. Ludlum, their clothes neatly packed in carpetbags, left a week later to assess the southern trees.

Fires of invention blazed through the country; new ideas and opportunities for innovation crammed the mail basket that Annag Duncan lugged in every morning. There were so many of them and it took so long to understand the complex explanations and diagrams that Mr. Pye suggested that Duke hire an educated man to assess the proposals and even that the Board arrange a meeting of these inventors. At such a meeting men who had worked out logging industry improvements or new machines might show scale models or drawings and diagrams. The Board would talk with the inventors.

"This could be promising," said Lavinia. "If something of value emerges Duke Logging can offer a fair price for the rights and then patent it. Let us set a date for the summer, when travel is less onerous. The company will put the inventors up, gratis, in the Hotel Great Lakes—a limit of twenty men. I believe it has a ballroom that may be ideal for exhibits. We will certainly find it interesting."

The next spring in Detroit, more than 250 miles east, Dieter Breitsprecher scissored out the half-page ad in the *Chicago Progress* calling for inventors to apply for Duke Logging's summer exhibit. The chance to mix with a collection of men whose brains buzzed with mechanics and machines was irresistible. Inventors did not write to Breitsprechers. He had a certain respect for Lavinia and remembered how quickly in the long-ago years she had learned the basics of scaling; he doubted she had ever used the knowledge—why should she?—she had competent employees, several lured away from the Breitsprechers. He wrote, asking if he might attend the exhibit, not as an inventor, not as a competitor, but as an interested friend. He offered to help defray the expenses of the gathering. He did not think she would refuse him; indeed, she wrote back cordially, refused his monetary offer and asked him to dine with her the Friday evening before the meeting.

This was their chance, she thought, to enfold Breitsprecher into Duke Logging. After their longest and most passionate meeting Duke's Board had suggested making Breitsprecher a buyout offer. The Breitsprecher logging concern was worth ten of the little independent cutters who cleared fifty acres and retired. But Lavinia sensed it might be more diplomatic to offer a partnership. Despite their peculiar ideas on clear-cutting and replanting stumpland, Breit-sprechers had the reputation of a highly reputable business that dealt fairly with loggers and dealers. And while Armenius was alive they had been successful. They also had the reputation of being honest, and while too much honesty could hold a company back, there were many people who still believed it a virtue. A partnership would add luster to Duke Logging, considered ruthless and devious by other timbermen. Lavinia was still grateful to Dieter for his help in teaching her how to read and apply the Scribner and Doyle scale rules to raw logs; and she was curious to know the details of Armenius's rumor-tainted death two years past. But would Dieter agree? He had always seemed rather aloof. So his request to attend the inventors' gathering seemed fortunate.

Two Civil War veterans, Parker Brace and Hudson Van Dipp, both from Cherokee County, Georgia, both house carpenters who had been friends before secession, fought for the south until they were captured at Shiloh and stuffed into Chicago's notorious Camp Douglas. They survived in the squalid pen where there was no medical treatment, no hygienic tubs or basins, where scurvied prisoners sat in apathy. Brace and Van Dipp did their best to survive by constructing a complicated trap from a piece of wire and a crushed tin cup and lived on rats. To stay sane they made a carpenter's game for themselves: through talk and scratched diagrams in the dirt they built an imaginary house from the foundation to the weather vane.

The dirty Yanks offered choices: be returned to the south as a prisoner of war; take an oath of allegiance and enlist in the U.S. Army or Navy; take the oath and be sent north to labor on public works; or take the oath and return home if that home lay within the Union Army lines. Brace and Van Dipp scorned these alternatives. But the day came when both showed symptoms of scurvy and Van Dipp said, "I am goin to take their goddamn oath and join their goddamn

army and get out a the goddamn rain, get the goddamn hell out a
here. Can't git much worse than this and maybe find somethin I kin
eat. Sick a goddamn raw rat." Both took the oath and the two new
Galvanized Yankees were sent off to fight the Indians in Texas. Van
Dipp had never imagined such a dry hard place existed in the world.
The sun rushed up in a tide of gilt that became the flat white of noon,
then the torpid decay of visibility in an evening dusk still throbbing
with accumulated heat. Brace was felled by arrows and lay for nine
hours in the dust hearing the scream of a redtail cut the incandescent
sky, but Van Dipp was never wounded. Mustered out, they went
back to Georgia briefly, recoiled from Reconstruction, found their
families recoiled from them and called them traitors.

Together they returned to Chicago, where the city was literally
exploding with demands for carpenters. Hundreds of people wanted
houses built yesterday. During a rare week of idleness Van Dipp said,
"Parker, let's don't wait until we got the next job. We-all kin make
up a stack of windows and doors beforehand. No telling what we'll
build, but I guarantee she'll have windows and a door." They added
cupboards and sets of stairs and even wall sections that could be
hauled to a site. It made putting up a house noticeably faster. It was
this habit of prefabrication that led to a partner and a grander idea.

One morning, as hot and humid as only a Chicago summer day
could be, a sharp-angled man in a wrinkled linen suit came into the
workshop and stood looking at the stacks of made-up windows and
staircases stored there.

"Good day. Do I have the pleasure of greeting Van Dipp and
Brace?"

"Don't guarantee how much pleasure is in it, but that's us," said
Van Dipp. "Who-all mought you be?"

"Charles Munster Weed, sir, an architect. I have a contract to
build a street of ten houses and I want good carpenters who will
work quickly. You have that reputation. Are you currently involved
in a construction project?" He looked pointedly at the extra windows
and stairs.

"Not much this minute. Them's frames and stairs we make up ahead to save us time. Doors and frames, pantry cupboards and such."

When Weed learned that several of his houses stood right in front of him only waiting for assembly, he hired the two carpenters on the spot. The work went as merrily as kittens playing with feathers.

They met again a week after Weed's houses were finished and the architect's almost rabid enthusiasm fertilized the Idea; he understood where their preconstruction process could go. "Why, you could build a town that way. You could have a dozen different designs of houses so people could pick the one they liked, you could pack one or more up and ship them to wherever on the railroad." His voice rose to an unmasculine pitch.

"We know where they-all need it, too," said Brace. "Out on them ol prairies. No trees, no wood, but they got a have houses. Some a them are a-buildin dirt houses, full a bugs and snakes. They want barns. They want churches. I guess they would buy a house all packaged, ready to go. But the problem is it takes money to git them packages built."

"And we ain't got it," said Van Dipp.

"Schoolhouses," raved the architect, rowing his arms back and forth. "Shops and courthouses. They need towns and this is a way to get one to them."

"We can bundle the parts up and ship by rail. Make the crates the right size fit in a farm wagon."

"Yes! Yes! I could design different models, let the customers choose what they want. You listen to me! I got some investment money. I'd like to work with you boys—if you are willing." They were willing and on the spot formed Van Dipp, Brace and Weed, and named their venture Prairie Homes.

More than a year had passed since Lavinia had sent the two genealogists out to search. Another autumn was closing in. Now she had a letter from R. R. Tetrazinni, who wrote that he had "discovered something you may find interesting" and wished an appointment. Lavinia named a day in late summer just before Duke's Inventor's Exhibition. To be fair she wrote to Sextus Bollard and asked what he had found. She was surprised when a letter came back from Bollard's nephew, Tom Bollard, saying Mr. Bollard had returned from foreign parts in a grave condition and had died shortly thereafter; he, Tom, had taken over the bookshop and would send on the papers his uncle had amassed for Lavinia. These arrived before Tetrazinni's visit, and Lavinia read that every one of Bollard's leads had played out in a dead end. Charles Duquet had left no trace in Parisian records and it was thought that any papers naming his people had likely burned in the French Revolution. Of the Dutch connection Lennart Vogel had been the last remaining relative.

R. R. Tetrazinni arrived punctually. His red beard was trimmed close and his spectacles transmuted to a gold-rimmed pince-nez. He carried two leather cases. Annag brought him a cup of coffee and put it near his elbow. He took out his papers and began a long recitation of his travels and discoveries. Annag Duncan sat near, taking a few notes. Lavinia listened with increasing impatience. Why could he not get to the point?

"Mr. Tetrazinni, let me ask you bluntly, have you found any Duke descendants?"

"Indeed I have. Though I fear you may not relish the disclosure of their identity." He cleared his throat and grinned, postponing the delicious moment. "I do not know how much you know of your family tree. In a nutshell. Charles Duquet adopted three sons, Nicolaus and Jan from an Amsterdam orphanage and another, Bernard, from the streets of La Rochelle. In those times adoptions were very informal, though he treated the boys as his sons and left them his goods in equal parts. You likely know that you are descended from Nicolaus, who married Mercy and with whom he had three children—Patience, Piet and Sedley, the last named your grandfather. In other words, you have *no Duquet blood flowing in your veins,* only that of the adopted son Nicolaus." He took a great swig of coffee and watched Lavinia's complexion redden.

"Back to Charles Duquet. After the adoption of those boys his Dutch wife, Cornelia Roos, bore him two legitimate children, Outger Duquet and Doortje Duquet. Doortje's line died out with the death of her only son, Lennart Vogel, an unmarried bachelor. Outger Duquet lived for some years in Penobscot Bay in Maine, and took an Indian concubine. She gave birth to a daughter, Beatrix Duquet, on whom her father lavished attention and education. But when he removed to Leiden the daughter remained in Maine. She eventually reverted to native ways and, as near as I can be sure, married a *métis* named Kuntaw Sel, descended from Mi'kmaq Indians and a French *habitant.*" Lavinia's cup clattered in its saucer.

"It seems Beatrix Duquet and Kuntaw Sel, who were legally married, had two sons—Josime Sel and Francis-Outger Sel. The only living bloodline descendants of Charles Duquet are the grandchildren of Josime and Francis-Outger. I have not finished my investigation as to these specific descendants' names and dwelling places. It would involve trips to Canada and contact with remnants of the Indian tribes. I did not endeavor to undertake this until I knew your wishes. However, these people would be the rightful heirs of Charles Duquet—if one counts only blood relationship as meaningful. I personally think the adopted sons' lines of descent have a stronger claim to the family fortune than the still-unidentified Indians. After all, we know that possession is nine points of the law. Here. It is all in my report." He handed her a sheaf of pages in an almost insolent manner and his tone indicated those unnamed Indians had a valid claim to the Duke empire.

She sat silent for a long minute, then said smoothly, "I think you need not disturb the Canadian situation. We will consider the investigation closed." She glanced at Annag, wishing she had not been present, and saw that the woman was frowning hotly at R. R. Tetrazinni. Good loyal Annag, thought Lavinia. She will keep her silence.

As soon as Tetrazinni left Lavinia tossed the report into the wastebin.

"I'll just put this into the stove," said Annag, carrying the bin into the front office, where she rattled the stove door but carefully placed Tetrazinni's report at the back of the supplies closet under her rain cape.

The Hotel Great Lakes owner, Simon Drimmel, fair-haired and handsome, was excited by his filled-up hotel and apprehensive about possible scratches on the ballroom floor. When several large crates labeled PRAIRIE HOMES arrived and Drimmel heard of the contents he ordered them unloaded on the south lawn.

"I can't have construction in the ballroom," he said. "It would scar the floor. It is essential we keep the floor in flawless condition fit for satin-soled slippers. Balls are our principal income."

"For all you know annual exhibits during the season when there are no balls may become a lucrative source of income," said Mr. Pye, who was managing the exhibition.

"Ah, perhaps." Drimmel smiled, hoping it was not to be. He very much liked the music, the perfume, excitement and beauty of the balls, the pretty gowns and shining ruddy faces.

"Quite all right," soothed Mr. Pye. "That particular exhibit belongs outside in any case."

At the end of the day, when everyone was drooping with fatigue, Lawyer Flense offered to drive Annag home "as it is on my way."

"Very kind, sir," murmured Annag, gathering her bags and traps.

Goosey Breeley, who usually dined with Lavinia, even when there was company, said, when she heard Dieter Breitsprecher was coming to dinner, that she would take her dinner in her room.

"That is hardly necessary, Goosey. Dine with us. It is no trouble. I had to invite him as a courtesy."

"No, I understand very well how such affairs work, dear Lavinia. You may wish to discuss business. It is my choice to dine in privacy. I rarely have a quiet repast free of responsibilities, so it will be a treat." Lavinia thought she was right. It would be easier with Dieter if she did not have to include Goosey in the conversation.

"Mr. Dieter Bridestretcher," said Libby the housemaid.

"Show him in." Lavinia, dressed in her customary black dress, sat on a crimson velvet sofa before the drawing room fire and steeled herself for the encounter. Rarely at a loss for words, she had no idea how to put the partnership offer. She should have written a letter.

"Dieter Breitsprecher, welcome. It has been a long time." She had not remembered he was so broad-shouldered and tall. His yellow hair was beginning to dull at the temples. His overlarge eyes, his whole smiling face seemed to her open and amiable. Immediately she felt awkward and wished the evening over and done.

"Certain, dear Miss Duke, it has been a long time." He spoke with almost no trace of an accent, held out a hedgerow bouquet of budded goldenrod, hawkweed, past-prime wild roses and grass-of-Parnassus. "It would have been tropical rarities—were there any." He saw a middle-aged woman, broad in the hips, buxom in the fitted black dress, but with the strong presence of the one in charge of the money.

"Dieter, please call me Lavinia. And thank you for the bouquet— although wild, it is handsome, and on this occasion I prefer natural- ism to artifice. Will you take a glass of wine? Or would you rather have spirits?" She would toss the weeds away after he left.

"To be truthful I would prefer whiskey—if you have it."

"If I have it! It is my own preference, one I adopted from my father." She went to the sideboard and poured two glasses of what purported to be aged Kentucky bourbon. They sat before the fire and at first said nothing, glancing at each other to get a measure.

"Well," said Lavinia, making the effort, "has business been good for you this year?"

"Yes, very good, despite the second loss to fire of our Robin's Nest Mill. I will never again hire a pipe smoker. The sawyer *would* knock his burning dottle into the sawdust despite a hundred admonitions. Sorrowfully the cause has been removed—he burned himself up in this one."

"How wretched," said Lavinia. "We, too, have lost mills to fire." Another lengthy silence stretched out. Lavinia thought of the subject of the presidential election—everyone knew General Grant would win. Instead she said, "Do you travel much? Back east? Or to Germany?"

"Once a year to New York or Boston. Or even Philadelphia, and one time to California to assess my cousin Armenius's unfortunate circumstances." There was an opening but she could not press her question about Armenius so soon for fear of looking an eager gossip.

"So you had a sawmill named Robin's Nest?"

"Yes. Every year a robin would build her nest on a rafter above the saw. I do not know if it was the same one. It very much worried the old pipe smoker, who feared the young ones would fall from the nest onto the saw."

Lavinia clenched one hand. "Oh, I hope that did not happen."

"It did not. That mill produced dozens of robins in its time."

"Mills do not seem to last long. There is always some catastrophe."

"You are quite right." He hitched his chair a little closer. He enjoyed talking about catastrophes and had seen a good many in the Michigan forests. "Most are entirely preventable, but men are careless and I think millmen are the most careless, though the owners and the show foreman can do a good deal of damage. For instance"—he peered earnestly at her—"I do not wish to bore you with accounts of misfortune?"

Again, an opening to inquire about Armenius, but instead she said, "Dieter, you do not bore me, pray continue. But first let me refresh your glass. Now go on."

"A Maine timberman told me of his reasons for coming out to Michigan. In Maine he had a big mill. He put his mill at the bottom of a steep hill covered with pine right to the water's edge. His plan was to cut the pine, make a slide for the logs that would carry them down into the mill, then load the lumber on ships docked in front, a very smooth and continuous operation that fell out just as he predicted. But he didn't understand what happens to a hill when you remove the trees."

Lavinia had no idea what he meant.

"What *does* happen to a hill with the trees removed?"

"Spring came and all began to thaw. He told me he was standing on a nearby spit of land in a position where he could admire his mill cutting as fast as the saws could run when he saw that entire treeless hill gather itself together like a cat and rush down in a landslide of mud. It buried the mill and mill hands, sank the ship waiting to be loaded. It made terrible big waves in the harbor. Never found anything that was in its path. A monstrous wet pile of mud and stumps."

"I had no idea such a thing could occur," said Lavinia. "I admire your knowledge of these dark mischances. I must send a bulletin to our sawyers not to place a mill at the bottom of a slope."

"Yes, or better still leave the trees in place. Tree roots hold down the soil. The branches shade the soil and protect it from heavy rain washouts."

"Miss Lavinia," said Libby in the doorway, "Cook says dinner is ready."

"Thank you, Libby. Dieter, shall we go in?"

Somehow they could not let go of catastrophes as a subject and over the roast lamb and fried potatoes went from landslides and fires to shipwrecks, crazy cooks, suicidal loggers, woods accidents, even a daring payroll holdup. Was this the time to ask about Armenius? Or the other, more important question? No.

"I have heard, Dieter, that you have bought up a good deal of cutover lands. Is that true?"

"It is. Such land can be had for almost nothing, and it gives me pleasure to replant and make it good and valuable forest again."

"But surely it will take many years before it can be cut, before it has value."

"Of course. But in Europe people consider the past and the future with greater seriousness. We have been managing forests for centuries and it is an ingrained habit to consider the future. Americans have no sense of years beyond three—last year, this year and next year. I suppose I keep to my old ways. I like to know that there will be a forest when I am gone."

"Very commendable, I am sure," she said. "Where do you find the young trees you plant?"

"We grow them. Breitsprechers started a pine seedling nursery some years ago. We employ Indians in spring and summer to plant for us. White woodsmen who cut trees scorn such work. But the Indians have a deeper understanding of nature and time, and we employ them when we can."

Lavinia thought that it was likely Indians were more glad of having paid work than of making forests for the future.

"Your care for forests is well known. And I have also heard that your logging camps have numerous small bunkhouses for four men instead of one great long building that can house a hundred?"

"Yes, it seems to me that more privacy will rest the men more thoroughly. These fellows labor greatly and appreciate small comforts."

She bit her tongue to keep from saying that many of Breitsprecher's woodsmen came to the crowded bunkhouses of Duke Logging because rough living challenged their male hardiness. They despised ease and comfort. That was certainly the wrong thing to say.

Lavinia fidgeted. She would have to make the Board's offer soon. And if he agreed she could ask openly about Armenius. They had reviewed catastrophes and she had missed her chance to find that out. By the time the dessert came—cream-filled éclairs dipped in chocolate with a huddle of sugared strawberries at one end—they were more comfortable with each other, and she was almost enjoying his company.

"Would you care for a stroll in the park before coffee and a liqueur?" asked Lavinia. She would ask him then.

"What park might that be?"

"It is a small forest park I have made with two neighbors," she said. "It is very pleasant on a summer evening and as it is still light we can enjoy the last rays."

They stepped into the woods, passing under a magnificent silver maple, its long-stemmed leaves showing their silvery undersides. Dieter was amazed. "Why, Lavinia, you have preserved this beautiful little forest. I commend you." He quoted from Uhland: "'The sweetest joys on earth are found / In forests green and deep,'" and thought that she was not entirely lost to the lust for money.

The park was ten acres of mixed hardwoods with another twenty of old virgin white pine at its east end, a remnant of the extensive shoreline trees cut by Duke Logging decades earlier. A pathway cleared of undergrowth wound through the trees, and as they crossed a log bridge he could see a rill coursing downslope into a pool lit by the sun, the evening insect hatch caught in the last rays. They walked to the pines in time to see the final orange slab fade into deep shadow.

Behind them sounded the day's final robin cries. The wind stirred the pine tops but they only heard the rich ringing calls *cheeriup cheerilee, cheeriup cheerilee.*

"They are telling us to be happy and cheerful," said Lavinia, caught in the perfumed memory of lying on Posey's silk pillow and listening to her hoarse low voice read of good Robin Red-breast.

"I wonder if you know how badly the robins are hurt when we cut down their trees," murmured Dieter. "We take their trees away and they are forced to build nests over whirling saws."

"Oh dear heaven," said Lavinia. "I never thought of it that way. Why do not they fly away to other trees?"

"They can, and do, but nests cannot be moved and then, when the young are just ready to fledge, come the choppers and fell the tree, dashing the infants to the ground." He stopped when he saw he was causing her real pain. "Dear Lavinia," he said. "You are very tenderhearted toward robins." He had discovered something.

"I know," she said nasally, trying not to bawl. "I love them so. Do you know that if someone dies in the woods the robins come and gather leaves, cover them over . . ." And the tears ran. What could he do? Gingerly Dieter put his hands on Lavinia's shoulders; she pressed her face against his shirt and they stood in amber afterglow with robins shouting all around them, adjuring them to cheer up, cheer up, for God's sake, cheer up.

She did not want his warmth even as she craved it, the smell of his shirt, her own weakness, and she pulled back. He looked at her, said nothing and they walked on, with considerable space between, to the house, to brandy and coffee in paper-thin porcelain cups, the liquid black until a spoon of cream made its miniature whirlpool.

Dieter Breitsprecher found her a great puzzle. She was like the perennial locked room containing unknown objects found in every great castle. He set down his brandy glass and opened his mouth to say something about the forest park, but she interrupted and said in a rush, "Dieter Breitsprecher, there is something I wish to ask you. The Board and I would like to offer you a partnership with Duke Logging, we value your knowledge, we wish you to join us on terms we both agree on, the Board, the Board and I, we have discussed this and we want you, I, I— Libby," she called without waiting for his response, "show Mr. Breitsprecher out." She stood swaying and then gabbled, "Let us talk here tomorrow, Dieter, after the exhibit. You can give me your answer then, your feelings— I have enjoyed the evening so much. And we can discuss the inventors, discuss everything for the Board and I value your opinion." And she rushed out of the room; there was no other word for it, she rushed away from him.

He stood flabbergasted. And although he had enough presence of mind to call after her that he, too, had enjoyed the evening, it had been more like spying through the keyhole into that locked room. "Unlikely I will sleep tonight," he said to himself. *"Verdammt noch mal!"*

By morning she had recovered her aplomb. Although she regretted her weak sniveling, Lavinia had finally said what she had to say. Now she would wait for his response. She was prepared for a refusal.

• • •

At the exhibit she noticed that Dieter Breitsprecher came in an hour after the doors opened. Annag Duncan moved through the murmuring crowd with a tray of cups, Miss Heinrich following her with the coffeepot.

David Neale took notes for his newspaper, or perhaps, thought Lavinia, he was one of Tappan's anonymous spies who reported on the characters of businessmen. Noah Ludlum and Glafford Jones seemed to be concentrating on a heavyset fellow with a jug of some thick tarry substance. Theodore Jinks and Axel Cowes had asked Mr. Drimmel to convert the cloakroom into a temporary office with chairs and table, and they sat there importantly, calling in the inventors one by one and quizzing them. She saw Dieter Breitsprecher approach Flense and Pye. They greeted each other and went outside, still talking. Flense looked at Lavinia and raised his eyebrows. What that meant she did not know. Should she follow them? Wait? Instead she went over to a lank-haired man in a rumpled linen suit who stood near the door with two other men.

"I am Lavinia Duke," she said. "Do you have an exhibit?" As soon as he said his name she remembered his letter. Weed, the architect, was a good talker, and he began to explain Prairie Homes. He beckoned her outside and pointed. "This is a quarter-size prebuilt model house, our Prairie Home Number One. It is small apurpose so that yesterday you could see the boxes. Today you see the model house. Did you see the boxes yesterday?"

"Alas, I did not," she said.

"Why, this house was all packed flat in those boxes yesterday. All of it." Lavinia gathered that it was an error not to have seen the packed-up boxes.

But she did see the miniature neat attractive cheap two-story instant house complete to weather vane and lightning rod that stood on the lawn.

"There they are," Weed said, pointing at empty crates lined up on the lawn. "The boxes. Each fits in a farm wagon. This house was inside the boxes yesterday." She looked at the model. Charming it was, but her first thought was to wonder how this applied to Duke Logging.

"Yes," said Weed, "and there are three other models and more to come." He stood expectantly, as if waiting for congratulation.

"Mr. Weed," said Lavinia, "I quite see it. But tell me about your plan for merchandising these." Mr. Weed was fairly dancing with eagerness to explain.

"People on the prairies need houses but got no trees. And farmers are no carpenters so they end up with a pile of sticks that falls with the first storm. If you are trying to start a farm why you can die before you get the roof over your head. But anybody can put one of our houses together, even a farmer." He shot a look at Mr. Drimmel, who was standing under a nearby beech tree watching hotel employees set up the picnic tables. "This model, if it was the full-size Prairie Home Number One, would cost four hundred and fifty dollars including rail delivery. Two men can put it together in about fourteen days. My partners and I are hoping Duke would supply us with lumber and investment money."

"Ah," said Lavinia. "But what have you reckoned about railroad transport costs? The prairies must have connection rails if they want these houses."

"Chicago is blossoming with railroads and the great transcontinental is very close to completion—they say within a year. Spurs will branch in every direction through the hinterlands. The railroads are coming. Put your men to cutting ties. They will be needed very soon."

At noon the Hotel Great Lakes served the alfresco picnic lunch of sliced ham, fried chicken, stuffed eggs and pie in the shade of the beech trees. Lavinia took her chicken leg to a bench on the far side of the beech.

"Thank you." His voice was already familiar to her. She looked up at Dieter Breitsprecher. "I spoke with your lawyer and accountant. I accept your offer provisionally. It will take some time to work out the details of what role I might play in such a partnership, and how best it might be done. I think Breitsprecher should close down its logging operations—perhaps sell them directly to Duke—but our cutover lands which I still own I want to keep so that I may continue my reforestation projects."

"Oh. Oh, Dieter. I am so glad." She stood up and grasped his fingers with her chicken-greased hand before snatching it away, blushing, dropping the gnawed drumstick to the ground, where ants rushed upon it. "After dinner tonight," she said, "we can walk in the park," for she had seen how much he liked the little woodland.

"Oh yes, wild horses could not stay me."

The second evening was easier. They talked as though they had been friends for many years—perhaps they had, thought Lavinia. They reviewed the inventors. Dieter did not like the thought of strychnine in the skid-road grease. "You have your robins," he said, "I have my bears." They agreed that the crated houses were smart and a sure success. Lavinia loved the little model house.

"It is our gift to you," Weed had said, and within an hour of the exhibition's close Lavinia had it placed under the great silver maple in her park. It stood as though waiting for small visitors, elves perhaps. Or children—she had read Lamb's "Dream Children" first with an ache, then with revulsion at her reaction. She quashed the silly weak thought.

A few days after the gathering the Duke Logging Corporation, for Lavinia had acted on Mr. Flense's advice to incorporate, formed a subsidiary they named the Prairie Home Division, which would handle all facets of the business, including transportation to the prairies, as well as supply all seasoned and milled lumber and stair rails, turned spindles, steam-bent balusters and decorative elements for the pre-built houses. Van Dipp, Brace and Weed would direct the construction and, as employees, would receive salaries from Duke. But a full partnership, which Weed wanted, was not agreeable to the Board.

"We are better able to handle the business end of this venture," said Flense. "Our offer of a ten-year contract at high salaries and a percentage of the income from the packaged buildings will ensure you stability and wealth. In ten years we can discuss the terms anew."

At dinner, Lavinia asked for an account of Armenius Breitsprecher's misfortune. Dieter sighed.

"If it is too painful, do not tell me," she said.

"It *is* painful, but offers many lessons. You know, Armenius was impetuous in nature. He was always interested in getting ahead, in adventurous risks. Our business was nothing compared to his passion when they discovered gold in California. He became a lunatic. Nothing I could say deterred him from packing his valise and wayfaring to California. He was there for a year and a half before I finally had a letter from him. From San Francisco. He said he had collected a fortune in nuggets, waited for a ship to New Orleans. From there he would make his way up the Mississippi to Chicago and so to Detroit. I waited; then, after two months I received an envelope, empty except for a newspaper clipping that read 'Timber King Fatally Wounded,' naming Armenius. I had no idea who had sent this lurid account. So I went to San Francisco and after considerable asking discovered the facts and the sad news that Armenius was truly dead. May I trouble you for a little more wine, Lavinia?"

"Of course." She poured it. "Go on. What had occurred?"

"He had flaunted his precious nuggets, bragging and showing them. Finally, he was accosted by two men in the alley behind a saloon, knocked unconscious, shot, robbed, and left for dead. But he was not dead and some Good Samaritans brought him into the saloon. They laid him on a table in the back room and called for a doctor. I heard that there were hundreds of doctors in San Francisco at that time on the hunt for gold, of course, and the man with whom I spoke, a fellow who knew Armenius from the hotel where they both were staying—it was he who had sent me the clipping—said many doctors crowded around him and fought for the privilege of treating him. I do not know whether they hoped for a fat fee or whether Armenius was considered, as the paper reported, a 'Timber King' whose cure would bring a doctor both money and fame. The doctor who seized him first cut open his shirt. The bullet had entered his chest and gone through his left lung. He was bleeding profusely. This doctor probed, then cut the wound further open to see how extensive the damage might be. He put a sponge in the gaping wound to stop the bleeding, then stitched up the incision. Armenius was brought to the hotel where he had been staying and put in his room. There he died four days later of a profound infection caused, I am sure of this, by the resident sponge."

"How dreadful," said Lavinia. "How very, very dreadful. Poor Armenius. Oh how sorry I am."

"Yes, it was one of the darkest hours of my own existence. In my opinion Armenius was murdered by the doctor. We were doing well in the timber business and my poor cousin left all that was good to run after minute particles of gold in a distant mountain stream and paid for it with his life."

They sat silent until Libby came in to clear the table and gasped when she saw them sitting in the dusk. "Sorry, miss, I thought you was outside."

"No, no, but I think we might go there. Dieter, will you walk with me in the forest?"

"Certain, Lavinia."

Dieter exuded a kind of calm surety. In his company she felt protected. The sun was down, the sky still suffused with peach and crushed strawberry light. They walked past the little house from the exhibition and Dieter smiled. Under the trees the air was still and close, tiny black mosquitoes rose languidly from the ground. Under the sultry pines it was nearly dark, a deep oceanic dusky green. There was a distant rumble of thunder. Dieter saw Lavinia in her black dress, the color of her dark hair absorbed by the shadow, everything concentrated in the pale intense face. A fragment of one of Catullus's poems came to him and he murmured " '*Montium domina, silvarumque virentium . . .*'"

He took her arm and they walked on slowly.

"Lavinia, why have you not married?"

His question startled her by its abrupt directness. She made a feeble sound like a cupboard hinge and said, "Oh, I never met anyone who took my attention in that direction. I am very selective in my friendships, I fear. And you?" A whip of lightning flicked through the sky.

"Much the same," he said. "I am too picky, too demanding of certain traits which I have never found in a female."

"And what traits might those be, Mr. Breitsprecher?"

"Why, grace, handsomeness, intelligence, the ability to tell red wine from white, a fondness for robins—and, rarest of all, the ability to scale logs."

She burst into a fit of laughter and he started as well; they stood whooping in the gloom until a shocked owl swooped soundlessly over their heads.

"Lavinia," he said when he could speak. "Shall we marry?"

"I think that is a very good question," she said. "I think we had better see to it."

Suddenly the thundercloud was upon them, blotting all the light. Veined lightning chased them to the house, the first fat drops rapping down as they came panting through the door. Has ever a woman had such a proposal? thought Lavinia. She was terrified, excited. Now, now would come answers to all her silent questions.

She pitched headlong into the most brutal and fierce love, the kind that could endure anything and that sometimes afflicted solitary women on the threshold of spinsterhood. She poured everything into this feeling. She scorched, she scorched. It was as if she had never been alive until Dieter. Since James's death she had never been close to another person, but now she was annealed to Dieter Breitsprecher. Of all people!

They planned to marry within the month but first came abstruse details of obligations and business, of rents and scheduled work. And Dieter had a commitment to go to New England to meet a man he much admired. "This man—George Marsh—is a Vermont farmer who is the first American I have discovered who recognizes the extreme threats hanging over the forests of this country. Second only to our marriage is my desire to converse with this observant and intelligent person. Some time ago we made an arrangement for me to come to him and see the waste laid the land by thoughtless felling of the noble maples and oaks for trivial potash and pearl-ash receipts. We have planned a small tour of the New England forests, where trees have been taken now for a century, to see the results. I must do this, my love." Lavinia was slightly amused at her betrothed's interest in denuded forests.

Lawyer Flense and Mr. Pye went to Detroit to meet Dieter's business manager, Maurice Mossbean, to work out the most sensible way of enfolding the Breitsprecher enterprise into Duke Logging and Lumber. "Indeed," said Mr. Mossbean, "the company's name had better change to Duke and Breitsprecher." The hundred details would be threshed out in Board meetings. Dieter Breitsprecher seemed curiously uninterested in the business end of forestry and relieved to turn all over to Duke Logging. It would give him time to develop his management plans, to expand his pine nursery and look into the hardwoods, which were so abundant and little-known. He thought he might write a paper on the Aceraceae, for maple trees interested him.

Days later, exhausted and red-eyed, Mr. Pye and Lawyer Flense sat in the rackety coach as the landscape flashed past. They smoked cigars and Mr. Flense had a silver hip flask he shared with Mr. Pye. "Do you not feel a little uncomfortable with this—merging?" he said.

"Very much so," said Mr. Pye, unscrewing the silver cap and taking a good swig of whiskey. "The possibilities for changes in the direction of our business are there. I applauded the idea of taking on Breitsprecher as a partner, but this marriage could bring deleterious changes to the way we do things. He may well persuade her to take up his conservative ideas of forestry and we shall see income drop even as it dropped for Breitsprechers when the cousin left."

Lawyer Flense said something so grossly raw that Mr. Pye had to pretend he had not heard it.

The betrothed agreed that they would live in Lavinia's house. "But I must have a library for thinking and reading," said Dieter. "A small greenhouse and laboratory would be a dream fulfilled. A man whose life has been solitary cannot immediately give up all his accustomed ways."

"I have been thinking," said Lavinia. "It would be best if we added a wing onto the house. The current arrangement of space is not suitable for a married couple. Goosey can have my old room. But I shall miss the cupola, where I often watched the ships."

"Let us have a cupola on the new wing—my dear girl must have her view of Lake Michigan shipping vessels."

"And you shall place your greenhouse wherever you wish. While you are gone to New England the time will pass quickly enough. I can oversee construction of the new wing with our new living quarters. Will we go abroad for a honeymoon? There is such a great deal to do."

He smiled. "A honeymoon! We shall go wherever you like. I leave it to you. I leave all such decisions to you. But consider if you would not like to see the results of untrammeled forest removal in the lands around the Mediterranean? It is what urged other countries to become mindful of forest care and management." He picked up her hand and suddenly licked her palm.

"Dieter!" She was startled, pretended offense and pulled her hand away although his hot mouth had given her a strange sensation. But a honeymoon looking at desolate lands was not tempting.

"Lavinia, I shall do my best to make you happy. I see nothing but joy in our future. I will get this visit to New England out of the way quickly. There are train connections much of the way to Albany, the rest by hired coach and whatever local railways exist. Vermont is still very rural. And I will write to you. I will write a long letter on the train, another when I arrive, still another when I go to bed and another when—"

"I think you have a grand sense of silliness."

She was in the old cupola looking out at the passing ships when she heard the crunch of wheels on gravel and looking down at the drive saw a carriage draw up at the front of the house. Mr. Pye and a tall thin man unknown to her got out. She heard the door knocker, heard Libby's voice, yet felt no presentiment until she reached the bottom of the stairs and looked at the unknown man who had taken off his hat, disclosing a dark shaven head, a cannonball skull looking like it had just emerged from the birth canal, the face long and narrow down to the point of jaw. Mr. Pye said, "Lavinia, you must sit down. This is Mr. Averso from the rail office. Lavinia, there has been an accident—" She heard without understanding, heard heard heard. This had happened with James. It could not happen again. She looked at Mr. Averso, that face, that head was imprinted on her memory for the rest of her life. Her heart froze and Averso's slowly opening mouth was the last thing she saw as she sank to the floor.

"Lavinia, we do not yet know!" shouted Mr. Pye. "Libby, fetch water!" He dashed the water into Lavinia's face, shook her, slapped her cheek. "We do not know! He was on the train, but we do not know if he was in the car that—the car that fell." What she did know was that Dieter had reserved a seat on an Albany-bound train. She heard Mr. Averso say that east of Cleveland the locomotive had steamed onto a high trestle bridge, the last car had somehow derailed, uncoupled, crashed into the chasm below.

"Lavinia!" shouted Mr. Pye. "Mr. Averso is telling us most of the people in the other cars survived, though some were injured. We must wait for news, Lavinia, we must wait! Hope is not lost. It is not sure who—who died or lived."

She stared at him. Stared at Averso. "It is not sure?" she asked.

"It is *not sure,*" said Mr. Averso. "I have come to offer you transport to the scene so we may determine if Mr. Breitsprecher was among the—the saved."

"It is not sure! I will come with you. I must know. Libby, Libby, my shawl. I am going to Dieter!"

So Lavinia learned that love came with a very high price and she sat clenched and bent in the seat as the special train rushed toward the accident. It was the familiar journey with Cyrus to find James frozen among the stumps. Once again she was rushing toward proof of the perils of modern life. Fate could not be so singularly cruel as to take Dieter from her.

Before dawn the next morning they reached a scene of horror lit by flickering bonfires and dim lanterns, the fallen car still smoldering in the rocks below the trestle. Blackened bodies lay in the stream below, the injured along the tracks moaning and calling. Where was help? All was the feeble chaos of the inept. Lavinia, Mr. Pye and Averso walked among the survivors looking for Dieter. She thought a huddled form had the wide shoulders of Dieter but the man turned his raw and bleeding face away. She could see one ear was torn so that it hung down below his jaw. His nose was a pulp and the swollen blackened features resembled a boiled hog face. She stumbled to the next one.

"*Lavinia!*" came a choking hoarse roar behind her. She turned. The hog-faced man, mouth agape, dribbling bloody froth croaked again, very low: ". . . viniaaaaa." She stared, trembling. Mr. Pye ran up, looked in the creature's face. "It's Dieter! Lavinia, it is Dieter Breitsprecher."

• • •

Goosey Breeley came into her element. She took on Dieter Breitsprecher's injuries as a mission. The guest suite in Lavinia's house
became his recovery room and Goosey his private Clara Barton. She
was indefatigable, dressing his wounds, changing bandages, airing
the room, reading to the patient for hours, concocting tasty dishes
famed as recuperative: oat porridge, beef broth, shredded chicken
breast, poached eggs and the like. "Sleep," she would say, "I am keeping watch, so sleep," and he slept.

He asked her one day if she would go to the little forest park and
bring him a sprig of pine; he thought the scent would refresh him.

Goosey asked Lavinia's permission first, for there was an unspo-
ken sense that the park was only for the use of Lavinia, Mr. Jinks and
Mr. Cowes.

"Of course, Goosey, you are quite free to ramble in those woods
all you like. Do bring him an armful of pine boughs."

Goosey was gone for more than an hour, but she went back every
day, occasionally bringing a fresh branch to the sickroom.

For Lavinia something important had changed. The foaming cataract of love that had coursed through her seemed to have shifted
into a subterranean channel. Dieter stitched and bandaged and lying
on pillows was not the Dieter against whose shirtfront she had wept.
This vulnerable man could not protect her. Their positions had been
reversed. Her desire for money and success swelled back into the
space vacated by Dieter—that at least was permanent.

The doctors said Dieter Breitsprecher would likely make a complete recovery but when she entered the sickroom and looked at the
swollen discolored face she could not quite believe it. When she sat
at his bedside she turned slightly away and spoke to the wall or window. She could not quell the atavistic feelings of being alone and surrounded by wolves that had plagued her since James's frozen death.

She plunged into work, leaving Dieter's care to Goosey except for the hour in the evening when she came and sat beside him and, looking at the wall, held his hand and told him sketchily of the day's business—too much detail might tire him. Although her feelings had changed she intended to go through with the marriage as soon as he was well. She liked him very much, she wanted a husband. But never had business been more absorbing: for the first time Duke was opening foreign markets.

59

lime leaf

If Lavinia cared less for Dieter Breitsprecher after his accident, he fell into a gyre of dangerous love. He could not escape. He sensed it would be a mistake if they married, but he was caught in the immediacy of the whirlpool and did not have the strength to stroke away. Some unsuspected need for Lavinia racked him. He knew it was irrational, knew her direction in life was injurious to his own beliefs. She would crush him. The unswallowable truth was that he wanted to be crushed. Although he would never say it to her, Lavinia returned him to his grandmother, that ruler-straight woman with the unlined face and black parted hair who knew the answers to everything and who ran a household that shone golden as the ormolu clock on the mantel. Her stringent rules, her commands and painful punishments, and the never-forgotten rare words of praise had arranged his emotions for Lavinia. So he lay abed, waiting for the scant hour when she came to his bedside and sat with face averted, talking of the day's business and weather signs.

"Mr. Pye, our good old accountant, has requested retirement on account of ill health. He has some painful gnawing in his vitals and his eyesight is not good. Annag has assured me she is able to keep the accounts as well as he."

"You would do well to give a little reception for him—a gold watch or a watch fob in the shape of a pinecone? What is the company policy?"

"I don't think we have one. My father was never a sentimental

568

man and I expect anyone who retired got a gold piece and a hand-shake. But I think you are right. We can arrange something pleasant for Mr. Pye, just a little collation in the boardroom. I'll tell Annag to take care of it."

To outsiders such changes seemed the mark of Dieter Breit-sprecher; he was a man of some mystery but since his entry into the affairs of Duke Logging outsiders believed him to be the source of all the company's deals. Lavinia's character and qualities were ascribed to him; his own reputation as an astute and fast-striking business-man grew.

To escape from his own feelings and thoughts during this con-valescence Dieter began to write letters to those men who seemed concerned with the disappearance of the North American forests, a concern that appeared more and more linked to a vague recognizance of national identity though he was not sure of this. Few now saw the forest as a great oppressive enemy; some even honored individual trees, especially those that were massive or stood as landmarks. A Unitarian minister in western Massachusetts gave a series of ser-mons on trees, sermons later published as a slender volume—*Trees of Life.* Dieter had a copy. Most stirring was the sermon on the cedars of Lebanon, *al Arz ar Rab,* great dark trees of God that had sheltered angels, trees felled by King Solomon's hundred thousand axmen. The sermon ended with a plea: "the cedars are now imperiled by ravenous goats that eat the young shoots. Queen Victoria herself has sent money to build a wall to protect the trees from capric destruc-tion." The congregation contributed a generous sum for the salva-tion of the cedars of Lebanon while continuing to quarter their own herds on public forestlands.

Dieter shied away from transcendental disputation but he was interested in the American shift from hatred of the forest to some-thing approaching veneration, a feeling he had known since his Ger-man childhood. After the deaths of his parents his grandmother had taken him to see the *Heede Riesenlinde.*

"A *Lindwurm*—dragon tree," she said in a low intense voice, her heavily beringed hand drawing him close to it. As they stood under the great carbuncled tree, its splayed trunk thick with emerald moss, she said, "This noble and ancient tree is a justice tree and much more." She told him the story of Siegfried, adapted for her own purposes, Siegfried the Bark-Skinned, who had acquired his horny covering after felling Fafnir, the dragon who lived in the lime tree. After swabbing himself with dragon's blood, Siegfried was armored, safe from harm except for a little place on his back where a lime leaf had stuck.

"This tree? The dragon lived in *this* lime tree?" asked Dieter, his eyes clenching the dark hollow in the roots, half-afraid the great serpent would appear.

"Yes, but it was a very long time ago. The dragon is dead, thanks be to Siegfried. And now you must think of yourself as Siegfried. The sadness you feel over the death of your mama and papa is a kind of dragon—*Sie müssen zurück schlagen*—you must quell this sorrow-dragon. You must harden yourself, overcome grief and form a protection of will against superfluous love. Then nothing can hurt you."

But Lavinia had found his lime leaf and pulled it away.

He wrote many letters to the Vermonter. Marsh was the best kind of farmer, for he noticed everything that happened in his world, the fall of tree branches, the depth of leaf mold in the woods and how rain was slowed by and caught in tree roots, tempered by the absorbent sponge of moss and decaying leaves. He saw what happened to soil when the trees were gone, how the birds disappeared when the pond was drained. When he traveled he compared landscapes and formed opinions. Dieter still hoped to visit him and see what the farmer had seen. As their correspondence went on he realized that George Perkins Marsh was considerably more than an observant Green Mountain farmer—linguist, congressman, diplomat, a traveler to foreign parts—one of the geniuses the young country seemed to throw out like seed grain.

• • •

The new wing would be added to Lavinia's house while they were on their honeymoon journey to New Zealand. When they returned all would be finished.

"A great deal of money," said Lavinia to herself. Still, one had to keep up appearances and Dieter must have his library and green-house. She put aside her black clothing and took up new fashions, form-hugging dresses with perky little bustles. And Goosey, that homely grey-haired matron who had been saving her stipend for years, had suddenly appeared in dresses of rich colors, unsparing of ruffles. Her hair was artfully plaited and wrapped into a crown.

At breakfast Goosey poured melted butter and maple syrup on her griddle cake. "Lavinia, I have meant to tell you for many a day but—"

"What is it, Goosey?" Lavinia preferred silence in the morning but this was not in Goosey's nature. She glanced at her distant cousin, saw her pink face and knotted brows. Goosey gave off a faint scent of orris root.

"I have accepted to marry Mr. Axel Cowes."

"But how do you come to know him?" Lavinia was greatly sur-prised. Goosey flared red and hunched her shoulders. It all came out. The day she had walked into the forest to cut a few pine twigs for Dieter she had encountered Mr. Cowes strolling with his dogs. They had chatted, they began to walk together, and over successive months they became daily walking companions, close friends and finally, betrothed. "He needs someone," said Goosey. Ah, thought Lavinia, so does everyone.

"I wish you every happiness, dear Goosey," she said, immediately planning to cut Goosey's bequest from her will.

Lavinia went early to the office and returned late. There was very much to do, two or three businessmen callers every day and the cor-respondence such a daily flood Annag Duncan and Miss Heinrich could not handle all of it. Though Annag looked like a prosperous and successful businesswoman, Miss Heinrich had changed little; she remained timid, hiding in the paper supply room when strangers came to the office.

"For heaven's sake," said Annag, "they won't bite you. It's just businessmen."

"I don't like that Mr. Wirehouse. He looks at me."

"He looks at everyone. You may look back at him, for a cat may look at a king." Lawyer Flense had presented her with an amusing book—*Alice's Adventures in Wonderland*. And this remark sent Miss Heinrich into tears. "I am not a cat!"

On one of Chicago's blowy old days Annag, trim in navy blue with a modest hem frill, came into Lavinia's office, her lips moving, rehearsing what she wanted to say.

"Miss Duke, the success of the company has made a great deal of work in the office. I feel we must hire two more clerks. The volume of mail is great. I suggest promoting Miss Heinrich to assistant director and getting two or even three new people to sort through and handle the letters, which she has done so far."

Lavinia said, "You are free to advertise for and hire new office people. We must train good people. And you know that Dieter and I will be abroad for nearly two years. I must have regular intelligence of everything, detailed weekly cables, and I believe all will go well. It does mean extra work for you. As for Miss Heinrich's promotion, do send her in to me and I will speak with her."

Only a few days earlier Miss Heinrich, the model of a man-fearing spinster, had come to Annag nervously rolling some papers in her hands.

"Mrs. Duncan, as you asked me to do I have reexamined the proposals from last summer's Inventor's Day and there is one that is particularly—interesting. But we did not proceed with it. I do not know if Miss Duke thought it promising . . ." Her voice trailed away.

"What proposal is that?"

"It is one from Maine, from a Mr. Stirrup. Illness kept him from the exhibit but he is trying anew. He was a rag merchant and now he has a paper mill in Maine on the Mattawannscot River. He once used only rags to make paper, but he says he has experimented in pulping some wood and blending the fibers with the rags. With great success, he says. And also he tried making paper with different wood pulps. Alone. No rags."

"That is interesting. I did not know of this proposal. Is there more to it than this?"

"Yes. He sent samples. Of the wood-pulp paper. He says he has made many experiments to find the best woods and the best processes. He writes of sulfite and sulfate processes. What does that mean?"

"I'm sure I don't know. Let me see the samples."

Annag Duncan examined the paper sheets, scratched a few inky words on several, folded and bent the pages. She handed everything back to Miss Heinrich then sat in her chair looking out the window onto the construction site of a museum, the gift of one of Chicago's many millionaires. At last she sighed, turned around and looked at her assistant. The poor thing was so nervous she was trembling.

"Miss Heinrich. I think you had better take this proposal in to Miss Duke and tell her that it caught your eye. She may not have read all the way through when it was first presented last year. I agree with you that there may be value here." She escorted her to Lavinia's office door, opened it and said, "Miss Duke, here is Miss Heinrich."

While Miss Heinrich stood like a snowwoman on the turkey carpet in front of the desk, Lavinia read the pages and examined the samples. "Very interesting. Miss Heinrich, I commend you. You shall have a promotion and a salary rise." Her mind was jumping ahead. Stirrup had mentioned that small logs, slash and otherwise unusable wood could be used for paper pulp—inexpensive paper made from waste wood. This, she thought, could open a lucrative market. Come to that, could not Duke & Breitsprecher build its own paper mill? "Take a letter, Miss Heinrich," she said. "Dear Mr. Stirrup. I have today read your proposal . . ." It was a move that would take Duke & Breitsprecher into the next century.

The marriage had a business advantage for Lavinia. Dieter became the company figurehead while she continued to manage and control, to build the great Duke empire by all means possible. Dieter had asked that the company not sell its cutover pinelands to speculators, but sequester and manage them through a separate division called Maintenance Timberland, which he would oversee, replant and manage. This was in addition to the acreage he had held back from the merger with Duke. So the first evidence of forest conservation tinged Duke & Breitsprecher's reputation.

"The day will come," Dieter explained to the Board, "though it be difficult for you to believe, when timber is scarce and becomes more valuable than we can project. You saw the promise in wood pulp for the paper market as Lavinia and Mr. Stirrup explained to us this morning. Holding Duke's Maine land for years was wise. If we ensure the continuation of our forestland, future wealth is guaranteed, whether for lumber or paper. We may have passed on by then but our work will be remunerative." No one could argue with this, for some of the old Breitsprecher lands he had planted twenty years earlier were bristling with sturdy trees and would indisputably be valuable timberland in another three or four decades. It forced the Board to think in new ways, on a scale of decades rather than months or a few years. Very frightening stuff.

Duke & Breitsprecher sent its first shipload of best pine to Sydney, Australia. Lawyer Flense went to San Francisco to meet with the buyer, an Englishman doing business in Australia, Harry Blustt, who wanted to arrange a contract for a decade of supply. Blustt wanted

Michigan pine, but said he also had an interest in the kauri trade—whatever kauri might be, thought Flense.

"We have a little of this wood in Australia, but most of it grows in New Zealand. We are interested in finding a logging partner to establish efficient lumber camps in that country." His ginger goatee rose and fell as he talked.

"I see," said Lawyer Flense. It was the first time he had heard the word *efficient* used in quite this way; he grasped the meaning immediately. "Of course Duke and Breitsprecher is interested in any overseas source of wood. We are ever interested in new timber supplies. And 'efficient' is our motto. But who are the New Zealand interests?"

Blustt laughed. "We arrange all that. We already have them—we have contacts with the right men. They look to Australia and London for advice and action in all things. But the native people are not satisfactory workers. We want American woodsmen who can use the ax and saw. Here is what the finished product looks like." He produced four small pieces of golden kauri wood.

"Ah," said Flense; the wood glowed as though sunlight were sequestered in every atom.

"Best house-building wood in the world," said Blustt.

Flense brought the samples back to Chicago and the Board passed the polished, blemish-free pieces from hand to hand. Kauri was a pine, and when they heard of the tree's generous manner of growth, enormous and straight for a hundred feet, all the limbs clustered at the top, they voted to know more. "It is reputed to be the most perfect tree on earth for the timberman," said Flense. "Or at least this fellow Blustt claims it is."

No one on the Board knew much about New Zealand. Lavinia wanted to meet Blustt, she wanted to see the kauri forests before the company made a leap into the dark. It might be the Michigan forests all over again. And so the journey was arranged. She and Dieter Breitsprecher, recovered though somewhat scarred, would travel to Sydney on their honeymoon trip, meet with Blustt, then continue to Auckland and for themselves see the kauri of the Coromandel peninsula.

Before they left Lavinia spent separate hours with Lawyer Flense and Axel Cowes.

"Mr. Flense," she said, "I think of you not only as my adviser and executor in all financial affairs, but as a friend. I have complete confidence in you. While Dieter and I are away I will give you a power of attorney to handle business matters. If you have doubts or questions on any matter please consult with Axel Cowes."

"Do not worry, dear Lavinia. All will be as you yourself might act." He smiled his curling smile, a gold tooth sparking. He took her right hand in his. "On my life," he said.

Both Lavinia and Dieter were prostrate with seasickness for the first weeks of the voyage. The captain (whose ship Duke & Breitsprecher owned) was at his wit's end in suggesting cures until the mate gathered remedies from the scuttlebutt. The one that worked came from the Chinese cook—ginger tea and walking the deck every other hour.

"Never go belowdecks," said the cook, bringing the invalids a great steaming pot reeking of ginger. Lavinia took three sweetened cups and walked for half an hour, her eyes on the horizon. Dieter found a single cup efficacious and by dinnertime the two vomiters were well enough to eat boiled beef and turnips. The shared illness somehow united them as the marriage ceremony had not and on board the bounding ship with a load of pine planks rubbing against each other in the hold Dieter and Lavinia began a sexual adventure. Dieter was delightedly astonished at how responsive and inventive Lavinia became in the narrow berth. The crew could hear laughter and occasional whoops from their quarters. The cook claimed it was another of the salubrious effects of ginger tea.

• • •

Harry Blustt met their ship. "Ah, a long voyage, what?" He explained that Sydney was still an infant city, both swampy and dusty, both crowded and empty, both brash and genteel.

"How interesting," said Lavinia. "But all I hope for at the moment is accommodations on immovable ground."

"Quite! Quite. Accommodations! You understand, guesthouses and inns are few—during the gold rush there were innumerable doss-houses, quite unsuitable. We have arranged for you to stay at a government official's house—he is in London until the turn of the year. I think you will be comfortable for the weeks before you sail to New Zealand. I have arranged several small dinners with men in the timber business."

The arranged dinners were all alike, vinous English businessmen hoping to strike deals to sell their lumber, most of which, Lavinia gathered, came from New Zealand, where choppers were bringing down the trees.

"Yas," said one bland fellow touching his lips with his napkin, "lumber ships crowd New Zealand harbors, ships take on kauri, totara and rimu. I say most are bound here for New South Wales, which is expanding like—like—like the very devil."

"But we are here to see about the possibilities of logging ourselves," said Lavinia. The men looked at Dieter as if to ask him to silence his wife—a woman had no place discussing logging nor lumber. They could not bring themselves to discuss anything with her, deferred instead to Dieter. Conversation languished; Lavinia and Dieter said good night as soon as they could without giving offense.

"I hope it is better in New Zeland," said Lavinia. "These fellows are small-time operators. They are only concerned to sell a load or two of their planks. They are supplying building material for New South Wales. That is their market. They do not understand serious logging." She waved her arm in a circle that included the fruit bats.

"It makes me question the abilities of Mr. Blustt. I hope it is not the same in Auckland."

"Let us first see the trees," said Dieter.

Before they had left Chicago, Dieter arranged—with advice from Mr. Marsh—the rental of a private house in Auckland for their monthlong stay. Their contact would be a man named Nashley Oval, an English artist, who had a government contract to paint panoramic views of New Zealand. "They are good people with interests that match our own," wrote Mr. Marsh, "but I will warn you that the wife's family keeps slaves, something the new government means to stamp out." When Dieter read this to Lavinia she made a face and said, "Slaves! Oh dear!"

The small ship, manned by tattooed Maori sailors, entered the great blue harbor at twilight. "Would it not be best to have a good night's rest and meet with Mr. Oval tomorrow?" asked Dieter, and Lavinia nodded, gazing down at the flashing paddles of men and women in carved canoes all around them. But Mr. Oval was waiting on the dock, a tall rumpled fellow with auburn hair and clear blue eyes.

"So pleased, so delighted," he murmured, kissing Lavinia's salt-chapped hand and shaking both of Dieter's. "I thought I would see you settled into Fern House. I have arranged a very simple dinner at my table this evening so we might sketch out a plan. If you are not too exhausted by the journey? Planning is important as a month is not nearly enough time to show you the wonders of New Zealand."

They went directly to his house in a garden of trees.

"What a majestic view," said Lavinia, admiring the harbor painted umber and violet with sunset dregs. A Maori servant—one of the slaves?—showed them into a sparsely furnished room, the walls melting away in shadow. Candles were the only illumination, which Dieter found very pleasant. He disliked both oil and gas lamps. A small round table was set for three. The servant brought in green-lipped mussels, poured a chilled white hock.

"Mr. Oval, delicious—it is reminiscent of German wines," said

Dieter, wondering how it was cooled. Did they have ice or snow in this place? He thought not.

"It *is* a German wine—imported, as all our wine. I doubt this climate could support vineyards, but some think otherwise. I had twenty cases of Bordeaux shipped a decade ago and it has taken too long a time to recover from the journey—really still not drinkable. I'm told reds can take twenty years or more. But the whites have been good and I've developed rather a preference for them, or so I think. To our coming journey together," he said and he raised his glass, smiled at Lavinia.

The mussel plates disappeared, replaced by a savory pie of the famous Bluff oysters.

"Tomorrow you can rest and get settled, and on Thursday I think it would be advantageous for us to sail to the Coromandel peninsula, where horses will carry us into the forests. Half a century ago horses were unknown here but they came in with the missionaries and the Maori took to them. Everyone rides. I understand, Mrs. Breitsprecher, that you especially wish to see the kauri. Did you bring riding clothes?" he asked Lavinia.

"No," said Lavinia. "I haven't been on a horse since I was a girl. It didn't occur to me to pack riding clothes."

"I think we can arrange a habit for you. My wife, of course, rides bareback. And in a pinch you can always wear men's trousers—women here on the frontier of civilization are not fashionable. If you are sanguine in temperament I feel we shall do well."

Lavinia's interest was piqued at the thought of an Englishwoman riding bareback and tried to imagine what such a woman would be like—an extravagant hoyden, no doubt. And was she herself expected to wear trousers? Was that what their host was suggesting?

She kept her jaw clenched against falling agape when Mrs. Oval entered the room. Nashley Oval stood up. Dieter rose, smiling. The woman who came toward them was tall and shapely, beautiful in balance and bone. She wore a costume of orange cotton skirt fringed with feathers, and on top a long garment of supple flax that left one shoulder bare. A river of black hair streamed to her waist. Her chin was tattooed with a curious design and a delicate tattooed line enhanced her shapely lips. Lavinia realized with a shock that she was a Maori.

"Welcome, welcome to our land," she said in perfect upper-class English, her soft voice dropping at the end of her sentence.

"May I present my wife, Ahorangi Oval. Dear heart, these are our guests, Lavinia and Dieter Breitsprecher, with whom we shall travel in your forests beginning on Thursday."

"I am so pleased," said Mrs. Oval in a soft fluid voice that reminded Dieter of a pigeon cote. "There is much to show you and I hope you will come to love this place as we do. We have learned about you both from our common friend, Mr. Marsh, whom we met in Italy several years ago."

Great heavens, thought Lavinia, Mr. Marsh again! He plays an invisible role in our lives.

A broad path climbed gradually up toward the forests. Ahorangi Oval, again in her orange skirt and flax blouse, sat astride a nervous bay mare dancing and shifting about. Lavinia, feeling constricted and slightly tortured in an ill-fitting riding habit, was on a tractable piebald mare. Dieter on a rangy gelding, and Mr. Oval on his Thoroughbred Queenie, rode behind the two women, talking of Mr. Marsh. Two bareback Maori men—the brothers of Ahorangi—rode in front, turning and calling out comments in good English. The servant and a packhorse laden with full *kete* baskets followed the party.

"You speak English very well," said Lavinia to Ahorangi.

"Yes, thank you. I went to school in London," she said.

At noon the brothers reined up near a stout tree with a self-important air. "A cabbage tree," said Ahorangi. "All parts are good to eat, we can thatch roofs, make our rain capes. It gives good medicines. It shows itself as different from other trees, so we plant them sometimes to mark a notable place. Let us have lunch here with the *ti kouka*."

• • •

The path rose and they entered a totara grove, the elegant trees rising high, showing needled spikes and red berries.

"This," said Ahorangi, gesturing with her expressive hands, "is the tree we esteem above all others."

"Even above the kauri?" asked Lavinia.

"Yes. The kauri is important and we revere it, but it is whitemen who love it to the exclusion of other trees. For them it is the ideal timber tree. But it is the totara with whom our lives and religion are even more deeply entwined. Like kauri, it is one of the great chieftain trees—also rimu and kahikatea and rata. Those are our royal trees."

"They remind me somewhat of yews," said Dieter, looking at the totara, "though they are much taller. Very tall indeed."

"Oh yes," said Mr. Oval. "They are a much-favored tree, both by the Maori and whites. The Maori prefer totara for carvings and war canoes, houses and so much else—framing timbers, even. The fruit is tasty and plentiful, a bark decoction controls fever. White men like it for its rot-resistant timber."

Ahorangi led Lavinia to a flounced rimu with drooping fronds. "This is my favorite," she said. "I love the rimu, but so do the timbermen." She touched a dangle of green. "The botanists say it is a pine, but it is different. It has no cones like European pines, but a good kind of berry. Kakapo—hear them?—like the berries very much."

In fact all the previous night in the Fern House, Lavinia had heard a smothered thumping sound like someone dropping cannonballs from the trees. Now she heard it again. Ahorangi told her it was the mating call of the kakapo, a fat puffy parrot that could not fly but spent its time in the rimu gorging on fruit—"usually they make this sound only at night, but I think this one may be rather ardent." Ahorangi touched Lavinia's arm and with a sad half smile said, "I must ask you something. I am afraid for the rimu. My husband says you are an important lady who owns a timber company and that you come here to look at the trees with a thought to cut them. I hope you will love our trees and not cut them. They are our lives. To live happily in this place we need the trees. I am afraid for them. You will not cut them, please?"

Lavinia said nothing, and in a few minutes Ahorangi understood the silence and walked back to her husband and brothers. For the rest of the day she stayed with them and made no effort to speak again with Lavinia.

Dieter rode up. "What is it?" he said, aware something was not right.

"She does not want us to cut any trees," said Lavinia. "She begged me not to cut them. I did not know what to say. There are so many trees here that there is no possibility they could be all removed as she seems to fear."

"Let us hope so," said Dieter. "That is my wish." And he, too, fell silent.

They passed through the rimu and followed a twisting trail that wound around a slope and into a grove. Lavinia and Dieter knew at once these were the kauri; they could be nothing else. Massively broad grey trunks with branches bunched at the top like the victims of a robbery throwing up their hands; but the staggering size of these monsters stunned them both.

"My God," said Dieter, "this is the enchanted forest from some ancient tale." He dismounted, tied his horse to a shrub and began to walk around a very, very large kauri. He was suddenly joyful. "They are too big to be cut," he said to Lavinia. "They cannot be brought down."

They can, Lavinia thought, they will be. Yet she, too, had been a little moved by the great silent trees, so immense, so helpless.

After dinner Lavinia tried to make amends. "Dear Mrs. Oval," she said.

"Please, call me Ahorangi."

"And you must call me Lavinia. I want to say that if I am here to look at the kauri trees for cutting, my husband is here because he believes in replanting what one takes. We wonder if it is possible to plant infant kauri trees, perhaps one for each large one that is cut, to care for the young trees as they grow and age?"

Ahorangi gave a small laugh. "The big kauri trees are very old—thousands of years. We will take you to see Kairaru of Tutamoe. It is the largest one. It would certainly be a hundred human generations before a seedling could replace one fallen mature kauri of such girth."

"One must have faith in the power of a seed," said Dieter. "We plant them knowing we will never see them when they are grown. We plant them for the health of the world rather than for people not yet born."

Nashley Oval leaned forward in his chair, his face tense and excited. "This—this idea of planting kauris. I like this very much. I wish to make a nursery—I suppose it would be a nursery—for starting young trees. I am not quite sure how they propagate . . ." He looked at his wife.

"They have cones and the cones carry the seeds. Many times you have seen the winged seeds spiraling down to the ground, riding on the wind, no?"

"Yes. So all one would have to do is gather those seeds and put them in a bed of soil?"

Dieter spoke up. "Likely one would get better results by gathering cones not quite ripe enough to disperse their seeds. And these should come from younger trees in vigorous good health. I know nothing of the germination rate of kauri seeds but there are bound to be variations. When do the winged seeds begin to disperse?"

"I would say February—March," said Ahorangi. "In the autumn, a few months hence."

"I should never get used to the seasons being opposite," said Lavinia.

"Oh, it's not difficult," said Nashley Oval. "It all falls into place quite naturally." He was quiet while the guests murmured over the roasted *hoki* fish with shallot sauce. "I plan to empty my glasshouse of lettuces and green pease and collect kauri seeds this coming February. I shall try my hand at starting young kauri trees."

"You will be the first in the world, dear Nashley," said Ahorangi, touching his hand.

Dieter spoke earnestly. "Mr. Oval, if you do such a thing allow me to congratulate you on a valuable hobbyhorse. You will find yourself lavishing your infant seedlings with affection and tender regard for their welfare. But pray do not give up your vegetables—if you can, do construct a glasshouse especially for the kauri. I would be most happy to contribute to such a venture in the interest of improving the future."

Ahorangi spoke to Lavinia. "You have not yet seen the young kauris—they call them rickers, and they look rather different than the mature trees. Tall and thin, like young girls before they—develop. They are a bit amusing. We shall see all ages while you are here."

Two weeks passed with excursions to kauri groves. Lavinia bought a large shoreline grove mixed with rimu and told Ahorangi and Nashley Oval that Duke & Breitsprecher would send men to begin cutting and milling these trees. It would take time to hire the right men, assemble the mill machinery and ship all to Auckland. No kauri in that grove would fall for a few more years. The woman sighed but nodded when Lavinia told her that Duke & Breitsprecher would pay Mr. Oval to set up a kauri nursery and maintain it, to plant young seedlings when the cut was finished.

Although Axel Cowes had known and worked with Lavinia for years, he chose to send his cable with news of the Chicago fire to Dieter, who came into the bedroom, where Lavinia sat writing in her notebook of expenses.

"My dear, we have had a cable from Axel Cowes. He says a great fire has burned half the city, even in the business district. People are ruined and homeless. There is much suffering."

Lavinia read the cable for herself. "We have lost warehouses—but on the other hand Axel says orders for milled lumber are pouring in. The ashes are not yet cold but rebuilding has begun. That is the famous Chicago spirit," she said. "But he does not detail our losses."

"I daresay it will take some weeks to understand the situation fully."

"He says Mr. Flense is away on business—he is not sure where—and so there is no comment from him. I very much wish there were. Mr. Flense could give some figures. One thing is clear, Dieter. We must go back as soon as we may," said Lavinia. "We are needed in Chicago. Though I dread the return voyage."

They left before the kauri cones were ripe, but Nashley Oval promised to send a bushel to Dieter, who was determined to learn the peculiarities of the plant. "We will write," said Dieter. Lavinia's mind was already in Chicago, responding to the city's desperate need of lumber.

If the trip from San Francisco to Sydney had been rough, the return was worse. Ginger tea did not help Lavinia, who spent most of her time lying green and thin in her berth. Dieter urged her to come up on deck and get some fresh air, and she tottered up and almost immediately retched and then fainted. The worst seemed to be over by midvoyage although she took very little except bread and tea.

"I will be better when we are on solid ground," she moaned. "Oh, speed the day."

Back at their renovated house the air still carried the stench of charred timbers from the city when the wind was right. Lavinia improved only slightly. Nauseated and dizzy she could not appreciate the new wing with its opulent suite and, in place of a cupola, a large balcony with a broad view of Lake Michigan. Dieter crowed over his glasshouse and potting shed and was pleased to wear crusty boots and a long canvas apron all day long, dressing only for dinner. Lavinia could no longer bear breakfast.

"Really, this can't continue. I am worried about you," said Dieter. "I have asked Dr. Honey to call and examine you this afternoon, get his opinion of your health. All is so beautiful here now I wish to enjoy it with you. I want us to walk together in the forest again, to admire the moon on the water. I want you well again."

But Lavinia knew what Dr. Honey would say. She had not expected it, but she knew. She waited until the doctor made his diagnosis and then, at the dinner table, eating only shreds of poached chicken breast, she told Dieter.

"I am going to have a child. This nausea will pass. I will be in health again. But I will be a mother and you a father."

Dieter laid down his fork and looked at her. He nodded but said nothing. After a long silence he looked at her, smiled and said *"hurra!"* loudly. The maid rushed in from the kitchen, saw them smiling at each other. Back in the kitchen she said to the cook, "Mr. Dieter is glad to be home again."

"I shall have to discover a first-rate nursemaid," said Lavinia.

Lavinia went to the office the next day feeling quite well and even pleased. She would know the mystery of motherhood. They would be parents. She felt she was, at last, a complete adult.

"Good morning, Annag," she said. "I'll look through the post for an hour. Come in at nine to take letters." The letters took all morning. One was rather annoying: a subcontractor logger wrote a rude note demanding the survey map of the Sticker River camps.

"This fellow sets out his demand as though he owns the property," said Lavinia.

"Oh, I'll deal with that, Miss Lavinia," said Annag. "It never should have been put in with your post. Mr. Flense knows all about it."

• • •

Lavinia expected the birth would be a frightful ordeal as she was not young and it was her first child, but she might have already produced half a dozen for all the difficulty. It was a quick and easy labor. The boy was healthy and perfect in form. Lavinia and Dieter had talked endlessly about names. Lavinia first suggested James Duke Breitsprecher, but Dieter made a face; next she suggested Charles Duke Breitsprecher, incorporating the name of the ancestor; Dieter asked why not use *his* father's name, Bardawulf, but Lavinia repeated, "Bardawulf Duke Breitsprecher? What a mouthful for the poor mite," and in the end Charles Duke prevailed. Dieter asked himself why humans reached into the ancestral pot for infant names, but found no answer.

She quickly regained her full health and went back to the office when Charles was ten days old, but not before she met with the elderly lawyer she and Dieter used for personal legal affairs and named Charles Duke Breitsprecher heir of her estate and business holdings. Now all was well; the future of the baby and the company was secure.

Her greater interest was not in the infant but in rotary lathes. Duke & Breitsprecher was entering the plywood market. Here was a use for birch, long despised as a weed tree. Her engineers were experimenting with various glued-up wood layers from different species. And they were discussing an interesting new wood, balsa wood from Ecuador, very light and very strong. She listened to their reports of its remarkable weight-strength ratio. The problem was that balsa trees did not constitute whole forests, but grew in scattered places throughout the dripping tropical forests. Finding the trees and getting the logs out was the difficulty. She thought it was not worth the effort, and balsa logging went on the shelf.

The day Lavinia went back to the office Dieter took the baby from his nurse and carried him into the park, laid him down under the newly leafed silver maple, propped himself on his elbow beside the child. Charles stared up into the quivering green, where dots of sunlight winked. But, wondered Dieter, how much could he see? Were the shapes of leaves sharp or was all a green massed blur? He picked the baby up and looked into his small pointed face seeing his expression change to one of interest as his eyes focused on Dieter's mustache. The baby's arms flew up in a nervous start.

"You see, Charles, it is a tree. Your life and fate are bound to trees. You will become the man of the forests who will stand by my side."

One morning Axel Cowes walked through the forest to the Breitsprecher kitchen door at six in the morning. "Good morning, Mrs. Balclop. Is Lavinia up?"

"Awake, I am sure, but likely not up and dressed. I have orders to send her coffeepot up at six thirty sharp." Lavinia had abandoned tea for cups of strong black coffee sweetened with honey.

"If you can add another cup I will take it up to her myself. There is most urgent business—a crisis I must discuss with her immediately."

At that moment Dieter came into the kitchen for his coffee mug. He would take it out to the potting shed and begin the morning's work.

"Axel! What brings you here at this early hour? A tree down in the forest?"

"In a manner of speaking. I came to break the news to Lavinia and to you that Mr. Flense has done a bunk." Mrs. Balclop tipped her head to hear everything.

"What does that mean, 'done a bunk'?"

"It means that he has left the city and the country for parts unknown—perhaps Texas, as they say of all absconders—with a great chunk of Duke and Breitsprecher funds in his pockets." There was a ringing silence. Cowes drew in his breath, said, "And Annag Duncan, too. She went with him."

"Oh oh oh," said Dieter. "Let us go up to Lavinia. She will take this hard."

IX

the shadow in the cup

1844–1960s

60

prodigal sons

The years had been hard on Aaron Sel, Jinot's only surviving son. When Jinot left for New Zealand with Mr. Bone, Aaron found his way to Mi'kma'ki and the family band of Kuntaw, his father's grandfather, who had after the death of his wife Beatrix left the Penobscot Bay house and returned to Nova Scotia hoping to live the old Mi'kmaw way. Aaron made an impression on Etienne, Kuntaw's grown son of twenty-six winters, as a brash youth with nothing of Jinot's reputation for merriness. Aaron had expected some kind of ceremonial welcome, the warmth of acceptance, had hoped for dissolving mysteries of who he was. He had expected young women. Now that he was here he did not know what he should do. He had no understanding of eel weirs, could not tell a blueberry from an enchantment. He could not hunt caribou or beaver. In any case there were no beaver or caribou.

"I have no friends here—everyone is against me," he said to Etienne in his most piteous voice.

"You have to learn. Come with me to the river and I show you how we repair the weir." But Aaron could not fit rocks together, could not hammer stakes in the right position.

"I need a gun," he said, but there were no guns for anyone without money.

"You want too much," said old Kuntaw, the Sel clan's elder and *sagmaw*. "Here you must learn to give, not take." But after two rest-

591

less years in Mi'kma'ki, Aaron went back to Boston, looked for Jinot, who was still in New Zealand, and drifted around the waterfront.

It was on the waterfront that two jovial men got into conversation with him, invited him to the alehouse and bought him drink. Later he had a misted memory of walking between his two new friends toward the docked ships, but no recollection at all of how he came to be aboard the *Elsie Jones*. He woke the next morning to the painful strike of the bosun's rope end.

"Git up, you stinkin Indan beggar brat." He was a green hand on the *Elsie Jones* bound to London with a cargo of spars and masts.

"You cannot do this! I know my rights. You cannot keep me against my will."

"What! Are you a sea lawyer? One of them always prating about 'rights' and 'free speech' and such? I'll learn you what your 'rights' are. You'll toe the mark and the mark will be high."

The bosun, James Crumble, instantly took a strong dislike to this young half-breed who spoke of "rights," put him in the hands of the crew for daily greenhorn instruction in the names and functions of the ropes, the tackle, the watches, the names and functions of the bewildering kinds of sails, the workings of the tackle fall, the daily duties beginning with the swabbing of the deck before the sun was up. They gave him tasks spangled with mortal dangers, sent him clambering up the futtock shrouds in great wind and icy rain, snarled confusing orders salted with vile epithets such as "toad-sucking gibcat," and "scabby jackeen," picked away relentlessly in faulting his lubberly errors. Nor did Crumble spare the rope's end, cracking it every time Aaron opened his mouth—"Shut yer gob, you hopeless fuckin hen turd of a fool or I'll spread your guts on the deck." *Crack!*

The trip was wretched, storm after storm and in the intervals between, rough seas. A set of monster waves cleaned the deck of the spars stored there and lightning struck their mainmast. Putting up a new mast in the heaving ship cost two men their lives and Aaron expected he would be the dreaded third man. He lay in his hammock trying to think how it would feel when he was pitched into that lurching brine, how long the drowning would take. He asked the old hands, who agreed there was sure to be a third death before they docked, and heard the comforting news that it would be over very quickly, just one or two water-choked gasps from the shock of the cold water, "and then you don't feel nothin." During the voyage Aaron grew in strength, knowledge and hatred for Crumble. He swore to himself that if he survived he would kill the man once they were ashore, but the bosun melted away as soon as his boots hit the London docks.

It took weeks, weeks of asking and walking warily along the great wharves in the odorous London fog before he found a ship though he cared not whether bound for Canada or Boston. Day after day the acid fog was so dense that men five feet away were wraiths. In those weeks he began to feel he had somehow changed, and in no minor way. Physically he felt well, strong and alert. He was nineteen, had become watchful, more inclined to read the body movements and faces of people around him. He wanted to go back to Kuntaw's Mi'kmaw band. "Likely old Kuntaw is dead by now," he said aloud. Maybe Etienne was in his place, one of the other men. He would try again with a more willing heart. His presumption of himself as the central figure in any scene had been scuttled by the bosun James Crumble.

In a grogshop one afternoon he heard two sailors talking coarsely about what they would do in Halifax. He moved closer, listened, said, "Halifax bound? Ship lookin for crew?"

They gazed at him, at his callused hands, tarry canvas pants. "*Excel* sails tomorrow mornin. Go talk to the bosun. He keeps aboard all night—Conny Binney."

Binney was a red-bearded good-natured fellow from Maine, for Maine men were as common as hempen ropes on the wharves of the world. "Wal, yes, sailin for Halifax, carryin China trade goods first for Halifax, a load a China dishes and some porcelain dawgs—at least they *call* 'em dawgs but look more like pawlywawgs to me. Cobblestone ballast. Ye ain't green, are ye? Not a landsman? Sailed afore the mast, have ye?" Aaron said he wasn't so very green as he'd sailed on the *Elsie Jones*. Binney raised his eyebrows.

"And so you attended Miss Crumble's Academy for Poor Sailor Lads?"

"I did, sir, and enjoyed a rigorous education. And survived."

Binney laughed. Aaron was hired as an able seaman. After Crumble, Conny Binney seemed too easy, giving orders in a pleasant voice. It seemed unnatural. The ship traveled against brisk westerlies, beating to windward all the way, and Aaron's spirits lifted with the exhilaration of sailing home, no matter what waited at the far end.

Going directly to Halifax would save him the torturous overland journey from Boston. He could walk to Pitu'pok, the Mi'kmaw settlement on the shore of the saltwater inland lake, in two or three days. He thought he could find Mi'kmaq there who would take him to K'taqmkuk. And the niggling question he had been pushing down kept kicking its way back into his thought: why was he going back to the Mi'kmaw life? He had a calling now, he could make a sailor's living. He could go back to the sea if he had to, as long as it wasn't a-whaling.

Long before land came in sight they could smell it—a mix of softwood smoke and drying cod blended with the familiar salt of the North Atlantic. A rushing flood of joy made Aaron grin foolishly at nothing. He got his pay, shook hands with Binney, who said, "If ye want a berth on the *Excel* again, we be back here come April or May. Nother v'yage t' China."

Aaron hurried through the knotted streets of Halifax, his mind filling with imagined conversations as he tried to explain why he had returned. Etienne had been angry when he left. Yet in his new sense of self he was glad to be back. He was ready to trap and construct weirs, to fish. He no longer expected his relatives to honor him simply because he had come to them, because he was Jinot's son. His sea skills might somehow find a use. He'd see what he'd see.

The trail through the forest he remembered was now mostly cleared land with settlements and a few farms, the too-familiar sight of settlers burning swathes of woodland. He met two whitemen children driving cattle along the shore. As they passed they began screaming "dirty Indan bug-eater" and threw clamshells at him. The ragged trail now showed trees again—sprouts growing up from stumps. This was the way he had taken five years earlier, after his father left with Mr. Bone. A Mi'kmaw family had fed him and given him a place to sleep, had told him Sels had all gone to K'taqmkuk, and that if he wanted them he should go to Sydney, the eastern-most port, and send word over the water. Someone would come. He remembered the man's name as Joe Funall. Just another mile he thought and he would see that *wikuom* near the trail. He walked far-ther than a mile and knew he had somehow missed it, turned back, looking hard into the scrappy woods. Some distance in he saw a few poles. That was the right place. He went toward them. Yes, it had been a *wikuom* once but was now weathered poles with rotted skins and bark at the base. They must have moved to the Mi'kmaw village a few miles farther on. He picked up his pace.

He was frightened by the village. Shabby *wikuoms* sat on rough ground amid slash and baked patches of bare earth. He saw smoke issuing from only one *wikuom*. There were no dogs, no people in sight. He walked slowly toward the *wikuom* making the smoke, but as he passed a derelict jumble of poles with only saplings instead of bark for a covering he heard someone cough, a retching, choking cough that sounded like it was tearing out someone's lungs. He bent to the opening. "Hello. Anybody there?" Stupid question. Of course there was someone there, someone dying of violent spasms of coughing. He peered into the gloom and saw a bundle of rags jerk forward and cough and cough and cough. The more he looked the more he saw—there were others in there, emaciated skeletal arms rose as if to ward him off, huge feverish eyes fixed him. An infant lay naked and dreadfully still on the ground. He went to the next *wikuom,* where a comatose man lay on the earth, only the very faint rise and fall of his

595

rib cage showing he lived. He did not speak. Farther along in the sole *wikuom* issuing smoke sat a man and woman, both very thin, but able to move and talk. The man said their names—Louis and Sarah Paul.

"What has happened?" asked Aaron, wondering what was wrong with himself. He was choking, hardly able to speak. He told them he wanted to find the way to K'taqmkuk, where others of his family lived. But here, in this ruined village, what had happened here, what had overcome these people, where were Joe Funall and his wife, who had been so kind to him years earlier? Whatever had occurred also might have befallen the Sel clan in K'taqmkuk.

"They die. Everybody sick, no food, die, die, die. Children all die. Mi'kmaw people now walk around, look for food, eat dirt, no firewood, whitemen shoot, say it their firewood. We make potato garden but too many rain. Potato all go rot. We come any place, try make *wikuom,* always whitemen come and set fire, come with clubs and sticks. They drive us on. Nowhere to go. Sometime good whiteman give food, coats. Only look for more good whitemen. Mi'kmaw people walk lookin, keep walkin. Now lie down and die."

Aaron knew that since the death of Amboise, his childhood brother, he had had a cold heart, but now, appalled, he felt it burning. He had no food but he had his wages. He reached for his money, his impulse was to thrust it into their hands, but he considered. They were too weak, he thought, to go buy food. But where was the nearest place? It would take him two days to go to and return from Halifax. Sydney was closer, and perhaps he would pass a whiteman farmer who would sell him food. "I will come back with food," he said and rushed forward on the trail.

Two miles along he saw a settler's house with a large garden, a cow and chickens. Before he could enter the gate a tall whiteman with glassy eyes and sprays of hair like black grass on the sides of his head came rushing around the corner of the house. "Git off 'n my propty!" he shouted. "Git! Damn Indan."

He walked on toward Sydney, passing settlers' houses and gardens. He tried once more to buy food and an angry man shot at him. Once more he tried. He walked around the corner of a small church to the pastor's house and saw the housewife on her knees weeding onions.

Poised to run he said, "Ma'am, I would like to buy some of your vegetables for some poor starving Indans down the trail."

"Why, them poor things," she said, "let me ask the pastor." And she went into the house. When she came out again the pastor was with her, his yellowish old face drawn into a stern expression.

"So, who is starvin? Indans, eh? You do not know how often I hear this complaint, but we do live in a time when the Red Man passes from the scene, replaced by the vigorous European settler. The Indan has to learn to work and earn his livin, grow a garden and put the harvest by against winter. Charity does but delay the inevitable." Then, taking in Aaron's posture and face, which suddenly looked less like that of a softhearted white man and more like the visage of a murderous Indian with a barely suppressed intent to kill, he stepped back a little. "Course we do try t' help, even knowin it—yes, course we sell you some vegetables. What will you, taters? Maggie, pull some taters and carrots for the poor Indans." Hastily the two pulled at stems, plucked young turnips from the ground, heaped the plunder on the ground for Aaron to pick up as best he could. He stuffed everything inside his shirt, the warm turnips scratching his skin. He stood up with the last potato in his hand and said, "This potato means life to those people." He held out his money. The pastor snatched it and with the passage of tender recovered from his fright and said, "I would say that the will of God, rather than a potato, decides the matter."

Aaron did not wait for the end of the sentence but was on his way back to the broken *wikuoms*. On the trail he saw movement under an elderberry shrub. He picked up a heavy maple stick from the slash pile alongside the trail. He came closer and saw the animal was one of the whiteman's favored creatures, a house cat. It had something—a bird—and he saw a wing rise and fall as the cat crunched the wing joint. Closer and closer, gripping the maple stick, came Aaron. The cat, intent on savaging the young partridge, which was large enough and still lively enough to escape, did not abandon the prey and Aaron crushed its head with the first blow. He then wrung the still-struggling young partridge's neck. "This is the will of your whiteman god," he murmured to the cat, taking it up by the hind legs and, with the limp partridge inside his bulging shirt, walked on toward the *wikuom* of Louis and Sarah Paul, left Louis making a fire and Sarah skinning the cat.

The next day in Sydney he saw five Mi'kmaw women sitting together on the dock. They seemed easy and content, joking with one another. They looked healthy. One of the women—he was almost sure it was Losa, the wife of Peter Sel, one of Kuntaw's sons, the older brother of Etienne. Round-faced with very red lips, Losa carried a single basket and the others, their handiwork sold, were chiding her for making something so clumsy no one wanted to buy it. She said something he could not hear. They laughed and it felt good to him to hear Mi'kmaw women laugh.

And there was Peter Sel's fishing smack at the far end of the wharf.

The basket makers began to board the vessel, chattering and laughing, still showing each other bits of finery or foods they had bought at the stores. Aaron, heavy in thought, and mentally rehears- ing a variety of pleas to Kuntaw and Etienne to come west to the ruined *wikuoms* and save the starving people and bring them back to K'taqmkuk, followed. As they left Sydney harbor and entered the grey ocean, Aaron went into the bow and faced east, taking bouquets of spray in the face, staring into the haze of distance. Why had he come back? What had changed him, he who cared for nothing but himself, who acted on fleeting impulse?

• • •

Peter Sel, who owned the boat, called to his son, "Alik, take the rudder. I go talk a little to that Aaron Sel who come back." He came up and stood beside Aaron for a few minutes looking east, said cautiously, "So you are back here. You are older."

"Yes, I am older. As are you."

"I heard that sad news about Jinot. Very sad."

"What sad news?" He looked at Peter.

"Etienne didn't find you? That Joe Dogg didn't find you?"

"Nobody found me. I been to sea on the ships. Years. I just come back now. Joe Dogg from the ax factory? What was he doing here?"

"Lookin for you. That Mr. Bone never come back so Joe Dogg wants to go find out what happen. He wants you to go with him, look for you in Boston but never find you. So he come here. Etienne said to him, 'I will go. I will find Jinot.' They go to New Zealand, very damn far. When they come back Etienne and Joe Dogg look for you again in Boston. Then Etienne come back here and said maybe Joe Dogg finds you."

"He did not find me. What happened?" Aaron knew of course with that much searching and travel that Jinot had to be dead.

"I only know Etienne said Jinot died with bad sickness in that sore leg. Mr. Bone dead, too, by a man in grass clothes."

There was a long silence. Aaron looked at the horizon. He felt an interior ripping as though something was pulling at his lungs. He forced a breath, looked at Peter Sel. He said, "The death of my father does not surprise me. He went away so many years ago. I grieve. I wish I had gone with him. I was a bad and stupid person before, maybe I still am that person but I think I am different."

"A man can get better," said Peter Sel. They stood silent while the sails filled and the boat took its course east. "Alik is my son."

"He is a good sailor," said Aaron.

"He is. He has eleven winters but he knows the boat. And the water." There was a long silence, then Peter said, "Sometimes good men start out very bad. I was bad like that. Wait when we dock. We can talk a little."

• • •

It was dusk when Peter's boat came alongside the wharf and the basket women raced ashore with their goods and money, and started the long trek home. Aaron did not follow them but waited. After some minutes Peter was there, lit his pipe, leaned on the rail. His son, Alik, coiled a rope a few feet away.

"You say you are changed," Peter said. "I, too, changed. Used to drink rum and wine, whiskey, all them poison stuff. Drink and fight. Fight ever night, ever day. I didn't have no boat then. I kill a man. Fight him very hard, drunk, smash his head. I try to break my own head. Just get headache. If I still live I got to change." Alik came closer, listened, gazing at his father. Aaron wondered if Peter had ever told him this story. It seemed not. After some minutes Aaron said, "Does Kuntaw still live?"

"Yes. He has too many winters now to count. There are not enough numbers for his winters. But he is my father and he is still very wise and leads us. He no longer hunts but tells stories of hunting."

"Let us go to Kuntaw and Etienne and the others. I want Etienne to tell me everything about the death of my father. And I have much to tell them."

"You go ahead. We come later," said Peter. He put his hand on his son's shoulder. "Alik and me got to finish clean the boat. Take care the boat, boat take care of you. Me and Etienne and Alik go out early morning catch fish for our celebrate. You want to come fish?"

"I do. I want this work. I help with the boat, too."

Old Kuntaw, half-asleep in the predawn pallid darkness when Aaron came into his *wikuom,* woke and stared, listened with mouth agape, put his hands up to his face and made a sound like a hurt moose. "Come here," he said, stretching out his stringy arms, "come and be embraced by one whose blood is running in circles with happiness. Call everyone," he said to his wife, Maudi, who was fumbling with the hide door. "Call everyone. Here is a Mi'kmaw son come home. Prepare food. Tomorrow we make a celebration. We will be happy!"

The next day Maudi built up her fire on the riverbank and dragged out her big cooking pots. In late morning Alik came carrying three big mackerel, Etienne and Peter following with more of the huge fat fish. Etienne embraced Aaron. The basket-making women Aaron had seen on the dock came from their *wikuoms* to help make the feast.

Aaron sat next to old Kuntaw and tried to explain that he had changed but the old man waved his hand as if driving off flies.

"I know how it is," he said. "I have felt this. Look you." He took up an empty wooden bowl, put in a dipper of water, asked Maudi to bring a dipper of mackerel oil from the pot and added it. He stirred the water and oil briskly with a forked twig until it whirled into an amalgam of froth. "Water is whiteman. Oil is Mi'kmaw. In the bowl is mix-up *métis*," he said, "whiteman and Mi'kmak. Now watch." They all stared at the bowl. The glistening mackerel oil rose and floated on top of the water. "That's how it was with me, long ago. I tried to be whiteman, but Mi'kmaw oil in me come to top. That same oil come up in you. Sometime I hope for this Canada that the Mi'kmaw oil will blend with the water and oil come to the top. We will hold our country again someday," he said, "but we will be a little bit changed—a little bit watery and the whitemen be a little bit oily."

Aaron and Etienne walked away some distance and sat on the ground, drawing strength from contact with the earth. Etienne said, "We look you in Boston. Never find."

Aaron said, "When I was here before I saw that old Kuntaw and the Sels thought they were making a Mi'kmaw place again, but I did not understand; it felt unsure, as when you take up a cup of tea and put it to your mouth and find that what looked to be tea was only the shadow in the cup."

"Do you feel this now?" asked Etienne.

"No. I drink the shadow now. I find it good."

• • •

They passed around the traditional talking stick all day and into the next night before voices slowed and they began to name problems—food, lost territory, the cruelty of whitemen's laws, the loss of good canoe makers. Suddenly Kuntaw's young wife, Maudi, very pregnant, who had been listening, said, "You men are foolish. You do not see the greatest problem of all. We need women here." There was silence for a minute and then Etienne said, "She is right. We need more women. I thought they would come if we made a good place, but they have not come. Why?"

"They have not heard we would welcome them," said Kuntaw. "In the old days women were important, they were the great deciders. They did everything, some even hunted like men. But over the years Mi'kmaw men begin to act like whitemen, who do not regard women as worthy. It is the old Mi'kmaw way to know women are of equal value as men."

Then Aaron spoke of the couple in the ruined village *wikuom,* the starving people, told what he had found in those *wikuoms.* "Those ones in the only unbroken *wikuom* are named Louis and Sarah Paul."

"How old are they?" asked Etienne.

"Old, I think," said Aaron.

Peter half-stood. "Old! They are not old. Louis is younger than me—a little. I knew that man once. He is a good man for weirs, none so careful as he. We used to call him Eel Man. And a good fisherman. I take him on my boat if he comes here. Very strong, knows the shoals and currents. He cannot be more than thirty winters. We must go there and get them, bring them here. Tomorrow."

Skerry Hallagher, Elise Sel's son who had gone to Dartmouth College for half a year, had come to Kuntaw's band much as Aaron. They were close in age, but where Aaron was muscular and hard-handed, Skerry was thin and intense, rarely said anything as he felt very much the outsider and was afraid of old Kuntaw, who told him he could never be a real Mi'kmaw man until he killed a moose. He did not think there was much mackerel oil in him. Now Skerry held out a dirty, creased envelope. "I did not say this before but my mother, Elise Hallagher, wishes to come in summer for a visit. Since my father died she is alone. She wishes to bring a young woman, Catherine Flute, a full-blood Mi'kmaw girl got brought to Boston by her parents when she was small. The parents are now dead with alcohol sickness and the girl is unhappy. My mother asks if we will take her here. She is fourteen or thereabouts. She says there are other lost Mi'kmaw girls in Boston. We could welcome them here?"

"Yes," said Etienne in the voice of a hot-blooded moose. "Tell your mother to bring all the girls she can find. I will personally marry them all."

Two days later Aaron, Etienne, Peter and Alik went back to the path west of Sydney to find the starving Mi'kmaw couple Aaron had seen and bring them to K'taqmkuk.

"I am sure this is the place where Louis and Sarah Paul had that *wikuom*," said Aaron to the others as they stood on the trail staring at five whitemen working with two oxen and a log puller, a dozen more heaping slash into a burning pile. There was no sign of any *wikuoms*, but at the back of the clearing a tiny wisp of smoke caught Etienne's eye. "There?" he said, and they walked over to the flat grey circles of ash. The *wikuoms* had been burned. They saw nothing of Louis and Sarah Paul.

"Ho!" shouted one of the whitemen. "Git out of there. Go on! Git goin!" He took up his shotgun, which had been leaning against a log, half-aimed it and pulled the trigger. A pellet went past Alik's ear with a sound like a hummingbird.

"We go," said Etienne. *"We go!"* This last he shouted angrily and the same whiteman did not like his tone and shot again.

"Eh!" said Etienne, hit in the back by a piece of shot.

"Those men," said Etienne later as Aaron pried the pellet out of his shoulder, "I seen them afore. They not settlers. They come and take any land they can get, clear it, burn it, however they can rid of trees and sell it. Some settler not want spend his life choppin trees buys it. It's a way whitemen make money. Take a lot of Kuntaw's oil to make *them* change." They walked on toward Sydney.

"And do Mi'kmaq not need money now?" asked Aaron. "How do you get your money?"

"Cooperin," said Etienne. "Didn't have time to show you yet but we make barrels. Whitemen buy from us. We got a workshop, forge, oak planks, steamer, plane, everything to make barrels, big ones, little ones, kegs, casks and tubs. We make the best barrels in Canada. Julian Cooko used to work in a cooper shop in Halifax, showed us how to make barrels, washtubs, all them things. He comes to live with us."

Elise Hallagher, widowed and aging, her hair white and stormy, arrived with two girls, Catherine Flute and Marie Antoinette Nevin. Skerry embraced his mother and it seemed to Aaron that his cousin clung to his mother rather childishly. He would never have survived Bosun Crumble. He smiled at Elise and when she smiled back he saw her likeness to Jinot. He looked at the two girls. Marie Antoinette had a cough and was sometimes distant in her manner but more often she laughed. She took refuge in laughter and silliness when Elise scolded her for her lazy ways. Marie Antoinette told Catherine Flute that she wanted to go back to Boston. She did not know any plants, failed to learn how to make baskets or sew, burned anything she tried to cook. She was good company, but that was it. The younger men liked her, and Alik Sel, Peter's son, spent as much time as he could following her around. Aaron saw his youthful self in her behavior.

At the end of the summer before the autumn storms began, Peter, Alik, Aaron, Etienne and his three boys, Molti, James and Joe-Paul, loaded Peter's boat with barrels to sell in Boston, where they got better prices. They sailed at dawn. Catherine Flute, who shared a *wikuom* with Elise and Marie Antoinette, said Marie had got up very early. Elise knew at once that the girl had gone on the boat, back to Boston, where she would surely take to drink and have a bad end.

The men came up the path loaded with bundles and boxes, all the supplies for winter, sacks of potatoes, candles and matches, coffee beans for Elise and Aaron, great tins of tea for the others, needles and bolts of wool and cotton. And there was Marie Antoinette Nevin, red-cheeked and laughing. And coughing.

She said, "I am here." She looked at Alik. Catherine Flute, who was shy and plain, a very quiet girl who had been starved and ill-treated by her parents, sat beside Joe-Paul. They married before the first snow. Even Elise found herself courted and she agreed to marry Julian Cooko, the man who had started the men making barrels years earlier, before he had been hurt in a woods accident. Now he had long spells of confusion and was no good for the barrel shop but sat by the fire and made eel traps.

Kuntaw died on the most beautiful day in a thousand years. The October air was sweet and every faint breath a pleasure. Wind stirred and he said, "Our wind reaching me here." A small cloud formed in the west. "Our small cloud coming to me." The hours passed and the small cloud formed a dark wall and approached. A drop fell, another, many, and Kuntaw said, "Our rain wetting my face." His people came near him, drawing him into their eyes, and he said, "Now . . . what . . ." The sun came out, the brilliant world sparkled, susurration, liquid flow, stems of striped grass what was it what was it the limber swish of a released branch. What, now what. Kuntaw opened his mouth, said nothing, and let the sunlight enter him.

61

talking stick

Over the next generation through isolated years of sickness and watchfulness Kuntaw's people tightened as a clan although they took in six or seven outsiders. Everyone now had English names, for the old Mi'kmaw names were fading out. Aaron married Lisal Jacko, the only young woman among the newcomers. As a group they avoided whitemen, but still fisher-hunter-missionaries found them. Some of these whitemen only pretended to be hunters; they were scouts on the lookout for timber and ores, anything of economic value. They asked casually to be taken where the big trees grew.

"They think we don't know they want to cut them trees down."

Their old continuing problem was that Mi'kmaw women rarely came to them. To find wives the Sels had to return to their remnant people at Shubenacadie, thin and listless people who sat staring at the ground.

"You see?" said one white settler to another. "They are lazy. If they starve it is because they refuse to work. Do not waste your pity on them. Do not give them food—it only delays the inevitable."

When Etienne heard of this he said, "But they are not lazy, only weak with hunger."

A year came when the Sels stopped making barrels, for whitemen had pushed them away from that trade by making cheaper ones, not as tight and sturdy, but at a lower price and, tellingly, with snowy curling letters stenciled on the side: WHITE RIBBON COOPERAGE. Some who had made barrels began to carve hockey sticks from the dense hardwood of hornbeam trees, whose grooved branches resembled muscular straining arms, but in a few years that enterprise, too, passed out of their hands and to a whiteman manufacturing company.

Another womanless Sel had drifted to them a few months after Kuntaw died—Édouard-Outger Sel, the oldest son of Francis-Outger, who himself was one of the two sons of Beatrix Duquet and Kuntaw, and so a grandson of the ancestor Dutchman Outger Duquet.

Édouard-Outger, who had been subjected to a Duquet education, left Penobscot Bay after his father's funeral, worked a few years in Boston and then began decades of wandering. By the time he came to his Mi'kmaw relatives he was in early middle age and rather peculiar. He spoke a garbled, halting old-fashioned kind of Mi'kmaw language mixed with unknown jargon and French words. At first no one knew how he had learned his antique version of the language and that information he kept to himself for a long time. Every few months he went away somewhere and came back grey and shaky, sometimes bandaged, but carrying a bag of flour or meal.

Little by little it came out. He said that after his father's death he had been a scrivener, a document copyist, in a Boston lawyer's office, hired for his clear legible hand, but then he was dismissed for tardiness and certain reasons he did not name. "I tell you something now," he said. "The world is very wide. I have traveled much, all the way to the western ocean." Slowly Édouard-Outger began to talk. He told how skilled horsemen of the Plains tribes were often shot by whitemen travelers for sport from moving trains as they shot running animals—dark waves of bison, huge skies stiff with birds. So rich in game were the vast plains that astonishing caravans of lordly hunting parties from Europe and England came with dogs and guns, cooks and special beds and tents. He did sometimes deviate from these sad tales with descriptions of curious adventures, which the Sels preferred to hear.

He was only a little strange, and that strangeness fell away. Although his skin was light in color, the shape of his features closely resembled Kuntaw's. He said it was because his mother was the daughter of a man who had married a Mi'kmaw woman. "So I am Mi'kmaw person on two sides," he said, laughing, "front and back sides," slapping his crotch and his hindquarters. It was this maternal Mi'kmaw grandmother who had taught him the language which sounded correct from a distance but was usually incomprehensible. Nor did it take long to discover what Édouard-Outger did when he went away every few months: he went on a reeling, mindless drunk and came back very quiet and humble with his penitential bags of flour. His one ability that drew the others to him was storytelling, his tales of what he had seen and done on his travels across the continent to the Pacific. He named some of the west ocean tribes—Nootka, Kwakiutl, Tlingit, Makah.

The Sels liked to hear stories of their West Coast counterparts. As Mi'kmaq had lived on the edge of the Atlantic for thousands of years without intrusive whitemen, those faraway people had lived on the Pacific; they felt a sense of counterbalance. They listened to Édouard-Outger's accounts of lives linked to huge cedar trees and the black canoes the western people made from them, of how they hunted giant whales in those canoes. He told of their communal houses as great buildings with lofty beams, decorated with carved animals and painted visages, and in front of the houses stood immense and gaudily colored poles with the heads of ravens and bears serving as memorials.

The men could scarcely believe his stories of how those people split great planks from living trees, how they fashioned boxes by steaming and bending flat boards, never cutting the wood. Édouard-Outger had one such small bentwood box with him to hold his tobacco and they passed it from hand to hand, examining it closely. It had a fearsome red face painted on one side that Édouard-Outger said was an eagle. Once they recognized the eagle it gave them the feeling of looking into a strange mind. Etienne wanted to know more about how they built the huge houses.

"I wish," said Etienne's wife, Alli, "that we could build such a great house, where we could all live safely and in harmony."

Peter spoke. "And those people on the western coast, do they live free from the incursions of whitemen?"

Édouard-Outger hesitated. He understood how badly his relatives wanted to hear of one place in the world where tribal lives continued unspoiled.

He sighed. "Those coast people have known whitemen for a long time just as we Mi'kmaw. They traded otter furs to whitemen for metal to make tools. Then the whitemen began to catch the otters themselves, and as they always take everything until it is gone they made the otter very scarce. The people's lives changed. And now the whitemen diseases are burning them up even as we suffered. Sickness comes in their own beautiful canoes on trading trips, for they are great visitors and traders, traveling up and down the coast with goods and to see their friends. The most skillful canoe makers have already died, and many carvers and artists, too. In only a few years they have lost too many of their people to count. They say their world has ceased to exist in a single generation." His listeners knew too well how this was. He changed the subject and for some time told how these people on the opposite ocean brought down huge trees without axes.

Kuntaw's people, most of them Sels, drifted back to Sipekne'katik, now called Shubenacadie, an old Mi'kmaw village location named a reserve in 1820, not because it was better; they went despite the worthless land the whitemen allowed them, despite the crowding and racist jeering, despite the massacres of the past, the onerous government rules. As Kuntaw had said they must live in two worlds, they went because inside they carried their old places hidden under the centuries, hidden as beetles under fallen leaves, as pebbles in a closed hand, hidden as memories. They were lonely for their own kind—and for women. There were women there. Beneath the reality of roads and square houses they saw their old sloping ground, saw their canoes drawn up onshore, pale smoke drifting from *wikuoms* decorated with double curves and pteridoid fronds, chevrons, arched frames and high color. Yet they could not ignore the reality that *wikuoms* could no longer be made and that whitemen settlers had built countless sawmills on the rivers, ruining the best places for eels. Everywhere, to feed the thousand sawmills countless trees went down.

After one St. Anne's Day celebration some tried to paddle back across the water to Kuntaw's old place, but their canoes were caught in a storm and they perished. There were fewer Mi'kmaq every year and whitemen laughed and said with satisfaction that in forty more years they would be gone, gone like the Beothuk, vanished from the earth. It seemed true. There had never been so few Mi'kmaq since the beginning of time, less than fifteen hundred, the remains of a people who had numbered more than one hundred thousand in the time before the whitemen came. Still the people clung to their home ground though they wandered often, looking for food, for a haven, for a cleft in the rock that would open into that world that had been torn from them.

Etienne spoke seriously and long.

"We got to do something. Our women can make their baskets but us men got to find wage work for money to buy food. Everybody says, 'Be that whiteman guide for fishing.' But that's not enough."

"I rather do guide for fish than hunt," said Peter. "They can't hurt you with that fish rod."

"Only other work for us Mi'kmaw is woods work. Plenty work there."

The whiteman timber kings were taking down the forests of Newfoundland, Nova Scotia, New Brunswick. Hundreds of sawmills stood on every river and stream that could be dammed. Once again Sels took up axes, and although everything was difficult they continued to talk together, to look for ways out of their troubles. Etienne built a whiteman log house and named his newest son Joseph Howe Sel to honor the fair-minded Commissioner for Indian Affairs. This took some explaining and in the evenings the remaining Sels gathered in the warmer log house to talk, each bringing a few sticks for the fire. It was a confining, immovable box, but it held the heat better than ragged *wikuoms* made without good bark, tanned skins or correct poles.

"Joseph Howe is one of them good whitemen. He looked and he saw our troubles," said Alli, who had shyly suggested the baby's name. "He tried help us. He saw us danger, all us land taken, us push away from river. Can't make eel weirs no more."

"Yes," said Etienne with something like a rare smile. "He saw we was cold, hungry, give us coats, blankets. He said these days we have to give up our *wikuom* as the bark gone with the big trees. No skin covers, them caribou and moose gone."

"Plenty logs and planks for a whiteman house but we got to buy them. With whiteman money," said Peter. He drew his face into a cruel mask. "Howe is a whiteman. If he is good to us it is to get something—more land—something. That is all I got to say bout that."

Alli asked a question. "Édouard-Outger, is it better in that Penobscot place where you come from? You got people there? Mi'kmaq already there?"

"Not anymore. No, Maine people don't like Mi'kmaw people. There are some Mi'kmaw people live there in Aroostook County. Good basket makers, not just women, men make those big baskets, too. But Penobscot? Same like here, woods all gone, whitemen got the land. My father, Francis-Outger Sel, had a sawmill"—he paused for a murmur of admiration—"but after he die in that sawmill somebody set it afire and it burned all down and the house. I was alone, family dead, went away out in the west. When I was gone the town took the property for taxes. My father he never pay taxes. He thought if you own property you own it. But you don't own it. You have to pay money every year to that town or they can take the land."

There was a hum of disbelief. "They took his land. Well, it was my land then but I didn't know about the tax. I wasn't there. When I come back it was all gone, you see. All gone. They laughed at me, said, 'Indian, you don't own no land here.'"

"Do whitemen here pay those tax?"

"I think so. Not know for sure. It is the way of whitemen that they must pay for everything, not one time but many many many times."

"We never did this thing with land—own it, buy it and pay and pay more tax."

"Yes, and that is why the Mi'kmaw people now have very little land. The whitemen get land with papers that secure it. You can see for yourself that now there are a hundred times more whitemen than Mi'kmaw people. If we want to secure any of our old land we have to do it the whiteman way with papers. And money. To learn those English laws we have to know how to read. Write. In English. The children must learn these ways if they live here. Or be wiped out."

"No. If we had a canoeful of money they would not let us own our own land. That is why there is the reserve."

There was muttering and a father in the back said, "It is true. We are so few in number that they can crush us with ease. One day of shooting and we would all lie dead. It is only a dream that they will someday go back to their old countries. They will never leave our country. They are with us for all time. And if we want to live we must be like them."

"It seems life is better for Indians in the States country?"

"No, it is not better for us anywhere. But here near Shubenacadie I think it is worse. Here the whitemen hate us very much."

Skerry Hallagher took the talking stick. "I know how to read and write. I know a little bit about the laws. If I can get books and paper I can teach the children and anyone who wants to learn this reading and writing. But it takes a long time. It is like learning to hunt."

"I, too, can help," said Elise.

Édouard-Outger cleared his throat and said softly, "And I. But where are all our children? I count only five." And he decided that he, too, would marry. It was one thing to talk, quite another to act.

Skerry Hallagher stood up. His eyes were weary and red. "Also. It is not only that the children must learn reading. Mi'kmaw men must take jobs and be paid."

"Jobs! What jobs?"

"The jobs whitemen don't want, the hardest jobs. Work in forest to cut trees. Cut firewood for settlers. Carry things for surveyors who mark out ways to take more of our land. Make our hunting paths into roads for whitemen wagons. Dig potato in Maine. More woods cutting there. We can do this. We can do these things. They will not crush us."

The young men agreed. They would go to the lumber camps and ask for work.

"At least in the lumber camps we will eat," said Alik, Peter's son.

"You are not going," said Peter. "I need you on the boat. Passengers. Fishing."

Etienne's oldest son, Molti, took the stick and said, "We can bring money to everyone."

At the end of the evening someone tossed the stick into the fire—it was only a stick. It was the last talking stick any Sel ever held. Talking sticks were the old way.

Alik said nothing to Peter, but slipped away in the night. In the end nine of the younger men went to lumber camps scattered across Nova Scotia, New Brunswick, Maine. It was easier for them in the woods camps. Men were valued and measured by what work they could do. And for Édouard-Outger that meant increasing Mi'kmaw numbers. He took a young wife, Maddil, and did what had to be done. Born in 1877, Lobert Sel was the oldest of Édouard-Outger's six children.

62

barkskins

For three generations the Sels worked in the woods of Nova Scotia and New Brunswick, down into Maine, falling and spudding trees, making booms, cranking booms from headworks, river driving, working the sawmills, building corduroy log roads, cutting cordwood, cutting pulp, cutting pit props. As Europe disgorged its people the logging camps, especially after the Great War, became polyglot assemblies of men—English, French, Americans, Germans, Swedes, Norwegians, a few men from Greenland, First Nation natives, even one or two Inuit. Injury and death were common enough in the northeast woods, but since the first logging days the most dangerous work was river driving, and until it ended it was work apportioned to Indians, those considered born to violent water.

"I'll tell you somethin, mister," a camp boss said to a company bookkeeper who had questioned his bateau and grub expenses. "Company wants its logs? Wants to git them to the sawmill? Water is everthing. Water moves the logs, powers the mills. They want their logs in the saw house they better swallow the drive expense cause ain't no other way to git 'em there." He jerked his thumb at the river where two Mi'kmaq and a Montagnais were dancing over the sticks, jabbing them along like sullen sheep.

The Sel barkskins saw the poll ax give way to the double-bitted ax, the double-bitted ax give way to the crosscut saw, the old up-and-down gang saws give way to circular saws and double circulars, to immensely long steel band saws that could cut the moon in half if they loaded it on a conveyor, saw the steady oxen give way to smart horses, horses replaced by stinking donkey engines and Shay-geared locomotives. As roads punched into forest distant from water, the tumultuous river drives ended in favor of trucks and roads. Loggers began to tend whirling, thumping, boiling, crashing machinery. The Sels suffered accidents and deaths in a profession where a man had to be watchful and lucky to live more than seven years.

The huge trees of the west were hard for puny axmen. It took years to learn how to handle the big stuff and slow learners did not have time to stay alive. But technology shaped crazy daydreams into real hissing screaming machines that leveled the last of the ancient forests on the continent.

After the talking stick had been thrown into the fire the young men left to take up woods work. Etienne Sel and Mike Jacko tried to watch out for their sons, but the boys resented a parental eye and escaped to more distant camps. Mike Jacko's son Blony, fifteen winters, and his younger brother, Pollo, started on a cutting crew for an outfit in Queens County. Blony had an inborn knack for the ax. When he wasn't chopping, Blony and a young Swede named Erto peeled bark with spudding irons made of old carriage springs, handled and honed. On his first drive Blony discovered he liked the dodging, leaping river work. He quickly understood the geometries of jams and relished picking them apart. Twice he fell in among the churning logs but knew better than to fight toward the shore—better to travel downstream with the sticks.

But still the hateful, cramping reservation was too close and Blony and Pollo moved west, worked for a winter in Idaho, where driving on cranky, twisted rivers was still the way to get logs to a sawmill. In the spring some men in the camp kept going to California, Oregon, Washington, where they said the trees were three hundred feet high.

A man he only knew as Shirt said to Blony, "Sonny, I'll learn you about them trees. The first Maine logger sailed up the coast and come near the shore seen a solid wooden wall a hunderd mile long with green stuff up around the clouds. Couldn't believe what he seen, fell down in a fit. He couldn't believe it. Nobody could believe it. But it was true. And that's where I'm goin."

Blony and Pollo were frightened the first time they saw the donkey engine at work. The engine was lashed to several stout trees and its steel haul cable lying loose and quiet on the ground. Five men stood casually around the engine. A signal came from somewhere distant and the puncher threw his lever; the donkey engine came to life. They watched the cable drum turn and the cable itself begin to wind on, tightening and tightening. The engine roared louder and there was a distant snapping of branches, a few faraway shouts, and in minutes the crackling and ground-shaking thumps grew louder and then out of the slash came a monstrous thirty-foot log springing into the air like a decapitated chicken in its final manic leaps, smashing down on stumps so hard they splintered, rebounding and coming straight for the donkey engine. "Holy Jesus!" yelled Blony to the delight of the puncher—the two greenhorns ran for their lives, followed by the haw-haws of the donkey crew. They looked back. The terrible log rested quietly a few feet short of the donkey engine. Pollo never imagined that a few months later he would be assigned as one of the steam kettle's crew and that an hour after he began work, ignorantly standing near a lazy curve in the cable already fastened to a faraway log, his left foot would be amputated by the tautened wire minutes after the engineer hit the lever with the heel of his callused hand.

His brother, Blony, and the engineer carried him spouting blood down to the bunkhouse. The second cook, Andre Mallet, served the camp as medic. He rested Pollo's leg on a junk of wood to elevate it, bound the bleeding stump above the ankle with a clean dishtowel soaked in melted lard, gave Pollo copious amounts of his medicinal whiskey for the pain and said he'd look in after the dinner hour. He sent Blony back with a cup of hot partridge broth and half a whiskey-soaked cake. This, in addition to certain Mi'kmaw sedatives—crinkleroot and lady's slipper root—that their mother had given

Blony "just in case," and the shock, shut Pollo down like a dry oil lamp. He slept. There followed weeks of pain and whiskey but slowly he began to heal.

"You stay here until you get around, but then I need your bunk for a workingman," the boss said. One of the choppers whittled out a pair of crutches. He was moving around the bunkhouse when Andre Mallet came in. "Hey, kid, boss cook cleared it so's you can help in the kitchen." What could he do but say yes? After a year he could scuttle around wearing a logger-whittled prosthesis. He was becoming a cook and some kind of permanent job might be there. But then Blony's death hit hard and he was the one who had to write the letter home.

Blony had wanted to be a river driver, but water work in Washington was salty, herding and corralling logs in tidewater. Because he was young he was a choker setter, the lowest job in the camp. After a few weeks in the high-lead logging camp he discovered a job even more daring than river work. He watched Napoleon Tessier, a skinny little Frenchman wearing climbing spurs and laden with saw, ax and rope, rush ten or twelve feet up the trunk of a big Douglas fir, dig in and casually flip his climbing loop to a higher position, scamper on again toward the top of a two-hundred-foot-tall tree. As he climbed he cut the limbs as flush as possible with his long-handled double-bitted ax, finally stopped thirty feet below the leader. His rope secure around the naked trunk and himself, his spurs jammed deep, he axed off the top (as large as a second-growth Maine pine); it tipped down with a crack and hiss, the wind rushing through the needles of the falling section. The bare spar, with Tessier hanging on, whipped back and forth. Tessier let out a screech and waved one arm, like a wild horse rider. Then he slid and kicked down so swiftly he blurred. On the ground he took a swig of cold tea, ate a handful of sugar and went back up to rig the pulley block, for Tessier was a rigger as well as a climber. When the job was done and the pulley block and guy lines in place they were ready to move giants.

Blony wanted to do this, to become a climber. He begged the boss to let him try. This man, a big perfect Swede with a mouth full of tobacco, did not like Blony or Pollo because they were East Coasters as well as half-breeds. But Blony kept asking, and finally Tessier said aloud that he *ought* to let the kid try, climbers were not plentiful, and finally the boss said, "Go ahead, Pocahontas."

Blony put on Tessier's spurs, buckled on the belt, tied his ax to it, got the climbing rope around the tree and himself, stuck his spurs into wood and tried to move up as Tessier had, to flip the loop up as Tessier had. Higher and higher, jamming in, flipping the rope and he reached the first branches.

Tessier, who was coaching, called up, "Don't cut your rope." Men had been known to make a quick misplaced slash and cut their own loop, a one-time-only mistake. Blony kept on, strong quick blows, paying no attention to the feathery scratching branch tips, up again, flip, chop, continue.

"High enough," yelled Tessier. "Top it." Blony topped it. The swinging ride as the limber spar swiped back and forth was the reward. He could see the distant ocean, he was above the world.

"*Très bien!* Done pretty good for a first climb," said Tessier. "Slow, but you done good." Blony couldn't get enough spar-tree climbing, and the more he did the faster he moved, trying to beat Tessier, who lately had struck a pose standing atop the fresh-trimmed spar while it was still quivering. So Blony had a stunt in mind as he climbed his last tree. Up he went, as squirrel-like as Tessier and about to do a trick that would show up the mustachioed Frenchman. He planned to top his tree, lift himself on top, stand on his head and whistle, but as the heavy-branched top he had just cut hinged over, the spar split and caught Blony in the cleft as a clothespin grips a tea towel. His scream was short, the air squeezed out of his collapsed lungs. It was Tessier's dreadful job to climb up and cut the spar a second time, this time below the dead boy, whose urine-drenched boots dangled in his face. Blony fell, still in the clasp of the Douglas fir, and they buried him that way.

• • •

Etienne's son Molti Sel, his cousin Alik Sel and the two Mius brothers, Noel and John, worked from Oregon to the Queen Charlotte Islands. Nimble and limber as they were, after Blony's death no one wanted to climb and rig tall trees. Molti stayed a choker setter for five or six seasons, his hands as hardened as lobster claws from gripping and heaving heavy chains; he was used to chains, didn't mind the weight. He signed on to work with Flannel Logging, a small gyppo outfit owned by Robbie and Glen Flannel, but only a few miles from a bobtail town offering some of the pleasures of life.

It was a bad crew. In his second week of work the three other choker setters stole the gyppo's chains and left in the night. Robbie Flannel drove his ailing log truck down the mountain to set the sheriff on the trail and to buy new chains. When he came back he had no chains but cheaper coils of cable and used haywire and two old drunks from the bar, who were the replacement choker setters.

"Cable lighter to use, easier to git it under a log," said Glen. "Use the haywire to move the cable. Forget about chains. Molti, you show these two stiffs what to do. They ain't no good but they're alive and anybody can be a choker setter, right?" Molti knew he should have walked off the job right then, but he didn't. They attached the haywire to the skyline cable and the donkey pulled it uphill. Someone released the haywire and one of the downslope stiffs fumbled with the excess. Molti fastened the haywire to another cable that had to be moved. He gave the signal to the donkey tender to pull and then saw the stiff was not clear, but standing in the cable's bight—that had been Pollo's mistake. He shouted to the drunk, who started a clumsy run, but the tangled haywire was still being drawn and it snarled, kinked, went tight and snapped. It lashed Molti's midriff with terrible force. The frightened stiffs helped him down to the bunkhouse, and there he lay with blood filling his mouth until ten o'clock that night, when he died. It was only Lobert Sel, Édouard-Outger's oldest son, trained to be cautious, who returned from the West Coast to his family unscarred, unbroken, happy to be reunited with his brother Jim, happy to find a wife, to take up the business of fatherhood and life.

• • •

Men could die in distant lands, as Aaron's oldest son, John, died across the ocean in trench mud in 1917 watching the slanting rain become the final mist. Men could die at home, as on the December morning in the same year when two ships, one packed with munitions and explosives for the war in Europe, collided in the Halifax narrows causing the world's largest explosion and a tsunami that wiped out the Mi'kmaw village in Tufts Cove. Among the mangled and drowned were Lobert's brother, Jim Sel, and four of his children.

"We go Shubenacadie," said grieving and frightened Lobert to his pregnant wife, Nanty, and they moved inland, to the reserve, though he never thought of the reserve as a safe haven. There they found a measure of balance although they were poor. Lobert worked for a timber company in exchange for pay in logs and used them to build a three-room house. When his son Edgar-Jim Sel—called Egga— was born he began to worry as his own father, Édouard-Outger, had worried over him. He did not want his sons to work in the forests nor his daughters to clean house for whitemen women. He saw no danger in the residential school, though he did not like the man who came to the house with paper and pen and said if he did not sign the consent forms his children would be taken by the welfare people. He signed. So, when Egga was ten years old he and his best friend, Johnny Stick, entered the residential school where Mi'kmaw children, their culture and language suffered a forty-year implosion as deadly as any munitions ship.

"You will get education, Egga. To read and write is important. You will get better work than cut trees," his father told him. And Lobert and Nanty visited him at the school every month, lugging a basket of home delicacies—smoked eel, Nanty's special bread, sardines and yellow cake. The priests and nuns smiled and spoke pleasantly. Lobert and Nanty were proud their son was getting an education and because of that pride and because of the false sweetness of the black-clad religious, Egga could not tell them that he never attended a class because the priests worked him all day long shoveling coal in the school's furnace room, where he learned to read only pressure gauges; that he was called a "lazy savage," frequently kicked. After a hard beating by fat Father O'Hoopy that left him deaf in one ear and with a broken arm that healed badly, Egga knew he was a slave, not a student. Johnny Stick worked beside him. Johnny's people never came to visit as they lived far away and Johnny got rough treatment from the priests. He was often called to Father Blink's room. Every boy knew what that meant as Father Blink (a hairy ill-smelling man whose black dress captured and held every stink his body produced) had perverse needs and those who did not satisfy them could expect beating, hunger, isolation, insults, hair pulling, doors slammed on fingers, arms twisted until they hung loose and unusable, kicks and public humiliation, being shaken awake in the night, screams directly in the face, being burned with sulfur-head matches—tortures not just for days, not just for weeks or months, but for years. Father Blink prided himself that he never forgot a boy who refused him.

Egga made a plan. He wanted to ask Johnny to come with him but never found the private moment to ask and he slipped away from the school on his own. Lobert and Nanty were awakened by thunderous pounding on their door.

"Where is he? Your stinking bad son ran off. We know he's here. You are in serious trouble for this!" They turned the log house upside down looking for Egga and came back at odd times for many months before giving up. Lobert and Nanty were miserable, and now began to hear certain stories about the school; they had failed to protect their son from harm. They were not the only bereft parents. Many, when bad news came that their child had died "after a long illness," accepted the lie. Not knowing what had happened to Egga, Nanty fell into a kind of prolonged sadness that took her to the grave, leaving Lobert with the blackest thoughts. For him the evils of the residential school and lack of government oversight permanently stained any English-Canadian claim to decency. It was all words. Yet some hopeful spark still burned and after the war he married Kate Googoo.

No one ever knew what Lobert had done, but when Paul, Alice and Mary May went to the resi school they suffered scorn and name-calling but were never beaten.

Runaway Egga, the direct descendant of Charles Duquet and René Sel, half-starved and ragged, walked by night and slept by day. The only place he had in mind was south. He did not know where he was going except away from Canada; attracted to watercraft he stowed aboard a fishing boat headed for Rockland, Maine, slipped off the boat in darkness and began to walk again. He followed the shoreline for many weeks, begging food or offering to work at farms he passed, slowly made his way to Barnstable and because he smelled frying fish from the galley begged a ride on a fishing boat headed to Martha's Vineyard. The fishermen gave him a hot chunk of scrod and he was theirs forever.

There were other homeless boys hanging around the docks where the fishing boats came in, running errands for the fishermen and helping unload fish. None of them were Mi'kmaw. Egga got his first real boat job learning to haul trap for weakfish and whiting. Captain Giff Peake, himself half Wampanoag, taught Egga how to read a few words, but watching the boy try to write was, he said, like watching a dog try to play the piano. Still, Egga was an eager worker, cheerful, every morning full of hope for a good day as escaped or released prisoners sometimes are.

Egga grew to adulthood aboard Captain Peake's boat, and when the old man retired to sit by his daughter's fire Egga signed on to bigger boats with men who worked the rich cod waters of Georges Bank. He put away his identification as Mi'kmaq and became a hybrid person. In the sweep of his twenty-first year he volunteered for U.S. military service and was turned down as an alien resident, applied for citizenship, met, courted and married Brenda, a Wampanoag girl.

Years later, reunited with his father, Lobert, he said, "What I loved about Bren right at the start was how fast she could count up—she was quick-minded with numbers and she could read right side up and upside down. She was workin for the fish dealers. But I got her away from them. Yes, I did so, everlasting joy." But their marriage wasn't easy; Bren had strong ideas and set them forward fearlessly.

Egga, determined to master reading, set himself the task of making his way through the newspapers every day. He subscribed to several Nova Scotia newspapers, including the *Amherst Daily,* and the *Yarmouth Herald,* and so he learned something of what he had left behind and over the years he and Bren talked about it. She had never been to Nova Scotia, but she had seen how it went with the Wampanoag. Sometimes Halifax men came down on fishing boats and Egga invited them to supper and asked for news. In this way they learned that between the wars Mi'kmaw workingmen went to Winnipeg to harvest grain, to Maine to pick apples, did whatever they could find. They worked as stevedores, emptied and dumped stinking ballast from ships. Many of them lived in lumber camps, away from the reservation except for occasional quiet visits to wives and children.

"I know what that does to their traditional ways," said Bren. "When the men go away to work it puts the responsibility for saving the language on the women." But it seemed that most of the women signed the papers sending their children to the residential schools, trusting they would be taught what they needed to live in the English culture. Few parents knew of the atrocities practiced on their boys and girls by genocidal nuns and priests. The children were never again wholly Mi'kmaw.

Molti Sel's grandsons, Blaise and Louis Sel, were loggers with chain saws and heavy machinery; trees were assembly-line products. Every year there were fewer men on the ground—the place of injuries and death; work was safer in the cab of a machine. They spread out, far distant from the reserve. The Mius and Sel brothers preferred tree-length logging setups and some of them worked in Minnesota and Wisconsin, some in Maine, some in British Columbia or Washington and Oregon states. The old bunkhouse camps were gone. They brought up their families in whiteman houses, listened to the radio, ate at the diner, drove to work and only went back to Nova Scotia for St. Anne's Day.

They knew how their grandfathers had lived. Blaise Sel, one of Molti's grandsons, a skilled feller-buncher operator, said, "Them old camps? You couldn't get me in one of them damn rat hovels for no amount a money, way the hell out in the sticks, nothin to do but work and pick your nose." His brother, Louis, ran the grapple skidder, hooking on to Blaise's bundles of trees, dragging them to the landing, where they went through the delimber, which stripped the branches. He didn't wait to see the logs loaded into the slasher and cut into preset lengths, nor did he care to see them loaded and hauled away to the pulp mill, but hurried back to Blaise for a fresh bouquet of stems. It was a job, it put food on his family's table, paid for his pickup truck, for his and his wife Astrid's house. Other Sels found jobs in the pulp and paper mills, in the plywood factories, in the cellulose-acetate plants, moving deeper into the world of plastics.

Noel Mius's youngest son, Chancey Mius, worked for an in-woods chipping company. But he remarked to his wife, Shelly, that chipping at the landing robbed the woods. "If you don't put those back, soils start to decline. Should do some nutrient replacement work where we took the trees. Think the company will do that? I don't."

"That's a shame," said his wife vaguely.

As if to balance this neglect, his brother Jackson in Maine ran an old-style two-man horse-logging outfit, slow, hard work, fresh air and enough danger to go around. Jackson cut the trees and his neighbor-partner, Sonny Hull, dragged them to the landing with his big draft horses. They had steady work from property owners who wanted a quiet operation that didn't rip up the land. But after a winter of almost no snow when Sonny Hull packed up and moved to Montana and the work was scarce, Jackson went back to school and earned a B.S. in forestry, kept going for a master's in wood management. He had never set foot on the old Mi'kmaw reservation at Shubenacadie through he knew he had people there. It was something he was going to do someday, some St. Anne's Day. To the Sel and Mius relatives St. Anne's Day had a value that outsiders could not understand.

"Worth the three-day drive if that's what it takes," said Blaise Sel, sitting relaxed and comfortable with second cousins and old aunties, belonging to the Mi'kmaw people if only for a day or two. His wife, Astrid, the granddaughter of Swedish immigrants, never came with him. "It's a little bit silly," she said, "you drivin all that way, sayin those Mi'kmaws are your blood kin. It's not like you to do that." But it was.

X

sliding into darkness

1886–2013

63

perfidy

Scrawny Miss Heinrich still sat at the front desk, the office anteroom unchanged since the company's near collapse decades earlier. She would never forget how everything had fallen wrong—the
depression, when construction fell off and lumber prices dropped.
Then, just as the timber business was recovering Lawyer Flense disappeared with Annag Duncan and the embezzled funds. It was the logging company's worst time. What an uproar! Miss Lavinia had called
in four special accountants, dark-eyed men with black mustaches.

"Miss Heinrich, could we please have the books for 'seventy-
three? Could we please have the Board meeting minutes for the last
three years?" Mr. Pye, aged and trembly, was called out of retirement to explain certain actions. The accountants spoke among themselves over dinner plates of steak and boiled potatoes—they strongly
suspected that old Mr. Pye might have set the whole scheme going
decades earlier and made his own nest comfortable.

When the accountants were finished they met with Dieter and
Lavinia.

"Mr. Breitsprecher, Mrs. Breitsprecher, from the beginning
Flense had extraordinary powers to acquire properties for Duke Logging. And to sell. There was no contract that limited his actions on
the company's behalf to acquisition. Yet he was an employee, not a
partner, nor a stockholder. There was nothing that prohibited him
from wrongdoing except moral responsibility."

"I always believed he was loyal to me personally as well as to the company. I never doubted that. I counted him as a friend and I trusted him. We did business as a gentleman's agreement. My father operated that way and was never defrauded," said Lavinia stiffly.

"This time you were defrauded. Flense made secret sales of the company's woodlands, lumber barges, warehouse contents." The accountants implied that the embezzlement was her own fault, that one's word counted for nothing.

The chief accountant inclined his head a little and said, "Mrs. Breitsprecher, may I recommend you to read Adam Smith? It is a truism that men do only what they are rewarded for doing. Flense received a rather modest salary for his legal work on behalf of the company. And in future keep in mind when doing business with Chicago lawyers—*homo homini lupus est*—man is a wolf to man."

They left Duke & Breitsprecher reduced to a skeleton staff and a lean future.

The company staggered and nearly fell. It was hard times nationally: stocks and land values plunged; industrious brooms of change swept out the markets. Men were no longer grateful for work—labor problems and strikes crippled every business, and the forests of the northwest were flash points for rebellious forest workers who preferred better pay to manly poverty. The entire country was in an irascible, sour mood. Lavinia, wanting to rid herself and the company of anything touching on Flense, voted with the remaining Board members to relinquish the incorporation charter. "When Duke was establishing itself as a major logging company we needed capital to build logging railroads, to purchase lumber barges and steamboats, build roads. But all that has changed. Henceforth we will return, although operating on a shoestring, to a sole proprietorship. Aside from all else, incorporation is better suited to canals and turnpikes, railroads and banks, not the timber industry—at least in the position we now find ourselves." A sense of being savagely cheated colored the atmosphere in the boardroom.

• • •

"Lavinia," Dieter said as they went over the details of Duke & Breit-sprecher's teetering position, "we will weather this storm. It is true that the company has lost a great deal of its value, but enough remains that we can start over."

Lavinia could barely speak for rage: "Dieter, my fortune—my *lost* fortune—came from the bonanza of Maine and Michigan lumber that we cut over the generations. No such rich woodlands exist these days. Flense took my ancestral heritage." But she exaggerated. Flense had not touched her personal property, had not sold her Chicago land holdings, now worth millions; it was the company assets he had rifled.

"My dear, please listen. The forests of the northwest are even more prodigious than those of Maine or the Great Lakes country. All will be well in a few years if the company builds up its timber acquisition again. And we are free to focus on our conservation policies as never before. We shall make a new reputation, a new name for Duke and Breitsprecher."

But Lavinia was not consoled. Especially her heart burned at the thought of Annag Duncan's perfidy. "I trusted her," she said. "I gave her a job when she had nothing and this is how she repaid me. I cannot understand how she fell into Flense's grasp." She clenched and unclenched her hands.

"Lavinia, did you never notice how attentive the lawyer was to her? He praised her cookies, brought her little bouquets, always had a smile and drove her home after long meetings. I believe she was smitten with his attentions. Neither I nor you praised her—we took her for granted—that was Flense's opportunity." He rubbed his chin. "And who can know? Perhaps he had an affection for her. She was a rather handsome woman." As soon as he spoke he knew he should not have said this.

"Indeed!" cried Lavinia in a passion. "I do not think so myself. But oh how I wish I could relive the years and keep a chain on his neck! And hers. However, I will engage Pinkerton's to look for the guilty parties. I'll see them in prison." She composed herself. There was nothing to do but go on. "And you are right, Dieter, the forests of the northwest are rich—if we can only get at the remoter areas. And we still have that kauri forestland in New Zealand."

"Do you remember our promise to the Ovals not to clean-cut and run away but remove judiciously and replant? I wish now that my experiments with the kauri seeds had flourished, but the soil conditions were inimical."

Lavinia could not resist her nature and sent orders to cut all the kauri, sparing none. That cut would begin to rebuild her fortune. And Dieter was right, there was still much that remained. Flense had not touched the plywood mills nor the paper mills, and both were drawing in money like dry sponges. They would take advantage of the new technical advances and milling machinery. Duke & Breitsprecher would survive.

"Our annual inventor's exposition must continue," said Lavinia. But the old Hotel Great Lakes had burned down. Lavinia tried to persuade the Board that an exposition hall on company property would attract inventors. "We made millions with the boxed houses and who knows what might come along these days when every man's head is whirring with logging machinery improvements? Let us use Mr. Jinks's old house and grounds as the central node. Participants will take pleasure in strolling through our little forest."

But fewer inventors applied to the Duke & Breitsprecher Exposition. Its day had passed. Men wanted to patent their ideas in their own names.

Dieter felt, too, that the golden days of logging when the forest was endless were over. Farmers who had cut off, burned down and worn out millions of acres of soil in the east were still rushing into the western timberlands to repeat their work, making huge pyres of prime trees and setting them alight, cursing when the scorched soil showed too rocky and poor for growing anything but weeds.

He suffered through the last quarter of the century as again and again Congress congratulated itself on enacting a series of logging laws—Timber Culture Act, Timber Cutting Act, Timber and Stone Act, all supposedly aimed at conservation but all written with more loopholes than a page of Spenserian calligraphy. "From what eggs do these fools hatch? They cannot see!" cried Dieter. "The greatest ill is waste. Only a minuscule fraction of the standing forest ever becomes lumber—most is burned or abandoned. *Mein Gott!*

"It is laughable," said Dieter. "It is criminal. The infamous 'land-lieu' clause that allows anyone to 'donate' woodland to a protected forest in exchange for an equal amount of land somewhere else. Lumbermen love this 'clause' that lets them swap their logged-off woods for acres of untouched timber. It makes me sick to see the way they send carloads of lobbyists to Washington to keep the good pay-days coming. This is the real American 'liberty'!" His solitary break-fast hour was filled with exasperated sighing as he read of successive waves of scandal from real estate men to legislatures. But he said nothing of this to Lavinia. He knew she employed lobbyists. And by association, so did he.

It seemed the two miscreants had gone in opposite directions. Month after month Pinkerton reported rumors of sightings of Flense in Peru, Athens (Georgia), Glasgow and Buenos Aires, but no actual hard evidence.

"Keep on, keep on," said Lavinia, paying the steep monthly detec-tive bills. Then came word that Flense had truly been tracked down to an alley behind the Mulo Rojo, a restaurant in Valparaiso, where he lay dead, stabbed and robbed. Of Annag Duncan there was no word. She had truly disappeared into the wilds of Scotland, where no stranger dared go.

One roaring wet morning the housemaid brought up Lavinia's pot of hot chocolate and trimmed toast. Lavinia was at the window, tying the belt of her rose silk dressing gown, looking out at the dark wind-streaked lake.

"Good morning, ma'am. Another nasty day. Mr. Dieter complains of a catarrh."

"He had better stay in then. I will look in on him after I dress."

The maid put the tray on the little breakfast table, poured the chocolate and left. Lavinia sat down, took up her cup, sipped once, turned to look out at the slanting rain and collapsed, chocolate drenching her thighs. When the doctor came he said heart attack, no one knew why these things happened. Sometimes people just—died. As did Lavinia. Dieter's catarrh became a lingering pleurisy that immobilized him for six weeks. Yet he managed to rise from his sickbed and meet with the stonemason, for, after a bit of tinkering, there was only one inscription for her stone:

> Call for the robin-redbreast
> Here lies a friend

She had made no changes in her will since the days before Annag Duncan's and Flense's scarper; bequests of properties and wealth no longer in existence made the reading of it painful to those who should have become wealthy but instead found themselves with barely enough to live modestly. She left eleven-year-old Charley the greatest part of her fortune, which he could not touch until he was forty—the age of reason in Lavinia's opinion. There was an odd addendum—that should a Canadian claimant come forth to seize a share of Duke-Breitsprecher assets that person should be resisted in every legal way. No one knew what this meant but it trailed a black thread through the day.

Dieter Breitsprecher, who seemed the ideal personality for a widower, surprised everyone by remarrying a year after Lavinia's death. His bride was the youngest daughter—Rallah Henge—of a preservationistminded timberman friend. The young woman with long chestnut-colored hair was thirty years younger than Dieter, and he treated her with elaborate courtesy as though she were a crystal goblet. She had a fluttery laugh and none of Lavinia's robust strengths and mannerisms. The logging business did not interest her; her hopes were all for children and eighteen months after the marriage she bore a son, James Bardawulf Breitsprecher. More than a decade later a daughter, Sophia Hannah, arrived but no more, for Rallah, she who had been so dainty and fragile, went into decline and died of stinking oozing breast cancer before Sophia could walk, before James Bardawulf had reached his teens. As for Charley, he had long before left home.

64

loser

When he remarried, Dieter sold Lavinia's old place and commissioned Burnham's to build him a house in the newly annexed town of Edison Park. Classical in appearance, it presented a calm front to the world with its orderly paired windows. Inside it was modern—wired for electric light and with two telephone lines.

Dieter had sent Charley to study forestry at Yale, where he ran up stairs three at a time, contradicted his professors. He was passionate about forests, but disappointed by the school's lack of similar enthusiasm; it was all about "management." He went to Germany to see firsthand the results of two hundred years of woodland supervision, but chafed under the lectures and begged Dieter and the Board to let him travel and learn the ways of forests through observation. They agreed on a stipend and he began a wandering journey.

He looked at beech woods and hornbeam, sought out the remnant chestnut groves of France, went to still-extant shreds of boreal forest in Scandinavia, to the scattered pieces of pine and birch woodlands in Scotland, the awkward corners of ash, oak and alder in Ireland and Wales. What preserved each was difficult accessibility. He took passage to Australia to see mutation-crazed eucalypts, to New Zealand, where he was embarrassed by Duke & Breitsprecher's vandalism of the ancient kauri and used a pseudonym rather than give his name. In a nightmare he had to lift and replace the fallen monsters on their bleeding stumps. But the day came when Dieter and the Board called him back to settle what his future with the company should be.

• • •

Returned to Chicago, he wandered around the city looking at the new skyscrapers, eating scrappy food from street vendors. His thoughts on forests were in shambles. He had seen too much and now believed that a managed forest was a criminal enslavement of nature. His views were unpopular. Nothing he could do but wait until the hourglass turned.

At breakfast one day Dieter said, dithering over his eternal dish of smoked salmon and two poached eggs, "Your sister and brother will visit next week. James Bardawulf has a very handsome wife, Caroline. His law practice is doing well. You have—"

"They are not my sister and brother, Father."

Dieter ignored the interruption and went on.

"—have not met Caroline. The last time you were here she was abroad with her mother. She and James Bardawulf have twin baby boys—Raphael and Claude. And Sophia married Andrew Harkiss in January. Perhaps I already told you that? She is somewhat young and I feel he will have a steadying effect. Harkiss attended Yale Forestry School, by the way, and started working for us four or five years ago. He revived our cutting operations, got us into Ecuador for the balsa. And after the great fire, into California redwood. He persuaded us to buy up a good deal of prime timber on the Oregon and Washington coasts. It seems the company is regaining its lost wealth."

"What great fire do you mean?"

"Why the great San Francisco fire after the earthquake—it destroyed every building two and a half miles north from the railroad freight sheds. They say it burned half the city. Surely you saw stories about it in the papers, wherever you were?"

"No. I rarely read the papers."

"The only buildings that survived were those constructed of redwood. Nothing could have better displayed its flame-resistant qualities. People demanded—still demand—redwood lumber to rebuild. Andrew accepted the challenge. He had men in the woods before the ashes were cold, and they worked every minute there was light to see. The mills ran twenty-four hours a day."

Charley faintly remembered Harkiss, who had been in the Yale forestry program during his own short time there.

"Andrew is very ambitious about restoring Breitsprecher to its former position. He dedicates himself to its improvement in every way." With no irony Dieter paraphrased Coué—"Every day, in every way, he strives to become better and better."

"Father, how do you feel about this logging enterprise? Better and better?"

"I give it my support, as we start replanting a year after they get out the cut. It is a balanced process."

"I can't imagine what you think will replace two-thousand-year-old redwoods—Scotch pine seedlings? And what of the diversity of species? What about the soil? Erosion? All those qualities you once cared about? Are you cutting old-growth fir and cedar and planting pine? You mentioned Oregon and Washington."

"I suppose I have become more practical through years with Lavinia. So, cutting whatever grows along the shoreline. The big timber in rough country remains untouched—we can't get that out without the great cost of rails and engines."

"What about the watershed protections? The hydrology will be severely compromised. I have been in that country. It is mountainous with steep slopes. And I know that not only redwoods, but those big cedars, can swell out twenty feet across at the bottom—your choppers likely have to use springboards, get up where the girth is ten foot less. The waste must be prodigious."

"Well. I suggest you talk to Andrew about that; he's the man with the ax." Dieter laughed.

"Oh God," said Charley at the thought of that dandified *homme chic* gripping an ax.

· · ·

When James Bardawulf and Caroline arrived, that youngest son went straight to the sideboard and made himself a whiskey highball; he did not ask anyone else what they would like. That was for Dieter to do—let him pour sherry, whiskey, more whiskey for Charley. Old familiar tensions seeped into the room.

Sophia and Andrew Harkiss were the family showpieces. Andrew's even-featured red face and intensely blue eyes, his slender but muscular body gave him an advantage. Yet under the fashionable exterior Dieter saw a hunger that made him think of a dog in the rain watching the master walk to and fro behind lighted windows. And there was James Bardawulf, baring his teeth in a caustic smile. His wife, Caroline, in a modish silk dress, Sophia very pretty. And Charley in his worn tweed lounge suit and unpolished boots. His children, thought Dieter, his dear, terrible children.

"So, Charles, you're paying us a visit," said Sophia. She was a certain type of beauty with upright posture and pale hair, her young face ornamented by a beautifully shaped mouth.

"Do you object?" He leaned forward, twiddled his fingers.

"It would hardly matter if I did," said Sophia. "You do as you please. You always have." She paused a minute, then delivered her dart. "That is, you have done as you please *so far.*"

They took their places at the table, handsome with its array of Spode plates and cut-crystal stemware.

Dieter said, "Is your room pleasant, Sophia?"

"It's very pleasant, Papa, as long as the wind doesn't come up. How a corner room makes the wind whistle."

"Well, that's it. It's a corner so the wind will catch on it as it changes direction," said Andrew. "It doesn't bother me."

The maid brought in a tureen of carrot soup, hot and spicy.

Conversation lagged, caught for a few minutes on Peary's claim for the pole, died away, touched on weather, on Andrew's house, being built by a local man with modernist ideas, on James Bardawulf's new Model T Ford.

"I don't know why anyone wants to go one hundred miles an hour," said Dieter. "It's folly."

"Father, if you tried an automobile I think you would see its advantages."

"What, go rocketing along by pressing one's foot on a knob? I find the idea effete. A man needs to acquire horsemanship, needs to *hold the reins!*"

"There is something to be said for the skill of handling and riding horses," agreed James Bardawulf, who was an indifferent equestrian but an avid collector. "But I am more interested in weapons. I recently acquired two Zulu shields said to be from the Isandlwana battle."

The conversation stuttered along. James Bardawulf asked Harkiss, "What are the main features of your new house?"

"Automobiles, houses—is not money our subject?" said Sophia in her offensive drawl. "I wonder we have not had a hash-through of the values of stocks and bonds, the excoriation of New York banks."

"Yes! And as to that," said Dieter, pleased with the subject, and missing the irony, "I propose a toast to Chicago. I daily rejoice that we settled here, not in New York. Only look at the differences in the last panic. New York was in turmoil, banks and trusts failed—that fellow at Knickerbocker Trust. But in Chicago we had a central clearinghouse and a special bank examiner to keep an eye on liquidity. The New York institutions fell short in these respects as well as on liquidity. That's when old Morgan had to push his way in and 'save the day.'"

"Some," said James Bardawulf, "say panics are unavoidable side effects of a free market."

"And there are those who say such events are the fault, not of the free market, but of unscrupulous individuals and unregulated proceedings, and that the only way to avoid periodic panics and financial failures is to have a government-controlled national bank as most European countries do."

"I expect there will be a time when that will come to pass, though I doubt I'll see it," said Dieter.

. . .

Over the almond pudding Dieter said, "Andrew, Charley was asking me about the West Coast operation—the redwood and cedars. He wonders—"

"I was hoping we could have a family dinner without talk of trees or forest management," interrupted Sophia, disappointed that the discussion of money had turned into a review of a distant New York panic. She enjoyed hearing about the company's increasing value, thanks to Andrew. As she had secured Andrew, it followed that she was the source for the company's improving fortunes.

"But there is no better subject than trees," put in Harkiss. "For this timber family it is the bread-and-butter subject."

James Bardawulf reached for the wine decanter, poured and then leaned back in his chair until it creaked ominously. He said, "No. Timberland discussion gets very hot if brother Charley is on hand. He knows everything about logging and forest management but does not condescend to speak until a mistaken apprehension is uttered and then he comes with sword and pistol and lays us all low."

Harkiss decided to laugh—a staccato bark—and Charley brushed his nose, his feet danced on the floor; he said, "James Bardawulf, I am indebted to you for your deep insights. I quite understand why you are such a success at the bar."

James Bardawulf, who did, in fact, drink rather much, turned maroon and half-stood, dropping his napkin atop his pudding.

"James Bardawulf," said Dieter. "You and Charley are not to start wrangling. Caroline, please tell us how the babies are doing."

She turned, raised her eyebrows as if surprised by the question. "Why, as well as they might do."

Charley studied Caroline Breitsprecher. She was attractive, even beautiful, a florid brunette, slightly plump, with grey eyes that were shrewd and penetrating. She looked at Charley, half-smiled and tipped him a wink.

He felt an electric current of desire. She had deliberately winked at him. Immediately he decided that she was a flirt and that he'd see how far she would go. His imagination jumped into bed with her. To fuck James Bardawulf's wife would be a double pleasure. He almost returned the wink.

But he said nothing of forests nor travel, even when questions were put to him. The next day he had that meeting with Dieter to explain how he was supposed to contribute to company capital. He had no doubt that James Bardawulf and Sophia, who both sat on the Board, were the primary sources of Dieter's summons that he return.

The spring wind off the lake was unseasonably cold. As Charley hurried along the street with his head down, he put one large Breitsprecher hand over each stinging ear. He lingered in the lower entrance foyer of the Duke Building to get warm, putting off the coming discussion with his father.

He climbed the stairs—so many polished oak stairs. He counted forty. Would they someday put in an elevator? He entered the familiar office, where Miss Heinrich, older than the redwoods, smiled bravely at him. "Go right in, Mr. Charley," she whispered. "I'll bring some coffee."

There sat Dieter at his desk, more of a table than a proper desk. Dieter waved at the chair on the other side of the table. His bald head caught the morning light. Charley wondered what he did to make it shine so. Dieter plunged directly in.

"I'm happy to say that many of my earlier ideas on forest care and management have become today's practice. I was pleased when Roosevelt created the Bureau of Forestry, after that vicious affair with the western senators who thought they'd scored well by forcing the abolishment of the forest reserves—that just got Roosevelt's dander up and he sequestered a hell of a lot of forest. The reserve system was always wide open to tinkering—it hardly slowed Weyerhaeuser down. Now he, too, is a colossus like Frick and Morgan. For years

I have been saying that if forestlands are to be protected there must be central government control. We are moving in that direction." He named his new heroes: Bernhard Fernow, who headed up the forestry school at Cornell, and a Maine man, Austin Cary, who struggled to make obstinate lumbermen and landowners grasp some basic forestry principles. And George Perkins Marsh, his old American ideal. Dieter said, "And what did you think of the German forests you saw? Did you look out our family connection to Graf von Rotstein?"

"I did make a search for that relative—no success. I was told the family died out some time ago."

Dieter snorted. He was proof that at least one distant family member survived, and, of course, the same blood ran in his children's veins.

"Tell me what you thought of the forests."

"I saw many, many plantations of pine in orderly rows. But I did not consider them to be forests."

"Indeed. Then what in your consideration *is* a forest?"

Charley said slowly, "I am sure that wild natural woodlands are the only true forests. The entire atmosphere—the surrounding air, the intertwined roots, the humble ferns and lichens, insects and diseases, the soil and water, weather. All these parts seem to play together in a kind of grand wild orchestra. A forest living for itself rather than the benefit of humankind." He stopped.

"I see, 'living for itself.' Yes, of course, but that is not managed land, where we plant and watch over trees to provide revenue to the owners, lifetime jobs to workers, shade and pleasure to nature lovers. Wild forests cannot be managed. That is why we cut them and benefit from their wood, then replace them with trees. Trees that can be managed. Your idea of a forest living for itself is not part of modern life. This is what Austin Cary is trying to teach—that timber can be grown as a crop that makes a good profit and can be renewed endlessly. On one side he has to persuade the men who want to cut as they always have and who see his talks as attacks to ruin their business. On the other side are people not unlike you who see the end of the forests, disaster for the rivers. Even changes in the weather. He has to convince them that forest crops are the way to keep a steady supply and control erosion."

They heard the light ticks of sleet on the window glass. Dieter narrowed his eyes. Chicago had long hard winters, and was it possible this one was persisting so deeply into spring? It was possible. Charley seemed not to notice the sleet but talked on in his low voice.

"I see little merit in rows of pine trees. There is no diversity and the vaunted utility is an illusion. What of the rural people who once went to the wild forest for a hundred reasons? Why do we assume they have no rights to continue their traditional woodland familiarities?" He noticed the fine layer of dust on everything in Dieter's office—globe, bookshelves, chair rungs, window ledges. There was dust on Dieter's ideas.

"Charley, you are missing my point. Here in America the cast of mind is fixed on taking all. My plea for replanting is still a peculiar idea to them. You may be right to say the old wild forests are imperiled, but this is, unfortunately, a matter of politics. You are wrong, too, when you say German forests are only managed plantations— there are no people in Europe as passionate for wild forests as the Germans. In you I see that Germanic streak, partly romantic, partly rebellious. And I wish you could understand that there are hidden complexities in the *managed* forest of which you know nothing."

"A pity you cannot grow barkless planks. It is no use, Father—I have seen what I have seen and cannot accept tree plantations as a greater good." He could see Dieter was working himself up; his bald pate shone red and he pinched his lips in and out.

"Then you had better become a *botanist*"—Dieter spat out the word—"and continue your adventuring." He got up and left the office.

Charley waited. Dieter's anger was rare but he was angry now. His temper would not last, never did last. He would come back. And in a while Charley heard the outer door open, heard Dieter say something to Miss Heinrich, heard her answer. He came in, spicules of melting ice on his shoulders. He nodded at Charley, drew out a bot-

644

tle, went to the cupboard and took out two glasses, poured for himself and Charley.

"Forgive me, Charley." He swallowed some whiskey. Sighed. "I had ideas and feelings similar to yours when I was young but over the years I learned that the entrepreneurial spirit of this country could not be dampened. We can't be wild animals. We are humans. We live in a world that is a certain way and forests must adapt to the overwhelming tide of men with axes, not the reverse. I came to believe that planting trees was a kind of forest continuation, not perfect but better than stumpland. We call such plots 'forest' and we believe that is what they are. Also, I have never thought that German management could be less than superior."

"Father, it reeks of the eighteenth century. It no longer fits. It is also true that there is too much cutting. The old forests are going and once they are gone we will have to wait a thousand years or more to see their like. Though nothing will be allowed such a generous measure of time to grow. Most wild American woodlands have already been savaged."

Dieter inhaled whiskey and erupted in spasmodic coughs. When he recovered, tears streaming, he changed the conversation and said, "Why don't you tell me what you have seen in your travels?"

Silence. The hissing lamp. Bursts of sleet on the window. How lined and weary was Charley's face, Dieter thought; he was old beyond his thirty-five years.

"You ask me about the company's cut in New Zealand. Where once a grove of the noble kauri grew I came upon acres of devastation. The killing ground could only be differentiated from the gum fields by the fresher stumps."

Dieter shuddered. The gum fields that he and Lavinia had seen were the most desolate landscapes, churned mud where nothing grew, great holes gouged in the wet earth, swamps without vegetation where moiling creatures clawed for bits of ancient resin to improve paint.

Charley talked, and when he paused Dieter asked, "What of New England, where my cousin Armenius first cruised the woods for James Duke? I have not been there since I visited Mr. Marsh a year or two after you were born."

"Why, northern New England is a world of denuded mountains scarred by railroad tracks and erosion. Slash, charred logs, millions of stumps and endless miles of washed-out roads. I don't see how fish can live in New England waters unless they can breathe silt. Large fires every summer, and still the rivers carry log drives—pitifully small sticks for the pulp mills and pressed-wood fabricators."

Dieter's voice was low. "Was all destruction? Did you see nothing good and beautiful?"

"Yes. I did. Brazil has the most profoundly diverse forests on earth!" For the first time since his return there was enthusiasm in Charley's voice. "The striking feature is the mix of species rather than large groves or aggregates of dominant trees. Foreigners are in constant wonderment. When they return to their countries they see how barren and meager are their homelands."

"I have always championed diversity."

"It is in the tropics, not only in Brazil but in Colombia, Costa Rica, Venezuela, in India and Malaysia—forests filled with mangoes, guava, passionfruit, starfruit, coconuts, bananas. The tropical forests are the most wondrous forests I ever saw. Spectacular forests, but now attracting men with pencils and measuring sticks, men seeking fruits to export. Cattle ranchers who cut and burn the forest for pasture. They are the places where the punitive *aviamento* system of the rubber business drives the economy. I take comfort in the thought that none of them can really harm that massive heart of the world. The rain forest is so large and rich it defeats all who try to conquer it."

Dieter felt he was drawing closer to Charley. "I would very much like to see these forests. But let me say that I heard the same complacent remarks about the Maine and New Hampshire woods, about the Michigan pine forest—too large to be irrecoverably harmed. And

I saw them fall. There is no such thing as being too large to fall. They all go down when men come."

"I hope you are wrong. Dear father, can you understand that I must go back to Brazil? What little I learned of the flowering and fruiting habits of the trees filled me with curiosity. Some seem to follow the rules of invisible seasons, but others flower from the time they sprout until they die. I want to learn why things happen as they do in that place." He looked at Dieter and said, "Tropical forest soil is rather poor—all the forest's richness is encased in its living trees. Is that not interesting?"

Dieter shook his head, asked, "Is such a thing possible?"

"It is. And in the level above the soil are shrubs and ferns, young trees, all dependent on shafts of light reaching them. They are not plants *in their own right* but the slaves of the large trees. Even stranger are the epiphytes, an entire world of parasitic plants that grow on the trees. That forest calls to me."

Dieter listened with consternation. Charley's preference for wild forests was disturbing. It was a proof that his older son was a sinking man, fated to be a loser. How to jolt him loose? How to involve him in the company's work?

"I'll do what I personally can to help you," said Dieter, "but you seem destined to observe, perhaps write a book—I do not see you holding a regular job or making a business success."

"There is no job that I have ever heard of that would be as honorable and interesting as going about and observing the lives of the trees and noting their peculiarities."

"Still, men must work—even you." The words came out so mournfully they both laughed.

"I need a real cause, Father, if I am to work at anything. I am no businessman. And I may indeed write a book. Although I know pitifully little and one lifetime is not enough to study even a single tropical forest tree. I want—how can I describe it? I want to discover the dynamo, the central force of the wild forest—all my interest lies in searching out that vital force."

But Dieter thought *dynamo* and *force* sounded too much like a romantic "meaning of life" quest. He had a painful thought—did he not scent the bitter fragrance of madness in Charley? "Why not think about all this over the winter? Stay here to get your bearings, do some reading and meet others interested in trees. We can talk again in a few months. And of course we want you here for the holidays." He was determined to understand and help this first son, but it seemed a heavy task; Dieter felt himself too old, lost in the forest of his own experience.

So Charley stayed the winter and spring to play a game of seduction with Mrs. James Bardawulf—Caroline—alternately beckoning and evasive; he was determined to get her, to spite his half brother, whom his father favored.

He was still trying in August, when the great 1910 fires in Montana, Idaho and eastern Washington burned more than three million acres of prime timber and settlements in two days, a raging blowup crown fire jumping and leapfrogging over hundreds of miles, a fire such as no human had ever seen. The country was shocked by headlines describing how the remote heart of America had been destroyed in forty-eight hours, for people believed that the wild essence of the country existed in its great forests somewhere out west. And now they had burned.

Dieter pled with pea-brained politicians and barely literate congressmen for more money and authority for the Forest Service. He spoke out against that governor who said forest fires were a good thing because they opened new country for settlers, and he cursed the congressman from a fire-plagued state who bellowed, "Not one cent for scenery!" He began a regimen of letter writing, wire sending and telephone calls; he volunteered to start new pine and fir seedling nurseries to replant the hideous blackened mountains and stem the landslides of burned soils. He tried to interest his older son.

"Charley, here's a cause for you—help rejuvenate the spoiled lands. I am meeting this evening at the house with James Bardawulf

and Andrew to discuss possible salvage of some of the burned timber. I hope you will join us." He did not think Charley could resist
the battle to heal the wrecked forest.

"It will just happen again," said Charley in a dismissive tone,
"until the yahoos have burned the country clear. You are pleading
with men who just don't care. As for salvage, it seems a bit like rifling
the pockets of a corpse." He left the door ajar as he went out.

Charley had had enough of Dieter's hopeless American forest projects and almost enough of the slippery Caroline. She enjoyed teasing
him and that, he promised himself, would be the key to getting her.
He would make one more effort and then leave. He telephoned.

"I'm leaving tomorrow morning," he said.

"Oh, Charley, where are you going? To the terrible fires in Idaho
and Montana?"

"No. The fires are ended. My interests pull me to the tropics. Let
me see you one last time. Will you not walk in the garden with me
for half an hour this evening?"

"I might if you are very, very good. None of your naughty ways."
She laughed, an often-rehearsed laugh that an earlier swain had told
her was like the music of a babbling brook.

"But you are so beautiful that I cannot make a promise. You have
a powerful effect on me. As a last favor please wear your exquisite
green dress."

"Oh, my Poiret. You have an eye for fashion. That is the most
expensive dress I own."

"The most beautiful," he murmured gallantly. He knew well that
it was a dress famously designed to be worn without a corset.

He came to the dark garden deliberately a little late, just as the moon
was rising, and saw her standing beside the redbud tree, the faded
heart-shaped leaves catching the lunar glow as did her pale dress.

She resembled the chrysalis of a luna moth. The watery moonlight seemed to solidify their bodies, to render shadows corporeal, as intense as stones.

"Here you are," she said and produced her rippling laugh. He seized her at once and lightly bit her neck.

"Oh don't! It will show!"

He bit again, harder.

"Stop, Charley. What has got into you?" She tried to push him away, but he was not having it and he was not playing her flirting game tonight. He pulled her to the garden bench. It took a few moments of sweet flattery and blandishment to ease her into position and gradually ruck high the green dress. He did this almost stealthily, not roughly, eased into her hot and responsive flesh and at the moment of discharge heard James Bardawulf's voice say, "Why, Charley, how thoughtful of you to drop in," and there was a tremendous concussive sound that his damaged brain told him was a moon bolt, very like being struck full force with a Zulu knobkerrie.

Caroline's shrieks brought servants from the house who pulled the club away from James Bardawulf, who then tore a rosebush out of the ground and began flailing the insensible form on the ground. Young Raphael, in his pajamas, ran for Dieter, who arrived still clutching his meeting notes.

"James Bardawulf, *anhalten, anhalten sofort!* Stop *halt* this stupidity! *Was ist los? Anhalten!* You will kill him!"

"I want to kill him! Let me go!"

The servants carried Charley to his room and two doctors came within the hour. Dr. Plate examined the unconscious Charley and said it was a grave injury. He might remain unconscious for some time—forever, even—might die without waking up. But he cleaned the wound, bandaged it and left the first of three nurses to watch over the wounded man. Dr. Scotbull examined the sobbing Caroline, who had been roughly used and violated but was otherwise unhurt. The moon-green dress was torn and dirty. "A few days in bed to rest and become calm. You must put the experience out of your mind and divert yourself with books or needlework," said the doctor, shooting sidelong glances at James Bardawulf, whose red eyes glared. The doctor steered him downstairs and poured him a glass of whiskey—watched him swallow it in a single glugging bolt. Within the half hour James Bardawulf went up to Caroline, hissing that if she liked rape so much that is what she would get, slapped her hard and mounted her.

The next day James Bardawulf was discovered in Dieter's house going up the stairs with the retrieved knobkerrie, and once again the servants disarmed him. Dieter had Charley moved to the hospital with a guard at the door. One son had tried to kill the other and it was clear he was going to keep trying until he was successful. James Bardawulf, now sexually excited, kept Caroline in bed for a week.

Dieter went to his younger son. "James Bardawulf, I know he wronged your wife, insulted your honor. If he recovers he will leave the family and live abroad. But I beg you to swallow your rage. You are young, and anger and desire to kill can sour you from the heart outward all the days of your life. I have lost one son—I cannot bear to lose you as well. I care for you deeply, James Bardawulf. And you must not blame Caroline. You must forgive." He embraced the rigid man, tears splashing on the younger son's shoulder. But James Bardawulf was anxious to get back to Caroline and go where his older half brother had been, and he pulled away from his father.

Remembrance began to seep in, fleet distorted images of falling, the smell of earth. Moonlight. The day came when Charley could get up and walk to the window. In early dusk he looked out. Soon, he thought, soon rather than late. The nights were chill, leafless trees disclosed their angular frames. When the bandage came off, by manipulating two mirrors he could see thick bristles of hair growing on each side of a furious dark scar.

"Father," he said to Dieter, whom he knew again, "what happened to me?"

"Something heavy fell on you in James Bardawulf's garden." A glass with a residue of sleeping powder stood on the night table.

"In James Bardawulf's garden? Why!" He turned the glass in his fingers.

"I see no point in keeping the information from you. You did something *schlecht*. You tried to—you ravished Caroline in the garden and James Bardawulf discovered you in the act. Your own brother's wife! He struck you."

"This is extremely painful to hear. I do not remember this. I think you must be mistaken."

Dieter looked at him. Was he willfully lying or did he truly not remember? He was lying. Worse, Dieter believed Charley's mind was unsound. And he must go.

Through intermediaries Dieter arranged the purchase of a small house for him in Lugar da Barra do Rio Negro, or Manaós, the city of the forest, where the wild tropical trees would be waiting for him. The house and a modest monthly sum of money were all he could do for this child he had long ago foretold, under the silver maple in Lavinia's park, would be a man of the trees.

In Amazonia, Charley discovered himself as nothing. What he did was nothing. He saw the rampant growth of vine, shoot, sprout, seedling, moist and dripping, swollen and bursting with vigor. He vividly, and without regret, remembered raping Caroline. The forest sounded with the constant patter and thump as leaves, twigs, petals and fruits, branches and weak old trees succumbed to gravity. When the storm wind called *friagem* generated by the Antarctic came, the noise increased, a bombardment of tree parts and fruits mixed with the hissing of the wind in the canopy.

Decomposition seemed as violent—the collapse of leaf structures, cells breaking down, liquefaction of solid wood into a mold squirming with lively bacteria and animalcula seething and transforming into energy. Yes, and insects and larvae, worms and rodents and everywhere the famous ants who ruled the tropics. He almost understood how the incomprehensible richness of Amazonia made humans clutch and rend in maenadic frenzies of destruction. Such a forest was an affront, standing there smirking, aloof from its destiny of improving men's lives.

Charley was slow in learning Portuguese. His first sentence was *"Você fala inglês?*—do you speak English?" But the answer was so often "I don't understand—*não compreendo"* that he struggled to master some useful words. In his first week in Manaós, making long walks around and through the town, he discovered a Portuguese paper goods shop, a *livraria,* that sold imported notebooks with fine French paper. He bought several.

Where to begin? Perhaps it was best to make a catalog of tree species. Two weeks of this and he realized it was beyond him. There were simply too many kinds of trees. He did not know them, could only observe their habits. He followed rubber tappers' paths, poor men in lifelong debt servitude, no better than slaves. He pitied them but it was not until he followed a smell into a small clearing and found a charred corpse that he could believe the ghastly rumor of punishment of those who tried to break free from the system; they were caught, wrapped around with ropes of flammable latex and set on fire. The forest encouraged cruelties and subjugation.

The furniture maker Senhor Davi Fagundes was the only person he knew who could identify the bark, flowers and branches he gathered. This hollow-eyed man when Charley had asked his usual "Do you speak English?" question had replied, "Yes, a little."

Charley wrote everything down in his notebooks. There were many species of mahogany, Brazilian rosewood, teak, bloodwood, exotic zebrawood, ipe and cambara woods, anigre and bubinga, cumaru and jatoba, lacewood and makore. And hundreds more without names. He felt fortunate if he could attach a name to one tree each week, draw its general shape, list some of its epiphytes and strangler vines.

"Why you want knowing this?" Fagundes asked.

"To learn the trees that grow in this kind of forest. Where I come from there are no such forests."

But more and more the cabinetmaker held up his hands and said *"Eu não sei!"* I don't know.

At the end of his first year Charley had sent the notebook to Dieter as he would every year until he learned of Conrad. He heard nothing back and wondered if Dieter had abandoned him. In fact, Dieter had abandoned everyone.

65

legacies

Not long after Charley's departure from Chicago, Dieter, the old pine, had gone down. "Mrs. Garfield," he said wearily on a Monday noon, "I'm going home early. I have a headache and think I need a night's sleep." Mrs. Garfield, who had replaced Miss Heinrich when she retired, clucked and said, "I hope you feel better tomorrow." But the next morning the headache was bad and he had a stiff neck. By the end of the week he was half-paralyzed, and the doctor diagnosed polio.

"I thought only children got polio," said Sophia.

"No, no, it can attack at any age. But keep children away from the house. It's contagious."

"Hard to breathe," Dieter whispered. It got harder. By Saturday pneumonia finished him.

"I don't care what it takes, we've got to find him," said James Bardawulf, striding to the grimy window and back. "He's a major heir in the will. The situation is crazy enough. That we don't know where the hell he is makes it worse. I'm going to get a private detective on it."

Andrew Harkiss made a sound that was almost a laugh. "You've been reading too many books, James Bardawulf. I'm sure Dieter had his address. Have you asked Mrs. Garfield? And isn't it likely that he gave the address to Mr. Grey when he made his will?" He picked up the telephone and dialed. "Mrs. Garfield, do we have Charley Breit-sprecher's address?"

"Yes sir. It's in the correspondence file. I'll get it."

"Well, good," said James Bardawulf. "We'll ask Mr. Grey to send someone from his office with the necessary papers. And I will enclose my personal letter." He had been composing the letter in his mind for several years and now he would write it.

The young lawyer, excited by the journey to the tropics (though after seeing dead monkeys in the market he wanted to be back in Chicago), had no trouble finding Charley Breitsprecher, disheveled and rather yellow, in the muddy river town. He told him Dieter had "passed" and handed him the envelope of documents. Charley sent the young man back to his hotel and arranged to meet him for dinner. When he was alone he read the lawyer's letter, read James Bardawulf's hand-written page, shook his head, wept and read it again.

James Bardawulf had written:

Dear Charley.

We both have very much to regret and resolve. I am deeply, deeply sorry for attacking you. I have suffered pangs of conscience ever since that night. And Caroline who blames herself for all. But as they say, there is no wind so ill that it does not bring some good. The good is our son Conrad. We love him. Our father, Dieter, taught me that holding on to anger is a great evil. If you return someday to your family in Chicago you will be received with affection.

Your brother, James Bardawulf Breitsprecher

"None more sorry than I am, James Bardawulf," said Charley to the letter.

Hours later he read the details of the will and after half a quart of brandy tore a page from his notebook and took up his pen.

"Dear Sir," he wrote to Mr. Grey. He disclaimed most of his portion of Dieter's estate, saying, "I would like it to go to my brother, James Bardawulf Breitsprecher, and his wife, Caroline Breitsprecher, for reasons they know."

A month later, when Dieter's will and Charley's letter were read, James Bardawulf caught his breath. How Charley had changed, down there in the jungle. But then, he, too, had altered.

In Brazil for the next seven or eight years Charley sent his notebooks not to Dieter but to the boy, Conrad Breitsprecher, often with a letter and a sketch of some comic tropical insect. His malaria attacks increased in ferocity. His fortieth birthday had brought him his mother's legacy, but he chose to stay in his little house. The work— which he would not leave even for an hour—was everything. Tenacity was in his bone marrow. Yet he dared make only short forays into the forest, for if he went deeper and the malaria laid him low he might be unable to struggle back to his house. Twice the attacks had led to seizures that left him half-dead on the floor.

He came into Senhor Fagundes's shop clutching a black twig with seven leaves. He was shaking and too ill to speak. He held out the branch to the man who had become something like a friend. The cabinetmaker took the shaking branch, twisted a leaf, looked in his dictionary.

"Leopardwood. Not same like lacewood but look almost—a little."

Charley swayed, put his hand out to take his twig and dropped to the floor, convulsed. Senhor Fagundes, shocked and afraid, hoping the man did not have a pestilent disease, called the hospital for an ambulance. Charley Duke Breitsprecher, ever a man of contradictions, died a week later of *Plasmodium falciparum* in Manaós, after writing in his last notebook:

Nothing in the natural world, no forest, no river, no insect nor leaf has any intrinsic value to men. All is worthless, utterly dispensable unless we discover some benefit to ourselves in it—even the most ardent forest lover thinks this way. Men behave as overlords. They decide what will flourish and what will die. I believe that humankind is evolving into a terrible new species and I am sorry that I am one of them.

The final sentence was his will—a scrawled request that this last notebook be sent to Conrad and all that he possessed, his fortune inherited from Lavinia, and Dieter's seedling nursery, be held in trust for the boy until he turned twenty-one.

The early months of the war in Europe did not much affect remote Chicago. As conflict sucked in country after country Americans went about their lives and voted to stay neutral. James Bardawulf and Caroline thought not of war, but of the future, and considered schools for Raphael, Claude and Conrad, handsome boys marked for success.

"This military academy in Indiana," said James Bardawulf, holding up a paper, "has a high reputation for educating young men of good character. Closer than eastern schools. I say we take a trip to Indiana to look it over."

James enrolled Raphael and Claude in the school and put down young Conrad's name—he was barely nine—to hold a place for him. And, as the yellow mists of chlorine gas spread over Ypres, James Bardawulf and Caroline returned to Chicago with their brochures and impressions.

"We got them where we want them," said Andrew Harkiss, recovered from the Spanish flu that had killed Chicagoans like chickens. Great rollers of change beat on national shores: newly independent but poor countries, once the colonial holdings of the great European powers, struggled to join the global scuffle. "What these countries have is the raw materials—forests and minerals and oil. We'd be fools not to get in on this, South America, Asia—all kinds of hardwood. It's our chance."

James Bardawulf, curious one day about the notebooks Charley had sent to Conrad, looked into them and found them filled with useful information on the qualities of tropical trees. He showed them to Andrew.

"Papa, I want my notebooks back," said young Conrad, who instead of reading Tom Swift stories found the grimy pages, punctuated with squashed gnat and mosquito corpses, interesting for their opaque originality and because this uncle he had never met had bequeathed him the notebooks and the seedling nursery business.

The company, now Breitsprecher-Duke, in league with banks, other timber outfits, the mining industry, coffee, cocoa, banana and mango importers, became part of the new colonialism. When the great onslaught on tropical forests began, they were in the van, taking all they could. Charley Breitsprecher's notebooks were used to plunder his forest.

At sixteen, after a summer on a cattle ranch where the work was considered character-building and healthful, Conrad fell ill with headaches and chills, painful joints and a deep weariness. He was diagnosed with undulant fever and kept in bed most of the fall and winter. He began to recover and in spring the doctor recommended three months rest at a hotel-sanatorium in the mountains of New Hampshire. There he experienced a day, never forgotten, that bound him forever to forests.

He fell in love with a local girl, Sally Shaw, a waitress in the dining room. Most of the visitors took breakfast in their rooms, but every morning he sat near his favorite east window and she brought him tea and the institution's famous popovers. She spoke to him in a teasing voice about the weather, or the breakfast offerings, but he felt strangely happy when she came to his table with the teapot. Her hands were small but deft, her nails lacquered, her black straight hair cut fashionably short. Very red lipstick outlined the rosebud shape of her mouth. She flirted. The room was quiet except for the swish of the door to the kitchen and the soft chink of silverware. The grey mountain slopes showed a frost of pale green, the buds of emerging leaves. When the sun struck they glowed a luminous gold-green. Conrad blurted out his wish that she would go walking with him on the mountain.

"I think you must know the best place to walk," he said.

"Say, do I ever! Tomorrow? I got the afternoon off." She had heard he was a rich man's son.

It was not a fair day. Heavy mist hung over the mountains. Yet the afternoon went in a direction he had not dared hope for. They walked up a steep trail, there was a clumsy kiss as they veered into sweet fern, her shrill laugh, then grappling and rolling on the ground. The perfume of crushed sweet fern fixed the experience. A light rain began. When he looked beyond her, he saw an army of perfect young white pine trees glistening in the wet mist, bursting with the urgency of growth. The rain, falling slant and silver, amplified their resinous fragrance. It was raining, the girl, her hair in ratty wet tails, was pulling at him to go back to the hotel, but he was happy. And somehow he was caught, not by the girl, but by the little pines.

After the crash of '29 the country staggered under the weight of economic depression and the rage of striking workers. Breitsprecher-Duke began to lose its footing. James Bardawulf told Conrad, now finished with school and with a degree that fitted him for nothing, that the family company would employ him if he wished, but without salary; after all he had money he could live on and Breitsprecher-Duke was enduring hard times. Raphael was counting on his smooth good looks for a job in films, and Claude worked for a real estate company specializing in western ranch properties. Since Roosevelt, cattle ranching had been popular with those who still had wealth.

"Let me think about it, Father," Conrad said. He thought instead of Dieter's old seedling nursery business. Could anything be done with it? It had been more of a hobby for Dieter with very few clients, but over the years he had kept on a single employee, Alfred McErlane, who managed the greenhouses. Perhaps it was time to evaluate the nursery, to talk with Mr. McErlane.

Conrad had been very young the first time he was in one of the greenhouses, a visit with his parents and brothers. He remembered a long, long wet concrete floor with hoses and watering cans in the aisle. There was a man in a yellow raincoat. Raphael and Claude had run down the aisle and were leaning over a tank at the end. Conrad followed them. When he looked into the dark water he saw huge slow-moving creatures, orange, spotted black and white like cows. James Bardawulf said they were koi, a kind of fish.

"Why are they so slow?" asked Raphael.

"Because they have seen everything in the tank, nothing new," James Bardawulf answered, and he laughed. But Caroline was upset and demanded that the koi be caught and brought to the pond in the garden.

"At least they will have a better life," she said. Two days later, though, Conrad saw a pair of great blue herons at the edge of the pond, and when he went closer to see if the fish were visibly enjoying their new freedom, the birds flew up, leaving behind the bones of the orange koi.

Very little had changed in the greenhouse. Al McErlane was not wearing a yellow raincoat, but hoses still stretched and coiled on the wet floor. As a child Conrad had not noticed the seedlings, but now he saw them: spruce and pine.

He looked first at the account books and client lists, for the nursery did a small but steady business.

"Al, it looks like our customers are mostly local parks and private landscape concerns. And just spruce and pine seedlings? I see very few lumber company clients. Tell me how you think our position stands and if you think it might be improved."

McErlane was surprised at Conrad's serious interest. He had expected Conrad to say the business would be sold or closed down.

"Well, you know, we go along. Timbermen that want to replant just leave a few seed trees and let the trees do the job. Nobody's got any money these hard times even if they believed in planting seedlings. Which they don't. But a guy from Weyerhaeuser come around a month or two ago asking questions about how we set up, where we get the seeds and all. I think they might be planning to get their own nursery going. They have the money to do it—they are the only timber people making a profit."

"And my grandfather Dieter was doing this fifty years ago. I wonder if there is not a real future for our seedling nursery."

"That would be my thought," said McErlane.

They talked and walked through the other glasshouses—there were five, all old and in poor shape. It didn't take Conrad long to discover that McErlane was as ignorant of new research and knowledge on seedling propagation, cloning, forest genetics and site preparation as Conrad himself. He was putting his hands on a finicky complicated business that called for extensive knowledge on the part of both the seedling grower and the planter.

"I have to back up," he said to McErlane. "I don't know what I need to know. I have to go to forestry school. I think we can keep the greenhouses running as they are for the clients that still depend on us until I learn enough to map out a new plan. One thing is sure. Seedlings are the best way to keep forests alive."

That night he made a list of questions. What would be the needs of future seedling buyers? McErlane had been raising and selling "will grow anywhere" pine and spruce bare-root seedlings, but there was evidence that most of these died when planted on rough logged-over sites. Site preparation would help, but what companies could afford the labor and machinery in these times? He strained to put his mind into the future, when the need for timber would press harder. Which species would timbermen demand, what were the diseases, what were the best planting sites and how should the sites be prepared? Nature's most dramatic way of replenishing the forest was fire. Loggers could duplicate such sites by clear-cutting and burning the slash. But which species did well in burned-over land? Which would suffer from possible invasion by wild grasses and plants?

He enrolled in forestry school, and as he studied he saw more and more difficulties. The real knot was the timber industry. He would have to persuade logging companies and lumbermen that their future was linked to his; if they wanted trees to cut in the future, they would have to plant new seedlings among the stumps. They would have to learn to think in decades and hundreds of years. They could not depend on leaving a few wild trees to seed the barren cuts—experience showed there was poor regeneration. Again and again, as he asked questions of college experiment stations and men who had tried reseeding, he came back to the same difficulty—site preparation was vital; timbermen had to see that doing the work and paying the costs was to their benefit. Conrad made a decision. Breitsprecher would offer site preparation as a service.

In the forestry school he heard of someone who had made kraft paper cylinders, filled them with soil and planted a seed in each. These seedlings did better than those with bare roots when set out on the same site. But was it practical to grow seedlings this way? Practical matters demanded experimentation. He had to include research in his plans. And there were costs. A square foot of nursery space could produce how many seedlings of what species with what labor and time and maintenance? Were there optimum or minimum sizes for seedlings? Were there limits? Yes, there were always limits—he had to find them. Finally, could the seedlings be priced to allow some profit or should he just hope to break even? For already he was inclining toward philanthropy, using his uncle Charley's legacy.

• • •

By 1939 he knew enough to work out a long-range plan. He built new greenhouses and set up a seedling experiment with eleven tree species. Al McErlane was busy with two new workers, Pedro Vaca, a young Mexican who told fanciful but amusing tales, and Hank Stone, the son of German immigrant grandparents who had changed their name from Stein during the Great War. A separate building was a small laboratory-office though he had not yet found the research horticulturist or plant breeder that he wanted. He had liked Elsie Guderian, one of the few women enrolled in the forestry school and interested in plant heredities, but she had another year before graduation. "Once I've got that degree . . ." she said, indicating she wanted the job. She was stocky, with hard red cheeks and horse legs, but a true researcher. What he wanted.

War was in the pure air once again, in the inky newspapers. It seemed to older people a continuation of the war they had grown up with, coming to a boil after just enough time to raise a new crop of sacrificial young men. A pattern was emerging—every twenty-five years or so another war would keep the human world stumbling along, a human boom and bust carried to deadly extremes. The Breitsprechers and Dukes had escaped military service for generations, but Conrad was called up. Both Raphael and Claude knew the right people. Conrad knew only Al McErlane and some forestry professors. Growing nursery seedlings was not a vital agricultural occupation.

He came back from the South Pacific in 1945, face and body damaged and changed, thoughts changed, ideas and beliefs changed. And when once more he shook Al McErlane's hand and walked through the seedling greenhouses, he thought that the rows of spiky, fresh green sturdy little pines were the most beautiful things he had ever seen.

66

her place in the sun

Plywood and fiberboard kept Breitsprecher-Duke alive. During the Second World War they experimented with interior and exterior hardboard siding, but after two years of moisture problems with different recipes—one unhappy trial involved seaweed and corn husk pulp—they dropped the product and concentrated on their plywood—Brite-Ply, made of culls and forest fire salvage. In the years after the war they caught the tail end of the building boom, but bigger companies supplied by cheaper Canadian wood sent them into decline, although the illusion of a productive, busy wood products company headed by two dynamic men—James Bardawulf Breitsprecher and Andrew Harkiss—persisted. Both men photographed well standing in front of a mountain of logs or the glittering rotary peeler, but like plywood these images were only a surface layer covering inferior material.

The younger generation of Breitsprechers wanted nothing to do with the plywood company. But Sophia Hannah Breitsprecher Harkiss, the youngest of Dieter's children, had her own idea of a place in the works. She found her brother and her husband annoyingly obtuse.

"Andrew! I do not understand why you and James Bardawulf don't let me into the company. For God's sake, it's the sixties, not the Dark Ages. I have no position." She had grown up listening to Dieter's stories of how Lavinia Duke, his first wife, apparently a reincarnation of Elizabeth I, had controlled the lumber business since her youth, and it seemed to Sophia, only vaguely aware of the company's decline, that she, too, should have a title. Her children were grown, why should she not have a career?

"You are a company director, you sit on the Board," said Andrew. "Very few companies have women on their boards. You have influence in that way and your comments are taken into consideration. What more do you want?"

"I want a position. I want an office and the responsibility of that office." She kept banging out this tune for more than a year until Harkiss said he would discuss it with James Bardawulf, who, as president of the company and paterfamilias, had the say. But she could not come up with a specific description of what her position might be.

"She wants to make a career move," Harkiss said gloomily to his brother-in-law. "You'd think she'd calm down, now that she's a grandmother. Instead she is like a rolling cannonball on the deck of a ship. She wants an office and her name on the door, a telephone and probably an expense account. Which she'll spend on clothes." He and James Bardawulf were having dinner at the Wild Goose in Sherman Oaks, James Bardawulf slashing at his veal cutlet Oskar, Andrew Harkiss picking gingerly at boned pheasant with a Kahlúa sauce.

"How's the pheasant?" asked James Bardawulf.

Harkiss made a face. "Unusual. I think I prefer gravy to Kahlúa." They were silent for a few minutes while the waiter hovered, filled their glasses with a sharp white wine. Harkiss drank greedily to rid his mouth of the Kahlúa.

"But what would Sophia *do*?" James Bardawulf wanted to resolve the issue.

"I don't know. For God's sake *she* doesn't know. It's the change of life—or something—and you know how they get." "They" made up the vaporish, flighty, talkative, scrambling world of women. Yet her husband understood that she had been biding her time for years, and that she would not let this drop. "I told her the company isn't the monolith she seems to think it is. I told her we had discussed selling out. She blew her top—how could we think of such a thing, ineffective management, lax ways, blah blah. I suppose I can put it to her that she has to draw up a formal request outlining the duties she would assume—tell her that vague wishes bear no fruit. I hope we can find something to quiet her down."

James Bardawulf glanced at the dessert wagon against the wall. The waiter saw the glance and hurried to snatch up two dessert menus. "How about something to do with the arts? She's always been interested in museums and concerts—she can do something cultural. Or civic. Community relations?"

"Sophia feels entitled to a place in the company."

"She's smart—I admit that. Too smart, maybe." Andrew Harkiss thought of his wife's years of correction of his appearance, how she sniped at his way of speaking, realigned the way he marshaled his facts. He sometimes felt he was married not to Sophia but to James Bardawulf; they spoke the same language. "She's not young but I can tell you that pointing that fact out to her will produce Vesuvius in action. Let's wait and see if she can come up with an idea on her own." Harkiss saw that Kahlúa sauce figured in two of the sweets on the dessert menu. He asked for butterscotch pie but even that came with an arabesque of the moody liqueur drizzled down the triangle. He sent it back, saying, "The chef must have stock in the company."

Andrew Harkiss told Sophia that James Bardawulf had asked that she write out a description of the job she wanted.

"Yes, yes," she said and went upstairs to her closet to sort out old, boring clothes that she would replace on a shopping trip to New York, for Chicago did not have really good garment shops. The specific position she wanted, whatever it was, would come to her.

• • •

The flight to New York bumped over a cloudscape that looked like trays packed with cauliflower heads. The air evened out later in the afternoon. As they flew toward darkness, approaching the cities of the east, the slender tangles of light below became great webs, the radiant country glittering in the night.

Sophia stayed at the Waldorf, as the Breitsprechers always did. From her room she telephoned her cousin Althea Evans, who had married a Wall Street stockbroker. She and Althea could shop together and have an elegant lunch. A maid answered the phone.

"Mrs. Evans is away. They are in Boca."

"Where?"

"Boca. Boca Raton. In Florida."

"Oh. Well, tell her her cousin Sophia called. Sophia Breitsprecher. From Chicago."

After a late New York breakfast of coffee and toast she went to Bonwit Teller, to Saks and Bergdorf's. She bought two Norell silk shirtwaist dresses. She tried on suits, even a pants suit, not liking the effect. On her last day she thought again about the position she had conjured up on the plane, rushed out to Henri Bendel and daringly tried on two Coco Chanel suits. Both horribly expensive, they were right for her, and damning the cost she bought them. They were what she imagined an ultrafashionable businesswoman would wear. And the position she was shaping in her mind meant stylized business rituals and the right costumes; Chanel suits were correct.

It amazed her how much alike were her husband and brother. They were almost interchangeable. She saw herself as the family intellectual; she took Book-of-the-Month Club selections and often read at least the first chapters of the books that arrived. She liked history and habitually skimmed the newspaper columns by "Old Timer" or

"Pioneer Jack." Dieter had been on the Board of the Chicago Public Library from the time after the Great Fire when Chicagoans were emotionally moved by the stooping gesture of the English intelligentsia who donated boxes of books for a new library. Dieter had continued to donate money to the library, first to get it out of that water tower, and then as a Good Work. This memory gave her the idea. If Dieter were still alive he certainly would give her the position and office she wanted.

It took her the entire return flight to write out the job description. The woman in the adjacent seat noticed her writing and said admiringly, "You must be a busy career woman!"

Sophia said, "Yes. Just returning from a business trip to Boca. Boca Raton. In Florida."

She sent the page to her brother, James Bardawulf Breitsprecher, President of Breitsprecher-Duke, rather than give it to Andrew, who might conveniently lose it. Or laugh meanly. Her brother would see the value. Then she waited.

Andrew met James Bardawulf for lunch at the members' club they both frequented. James smiled broadly and said, "That was easy enough. We can give her the job."

"What job?"

"Sophia. The position she wanted. I got her letter this morning. It will suit her and keep her out of business deals."

"What the hell? She didn't send *me* any letter."

"Maybe she wanted it to be a surprise. Don't worry, she only wants to be the company historian. She wants to write a history of Breitsprecher-Duke. She wants all the old journals and letters, copies of wires and telegraphs, whatever papers didn't get burned or thrown out. There are boxes of that stuff in one of the storage rooms. She calls all that junk 'the Breitsprecher-Duke archives.' I'm happy to have a door painted with her name and 'Archival Research'—which is what she wants."

"Knock me over. She said nothing to me. Is there anything to write about?"

"Oh yes. Dieter, of course, and Lavinia—working back to old Charles Duke, who started the company—Charles Duke—Canada, Holland. All over. Yes, there's a lot back there we don't know. Have to say I'm interested myself to see if she turns up anything useful. There could be some nice publicity that we could work into ads— you know, 'Venerable Old Company. Leader in wood products for over two centuries.'"

"Oh boy," said Andrew.

There were several unused rooms in the building, any one of which could be cleared out to become Sophia's office. She looked them over. Four dusty conjoined rooms, once the kingdom of Lawyer Flense, with a view of the lake would do very well—an anteroom for her secretary, her inner sanctum, two meeting rooms. They would have to be cleared, cleaned, repainted. She telephoned her son, Robert, who had recently opened his office, Harkiss Interiors.

"Robert, I need your help. Are you very busy?" Robert, who had had only a single commission—the guest room in the apartment of Mrs. Grainley Wiley, with whom he was having an affair—was sick with worry over his upcoming office rent. He needed another commission. He made the usual noises of "let me see" and "I think I can squeeze you in" before he agreed.

"This is rather good, Mother, a very workable space. Your renovation ideas are not bad but I would suggest opening out this wall"— he pointed at the separation between the two meeting rooms—"and giving yourself a really large office. Make that room you had picked for your office a meeting room. And we can put in carpet. You'll be amazed how much carpet softens the atmosphere."

"I haven't been living under a stone for the past fifty years, Robert. I have actually heard about carpet." But she liked the idea of a larger office. Together they shopped for Danish modern office furniture in oil-rubbed teak, beige wool carpet, a big leather Eames chair.

The day came when Sophia, installed in her new office, began reading through pages and pages of crabbed handwriting and atrocious spelling, trying to sort out mysterious characters whose connections to the family were unclear. She hired a secretary, a potato-faced blonde named Debra Strong (niece of Mrs. Garfield, the company secretary), who said her last job had been at a women's magazine. Debra sorted the papers into rough time periods, put them into neatly labeled folders. Sophia's plan was to tell of the early travails of a pioneer enterprise that became successful through hard work, and went on to enjoy the fame and fortune of being one of the oldest and most successful logging companies in the nation.

Obscurity, and French, like thick blankets, befogged the papers. Was Charles Duke the same person as Charles Duquet, whose name appeared on what might be a promissory note signed by someone named Dred-Peacock; it was signed with an X indicating Charles Duquet was illiterate—or was it Dred-Peacock? Later correspondence was clearly signed by Charles Duke. So she was sure Dred-Peacock, whoever he was, was the illiterate. There was too much French for her. She hired a student to translate the difficult pages but found the lists of old deals and accounts tedious and put them aside as immaterial.

After a year of scratching through the papers a story began to take shape. Charles Duke, a poor French boy, set out for the New World to escape a harsh life on a French farm. Once in North America he began to make his way by hard work and eventually, with the money he earned, bought timberland and opened a sawmill. The correspondence with Dred-Peacock ended abruptly, though in the next batch of material there were nearly forty letters to his sons. These made tiresome reading as they were loaded with advice and maxims and shed no light on Charles Duke's character beyond commanding his sons to do what he told them to do. He seemed a serious fellow, but one who doted on his children. She skipped over James Duke, a dull stick. Lavinia, alas, had left behind hundreds of boxes of business correspondence and notes on the lumber industry. Sophia did not understand most of Dieter's first wife's descriptions of inventions, meetings, numbers of board feet taken from various forests and shipped to distant destinations. It was enough to say she was a highly respected businesswoman. And, thought Sophia, an insanely busy scribbler.

She came on a folder that Debra Strong had labeled "Genealogy?" containing some torn and yellowed pages. This, she thought, might be useful. She matched the torn pieces together. A letter from R. R. Tetrazinni in Philadelphia said only that the investigation was complete to the point set out in his report and that if Lavinia Duke Breitsprecher wished to follow up with further investigation of the names and addresses of the heirs she should contact him as soon as practicable as he had other work to hand. The report puzzled Sophia. What heirs?

She telephoned James Bardawulf. "I've come on something that I don't quite understand. It's a report from a private investigator to Dieter's first wife, Lavinia Duke. I wish you would take a look at it. I think it says there are some unknown heirs. But I don't know who they are or what they have inherited."

"It's probably a fraud letter. People claiming to be heirs to fortunes and long-lost cousins are not uncommon. Can you send it over to me?"

"I'd rather show it to you here. Why don't you come over this afternoon and look at it? And we can go have a drink and talk. Some outdoor place on the lake—it's so hot this summer. I haven't seen you for months."

67

a little problem

It was Breitsprecher-Duke's most peculiar meeting, so divided in content it was as though strangers had been swept up from the hot streets and ordered to conduct business. They sat around the mahogany table in Breitsprecher-Duke's meeting room with a portrait of Lavinia Duke on the south wall and one of Dieter on the north. The old air conditioner was gasping as though fighting off its own heatstroke. On the table was a tray of cream cheese sandwiches with the bread curling up, paper napkins from the old days stamped with the letters DUKE LOGGING and the image of an ax. Although the room was swollen with August heat, a coffee urn hissed on the side table.

Sophia, in the grey wool Chanel despite the heat, made a rambling speech about the company history and passed out copies of the fruits of her labors—sixteen pages of company fantasy bound in leather and stamped *Breitsprecher-Duke, the Story of a Forest Giant.* She waited for congratulations, but James Bardawulf had already told the others of the old Tetrazinni report and his own weeks of dead-end work to prove it a hoax. The company's legal adviser, Hazelton Culross, was present. James Bardawulf, in an acid-tinged voice, went straight to the problem.

"Mr. Tetrazinni is long gone. His son, Chandler Tetrazinni, with whom I spoke at length, inherited the business. He is a lawyer."

Raphael, who knew his father well, recognized the danger signal. If James had respected Tetrazinni he would have said "attorney." "Lawyer" meant something with greater elements of python. The

673

room was hot and the August sun eating at the begrimed window glass seemed to have found a way through it.

James Bardawulf's harsh voice continued. "Frankly, I wish I hadn't contacted him. He heads up Tetrazinni Search Services, which specializes in tracing missing and unknown heirs. He was surprised to hear from me and said he would look in the files. Two days later he called and said he had found the relevant papers and that the case was far from dead. I'm afraid my questions led him to this almost forgotten affair and he smelled the possibility of money. I regret to say that I think that if I had not called him he would never have heard of Breitsprecher. But we can't undo the situation. I learned from Hazelton that Tetrazinni's outfit works for a percentage of the inheritance, and to me that means that he now intends to go to the heirs and offer them a contract. A champertous contract, which is, unfortunately, quite legal these days. Lavinia Duke initiated this search decades ago"—he glanced up at her portrait—"just why she did this is far from clear as she should have been advised to ignore sleeping dogs. Tetrazinni, the man she hired, claimed to have found legitimate heirs to the Duke fortune, heirs who actually had a more valid claim than Lavinia herself—that is if blood relationship is the criterion."

"How can that be?" said Sophia, pushing the extra copies of *The Story of a Forest Giant* away. "Surely it can't mean anything. Breitsprecher and Duke have owned the business for generations! It's accepted, it's known." She patted her forehead with one of the napkins. "This air conditioner is useless."

"A suit may be forthcoming if those heirs proceed," said James Bardawulf morosely.

"Proceed! Have they begun an action?" Andrew Harkiss got up and poured his sixth cup of coffee since breakfast. Coffee gave him jitters and palpitations, forcing him to drink gin at night to calm down. "And are you going to tell us who these 'putative heirs' might be?"

"Believe it or not, they are some Indians up in Canada."

"Oh no, oh no," said Conrad Breitsprecher suddenly, his face so drained of color that his black eyebrows seemed drawn on his forehead with charcoal. "That could break up the company." James Bardawulf was surprised at his agitation. What did *he* have to worry about? The seedling nurseries were making money as though they had a printing press in the cellar. No red ink there, no covetous Indians with their hands held out. And Conrad took no profits, but poured every penny back into his damn seedlings. His obsession.

Claude Breitsprecher also noticed Conrad's anxiety. Pure ego, he thought. Conrad believed the reputation of Breitsprecher-Duke rested entirely on the seedling nursery division, which wasn't even part of the company. As a young man Dieter had set it up with his cousin Armenius Breitsprecher and made it into a hobby that he fondly believed was an innovative business. But Conrad had, for all his eccentricities and peculiar ways, turned it into a success. How did *that* happen?

"Break up the company? I doubt that. In any case your nursery business is and always has been quite separate."

"Of course. But—it's the thought that someone you don't know can come in and take all you've built up. Once they get their hooks into you they'll keep on until they've got everything. They'll come after my nurseries! They carry the name Breitsprecher!" Conrad was clenching his fists.

Conrad is really upset, thought Sophia. She made a suggestion. "Can't we just rip up the report and forget we ever saw it? Actually part of it *was* ripped when I found it."

Hazelton Culross laughed. "Not now. James Bardawulf contacted Mr. Tetrazinni and they discussed the report, so Mr. Tetrazinni knows and he knows James Bardawulf and all of you also know. You are no longer ignorant of the report's existence."

James Bardawulf gave his copy of *The Story of a Forest Giant* a little dismissive flick with his finger. Sophia clenched her fists.

"We can sell, can't we?" asked Harkiss. "International Paper has been after us for a year. Shouldn't we accept their offer, divide the money and reorganize our lives? Most of us active in the company are near retirement age in any case. To me it seems a good time to sell."

James Bardawulf stuck out his lower lip. "Doing so will not stop

675

Tetrazinni and the so-called heirs. Even if we sold, those heirs could still come after each of us."

Sophia began to snivel.

But Hazelton Culross asked the big question. "How much do you know about the assumed heirs?"

"According to Tetrazinni's report to Lavinia Duke the heirs would be Mi'kmaq Indians. Canadian Indian. We do not have the names of the present-day descendants."

"Well, none of those people were in the company papers," said Sophia. "How was I expected to know? I only saw something about a large table in the Penobscot Bay house. No idea what that referred to."

"In fact," said Andrew Harkiss, ignoring her, "the line may have died out? The problem may have solved itself? That report is old."

"Perhaps. We just don't know. And the original report found that the Duke descendants as *we* know them"—he touched his copy of *The Story of a Forest Giant*—"were only through Charles Duquet's *adopted* sons. His only legitimate son was Outger Duquet, Beatrix's father. That's where the trouble comes. So Lavinia herself had no direct claim to Duquet ancestry." There was a touch of triumph in James Bardawulf's voice.

"Before you start to worry," said Hazelton Culross, sensing the waves of anxiety crashing around him, "consider that Tetrazinni himself may not know if there are any current presumed heirs. He would have to do the legwork to establish names and whereabouts. And if and when he finds them he would have to persuade them that they have a claim worth pursuing. He would likely get them to sign a contract with him and only then would things go forward. If these heirs are Canadian it is another layer of difficulty for Tetrazinni to work through. All those things take time and money and *the lawyer* would have to bear the cost. And *then* he would come up against a company that for centuries has been directed and led first by the Dukes, then by the Breitsprechers, accepted as the legitimate owners of the properties and the operators of a legitimate business for almost three hundred years. Even if he put the effort and money into finding any living heirs, Tetrazinni would have the slimmest chance of getting anywhere with this. I would put it out of my mind and continue as you always have."

There was a silence, a grateful silence. Andrew took a deep breath and said, "But we have discussed selling the company. International Paper is interested. Except for the seedling division," he added hastily as Conrad half-stood.

"But there's still a chance the heirs could sue us, right?" he asked, fixed and tense.

"Well, yes. Anything is possible. But I don't think any court would give them the time of day."

"Well, *I* give them the time of day," said Conrad. "I find all this very disturbing." And he rushed from the room.

Hazelton Culross looked at James Bardawulf, at Sophia and Andrew. "He really seems to see this as a threat. He is overreacting."

Claude said, "He has never been right since his war experience. It may sound far-fetched but I have heard of delayed reactions to war experiences."

Hazelton's advice was simple: "Stay away from Tetrazinni. Don't go looking for trouble."

Almost two weeks later Sophia found a memo from James Bardawulf on her desk. "Call me." It was still ungodly hot. She worried about sweat stains on her silk blouse. The air conditioner sent out a tepid waft of mold-scented air. She dialed her brother's number, got his snotty new secretary with her English-accented "May I say who is calling please?"

"Tell him it's his old mistress."

There was an intake of breath, a lengthy silence, then James Bardawulf's cautious little "Hello?"

"I got your memo," she said. "What's going on?"

"Sophia! Don't ever say that kind of thing to Miss Greenberry. She believed you!"

"Englishwomen have no sense of humor." She cut off James Bardawulf's roars and huffs. "Calm down. Why did you want me to call you?"

"To give you some very interesting news. For us, anyway. Hazelton Culross, who takes *The Philadelphia Inquirer,* called me this morning. He said there's a back-page story in today's paper saying that a law-yer named Tetrazinni died in a fight with a burglar over the week-end. The office was wrecked, file cabinets overturned, desk drawers pulled out and the safe wide open. Tetrazinni shot. I don't know yet if there is anything in the Chicago papers. I've sent out for a *Trib.*"

"My God. That's extraordinary. You might even think—" A deep breath. "Have you let the others know?"

"Just you so far. I was going to call them after I talked with you. After all, you are the one who opened the whole can of worms. The primary instigator."

Sophia let that pass. It was James Bardawulf who had started the wheels turning. "Let poor Conrad know. He was so upset that day."

Another of James Bardawulf's long silences. Then the little voice again. "Maybe he already knows."

"James, what do you mean? James Bardawulf!"

"I only mean he might have seen the papers already. What did you think I meant?"

"Not important," she said. "Talk to you later."

His last remark floated out of the receiver: "We can proceed with the sale."

And so, over the centuries Breitsprecher-Duke had risen and fallen like a boat on the tides. Now the tide was out. And International Paper was in. Only boxes of papers and several portraits remained of the old company. And a separate entity called Breitsprecher Seedlings.

68

Egga's daughters

There was no going back after World War II: women were edging into jobs men had always done. Feminist rhetoric floated in the air. Bren Sel thought it should be this way, and shot a combative look at her husband, Edgar-Jim Sel, called Egga, an unaware man. She believed the new ideas were a release from the bondage of history and tried to explain this to him, but Egga did not see a parallel between feminist emergence from an oppressive past and his own life and renunciation of Mi'kmaw particularity. He had come down to Martha's Vineyard as a runaway boy escaping the residential Indian school at Shubenacadie in Nova Scotia, found work as a fisherman and later found Brenda Hingham.

When he proposed she said yes, and then, "I am marrying an enemy."

"Enemy? How am I your enemy?"

"Do you not know that the Mi'kmaq came here and fought my people? Before the whitemen?"

"I did not know this. Was it a battle?"

"A battle? It was a war. Mi'kmaw warriors took the whole New England coast. For a little time."

"And now this Mi'kmaw wins again." He flashed a guess that likely there had been a little infusion of Mi'kmaw into the Wôpanâak in that long-ago time.

• • •

They were an awkward match. "You don't understand," she said to him often.

"What don't I understand?" he asked.

"If you don't know I can't tell you."

The central problem, she believed, was Egga's refusal to be Mi'kmaq.

He said, "It made my life very bad, being a Mi'kmaw person. I have put it away."

"You can't put away what you are. Your parents, your brothers and sisters. And all the generations behind them, your people. You cannot rinse out your blood like a dirty shirt and say it is a—a pineapple! It is you, your heritage, what you came from, it *cannot* be something else. And now it is part of our children and they must know it." Egga rolled his eyes—this was what came from marrying into the matrilineal Wôpanâak.

Bren wanted to guide their two daughters toward being a new kind of woman—whiteman, Wôpanâak and Mi'kmaw mix of genes, ideas, careers, perceptions of the world. Both girls were strong-minded and smart, both sassy children who gave Egga bizarre thoughts of the residential school with its punishing nuns and priests. If his womenfolk were dropped into such a school the place would be in riot within a day, Bren, Marie and Sapatisia leading the charge, nuns and priests begging mercy. He enjoyed this vision and when one of his rambunctious girls was particularly audacious he was pleased, comparing them to the pitifully fearful Mi'kmaw children at the resi school. He wanted bold children. Very gradually, very slowly he began to talk about his old life, surprised at the sharp interest his children and wife took in his stories. When he told his parents' names—Lobert and Nanty Sel—they wanted to write letters, go to Shubenacadie, to Lobert's log house. They wanted to love these unknown relatives. And perhaps, thought Egga, so did he. Bren's nagging made him wonder what being Mi'kmaq could mean beyond pain and humiliation. Bren herself was enthusiastically Wôpanâak, and again he imagined lustful and ancient Mi'kmaw warriors surging into Wôpanâak villages and women. He laughed.

"What is so funny?" asked Bren.

"If you don't know I can't tell you," he said.

In Shubenacadie a few years after his wife Nanty died, Egga's father, Lobert Sel, remarried a young widow, Kate Googoo, already pregnant with their first child. The year after Paul was born, Alice Sel arrived, and the last baby, Mary May. Egga, down in Martha's Vineyard, knew nothing about these younger siblings.

Bren insisted on a serious commitment to homework. "I want you girls to go to university. I will make the money to send you." Although from childhood she had wanted to study linguistics with the vague hope of resurrecting the old native Wôpanâak language (which she did not speak), there had been no money in her family for such schooling. When Sapatisia, her older child, started school Bren got the only job available—night shift at the fish plant, socking almost all of her paycheck into their education account. Her girls would have lives of value.

"They'll never have to work at a fish plant," she said to Egga. "Or a tourist motel."

Nothing had prepared either Egga or Bren for the intensity of their first child, Sapatisia, named for Egga's mother's mother. The child fixed obsessively on subjects and people; did everything with intensity—there seemed no middle way for her. If Egga was late coming in from the water she stood at the window watching until she saw him climbing up the gravel path. He came through the door and she clung to his leg like a barnacle.

"She won't be left," said Bren. "I can't go out of her sight. And she's the same about you if you don't get home on time. I don't know how it will be when she starts school."

"You know I can't always tell when I'll get back—weather could keep me out—even for days. The fish don't have clocks. And boats don't have telephones."

"She'd keep watching," said Bren.

The incident with a baby chicken rattled both parents. Bren had decided to raise a dozen hens for eggs and meat, save on groceries, make a change from fried cod. She ordered twenty chicks by mail and when they came she put the box behind the stove to keep them warm. She showed the little balls of fluff to Sapatisia, who was enchanted. She let her hold one.

"Be careful. It's delicate."

But Sapatisia loved the warm little peeping creature and in her immoderate affection squeezed it and squeezed, then shrieked when the dead chick hung limp.

"For that you must be punished," said Bren, and Sapatisia roared with the insult of her first spanking.

"That is how she is," said Egga. "She can't help it. God save any man she loves. She'll eat him alive and throw the bones out the window."

Bren's fear of Sapatisia throwing a fit her first day at school dissolved. It was as if the child had steeled herself for it. She did not cry when Bren left her in the little kindergarten chair, nor would she move to a different chair despite the teacher's coaxing. Left alone she was tractable; commanded to do something—anything—she was impossible.

"I don't know what's going on in that little head," said the teacher.

"Welcome to the knitting circle," said Bren.

Still, Sapatisia made it through all the grades, occasionally striking off sparks of brilliance. She seemed happiest, thought Egga, when, on a Sunday, they hiked along the shore. She came home carrying handfuls of wilted grasses, water-smooth rocks with flecks of mica.

In her freshman year at college Sapatisia, given to instant love or hate, fastened her affections first on the subject of plants and then on a married ecology professor. The man was flattered; there was an affair; he tried to disengage and Sapatisia appeared at his door gripping a hunting knife. She lunged at the professor, who twisted adroitly and the knife plunged into the wood doorframe. She was muscular and strong but the professor was stronger and, shouting to his wife to call the police, he held Sapatisia down until they arrived. The next day Egga came to the jail to take her home.

"You know you are expelled from school," he said.

"Yes."

"I won't ask you why you did this. I know why. You are like I was when I ran away from the resi school."

"I am *not* like you," she said. "I am different. And my reasons were different."

"Oh," said Egga. "Different from me, different from everybody. But you have to live in this world. Accept some of the rules that keep it in balance. Make an adjustment. Or you will die young."

"I want to go to Shubenacadie," she said. "I want to see those Sel people. I want to know who I am."

Egga and Bren had heard nothing about a professor of ecology or botany, only of Sapatisia's burning interest in the plants and forests of the earth. She seemed to feel personal guilt for eroded slopes and dirty rivers. If she looked up she saw not heaven's blue but apocalyptic clouds in an aircraft-gouged sky.

"She has a female urge to repair the damage humans have done to nature," said Bren that evening after Sapatisia was up in her old room.

"Yes, and a female urge to destroy men. We are lucky the professor did not press charges." Silence in the room except for their breathing. Egga sighed and said, "What do you think about letting her go to Nova Scotia?"

"Oh, Egga, *let* her go? She will go there no matter what. I'll talk to her, but brace yourself."

• • •

"You'll have to find work to live on, a scholarship to finish your studies," Bren told her in a chill voice. This daughter absorbed too much of her energy. "We have Marie to think about, too, you know."

Sapatisia left the next day on a northbound bus.

Egga and Bren heard nothing for months until a rare letter, postmarked Halifax, Nova Scotia, arrived from their firstborn daughter.

I haven't met Uncle Paul yet or his daughter Jeanne. Aunt Mary May Mius is shy and seems pretty fussy about her son Felix. Felix is nothing to be fussy about! The best one is Aunt Alice. I liked her. It is a pretty big family. Going to Winnipeg next week to study forestry, doing o.k., love, S

And only a few days later an ink-blotched letter arrived for Egga from his father, Lobert Sel.

It means so much to us that our strong young granddaughter Sapatisia visited us. She ask many questions about our people and old Sel stories. Egga it has been many years since you left. Can you or other granddaughter Marie come here one time? I grow old. Wish to see you. That bad school that hurt you is closed and burned up. Come home.

These letters made Egga tearful and he planned a trip to Shubenacadie. He wrote to Lobert that he would come—yes, he and Bren—the next St. Anne's Day. But from Sapatisia they heard little more than occasional cards postmarked from different cities.

How different was their younger daughter, Marie.

"She should have been a boy," said Egga to Bren, thinking of the time when his greasy little toddler had partially disassembled an electric motor and put it back together enlivened with pink plastic stacking rings from her toy box. Nothing mechanical in the house was safe from Marie's inquiring fingers and she was the easiest person in the world to please at birthdays and holidays with gifts of ship and plane models. She was outspoken and a little brash, but that was a proof to Egga that his younger daughter would not be trodden down. She spent a college summer running a CTL, the cut-to-length wonder tool that felled and delimbed trees in front of itself so the detritus formed a mat for it to move on; it was her hero-machine.

She fell hard for Davey Jones, a bowlegged young lobsterman who wrote poetry, danced reels and strathspeys, played poker and had kept a weather notebook since he was nine. In December of 1978 she married him.

"Yes," she said, when he proposed, "but I want to keep my job. I like my job."

"I like mine, too, so no argument."

After the wedding night the first thing she told her new husband was "There is less soil compaction with the CTL than even a horse team."

"What makes you think I care?" he said. "Come here and I'll tell you about lobster pots."

69

boreal forest

Jeanne Sel and Felix Mius grew up together, knew each other's childhood thoughts and feelings; as they grew older these diverged as a mountain rill bifurcates in rocky terrain and becomes two streams. Felix had quiet ways that disguised an agile and explorative mind. His complexion was rough and he was inclined to fall in love with unattainable older women who raised their eyebrows at him but never their skirts. Jeanne's close-set eyes and thin lips convinced her she was above the fray of love entanglements.

Jeanne remembered her mother on a ferry, leaning over the rail waving good-bye, good-bye, until the vessel melted away in heavy fog where a few hours later it collided with a coal barge; both went down in deep water. Her father, Paul Sel, told her that Mama could not come back, but his own weeping indicated something very terrible.

"I don't know, Mary May," Paul said to his sister, whose son, Felix, was a year younger than Jeanne. "I don't know what to do. She won't talk or play with other kids—except here with Felix."

"That's a good sign," Mary May said. "Let them be together. Little kids sort things out. I think better Jeanne come stay with us. And I think a picnic trip. Help her get over losing Marta. Help *you*, Paul."

"Nothing can help me," said her brother, but he didn't object when Mary May called, "Felix and Jeanne, come on. We are going on a picnic."

They headed away from the reservation crowded together like

buns in a package in Paul's decrepit grey truck. The interior smelled of mold and a dog that Paul had once owned.

"Where we goin, where we goin?" Felix asked over and over, excited.

"Where we goin?" said Jeanne.

"You'll see when we get there."

"There" was Kejimkujik Provincial Park. Mary May said to them, "Long time ago this was Mi'kmaw place." Jeanne and Felix, after hours of riding until their legs became paralyzed sticks, jumped and ran under the huge old-growth hemlock. There was a garden of boulders under lustrous blue-green trees.

Felix discovered that the undersides of the branches shone silver, in the deep shade grew maidenhair fern, graceful ebon-black curved branches and tiny mitten-like leaves. The hemlocks sighed very gently. He engaged with *Tsuga canadensis.*

"I wish Mama could see this," Jeanne said, admiring the gleaming stems of the fern, smelling the musky odor. At the edge of the water she found a forest of mathematically perfect ebony spleenwort and looking around encountered myriad tones of green: citrine, viridian, emerald. It was a fine and satisfying day that was never forgotten by the children.

In high school teachers talked of careers. Jeanne learned that botanists lived in a world of stem and leaf. There would not be an oil or gas job with Encana or Mime'j Seafoods for Felix Mius; he intended to get into forestry school—everyone knew about Jackson Mius, who had logged with a horse team in Maine back in the sixties, then went to the University of Maine and got a degree and a job with the state in forest research. He had done it, so would Felix. The cousins set the goal of getting into university. They had to complete two years at the community college before they could apply. The odds were against them.

After high school graduation they moved to Aunt Alice Sel's

house in Dartmouth, her child-care center and home for an occasional young Mi'kmaw trying out urban life. They enrolled at the community college and worked part-time jobs.

The lower level of Alice's kitchen traffic was always congested with toddlers; the upper level with friends and relatives, chaos exemplified. Jeanne thought it a madhouse until one September Saturday she came downstairs and found the kitchen empty, the house silent. A syrup of honey-colored autumnal sunlight fell on the scrubbed table and old mismatched chairs. Alice's kitchen was beautiful.

"Those two, they're sure tryin hard at their schoolwork. I guess it's good they got each other. Like brother and sister," remarked Alice to her sister, Mary May. They sat at the crowded kitchen table with teapot and cups.

"Well, I just hope it don't get—funny. That kind of worries me, them bein so close. You know, cousins and all. I pray they don't do nothin wrong."

Alice gave her sister her dry look. "Quit worryin. He just watches out for her. That Jeanne, I think, she won't never get romantic about nobody. And Felix takes girls to the movies if he can afford it. But not Jeanne—she wants to see a movie she goes by herself."

The cousins struggled with the college course work: they couldn't get into university without the credits. Neither spoke Mi'kmaw fluently; English had come first, but some early mornings they sat together at the computer to learn Mi'kmaw words, following the Listuguj speakers' pronunciations. Then Alice would come in and ruin everything by criticizing their efforts.

On Saturdays, Jeanne hauled laundry to the Bucket O' Suds. While the clothes churned she flipped through a stack of ragged magazines and old newsletters that featured profiles of people in the province. One interested her; she tore the page out.

That evening, drinking tea after supper to wash down the store-bought cake, she showed it to the others. "It's an article on this woman, Sapatisia Sel. Suppose she is a relation?"

Felix said, "If every Sel relative gave us a dollar we'd be rich. What about this Sapatisia Sel?"

"It says she collects medicine plants and trees."

"Another one?" said Felix scornfully. *Medicine plants!* Over the years a stream of white people had come to "study" Mi'kmaw medicine plants and the older women on the reservation were used to being quizzed about traditional cures.

"I know Sapatisia," said Alice, reaching for the page. She read a minute, studied the picture. "That's Egga's daughter. She's a relative from the States. She come here once. This says she knows about old-time medicine plants."

"And she plants trees."

Felix hated the required remedial English grammar and composition that seemed unnecessary to a future study of forestry. It was not that he disliked learning—he and Jeanne stuffed their brains. The relentless reading and studying wore them down and they decided to make a rare free evening and hear Dr. Alfred Onehube from Manitoba lecture on the state of the world's forests.

Onehube disclosed himself as a militant ecoconservationist. Several people connected with forest production and timber sales got up and walked out. But Felix and Jeanne sat on the edges of their seats drinking in the named sins against the forest.

"Budworm, for example," said Dr. Onehube at AK-47 velocity. "Natural cycles of budworm infestation, roughly every thirty or forty years. When the insects outstripped their food supply they disappeared. Dead trees fell, waited for the fire. Fire came, new trees grew from the ashes. But after the Second World War we wanted all the trees we could get for wood pulp and paper. Everybody had new chemical weapons, and war surplus planes. So when spruce bud-worm invaded the boreal forests in the 1940s, the Forest Service sprayed DDT. Our Miramichi River, home of the greatest Atlantic salmon run on earth, turned into a death river as the DDT killed all the tiny water animalcules that fed the salmon."

He stopped and drank half the glass of water on the podium, spill-ing some down his jacket, where the drops sparkled in the light until they were absorbed by the cloth. He looked up into the lights, seemed to draw breath, then continued in his earnest rapid-fire baritone.

"We know better about DDT now. But what makes us think we are any smarter about the effects of vast clear-cutting of a very fragile ecosystem? Hah? There are countless unknowns here. And we don't even know how much we don't know."

Finally, when listeners began looking at their watches and some in the rear sidled guiltily out of the hall, he came to an end: "Incompe-tent forest . . . *ignorance . . . wood fiber,* battles . . . disturbances . . . *chemical destruction* . . . slow-growing . . . *unstoppable.*" He lowered his voice dra-matically, paused and then whispered into the microphone, "Now we are finishing off the cold land of little sticks, the great breeding grounds for millions of birds, the cleansing breath of the earth, the spring nutri-ent runoff to the ocean that revitalizes everything—the beginning of the great food chain. You people," he said, looking at the audience. "We are *killing . . . the . . . great . . . boreal . . . forest.*" There was a frictional hissing sound as people moved in their seats, then small applause and the noise of seats folding back into place as everyone rose. A college official came out and announced that Dr. Onehube would speak at noon the next day on overpopulation—a lecture titled "SRO—Standing Room Only."

As they left the auditorium Felix heard a man behind him say, "Another tree-hugging eco-nut." Jeanne's face was stiff. Without look-ing at Felix she said, "I feel completely stupid, helpless. What are we doing but cramming our heads with words? Felix, what can we do?"

"I don't know." They walked in silence. The rain was finished, pushed along by the rising wind, its raw edge slicing off the water.

• • •

Impossible to go back to the study schedule after the call to activism, but where to begin? Jeanne reorganized the stacks of paper and books on her study table. She came on the profile of Sapatisia Sel torn from the power company's newsletter and read it with fresh interest.

"Felix, I want to know why she said that the old Mi'kmaw medicine plants can't be used anymore. I bet she knows how to help the forest. The article says she lives on Cape George. Let's go find her."

"How can we get there? No car."

They left it there for several days. Alice came down with the flu and Jeanne stayed home from classes to run the child care and cook. Alice's reservation friends brought Mi'kmaw medicines for the sick woman. Jeanne was delighted to see the medicines in use and to hear their clicking names even if she didn't know what they meant: *wijok'jemusi, wisowtakjijkl, pako'si-jipisk, pko'kmin, miti, pakosi, tupsi, l'mu'ji'jmanaqsi, kjimuatkw, stoqon.* Morning, noon and night Alice was inundated with washes, gargles, tisanes, decoctions, brews, teas and infusions.

"You see," said Jeanne to Felix. "The medicines are still used! That Sapatisia has some explaining to do."

Another week and Alice was on her feet again, cured. "Layin there in bed I decided to give up meetins of the Child Help Program. Just too tired at the end of the day," she said, and looked it, her round face mottled and puffy as a cheese soufflé.

"Hitchhike," whispered Jeanne to Felix, who was struggling into his old torn jacket.

"You just won't give up, will you?" And he was out into the early darkness.

Alice found the way. "You can get a ride. It seems like," she said, "Johnny Stick is goin that way. He's pretty good company now. He started goin to those 'truth and reconciliation' meetings a few years ago. Helps to know you are not alone in the boat."

"What was the matter with him?" asked Felix, who picked up a tone in her voice.

"Oh, that bad stuff from years ago when he was a kid. The resi school."

"Mr. Stick is all right to take a ride with?"

"Yes. He's fine. He's got a carpenter job up there fixin the handrail in the old lighthouse. It hasn't blinked a blink for sailors for eighty years but the tourists like it. In the summer there's a chips truck in the parking lot, does good business, so that shaky old handrail, got chip grease and salt all over it. He said be ready tomorrow mornin. Early. Bring your blankets. You can rough it a few nights."

Mr. Stick was in his late middle years, his dark jowls clean-shaven. The back of his pickup held an enormous red cooler and under a tarp the handrail sections for the lighthouse. He said, "Nice maple rail. Same finish like one of them no-stick fry pans. So where do y'want to go on the Cape?"

"We don't know. I mean, we're looking for a woman named Sapatisia Sel. But we don't know exactly where she lives."

"Here's the deal. You help me put that rail in place you'll get a round trip and a place to sleep. And your dinner."

Jeanne nodded. Mr. Stick gazed out at the horizon for a long minute before he snapped to and said gruffly, "Then let's get goin. Hop in!" He talked as he drove. "I know who you mean. Egga Sel's daughter. Sapatisia. There's not too many live out on the Cape except motel and restaurant people in the tourist season. I guess she's got a place out there. Somewhere." They all knew everything was for the tourists, the despised tourists who kept Nova Scotia alive.

"She knows about the old Mi'kmaw medicines. That's why we want to talk to her," said Jeanne.

"Seen a woman go along the cliffs with a basket. I thought she was a berry picker first time I see her, but it wasn't the season. I never seen her up close to talk to. I knew Egga pretty good. Long ago. At least I think it was her. Not sure. Cliff path below the lighthouse. Seen her when I was measurin for the handrail. Stayed three nights, slept in the truck and I seen this woman couple times. Must be good stuff grows down there."

Mr. Stick said, "She's a Sel. Try and find a Mi'kmaq ain't related to a Sel! Get up pretty early in the mornin for that. I got some *gneg wetagutijig* cousin Sels."

Driving slowly in the thickening fog, he said that Felix and Jeanne, between times of helping him, could watch for the woman. "Sapatisia, she went to university, travel all over the world. But I don't know if you'll see her, way the fog's workin up. Not much hope for today," he said as he turned onto the gravel drive to the lighthouse.

"Look!" said Jeanne, pointing at the storage building. They all saw a fading movement.

"No, no! I see her yet. *Ala'tett.* Way over there." Mr. Stick pointed at a blob that was gone as soon as he spoke. "Wait for mornin. I think she comes back."

He made a fire in the parking lot, cooked hot dogs in a dirty cast-iron frying pan. Then, yawning, he said good night and retired to his truck, where they could see the glint of a bottle as he tilted it up. The cousins went into the lighthouse, unrolled their sleeping bags.

All the next day the fog hung heavy and unmoving. Felix and Jeanne held the railing steady while Mr. Stick bolted the sections to the braces. He fussed with joins and angles, took the sections down again and made minute adjustments. He worked without talking. The light was dimming when he was satisfied with the railing.

The next morning sprang open brilliantly clear with a snapping wind shooting up their jacket sleeves. Mr. Stick ate dry bread for breakfast, didn't offer any to them but drank deeply from his thermos of stone-cold black tea, then smoked his pipe. "Got to clean her up a little," he said, meaning the railing. Jeanne and Felix climbed to the top of the lighthouse.

"Some view. I see two tankers. No, one's the ferry."

"I see Sapatisia Sel," said Felix. "Down there on the rocks."

The woman in canvas overalls and jacket was digging with a trowel. A notebook lay open on a boulder and the wind riffled the pages.

"Hello," called Jeanne. The woman looked up at them. She was short and sturdy, black long hair in a single braid. Her narrow eyes looked Asian; she said nothing.

"Are you Sapatisia Sel?"

The woman picked up the book and set off rapidly down the shore with a plant still in her grasp, fragments of soil falling from the roots.

"Please wait! We want to talk to you."

In a few minutes they heard a distant engine start up. By the time they reached the bottom of the lighthouse the red pickup was roaring along the road. Gone.

"I'd say she don't feel like talkin," said Mr. Stick. "Ten more minutes then I'm headin back to Dartmouth. You want a ride? Or stay?"

"Yes to a ride," said Jeanne, not looking forward to the fumigation, hoping Mr. Stick would stop at a store along the way. But he did not, drove faster and faster through the fog that had erased Sapatisia Sel.

Mr. Stick, feeling obscurely responsible for the cousins' thwarted search, had gone to Lobert Sel, whose mind was failing, yet he seemed to know where Sapatisia's little house stood. He put his trembling finger on an inlet he said was Pussle Cove. "Couple kilometers east the lighthouse. No road sign." Mr. Stick gave the smirched paper to Alice, who put it beside Jeanne's plate that evening. So she had an address. And to get there she took money from her savings account at the East Coast Credit Union and gave it to Felix, asked him to rent a car. She had no license.

The rain didn't matter and the cousins had a sense of holiday freedom. The rental car hummed along, the wet roadside unfurled and the windshield wipers beat a slow march. They shared a bag of jelly donuts Felix bought at Tim Hortons. They passed the Wreck Point lighthouse and he slowed.

"That's it. Has to be." Jeanne pointed at a faint trackway that sidled shyly off the main road directly into a patch of wind-racked black spruce. "I see car tracks."

Felix turned cautiously into the watery ruts dimpled by raindrops and inched slowly between clawing branches. They looked down at a small unpainted house on the edge of the sea, smoke barely clearing the chimney. Nearby a wind-twisted spruce and an outhouse leaned west. A northern harrier huddled in the tree.

Before they could knock, the door opened and Sapatisia Sel, wearing a heavy grey sweater that looked like it had been knitted from fog and briars, stood staring at them without expression. She was not old but weathered, a plank washed up on shore.

"All right," she said in a low voice. "Here you are. Again. Why? Who are you and what do you want? Ever hear of privacy?"

"We come up from Dartmouth," said Jeanne and waited as though she had explained everything.

"I guessed that. Why are you bothering me?"

"I am Jeanne Sel, and this is my cousin Felix. Also Sel. We are students. I read this article"—she held the limp cutting out—"about you and I have a question."

"What question?" She did not take the clip.

"Well, you say that Mi'kmaw medicine plants from long ago can't be used now. Why not? I mean, if we know that a certain plant cured aches or itches, why wouldn't it be good to use it now? Our aunt Alice just had the flu and everybody brought her Mi'kmaw medicine and she got better."

Sapatisia Sel made a sound halfway between a moan and a sigh. "Good God, you came all this way to ask that?"

Salt-dimmed windows faced the Atlantic and the ocean itself seemed hung in space. The only table in the room looked like it had been stolen from a provincial park. Near the door stood an immense cupboard, painted red.

"Used to be a fisherman's house," said Sapatisia. "Fixed it up. Suits me the few months I'm here."

On the west wall Jeanne saw a bench cluttered with botanical instruments, a large microscope, a battered and age-blackened plant press layered with drying papers, dark stem ends protruding.

"Sit," said Sapatisia Sel, jerking her thumb at the table. "So. You want to know so badly why we can't use the old medicine plants that you drive a hundred kilometers on a stormy day to ask me, who you don't know? Maybe you think I have an answer. I don't."

Her unbraided hair straggled over her shoulders. "Since the conquest the air has been filled with pesticides and chemical fertilizers, with exhaust particles and smoke. We have acid rain. The deep forests are gone and now the climate shifts. Can you figure out for yourselves that the old medicine plants grew in a different world?" Felix, who had had many school-yard fights, liked her low voice, but not her combative posture.

"Those plants were surrounded by strong healthy trees, trees that no longer exist, trees replaced by weak and diseased specimens. We can only guess at the symbiotic relationships between those plants and the trees and shrubs of their time." She looked out the window, tapped her foot. "And I must say you are unusual young people to come here looking for answers. Are you botany students?"

They began to explain their lives to her, Alice's house and how they came to be there.

"You deluded idiots," said Sapatisia Sel. "And now you will go back and continue your studies?"

"We have to pass the exams. So we can get into university."

"Why do you want that?"

"To have careers. To be somebody."

"You are already somebody. Do you mean somebody more important than poor Mi'kmaw students?"

"Yes. I guess so," said Jeanne, and Felix, who did not want to nod, nodded.

"It's not just ourselves," said Jeanne. "Felix cares about the forests," she said. "And I care. We want to do something."

Felix saw the woman's rigid shoulders drop a little. He told her about hearing Dr. Onehube's lecture on the boreal forest.

"Well, Alfred does get people going."

"Do you know him?"

"We've worked together on projects." She got up and walked around, went to the door, opened and closed it. "You two are beginning to interest me now that we're past the medicine plants. You are young and green, you do not know how the world works or that you will be punished for your temerity in wanting careers." Outside the window in the gathering twilight Felix saw the northern harrier fly to its tree, something limp in its talons.

Felix thought of the long drive back. "You sound like a teacher. Are you a teacher?"

"I've done the university things, teaching and lecturing. I, too, wanted a career, I had a career, I left the career. I've learned enough to know that today the world we have made is desperate for help. Help that isn't coming. I don't teach now. I have a project and I work at it. With others. My interests are overlapping ecosystems, the difficulties in understanding the fabric of the natural world. So if you came here looking for a discussion of research on medicinal plant genomes you're in the wrong place."

Felix did not like her, but there was something—and Jeanne sat with her mouth open, staring hungrily at Sapatisia Sel, waiting for the next sentence.

"We look at models, examine causation and apparent effect, we struggle with the wild cards, worry about population growth. Humans now outnumber every mammalian form of life that has ever existed. Maybe unstoppable. We have nightmares about oceanic currents and sea star die-off, melting ice, more violent winter storms. And we think about forest degradation. Forest, the beginning and likely end. As Onehube says." And then in that low voice that sounded as though she were talking to herself she said, "But others now suggest more frightening problems and ends than Alfred Onehube ever dreamed."

She seemed done with talking, thrust a notebook at them and said, "Write down your address. I'll be in touch." Then she sent them on their way.

70

moonlight

Autumn lurched clumsily out of the equinox, black ice one day, sunlight polishing tree branches the next. A few straggler tourists were still underfoot, as irritating as gravel. Jeanne, who worked weekends at an information kiosk, collected (as everyone did) their idiotic questions, especially those from the Americans who thought it might be shorter to drive from Halifax to Antigonish counting miles rather than kilometers.

"I'm late, I'm late," muttered Felix, a white rabbit running through the kitchen, snatching a half-cooked pork chop from the pan and dashing up the stairs.

"Don't eat that pork—it's still raw," shouted Alice. "Use some sense. And you got some mail." Felix, simultaneously changing clothes and chewing on the red pork, looked at the clock. On his way to the back door through the kitchen he dropped the pork chop back in the pan and picked up the buff envelope, saw "Breitsprecher Tree Project" and a Chicago address in the upper left corner. He stopped, turned the envelope over.

"Jeanne get one, too, just like that," said Alice, nodding at Jeanne's plate, the envelope standing against it. "Late again—something she has to do at the school."

Felix tore the end off the envelope and pulled out a letter. Something fell out as he unfolded it and fluttered under the table. He read the letter and read it again, not understanding. It informed him that he was the recipient of a five-thousand-dollar fellowship from the Breitsprecher Tree Project and was signed by someone named Jason Bloodroot. What did it mean? Once more he read the letter, retrieved the check from the floor. It was made out to Felix Sel, it looked real. The letter said he was to contact Dr. Sapatisia Sel within ten days for further information about the project.

"I'll be double damn," he said. "*Doctor* Sapatisia Sel." There was her address and her cell phone number. He whooped so loudly that Jeanne, outside in the street, heard. She came in to find them dancing around the table, tore open her identical letter.

"You call her," said Felix. "It's you who connected us with her. So you phone."

The next day over the supper plates Felix studied the provincial highway map looking for an alternate route. "The trip was too long last time. But how about this"—he jabbed his pencil into the map—"a shortcut." Jeanne was old enough to know that no man on earth could be deterred from taking an unknown shortcut.

And now the lime-green rental car thumped into the darkening morning. The coast road would have been better. The shortcut was like driving up a dry river bed. Despite the rental car's chopped-off look (as though a log slasher had got it), Jeanne thought it a technological marvel. She began poking at the GPS touch screen.

The back road was a roller coaster of broken asphalt. The car could not catch the rhythm of the frost heaves. There were no towns, no houses, only third-growth spruce and brush representing the great forest of an earlier century. At the height of land they could see the dulled ocean and its grey line of rain. Tiny drops speckled the windshield.

"I don't think this is the tourist route," said Felix, steering around a dead branch. "Not sure where we are. And this city car doesn't like it."

"But we can see the water, so the highway has to be between us and the shore. When you see a right turn, take it."

"What time is it?"

"Almost eleven. We'll be late."

The car scraped through a series of potholes. Something dark and thin ran across the road.

"What was that?"

"Mink, one of those big escaped ones from the mink farms."

"You remember what Dr. Onehube said about those farms—pollute the rivers and the minks get out and breed with wild minks and make bad genetic changes?" The road degenerated into a stew of stones and mud. Felix clenched the wheel, drove very slowly, and the car struggled forward.

"You know," Felix said, "I found out something interesting about Dr. Sapatisia Sel. Guess."

"What, she was elected prom queen back in the day?"

"Not likely. She was married. Married to somebody we know."

"Who!" Jeanne did not believe it. How could her hero have married anyone?

"Well, not somebody we actually know—someone we heard talk."

"No, you don't mean that Onehube?"

"Yes. She was his student. And they got married."

Jeanne shuddered. She preferred to think of Sapatisia as a Lone Heroine.

"Anyway, what difference does it make? They were divorced."

Jeanne said nothing.

"Onehube's okay. He got us going."

"Wonder why they split up."

They descended the hill, passed assemblages of motley boards and corrugated roofing, one with a hopeless FOR SALE sign. Abruptly the clouds began to rip open like rotten cloth, showing bright blue under-skirts. As a slice of sunlight painted the drenched countryside, touched the sea, a flight of migrating birds cut the sky like crazy little scissors.

"We'll get there pretty soon," said Felix. "But I don't know where we are."

Jeanne began tracing her finger over the GPS touch screen. A tiny red dot on a crumpled string of a road appeared. "Look, Felix! It shows us on this road!"

"All right!" said Felix. Jeanne promised herself she would buy this model of car if she ever had the money. Suddenly a loud female voice said, "In a half kilometer turn right." Jeanne shrieked.

"You don't get out into the world enough," said Felix, swinging onto the wet highway. The sun changed the macadam surface to black lacquer and in a few kilometers they passed the lighthouse.

There was Sapatisia Sel's red pickup, beside it a rust-blotched sedan and a jeep so muddy it had no other color. Felix parked next to the jeep. At the lee side of the house they saw two large tents. A sign on one read MEN.

"The other one must be for women," said Jeanne. "Are they toilets?"

"Now *you* sound like a tourist. The outhouse is over there," he told her and jerked his thumb toward the unmistakable small building on the cliff. The northern harrier sat on its branch, eyeing them. "I say the tents are for sleeping."

"Let's go in." The harrier rattled a loud *tektektektek*.

The room looked different, richer in a homely way. The stolen picnic table was cluttered with papers, two laptops, a carton of almond milk and some plastic plates. Sapatisia, two young women—one with elaborately coiffed black hair, the other white-blond—and a sun-darkened man in a checked lumberjack shirt sat at the table drinking tea—wintergreen, thought Jeanne, catching the sprightly aroma—and eating take-out fried chicken legs.

"You made it," said Sapatisia. She was still in dirty jeans and the heavy grey sweater. "Sit down and have something. The coleslaw— where is it—" She half-rose.

"I've got it," said the man. His eyes looked bruised. He was older than the others, tall and thin, with a scar that torqued his mouth into a crooked slant. He stretched out a long arm and pushed the coleslaw bowl down the table. He looked at Jeanne and Felix.

"That's Tom Paulin," said Sapatisia, and she made sketchy introductions: "Jeanne Sel, Felix Sel, Tom Paulin, Hugdis Sigurdsson and Charlene Lopez. Let's eat now and then talk about the project." Her knotty dark hair was held back in a ponytail that resembled a Percheron's fly whisk; her eyes reflected the window light with a pale flash. Felix repeated "Tom Paulin" to himself, Tom Paulin the coleslaw passer. There was something about the man's straight back and the way he moved that indicated tension.

They tossed the gnawed chicken bones into the stove; Jeanne smelled them scorching.

Sapatisia said, "So then. Briefly, the Breitsprecher Tree Project does forest replanting. We have ties with as many as thirty conservation groups and we often work within their programs. The six of us make a work group. We like to have ten, but this time we have six. A few more might come later. We will be the only team working in Nova Scotia this season and there is a lot to do. We'll plant trees and monitor several test plots outplanted three years ago. We keep detailed notes on how well they are doing for up to ten years. One particular plot was showing a lot of chlorosis last year. Dozens of variables. I have a pet site where we're looking for the effects of mycorrhizal fungi on seedling growth. Burned soil is deficient in mycorrhizae and seedlings do not do well without them—their presence increases nutrient and mineral intake."

Sapatisia looked down the table at Jeanne and Felix scribbling notes, Charlene staring back at her, Tom Paulin in his private distance. She said, "Come back to us, Tom." She spoke softly. She knew a little about him: that he had been through deadly experiences in Afghanistan years earlier, and that after he came home, somehow trees had saved him. He looked at her, cracked out a blink of a smile like someone working a mirror against the sun. She went on.

"Whenever we can we'll visit the province's ecoregions, starting tomorrow with the highland plateau. It's useful to have a grasp of small areas, to know what is special about each. Once you understand how to assess different geographies, soils and hydrologies, sizing up new places will become second nature."

Felix said, "You mentioned different countries—will we go to other places or just stay here?" Tom Paulin nodded, poured more tea into his personal cup marked with *mù*, the Chinese ideogram for tree.

"For this three-month session you stay here. Next year you may work in a tropical rain forest." Jeanne noticed that Sapatisia's hands were dark, the nails broken. She looked at her own white, useless hands. The room was quiet and they could faintly hear the relentless cry of the harrier.

"If you like a particular kind of work you might specialize—Tom knows about wildfires and deforestation. Charlene is our expert on planting techniques." She nodded at the handsome hawk-nosed woman whose hair was twisted into an intricate knot at the back of her head. Jeanne wondered how she managed it in a tent.

Sapatisia said, "So. Essential information for our newcomers. The Tree Project will supply you with room and board and pay for your travel and all equipment and tools. Sometimes you will be living in tents, sometimes in hotels or with a host family. This month it's tents. The team will work together on the same plot. The work is hard and dirty. Next week Charlene will show Jeanne, Felix and Hugdis how we plant trees—we'll be doing spruce, birch, fir, maples, hemlock on several cutover degraded plots—and the burned plots—all near enough so we can use this place for our camp. We'll share the cooking, kitchen and cleanup chores."

"Then this project is not about medicinal plants?" asked Felix. He had noticed that Sapatisia often glanced at Charlene. What was that about?

"It can be medicinal plants where they are natural constituents of an area. Don't jump to the conclusion that medicinal plants only benefit humans—animals and other plants also use natural medicines. We often have to guess what understory plants belong in the mix because on badly degraded land we are not entirely sure what was there before the cut. You'll see as we go along." The male harrier flew from the tree and his shadow crossed the window.

Sapatisia said, "Tomorrow we will be on the plateau to examine the mixed-wood forests." From the red cupboard she took a stack of notebooks stamped BREITSPRECHER TREE PROJECT. "For field notes. Don't forget to consult the project's online library. A huge amount of information is available." She took up a sheaf of papers.

"Here are thumbnail descriptions of the geology and soils we'll see tomorrow. Add your personal observations to these notes. And remember that where there are highlands, there must be lowlands with bogs and marshes—they are not discrete."

"And moose," murmured Felix. He was here. He'd welcome anything he could learn.

"Yes, and otters and beaver, muskrats and dragonflies, mosquitoes, beetles and worms, and how do they all fit into the forest's life? Try to approach questions from the viewpoint of the forest." She looked at Tom Paulin as she said this. Then, more briskly, "If you have questions about fires and soils, ask Tom. Always share your knowledge."

On the pages she passed out Felix saw a jumble of new words—glacial till, ferro-humic podzols, Proterozoic intrusives, gleysols, fibrisols. He was excited by the names of the soils. This was real knowledge.

Jeanne had a question that had plagued her since she opened the envelope and saw the check fall out. "Why us?" she asked. "Why do you think Mi'kmaw people should do this?" Tom Paulin looked at Jeanne as if he were on a voyage of discovery and seeing a new land for the first time.

"It is not just Mi'kmaw people working on the project. Some are Mi'kmaw, we are even related as I'm sure you know, but Hugdis comes from Iceland and Charlene from Mexico. Tom is from the

American south. In Brazil, Peru, Colombia, Cambodia, Sumatra, Vietnam, United States West Coast, many of the people working to replant forests and resurrect damaged rivers are the children of indigenous forest residents. Dispossessed people who lived in forests for millennia until recently are the ones who step forward to do the repair work. They are the ones who best understand how to heal the forest.

"It will take thousands of years for great ancient forests to return. None of us here will see the mature results of our work, but we must try, even if it is only one or two people with buckets of seedlings working to put forest pieces back together. It is terribly important to all of us humans—I can't find the words to say how important—to help the earth regain its vital diversity of tree cover. And the forests will help us. They are old hands at restoring themselves.

"Now I'm going out to Sobeys market. Let's try for supper at five thirty?" She left and they heard the red pickup charge up the hill.

"When she mentioned forest people," said Jeanne to Hugdis, "I was going to ask if that idea of idyllic tribes living in wild forestland isn't a myth, like the myth of pristine primeval forest before the whitemen came. And actually isn't it a favor to bring those people into modern life now?"

"Jeanne!" cried Felix. "You don't think it was a *favor* for the French and English to 'bring' the Mi'kmaq into their idea of modern life. I know you don't."

Jeanne blushed and tensed in embarrassment. "That was different."

Hugdis changed the subject by telling the bizarre story of how the crazy Nazis tried to make the Bialowieza forest in Poland into the great primeval wilderness, about their efforts in back-breeding cattle to something they imagined was the extinct aurochs. And that started Tom on the sadness of Afghan people chopping down their last pitiful trees to sell for firewood; they talked until they heard the red truck come down the hill. One thing about this group, thought Felix, they really like talking about trees.

• • •

"Spaghetti tonight," said Sapatisia, coming in with bags of food and bottles of wine. "If you don't like the food you get to be the next cook."

Tom Paulin refilled the woodbox, stoked the stove, Charlene put a great pot of water on to boil, Jeanne and Hugdis chopped onions and green peppers, Felix sliced a large wrinkled pepperoni sausage into near-translucent disks and found bowls and forks. When Sapatisia mixed the sauce into the pasta she set the pot directly on the table.

As they ate they talked of their lives and families, but everyone kept looking at Sapatisia. To Jeanne, who had become an instant disciple, she seemed to stand for all that was good.

It was almost dark when they finished. Tom Paulin went outside while the rest of them cleared the table and Sapatisia rinsed out the teapot. Jeanne began to wash the dishes. Tom came back in and said, "The moon is coming up." In the window they all saw the red moon, made ragged by sea fog, rising swiftly out of the ocean, paling as it climbed. It looked close enough to hit with a harpoon and seemed to draw farther away as it rose. Jeanne knew the moon's apparent recession was only its rise above the distorting atmosphere, but suppose, she thought, that this time it kept going, becoming smaller and more distant like the waving hand of someone on a ferry.

The old stove radiated heat as they sat with their cups of tea and talked on, picking up on their earlier conversation about the tropics.

"It seems," said Sapatisia, "you are all more interested in tropical than boreal woodlands?"

"They are more endangered, aren't they? I keep reading that the forests of Sumatra will be gone in twenty years," said Jeanne. "There is a sense of urgency."

"And you think boreal forests are less threatened? A misapprehension. You are attracted to the romance of the tropics. There has been a lot of media attention lately—Disney Company roasted for using wood pulp from poached tropical trees to make children's books. Hardwood floor companies suddenly swearing that they only use ecologically sound plantation-grown trees."

She went on. "Charlene, you've spent time in Brazil and Colombia. How many trees and how many tree species would you say grow in Amazonia?"

"My God, who knows! The diversity is so great and the different species so scattered—"

Tom interrupted. "I read the Field Museum's report last year that said *sixteen thousand species* and I don't remember how many million trees."

Sapatisia nodded. "And they estimate around three hundred and ninety billion individual trees in the Amazon basin."

Tom looked at her. "How the hell can we understand those numbers? North America only has one thousand species. Sixteen thousand!"

Sapatisia crooked her mouth in a wry smile. "Yes, how *do* we grasp these enormous diverse numbers? But the report also said that half the trees actually belong to a much smaller count of two hundred twenty-seven species—the predominants, including cacao, rubber, açai berries, Brazil nuts."

Charlene poured more tea. "Those are the trees humans have been growing for centuries. Aren't there more of those species because human have nurtured them?"

Sapatisia shrugged. "Possibly. We just don't know. Some people are sure those hyperdominants were in the catbird seat because preconquest indigenous people grew them. On the other hand, some think they were always dominant and are in a naturally stable state. Quite a nice little puzzle.

"And that's the allure," she went on. "The slippery composition of ecosystems in general. It is uncomfortable to live in a spinning world of hallucinatory change. But how interesting it is."

Tom Paulin leaned forward. Felix thought he had loosened up since dinner—maybe it was the wine. "I'm thinking about the other end of the Amazonian stick—not the hyperdominant species but the rarities. The extinct species. I'm thinking about 'dark diversity.' Like dark matter."

"Dark diversity?" Felix liked the sound of this.

"A little like absent presence—when you pry a sunken stone from the ground the shape of the stone is still there in the hollow—absent presence. Say there is a particular rare plant that influences the trees and plants near it. Say conditions change and our rare plant goes extinct and its absence affects the remaining plants—dark diversity."

"But if conditions change again will the absent plant return?" asked Jeanne. "Are you saying extinction is not forever?"

"Sit next to me in the van tomorrow and we'll figure out dark diversity *and* dark matter. Right now I need sleep." He thought that she was not pretty but she had that soft beautiful skin color. And feelings. And a mind.

No one could sleep under such a moon. Its bitter white light destroyed repose. It was like acid poured over the landscape, seeping into every crevice.

Felix thought first of soil types, then of the unborn millions of tree cutters to come. And Sapatisia's emphasis on how enormously important the work was, not just a job but a cause, a lifework. He had listened to Onehube—was this the big thing he, Felix, could do? A drowsy thought swam to the surface—he might now actually be doing it—forest work. Had he gotten around the barrier of college and even the university? Yes, he was at the edge of the forest. This was his start. They could not pull him back.

And Jeanne felt a stream of joy like a narrow sun ray breaking through heavy overcast, a sense that in this one day her life had become filled with leafy meaning. Because of Sapatisia Sel.

• • •

Tom Paulin in his travel-worn sleeping bag was remembering Afghanistan and lost comrades, men welded tightly by searing experiences that outsiders could never understand. There was dark diversity for you. He found civilian life unbearably lonely; he tasted the sour flavor of belonging nowhere but with the old broken group, forever stitched to each other like parts of a coat—the loneliness of a ripped-out sleeve, he thought. And then at Seeley Lake he had found the larches. Running from suicidal despair he had joined a work crew in an old-growth larch forest where lightning storms fried the summer skies. The Indians had burned underbrush to encourage grassy meadows for deer, but in the last century thickets of Doug fir crowded out larch sprouts. He touched one tree's soft needles. A thought, unbidden, came—that one of his lost friends was inside that young tree. The burn of anxious grief for that fallen friend began to soften. The work crew had fired the built-up fuel load around the old larches, and the next year seedlings surged up in their thousands. He went on to different forests and in each of the young trees he saw the brothers he had lost. The more seedlings he planted, the more of them he resurrected.

Sapatisia tossed on her bed in the sleeping loft where once fishermen had stored their gear. It emitted a faint odor of stale bedding and old wool, of ancient seaboots and the wood handles of scaling knives. Every place in the world, she thought, had its own distinctive smell. The smell of old Mi'kma'ki must have been wet stones, sea wrack, pine and spruce, mellowing needle duff under the trees, a smell of salted wind and sassafras, of river fish and the people who lived in it, hair and limbs cleansed in the ever-flowing aromatic air. She rolled onto her side and looked down through a gap in the floorboards and saw moonlight shining on the teacups. She turned again and looked at the glowing sea.

Her thoughts surged like the bubbles rising up the sides of a boiling pot. Nothing done. Everything still unsaid, nothing ready. She had not yet told them of the dangers, that forest restoration workers were attacked and killed, that any kind of interruption to the profitable destruction of forests invited reprisal. She had not mentioned the floods of propaganda and lies that would drown them. She had not told them about the devouring fires, the rich peat-bog carbon mass of the boreal Canadian forests that burned hotter than those of Eurasia, the uncontrollable crown fires were changing the earth's albedo. In the morning she had to tell them.

New thoughts rushed in. Would they work as a group? Not everyone was suited to the life. She thought Felix would be good—he was hungry for the work. Tom Paulin was her rock, he would carry this group—if he stayed alive. Jeanne might be the finest kind once she found her way. Wait and see. Hugdis would leave in November. And there was Charlene, Charlene sulking again over some imagined wrong. And Mayara—no, she did not want to remember, she would not! But there was Mayara, rising in her memory, dark mestizo activist Mayara, sister, daughter, lover. Yes, and beautiful, too. And the treacherous memory would not stop there but leapt to Mayara on the day she had taken the foreign journalist to see a savagely destructive cut in a protected sanctuary, red mahogany logs lying on the ground, the butts still wet, when the cutters returned carrying guns instead of chain saws. As if they had known. Of course they had known. It was over in seconds, short bursts of gunfire. The photographs had shown Mayara cut in half, folded as though she were trying to kiss her own knees. Her knees! Her beautiful brown, rounded knees.

There followed ten terrible days as Sapatisia and Alfred Onehube staggered through a minefield of pain, confessions of betrayal, grief like a heated knife, until their throats were raw, until they were both exhausted by the enormity of what they had lost. And crushing this was the knowledge of another loss so great it obliterated personal dissolution. For after the divorce she had gone to the ice.

• • •

On the Greenland glaciers with ice scientists she suffered a full-force shock of recognition—the coming disappearance of a world believed immutable. She had heard for years that the earth and its life-forms were sensitive to slight temperature changes, that species prospered and disappeared as weather and climate varied, but dismissed these alarms as environmental determinism. On the ice her thinking shifted as the moon shifts its position in the sky. Historical evidence and the intense scrutiny of contemporary changes sent signals like fiery arrows; the earth was exquisitely sensitive to solar flares, the shadow of volcanic ash, electromagnetic space storms, subterranean magma movement. All her life she had assumed polar ice was a permanent feature of earth. She had not understood. "My God, how violently it is melting," she had whispered to herself. Great fissures thousands of feet deep opened by meltwater that eroded the hard blue ice, fissures that gaped open to receive the cataract's plunge, down to the rock beneath the great frozen bed, forcing its under-ice way to the sea, lubricating the huge cap from below. Standing near the brink of one ghastly thundering abyss someone said, "We are looking at something never before seen." That night, back at the camp, everyone admitted being shaken by the living evidence.

"A great crisis is just ahead," said one scientist. "What we saw this last week—" he muttered. Sapatisia Sel thought he meant that they had been looking at human extinction. She wanted to cry out, "The forests, the trees, they can change everything!" but her voice froze in her throat.

The ice had frightened her badly and the next day she called him from the airport: "Can't we try again? Can't we fix what we broke? I need to be with you. Our lives and our work. I understand now that the work is the most important thing." Onehube had said—"Some broken things can't be fixed."

• • •

She, Sapatisia Sel, was here now and she hadn't given up, but she had to sleep, had to, had to sleep. "What can I do but keep on trying? But what if it was all for nothing? What if it was already too late when the first hominid rose up and stared at the world? No!" What she and so many others were doing was working, it had to work. So many people trying to repair the damage, so selfless many of them caring and trying. And the forests themselves trying to grow back. "Oh God," she groaned, "oh God! Put out the moon!"

In the eastern quadrant of the sky the moon was small and very white and its impersonal brilliance showed the rocky coast, ravaged forests, silent feller bunchers, a black glowering mass of peat bog and spiky forest like old negatives. It showed Onehube's white-knuckled grip on the steering wheel. The sea lifted itself toward the light. And kept on lifting.

Acknowledgments

It is not possible to list all of the people who helped with suggestions and resources during the work on *Barkskins,* but here are a few of the many.

Portions of two chapters appeared in somewhat different form in *Brick* and *The New Yorker.*

The writing of this book was supported in part by a Ford Fellowship and United States Artists, and in part by my publisher Scribner. Parts of this work were written during a residency in the International House of Literature Passa Porta (Brussels) as part of the program Residences in Flanders and Brussels, organized by the literary organization Het beschrijf and the Department of Culture of the Flemish Community of Belgium. Special thanks to Ilke Froyen and the Passa Porta staff and their excellent bookstore. Thanks also to Isolde Bouten, who gave me a first taste of speaking and hearing and reading Nederlands. I am grateful to my publisher Erik Visser of De Geus, and my editor Nele Hendrickx, for their encouragement and scrutiny of my dictionary Dutch.

In New Zealand

Writer Jenny and musician Laughton Pattrick, friends and guides, tui enthusiasts, exemplars of joie de vivre took me into the rich Wilton's Bush (a.k.a. Otari) forest reserve in Wellington to see rimu, totara, kahikatea, rewarewa, tree ferns—a moist forest world of yesteryear. The New Zealand Maritime Museum Library and Archives was

ACKNOWLEDGMENTS

helpful. Betty Nelley, Curator, and Andrea Hemmins, Collections Manager of the Kauri Museum, Matakohe, Northland, were welcoming and enormously helpful. I enjoyed the help of Rita Havell, Research Librarian at the Alexander Turnbull Library, Wellington. Karren Beanland of the Michael King Writers' Centre helped with information and connections. One of those connections was Liz Allen, a center trustee, who took several days from her busy schedule to drive me up to the Hokianga to visit kauri museums and one of the few remaining kauri forests. In the Hokianga, Betty Nelley of the stunning Kauri Museum arranged a night foray into the forest to see the great trees by moonlight. Our guide was Kyle Tuwhekaea Ranga Chapman, who added to the drama of the experience with flute, bull-roarer, chant, story and lurid denunciations of stoats and possums that prey on kiwis.

In Nova Scotia

Grateful thanks to Roger Lewis, Mi'kmaw scholar, Curator, archaeologist, ethnologist and mesmerizing raconteur, of the Nova Scotia Museum: Museum of Natural History, for reading parts of the novel and explaining the importance of rivers to Mi'kmaw people. And thanks to my sister Roberta Roberts, who spent a week with me in that province.

In United States

The encouragement and support of my agent, Liz Darhansoff, and editor, Nan Graham, carried through several time extensions. I am grateful to Susan M. S. Brown for Herculean labors on the manuscript and for arranging three hundred years' worth of characters in an understandable family tree. It would have killed me to do this hard job. Cheryl Oakes, Librarian at the Forest History Society,

716

ACKNOWLEDGMENTS

came up with hard-to-find articles and references, and Cort Conley of the Idaho Commission on the Arts helped with books on western logging. In Vermont, Dr. John P. Lawrence aided me with some characters' medical details. Artist David Bradley of Santa Fe linked me to reports on the struggles of indigenous forest people forced out of their traditional territory by logging, cattle ranching, palm oil farms and mining. I found many scarce books through the myriad booksellers who list their wares on AbeBooks, and of course the indispensable Internet, especially the Google search engine, brought many obscure personalities and events to the surface. Coe Library at the University of Wyoming was my starting point for many scarce or hard to find books. Thanks also to Morgan Lang for help with the technical end of handling a large manuscript.

⇒⊱ Sel Family Tree ⊰⇐

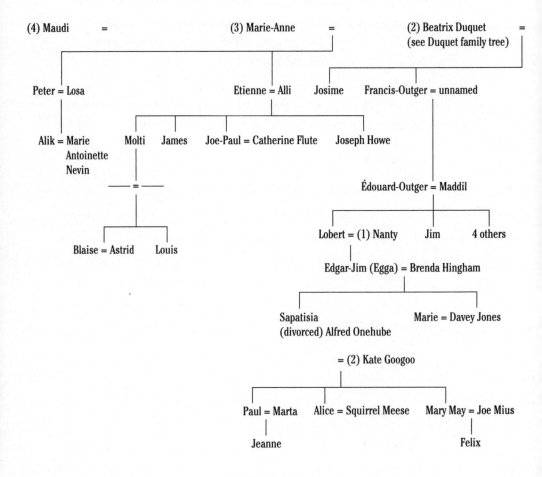

Achille

(4) Maudi = (3) Marie-Anne = (2) Beatrix Duquet (see Duquet family tree) =

Peter = Losa

Etienne = Alli   Josime   Francis-Outger = unnamed

Alik = Marie Antoinette Nevin   Molti   James   Joe-Paul = Catherine Flute   Joseph Howe

Édouard-Outger = Maddil

—— = ——

Lobert = (1) Nanty   Jim   4 others

Blaise = Astrid   Louis

Edgar-Jim (Egga) = Brenda Hingham

Sapatisia (divorced) Alfred Onehube   Marie = Davey Jones

= (2) Kate Googoo

Paul = Marta   Alice = Squirrel Meese   Mary May = Joe Mius

Jeanne   Felix

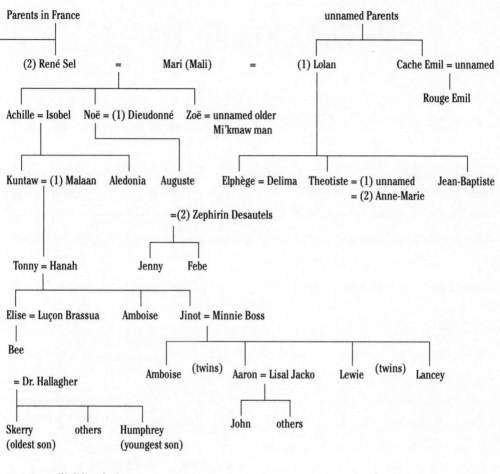

Parents in France   unnamed Parents

(2) René Sel   =   Mari (Mali)   =   (1) Lolan   Cache Emil = unnamed

Rouge Emil

Achille = Isobel   Noë = (1) Dieudonné   Zoë = unnamed older Mi'kmaw man

Kuntaw = (1) Malaan   Aledonia   Auguste   Elphège = Delima   Theotiste = (1) unnamed   Jean-Baptiste
                                       = (2) Anne-Marie

=(2) Zephirin Desautels

Tonny = Hanah   Jenny   Febe

Elise = Luçon Brassua   Amboise   Jinot = Minnie Boss

Bee

                 Amboise   (twins)   Aaron = Lisal Jacko   Lewie   (twins)   Lancey

= Dr. Hallagher

Skerry   others   Humphrey   John   others
(oldest son)   (youngest son)

= (3) Julian Cooko

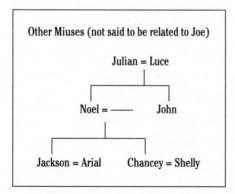

Other Miuses (not said to be related to Joe)

Julian = Luce

Noel = —— John

Jackson = Arial   Chancey = Shelly

⤜ Duke Family Tree ⥤

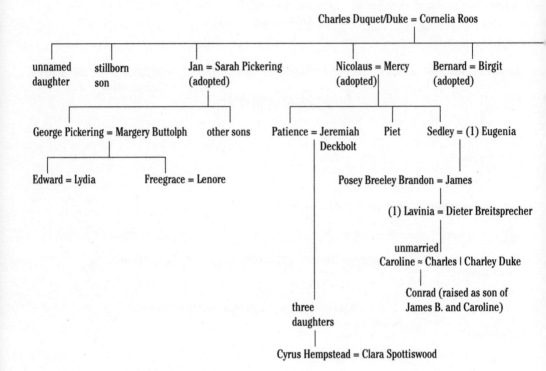

Charles Duquet/Duke = Cornelia Roos

| unnamed daughter | stillborn son | Jan = Sarah Pickering (adopted) | | Nicolaus = Mercy (adopted) | Bernard = Birgit (adopted) |

George Pickering = Margery Buttolph   other sons   Patience = Jeremiah Deckbolt   Piet   Sedley = (1) Eugenia

Edward = Lydia   Freegrace = Lenore

Posey Breeley Brandon = James

(1) Lavinia = Dieter Breitsprecher

unmarried
Caroline ≈ Charles | Charley Duke

Conrad (raised as son of
three   James B. and Caroline)
daughters

Cyrus Hempstead = Clara Spottiswood

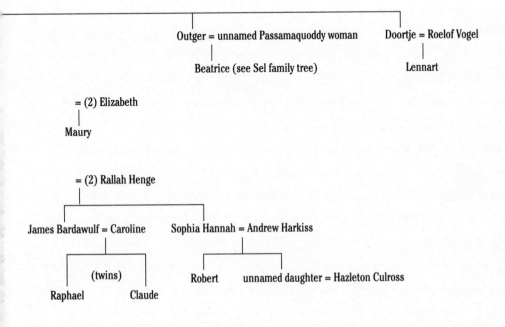

Outger = unnamed Passamaquoddy woman   Doortje = Roelof Vogel

Beatrice (see Sel family tree)   Lennart

= (2) Elizabeth

Maury

= (2) Rallah Henge

James Bardawulf = Caroline   Sophia Hannah = Andrew Harkiss

(twins)

Raphael   Claude   Robert   unnamed daughter = Hazleton Culross